BRIDGERTON

IT'S IN HIS KISS

ON THE WAY TO THE WEDDING

By Julia Quinn

THE BRIDGERTON PREQUELS

Because of Miss Bridgerton
The Girl with the Make-Believe Husband
The Other Miss Bridgerton
First Comes Scandal

THE BRIDGERTON SERIES

The Duke and I
The Viscount Who Loved Me
An Offer from a Gentleman
Romancing Mister Bridgerton
To Sir Phillip, With Love
When He Was Wicked
It's in His Kiss
On the Way to the Wedding
The Bridgertons: Happily Ever After

ANTHOLOGIES

The Further Observations of Lady Whistledown
Lady Whistledown Strikes Back

THE SMYTHE-SMITH QUARTET

Just Like Heaven
A Night Like This
The Sum of All Kisses
The Secrets of Sir Richard Kenworthy

THE BEVELSTOKE SERIES

The Secret Diaries of Miss Miranda Cheever
What Happens in London
Ten Things I Love About You

THE TWO DUKES OF WYNDHAM

The Lost Duke of Wyndham
Mr. Cavendish, I Presume

AGENTS OF THE CROWN

To Catch an Heiress
How to Marry a Marquis

THE LYNDON SISTERS

Everything and the Moon
Brighter Than the Sun

THE SPLENDID TRILOGY

Splendid
Dancing at Midnight
Minx

BRIDGERTON

IT'S IN HIS KISS

ON THE WAY TO THE WEDDING

JULIA QUINN

An Imprint of HarperCollins*Publishers*

"It's in His Kiss: The 2nd Epilogue" was originally published as an e-book.

"On the Way to the Wedding: The 2nd Epilogue" was originally published as an e-book.

HarperCollins books may be purchased for educational, business, or sales promotional use. For information, please email the Special Markets Department at SP-sales@harpercollins.com.

Originally published separately as *It's in His Kiss* and *On the Way to the Wedding* in the United States by Avon Books in 2005 and 2006.

Bridgerton Family Tree designed by Emily Cotler, Waxcreative Design

Library of Congress Cataloging-in-Publication Data has been applied for.

ISBN 978-0-06-338373-9

10 9 8 7 6 5 4 3 2 1

Table of Contents

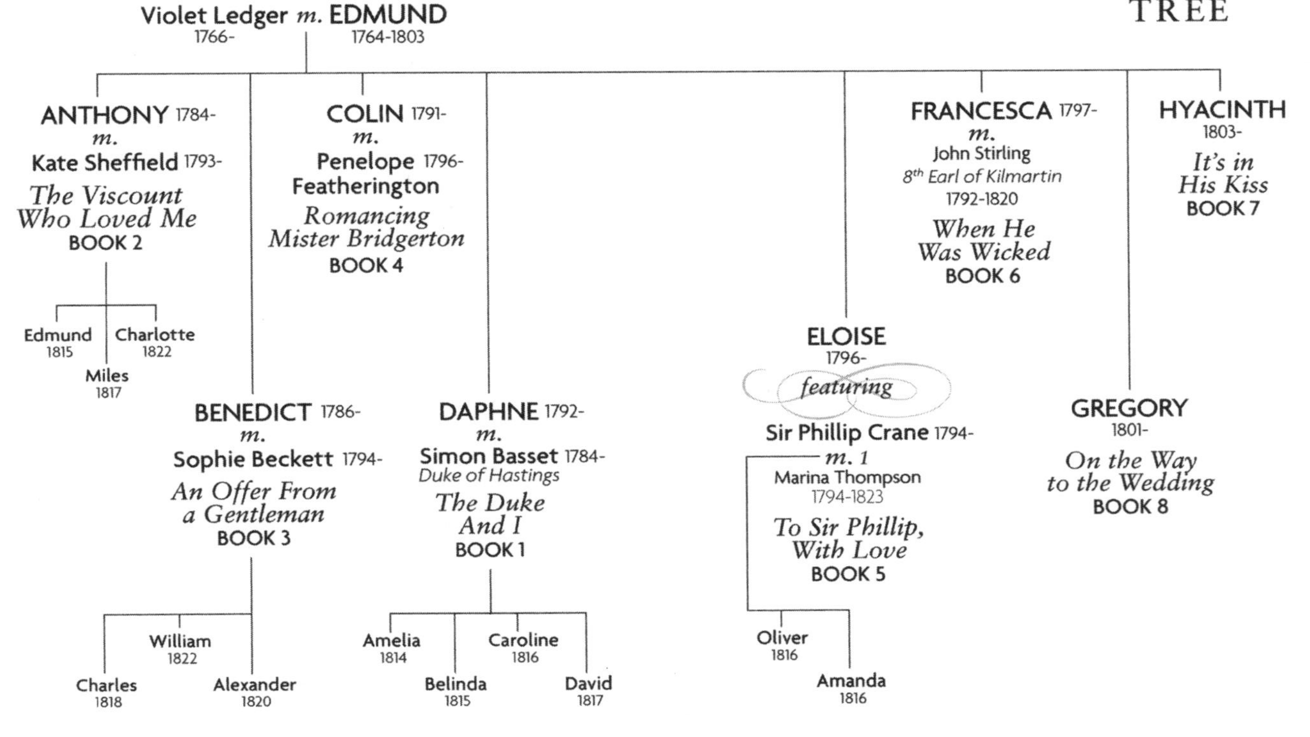
Bridgerton
FAMILY
TREE
Violet Ledger m. EDMUND
1766-
1764-1803
ANTHONY 1784-
m.
Kate Sheffield 1793-
The Viscount
Who Loved Me
BOOK 2
Edmund
1815
Charlotte
1822
Miles
1817
COLIN 1791-
m.
Penelope 1796-
Featherington
Romancing
Mister Bridgerton
BOOK 4
BENEDICT 1786-
m.
Sophie Beckett 1794-
An Offer From
a Gentleman
BOOK 3
Charles
1818
William
1822
Alexander
1820
DAPHNE 1792-
m.
Simon Basset 1784-
Duke of Hastings
The Duke
And I
BOOK 1
Amelia
1814
Belinda
1815
Caroline
1816
David
1817
ELOISE
1796-
featuring
Sir Phillip Crane 1794-
m. 1
Marina Thompson
1794-1823
To Sir Phillip,
With Love
BOOK 5
Oliver
1816
Amanda
1816
FRANCESCA 1797-
m.
John Stirling
8th Earl of Kilmartin
1792-1820
When He
Was Wicked
BOOK 6
GREGORY
1801-
On the Way
to the Wedding
BOOK 8
HYACINTH
1803-
It's in
His Kiss
BOOK 7

BRIDGERTON

IT'S IN HIS KISS

For Steve Axelrod, for a hundred different reasons. (But especially the caviar!)

And also for Paul, even though he seems to think I'm the sort of person who likes to share caviar.

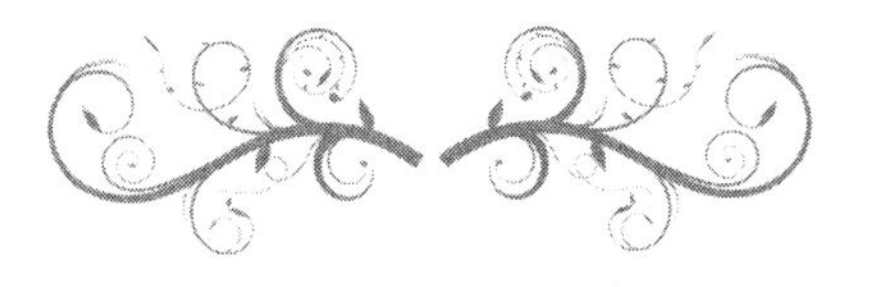

Acknowledgments

The author wishes to thank Eloisa James and Alessandro Vettori for their expertise in all things Italian.

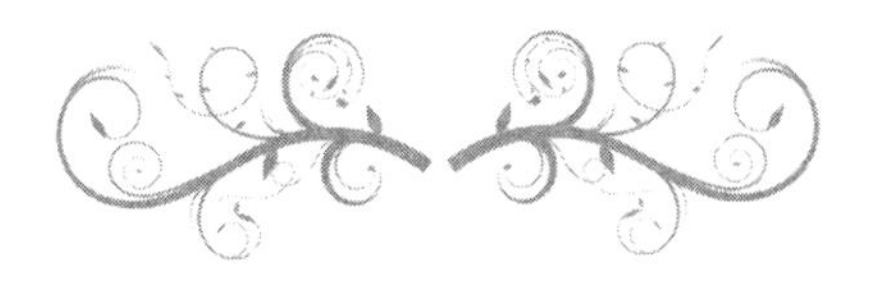

Prologue

1815, ten years before our story begins in earnest . . .

There were four principles governing Gareth St. Clair's relationship with his father that he relied upon to maintain his good humor and general sanity.

One: They did not converse unless absolutely necessary.

Two: All absolutely necessary conversations were to be kept as brief as possible.

Three: In the event that more than the simplest of salutations was to be spoken, it was always best to have a third party present.

And finally, four: For the purpose of achieving points one, two, and three, Gareth was to conduct himself in a manner so as to garner as many invitations as possible to spend school holidays with friends.

In other words, not at home.

In more precise words, away from his father.

All in all, Gareth thought, when he bothered to think about it, which wasn't often now that he had his avoidance tactics down to a science, these principles served him well.

And they served his father just as well, since Richard St. Clair liked his younger son about as much as his younger son liked him. Which was why, Gareth thought with a frown, he'd been so surprised to be summoned home from school.

And with such force.

His father's missive had held little ambiguity. Gareth was to report to Clair Hall immediately.

It was dashed irritating, this. With only two months left at Eton, his life was in full swing at school, a heady mix of games and studies, and of course the occasional surreptitious foray to the local public house, always late at night, and always involving wine and women.

Gareth's life was exactly as a young man of eighteen years would wish it. And he'd been under the assumption that, as long as he managed to remain out of his father's line of sight, his life at nineteen would be similarly blessed. He was to attend Cambridge in the fall, along with all of his closest friends, where he had every intention of pursuing his studies and social life with equal fervor.

As he glanced around the foyer of Clair Hall, he let out a long sigh that was meant to sound impatient but came out more nervous than anything else. What on earth could the baron—as he had taken to calling his father—want with him? His father had long since announced that he had washed his hands of his younger son and that he was only paying for his education because it was expected of him.

Which everyone knew really meant: It would look bad to their friends and neighbors if Gareth wasn't sent to a proper school.

When Gareth and his father *did* cross paths, the baron usually spent the entire time going on about what a disappointment the boy was.

Which only made Gareth wish to upset his father even more. Nothing like living down to expectations, after all.

Gareth tapped his foot, feeling rather like a stranger in his own home as he waited for the butler to alert his father as to his arrival. He'd spent so little time here in the last nine years it was difficult to feel much in the way of attachment. To him, it was nothing but a pile of stones that belonged to his father and would eventually go to his elder brother, George. Nothing of the house, and nothing of the St. Clair fortunes would come to Gareth, and he knew that his lot was to make his own way in the world. He supposed he would enter the military after Cambridge; the only other acceptable avenue of vocation was the clergy, and heaven knew he wasn't suited for *that*.

Gareth had few memories of his mother, who had died in an accident when he was five, but even he could recall her tousling his hair and laughing about how he was never serious.

"My little imp, you are," she used to say, followed by a whispered, "Don't lose that. Whatever you do, don't lose it."

He hadn't. And he rather doubted the Church of England would wish to welcome him into their ranks.

"Master Gareth."

Gareth looked up at the sound of the butler's voice. As always, Guilfoyle spoke in flat sentences, never queries.

"Your father will see you now," Guilfoyle intoned. "He is in his study."

Gareth nodded at the aging butler and made his way down the hall toward his father's study, always his least favorite room in the house. It was where his father delivered his lectures, where his father told him he would never amount to anything, where his father icily speculated that he should never have had a second son, that

Gareth was nothing but a drain on the family finances and a stain on their honor.

No, Gareth thought as he knocked on the door, no happy memories here.

"Enter!"

Gareth pushed open the heavy oak door and stepped inside. His father was seated behind his desk, scribbling something on a sheet of paper. He looked well, Gareth thought idly. His father always looked well. It would have been easier had he turned into a ruddy caricature of a man, but no, Lord St. Clair was fit and strong and gave the appearance of a man two decades younger than his fifty-odd years.

He looked like the sort of man a boy like Gareth ought to respect.

And it made the pain of rejection all the more cruel.

Gareth waited patiently for his father to look up. When he didn't, he cleared his throat.

No response.

Gareth coughed.

Nothing.

Gareth felt his teeth grinding. This was his father's routine—ignoring him for just long enough to act as a reminder that he found him beneath notice.

Gareth considered saying, "Sir." He considered saying, "My lord." He even considered uttering the word "Father," but in the end he just slouched against the doorjamb and started to whistle.

His father looked up immediately. "Cease," he snapped.

Gareth quirked a brow and silenced himself.

"And stand up straight. Good God," the baron said testily, "how many times have I told you that whistling is ill-bred?"

Gareth waited a second, then asked, "Am I meant to answer that, or was it a rhetorical question?"

His father's skin reddened.

Gareth swallowed. He shouldn't have said that. He'd known that his deliberately jocular tone would infuriate the baron, but sometimes it was so damned hard to keep his mouth shut. He'd spent years trying to win his father's favor, and he'd finally given in and given up.

And if he took some satisfaction in making the old man as miserable as the old man made him, well, so be it. One had to take one's pleasures where one could.

"I am surprised you're here," his father said.

Gareth blinked in confusion. "You asked me to come," he said. And the miserable truth was—he'd never defied his father. Not really. He poked, he prodded, he added a touch of insolence to his every statement and action, but he had never behaved with out-and-out defiance.

Miserable coward that he was.

In his dreams, he fought back. In his dreams, he told his father exactly what he thought of him, but in reality, his defiance was limited to whistles and sullen looks.

"So I did," his father said, leaning back slightly in his chair. "Nonetheless, I never issue an order with the expectation that you will follow it correctly. You so rarely do."

Gareth said nothing.

His father stood and walked to a nearby table, where he kept a decanter of brandy. "I imagine you're wondering what this is all about," he said.

Gareth nodded, but his father didn't bother to look at him, so he added, "Yes, sir."

The baron took an appreciative sip of his brandy, leaving Gareth waiting while he visibly savored the amber liquid. Finally, he turned, and with a coolly assessing stare said, "I have finally discovered a way for you to be useful to the St. Clair family."

Gareth's head jerked in surprise. "You have? Sir?"

His father took another drink, then set his glass down. "Indeed." He turned to his son and looked at him directly for the first time during the interview. "You will be getting married."

"Sir?" Gareth said, nearly gagging on the word.

"This summer," Lord St. Clair confirmed.

Gareth grabbed the back of a chair to keep from swerving. He was eighteen, for God's sake. Far too young to marry. And what about Cambridge? Could he even attend as a married man? And where would he put his wife?

And, good God above, *whom* was he supposed to marry?

"It's an excellent match," the baron continued. "The dowry will restore our finances."

"Our finances, sir?" Gareth whispered.

Lord St. Clair's eyes clamped down on his son's. "We're mortgaged to the hilt," he said sharply. "Another year, and we will lose everything that isn't entailed."

"But . . . how?"

"Eton doesn't come cheap," the baron snapped.

No, but surely it wasn't enough to beggar the family, Gareth thought desperately. This couldn't be *all* his fault.

"Disappointment you may be," his father said, "but I have not shirked my responsibilities to you. You have been educated as a gentleman. You have been given a horse, clothing, and a roof over your head. Now it is time you behaved like a man."

"Who?" Gareth whispered.

"Eh?"

"Who," he said a little louder. Whom was he meant to marry?

"Mary Winthrop," his father said in a matter-of-fact voice.

Gareth felt the blood leave his body. "Mary . . ."

"Wrotham's daughter," his father added.

As if Gareth didn't know that. "But Mary . . ."

"Will be an excellent wife," the baron continued. "Biddable, and you can dump her in the country should you wish to gad about town with your foolish friends."

"But Father, Mary—"

"I accepted on your behalf," his father stated. "It's done. The agreements have been signed."

Gareth fought for air. This couldn't be happening. Surely a man could not be forced into marriage. Not in this day and age.

"Wrotham would like to see it done in July," his father added. "I told him we have no objections."

"But . . . Mary . . ." Gareth gasped. "I can't marry Mary!"

One of his father's bushy brows inched toward his hairline. "You can, and you will."

"But Father, she's . . . she's . . ."

"Simple?" the baron finished for him. He chuckled. "Won't make a difference when she's under you in bed. And you don't have to have anything to do with her otherwise." He walked toward his son until they were uncomfortably close. "All you need to do is show up at the church. Do you understand?"

Gareth said nothing. He didn't *do* much of anything, either. It was all he could manage just to breathe.

He'd known Mary Winthrop his entire life. She was a year his elder, and their families' estates had bordered on one another's for over a century. They'd been playmates as young children, but it soon became apparent that Mary wasn't quite right in the head. Gareth had remained her champion whenever he was in the district; he'd bloodied more than one bully who had thought to call her names or take advantage of her sweet and unassuming nature.

But he couldn't *marry* her. She was like a child. It had to be a sin. And even if it wasn't, he could never stomach it. How could she possibly understand what was meant to transpire between them as man and wife?

He could never bed her. Never.

Gareth just stared at his father, words failing him. For the first time in his life, he had no easy reply, no flip retort.

There were no words. Simply no words for such a moment.

"I see we understand each other," the baron said, smiling at his son's silence.

"No!" Gareth burst out, the single syllable ripping itself from his throat. "No! I can't!"

His father's eyes narrowed. "You'll be there if I have to tie you up."

"No!" He felt like he was choking, but somehow he got the words out. "Father, Mary is . . . Well, she's a child. She'll never be more than a child. You know that. I can't marry her. It would be a sin."

The baron chuckled, breaking the tension as he turned swiftly away. "Are you trying to convince me that you, of all people, have suddenly found religion?"

"No, but—"

"There is nothing to discuss," his father cut in. "Wrotham has been extremely generous with the dowry. God knows he has to be, trying to unload an idiot."

"Don't speak of her that way," Gareth whispered. He might not want to marry Mary Winthrop, but he'd known her all his life, and she did not deserve such talk.

"It is the best you will ever do," Lord St. Clair said. "The best you will ever have. Wrotham's settlement is extraordinarily generous, and I will arrange for an allowance that will keep you comfortable for life."

"An allowance," Gareth echoed dully.

His father let out one short chuckle. "Don't think I would trust you with a lump sum," he said. "You?"

Gareth swallowed uncomfortably. "What about school?" he whispered.

"You can still attend," his father said. "In fact, you have your new bride to thank for that. Wouldn't have had the blunt to send you without the marriage settlement."

Gareth stood there, trying to force his breathing into something that felt remotely even and normal. His father knew how much it meant to him to attend Cambridge. It was the one thing upon which the two of them agreed: A gentleman needed a gentleman's education. It didn't matter that Gareth craved the entire experience, both social and academic, whereas Lord St. Clair saw it merely as something a man had to do to keep up appearances. It had been decided upon for years—Gareth would attend and receive his degree.

But now it seemed that Lord St. Clair had known that he could not pay for his younger son's education. When had he planned to tell him? As Gareth was packing his bags?

"It's done, Gareth," his father said sharply. "And it has to be you. George is the heir, and I can't have him sullying the bloodlines. Besides," he added with pursed lips, "I wouldn't subject him to this, anyway."

"But you would me?" Gareth whispered. Was this how much his father hated him? How little he thought of him? He looked up at his father, at the face that had brought him so much unhappiness. There had never been a smile, never an encouraging word. Never a—

"Why?" Gareth heard himself saying, the word sounding like a wounded animal, pathetic and plaintive. "Why?" he said again.

His father said nothing, just stood there, gripping the edge of his desk until his knuckles grew white. And Gareth could do nothing but stare, somehow transfixed by the ordinary sight of his father's hands. "I'm your son," he whispered, still unable to move his gaze from his father's hands to his face. "Your son. How could you do this to your own son?"

And then his father, who was the master of the cutting retort, whose anger always came dressed in ice rather than fire, exploded. His hands flew from the table, and his voice roared through the room like a demon.

"By God, how could you not have figured it out by now? You are not my son! You have never been my son! You are nothing but a by-blow, some mangy whelp your mother got off another man while I was away."

Rage poured forth like some hot, desperate thing, too long held captive and repressed. It hit Gareth like a wave, swirling around him, squeezing and choking until he could barely breathe. "No," he said, desperately shaking his head. It was nothing he hadn't considered, nothing he hadn't even hoped for, but it couldn't be true. He *looked* like his father. They had the same nose, didn't they? And—

"I have fed you," the baron said, his voice low and hard. "I have clothed you and presented you to the world as my son. I have supported you when another man would have tossed you into the street, and it is well past time that you returned the favor."

"No," Gareth said again. "It can't be. I look like you. I—"

For a moment Lord St. Clair remained silent. Then he said, bitterly, "An unhappy coincidence, I assure you."

"But—"

"I could have turned you out at your birth," Lord St. Clair cut in, "sent your mother packing, tossed you both into the street. But I did not." He closed the distance between them and put his face very close to Gareth's. "You have been acknowledged, and you are legitimate." And then, in a voice furious and low: "You owe me."

"No," Gareth said, his voice finally finding the conviction he was going to need to last him through the rest of his days. "No. I won't do it."

"I will cut you off," the baron warned. "You won't see another penny from me. You can forget your dreams of Cambridge, your—"

"No," Gareth said again, and he sounded different. He felt changed. This was the end, he realized. The end of his childhood, the end of his innocence, and the beginning of—

God only knew what it was the beginning of.

"I am through with you," his father—no, not his father—hissed. "Through."

"So be it," Gareth said.

And he walked away.

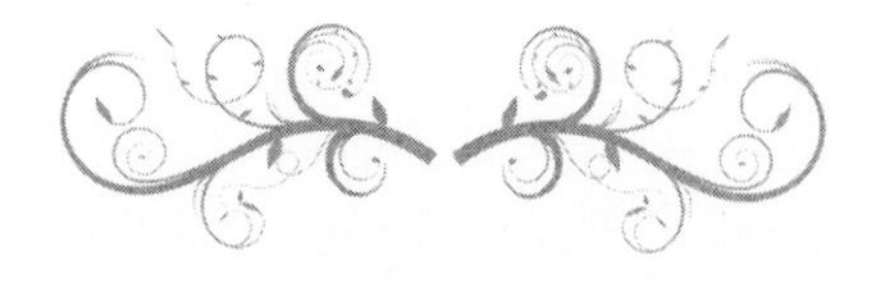

Chapter 1

Ten years have passed, and we meet our heroine, who, it must be said, has never been known as a shy and retiring flower. The scene is the annual Smythe-Smith musicale, about ten minutes before Mr. Mozart begins to rotate in his grave.

"Why do we do this to ourselves?" Hyacinth Bridgerton wondered aloud.

"Because we are good, kind people," her sister-in-law replied, sitting in—God help them—a front-row seat.

"One would think," Hyacinth persisted, regarding the empty chair next to Penelope with the same excitement she might show a sea urchin, "that we would have learned our lesson last year. Or perhaps the year before that. Or maybe even—"

"Hyacinth?" Penelope said.

Hyacinth swung her gaze to Penelope, lifting one brow in question.

"Sit."

Hyacinth sighed. But she sat.

The Smythe-Smith musicale. Thankfully, it came around just

once per year, because Hyacinth was quite certain it would take a full twelve months for her ears to recover.

Hyacinth let out another sigh, this one louder than the last. "I'm not entirely certain that I'm either good or kind."

"I'm not certain, either," Penelope said, "but I have decided to have faith in you nevertheless."

"Rather sporting of you," Hyacinth said.

"I thought so."

Hyacinth glanced at her sideways. "Of course you did not have any choice in the matter."

Penelope turned in her seat, her eyes narrowing. "Meaning?"

"Colin refused to accompany you, didn't he?" Hyacinth said with a sly look. Colin was Hyacinth's brother, and he'd married Penelope a year earlier.

Penelope clamped her mouth into a firm line.

"I do love it when I am right," Hyacinth said triumphantly. "Which is fortunate, since I so often am."

Penelope just looked at her. "You do know that you are insufferable."

"Of course." Hyacinth leaned toward Penelope with a devilish smile. "But you love me, anyway, admit it."

"I admit nothing until the end of the evening."

"After we have both gone deaf?"

"After we see if you behave yourself."

Hyacinth laughed. "You married into the family. You have to love me. It's a contractual obligation."

"Funny how I don't recall that in the wedding vows."

"Funny," Hyacinth returned, "I remember it perfectly."

Penelope looked at her and laughed. "I don't know how you do it, Hyacinth," she said, "but exasperating as you are, you somehow always manage to be charming."

"It's my greatest gift," Hyacinth said demurely.

"Well, you do receive extra points for coming with me tonight," Penelope said, patting her on the hand.

"Of course," Hyacinth replied. "For all my insufferable ways, I am in truth the soul of kindness and amiability." And she'd have to be, she thought, as she watched the scene unfolding on the small, makeshift stage. Another year, another Smythe-Smith musicale. Another opportunity to learn just how many ways one could ruin a perfectly good piece of music. Every year Hyacinth swore she wouldn't attend, then every year she somehow found herself at the event, smiling encouragingly at the four girls on the stage.

"At least last year I got to sit in the back," Hyacinth said.

"Yes, you did," Penelope replied, turning on her with suspicious eyes. "How did you manage that? Felicity, Eloise, and I were all up front."

Hyacinth shrugged. "A well-timed visit to the ladies' retiring room. In fact—"

"Don't you dare try that tonight," Penelope warned. "If you leave me up here by myself . . ."

"Don't worry," Hyacinth said with a sigh. "I am here for the duration. But," she added, pointing her finger in what her mother would surely have termed a most unladylike manner, "I want my devotion to you to be duly noted."

"Why is it," Penelope asked, "that I am left with the feeling that you are keeping score of something, and when I least expect it, you will jump out in front of me, demanding a favor?"

Hyacinth looked at her and blinked. "Why would I need to jump?"

"Ah, look," Penelope said, after staring at her sister-in-law as if she were a lunatic, "here comes Lady Danbury."

"Mrs. Bridgerton," Lady Danbury said, or rather barked. "Miss Bridgerton."

"Good evening, Lady Danbury," Penelope said to the elderly countess. "We saved you a seat right in front."

Lady D narrowed her eyes and poked Penelope lightly in the ankle with her cane. "Always thinking of others, aren't you?"

"Of course," Penelope demurred. "I wouldn't dream of—"

"Ha," Lady Danbury said.

It was, Hyacinth reflected, the countess's favorite syllable. That and *hmmmph*.

"Move over, Hyacinth," Lady D ordered. "I'll sit between you."

Hyacinth obediently moved one chair to the left. "We were just pondering our reasons for attending," she said as Lady Danbury settled into her seat. "I for one have come up blank."

"I can't speak for you," Lady D said to Hyacinth, "but *she*"—at this she jerked her head toward Penelope—"is here for the same reason I am."

"For the music?" Hyacinth queried, perhaps a little too politely.

Lady Danbury turned back to Hyacinth, her face creasing into what might have been a smile. "I've always liked you, Hyacinth Bridgerton."

"I've always liked you, too," Hyacinth replied.

"I expect it is because you come and read to me from time to time," Lady Danbury said.

"Every week," Hyacinth reminded her.

"Time to time, every week . . . pfft." Lady Danbury's hand cut a dismissive wave through the air. "It's all the same if you're not making it a daily endeavor."

Hyacinth judged it best not to speak. Lady D would surely find some way to twist her words into a promise to visit every afternoon.

"And I might add," Lady D said with a sniff, "that you were most unkind last week, leaving off with poor Priscilla hanging from a cliff."

"What are you reading?" Penelope asked.

"*Miss Butterworth and the Mad Baron*," Hyacinth replied. "And she wasn't hanging. Yet."

"Did you read ahead?" Lady D demanded.

"No," Hyacinth said with a roll of her eyes. "But it's not difficult to forecast. Miss Butterworth has already hung from a building and a tree."

"And she's still living?" Penelope asked.

"I said hung, not hanged," Hyacinth muttered. "More's the pity."

"Regardless," Lady Danbury cut in, "it was most unkind of you to leave *me* hanging."

"It's where the author ended the chapter," Hyacinth said unrepentantly, "and besides, isn't patience a virtue?"

"Absolutely not," Lady Danbury said emphatically, "and if you think so, you're less of a woman than I thought."

No one understood why Hyacinth visited Lady Danbury every Tuesday and read to her, but she enjoyed her afternoons with the countess. Lady Danbury was crotchety and honest to a fault, and Hyacinth adored her.

"The two of you together are a menace," Penelope remarked.

"My aim in life," Lady Danbury announced, "is to be a menace to as great a number of people as possible, so I shall take that as the highest of compliments, Mrs. Bridgerton."

"Why is it," Penelope wondered, "that you only call me Mrs. Bridgerton when you are opining in a grand fashion?"

"Sounds better that way," Lady D said, punctuating her remark with a loud thump of her cane.

Hyacinth grinned. When she was old, she wanted to be exactly like Lady Danbury. Truth be told, she liked the elderly countess better than most of the people she knew her own age. After three seasons on the marriage mart, Hyacinth was growing just a little bit weary of the same people day after day. What had once been exhilarating—the balls, the parties, the suitors—well, it was still enjoyable—that much she had to concede. Hyacinth certainly wasn't one of those girls who complained about all of the wealth and privilege she was forced to endure.

But it wasn't the same. She no longer held her breath each time she entered a ballroom. And a dance was now simply a dance, no longer the magical swirl of movement it had been in years gone past.

The excitement, she realized, was gone.

Unfortunately, every time she mentioned this to her mother, the reply was simply to find herself a husband. That, Violet Bridgerton took great pains to point out, would change everything.

Indeed.

Hyacinth's mother had long since given up any pretense of subtlety when it came to the unmarried state of her fourth and final daughter. It had, Hyacinth thought grimly, turned into a personal crusade.

Forget Joan of Arc. Her mother was Violet of Mayfair, and neither plague nor pestilence nor perfidious paramour would stop her in her quest to see all eight of her children happily married. There were only two remaining, Gregory and Hyacinth, but Gregory was still just twenty-four, which was (rather unfairly, in Hyacinth's opinion) considered a perfectly acceptable age for a gentleman to remain a bachelor.

But Hyacinth at twenty-two? The only thing staving off her mother's complete collapse was the fact that her elder sister Eloise had waited until the grand old age of twenty-eight before finally becoming a bride. By comparison, Hyacinth was practically in leading strings.

No one could say that Hyacinth was hopelessly on the shelf, but even she had to admit that she was edging toward that position. She had received a few proposals since her debut three years earlier, but not as many as one would think, given her looks—not the prettiest girl in town but certainly better than at least half—and her fortune—again, not the largest dowry on the market, but certainly enough to make a fortune hunter look twice.

And her connections were, of course, nothing short of impeccable. Her brother was, as their father had been before him, the Viscount Bridgerton, and while theirs might not have been the loftiest title in the land, the family was immensely popular and influential. And if that weren't enough, her sister Daphne was the Duchess of Hastings, and her sister Francesca was the Countess of Kilmartin.

If a man wanted to align himself with the most powerful families in Britain, he could do a lot worse than Hyacinth Bridgerton.

But if one took the time to reflect upon the timing of the proposals she had received, which Hyacinth didn't care to admit that she had, it was starting to look damning indeed.

Three proposals her first season.

Two her second.

One last year.

And none thus far this time around.

It could only be argued that she was growing less popular. Unless, of course, someone was foolish enough actually to *make* the argument, in which case Hyacinth would have to take the other side, facts and logic notwithstanding.

And she'd probably win the point, too. It was a rare man—or woman—who could outwit, outspeak, or outdebate Hyacinth Bridgerton.

This might, she'd thought in a rare moment of self-reflection, have something to do with why her rate of proposals was declining at such an alarming pace.

No matter, she thought, watching the Smythe-Smith girls mill about on the small dais that had been erected at the front of the room. It wasn't as if she should have accepted any of her six proposals. Three had been fortune hunters, two had been fools, and one had been quite terminally boring.

Better to remain unmarried than shackle herself to someone who'd bore her to tears. Even her mother, inveterate matchmaker that she was, couldn't argue that point.

And as for her current proposal-free season—well, if the gentlemen of Britain couldn't appreciate the inherent value of an intelligent female who knew her own mind, that was their problem, not hers.

Lady Danbury thumped her cane against the floor, narrowly missing Hyacinth's right foot. "I say," she said, "have either of you caught sight of my grandson?"

"Which grandson?" Hyacinth asked.

"Which grandson," Lady D echoed impatiently. "Which grandson? The only one I like, that's which."

Hyacinth didn't even bother to hide her shock. "Mr. St. Clair is coming tonight?"

"I know, I know," Lady D cackled. "I can hardly believe it myself. I keep waiting for a shaft of heavenly light to burst through the ceiling."

Penelope's nose crinkled. "I think that might be blasphemous, but I'm not sure."

"It's not," Hyacinth said, without even looking at her. "And why is he coming?"

Lady Danbury smiled slowly. Like a snake. "Why are you so interested?"

"I'm *always* interested in gossip," Hyacinth said quite candidly. "About anyone. You should know that already."

"Very well," Lady D said, somewhat grumpily after having been thwarted. "He's coming because I blackmailed him."

Hyacinth and Penelope regarded her with identically arched brows.

"Very well," Lady Danbury conceded, "if not blackmail, then a heavy dose of guilt."

"Of course," Penelope murmured, at the exact time Hyacinth said, "*That* makes much more sense."

Lady D sighed. "I might have told him I wasn't feeling well."

Hyacinth was dubious. "*Might* have?"

"Did," Lady D admitted.

"You must have done a very good job of it to get him to come tonight," Hyacinth said admiringly. One had to appreciate Lady Danbury's sense of the dramatic, especially when it resulted in such impressive manipulation of the people around her. It was a talent Hyacinth cultivated as well.

"I don't think I have ever seen him at a musicale before," Penelope remarked.

"Hmmmph," Lady D grunted. "Not enough loose women for him, I'm sure."

From anyone else, it would have been a shocking statement. But this was Lady Danbury, and Hyacinth (and the rest of the *ton* for that matter) had long since grown used to her rather startling turns of phrase.

And besides, one did have to consider the man in question.

Lady Danbury's grandson was none other than the notorious Gareth St. Clair. Although it probably wasn't entirely his fault that he had gained such a wicked reputation, Hyacinth reflected. There were plenty of other men who behaved with equal lack of propriety, and more than a few who were as handsome as sin, but Gareth St. Clair was the only one who managed to combine the two to such success.

But his reputation was abominable.

He was certainly of marriageable age, but he'd never, not even once, called upon a proper young lady at her home. Hyacinth was quite sure of *that*; if he'd ever even hinted at courting someone, the rumor mills would have run rampant. And furthermore, Hyacinth would have heard it from Lady Danbury, who loved gossip even more than she did.

And then, of course, there was the matter of his father, Lord St. Clair. They were rather famously estranged, although no one knew why. Hyacinth personally thought it spoke well of Gareth that he did not air his familial travails in public—especially since she'd met his father and thought him a boor, which led her to believe that whatever the matter was, the younger St. Clair was not at fault.

But the entire affair lent an air of mystery to the already charismatic man, and in Hyacinth's opinion made him a bit of a challenge to the ladies of the *ton*. No one seemed quite certain how to view him. On the one hand, the matrons steered their daughters away; surely a connection with Gareth St. Clair could not enhance a girl's reputation. On the other hand, his brother had died tragically young, almost a year earlier, and now he was the heir to the barony. Which had only served to make him a more romantic—and eligible—figure. Last month Hyacinth had seen a girl swoon—or at least pretend to—when he had deigned to attend the Bevelstoke Ball.

It had been appalling.

Hyacinth had *tried* to tell the foolish chit that he was only there because his grandmother had forced him into it, and of course because his father was out of town. After all, everyone knew that he only consorted with opera singers and actresses, and certainly not any of the ladies he might meet at the Bevelstoke Ball. But the girl would not be swayed from her overemotional state, and eventually she had collapsed onto a nearby settee in a suspiciously graceful heap.

Hyacinth had been the first to locate a vinaigrette and shove it under her nose. Really, some behavior just couldn't be tolerated.

But as she stood there, reviving the foolish chit with the noxious fumes, she had caught sight of him staring at her in that vaguely mocking way of his, and she couldn't shake the feeling that he found her amusing.

Much in the same way she found small children and large dogs amusing.

Needless to say, she hadn't felt particularly complimented by his attention, fleeting though it was.

"Hmmph."

Hyacinth turned to face Lady Danbury, who was still searching the room for her grandson. "I don't think he's here yet," Hyacinth said, then added under her breath, "No one's fainted."

"Enh? What was that?"

"I said I don't think he's here yet."

Lady D narrowed her eyes. "I heard that part."

"It's all I said," Hyacinth fibbed.

"Liar."

Hyacinth looked past her to Penelope. "She treats me quite abominably, did you know that?"

Penelope shrugged. "Someone has to."

Lady Danbury's face broke out into a wide grin, and she turned to Penelope, and said, "Now then, I must ask—" She looked over at the stage, craning her neck as she squinted at the quartet. "Is it the same girl on cello this year?"

Penelope nodded sadly.

Hyacinth looked at them. "What are you talking about?"

"If you don't know," Lady Danbury said loftily, "then you haven't been paying attention, and shame on you for that."

Hyacinth's mouth fell open. "Well," she said, since the alternative was to say nothing, and she never liked to do *that.* There was nothing more irritating than being left out of a joke. Except, perhaps, being scolded for something one didn't even understand. She turned back to the stage, watching the cellist more closely. Seeing nothing out of the ordinary, she twisted again to face her companions and opened her mouth to speak, but they were already deep in a conversation that did not include her.

She hated when that happened.

"Hmmmph." Hyacinth sat back in her chair and did it again. "Hmmmph."

"You sound," came an amused voice from over her shoulder, "exactly like my grandmother."

Hyacinth looked up. There he was, Gareth St. Clair, inevitably at the moment of her greatest discomfiture. And, of course, the only empty seat was next to her.

"Doesn't she, though?" Lady Danbury asked, looking up at her grandson as she thumped her cane against the floor. "She's quickly replacing you as my pride and joy."

"Tell me, Miss Bridgerton," Mr. St. Clair asked, one corner of his lips curving into a mocking half smile, "is my grandmother remaking you in her image?"

Hyacinth had no ready retort, which she found profoundly irritating.

"Move over again, Hyacinth," Lady D barked. "I need to sit next to Gareth."

Hyacinth turned to say something, but Lady Danbury cut in with, "Someone needs to make sure he behaves."

Hyacinth let out a noisy exhale and moved over another seat.

"There you go, my boy," Lady D said, patting the empty chair with obvious glee. "Sit and enjoy."

He looked at her for a long moment before finally saying, "You owe me for this, Grandmother."

"Ha!" was her response. "Without me, you wouldn't exist."

"A difficult point to refute," Hyacinth murmured.

Mr. St. Clair turned to look at her, probably only because it enabled him to turn away from his grandmother. Hyacinth smiled at him blandly, pleased with herself for showing no reaction.

He'd always reminded her of a lion, fierce and predatory, filled with restless energy. His hair, too, was tawny, hovering in that curious state between light brown and dark blond, and he wore it rakishly, defying convention by keeping it just long enough to tie in a short queue at the back of his neck. He was tall, although not overly so, with an athlete's grace and strength and a face that was just imperfect enough to be handsome, rather than pretty.

And his eyes were blue. Really blue. Uncomfortably blue.

Uncomfortably blue? She gave her head a little shake. That had to be quite the most asinine thought that had ever entered her head. Her own eyes were blue, and there was certainly nothing uncomfortable about *that*.

"And what brings you here, Miss Bridgerton?" he asked. "I hadn't realized you were such a lover of music."

"If she loved music," Lady D said from behind him, "she'd have already fled to France."

"She does hate to be left out of a conversation, doesn't she?" he murmured, without turning around. "Ow!"

"Cane?" Hyacinth asked sweetly.

"She's a threat to society," he muttered.

Hyacinth watched with interest as he reached behind him, and without even turning his head, wrapped his hand around the cane and wrenched it from his grandmother's grasp. "Here," he said, handing it to her, "you will look after this, won't you? She won't need it while she's sitting down."

Hyacinth's mouth fell open. Even she had never dared to interfere with Lady Danbury's cane.

"I see that I have finally impressed you," he said, sitting back in his chair with the expression of one who is quite pleased with himself.

"Yes," Hyacinth said before she could stop herself. "I mean, no. I mean, don't be silly. I certainly haven't been *not* impressed by you."

"How gratifying," he murmured.

"What I meant," she said, grinding her teeth together, "was that I haven't really thought about it one way or the other."

He tapped his heart with his hand. "Wounded," he said flippantly. "And right through the heart."

Hyacinth gritted her teeth. The only thing worse than being made fun of was not being sure if one was being made fun of. Everyone else in London she could read like a book. But with Gareth St. Clair, she simply never knew. She glanced past him to see if Penelope was listening—not that she was sure why that mattered one way or another—but Pen was busy placating Lady Danbury, who was still smarting over the loss of her cane.

Hyacinth fidgeted in her seat, feeling uncommonly closed-in. Lord Somershall—never the slenderest man in the room—was on her left, spilling onto her chair. Which only forced her to scoot a little to the right, which of course put her in even closer proximity to Gareth St. Clair, who was positively radiating heat.

Good God, had the man smothered himself in hot-water bottles before setting out for the evening?

Hyacinth picked up her program as discreetly as she was able and used it to fan herself.

"Is something amiss, Miss Bridgerton?" he inquired, tilting his head as he regarded her with curious amusement.

"Of course not," she answered. "It's merely a touch warm in here, don't you think?"

He eyed her for one second longer than she would have liked, then turned to Lady Danbury. "Are you overheated, Grandmother?" he asked solicitously.

"Not at all," came the brisk reply.

He turned back to Hyacinth with a tiny shrug. "It must be you," he murmured.

"It must," she ground out, facing determinedly forward. Maybe there still was time to escape to the ladies' retiring room. Penelope would want to have her drawn and quartered, but did it really count as abandonment when there were two people seated between them? Besides, she could surely use Lord Somershall as an excuse. Even now he was shifting in his seat, bumping up against her in a way that Hyacinth wasn't entirely certain was accidental.

Hyacinth shifted slightly to the right. Just an inch—not even. The last thing she wanted was to be pressed up against Gareth St. Clair. Well, the second-to-last, anyway. Lord Somershall's portly frame was decidedly worse.

"Is something amiss, Miss Bridgerton?" Mr. St. Clair inquired.

She shook her head, getting ready to push herself up by planting the heels of her hands on the chair on either side of her lap. She couldn't—

Clap.

Clap clap clap.

Hyacinth nearly groaned. It was one of the Ladies Smythe-Smith, signaling that the concert was about to begin. She'd lost her moment of opportunity. There was no way she could depart politely now.

But at least she could take some solace in the fact that she wasn't the only miserable soul. Just as the Misses Smythe-Smith lifted their bows to strike their instruments, she heard Mr. St. Clair let out a very quiet groan, followed by a heartfelt, "God help us all."

Chapter 2

Thirty minutes later, and somewhere not too far away, a small dog is howling in agony. Unfortunately, no one can hear him over the din . . .

There was only one person in the world for whom Gareth would sit politely and listen to really bad music, and Grandmother Danbury happened to be it.

"Never again," he whispered in her ear, as something that might have been Mozart assaulted his ears. This, after something that might have been Haydn, which had followed something that might have been Handel.

"You're not sitting politely," she whispered back.

"We could have sat in the back," he grumbled.

"And missed all the fun?"

How anyone could term a Smythe-Smith musicale fun was beyond him, but his grandmother had what could only be termed a morbid love for the annual affair.

As usual, four Smythe-Smith girls were seated on a small dais, two with violins, one with a cello, and one at a pianoforte, and the noise they were making was so discordant as to be almost impressive.

Almost.

"It's a good thing I love you," he said over his shoulder.

"Ha," came her reply, no less truculent for its whispered tone. "It's a good thing I love *you*."

And then—thank God—it was over, and the girls were nodding and making their curtsies, three of them looking quite pleased with themselves, and one—the one on the cello—looking as if she might like to hurl herself through a window.

Gareth turned when he heard his grandmother sigh. She was shaking her head and looking uncharacteristically sympathetic.

The Smythe-Smith girls were notorious in London, and each performance was somehow, inexplicably, worse than the last. Just when one thought there was no possible way to make a deeper mockery of Mozart, a new set of Smythe-Smith cousins appeared on the scene, and proved that yes, it could be done.

But they were nice girls, or so he'd been told, and his grandmother, in one of her rare fits of unabashed kindness, insisted that someone had to sit in the front row and clap, because, as she put it, "Three of them couldn't tell an elephant from a flute, but there's always one who is ready to melt in misery."

And apparently Grandmother Danbury, who thought nothing of telling a duke that he hadn't the sense of a gnat, found it vitally important to clap for the one Smythe-Smith girl in each generation whose ear wasn't made of tin.

They all stood to applaud, although he suspected his grandmother did so only to have an excuse to retrieve her cane, which Hyacinth Bridgerton had handed over with no protest whatsoever.

"Traitor," he'd murmured over his shoulder.

"They're your toes," she'd replied.

He cracked a smile, despite himself. He had never met anyone quite like Hyacinth Bridgerton. She was vaguely amusing, vaguely annoying, but one couldn't quite help but admire her wit.

Hyacinth Bridgerton, he reflected, had an interesting and unique reputation among London socialites. She was the youngest of the Bridgerton siblings, famously named in alphabetical order, A-H. And she was, in theory at least and for those who cared about such things, considered a rather good catch for matrimony. She had never been involved, even tangentially, in a scandal, and her family and connections were beyond compare. She was quite pretty, in wholesome, unexotic way, with thick, chestnut hair and blue eyes that did little to hide her shrewdness. And perhaps most importantly, Gareth thought with a touch of the cynic, it was whispered that her eldest brother, Lord Bridgerton, had increased her dowry last year, after Hyacinth had completed her third London season without an acceptable proposal of marriage.

But when he had inquired about her—not, of course, because he was interested; rather he had wanted to learn more about this young lady who seemed to enjoy spending a great deal of time with his grandmother—his friends had all shuddered.

"Hyacinth Bridgerton?" one had echoed. "Surely not to marry? You must be mad."

Another had called her terrifying.

No one actually seemed to dislike her—there was a certain charm to her that kept her in everyone's good graces—but the consensus was that she was best in small doses. "Men don't like women who are more intelligent than they are," one of his shrewder friends had commented, "and Hyacinth Bridgerton isn't the sort to feign stupidity."

She was, Gareth had thought on more than one occasion, a younger version of his grandmother. And while there was no one in the world he adored more than Grandmother Danbury, as far as he was concerned, the world needed only one of her.

"Aren't you glad you came?" the elderly lady in question asked, her voice carrying quite well over the applause.

No one ever clapped as loudly as the Smythe-Smith audience. They were always so glad that it was over.

"Never again," Gareth said firmly.

"Of course not," his grandmother said, with just the right touch of condescension to show that she was lying through her teeth.

He turned and looked her squarely in the eye. "You will have to find someone else to accompany you next year."

"I wouldn't dream of asking you again," Grandmother Danbury said.

"You're lying."

"What a terrible thing to say to your beloved grandmother." She leaned slightly forward. "How did you know?"

He glanced at the cane, dormant in her hand. "You haven't waved that thing through the air once since you tricked Miss Bridgerton into returning it," he said.

"Nonsense," she said. "Miss Bridgerton is too sharp to be tricked, aren't you, Hyacinth?"

Hyacinth shifted forward so that she could see past him to the countess. "I beg your pardon?"

"Just say yes," Grandmother Danbury said. "It will vex him."

"Yes, of course, then," she said, smiling.

"And," his grandmother continued, as if that entire ridiculous exchange had not taken place, "I'll have you know that I am the soul of discretion when it comes to my cane."

Gareth gave her a look. "It's a wonder I still have my feet."

"It's a wonder you still have your ears, my dear boy," she said with lofty disdain.

"I will take that away again," he warned.

"No you won't," she replied with a cackle. "I'm leaving with Penelope to find a glass of lemonade. You keep Hyacinth company."

He watched her go, then turned back to Hyacinth, who was glancing about the room with slightly narrowed eyes.

"Who are you looking for?" he asked.

"No one in particular. Just examining the scene."

He looked at her curiously. "Do you always sound like a detective?"

"Only when it suits me," she said with a shrug. "I like to know what is going on."

"And is anything 'going on'?" he queried.

"No." Her eyes narrowed again as she watched two people in a heated discussion in the far corner. "But you never know."

He fought the urge to shake his head. She was the *strangest* woman. He glanced at the stage. "Are we safe?"

She finally turned back, her blue eyes meeting his with uncommon directness. "Do you mean is it over?"

"Yes."

Her brow furrowed, and in that moment Gareth realized that she had the lightest smattering of freckles on her nose. "I think so," she said. "I've never known them to hold an intermission before."

"Thank God," he said, with great feeling. "Why do they do it?"

"The Smythe-Smiths, you mean?"

"Yes."

For a moment she remained silent, then she just shook her head, and said, "I don't know. One would think . . ."

Whatever she'd been about to say, she thought the better of it. "Never mind," she said.

"Tell me," he urged, rather surprised by how curious he was.

"It was nothing," she said. "Just that one would think that someone would have told them by now. But actually . . ." She glanced around the room. "The audience has grown smaller in recent years. Only the kindhearted remain."

"And do you include yourself among those ranks, Miss Bridgerton?"

She looked up at him with those intensely blue eyes. "I wouldn't have thought to describe myself as such, but yes, I suppose I am. Your grandmother, too, although she would deny it to her dying breath."

Gareth felt himself laugh as he watched his grandmother poke the Duke of Ashbourne in the leg with her cane. "Yes, she would, wouldn't she?"

His maternal grandmother was, since the death of his brother George, the only person left in the world he truly loved. After his father had booted him out, he'd made his way to Danbury House in Surrey and told her what had transpired. Minus the bit about his bastardy, of course.

Gareth had always suspected that Lady Danbury would have stood up and cheered if she knew he wasn't really a St. Clair. She'd never liked her son-in-law, and in fact routinely referred to him as "that pompous idiot." But the truth would reveal his mother—Lady Danbury's youngest daughter—as an adulteress, and he hadn't wanted to dishonor her in that way.

And strangely enough, his father—funny how he still called him that, even after all these years—had never publicly denounced him. This had not surprised Gareth at first. Lord St. Clair was a proud man, and he certainly would not relish revealing himself as a cuckold. Plus, he probably still hoped that he might eventually rein Gareth in and bend him to his will. Maybe even get him to marry Mary Winthrop and restore the St. Clair family coffers.

But George had contracted some sort of wasting disease at the age of twenty-seven, and by thirty he was dead.

Without a son.

Which had made Gareth the St. Clair heir. And left him, quite simply, stuck. For the past eleven months, it seemed he had done nothing but wait. Sooner or later, his father was going to announce to all who would listen that Gareth wasn't really his son. Surely the baron, whose third-favorite pastime (after hunting and raising hounds) was tracing the St. Clair family tree back to the Plantagenets, would not countenance his title going to a bastard of uncertain blood.

Gareth was fairly certain that the only way the baron could remove him as his heir would be to haul him, and a pack of witnesses as well, before the Committee for Privileges in the House of Lords. It would be a messy, detestable affair, and it probably wouldn't work, either. The baron had been married to Gareth's mother when she had given birth, and that rendered Gareth legitimate in the eyes of the law, regardless of his bloodlines.

But it would cause a huge scandal and quite possibly ruin Gareth in the eyes of society. There were plenty of aristocrats running about who got their blood and their names from two different men, but the *ton* didn't like to talk about it. Not publicly, anyway.

But thus far, his father had said nothing.

Half the time Gareth wondered if the baron kept his silence just to torture him.

Gareth glanced across the room at his grandmother, who was accepting a glass of lemonade from Penelope Bridgerton, whom she'd somehow coerced into waiting on her hand and foot. Agatha, Lady Danbury, was most usually described as crotchety, and that was by the people who held her in some affection. She was a lioness among the *ton*, fearless in her words and willing to poke fun at the most august of personages, and even, occasionally, herself. But for all her acerbic ways, she was famously loyal to the ones she loved, and Gareth knew he ranked at the top of that list.

When he'd gone to her and told her that his father had turned him out, she had been livid, but she had never attempted to use her power as a countess to force Lord St. Clair to take back his son.

"Ha!" his grandmother had said. "I'd rather keep you myself."

And she had. She'd paid Gareth's expenses at Cambridge, and when he'd graduated (not with a first, but he had acquitted himself well), she had informed him that his mother had left him a small bequest. Gareth hadn't been aware that she'd had any money of her own, but Lady Danbury had just twisted her lips and said, "Do you really think I'd let that idiot have complete control of her money? I wrote the marriage settlement, you know."

Gareth didn't doubt it for an instant.

His inheritance gave him a small income, which funded a very small suite of apartments, and Gareth was able to support himself. Not lavishly, but well enough to make him feel he wasn't a complete wastrel, which, he was surprised to realize, mattered more to him than he would have thought.

This uncharacteristic sense of responsibility was probably a good thing, too, since when he did assume the St. Clair title, he was going to inherit a mountain of debt along with it. The baron had obviously been lying when he'd told Gareth that they would lose everything that wasn't entailed if he didn't marry Mary Winthrop, but still, it was clear that the St. Clair fortune was meager at best. Furthermore, Lord St. Clair didn't appear to be managing the family finances any better than he had when he'd tried to force Gareth into marriage. If anything, he seemed to be systematically running the estates into the ground.

It was the one thing that made Gareth wonder if perhaps the

baron *didn't* intend to denounce him. Surely the ultimate revenge would be to leave his false son riddled with debt.

And Gareth knew—with every fiber of his being he knew—that the baron wished him no happiness. Gareth didn't bother with most *ton* functions, but London wasn't such a large city, socially speaking, and he couldn't always manage to avoid his father completely. And Lord St. Clair never made any effort to hide his enmity.

As for Gareth—well, he wasn't much better at keeping his feelings to himself. He always seemed to slip into his old ways, doing something deliberately provoking, just to make the baron angry. The last time they'd found themselves in each other's company, Gareth had laughed too loudly, then danced far too closely with a notoriously merry widow.

Lord St. Clair had turned very red in the face, then hissed something about Gareth being no better than he should be. Gareth hadn't been exactly certain to what his father had been referring, and the baron had been drunk, in any case. But it had left him with one powerful certainty—

Eventually, the other shoe was going to drop. When Gareth least expected it, or perhaps, now that he'd grown so suspicious, precisely when he most suspected it. But as soon as Gareth attempted to make a change in his life, to move forward, to move up . . .

That was when the baron would make his move. Gareth was sure of it.

And his world was going to come crashing down.

"Mr. St. Clair?"

Gareth blinked and turned to Hyacinth Bridgerton, whom, he realized somewhat sheepishly, he'd been ignoring in favor of his own thoughts. "So sorry," he murmured, giving her the slow and easy smile that seemed to work so well when he needed to placate a female. "I was woolgathering."

At her dubious expression, he added, "I *do* think from time to time."

She smiled, clearly despite herself, but he counted that as a success. The day he couldn't make a woman smile was the day he ought to just give up on life and move to the Outer Hebrides.

"Under normal circumstances," he said, since the occasion seemed to call for polite conversation, "I would ask if you enjoyed the musicale, but somehow that seems cruel."

She shifted slightly in her seat, which was interesting, since most young ladies were trained from a very young age to hold themselves with perfect stillness. Gareth found himself liking her the better for her restless energy; he, too, was the sort to find himself drumming his fingers against a tabletop when he didn't realize it.

He watched her face, waiting for her to reply, but all she did was look vaguely uncomfortable. Finally, she leaned forward and whispered, "Mr. St. Clair?"

He leaned in as well, giving her a conspiratorial quirk of his brow. "Miss Bridgerton?"

"Would you mind terribly if we took a turn about the room?"

He waited just long enough to catch her motioning over her shoulder with the tiniest of nods. Lord Somershall was wiggling slightly in his chair, and his copious form was edged right up next to Hyacinth.

"Of course," Gareth said gallantly, rising to his feet and offering her his arm. "I need to save Lord Somershall, after all," he said, once they had moved several paces away.

Her eyes snapped to his face. "I beg your pardon?"

"If I were a betting man," he said, "I'd lay the odds four-to-one in your favor."

For about half a second she looked confused, and then her face slid into a satisfied smile. "You mean you're not a betting man?" she asked.

He laughed. "I haven't the blunt to be a betting man," he said quite honestly.

"That doesn't seem to stop most men," she said pertly.

"Or most women," he said, with a tilt of his head.

"*Touché*," she murmured, glancing about the room. "We are a gambling people, aren't we?"

"And what about you, Miss Bridgerton? Do you like to wager?"

"Of course," she said, surprising him with her candor. "But only when I know I will win."

He chuckled. "Strangely enough," he said, guiding her toward the refreshment table, "I believe you."

"Oh, you should," she said blithely. "Ask anyone who knows me."

"Wounded again," he said, offering her his most engaging smile. "I thought *I* knew you."

She opened her mouth, then looked shocked that she didn't have a reply. Gareth took pity on her and handed her a glass of lemonade. "Drink up," he murmured. "You look thirsty."

He chuckled as she glowered at him over the rim of her glass, which of course only made her redouble her efforts to incinerate him with her glare.

There was something very amusing about Hyacinth Bridgerton, he decided. She was smart—very smart—but she had a certain air about her, as if she was used to always being the most intelligent person in the room. It wasn't unattractive; she was quite charming in her own way, and he imagined that she would have to have learned to speak her own mind in order to be heard in her family—she was the youngest of eight, after all.

But it did mean that he rather enjoyed seeing her at a loss for words. It was *fun* to befuddle her. Gareth didn't know why he didn't make a point of doing it more often.

He watched as she set her glass down. "Tell me, Mr. St. Clair," she said, "what did your grandmother say to you to convince you to attend this evening?"

"You don't believe I came of my own free will?"

She lifted one brow. He was impressed. He'd never known a female who could do that.

"Very well," he said, "there was a great deal of hand fluttering, then something about a visit to her physician, and then I believe she sighed."

"Just once?"

He quirked a brow back at her. "I'm made of stronger stuff than that, Miss Bridgerton. It took a full half hour to break me."

She nodded. "You *are* good."

He leaned toward her and smiled. "At many things," he murmured.

She blushed, which pleased him mightily, but then she said, "I've been warned about men like you."

"I certainly hope so."

She laughed. "I don't think you're nearly as dangerous as you'd like to be thought."

He tilted his head to the side. "And why is that?"

She didn't answer right away, just caught her lower lip between her teeth as she pondered her words. "You're far too kind to your grandmother," she finally said.

"Some would say she's too kind to me."

"Oh, many people say that," Hyacinth said with a shrug.

He choked on his lemonade. "You haven't a coy bone in your body, do you?"

Hyacinth glanced across the room at Penelope and Lady Danbury before turning back to him. "I keep trying, but no, apparently not. I imagine it's why I am still unmarried."

He smiled. "Surely not."

"Oh, indeed," she said, even though it was clear he was funning her. "Men need to be trapped into marriage, whether they realize it or not. And I seem to be completely lacking in the ability."

He grinned. "You mean you're not underhanded and sly?"

"I'm both those things," she admitted, "just not subtle."

"No," he murmured, and she couldn't decide whether his agreement bothered her or not.

"But tell me," he continued, "for I'm most curious. Why do you think men must be trapped into marriage?"

"Would *you* go willingly to the altar?"

"No, but—"

"You see? I am affirmed." And somehow that made her feel a great deal better.

"Shame on you, Miss Bridgerton," he said. "It's not very sporting of you not to allow me to finish my statement."

She cocked her head. "Did you have anything interesting to say?"

He smiled, and Hyacinth felt it down to her toes. "I'm always interesting," he murmured.

"*Now* you're just trying to scare me." She didn't know where this was coming from, this crazy sense of daring. Hyacinth wasn't shy, and she certainly wasn't as demure as she ought to have been, but nor was she foolhardy. And Gareth St. Clair was not the sort of man with whom one ought to trifle. She was playing with fire, and she knew it, but somehow she couldn't stop herself. It was as if each statement from his lips was a dare, and she had to use her every faculty just to keep up.

If this was a competition, she wanted to win.

And if any of her flaws was going to prove to be fatal, this was surely it.

"Miss Bridgerton," he said, "the devil himself couldn't scare you."

She forced her eyes to meet his. "That's not a compliment, is it?"

He lifted her hand to his lips, brushing a feather-light kiss across her knuckles. "You'll have to figure that out for yourself," he murmured.

To all who observed, he was the soul of propriety, but Hyacinth caught the daring gleam in his eye, and she felt the breath leave her body as tingles of electricity rushed across her skin. Her lips parted, but she had nothing to say, not a single word. There was nothing but air, and even that seemed in short supply.

And then he straightened as if nothing had happened and said, "Do let me know what you decide."

She just stared at him.

"About the compliment," he added. "I am sure you will wish to let me know how I feel about you."

Her mouth fell open.

He smiled. Broadly. "Speechless, even. I'm to be commended."

"You—"

"No. No," he said, lifting one hand in the air and pointing toward her as if what he really wanted to do was place his finger on her lips and shush her. "Don't ruin it. The moment is too rare."

And she could have said something. She should have said something. But all she could do was stand there like an idiot, or if not that, then like someone completely unlike herself.

"Until next time, Miss Bridgerton," he murmured.

And then he was gone.

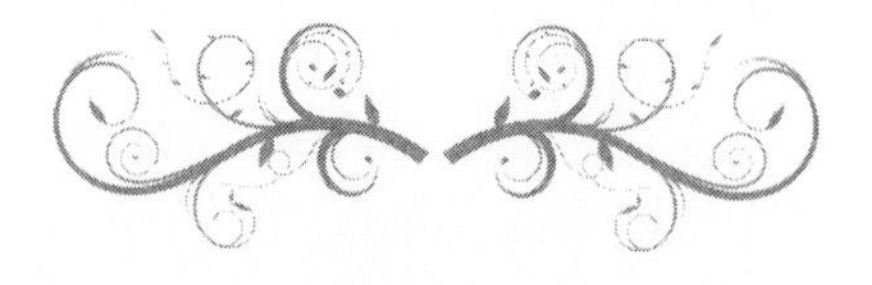

Chapter 3

Three days later, and our hero learns that one can never really escape one's past.

"There is a woman to see you, sir."

Gareth looked up from his desk, a huge mahogany behemoth that took up nearly half of his small study. "A woman, you say?"

His new valet nodded. "She said she is your brother's wife."

"Caroline?" Gareth's attention snapped into sharp focus. "Show her in. Immediately."

He rose to his feet, awaiting her arrival in his study. He hadn't seen Caroline in months, only once since George's funeral, truth be told. And Lord knew that hadn't been a joyful affair. Gareth had spent the entire time avoiding his father, which had added stress on top of his already crushing grief.

Lord St. Clair had ordered George to cease all brotherly relations with Gareth, but George had never cut him off. In all else, George had obeyed his father, but never that. And Gareth had loved him all the more for it. The baron hadn't wanted Gareth to attend the ceremony, but when Gareth had pushed his way into the church, even he hadn't been willing to make a scene and have him evicted.

"Gareth?"

He turned away from the window, unaware that he'd even been looking out. "Caroline," he said warmly, crossing the room to greet his sister-in-law. "How have you been?"

She gave a helpless little shrug. Hers had been a love match, and Gareth had never seen anything quite as devastating as Caroline's eyes at her husband's funeral.

"I know," Gareth said quietly. He missed George, too. They had been an unlikely pair—George, sober and serious, and Gareth, who had always run wild. But they had been friends as well as brothers, and Gareth liked to think that they had complemented each other. Lately Gareth had been thinking that he ought to try to lead a somewhat tamer life, and he had been looking to his brother's memory to guide his actions.

"I was going through his things," Caroline said. "I found something. I believe that it is yours."

Gareth watched curiously as she reached into her satchel and pulled out a small book. "I don't recognize it," he said.

"No," Caroline replied, handing it to him. "You wouldn't. It belonged to your father's mother."

Your father's mother. Gareth couldn't quite prevent his grimace. Caroline did not know that Gareth was not truly a St. Clair. Gareth had never been certain if George had known the truth, either. If he had, he'd never said anything.

The book was small, bound with brown leather. There was a little strap that reached from back to front, where it could be fastened with a button. Gareth carefully undid it and turned the book open, taking extra care with the aged paper. "It's a diary," he said with surprise. And then he had to smile. It was written in Italian. "What does it say?"

"I don't know," Caroline said. "I didn't even know it existed until I found it in George's desk earlier this week. He never mentioned it."

Gareth looked down at the diary, at the elegant handwriting forming words he could not understand. His father's mother had been the daughter of a noble Italian house. It had always amused Gareth that his father was half-Italian; the baron was so insufferably proud of his St. Clair ancestry and liked to boast that they had been in England since the Norman Invasion. In fact, Gareth couldn't recall him ever making mention of his Italian roots.

"There was a note from George," Caroline said, "instructing me to give this to you."

Gareth glanced back down at the book, his heart heavy. Just one more indication that George had never known that they were not full brothers. Gareth bore no blood relationship to Isabella Marinzoli St. Clair, and he had no real right to her diary.

"You shall have to find someone to translate it," Caroline said with a small, wistful smile. "I'm curious as to what it says. George always spoke so warmly of your grandmother."

Gareth nodded. He remembered her fondly as well, though they hadn't spent very much time together. Lord St. Clair hadn't gotten on very well with his mother, so Isabella did not visit very often. But she had always doted upon her *due ragazzi*, as she liked to call her two grandsons, and Gareth recalled feeling quite crushed when, at the age of seven, he'd heard that she had died. If affection was anywhere near as important as blood, then he supposed the diary would find a better home in his hands than anyone else's.

"I'll see what I can do," Gareth said. "It can't be that difficult to find someone who can translate from the Italian."

"I wouldn't trust it to just anyone," Caroline said. "It is your grandmother's diary, after all. Her personal thoughts."

Gareth nodded. Caroline was right. He owed it to Isabella to find someone discreet to translate her memoirs. And he knew exactly where to start in his search.

"I'll take this to Grandmother Danbury," Gareth suddenly said, allowing his hand to bob up and down with the diary, almost as if he was testing its weight. "She'll know what to do."

And she would, he thought. Grandmother Danbury liked to say that she knew everything, and the annoying truth was, she was most often right.

"Do let me know what you find out," Caroline said, as she headed for the door.

"Of course," he murmured, even though she was already gone. He looked down at the book. *10 Settembre, 1793 . . .*

Gareth shook his head and smiled. It figured his one bequest from the St. Clair family coffers would be a diary he couldn't even read.

Ah, irony.

Meanwhile, in a drawing room not so very far away . . .

"Enh?" Lady Danbury screeched. "You're not speaking loudly enough!"

Hyacinth allowed the book from which she was reading to fall closed, with just her index finger stuck inside to mark her place. Lady Danbury liked to feign deafness when it suited her, and it seemed to suit her every time Hyacinth got to the racy parts of the lurid novels that the countess enjoyed so well.

"I said," Hyacinth said, leveling her gaze onto Lady Danbury's face, "that our dear heroine was breathing hard, no, let me check, she was *breathy* and *short of breath*." She looked up. "Breathy *and* short of breath?"

"Pfft," Lady Danbury said, waving her hand dismissively.

Hyacinth glanced at the cover of the book. "I wonder if English is the author's first language?"

"Keep reading," Lady D ordered.

"Very well, let me see, *Miss Bumblehead ran like the wind as she saw Lord Savagewood coming toward her*."

Lady Danbury narrowed her eyes. "Her name isn't Bumblehead."

"It ought to be," Hyacinth muttered.

"Well, that's true," Lady D agreed, "but we didn't write the story, did we?"

Hyacinth cleared her throat and once again found her place in the text. "*He was coming closer*," she read, "*and Miss Bumbleshoot—*"

"Hyacinth!"

"Butterworth," Hyacinth grumbled. "Whatever her name is, she ran for the cliffs. End of chapter."

"The cliffs? Still? Wasn't she running at the end of the last chapter?"

"Perhaps it's a long way."

Lady Danbury narrowed her eyes. "I don't believe you."

Hyacinth shrugged. "It is certainly true that I would lie to you to get out of reading the next few paragraphs of Priscilla Butterworth's remarkably perilous life, but as it happens, I'm telling the truth." When Lady D didn't say anything, Hyacinth held out the book, and asked, "Would you like to check for yourself?"

"No, no," Lady Danbury said, with a great show of acceptance. "I believe you, if only because I have no choice."

Hyacinth gave her a pointed look. "Are you blind now, as well as deaf?"

"No." Lady D sighed, letting one hand flutter until it rested palm out on her forehead. "Just practicing my high drama."

Hyacinth laughed out loud.

"I do not jest," Lady Danbury said, her voice returning to its usual sharp tenor. "And I am thinking of making a change in life. I could do a better job on the stage than most of those fools who call themselves actresses."

"Sadly," Hyacinth said, "there doesn't seem to be much demand for aging countess roles."

"If anyone else said that to me," Lady D said, thumping her cane against the floor even though she was seated in a perfectly good chair, "I'd take it as an insult."

"But not from me?" Hyacinth queried, trying to sound disappointed.

Lady Danbury chuckled. "Do you know why I like you so well, Hyacinth Bridgerton?"

Hyacinth leaned forward. "I'm all agog."

Lady D's face spread into a creased smile. "Because you, dear girl, are exactly like me."

"Do you know, Lady Danbury," Hyacinth said, "if you said that to anyone else, she'd probably take it as an insult."

Lady D's thin body quivered with mirth. "But not you?"

Hyacinth shook her head. "Not me."

"Good." Lady Danbury gave her an uncharacteristically grandmotherly smile, then glanced up at the clock on the mantel. "We've time for another chapter, I think."

"We agreed, one chapter each Tuesday," Hyacinth said, mostly just to be vexing.

Lady D's mouth settled into a grumpy line. "Very well, then," she said, eyeing Hyacinth in a sly manner, "we'll talk about something else."

Oh, dear.

"Tell me, Hyacinth," Lady Danbury said, leaning forward, "how are your prospects these days?"

"You sound like my mother," Hyacinth said sweetly.

"A compliment of the highest order," Lady D tossed back. "I like your mother, and I hardly like anyone."

"I'll be sure to tell her."

"Bah. She knows that already, and you're avoiding the question."

"My prospects," Hyacinth replied, "as you so delicately put it, are the same as ever."

"Such is the problem. You, my dear girl, need a husband."

"Are you quite certain my mother isn't hiding behind the curtains, feeding you lines?"

"See?" Lady Danbury said with a wide smile. "I *would* be good on the stage."

Hyacinth just stared at her. "You have gone quite mad, did you know that?"

"Bah. I'm merely old enough to get away with speaking my mind. You'll enjoy it when you're my age, I promise."

"I enjoy it now," Hyacinth said.

"True," Lady Danbury conceded. "And it's probably why you're still unmarried."

"If there were an intelligent unattached man in London," Hyacinth said with a beleaguered sigh, "I assure you I would set my cap for him." She let her head cock to the side with a sarcastic tilt. "Surely you wouldn't see me married to a fool."

"Of course not, but—"

"And *stop* mentioning your grandson as if I weren't intelligent enough to figure out what you're up to."

Lady D gasped in full huff. "I didn't say a *word*."

"You were about to."

"Well, he's perfectly nice," Lady Danbury muttered, not even trying to deny it, "and more than handsome."

Hyacinth caught her lower lip between her teeth, trying not to remember how very strange she'd felt at the Smythe-Smith musicale with Mr. St. Clair at her side. That was the problem with him, she realized. She didn't feel like herself when he was near. And it was the most disconcerting thing.

"I see you don't disagree," Lady D said.

"About your grandson's handsome visage? Of course not," Hyacinth replied, since there was little point in debating it. There were some people for whom good looks were a fact, not an opinion.

"And," Lady Danbury continued in grand fashion, "I'm happy to say that he inherited his brain from *my* side of the family, which, I might regretfully add, isn't the case with all of my progeny."

Hyacinth glanced up at the ceiling in an attempt to avoid comment. Lady Danbury's eldest son had famously gotten his head stuck between the bars of the front gate of Windsor Castle.

"Oh, go ahead and say it," Lady D grumbled. "At least two of my children are half-wits, and heaven knows about *their* children. I flee in the opposite direction when they come to town."

"I would never—"

"Well, you were thinking it, and rightly you should. Serves me right for marrying Lord Danbury when I knew he hadn't two thoughts to bang together in his head. But Gareth *is* a prize, and you're a fool if you don't—"

"Your grandson," Hyacinth cut in, "isn't the least bit interested in me or any marriageable female, for that matter."

"Well, that *is* a problem," Lady Danbury agreed, "and for the life of me, I don't know why the boy shuns your sort."

"My *sort*?" Hyacinth echoed.

"Young, female, and someone he would actually have to marry if he dallied with."

Hyacinth felt her cheeks burn. Normally this would be exactly the sort of conversation she relished—it was far more fun to be improper than otherwise, within reason, of course—but this time it was all she could do to say, "I hardly think you should be discussing such things with me."

"Bah," Lady D said, gesturing dismissively with her hand. "Since when have you become so missish?"

Hyacinth opened her mouth, but thankfully, Lady Danbury didn't seem to desire an answer. "He's a rogue, it's true," the countess sailed on, "but it's nothing you can't overcome if you put your mind to it."

"I'm not going to—"

"Just yank your dress down a little when next you see him," Lady D cut in, waving her hand impatiently in front of her face. "Men lose all sense at the sight of a healthy bosom. You'll have him—"

"Lady Danbury!" Hyacinth crossed her arms. She did have her pride, and she wasn't about to go chasing after a rake who clearly had no interest in marriage. That sort of public humiliation she could do without.

And besides, it would require a great deal of imagination to describe her bosom as healthy. Hyacinth knew she wasn't built like a boy, thank goodness, but nor did she possess attributes that would cause any man to look twice in the area directly below her neck.

"Oh, very well," Lady Danbury said, sounding exceedingly grumpy, which, for her, was exceeding indeed. "I won't say another word."

"Ever?"

"Until," Lady D said firmly.

"Until when?" Hyacinth asked suspiciously.

"I don't know," Lady Danbury replied, in much the same tone.

Which Hyacinth had a feeling meant five minutes hence.

The countess was silent for a moment, but her lips were pursed, signaling that her mind was up to something that was probably devious in the extreme. "Do you know what I think?" she asked.

"Usually," Hyacinth replied.

Lady D scowled. "You are entirely too mouthy."

Hyacinth just smiled and ate another biscuit.

"I think," Lady Danbury said, apparently over her pique, "that we should write a book."

To Hyacinth's credit, she didn't choke on her food. "I beg your pardon?"

"I need a challenge," Lady D said. "Keeps the mind sharp. And surely we could do better than *Miss Butterworth and the Mealy-mouthed Baron*."

"*Mad Baron*," Hyacinth said automatically.

"Precisely," Lady D said. "Surely we can do better."

"I'm sure we could, but it does beg the question—why would we want to?"

"Because we *can*."

Hyacinth considered the prospect of a creative liaison with Lady Danbury, of spending hours upon hours—

"No," she said, quite firmly, "we can't."

"Of course we can," Lady D said, thumping her cane for what was only the second time during the interview—surely a new record of restraint. "I'll think up the ideas, and you can figure out how to word it all."

"It doesn't sound like an equitable division of labor," Hyacinth remarked.

"And why should it be?"

Hyacinth opened her mouth to reply, then decided there was really no point.

Lady Danbury frowned for a moment, then finally added, "Well, think about my proposal. We'd make an excellent team."

"I shudder to think," came a deep voice from the doorway, "what you might be attempting to browbeat poor Miss Bridgerton into now."

"Gareth!" Lady Danbury said with obvious pleasure. "How nice of you *finally* to come visit me."

Hyacinth turned. Gareth St. Clair had just stepped into the room, looking alarmingly handsome in his elegant afternoon clothing. A shaft of sunlight was streaming through the window, landing on his hair like burnished gold.

His presence was most surprising. Hyacinth had been visiting every Tuesday for a year now, and this was only the second time their paths had crossed. She had begun to think he might be purposefully avoiding her.

Which begged the question—why was he here now? Their conversation at the Smythe-Smith musicale was the first they had ever shared that went beyond the most basic of pleasantries, and suddenly he was here in his grandmother's drawing room, right in the middle of their weekly visit.

"Finally?" Mr. St. Clair echoed with amusement. "Surely you haven't forgotten my visit last Friday." He turned to Hyacinth, his face taking on a rather convincing expression of concern. "Do you think she might be beginning to lose her memory, Miss Bridgerton? She is, what can it be now, ninety—"

Lady D's cane came down squarely on his toes. "Not even close, my dear boy," she barked, "and if you value your appendages, you shan't blaspheme in such a manner again."

"The Gospel according to Agatha Danbury," Hyacinth murmured.

Mr. St. Clair flashed her a grin, which surprised her, first because she hadn't thought he would hear her remark, and second because it made him seem so boyish and innocent, when she knew for a fact that he was neither.

Although . . .

Hyacinth fought the urge to shake her head. There was always an *although*. Lady D's "finallys" aside, Gareth St. Clair *was* a frequent visitor at Danbury House. It made Hyacinth wonder if he was truly the rogue society made him out to be. No true devil would be so devoted to his grandmother. She'd said as much at the Smythe-Smith musicale, but he'd deftly changed the subject.

He was a puzzle. And Hyacinth hated puzzles.

Well, no, in truth she loved them.

Provided, of course, that she solved them.

The puzzle in question ambled across the room, leaning down to drop a kiss on his grandmother's cheek. Hyacinth found herself staring at the back of his neck, at the rakish queue of hair brushing up against the edge of his bottle green coat.

She knew he hadn't a great deal of money for tailors and such, and she knew he never asked his grandmother for anything, but lud, that coat fit him to perfection.

"Miss Bridgerton," he said, settling onto the sofa and allowing one ankle to rest rather lazily on the opposite knee. "It must be Tuesday."

"It must," Hyacinth agreed.

"How fares Priscilla Butterworth?"

Hyacinth lifted her brows, surprised that he knew which book they were reading. "She is running for the cliffs," she replied.

"I fear for her safety, if you must know. Or rather, I would," she added, "if there were not eleven chapters still to be read."

"Pity," he remarked. "The book would take a far more interesting turn if she was killed off."

"Have you read it, then?" Hyacinth queried politely.

For a moment it seemed he would do nothing but give her a *Surely You Jest* look, but he punctuated the expression with, "My grandmother likes to recount the tale when I see her each Wednesday. Which I *always do*," he added, sending a heavy-lidded glance in Lady Danbury's direction. "And most Fridays and Sundays as well."

"Not last Sunday," Lady D said.

"I went to church," he deadpanned.

Hyacinth choked on her biscuit.

He turned to her. "Didn't you see the lightning strike the steeple?"

She recovered with a sip of tea, then smiled sweetly. "I was listening too devotedly to the sermon."

"Claptrap last week," Lady D announced. "I think the priest is getting old."

Gareth opened his mouth, but before he could say a word, his grandmother's cane swung around in a remarkably steady horizontal arc. "Don't," she warned, "make a comment beginning with the words, 'Coming from you . . . ' "

"I wouldn't dream of it," he demurred.

"Of course you would," she stated. "You wouldn't be my grandson if you wouldn't." She turned to Hyacinth. "Don't you agree?"

To her credit, Hyacinth folded her hands in her lap and said, "Surely there is no right answer to that question."

"Smart girl," Lady D said approvingly.

"I learn from the master."

Lady Danbury beamed. "Insolence aside," she continued determinedly, gesturing toward Gareth as if he were some sort of zoological specimen, "he really is an exceptional grandson. Couldn't have asked for more."

Gareth watched with amusement as Hyacinth murmured something that was meant to convey her agreement without actually doing so.

"Of course," Grandmother Danbury added with a dismissive wave of her hand, "he hasn't much in the way of competition. The rest of them have only three brains to share among them."

Not the most ringing of endorsements, considering that she had twelve living grandchildren.

"I've heard some animals eat their young," Gareth murmured, to no one in particular.

"This being a *Tuesday*," his grandmother said, ignoring his comment completely, "what brings you by?"

Gareth wrapped his fingers around the book in his pocket. He'd been so intrigued by its existence since Caroline had handed it over that he had completely forgotten about his grandmother's weekly visit with Hyacinth Bridgerton. If he'd been thinking clearly, he would have waited until later in the afternoon, after she had departed.

But now he was here, and he had to give them some reason for his presence. Otherwise—God help him—his grandmother would assume he'd come *because* of Miss Bridgerton, and it would take months to dissuade her of the notion.

"What is it, boy?" his grandmother asked, in her inimitable way. "Speak up."

Gareth turned to Hyacinth, slightly pleased when she squirmed a little under his intent stare. "Why do you visit my grandmother?" he asked.

She shrugged. "Because I like her."

And then she leaned forward and asked, "Why do *you* visit her?"

"Because she's my—" He stopped, caught himself. He didn't visit just because she was his grandmother. Lady Danbury was a number of things to him—trial, termagant, and bane of his existence sprang to mind—but never a duty. "I like her, too," he said slowly, his eyes never leaving Hyacinth's.

She didn't blink. "Good."

And then they just stared at each other, as if trapped in some sort of bizarre contest.

"Not that I have any complaints with this particular avenue of conversation," Lady Danbury said loudly, "but what the devil are the two of you talking about?"

Hyacinth sat back and looked at Lady Danbury as if nothing had happened. "I have no idea," she said blithely, and proceeded to sip at her tea. Setting the cup back in its saucer, she added, "He asked me a question."

Gareth watched her curiously. His grandmother wasn't the easiest person to befriend, and if Hyacinth Bridgerton happily sacrificed her Tuesday afternoons to be with her, that was certainly a point in her favor. Not to mention that Lady Danbury hardly liked anyone, and she raved about Miss Bridgerton at every possible opportunity. It was, of course, partly because she was trying to pair the two of them up; his grandmother had never been known for her tact or subtlety.

But still, if Gareth had learned one thing over the years, it was that his grandmother was a shrewd judge of character. And besides, the diary was written in Italian. Even if it did contain some indiscreet secret, Miss Bridgerton would hardly know.

His decision made, he reached into his pocket and pulled out the book.

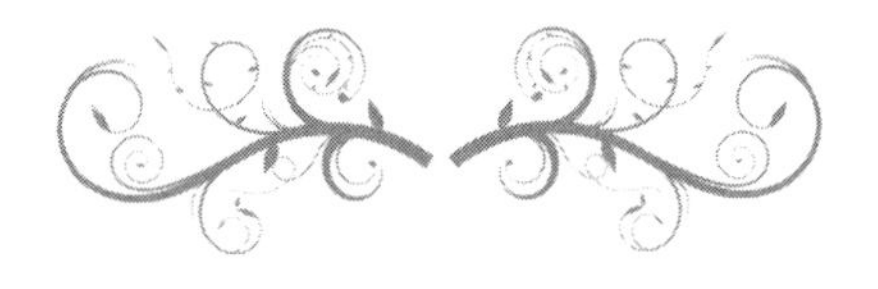

Chapter 4

At which point Hyacinth's life finally becomes almost as exciting as Priscilla Butterworth's. Minus the cliffs, of course . . .

Hyacinth watched with interest as Mr. St. Clair appeared to hesitate. He glanced over at her, his clear blue eyes narrowing almost imperceptibly before he turned back to his grandmother. Hyacinth tried not to look too interested; he was obviously trying to decide if he should mention his business in her presence, and she suspected that any interference on her part would cause him to keep his counsel.

But apparently she passed muster, because after a brief moment of silence, he reached into his pocket and pulled out what appeared to be a small, leather-bound book.

"What is this?" Lady Danbury asked, taking it into her hands.

"Grandmother St. Clair's diary," he replied. "Caroline brought it over this afternoon. She found it among George's effects."

"It's in Italian," Lady D said.

"Yes, I was aware."

"I meant, why did you bring it to *me*?" she asked, somewhat impatiently.

Mr. St. Clair gave her a lazy half smile. "You are always telling me you know everything, or if not everything, then everyone."

"You said that to me earlier this afternoon," Hyacinth put in helpfully.

Mr. St. Clair turned to her with a vaguely patronizing, "Thank you," which arrived at precisely the same moment as Lady Danbury's glare.

Hyacinth squirmed. Not at Lady D's glare—she was quite impervious to those. But she hated this feeling that Mr. St. Clair thought her deserving of condescension.

"I was hoping," he said to his grandmother, "that you might know of a reputable translator."

"For Italian?"

"It would seem to be the required language."

"Hmmph." Lady D tap tap tapped her cane against the carpet, much the way a normal person would drum fingers atop a table. "Italian? Not nearly as ubiquitous as French, which of course any decent person would—"

"I can read Italian," Hyacinth interrupted.

Two identical pairs of blue eyes swung her direction.

"You're joking," Mr. St. Clair said, coming in a mere half second before his grandmother barked, "You can?"

"You don't know everything about me," Hyacinth said archly. To Lady Danbury, of course, since Mr. St. Clair could hardly make that claim.

"Well, yes, of course," Lady D blustered, "but Italian?"

"I had an Italian governess when I was small," Hyacinth said with a shrug. "It amused her to teach me. I'm not fluent," she allowed, "but given a page or two, I can make out the general meaning."

"This is quite more than a page or two," Mr. St. Clair said, tilting his head toward the diary, which still rested in his grandmother's hands.

"Clearly," Hyacinth replied peevishly. "But I'm not likely to read more than a page or two at a time. And she didn't write it in the style of the ancient Romans, did she?"

"That would be Latin," Mr. St. Clair drawled.

Hyacinth clamped her teeth together. "Nevertheless*less*," she ground out.

"For the love of God, boy," Lady Danbury cut in, "give her the book."

Mr. St. Clair forbore to point out that she was still holding it, which Hyacinth thought showed remarkable restraint on his part. Instead, he rose to his feet, plucked the slim volume from his grandmother's hands, and turned toward Hyacinth. He hesitated then—just for a moment, and Hyacinth would have missed it had she been looking anywhere but directly at his face.

He brought the book to her then, holding it out with a softly murmured, "Miss Bridgerton."

Hyacinth accepted it, shivering against the odd feeling that she had just done something far more powerful than merely taking a book into her hands.

"Are you cold, Miss Bridgerton?" Mr. St. Clair murmured.

She shook her head, using the book as a means to avoid looking at him. "The pages are slightly brittle," she said, carefully turning one.

"What does it say?" Mr. St. Clair asked.

Hyacinth gritted her teeth. It was never fun to be forced to perform under pressure, and it was nigh near impossible with Gareth St. Clair breathing down her neck.

"Give her some room!" Lady D barked.

He moved, but not enough to make Hyacinth feel any more at ease.

"Well?" he demanded.

Hyacinth's head bobbed slightly back and forth as she worked out the meaning. "She's writing about her upcoming wedding," she said. "I think she's due to marry your grandfather in"—she bit her lip as she scanned down the page for the appropriate words—"three weeks. I gather the ceremony was in Italy."

Mr. St. Clair nodded once before prodding her with, "And?"

"And . . ." Hyacinth wrinkled her nose, as she always did when she was thinking hard. It wasn't a terribly attractive expression, but the alternative was simply not to think, which she didn't find appealing.

"What did she say?" Lady Danbury urged.

"*Orrendo orrendo* . . . ," Hyacinth murmured. "Oh, right." She looked up. "She's not very happy about it."

"Who *would* be?" Lady D put in. "The man was a bear, apologies to those in the room sharing his blood."

Mr. St. Clair ignored her. "What else?"

"I told you I'm not fluent," Hyacinth finally snapped. "I need time to work it out."

"Take it home," Lady Danbury said. "You'll be seeing him tomorrow night, anyway."

"I am?" Hyacinth asked, at precisely the moment Mr. St. Clair said, "She will?"

"You're accompanying me to the Pleinsworth poetry reading," Lady D told her grandson. "Or have you forgotten?"

Hyacinth sat back, enjoying the sight of Gareth St. Clair's mouth opening and closing in obvious distress. He looked a bit like a fish, she decided. A fish with the features of a Greek god, but still, a fish.

"I really . . ." he said. "That is to say, I can't—"

"You can, and you will be there," Lady D said. "You promised."

He regarded her with a stern expression. "I cannot imagine—"

"Well, if you didn't promise, you should have done, and if you love me . . ."

Hyacinth coughed to cover her laugh, then tried not to smirk when Mr. St. Clair shot a dirty look in her direction.

"When I die," he said, "surely my epitaph will read, 'He loved his grandmother when no one else would.' "

"And what's wrong with that?" Lady Danbury asked.

"I'll be there," he sighed.

"Bring wool for your ears," Hyacinth advised.

He looked aghast. "It cannot possibly be worse than last night's musicale."

Hyacinth couldn't quite keep one corner of her mouth from tilting up. "Lady Pleinsworth used to *be* a Smythe-Smith."

Across the room, Lady Danbury chortled with glee.

"I had best be getting home," Hyacinth said, rising to her feet. "I shall try to translate the first entry before I see you tomorrow evening, Mr. St. Clair."

"You have my gratitude, Miss Bridgerton."

Hyacinth nodded and crossed the room, trying to ignore the strangely giddy sensation growing in her chest. It was just a book, for heaven's sake.

And he was just a man.

It was annoying, this strange compulsion she felt to impress him. She wanted to do something that would prove her intelligence and wit, something that would force him to look at her with an expression other than vague amusement.

"Allow me to walk you to the door," Mr. St. Clair said, falling into step beside her.

Hyacinth turned, then felt her breath stop short in surprise. She hadn't realized he was standing so close. "I . . . ah . . ."

It was his eyes, she realized. So blue and clear she ought to have felt she could read his thoughts, but instead she rather thought he could read hers.

"Yes?" he murmured, placing her hand on his elbow.

She shook her head. "It's nothing."

"Why, Miss Bridgerton," he said, guiding her into the hall. "I don't believe I've ever seen you at a loss for words. Except for the other night," he added, cocking his head ever so slightly to the side.

She looked at him, narrowing her eyes.

"At the musicale," he supplied helpfully. "It was lovely." He smiled, most annoyingly. "Wasn't it lovely?"

Hyacinth clamped her lips together. "You barely know me, Mr. St. Clair," she said.

"Your reputation precedes you."

"As does yours."

"*Touché*, Miss Bridgerton," he said, but she didn't particularly feel she'd won the point.

Hyacinth saw her maid waiting by the door, so she extricated her hand from Mr. St. Clair's elbow and crossed the foyer. "Until tomorrow, Mr. St. Clair," she said.

And as the door shut behind her, she could have sworn she heard him reply, "*Arrivederci.*"

Hyacinth arrives home.
Her mother has been waiting for her.
This is not good.

"Charlotte Stokehurst," Violet Bridgerton announced, "is getting married."

"Today?" Hyacinth queried, taking off her gloves.

Her mother gave her a look. "She has become engaged. Her mother told me this morning."

Hyacinth looked around. "Were you waiting for me in the hall?"

"To the Earl of Renton," Violet added. "Renton."

"Have we any tea?" Hyacinth asked. "I walked all the way home, and I'm thirsty."

"Renton!" Violet exclaimed, looking about ready to throw up her hands in despair. "Did you hear me?"

"Renton," Hyacinth said obligingly. "He has fat ankles."

"He's—" Violet stopped short. "Why were you looking at his ankles?"

"I couldn't very well miss them," Hyacinth replied. She handed her reticule—which contained the Italian diary—to a maid. "Would you take this to my room, please?"

Violet waited until the maid scurried off. "I have tea in the drawing room, and there is nothing wrong with Renton's ankles."

Hyacinth shrugged. "If you like the puffy sort."

"Hyacinth!"

Hyacinth sighed tiredly, following her mother into the drawing room. "Mother, you have six married children, and they all are quite happy with their choices. Why must you try to push *me* into an unsuitable alliance?"

Violet sat and prepared a cup of tea for Hyacinth. "I'm not," she said, "but Hyacinth, couldn't you even look?"

"Mother, I—"

"Or for my sake, pretend to?"

Hyacinth could not help but smile.

Violet held the cup out, then took it back and added another spoonful of sugar. Hyacinth was the only one in the family who took sugar in her tea, and she'd always liked it extra sweet.

"Thank you," Hyacinth said, tasting the brew. It wasn't quite as hot as she preferred, but she drank it anyway.

"Hyacinth," her mother said, in that tone of voice that always made Hyacinth feel a little guilty, even though she knew better, "you know I only wish to see you happy."

"I know," Hyacinth said. That was the problem. Her mother did only wish her to be happy. If Violet had been pushing her toward marriage for social glory or financial gain, it would have been much easier to ignore her. But no, her mother loved her and truly did want her to be happy, not just married, and so Hyacinth tried her best to maintain her good humor through all of her mother's sighs.

"I would never wish to see you married to someone whose company you did not enjoy," Violet continued.

"I know."

"And if you never met the right person, I would be perfectly happy to see you remain unwed."

Hyacinth eyed her dubiously.

"Very well," Violet amended, "not *perfectly* happy, but you know I would never pressure you to marry someone unsuitable."

"I know," Hyacinth said again.

"But darling, you'll never find anyone if you don't look."

"I look!" Hyacinth protested. "I have gone out almost every night this week. I even went to the Smythe-Smith musicale last night. Which," she said quite pointedly, "I might add *you* did not attend."

Violet coughed. "Bit of a cough, I'm afraid."

Hyacinth said nothing, but no one could have mistaken the look in her eyes.

"I heard you sat next to Gareth St. Clair," Violet said, after an appropriate silence.

"Do you have spies *every*where?" Hyacinth grumbled.

"Almost," Violet replied. "It makes life so much easier."

"For you, perhaps."

"Did you like him?" Violet persisted.

Like him? It seemed such an odd question. Did she like Gareth St. Clair? Did she like that it always felt as if he was silently laughing at her, even after she'd agreed to translate his grandmother's diary? Did she like that she could never tell what he was thinking, or that he left her feeling unsettled, and not quite herself?

"Well?" her mother asked.

"Somewhat," Hyacinth hedged.

Violet didn't say anything, but her eyes took on a gleam that terrified Hyacinth to her very core.

"*Don't*," Hyacinth warned.

"He would be an excellent match, Hyacinth."

Hyacinth stared at her mother as if she'd sprouted an extra head. "Have you gone mad? You know his reputation as well as I."

Violet brushed that aside instantly. "His reputation won't matter once you're married."

"It would if he continued to consort with opera singers and the like."

"He wouldn't," Violet said, waving her hand dismissively.

"How could you possibly know that?"

Violet paused for a moment. "I don't know," she said. "I suppose it's a feeling I have."

"Mother," Hyacinth said with a great show of solicitude, "you know I love you dearly—"

"Why is it," Violet pondered, "that I have come to expect nothing good when I hear a sentence beginning in that manner?"

"But," Hyacinth cut in, "you must forgive me if I decline to marry someone based upon a feeling you might or might not have."

Violet sipped her tea with rather impressive nonchalance. "It's the next best thing to a feeling *you* might have. And if I may say so myself, my feelings on these things tend to be right on the mark." At Hyacinth's dry expression, she added, "I haven't been wrong yet."

Well, that was true, Hyacinth had to acknowledge. To herself, of course. If she actually admitted as much out loud, her mother would take that as a *carte blanche* to pursue Mr. St. Clair until he ran screaming for the trees.

"Mother," Hyacinth said, pausing for slightly longer than normal to steal a bit of time to organize her thoughts, "I am not going to chase after Mr. St. Clair. He's not at all the right sort of man for me."

"I'm not certain you'd know the right sort of man for you if he arrived on our doorstep riding an elephant."

"I would think the elephant would be a fairly good indication that I ought to look elsewhere."

"*Hyacinth.*"

"And besides that," Hyacinth added, thinking about the way Mr. St. Clair always seemed to look at her in that vaguely condescending manner of his, "I don't think he likes me very much."

"Nonsense," Violet said, with all the outrage of a mother hen. "Everyone likes you."

Hyacinth thought about that for a moment. "No," she said, "I don't think everyone does."

"Hyacinth, I am your mother, and I know—"

"Mother, you're the *last* person anyone would tell if they didn't like me."

"Nevertheless—"

"Mother," Hyacinth cut in, setting her teacup firmly in its saucer, "it is of no concern. I don't mind that I am not universally adored. If I wanted everyone to like me, I'd have to be kind and charming and bland and boring all the time, and what would be the fun in that?"

"You sound like Lady Danbury," Violet said.

"I like Lady Danbury."

"I like her, too, but that doesn't mean I want her as my daughter."

"Mother—"

"You won't set your cap for Mr. St. Clair because he scares you," Violet said.

Hyacinth actually gasped. "That is not true."

"Of course it is," Violet returned, looking vastly pleased with herself. "I don't know why it hasn't occurred to me sooner. And he isn't the only one."

"I don't know what you're talking about."

"Why have you not married yet?" Violet asked.

Hyacinth blinked at the abruptness of the question. "I beg your pardon."

"Why have you not married?" Violet repeated. "Do you even want to?"

"Of course I do." And she did. She wanted it more than she would ever admit, probably more than she'd ever realized until that very moment. She looked at her mother and she saw a matriarch, a woman who loved her family with a fierceness that brought tears to her eyes. And in that moment Hyacinth realized that she wanted to love with that fierceness. She wanted children. She wanted a family.

But that did not mean that she was willing to marry the first man who came along. Hyacinth was nothing if not pragmatic; she'd be happy to marry someone she didn't love, provided he suited her in almost every other respect. But good heavens, was it so much to ask for a gentleman with some modicum of intelligence?

"Mother," she said, softening her tone, since she knew that Violet meant well, "I do wish to marry. I swear to you that I do. And clearly I have been looking."

Violet lifted her brows. "Clearly?"

"I have had six proposals," Hyacinth said, perhaps a touch defensively. "It's not my fault that none was suitable."

"Indeed."

Hyacinth felt her lips part with surprise at her mother's tone. "What do you mean by that?"

"Of *course* none of those men was suitable. Half were after your fortune, and as for the other half—well, you would have reduced them to tears within a month."

"Such tenderness for your youngest child," Hyacinth muttered. "It quite undoes me."

Violet let out a ladylike snort. "Oh, *please*, Hyacinth, you know exactly what I mean, and you know that I am correct. None of those men was your match. You need someone who is your equal."

"That is exactly what I have been trying to tell you."

"But my question to you is—*why* are the wrong men asking for your hand?"

Hyacinth opened her mouth, but she had no answer.

"You say you wish to find a man who is your match," Violet said, "and I think you think you do, but the truth is, Hyacinth—every time you meet someone who can hold his own with you, you push him away."

"I don't," Hyacinth said, but not very convincingly.

"Well, you certainly don't encourage them," Violet said. She leaned forward, her eyes filled with equal parts concern and remonstration. "You know I love you dearly, Hyacinth, but you do like to have the upper hand in the conversation."

"Who doesn't?" Hyacinth muttered.

"Any man who is your equal is not going to allow you to manage him as you see fit."

"But that's not what I want," Hyacinth protested.

Violet sighed. But it was a nostalgic sound, full of warmth and love. "I wish I could explain to you how I felt the day you were born," she said.

"Mother?" Hyacinth asked softly. The change of subject was sudden, and somehow Hyacinth knew that whatever her mother said to her, it was going to matter more than anything she'd ever heard in her life.

"It was so soon after your father died. And I was so sad. I can't even begin to tell you how sad. There's a kind of grief that just eats one up. It weighs one down. And one can't—" Violet stopped, and her lips moved, the corners tightening in that way they did when a person was swallowing . . . and trying not to cry. "Well, one can't do anything. There's no way to explain it unless you've felt it yourself."

Hyacinth nodded, even though she knew she could never truly understand.

"That entire last month I just didn't know how to feel," Violet continued, her voice growing softer. "I didn't know how to feel about you. I'd had seven babies already; one would think I would be an expert. But suddenly everything was new. You wouldn't have a father, and I was so scared. I was going to have to be everything to you. I suppose I was going to have to be everything to your brothers and sisters as well, but somehow that was different. With you . . ."

Hyacinth just watched her, unable to take her eyes from her mother's face.

"I was scared," Violet said again, "terrified that I might fail you in some way."

"You didn't," Hyacinth whispered.

Violet smiled wistfully. "I know. Just look how well you turned out."

Hyacinth felt her mouth wobble, and she wasn't sure whether she was going to laugh or cry.

"But that's not what I'm trying to tell you," Violet said, her eyes taking on a slightly determined expression. "What I'm trying to say is that when you were born, and they put you into my arms—it's strange, because for some reason I was so convinced you would look just like your father. I thought for certain I would look down and see his face, and it would be some sort of sign from heaven."

Hyacinth's breath caught as she watched her, and she wondered why her mother had never told her this story. And why she'd never asked.

"But you didn't," Violet continued. "You looked rather like me. And then—oh my, I remember this as if it were yesterday—you looked into my eyes, and you blinked. Twice."

"Twice?" Hyacinth echoed, wondering why this was important.

"Twice." Violet looked at her, her lips curving into a funny little smile. "I only remember it because you looked so *deliberate*. It was the strangest thing. You gave me a look as if to say, 'I know exactly what I'm doing.' "

A little burst of air rushed past Hyacinth's lips, and she realized it was a laugh. A small one, the kind that takes a body by surprise.

"And then you let out a *wail*," Violet said, shaking her head. "My heavens, I thought you were going to shake the paint right off the walls. And I smiled. It was the first time since your father died that I smiled."

Violet took a breath, then reached for her tea. Hyacinth watched as her mother composed herself, wanting desperately to ask her to continue, but somehow knowing the moment called for silence.

For a full minute Hyacinth waited, and then finally her mother said, softly, "And from that moment on, you were so dear to me. I love all my children, but you . . ." She looked up, her eyes catching Hyacinth's. "You saved me."

Something squeezed in Hyacinth's chest. She couldn't quite move, couldn't quite breathe. She could only watch her mother's face, listen to her words, and be so very, very grateful that she'd been lucky enough to be her child.

"In some ways I was a little too protective of you," Violet said, her lips forming the tiniest of smiles, "and at the same time too lenient. You were so exuberant, so completely sure of who you were and how you fit into the world around you. You were a force of nature, and I didn't want to clip your wings."

"Thank you," Hyacinth whispered, but the words were so soft, she wasn't even sure she'd said them aloud.

"But sometimes I wonder if this left you too unaware of the people around you."

Hyacinth suddenly felt awful.

"No, no," Violet said quickly, seeing the stricken expression on Hyacinth's face. "You are kind, and you're caring, and you are far more thoughtful than I think anyone realizes. But—oh dear, I don't know how to explain this." She took a breath, her nose wrinkling as she searched for the right words. "You are so used to being completely comfortable with yourself and what you say."

"What's wrong with that?" Hyacinth asked. Not defensively, just quietly.

"Nothing. I wish more people had that talent." Violet clasped her hands together, her left thumb rubbing against her right palm. It was a gesture Hyacinth had seen on her mother countless times, always when she was lost in thought.

"But what I think happens," Violet continued, "is that when

you *don't* feel that way—when something happens to give you unease—well, you don't seem to know how to manage it. And you run. Or you decide it isn't worth it." She looked at her daughter, her eyes direct and perhaps just a little bit resigned. "And that," she finally said, "is why I'm afraid you will never find the right man. Or rather, you'll find him, but you won't know it. You won't let yourself know it."

Hyacinth stared at her mother, feeling very still, and very small, and very unsure of herself. How had this happened? How had she come in here, expecting the usual talk of husbands and weddings and the lack thereof, only to find herself laid bare and open until she wasn't quite certain who she was anymore.

"I'll think about that," she said to her mother.

"That's all I can ask."

And it was all she could promise.

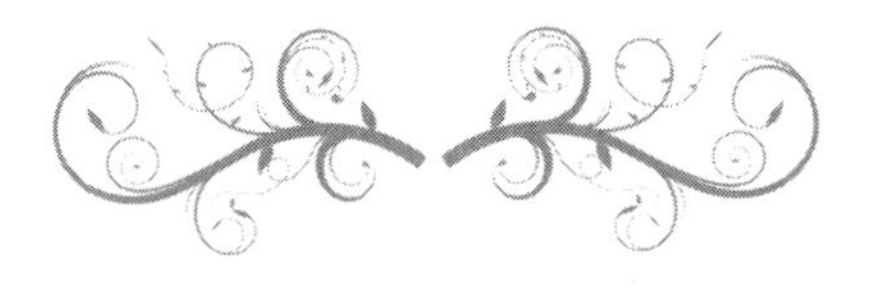

Chapter 5

The next evening, in the drawing room of the estimable Lady Pleinsworth. For some strange reason, there are twigs attached to the piano. And a small girl has a horn on her head.

"People will think you're courting me," Hyacinth said, when Mr. St. Clair walked directly to her side without any pretense of glancing about the room first.

"Nonsense," he said, sitting down in the empty chair next to her. "Everyone knows I don't court respectable women, and besides, I should think it would only enhance your reputation."

"And here I thought modesty an overrated virtue."

He flashed her a bland smile. "Not that I wish to give you any ammunition, but the sad fact of it is—most men are sheep. Where one goes, the rest will follow. And didn't you say you wished to be married?"

"Not to someone who follows you as the lead sheep," she replied.

He grinned at that, a devilish smile that Hyacinth had a feeling he had used to seduce legions of women. Then he looked about, as if intending to engage in something surreptitious, and leaned in.

Hyacinth couldn't help it. She leaned in, too. "Yes?" she murmured.

"I am about *this* close to bleating."

Hyacinth tried to swallow her laugh, which was a mistake, since it came out as an exceedingly inelegant splutter.

"How fortunate that you weren't drinking a glass of milk," Gareth said, sitting back in his chair. He was still the picture of perfect composure, drat the man.

Hyacinth tried to glare at him, but she was fairly certain she wasn't able to wipe the humor out of her eyes.

"It would have come out your nose," he said with a shrug.

"Hasn't anyone ever told you that's not the sort of thing you say to impress a woman?" she asked, once she'd regained her voice.

"I'm not trying to impress you," he replied, glancing up at the front of the room. "Gads," he said, blinking in surprise. "What is *that*?"

Hyacinth followed his gaze. Several of the Pleinsworth progeny, one of whom appeared to be costumed as a shepherdess, were milling about.

"Now that's an interesting coincidence," Gareth murmured.

"It might be time to start bleating," she agreed.

"I thought this was meant to be a poetry recitation."

Hyacinth grimaced and shook her head. "An unexpected change to the program, I'm afraid."

"From iambic pentameter to Little Bo Peep?" he asked doubtfully. "It does seem a stretch."

Hyacinth gave him a rueful look. "I think there will still be iambic pentameter."

His mouth fell open. "From Peep?"

She nodded, holding up the program that had been resting in

her lap. "It's an original composition," she said, as if that would explain everything. "By Harriet Pleinsworth. *The Shepherdess, the Unicorn, and Henry VIII.*"

"All of them? At once?"

"I'm not jesting," she said, shaking her head.

"Of course not. Even you couldn't have made this up."

Hyacinth decided to take that as a compliment.

"Why didn't I receive one of these?" he asked, taking the program from her.

"I believe it was decided not to hand them out to the gentlemen," Hyacinth said, glancing about the room. "One has to admire Lady Pleinsworth's foresight, actually. You'd surely flee if you knew what was in store for you."

Gareth twisted in his seat. "Have they locked the doors yet?"

"No, but your grandmother has already arrived."

Hyacinth wasn't sure, but it sounded very much like he groaned.

"She doesn't seem to be coming this way," Hyacinth added, watching as Lady Danbury took a seat on the aisle, several rows back.

"Of course not," Gareth muttered, and Hyacinth knew he was thinking the same thing she was.

Matchmaker.

Well, it wasn't as if Lady Danbury had ever been especially subtle about it.

Hyacinth started to turn back to the front, then halted when she caught sight of her mother, for whom she'd been holding an empty seat to her right. Violet pretended (rather badly, in Hyacinth's opinion) not to see her, and she sat down right next to Lady Danbury.

"Well," Hyacinth said under her breath. Her mother had never been known for her subtlety, either, but she would have thought that after their conversation the previous afternoon, Violet wouldn't have been *quite* so obvious.

A few days to reflect upon it all might have been nice.

As it was, Hyacinth had spent the entire past two days pondering her conversation with her mother. She tried to think about all the people she had met during her years on the Marriage Mart. For the most part, she had had a fine time. She'd said what she wished and made people laugh and had rather enjoyed being admired for her wit.

But there had been a few people with whom she had not felt completely comfortable. Not many, but a few. There had been a gentleman during her first season with whom she'd been positively tongue-tied. He had been intelligent and handsome, and when he'd looked at her, Hyacinth had thought her legs might give out. And then just a year ago her brother Gregory had introduced her to one of his school friends who, Hyacinth had to admit, had been dry and sarcastic and more than her match. She'd told herself she hadn't liked him, and then she'd told her mother that she thought he seemed the sort to be unkind to animals. But the truth was—

Well, she didn't know what the truth was. She didn't know everything, much as she tried to give the impression otherwise.

But she had avoided those men. She'd said she didn't like them, but maybe that wasn't it. Maybe she just hadn't liked herself when she was with them.

She looked up. Mr. St. Clair was leaning back in his seat, his face looking a little bit bored, a little bit amused—that sophisticated and urbane sort of expression men across London sought to emulate. Mr. St. Clair, she decided, did it better than most.

"You look rather serious for an evening of bovine pentameter," he remarked.

Hyacinth looked over at the stage in surprise. "Are we expecting cows as well?"

He handed the small leaflet back to her and sighed. "I'm preparing myself for the worst."

Hyacinth smiled. He really *was* funny. And intelligent. And very, very handsome, although that had certainly never been in doubt.

He was, she realized, everything she'd always told herself she was looking for in a husband.

Good *God*.

"Are you all right?" he asked, sitting up quite suddenly.

"Fine," she croaked. "Why?"

"You looked . . ." He cleared his throat. "Well, you looked . . . ah . . . I'm sorry. I can't say it to a woman."

"Even one you're not trying to impress?" Hyacinth quipped. But her voice sounded a little bit strained.

He stared at her for a moment, then said, "Very well. You looked rather like you were going to be sick."

"I'm never sick," she said, looking resolutely forward. Gareth St. Clair was *not* everything she'd ever wanted in a husband. He couldn't be. "And I don't swoon, either," she added. "Ever."

"*Now* you look angry," he murmured.

"I'm not," she said, and she was rather pleased with how positively sunny she sounded.

He had a terrible reputation, she reminded herself. Did she really wish to align herself with a man who'd had relations with so many women? And unlike most unmarried women, Hyacinth actually knew what "relations" entailed. Not firsthand, of course, but she'd managed to wrench the most basic of details from her older married sisters. And while Daphne, Eloise, and Francesca assured her it was all very enjoyable with the right sort of husband, it stood to reason that the right sort of husband was one who remained faithful to one's wife. Mr. St. Clair, in contrast, had had relations with *scores* of women.

Surely such behavior couldn't be healthy.

And even if "scores" was a bit of an exaggeration, and the true number was much more modest, how could she compete? She knew for a fact that his last mistress had been none other than Maria Bartolomeo, the Italian soprano as famed for her beauty as she was for her voice. Not even her own mother could claim that Hyacinth was anywhere near as beautiful as *that*.

How horrible that must be, to enter into one's wedding night, knowing that one would suffer by comparison.

"I think it's beginning." She heard Mr. St. Clair sigh.

Footmen were crisscrossing the room, snuffing candles to dim the light. Hyacinth turned, catching sight of Mr. St. Clair's profile. A candelabrum had been left alive over his shoulder, and in the flickering light his hair appeared almost streaked with gold. He was wearing his queue, she thought idly, the only man in the room to do so.

She liked that. She didn't know why, but she liked it.

"How bad would it be," she heard him whisper, "if I ran for the door?"

"Right now?" Hyacinth whispered back, trying to ignore the tingling feeling she got when he leaned in close. "Very bad."

He sat back with a sad sigh, then focused on the stage, giving every appearance of the polite, and only very slightly bored, gentleman.

But it was only one minute later when Hyacinth heard it. Soft, and for her ears only:

"Baaa.

"Baaaaaaaaa."

Ninety mind-numbing minutes later, and sadly, our hero was right about the cows.

"Do you drink port, Miss Bridgerton?" Gareth asked, keeping his eyes on the stage as he stood and applauded the Pleinsworth children.

"Of course not, but I've always wanted to taste it, why?"

"Because we both deserve a drink."

He heard her smother a laugh, then say, "Well, the unicorn was rather sweet."

He snorted. The unicorn couldn't have been more than ten years old. Which would have been fine, except that Henry VIII had insisted upon taking an unscripted ride. "I'm surprised they didn't have to call for a surgeon," he muttered.

Hyacinth winced. "She did seem to be limping a bit."

"It was all I could do not to whinny in pain on her behalf. Good God, who—Oh! Lady Pleinsworth," Gareth said, pasting a smile on his face with what he thought was admirable speed. "How nice to see you."

"Mr. St. Clair," Lady Pleinsworth said effusively. "I'm so delighted you could attend."

"I wouldn't have missed it."

"And Miss Bridgerton," Lady Pleinsworth said, clearly angling for a bit of gossip. "Do I have you to thank for Mr. St. Clair's appearance?"

"I'm afraid his grandmother is to blame," Hyacinth replied. "She threatened him with her cane."

Lady Pleinsworth didn't seem to know quite how to respond to this, so she turned back to Gareth, clearing her throat a few times before asking, "Have you met my daughters?"

Gareth managed not to grimace. This was exactly why he tried to avoid these things. "Er, no, I don't believe I've had the pleasure."

"The shepherdess," Lady Pleinsworth said helpfully.

Gareth nodded. "And the unicorn?" he asked with a smile.

"Yes," Lady Pleinsworth replied, blinking in confusion, and quite possibly distress, "but she's a bit young."

"I'm sure Mr. St. Clair would be delighted to meet Harriet," Hyacinth cut in before turning to Gareth with an explanatory, "The shepherdess."

"Of course," he said. "Yes, delighted."

Hyacinth turned back to Lady Pleinsworth with a smile that was far too innocent. "Mr. St. Clair is an expert on all things ovine."

"Where is *my* cane when I need it?" he murmured.

"I beg your pardon?" Lady Pleinsworth said, leaning forward.

"I would be honored to meet your daughter," he said, since it seemed the only acceptable statement at that point.

"Wonderful!" Lady Pleinsworth exclaimed, clapping her hands together. "I know she will be so excited to meet you." And then, saying something about needing to see to the rest of her guests, she was off.

"Don't look so upset," Hyacinth said, once it was just the two of them again. "You're quite a catch."

He looked at her assessingly. "Is one meant to say such things quite so directly?"

She shrugged. "Not to men one is trying to impress."

"*Touché*, Miss Bridgerton."

She sighed happily. "My three favorite words."

Of that, he had no doubt.

"Tell me, Miss Bridgerton," he said, "have you begun to read my grandmother's diary?"

She nodded. "I was surprised you didn't ask earlier."

"Distracted by the shepherdess," he said, "although please don't say as much to her mother. She'd surely take it the wrong way."

"Mothers always do," she agreed, glancing around the room.

"What are you *looking* for?" he asked.

"Hmmm? Oh, nothing. Just looking."

"For what?" he persisted.

She turned to him, her eyes wide, unblinking, and startlingly blue. "Nothing in particular. Don't you like to know everything that is going on?"

"Only as it pertains to me."

"Really?" She paused. "I like to know everything."

"So I'm gathering. And speaking of which, what have you learned of the diary?"

"Oh, yes," she said, brightening before his eyes. It seemed an odd sort of metaphor, but it was true. Hyacinth Bridgerton positively sparkled when she had the opportunity to speak with authority. And the strangest thing was, Gareth thought it rather charming.

"I have only read twelve pages, I'm afraid," she said. "My mother required my assistance with her correspondence this afternoon, and I did not have the time I would have wished to work on it. I didn't tell her about it, by the way. I wasn't sure if it was meant to be a secret."

Gareth thought of his father, who would probably want the diary, if only because Gareth had it in his possession. "It's a secret," he said. "At least until I deem otherwise."

She nodded. "It's probably best not to say anything until you know what she wrote."

"What did you find out?"

"Well . . ."

He watched her as she grimaced. "What is it?" he asked.

Both corners of her mouth stretched out and down in that expression one gets when one is trying not to deliver bad news. "There's really no polite way to say it, I'm afraid," she said.

"There rarely is, when it comes to my family."

She eyed him curiously, saying, "She didn't particularly wish to marry your grandfather."

"Yes, you said as much this afternoon."

"No, I mean she *really* didn't want to marry him."

"Smart woman," he muttered. "The men in my family are bull-headed idiots."

She smiled. Slightly. "Yourself included?"

He should have anticipated that. "You couldn't resist, could you?" he murmured.

"Could *you*?"

"I imagine not," he admitted. "What else did she say?"

"Not a great deal more," Hyacinth told him. "She was only seventeen at the beginning of the diary. Her parents forced the match, and she wrote three pages about how upset she was."

"Upset?"

She winced. "Well, a bit more than upset, I must say, but—"

"We'll leave it at 'upset.'"

"Yes," she agreed, "that's best."

"How did they meet?" he asked. "Did she say?"

Hyacinth shook her head. "No. She seems to have begun the journal after their introduction. Although she did make reference to a party at her uncle's house, so perhaps that was it."

Gareth nodded absently. "My grandfather took a grand tour," he said. "They met and married in Italy, but that's all I've been told."

"Well, I don't think he compromised her, if that's what you wish to know," Hyacinth said. "I would think she'd mention *that* in her diary."

He couldn't resist a little verbal poke. "Would *you*?"

"I beg your pardon?"

"Would you write about it in your diary if someone compromised you?"

She blushed, which delighted him. "I don't keep a diary," she said.

Oh, he was loving this. "But if you did . . ."

"But I *don't*," she ground out.

"Coward," he said softly.

"Would you write all of your secrets down in a diary?" she countered.

"Of course not," he said. "If someone found it, that would hardly be fair to the people I've mentioned."

"People?" she dared.

He flashed her a grin. "Women."

She blushed again, but it was softer this time, and he rather doubted she even knew she'd done it. It tinged her pink, played with the light sprinkling of freckles across her nose. At this point, most women would have expressed their outrage, or at least pretended to, but not Hyacinth. He watched as her lips pursed slightly—maybe to hide her embarrassed expression, maybe to bite off a retort, he wasn't sure which.

And he realized that he was enjoying himself. It was hard to believe, since he was standing next to a piano covered with twigs, and he was well aware that he was going to have to spend the rest of the evening avoiding a shepherdess and her ambitious mother, but he was enjoying himself.

"Are you really as bad as they say?" Hyacinth asked.

He started in surprise. He hadn't expected that. "No," he admitted, "but don't tell anyone."

"I didn't think so," she said thoughtfully.

Something about her tone scared him. He didn't want Hyacinth Bridgerton thinking so hard about him. Because he had the oddest feeling that if she did, she might see right through him.

And he wasn't sure what she'd find.

"Your grandmother is coming this way," she said.

"So she is," he said, glad for the distraction. "Shall we attempt an escape?"

"It's far too late for that," Hyacinth said, her lips twisting slightly. "She's got my mother in tow."

"Gareth!" came his grandmother's strident voice.

"Grandmother," he said, gallantly kissing her hand when she reached his side. "It is always a pleasure to see you."

"Of course it is," she replied pertly.

Gareth turned to face an older, slightly fairer, version of Hyacinth. "Lady Bridgerton."

"Mr. St. Clair," said Lady Bridgerton warmly. "It has been an age."

"I don't often attend such recitations," he said.

"Yes," Lady Bridgerton said frankly, "your grandmother told me she was forced to twist your arm to attend."

He turned to his grandmother with raised brows. "You are going to ruin my reputation."

"You've done that all on your own, m'dear boy," Lady D said.

"I think what he means," Hyacinth put in, "is that he's not likely to be thought dashing and dangerous if the world knows how well he dotes upon you."

A slightly awkward silence fell over the group as Hyacinth realized that they had all understood his remark. Gareth found himself taking pity on her, so he filled the gap by saying, "I do have another engagement this evening, however, so I'm afraid I must take my leave."

Lady Bridgerton smiled. "We will see you Tuesday evening, however, yes?"

"Tuesday?" he queried, realizing that Lady Bridgerton's smile was nowhere near as innocent as it looked.

"My son and his wife are hosting a large ball. I'm sure you received an invitation."

Gareth was sure he had, too, but half the time he tossed them aside without looking at them.

"I promise you," Lady Bridgerton continued, "there will be no unicorns."

Trapped. And by a master, too. "In that case," he said politely, "how could I refuse?"

"Excellent. I'm sure Hyacinth will be delighted to see you."

"I am quite beside myself with glee," Hyacinth murmured.

"Hyacinth!" Lady Bridgerton said. She turned to Gareth. "She doesn't mean that."

He turned to Hyacinth. "I'm crushed."

"Because I'm beside myself, or because I'm not?" she queried.

"Whichever you prefer." Gareth turned to the group at large. "Ladies," he murmured.

"Don't forget the shepherdess," Hyacinth said, her smile sweet and just a little bit wicked. "You *did* promise her mother."

Damn. He'd forgotten. He glanced across the room. Little Bo Peep had begun to point her crook in his direction, and Gareth had the unsettling feeling that if he got close enough, she might loop it round and reel him in.

"Aren't the two of you friends?" he asked Hyacinth.

"Oh, no," she said. "I hardly know her."

"Wouldn't you like to *meet* her?" he ground out.

She tapped her finger against her jaw. "I . . . No." She smiled blandly. "But I will watch you from afar."

"Traitor," he murmured, brushing past her on the way to the shepherdess.

And for the rest of the night, he couldn't quite forget the smell of her perfume.

Or maybe it was the soft sound of her chuckle.

Or maybe it was neither of those things. Maybe it was just her.

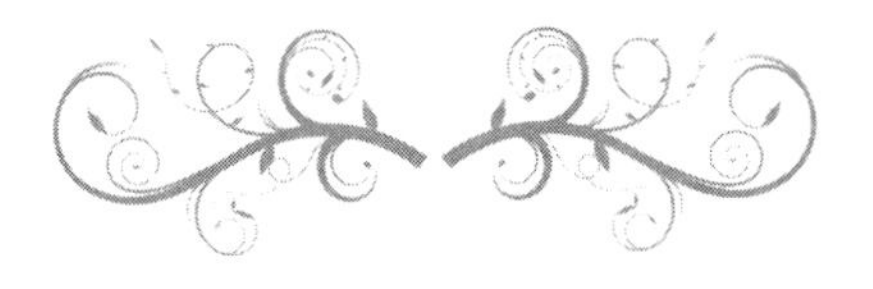

Chapter 6

The following Tuesday, in the ballroom at Bridgerton House. The candles are lit, music fills the air, and the night seems made for romance

But not, however, for Hyacinth, who is learning that friends can be just as vexing as family

Sometimes more so.

"Do you know whom I think you should marry? I think you should marry Gareth St. Clair."

Hyacinth looked at Felicity Albansdale, her closest friend, with an expression that hovered somewhere between disbelief and alarm. She absolutely, positively, was not prepared to say that she should marry Gareth St. Clair, but on the other hand, she had begun to wonder if perhaps she ought to give it just a touch of consideration.

But still, was she so transparent?

"You're mad," she said, since she wasn't about to tell anyone that she might be developing a bit of a *tendre* for the man. She didn't like to do anything if she didn't do it well, and she had a sinking feeling that she did not know how to pursue a man with anything resembling grace or dignity.

"Not at all," Felicity said, eyeing the gentleman in question from across the ballroom. "He would be perfect for you."

As Hyacinth had spent the last several days thinking of nothing but Gareth, his grandmother, and his other grandmother's diary, she had no choice but to say, "Nonsense. I hardly know the man."

"No one does," Felicity said. "He's an enigma."

"Well, I wouldn't say *that*," Hyacinth muttered. *Enigma* sounded far too romantic, and—

"Of course he is," Felicity said, cutting into her thoughts. "What do we know about him? Nothing. Ergo—"

"Ergo nothing," Hyacinth said. "And I'm certainly not going to marry him."

"Well, you have to marry somebody," Felicity said.

"This is what happens when people get married," Hyacinth said disgustedly. "All they want is to see everyone else married."

Felicity, who had wed Geoffrey Albansdale six months earlier, just shrugged. "It's a noble goal."

Hyacinth glanced back at Gareth, who was dancing with the very lovely, very blond, and very petite Jane Hotchkiss. He appeared to be hanging on her every word.

"I am *not*," she said, turning to Felicity with renewed determination, "setting my cap for Gareth St. Clair."

"Methinks the lady doth protest too much," Felicity said airily.

Hyacinth gritted her teeth. "The lady protested *twice*."

"If you stop to think about it—"

"Which I won't do," Hyacinth interjected.

"—you'll see that he is a perfect match."

"And how is that?" Hyacinth asked, even though she knew it would only encourage Felicity.

Felicity turned to her friend and looked her squarely in the eye. "He is the only person I can think of who you wouldn't—or rather, couldn't—run into the ground."

Hyacinth looked at her for a long moment, feeling unaccountably stung. "I am unsure of whether to be complimented by that."

"Hyacinth!" Felicity exclaimed. "You know I meant no insult. For heaven's sake, what is the matter with you?"

"It's nothing," Hyacinth mumbled. But between this conversation and the one the previous week with her mother, she was beginning to wonder how, exactly, the world saw her.

Because she wasn't so certain it corresponded with how she saw herself.

"I wasn't saying that I want you to change," Felicity said, taking Hyacinth's hand in a gesture of friendship. "Goodness, no. Just that you need someone who can keep up with you. Even you must confess that most people can't."

"I'm sorry," Hyacinth said, giving her head a little shake. "I overreacted. I just . . . I haven't felt quite like myself the last few days."

And it was true. She hid it well, or at least she thought she did, but inside, she was in a bit of a turmoil. It was that talk with her mother. No, it was that talk with Mr. St. Clair.

No, it was everything. Everything all at once. And she was left feeling as if she wasn't quite sure who she was anymore, which was almost impossible to bear.

"It's probably a sniffle," Felicity said, looking back out at the ballroom floor. "Everyone seems to have one this week."

Hyacinth didn't contradict her. It would have been nice if it was just a sniffle.

"I know you are friendly with him," Felicity continued. "I heard you sat together at both the Smythe-Smith musicale and the Pleinsworth poetry recitation."

"It was a play," Hyacinth said absently. "They changed it at the last moment."

"Even worse. I would have thought you'd have managed to get out of attending at least one."

"They weren't so awful."

"Because you were sitting next to Mr. St. Clair," Felicity said with a sly smile.

"You are terrible," Hyacinth said, refusing to look at her. If she did, Felicity was sure to see the truth in her eyes. Hyacinth was a good liar, but not that good, and not with Felicity.

And the worst of it was—she could hear herself in Felicity's words. How many times had she teased Felicity in the very same way before Felicity had married? A dozen? More?

"You should dance with him," Felicity said.

Hyacinth kept her eyes on the ballroom floor. "I can't do anything if he does not ask."

"Of course he'll ask. You have only to stand on the other side of the room, where he is more likely to see you."

"I'm not going to *chase* him."

Felicity's smile spread across her face. "You do like him! Oh, this is lovely! I have never seen—"

"I don't like him," Hyacinth cut in. And then, because she realized how juvenile that sounded, and that Felicity would never believe her, she added, "I merely think that perhaps I ought to see if I *might* like him."

"Well, that's more than you've ever said about any other gentleman," Felicity pointed out. "And you have no need to chase him. He wouldn't dare ignore you. You are the sister of his host, and besides, wouldn't his grandmother take him to task if he didn't ask you to dance?"

"Thank you for making me feel like such a prize."

Felicity chuckled. "I have never seen you like this, and I must say, I'm enjoying it tremendously."

"I'm glad one of us is," Hyacinth grumbled, but her words were lost under the sharp sound of Felicity's gasp.

"What is it?" Hyacinth asked.

Felicity tilted her head slightly to the left, motioning across the room. "His father," she said in a low voice.

Hyacinth turned around sharply, not even trying to conceal her interest. Good heavens, Lord St. Clair was here. All of London knew that father and son did not speak, but invitations to parties were still issued to both. The St. Clair men seemed to have a remarkable talent for not appearing where the other might be, and so hostesses were generally spared the embarrassment of having them attend the same function.

But obviously, something had gone wrong this evening.

Did Gareth know his father was there? Hyacinth looked quickly back to the dance floor. He was laughing at something Miss Hotchkiss was saying. No, he didn't know. Hyacinth had witnessed him with his father once. It had been from across the room, but there had been no mistaking the strained expression on his face.

Or the way both had stormed off to separate exits.

Hyacinth watched as Lord St. Clair glanced around the room. His eyes settled on his son, and his entire face hardened.

"What are you going to do?" Felicity whispered.

Do? Hyacinth's lips parted as she glanced from Gareth to his father. Lord St. Clair, still unaware of her regard, turned on his heel and walked out, possibly in the direction of the card room.

But there was no guarantee he wouldn't be back.

"You're going to do something, aren't you?" Felicity pressed. "You have to."

Hyacinth was fairly certain *that* wasn't true. She had never done anything before. But now it was different. Gareth was . . . Well, she supposed he was her friend, in a strange, unsettling sort of way. And she did need to speak with him. She'd spent the entire morning and most of the afternoon in her room, translating his grandmother's diary. Surely he would wish to know what she had learned.

And if she managed to prevent an altercation in the process . . . Well, she was always happy to be the heroine of the day, even if no one but Felicity would be aware of it.

"I will ask him to dance," Hyacinth announced.

"You will?" Felicity asked, eyes bugging out. Hyacinth was certainly known as An Original, but even she had never dared to ask a gentleman to dance.

"I shan't make a big scene about it," Hyacinth said. "No one will know but Mr. St. Clair. And you."

"And whoever happens to be standing next to him. And whomever *they* tell, and whoever—"

"Do you know what is nice about friendships as long-standing as ours?" Hyacinth interrupted.

Felicity shook her head.

"You won't take permanent offense when I turn my back and walk away."

And then Hyacinth did just that.

But the drama of her exit was considerably diminished when she heard Felicity chuckle and say, "Good luck!"

Thirty seconds later. It doesn't take very long to cross a ballroom, after all.

Gareth had always liked Jane Hotchkiss. Her sister was married to his cousin, and as a result they saw each other from time to time at Grandmother Danbury's house. More importantly, he knew he could ask her to dance without her wondering if there was some sort of ulterior matrimonial purpose.

But on the other hand—she knew him well. Or at least well enough to know when he was acting out of character.

"What are you looking for?" she asked, as their quadrille was drawing to a close.

"Nothing," he answered.

"Very well," she said, her pale blond brows coming together in a slightly exasperated expression. "*Who* are you looking for, then? And don't say no one, because you have been craning your neck throughout the dance."

He swung his head around so that his gaze was firmly fixed on her face. "Jane," he said, "your imagination knows no bounds."

"Now I know you're lying."

She was right, of course. He'd been looking for Hyacinth Bridgerton since he had walked through the door twenty minutes earlier. He'd thought he caught sight of her before he'd stumbled upon Jane, but it had turned out to be one of her numerous sisters. All the Bridgertons looked devilishly alike. From across the room, they were practically indistinguishable.

As the orchestra played the last notes of their dance, Gareth took Jane's arm and led her to the side of the room. "I would never lie to you, Jane," he said, giving her a jaunty half smile.

"Of course you would," she returned. "And anyway, it's as obvious as day. Your eyes give you away. The only time they ever look serious is when you're lying."

"That can't be—"

"It's true," she said. "Trust me. Oh, good evening, Miss Bridgerton."

Gareth turned sharply to see Hyacinth, standing before them

like a vision in blue silk. She looked especially lovely this evening. She'd done something different with her hair. He wasn't sure what; he was rarely observant enough to notice such minutiae. But it was altered somehow. It must have framed her face differently, because something about her didn't look quite the same.

Maybe it was her eyes. They looked determined, even for Hyacinth.

"Miss Hotchkiss," Hyacinth said with a polite nod. "How lovely to see you again."

Jane smiled warmly. "Lady Bridgerton always hosts such lovely parties. Please convey my regards."

"I shall. Kate is just over there by the champagne," Hyacinth said, referring to her sister-in-law, the current Lady Bridgerton. "In case you wished to tell her yourself."

Gareth felt his eyebrows rise. Whatever Hyacinth was up to, she wanted to speak with him alone.

"I see," Jane murmured. "I had best go speak with her, then. I wish you both a pleasant evening."

"Smart girl," Hyacinth said, once they were alone.

"You weren't exactly subtle," Gareth said.

"No," she replied, "but then, I rarely am. It's a skill one must be born with, I'm afraid."

He smiled. "Now that you have me all to yourself, what do you wish to do with me?"

"Don't you wish to hear about your grandmother's diary?"

"Of course," he said.

"Shall we dance?" she suggested.

"You're asking *me*?" He rather liked this.

She scowled at him.

"Ah, there is the real Miss Bridgerton," he teased. "Shining through like a surly—"

"Would you care to dance with me?" she ground out, and he realized with surprise that this wasn't easy for her. Hyacinth Bridgerton, who almost never gave the impression of being at odds with anything she did, was scared to ask him to dance.

How fun.

"I'd be delighted," he said immediately. "May I guide you onto the floor, or is that a privilege reserved for the one doing the asking?"

"You may lead," she said, with all the hauteur of a queen.

But when they reached the floor, she seemed a little less sure of herself. And though she hid it quite well, her eyes were flicking around the room.

"Who are you looking for?" Gareth asked, letting out an amused snuff of air as he realized he was echoing Jane's exact words to him.

"No one," Hyacinth said quickly. She snapped her gaze back to his with a suddenness that almost made him dizzy. "What is so amusing?"

"Nothing," he countered, "and you were most certainly looking for someone, although I will compliment you on your ability to make it seem like you weren't."

"That's because I wasn't," she said, dipping into an elegant curtsy as the orchestra began the first strains of a waltz.

"You're a good liar, Hyacinth Bridgerton," he murmured, taking her into his arms, "but not quite as good as you think you are."

Music began to float through the air, a soft, delicate tune in three-four time. Gareth had always enjoyed dancing, particularly with an attractive partner, but it became apparent with the first—no, one must be fair, probably not until the sixth—step that this would be no ordinary waltz.

Hyacinth Bridgerton, he was quite amused to note, was a clumsy dancer.

Gareth couldn't help but smile.

He didn't know why he found this so entertaining. Maybe it was because she was so capable in everything else she did; he'd heard that she'd recently challenged a young man to a horse race in Hyde Park and won. And he was quite certain that if she ever found someone willing to teach her to fence, she'd soon be skewering her opponents through the heart.

But when it came to dancing . . .

He should have known she'd try to lead.

"Tell me, Miss Bridgerton," he said, hoping that a spot of conversation might distract her, since it always seemed that one danced with more grace when one wasn't thinking quite so hard about it. "How far along are you with the diary?"

"I've only managed ten pages since we last spoke," she said. "It might not seem like much—"

"It seems like quite a lot," he said, exerting a bit more pressure on the small of her back. A little more, and maybe he could force . . . her . . . to turn . . .

Left.

Phew.

It was quite the most exerting waltz he'd ever danced.

"Well, I'm not fluent," she said. "As I told you. So it's taking me much longer than if I could just sit down and read it like a book."

"You don't need to make excuses," he said, wrenching her to the right.

She stepped on his toe, which he ordinarily would have taken as retaliation, but under the present circumstances, he rather thought it was accidental.

"Sorry," she muttered, her cheeks turning pink. "I'm not usually so clumsy."

He bit his lip. He couldn't possibly laugh at her. It would break her heart. Hyacinth Bridgerton, he was coming to realize, didn't like to do anything if she didn't do it well. And he suspected that she had no idea that she was such an abysmal dancer, not if she took the toe-stomping as such an aberration.

It also explained why she felt the need to continually remind him that she wasn't fluent in Italian. She couldn't possibly bear for him to think she was slow without a good reason.

"I've had to make a list of words I don't know," she said. "I'm going to send them by post to my former governess. She still resides in Kent, and I'm sure she'll be happy to translate them for me. But even so—"

She grunted slightly as he swung her to the left, somewhat against her will.

"Even so," she continued doggedly, "I'm able to work out most of the meaning. It's remarkable what you can deduce with only three-quarters of the total."

"I'm sure," he commented, mostly because some sort of agreement seemed to be required. Then he asked, "Why don't you purchase an Italian dictionary? I will assume the expense."

"I have one," she said, "but I don't think it's very good. Half the words are missing."

"Half?"

"Well, some," she amended. "But truly, that's not the problem."

He blinked, waiting for her to continue.

She did. Of course. "I don't think Italian is the author's native tongue," she said.

"The author of the dictionary?" he queried.

"Yes. It's not terribly idiomatic." She paused, apparently deep in whatever odd thoughts were racing through her mind. Then she gave a little shrug—which caused her to miss a step in the waltz, not that she noticed—and continued with, "It's really of no matter. I'm making fair progress, even if it is a bit slow. I'm already up to her arrival in England."

"In just ten pages?"

"Twenty-two in total," Hyacinth corrected, "but she doesn't make entries every day. In fact, she often skips several weeks at a time. She only devoted one paragraph to the sea crossing—just enough to express her delight that your grandfather was afflicted by seasickness."

"One must take one's happiness where one can," Gareth murmured.

Hyacinth nodded. "And also, she, ah, declined to mention her wedding night."

"I believe we may consider that a small blessing," Gareth said. The only wedding night he wanted to hear about less than Grandmother St. Clair's would have to be Grandmother Danbury's.

Good God, that would send him right over the edge.

"What has you looking so pained?" Hyacinth asked.

He just shook his head. "There are some things one should never know about one's grandparents."

Hyacinth grinned at that.

Gareth's breath caught for a moment, then he found himself grinning back. There was something infectious about Hyacinth's smiles, something that forced her companions to stop what they were doing, even what they were thinking, and just smile back.

When Hyacinth smiled—when she really smiled, not one of those faux half smiles she did when she was trying to be clever—it transformed her face. Her eyes lit, her cheeks seemed to glow, and—

And she was beautiful.

Funny how he'd never noticed it before. Funny how no one had noticed it. Gareth had been out and about in London since she'd made her nod several years earlier, and while he'd never heard anyone speak of her looks in an uncomplimentary manner, nor had he heard anyone call her beautiful.

He wondered if perhaps everyone was so busy trying to keep up with whatever it was she was saying to stop and actually look at her face.

"Mr. St. Clair? Mr. St. Clair?"

He glanced down. She was looking up at him with an impatient expression, and he wondered how many times she'd uttered his name.

"Under the circumstances," he said, "you might as well use my given name."

She nodded approvingly. "A fine idea. You may of course use mine as well."

"Hyacinth," he said. "It suits you."

"It was my father's favorite flower," she explained. "Grape hyacinths. They bloom like mad in spring near our home in Kent. The first to show color every year."

"And the exact color of your eyes," Gareth said.

"A happy coincidence," she admitted.

"He must have been delighted."

"He never knew," she said, looking away. "He died before my birth."

"I'm sorry," Gareth said quietly. He did not know the Bridgertons well, but unlike the St. Clairs, they seemed to actually like each other. "I knew he had passed on some time ago, but I was not aware that you never knew him."

"It shouldn't matter," she said softly. "I shouldn't miss what I never had, but sometimes . . . I must confess . . . I do."

He chose his words carefully. "It's difficult . . . I think, not to know one's father."

She nodded, looking down, then over his shoulder. It was odd, he thought, but still somewhat endearing that she didn't wish to look at him during such a moment. Thus far their conversations had been all sly jokes and gossip. This was the first time they had ever said anything of substance, anything that truly revealed the person beneath the ready wit and easy smile.

She kept her eyes fixed on something behind him, even after he'd expertly twirled her to the left. He couldn't help but smile. She was a much better dancer now that she was distracted.

And then she turned back, her gaze settling on his face with considerable force and determination. She was ready for a change of subject. It was clear.

"Would you like to hear the remainder of what I've translated?" she inquired.

"Of course," he said.

"I believe the dance is ending," she said. "But it looks as if there is a bit of room over there." Hyacinth motioned with her head to the far corner of the ballroom, where several chairs had been set up for those with weary feet. "I am sure we could manage a few moments of privacy without anyone intruding."

The waltz drew to a close, and Gareth took a step back and gave her a small bow. "Shall we?" he murmured, holding out his arm so that she might settle her hand in the crook of his elbow.

She nodded, and this time, he let *her* lead.

Chapter 7

Ten minutes later, and our scene has moved to the hall.

Gareth generally had little use for large balls; they were hot and crowded, and much as he enjoyed dancing, he'd found that he usually spent the bulk of his time making idle conversation with people in whom he wasn't particularly interested. But, he thought as he made his way into the side hall of Bridgerton House, he was having a fine time this evening.

After his dance with Hyacinth, they had moved to the corner of the ballroom, where she'd informed him of her work with the diary. Despite her excuses, she had made good progress, and had in fact just reached the point of Isabella's arrival in England. It had not been auspicious. His grandmother had slipped while exiting the small dinghy that had carried her to shore, and thus her first connection with British soil had been her bottom against the wet sludge of the Dover shore.

Her new husband, of course, hadn't lifted a hand to help her.

Gareth shook his head. It was a wonder she hadn't turned tail and run back to Italy right then. Of course, according to Hyacinth, there wasn't much waiting for her there, either. Isabella had repeatedly begged her parents not to make her marry an Englishman, but they had insisted, and it did not sound as if they would have been particularly welcoming if she had run back home.

But there was only so long he could spend in a somewhat secluded corner of the ballroom with an unmarried lady without causing talk, and so once Hyacinth had finished the tale, he had bid her farewell and handed her off to the next gentleman on her dance card.

His objectives for the evening accomplished (greeting his hostess, dancing with Hyacinth, discerning her progress with the diary), he decided he might as well leave altogether. The night was still reasonably young; there was no reason he couldn't go to his club or a gambling hell.

Or, he thought with a bit more anticipation, he hadn't seen his mistress in some time. Well, not a mistress, exactly. Gareth hadn't enough money to keep a woman like Maria in the style to which she was accustomed, but luckily one of her previous gentlemen had given her a neat little house in Bloomsbury, eliminating the need for Gareth to do the same. Since he wasn't paying her bills, she felt no need to remain faithful, but that hardly signified, since he didn't, either.

And it had been a while. It seemed the only woman he'd spent any time with lately was Hyacinth, and the Lord knew he couldn't dally there.

Gareth murmured his farewells to a few acquaintances near the ballroom door, then slipped out into the hall. It was surprisingly empty, given the number of people attending the party. He started to walk toward the front of the house, but then stopped. It was a long way to Bloomsbury, especially in a hired hack, which was what he was going to need to use, since he'd gained a ride over with his grandmother. The Bridgertons had set aside a room in the back for gentlemen to see to their needs. Gareth decided to make use of it.

He turned around and retraced his steps, then bypassed the ballroom door and headed farther down the hall. A couple of laughing gentlemen stepped out as he reached the door, and Gareth nodded his greetings before entering.

It was one of those two-room chambers, with a small waiting area outside an inner sanctum to afford a bit more privacy. The door to the second room was closed, so Gareth whistled softly to himself as he waited his turn.

He loved to whistle.

My bonnie lies over the ocean . . .

He always sang the words to himself as he whistled.

My bonnie lies over the sea. . . .

Half the songs he whistled had words he couldn't very well sing aloud, anyway.

My bonnie lies over the ocean . . .

"I should have known it was you."

Gareth froze, finding himself face-to-face with his father, who, he realized, had been the person for whom he had been waiting so patiently to relieve himself.

"So bring back my bonnie to me," Gareth sang out loudly, giving the final word a nice, dramatic flourish.

He watched his father's jaw set into an uncomfortable line. The baron hated singing even more than he did whistling.

"I'm surprised they let you in," Lord St. Clair said, his voice deceptively placid.

Gareth shrugged insolently. "Funny how one's blood remains so conveniently hidden inside, even when it's not quite blue." He gave the older man a game smile. "All of the world thinks I am yours. Is that not just the most—"

"Stop," the baron hissed. "Good God, it's enough just to look at you. Listening makes me ill."

"Strangely enough, I remain unbothered."

But inside, Gareth could feel himself beginning to change. His heart was beating faster, and his chest had taken on a strange, shaky feeling. He felt unfocused, restless, and it took all of his self-control to hold his arms still at his sides.

One would think he'd have grown used to this, but every time, it took him by surprise. He always told himself that this would be the time he would see his father and it just wouldn't matter, but no . . .

It always did.

And Lord St. Clair wasn't even really his father. That was the true rub. The man had the ability to turn him into an immature idiot, and he wasn't even really his father. Gareth had told himself, time and again, that it didn't matter. *He* didn't matter. They weren't related by blood, and the baron should not mean any more to him than a stranger on the street.

But he did. Gareth didn't want his approval; he'd long since given up on that, and besides, why would he want approbation from a man he didn't even respect?

It was something else. Something much harder to define. He saw the baron and he suddenly had to assert himself, to make his presence known.

To make his presence felt.

He had to *bother* the man. Because the Lord knew, the man bothered him.

He felt this way whenever he saw him. Or at least when they were forced into conversation. And Gareth knew that he had to end the contact now, before he did something he might regret.

Because he always did. Every time he swore to himself that

he would learn, that he'd be more mature, but then it happened again. He saw his father, and he was fifteen again, all smirky smiles and bad behavior.

But this time he was going to try. He was in Bridgerton House, for God's sake, and the least he could do was try to avoid a scene.

"If you'll excuse me," he said, trying to brush past him.

But Lord St. Clair stepped to the side, forcing their shoulders to collide. "She won't have you, you know," he said, chuckling under the words.

Gareth held himself very still. "What are you talking about?"

"The Bridgerton chit. I saw you panting after her."

For a moment Gareth didn't move. He hadn't even realized his father had been in the ballroom. Which bothered him. Not that it should have done. Hell, he should have been whooping with joy that he'd finally managed to enjoy an event without being needled by Lord St. Clair's presence.

But instead he just felt somehow deceived. As if the baron had been hiding from him.

Spying on him.

"Nothing to say?" the baron taunted.

Gareth just lifted a brow as he looked through the open door to the chamber pot. "Not unless you wish me to aim from here," he drawled.

The baron turned, saw what he meant, then said disgustedly, "You would do it, too."

"You know, I believe I would," Gareth said. Hadn't really occurred to him until that moment—his comment had been more of a threat than anything else—but he might be willing to engage in a bit of crude behavior if it meant watching his father's veins nearly burst with fury.

"You are revolting."

"You raised me."

A direct hit. The baron seethed visibly before he shot back with, "Not because I wanted to. And I certainly never dreamed I would have to pass the title on to you."

Gareth held his tongue. He would say a lot of things to anger his father, but he would not make light of his brother's death. Ever.

"George must be spinning in his grave," Lord St. Clair said in a low voice.

And Gareth snapped. One moment he was standing in the middle of the small room, his arms hanging stiffly at his sides, and the next he had his father pinned up against the wall, one hand on his shoulder, the other at his throat.

"He was my brother," Gareth hissed.

The baron spit in his face. "He was my son."

Gareth's lungs were beginning to shake. It felt as if he couldn't get enough air. "He was my brother," he repeated, putting every ounce of his will into keeping his voice even. "Maybe not through you, but through our mother. And I loved him."

And somehow the loss felt all the more severe. He had mourned George since the day he'd died, but right now it felt like a big, gaping hole was yawning within him, and Gareth didn't know how to fill it.

He was down to one person now. Just his grandmother. Just one person he could honestly say he loved.

And loved him in return.

He hadn't realized this before. Maybe he hadn't wanted to. But now, standing here with the man he'd always called Father, even after he'd learned the truth, he realized just how alone he was.

And he was disgusted with himself. With his behavior, with what he became in the baron's presence.

Abruptly, he let go, backing up as he watched the baron catch his breath.

Gareth's own breathing wasn't so steady, either.

He should go. He needed to get out, away, be anywhere but here.

"You'll never have her, you know," came his father's mocking voice.

Gareth had taken a step toward the door. He hadn't even realized he'd moved until the baron's words caused him to freeze.

"Miss Bridgerton," his father clarified.

"I don't want Miss Bridgerton," Gareth said carefully.

This made the baron laugh. "Of course you do. She is everything you're not. Everything you could never hope to be."

Gareth forced himself to relax, or at least give the appearance of it. "Well, for one thing," he said with the cocky little smile he knew his father hated, "she's female."

His father sneered at his feeble attempt at humor. "She will never marry you."

"I don't recall asking her."

"Bah. You've been lapping at her heels all week. Everyone's been commenting on it."

Gareth knew that his uncharacteristic attention paid to a proper young lady had raised a few eyebrows, but he also knew that the gossip wasn't anywhere near what his father intimated.

Still, it gave him a sick sort of satisfaction to know that his father was as obsessed with him and his doings as the other way around.

"Miss Bridgerton is a good friend of my grandmother's," Gareth said lightly, enjoying the slight curl of his father's lip at the mention of Lady Danbury. They had always hated each other, and when they'd still spoken, Lady D had never ceded the upper hand.

She was the wife of an earl, and Lord St. Clair a mere baron, and she never allowed him to forget it.

"Of course she's a friend of the countess," the baron said, recovering quickly. "I'm sure it's why she tolerates your attentions."

"You would have to ask Miss Bridgerton," Gareth said lightly, trying to brush off the topic as inconsequential. He certainly wasn't about to reveal that Hyacinth was translating Isabella's diary. Lord St. Clair would probably demand that he hand it over, and that was one thing Gareth absolutely did not intend to do.

And it wasn't just because it meant that he possessed something his father might desire. Gareth truly wanted to know what secrets lay in the delicate handwritten pages. Or maybe there were no secrets, just the daily monotony of a noblewoman married to a man she did not love.

Either way, he wanted to hear what she'd had to say.

So he held his tongue.

"You can try," Lord St. Clair said softly, "but they will never have you. Blood runs true. It always does."

"What do you mean by that?" Gareth asked, his tone carefully even. It was always difficult to tell whether his father was threatening him or just expounding upon his most favorite of subjects—bloodlines and nobility.

Lord St. Clair crossed his arms. "The Bridgertons," he said. "They will never allow her to marry you, even if she is foolish enough to fancy herself in love with you."

"She doesn't—"

"You're uncouth," the baron burst out. "You're stupid—"

It shot out of his mouth before he could stop himself: "I am *not*—"

"You behave stupidly," the baron cut in, "and you're certainly not good enough for a Bridgerton girl. They'll see through you soon enough."

Gareth forced himself to get his breathing under control. The baron loved to provoke him, loved to say things that would make Gareth protest like a child.

"In some ways," Lord St. Clair continued, a slow, self-satisfied smile spreading across his face, "it's an interesting question."

Gareth just stared at him, too angry to give him the satisfaction of asking what he meant.

"Who, pray tell," the baron mused, "is your father?"

Gareth caught his breath. It was the first time the baron had ever come out and asked it so directly. He'd called Gareth a by-blow, he'd called him a mongrel and a mangy whelp. And he had called Gareth's mother plenty of other, even less flattering things. But he'd never actually come out and pondered the question of Gareth's paternity.

And it made him wonder—had he learned the truth?

"You'd know better than I," Gareth said softly.

The moment was electric, with silence rocking the air. Gareth didn't breathe, would have stopped his heart from beating if he could have done, but in the end all Lord St. Clair said was "Your mother wouldn't say."

Gareth eyed him warily. His father's voice was still laced with bitterness, but there was something else there, too, a certain probing, testing quality. Gareth realized that the baron was feeling him out, trying to see if Gareth had learned something of his paternity.

"It's eating you alive," Gareth said, unable to keep from smiling. "She wanted someone else more than you, and it's killing you, even after all these years."

For a moment he thought the baron might strike him, but at the last minute, Lord St. Clair stepped back, his arms stiff at his sides. "I didn't love your mother," he said.

"I never thought you had," Gareth replied. It had never been about love. It had been about pride. With the baron, it was always about pride.

"I want to know," Lord St. Clair said in a low voice. "I want to know who it was, and I will give you the satisfaction of admitting to that desire. I have never forgiven her for her sins. But you . . . you . . ." He laughed, and the sound shivered right into Gareth's soul.

"You *are* her sins," the baron said. He laughed again, the sound growing more chilling by the second. "You'll never know. You will never know whose blood passes through your veins. And you'll never know who didn't love you well enough to claim you."

Gareth's heart stopped.

The baron smiled. "Think about that the next time you ask Miss Bridgerton to dance. You're probably nothing more than the son of a chimney sweep." He shrugged, the motion purposefully disdainful. "Maybe a footman. We always did have strapping young footmen at Clair Hall."

Gareth almost slapped him. He wanted to. By God, he itched to, and it took more restraint than he'd ever known he possessed not to do it, but somehow he managed to remain still.

"You're nothing but a mongrel," Lord St. Clair said, walking to the door. "That's all you'll ever be."

"Yes, but I'm *your* mongrel," Gareth said, smiling cruelly. "Born in wedlock, even if not by your seed." He stepped forward, until they were nearly nose to nose. "I'm yours."

The baron swore and moved away, grasping the doorknob with shaking fingers.

"Doesn't it just slay you?"

"Don't attempt to be better than you are," the baron hissed. "It's too painful to watch you try."

And then, before Gareth could get in the last word, the baron stormed out of the room.

For several seconds Gareth didn't move. It was as if something in his body recognized the need for absolute stillness, as if a single motion might cause him to shatter.

And then—

His arms pumped madly through the air, his fingers curling into furious claws. He clamped his teeth together to keep from screaming, but sounds emerged all the same, low and guttural.

Wounded.

He hated this. Dear God, why?

Why why why?

Why did the baron still have this sort of power over him? He wasn't his father. He'd never been his father, and damn it all, Gareth should have been glad for that.

And he was. When he was in his right mind, when he could think clearly, he was.

But when they were face-to-face, and the baron was whispering all of Gareth's secret fears, it didn't matter.

There was nothing but pain. Nothing but the little boy inside, trying and trying and trying, always wondering why he was never quite good enough.

"I need to leave," Gareth muttered, crashing through the door into the hall. He needed to leave, to get away, to not be with people.

He wasn't fit company. Not for any of the reasons his father said, but still, he was likely to—

"Mr. St. Clair!"

He looked up.

Hyacinth.

She was standing in the hall, alone. The light from the candles seemed to leap against her hair, bringing out rich red undertones. She looked lovely, and she somehow looked . . . complete.

Her life was full, he realized. She might not have been married, but she had her family.

She knew who she was. She knew where she belonged.

And he had never felt more jealous of another human being than he did in that moment.

"Are you all right?" she asked.

He didn't say anything, but that never stopped Hyacinth. "I saw your father," she said softly. "Down the hall. He looked angry, and then he saw me, and he laughed."

Gareth's fingernails bit into his palms.

"Why would he laugh?" Hyacinth asked. "I hardly know the man, and—"

He had been staring at a spot past her shoulder, but her silence made his eyes snap back to her face.

"Mr. St. Clair?" she asked softly. "Are you sure there is nothing wrong?" Her brow was crinkled with concern, the kind one couldn't fake, then she added, more softly, "Did he say something to upset you?"

His father was right about one thing. Hyacinth Bridgerton was good. She may have been vexing, managing, and often annoying as hell, but inside, where it counted, she was good.

And he heard his father's voice.

You'll never have her.

You're not good enough for her.

You'll never—

Mongrel. Mongrel. Mongrel.

He looked at her, really looked at her, his eyes sweeping from her face to her shoulders, laid bare by the seductive décolletage of her dress. Her breasts weren't large, but they'd been pushed up, surely by some contraption meant to tease and entice, and he could see the barest hint of her cleavage, peeking out at the edge of the midnight blue silk.

"Gareth?" she whispered.

She'd never called him by his given name before. He'd told her she could, but she hadn't yet done so. He was quite certain of that.

He wanted to touch her.

No, he wanted to consume her.

He wanted to use her, to prove to himself that he was every bit as good and worthy as she was, and maybe just to show his father that he *did* belong, that he wouldn't corrupt every soul he touched.

But more than that, he just plain wanted her.

Her eyes widened as he took a step toward her, halving the distance between them.

She didn't move away. Her lips parted, and he could hear the soft rush of her breath, but she didn't move.

She might not have said yes, but she didn't say no.

He reached out, snaking his arm around her back, and in an instant she was pressed against him. He wanted her. God, how he wanted her. He needed her, for more than just his body.

And he needed her now.

His lips found hers, and he was none of the things one should be the first time. He wasn't gentle, and he wasn't sweet. He did no seductive dance, idly teasing her until she couldn't say no.

He just kissed her. With everything he had, with every ounce of desperation coursing through his veins.

His tongue parted her lips, swooped inside, tasting her, seeking her warmth. He felt her hands at the back of his neck, holding on for all she was worth, and he felt her heart racing against his chest.

She wanted him. She might not understand it, she might not know what to do with it, but she wanted him.

And it made him feel like a king.

His heart pounded harder, and his body began to tighten. Somehow they were against a wall, and he could barely breathe as his hand crept up and around, skimming over her ribs until he reached the soft fullness of her breast. He squeezed—softly, so as not to scare her, but with just enough strength to memorize the shape of her, the feel, the weight in his hand.

It was perfect, and he could feel her reaction through her dress.

He wanted to take her into his mouth, to peel the dress from her body and do a hundred wicked things to her.

He felt the resistance slip from her body, heard her sigh against his mouth. She'd never been kissed before; he was quite certain of that. But she was eager, and she was aroused. He could feel it in the way her body pressed against his, the way her fingers clutched desperately at his shoulders.

"Kiss me back," he murmured, nibbling at her lips.

"I *am*," came her muffled reply.

He drew back, just an inch. "You need a lesson or two," he said with a smile. "But don't worry, we'll get you good at this."

He leaned in to kiss her once more—dear God, he was enjoying this—but she wriggled away.

"Hyacinth," he said huskily, catching her hand in his. He tugged, intending to pull her back against him, but she yanked her hand free.

Gareth raised his brows, waiting for her to say something.

This was Hyacinth, after all. Surely she'd say something.

But she just looked stricken, sick with herself.

And then she did the one thing he never would have thought she'd do.

She ran away.

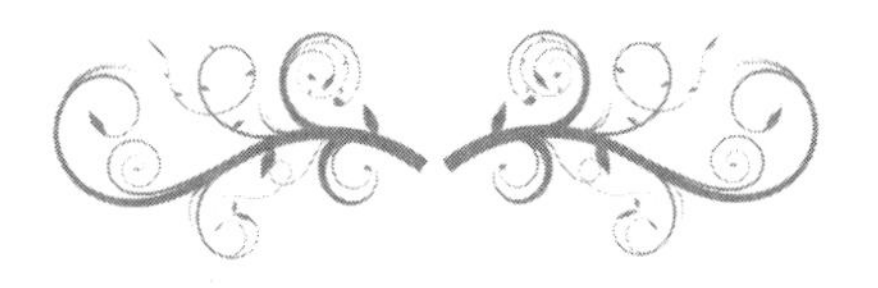

Chapter 8

The next morning. Our heroine is sitting on her bed, perched against her pillows. The Italian diary is at her side, but she has not picked it up.

She has relived the kiss in her mind approximately forty-two times.

In fact, she is reliving it right now:

Hyacinth would have liked to think that she would be the sort of woman who could kiss with aplomb, then carry on for the rest of the evening as if nothing had happened. She'd have liked to think when the time came to treat a gentleman with well-deserved disdain, that butter wouldn't melt in her mouth, her eyes would be perfect chips of ice, and she would manage a cut direct with style and flair.

And in her imagination, she did all of that and more.

Reality, however, had not been so sweet.

Because when Gareth had said her name and tried to tug her back to him for another kiss, the only thing she could think to do was run.

Which was not, she had assured herself, for what had to be the forty-third time since his lips had touched hers, in keeping with her character.

It couldn't be. She couldn't let it be. She was Hyacinth Bridgerton.

Hyacinth.

Bridgerton.

Surely that had to mean something. One kiss could not turn her into a senseless ninny.

And besides, it wasn't the kiss. The kiss hadn't bothered her. The kiss had, in fact, been rather nice. And, to be honest, long overdue.

One would think, in her world, among her society, that she would have taken pride in her untouched, never-been-kissed status. After all, the mere hint of impropriety was enough to ruin a woman's reputation.

But one did not reach the age of two-and-twenty, or one's fourth London season, without feeling the littlest bit rejected that no one had thus far attempted a kiss.

And no one had. Hyacinth wasn't asking to be *ravished*, for heaven's sake, but no one had even leaned in, or dropped a heavy gaze to her lips, as if he was thinking about it.

Not until last night. Not until Gareth St. Clair.

Her first instinct had been to jump with surprise. For all Gareth's rakish ways, he hadn't shown any interest in extending his reputation as a rogue in her direction. The man had an opera singer tucked away in Bloomsbury, after all. What on earth would he need with *her*?

But then . . .

Well, good heavens, she still didn't know how it had all come about. One moment she was asking him if he was unwell—he'd looked very odd, after all, and it was obvious he'd had some sort of altercation with his father, despite her efforts to separate the two—and then the next he was staring at her with an intensity that had made her shiver. He'd looked possessed, consumed.

He'd looked as if he wanted to consume *her*.

And yet Hyacinth couldn't shake the feeling that he hadn't really meant to kiss her. That maybe any woman happening across him in the hall would have done just as well.

Especially after he'd laughingly told her that she needed improvement.

She didn't think he had meant to be cruel, but still, his words had stung.

"Kiss me back," she said to herself, her voice a whiny mimic of his. "Kiss me back."

She flopped back against her pillows. "I *did*." Good heavens, what did it say about her if a man couldn't even tell when she was trying to kiss him back?

And even if she hadn't been doing such a good job of it—and Hyacinth wasn't quite ready to admit to *that*—it seemed the sort of thing that ought to come naturally, and certainly the sort of thing that ought to have come naturally to *her*. Well, still, what on earth was she expected to do? Wield her tongue like a sword? She'd put her hands on his shoulders. She hadn't struggled in his arms. What else was she supposed to have done to indicate that she was enjoying herself?

It seemed a wretchedly unfair conundrum to her. Men wanted their women chaste and untouched, then they mocked them for their lack of experience.

It was just . . . it was just . . .

Hyacinth chewed on her lip, horrified by how close to tears she was.

It was just that she'd thought her first kiss would be magical.

And she'd *thought* that the gentleman in question would emerge from the encounter if not impressed then at least a little bit pleased by her performance.

But Gareth St. Clair had been his usual mocking self, and Hyacinth hated that she'd allowed him to make her feel small.

"It's just a kiss," she whispered, her words floating through the empty room. "Just a kiss. It doesn't mean a thing."

But she knew, even as she tried so hard to lie to herself about it, that it had been more than a kiss.

Much, much more.

At least that was how it had been for her. She closed her eyes in agony. Dear God, while she'd been lying on her bed thinking and thinking, then rethinking and thinking again, he was probably sleeping like a baby. The man had kissed—

Well, she didn't care to speculate on how many women he had kissed, but it certainly had to have been enough to make her seem the greenest girl in London.

How was she going to face him? And she was going to have to face him. She was translating his grandmother's diary, for heaven's sake. If she tried to avoid him, it would seem so obvious.

And the last thing she wanted to do was allow him to see how upset he had made her. There were quite a few things in life a woman needed a great deal more than pride, but Hyacinth figured that as long as dignity was still an option, she might as well hang on to it.

And in the meantime . . .

She picked up his grandmother's diary. She hadn't done any work on it for a full day. She was only twenty-two pages in; there were at least a hundred more to go.

She looked down at the book, lying unopened on her lap. She supposed she could send it back. In fact, she probably *should* send it back. It would serve him right to be forced to find another translator after his behavior the night before.

But she was enjoying the diary. Life didn't toss very many challenges in the direction of well-bred young ladies. Frankly, it would be nice to be able to say she had translated an entire book from the Italian. And it would probably be nice to actually do it, too.

Hyacinth fingered the small bookmark she'd used to hold her place and opened the book. Isabella had just arrived in England in the middle of the season, and after a mere week in the country, her new husband had dragged her off to London, where she was expected—without the benefit of fluent English—to socialize and entertain as befitted her station.

To make matters worse, Lord St. Clair's mother was in residence at Clair House and was clearly unhappy about having to give up her position as lady of the house.

Hyacinth frowned as she read on, stopping every now and then to look up an unfamiliar word. The dowager baroness was interfering with the servants, countermanding Isabella's orders and making it uncomfortable for those who accepted the new baroness as the woman in charge.

It certainly didn't make marriage look terribly appealing. Hyacinth made a mental note to try to marry a man without a mother.

"Chin up, Isabella," she muttered, wincing as she read about the latest altercation—something about an addition of mussels to the menu, despite the fact that shellfish made Isabella develop hives.

"You need to make it clear who's in charge," Hyacinth said to the book. "You—"

She frowned, looking down at the latest entry. This didn't make sense. Why was Isabella talking about her *bambino?*

Hyacinth read the words three times before thinking to glance back up at the date at top. *24 Ottobre 1766.*

1766? Wait a minute . . .

She flipped back one page.

1764.

Isabella had skipped two years. Why would she do that?

Hyacinth looked quickly through the next twenty or so pages. *1766 . . . 1769 . . . 1769 . . . 1770 . . . 1774 . . .*

"You're not a very dedicated diarist," Hyacinth murmured. No wonder Isabella had managed to fit decades into one slim volume; she frequently went years between entries.

Hyacinth turned back to the passage about the *bambino*, continuing her laborious translation. Isabella was back in London, this time without her husband, which didn't seem to bother her one bit. And she seemed to have gained a bit of self-confidence, although that might have been merely the result of the death of the dowager, which Hyacinth surmised had happened a year earlier.

I found the perfect spot, Hyacinth translated, jotting the words down on paper. *He will never . . .* She frowned. She didn't know the rest of the sentence, so she put some dashes down on her paper to indicate an untranslated phrase and moved on. *He does not think I am intelligent enough*, she read. *And so he won't suspect . . .*

"Oh, my goodness," Hyacinth said, sitting up straight. She flipped the page of the diary, reading it as quickly as she could, her attempts at a written translation all but forgotten.

"Isabella," she said with admiration. "You sly fox."

An hour or so later, an instant before Gareth knocks on Hyacinth's door.

Gareth sucked in a deep breath, summoning the courage to wrap his fingers around the heavy brass knocker that sat on the front door of Number Five, Bruton Street, the elegant little house Hyacinth's mother had purchased after her eldest son had married and taken over Bridgerton House.

Then he tried not to feel completely disgusted with himself for feeling he needed the courage in the first place. And it wasn't really courage he needed. For God's sake, he wasn't *afraid*. It was . . . well, no, it wasn't quite dread. It was—

He groaned. In every life, there were moments a person would do just about anything to put off. And if it meant he was less of a man because he *really* didn't feel like dealing with Hyacinth Bridgerton . . . well, he was perfectly willing to call himself a juvenile fool.

Frankly, he didn't know anyone who'd want to deal with Hyacinth Bridgerton at a moment like this.

He rolled his eyes, thoroughly impatient with himself. This shouldn't be difficult. He shouldn't feel strained. Hell, it wasn't as if he had never kissed a female before and had to face her the next day.

Except . . .

Except he'd never kissed a female like Hyacinth, one who A) hadn't been kissed before and B) had every reason to expect that a kiss might mean something more.

Not to mention C) was Hyacinth.

Because one really couldn't discount the magnitude of that. If there was one thing he had learned in this past week, it was that Hyacinth was quite unlike any other woman he'd ever known.

At any rate, he'd sat at home all morning, waiting for the package that would surely arrive, escorted by a liveried footman, returning his grandmother's diary. Hyacinth couldn't possibly wish to translate it now, not after he had insulted her so grievously the night before.

Not, he thought, only a little bit defensively, that he'd meant to insult her. In truth, he hadn't meant anything one way or another. He certainly hadn't meant to kiss her. The thought hadn't even occurred to him, and in fact he rather thought it *wouldn't* have occurred to him except that he had been so off-balance, and then she'd somehow been there, right in the hallway, almost as if summoned by magic.

Right after his father had taunted him about her.

What the hell else was he expected to do?

And it hadn't meant anything. It was enjoyable—certainly more enjoyable than he would have imagined, but it hadn't meant a thing.

But women tended to view these things badly, and her expression when she broke it off had not been terribly inviting.

If anything, she had looked horrified.

Which had made him feel a fool. He'd never disgusted a woman with his kiss before.

And it had all been magnified later that night, when he'd overheard someone asking her about him, and she had brushed it off with a laugh, saying that she couldn't possibly have refused to dance with him; she was far too good friends with his grandmother.

Which was true, and he certainly understood that she was attempting to save face, even if she hadn't known that he could hear, but all the same, it was too close an echo of his father's words for him not to feel it.

He let out a sigh. There was no putting it off any longer. He lifted his hand, intending to grasp the knocker—

And then quite nearly lost his balance when the door flew open.

"For heaven's sake," Hyacinth said, looking at him through impatient eyes, "were you ever going to knock?"

"Were you watching for me?"

"Of course I was. My bedroom is right above. I can see everyone."

Why, he wondered, did this not surprise him?

"And I did send you a note," she added. She stood aside, motioning for him to come in. "Recent behavior notwithstanding," she continued, "you do seem to possess manners enough not to refuse a direct written request from a lady."

"Er . . . yes," he said. It was all he could seem to think of, faced as he was by the whirlwind of energy and activity standing across from him.

Why wasn't she angry with him? Wasn't she *supposed* to be angry?

"We need to talk," Hyacinth said.

"Of course," he murmured. "I must apologize—"

"Not about that," she said dismissively, "although . . ." She looked up, her expression somewhere between thoughtful and peeved. "You certainly *should* apologize."

"Yes, of course, I—"

"But that's not why I summoned you," she cut in.

If it had been polite, he would have crossed his arms. "Do you wish for me to apologize or not?"

Hyacinth glanced up and down the hall, placing one finger to her lips with a soft, "Shhh."

"Have I suddenly been transported into a volume of *Miss Butterworth and the Mad Baron*?" Gareth wondered aloud.

Hyacinth scowled at him, a look that he was coming to realize was quintessentially her. It was a frown, yes, but with a hint—no, make that three hints—of impatience. It was the look of a woman who had spent her life waiting for people to keep up with her.

"In here," she said, motioning toward an open doorway.

"As you wish, my lady," he murmured. Far be it for him to complain about not having to apologize.

He followed her into what turned out to be a drawing room, tastefully decorated in shades of rose and cream. It was very delicate and very feminine, and Gareth half wondered if it had been designed for the sole purpose of making men feel overlarge and ill at ease.

Hyacinth waved him over to a sitting area, so he went, watching her curiously as she carefully maneuvered the door until it was shut most of the way. Gareth eyed the four-inch opening with amusement. Funny how such a small space could mean the difference between propriety and disaster.

"I don't want to be overheard," Hyacinth said.

Gareth just lifted his brows in question, waiting for her to seat herself on the sofa. When he was satisfied that she wasn't going to jump up and check behind the drapes for an eavesdropper, he sat in a Hepplewhite armchair that was catercorner to the sofa.

"I need to tell you about the diary," she said, her eyes alight with excitement.

He blinked with surprise. "You're not going to return it, then?"

"Of course not. You don't think I—" She stopped, and he noticed that her fingers were twisting spirals in the soft green fabric of her skirt. For some reason this pleased him. He was rather relieved that she was not furious with him for kissing her—like any man, he'd go to great lengths to avoid any sort of hysterical feminine scene. But at the same time, he didn't wish for her to be completely unaffected.

Good God, he was a better kisser than *that*.

"I *should* return the diary," she said, sounding rather like herself again. "Truly, I should force you to find someone else to translate it. You deserve no less."

"Absolutely," he demurred.

She gave him a look, saying that she didn't appreciate such perfunctory agreement. *"However,"* she said, as only she could say it.

Gareth leaned forward. It seemed expected.

"However," she said again, "I rather like reading your grandmother's diary, and I see no reason to deprive myself of an enjoyable challenge simply because you have behaved recklessly."

Gareth held silent, since his last attempt at agreement had been so ill received. It soon became apparent, however, that this time he was expected to make a comment, so he quickly chimed in with, "Of course not."

Hyacinth nodded approvingly, then added, "And besides"—and here she leaned forward, her bright blue eyes sparkling with excitement—*"it just got interesting."*

Something turned over in Gareth's stomach. Had Hyacinth discovered the secret of his birth? It hadn't even occurred to him that Isabella might have known the truth; she'd had very little contact with her son, after all, and rarely visited.

But if she did know, she very well might've written it down.

"What do you mean?" he asked carefully.

Hyacinth picked up the diary, which had been sitting on a nearby end table. "Your grandmother," she said, her entire bearing radiating excitement, "had a secret." She opened the book—she'd marked a page with an elegant little bookmark—and held it out, pointing with her index finger to a sentence in the middle of the page as she said, *"Diamanti. Diamanti."* She looked up, unable to contain an exhilarated grin. "Do you know what that means?"

He shook his head. "I'm afraid not."

"Diamonds, Gareth. It means diamonds."

He found himself looking at the page, even though he couldn't possibly understand the words. "I beg your pardon?"

"Your grandmother had jewels, Gareth. And she never told your grandfather about them."

His lips parted. "What are you saying?"

"*Her* grandmother came to visit shortly after your father was born. And she brought with her a set of jewels. Rings, I think. And a bracelet. And Isabella never told anyone."

"What did she do with them?"

"She hid them." Hyacinth was practically bouncing off the sofa now. "She hid them in Clair House, right here in London. She wrote that your grandfather didn't much like London, so there would be less chance he'd discover them here."

Finally, some of Hyacinth's enthusiasm began to seep into him. Not much—he wasn't going to allow himself to get too excited by what was probably going to turn out to be a wild-goose chase. But her fervor was infectious, and before he realized it, he was leaning forward, his heart beginning to beat just a little bit faster. "What are you saying?" he asked.

"I'm saying," she said, as if she was repeating something she'd uttered five times already, in every possible permutation, "that those jewels are probably still there. Oh!" She stopped short, her eyes meeting his with an almost disconcerting suddenness. "Unless you already know about them. Does your father already have them in his possession?"

"No," Gareth said thoughtfully. "I don't think so. At least, not that I've ever been told."

"You see? We can—"

"But I'm rarely told of anything," he cut in. "My father has never considered me his closest confidant."

For a moment her eyes took on a sympathetic air, but that was quickly trampled by her almost piratical zeal. "Then they're still there," she said excitedly. "Or at least there is a very good chance that they are. We have to go get them."

"What—*We?*" Oh, no.

But Hyacinth was too lost in her own excitement to have noticed his emphasis. "Just think, Gareth," she said, clearly now perfectly comfortable with the use of his given name, "this could be the answer to all of your financial problems."

He drew back. "What makes you think I have financial problems?"

"Oh, please," she scoffed. "Everyone knows you have financial problems. Or if you don't, you will. Your father has run up debts from here to Nottinghamshire and back." She paused, possibly for air, then said, "Clair Hall is in Nottinghamshire, isn't it?"

"Yes, of course, but—"

"Right. Well. You're going to inherit those debts, you know."

"I'm aware."

"Then what better way to ensure your solvency than to secure your grandmother's jewels before Lord St. Clair finds them? Because we both know that he will only sell them and spend the proceeds."

"You seem to know a great deal about my father," Gareth said in a quiet voice.

"Nonsense," she said briskly. "I know nothing about him except that he detests you."

Gareth cracked a smile, which surprised him. It wasn't a topic about which he usually possessed a great deal of humor. But then again, no one had ever dared broach it with such frankness before.

"I could not speak on your behalf," Hyacinth continued with a shrug, "but if *I* detested someone, you can be sure I would go out of my way to make certain he didn't get a treasure's worth of jewels."

"How positively Christian of you," Gareth murmured.

She lifted a brow. "I never said I was a model of goodness and light."

"No," Gareth said, feeling his lips twitch. "No, you certainly did not."

Hyacinth clapped her hands together, then set them both palms down on her lap. She looked at him expectantly. "Well, then," she said, once it was apparent that he had no further comment, "when shall we go?"

"Go?" he echoed.

"To look for the diamonds," she said impatiently. "Haven't you been listening to anything I've said?"

Gareth suddenly had a terrifying vision of what it must be like inside her mind. She was dressed in black, clearly, and—good God—almost certainly in men's clothing as well. She'd probably insist upon lowering herself out her bedroom window on knotted sheets, too.

"*We* are not going anywhere," he said firmly.

"Of course we are," she said. "You must get those jewels. You can't let your father have them."

"*I* will go."

"You're not leaving *me* behind." It was a statement, not a question. Not that Gareth would have expected otherwise from her.

"*If* I attempt to break into Clair House," Gareth said, "and that is a rather large *if*, I will have to do so in the dead of night."

"Well, of course."

Good God, did the woman *never* cease talking? He paused, waiting to make sure that she was done. Finally, with a great show of exaggerated patience, he finished with, "I am not dragging you around town at midnight. Forget, for one moment, about the danger, of which I assure you there is plenty. If we were caught, I would be required to marry you, and I can only assume your desire for that outcome evenly matches mine."

It was an overblown speech, and his tone had been rather pompous and stuffy, but it had the desired effect, forcing her to close her mouth for long enough to sort through the convoluted structure of his sentences.

But then she opened it again, and said, "Well, you won't have to drag me."

Gareth thought his head might explode. "Good God, woman, have you been listening to anything I've said?"

"Of course I have. I have four older brothers. I can recognize a supercilious, pontificating male when I see one."

"Oh, for the love of—"

"You, Mr. St. Clair, aren't thinking clearly." She leaned forward, lifting one of her brows in an almost disconcertingly confident manner. "You need me."

"Like I need a festering abscess," he muttered.

"I am going to pretend I didn't hear that," Hyacinth said. Between her teeth. "Because if I did otherwise, I would not be inclined to aid you in your endeavors. And if I did not aid you—"

"Do you have a *point?*"

She eyed him coolly. "You are not nearly as sensible a person as I thought you."

"Strangely enough, you are *exactly* as sensible as I thought you."

"I will pretend I didn't hear *that* as well," she said, jabbing her index finger in his direction in a most unladylike manner. "You seem to forget that of the two of us, I am the only one who reads Italian. And I don't see how you are going to find the jewels without my aid."

His lips parted, and when he spoke, it was in a low, almost terrifyingly even voice. "You would withhold the information from me?"

"Of course not," Hyacinth said, since she couldn't bring herself to lie to him, even if he did deserve it. "I do have *some* honor. I was merely trying to explain that you will need me *there*, in the house. My knowledge of the language isn't perfect. There are some words that could be open to interpretation, and I might need to see the actual room before I can tell exactly what she was talking about."

His eyes narrowed.

"It's the truth, I swear!" She quickly grabbed the book, flipping a page, then another, then going back to the original. "It's right here, see? *Armadio.* It could mean cabinet. Or it could mean wardrobe. Or—" She stopped, swallowing. She hated to admit that she wasn't quite sure what she was talking about, even if that deficiency was the only thing that was going to secure her a place by his side when he went to look for the jewels. "If you must know," she said, unable to keep her irritation out of her voice, "I'm not precisely certain what it means. Precisely, that is," she added, because the truth was, she *did* have a fairly good idea. And it just wasn't in her character to admit to faults she didn't have.

Good gracious, she had a difficult enough time with faults she did possess.

"Why don't you look it up in your Italian dictionary?"

"It's not listed," she lied. It wasn't really *such* an egregious fib. The dictionary had listed several possible translations, certainly enough for Hyacinth to truthfully claim an imprecise understanding.

She waited for him to speak—probably not as long as she should have done, but it seemed like an eternity. And she *just* couldn't keep quiet. "I could, if you wish, write to my former governess and ask for a more exact definition, but she's not the most reliable of correspondents—"

"Meaning?"

"Meaning I haven't written to her in three years," Hyacinth admitted, "although I'm quite certain she would come to my aid now. It's just that I have no idea how busy she is or when she might find the time to reply—the last I'd heard she'd given birth to twins—"

"Why does this not surprise me?"

"It's true, and heaven only knows how long it will take her to respond. Twins are an uncommon amount of work, or so I'm told, and . . ." Her voice lost some of its volume as it became apparent he wasn't listening to her. She stole a glance at his face and finished, anyway, mostly because she'd already thought of the words, and there wasn't much point in *not* saying them. "Well, I don't think she has the means for a baby nurse," she said, but her voice had trailed off by the end of it.

Gareth held silent for what seemed an interminably long time before finally saying, "If what you say is correct, and the jewels are still hidden—and that is no certainty, given that she hid them"—his eyes floated briefly up as he did the math—"over sixty years ago, then surely they will remain in place until we can get an accurate translation from your governess."

"You could wait?" Hyacinth asked, feeling her entire head move forward and down with disbelief. "You could actually *wait*?"

"Why not?"

"Because they're *there*. Because—" She cut herself off, unable to do anything other than stare at him as if he were mad. She knew that people's minds did not work the same way. And she'd long since learned that hardly anyone's mind worked the way hers did. But she couldn't imagine that *any*one could wait when faced with *this*.

Good heavens, if it were up to her, they'd be scaling the wall of Clair House that night.

"Think about this," Hyacinth said, leaning forward. "If he finds those jewels between now and whenever you find the time to go look for them, you are never going to forgive yourself."

He said nothing, but she could tell that she'd finally got through to him.

"Not to mention," she continued, "that *I* would never forgive you were that to happen."

She stole a glance at him. He seemed unmoved by that particular argument.

Hyacinth waited quietly while he thought about what to do. The silence was horrible. While she'd been going on about the diary, she'd been able to forget that he'd kissed her, that she'd enjoyed it, and that he apparently hadn't. She'd thought that their next meeting would be awkward and uncomfortable, but with a goal and a mission, she'd felt restored to her usual self, and even if he didn't take her along to find the diamonds, she supposed she still owed Isabella thanks for that.

But all the same, she rather thought she'd die if he left her behind. Either that or kill him.

She gripped her hands together, hiding them in the folds of her skirt. It was a nervous gesture, and the mere fact that she was doing it set her even more on edge. She hated that she was nervous, hated that he made her nervous, hated that she had to sit there and not say a word while he pondered her options. But contrary to popular belief, she did occasionally know when to keep her mouth shut, and it was clear that there was nothing more she could say that would sway him one way or the other. Except maybe . . .

No, even she wasn't crazy enough to threaten to go by herself.

"What were you going to say?" Gareth asked.

"I beg your pardon?"

He leaned forward, his blue eyes sharp and unwavering. "What were you going to say?"

"What makes you think I was going to say something?"

"I could see it in your face."

She cocked her head to the side. "You know me that well?"

"Frightening though it may seem, apparently I do."

She watched as he sat back in his seat. He reminded her of her brothers as he shifted in the too-small chair; they were forever complaining that her mother's sitting room was decorated for tiny females. But that was where the resemblance ended. None of her brothers had ever possessed the daring to wear his hair back in such a rakish queue, and none of them ever looked at her with that blue-eyed intensity that made her forget her own name.

He seemed to be searching her face for something. Or maybe he was just trying to stare her down, waiting for her to crack under the pressure.

Hyacinth caught her lower lip between her teeth—she wasn't strong enough to maintain the perfect picture of composure. But she did manage to keep her back straight, and her chin high, and perhaps most importantly, her mouth shut as he pondered his options.

A full minute went by. Very well, it was probably no more than ten seconds, but it felt like a minute. And then finally, because she could stand it no longer, she said (but very softly), "You need me."

His gaze fell to the carpet for a moment before turning back to her face. "If I take you—"

"Oh, thank you!" she exclaimed, just barely resisting the urge to jump to her feet.

"I said *if* I take you," he said, his voice uncommonly stern.

Hyacinth silenced herself immediately, looking at him with an appropriately dutiful expression.

"If I take you," he repeated, his eyes boring into hers, "I expect you to follow my orders."

"Of course."

"We will proceed as I see fit."

She hesitated.

"Hyacinth."

"Of course," she said quickly, since she had a feeling that if she didn't, he would call it off right then and there. "But if I have a good idea . . ."

"Hyacinth."

"As pertains to the fact that I understand Italian and you don't," she added quickly.

The look he gave her was as exhausted as it was austere.

"You don't have to do what I ask," she finally said, "just listen."

"Very well," he said with a sigh. "We will go Monday night."

Hyacinth's eyes widened with surprise. After all the fuss he'd made, she hadn't expected him to elect to go so soon. But she wasn't about to complain. "Monday night," she agreed.

She could hardly wait.

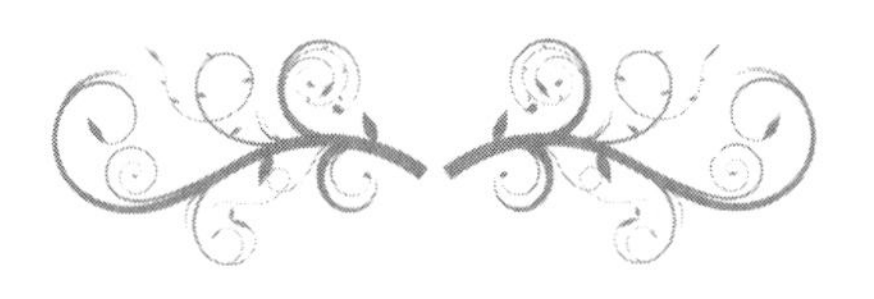

Chapter 9

Monday night. Our hero, who has spent much of his life in reckless abandon, is discovering the rather odd sensation of being the more sensible member of a duo.

There were a number of reasons, Gareth decided as he stole around to the back of Hyacinth's house, why he should question his sanity.

One: It was after midnight.

Two: They would be quite alone.

Three: They were going to the baron's house to:

Four: Commit larceny.

As far as bad ideas went, this stole the prize.

But no, somehow she had talked him into it, and so here he was, against all better judgment, ready to lead a proper young miss out of her house, into the night, and quite possibly into danger.

Not to mention that if anyone caught wind of this, the Bridgertons would have him standing up before a priest before he could catch his breath, and they'd be shackled to each other for life.

He shivered. The thought of Hyacinth Bridgerton as his lifelong companion . . . He stopped for a moment, blinking in surprise.

Well, it wasn't horrible, actually, but at the same time, it did leave a man feeling very, very uneasy.

He knew she thought she'd talked him into doing this, and maybe she had contributed in some degree to his decision, but the truth was, a man in Gareth's financial position couldn't afford to turn his nose up when faced with an opportunity such as this. He'd been a little startled at Hyacinth's frank assessment of his financial situation. Forget for a moment that such matters were not considered polite conversation (he wouldn't have expected her to adhere to such normal notions of propriety in any case). But he'd had no idea that his state of affairs was such common knowledge.

It was disconcerting, that.

But what was even more compelling, and what was really egging him on to look for the jewels now, as opposed to waiting until Hyacinth could obtain a better translation of the diary, was the delicious thought that he might actually snatch the diamonds right from under his father's nose.

It was difficult to pass up an opportunity like *that*.

Gareth edged along the back of Hyacinth's house to the servants' entrance, located in the rear, across from the mews. They had agreed to meet there at precisely half one, and he had no doubt that she would be ready and waiting for him, dressed as he had instructed, all in black.

And sure enough, there she was, holding the back door an inch ajar, peeking out through the crack.

"You're right on time," she said, slipping outside.

He stared at her in disbelief. She'd taken his order to heart and was dressed head to toe in unrelenting black. Except that no skirt swirled about her feet. Instead, she wore breeches and a waistcoat.

He'd *known* she was going to do this. He'd known it, and yet still, he couldn't contain his surprise.

"It seemed more sensible than a dress," Hyacinth said, correctly interpreting his silence. "And besides, I don't own anything in pure black. Haven't ever been in mourning, thank goodness."

Gareth just stared. There was a reason, he was coming to realize, why women didn't wear breeches. He didn't know where she'd acquired her costume—it had probably belonged to one of her brothers in his youth. It hugged her body in a most scandalous fashion, outlining her curves in a manner Gareth would really rather not have seen.

He didn't want to know that Hyacinth Bridgerton had a delectable figure. He didn't want to know that her legs were quite long for her somewhat petite height or that her hips were gently rounded and that they twitched in the most mesmerizing fashion when they weren't hidden beneath the silky folds of a skirt.

It was bad enough that he'd kissed her. He didn't need to want to do it again.

"I can't believe I'm doing this," he muttered, shaking his head. Good God, he sounded like a stick, like all those sensible friends he'd dragged into mischief as a youth.

He was beginning to think they'd actually known what they were talking about.

Hyacinth looked at him with accusing eyes. "You cannot back out now."

"I wouldn't dream of it," he said with a sigh. The woman would probably chase him down with a club if he did. "Come along, let's be off before someone catches us right here."

She nodded, then followed his lead down Barlow Place. Clair House was located less than a quarter mile away, and so Gareth had plotted a route for them to travel on foot, sticking, whenever they could, to the quiet side streets where they'd be less likely to be spotted by a member of the *ton*, traveling home via carriage from a party.

"How did you know your father wouldn't be home this evening?" Hyacinth whispered as they approached the corner.

"I'm sorry?" He peered around the corner, making sure the coast was clear.

"How did you know your father wouldn't be home?" she said again. "I was surprised that you would have knowledge of such a thing. I can't imagine he makes you privy to his schedule."

Gareth gritted his teeth, surprised by the bubble of irritation her question brought up inside of him. "I don't know," he muttered. "I just do." It was damned annoying, actually, that he was always so aware of his father's movements, but at least he could take some satisfaction in knowing that the baron was similarly afflicted.

"Oh," Hyacinth said. And it was all she said. Which was nice. Out of character, but nice.

Gareth motioned for her to follow as they made their way the short distance up Hay Hill, and then finally they were on Dover Street, which led to the alleyway behind Clair House.

"When was the last time you were here?" Hyacinth whispered as they crept up to the back wall.

"On the inside?" he asked brusquely. "Ten years. But if we're lucky, that window"—he pointed to a ground-floor aperture, only a little out of their reach—"will still have a broken latch."

She nodded appreciatively. "I was wondering how we were going to get in."

They both held silent for a moment, looking up at the window.

"Higher than you remembered?" asked Hyacinth. But then, of

course, she didn't wait for an answer before adding, "It's a good thing you brought me along. You can boost me up."

Gareth looked from her to the window and back. It somehow seemed wrong to send her into the house first. He hadn't considered this, though, when planning his entry.

"I'm not going to boost *you* up," Hyacinth said impatiently. "So unless you've a crate hidden away somewhere, or perhaps a small ladder—"

"Just go," Gareth practically growled, making a step for her with his hands. He had done this before, plenty of times. But it was a far different thing with Hyacinth Bridgerton brushing alongside his body than one of his school-chums.

"Can you reach?" he asked, hoisting her up.

"Mmm hmm" was the reply.

Gareth looked up. Right at her bottom. He decided to enjoy the view as long as she had no idea she was providing it.

"I just need to get my fingers under the edge," she whispered.

"Go right ahead," he said, smiling for the first time all night.

She twisted immediately around. "Why do you suddenly sound so equable?" she asked suspiciously.

"Just appreciating your usefulness."

"I—" She pursed her lips together. "Do you know, I don't think I trust you."

"Absolutely you shouldn't," he agreed.

He watched as she jiggled the window, then slid it up and open.

"Did it!" she said, sounding triumphant even through her whisper.

He gave her an appreciative nod. She was fairly insufferable, but it seemed only fair to give credit where credit was due. "I'm going to push you up," he said. "You should be able to—"

But she was already in. Gareth couldn't help but stand back in admiration. Hyacinth Bridgerton was clearly a born athlete.

Either that or a cat burglar.

Her face appeared in the open window. "I don't think anyone heard," she whispered. "Can you get up by yourself?"

He nodded. "As long as the window is already open, it's no trouble." He'd done this before, several times, when he'd been a schoolboy, home on holiday. The exterior wall was made of stone, and there were a few rough spots, with outcroppings just long enough to wedge his foot. Add that to the one knobby bit he could grasp with his hand . . .

He was inside in under twenty seconds.

"I'm impressed," Hyacinth said, peering back out the window.

"You're impressed by strange things," he said, brushing himself off.

"Anyone can bring flowers," she said with a shrug.

"Are you saying all a man needs to do to win your heart is scale a building?"

She looked back out the window. "Well, he'd have to do a bit more than this. Two stories, at the very least."

He shook his head, but he couldn't help but smile. "You said that the diary mentioned a room decorated in shades of green?"

She nodded. "I wasn't entirely certain of the meaning. It could have been a drawing room. Or maybe a study. But she did mention a small, round window."

"The baroness's office," he decided. "It's on the second floor, right off the bedroom."

"Of course!" She was whispering, but her excitement still rang through. "That would make perfect sense. Especially if she wanted to keep it from her husband. She wrote that he never visited her rooms."

"We'll go up the main stairs," Gareth said quietly. "We'll be less likely to be heard. The back ones are too close to the servants' quarters."

She nodded her agreement, and together they crept through the house. It was quiet, just as Gareth would have expected. The baron lived alone, and when he was out, the servants retired early.

Except one. Gareth stopped short, needing a moment to reassess. The butler would be awake; he never went to bed when Lord St. Clair was still expected back and might require assistance.

"This way," Gareth mouthed to Hyacinth, doubling back to take a different route. They would still take the main stairs, but they would go the long way around to get there.

Hyacinth followed his lead, and a minute later they were creeping up the stairs. Gareth pulled her to the side; the steps had always creaked in the center, and he rather doubted his father possessed the funds to have them repaired.

Once in the upstairs hall, he led Hyacinth to the baroness's office. It was a funny little room, rectangular with one window and three doors, one to the hall, one to the baroness's bedroom, and the last to a small dressing room that was more frequently used for storage since there was a much more comfortable dressing area directly off the bedchamber.

Gareth motioned Hyacinth inside, then stepped in behind her, closing the door carefully, his hand tight on the doorknob as it turned.

It shut without a click. He let out a breath.

"Tell me exactly what she wrote," he whispered, pulling back the drapes to allow in a bit of moonlight.

"She said it was in the *armadio*," Hyacinth whispered back. "Which is probably a cabinet. Or maybe a set of drawers. Or—" Her eyes fell on a tall but narrow curio cabinet. It was triangular in shape, tucked into one of the rear corners. The wood was a dark, rich hue, and it stood on three spindly legs, leaving about two feet of space under its base. "This is it," Hyacinth whispered excitedly. "It has to be."

She was across the room before Gareth even had a chance to move, and by the time he joined her, she had one of the drawers open and was searching through.

"Empty," she said, frowning. She knelt and pulled open the bottom drawer. Also empty. She looked up at Gareth and said, "Do you think someone removed her belongings after she passed away?"

"I have no idea," he said. He gave the cabinet door a gentle tug and pulled it open. Also empty.

Hyacinth stood, planting her hands on her hips as she regarded the cabinet. "I can't imagine what else . . ." Her words trailed off as she ran her fingers over the decorative carvings near the top edge.

"Maybe the desk," Gareth suggested, crossing the distance to the desk in two strides.

But Hyacinth was shaking her head. "I don't think so," she said. "She wouldn't have called a desk an *armadio*. It would have been a *scrivania*."

"It still has drawers," Gareth muttered, pulling them open to inspect the contents.

"There's something about this piece," Hyacinth murmured. "It looks rather Mediterranean, don't you think?"

Gareth looked up. "It does," he said slowly, coming to his feet.

"If she brought this from Italy," Hyacinth said, her head tilting slightly to the side as she eyed the cabinet assessingly, "or if her grandmother brought it on her visit . . ."

"It would stand to reason that she would know if there was a secret compartment," Gareth finished for her.

"And," Hyacinth said, her eyes alight with excitement, "her husband *wouldn't*."

Gareth quickly set the desk to rights and returned to the curio cabinet. "Stand back," he instructed, wrapping his fingers around the lower lip so that he could pull it away from the wall. It was heavy, though, much heavier than it looked, and he was only able to move it a few inches, just far enough so that he could run his hand along the back.

"Do you feel anything?" Hyacinth whispered.

He shook his head. He couldn't reach very far in, so he dropped to his knees and tried feeling the back panel from underneath.

"Anything there?" Hyacinth asked.

He shook his head again. "Nothing. I just need to—" He froze as his fingers ran across a small, rectangular outcropping of wood.

"What is it?" she asked, trying to peer around the back.

"I'm not certain," he said, stretching his arm a half inch farther. "It's a knob of some sort, maybe a lever."

"Can you move it?"

"I'm trying," he nearly gasped. The knob was almost out of his reach, and he had to contort and twist just to catch it between his fingers. The lower front edge of the cabinet was digging painfully into the muscles of his upper arm, and his head was twisted awkwardly to the side, his cheek pressing up against the cabinet door.

All in all, not the most graceful of positions.

"What if I do this?" Hyacinth wedged herself next to the cabinet and slid her arm around back. Her fingers found the knob easily.

Gareth immediately let go and pulled his arm out from under the cabinet.

"Don't worry," she said, somewhat sympathetically, "you couldn't have fit your arm back here. There isn't much room."

"I don't care which of us can reach the knob," he said.

"You don't? Oh." She shrugged. "Well, I would."

"I know," he said.

"Not that it really matters, of course, but—"

"Do you feel anything?" he cut in.

She shook her head. "It doesn't seem to be moving. I've tried it up and down, and side to side."

"Push it in."

"That doesn't do it, either. Unless I—" Her breath caught.

"What?" Gareth asked urgently.

She looked up at him, her eyes shining, even in the dim light of the moon. "It twisted. And I felt something click."

"Is there a drawer? Can you pull it out?"

Hyacinth shook her head, her mouth scrunching into an expression of concentration as she moved her hand along the back panel of the cabinet. She couldn't find any cracks or cutouts. Slowly, she slid down, bending at the knees until her hand reached the lower edge. And then she looked down. A small piece of paper lay on the floor.

"Was this here before?" she asked. But the words were mere reflex; she knew it hadn't been.

Gareth dropped to his knees beside her. "What is it?"

"This," she said, unfolding the small piece of paper with trembling hands. "I think it fell from somewhere when I twisted the knob." Still on hands and knees, she moved about two feet so that the paper caught the narrow shaft of moonlight flowing through the window. Gareth crouched beside her, his body warm and hard and overwhelmingly close as she smoothed the brittle sheet open.

"What does it say?" he asked, his breath dancing across her neck as he leaned in.

"I-I'm not sure." She blinked, forcing her eyes to focus on the words. The handwriting was clearly Isabella's, but the paper had been folded and refolded several times, making it difficult to read. "It's in Italian. I think it might be another clue."

Gareth shook his head. "Trust Isabella to turn this into a fancy hunt."

"Was she very crafty, then?"

"No, but inordinately fond of games." He turned back to the cabinet. "I'm not surprised she would have a piece like this, with a secret compartment."

Hyacinth watched as he ran his hand along the underside of the cabinet. "There it is," he said appreciatively.

"Where?" she asked, moving beside him.

He took her hand and guided it to a spot toward the back. A piece of wood seemed to have rotated slightly, just enough to allow a scrap of paper to slide through and float to the ground.

"Do you feel it?" he murmured.

She nodded, and she couldn't be sure whether she was referring to the wood, or the heat of his hand over hers. His skin was warm, and slightly rough, as if he'd been out and about without his gloves. But mostly his hand was large, covering hers completely.

Hyacinth felt enveloped, swallowed whole.

And dear God, it was just his hand.

"We should put this back," she said quickly, eager for anything that forced her mind to focus on something else. Pulling her hand from his, she reached out and turned the wood back into place. It seemed unlikely that anyone would notice the change in the underside of the cabinet, especially considering that the secret compartment had gone undetected for over sixty years, but all the same, it seemed prudent to leave the scene as they had found it.

Gareth nodded his agreement, then motioned for her to move

aside as he pushed the cabinet back against the wall. "Did you find anything useful in the note?" he asked.

"The note? Oh, the note," she said, feeling like the veriest fool. "Not yet. I can hardly read a thing with only the moonlight to see by. Do you think it would be safe to light a—"

She stopped. She had to. Gareth had clamped his hand unrelentingly over her mouth.

Eyes wide, she looked up at his face. He was holding one finger to his lips and motioning with his head toward the door.

And then Hyacinth heard it. Movement in the hall. "Your father?" she mouthed, once he had removed his hand. But he wasn't looking at her.

Gareth stood, and on careful and silent feet moved to the door. He placed his ear against the wood, and then, barely a second later, stepped quickly back, jerking his head to the left.

Hyacinth was at his side in an instant, and before she knew what was happening, he'd pulled her through a door into what seemed to be a large closet filled with clothes. The air was black as pitch, and there was little room to move about. Hyacinth was backed up against what felt like a brocaded gown, and Gareth was backed up against her.

She wasn't sure she knew how to breathe.

His lips found her ear, and she felt more than she heard, "Don't say a word."

The door connecting the office to the hall clicked open, and heavy footsteps thudded across the floor.

Hyacinth held her breath. Was it Gareth's father?

"That's odd," she heard a male voice say. It sounded like it was coming from the direction of the window, and—

Oh, *no*. They'd left the drapes pulled back.

Hyacinth grabbed Gareth's hand and squeezed hard, as if that might somehow impart this knowledge to him.

Whoever was in the room took a few steps, then stopped. Terrified at the prospect of being caught, Hyacinth reached carefully behind her with her hand, trying to gauge how far back the closet went. Her hand didn't touch another wall, so she wiggled between two of the gowns and positioned herself behind them, giving Gareth's hand a little tug before letting go so that he could do the same. Her feet were undoubtedly still visible, peeking out from under the hems of the dresses, but at least now, if someone opened the closet door, her face wouldn't be right there at eye level.

Hyacinth heard a door opening and closing, but then the footsteps moved across the carpet again. The man in the room had obviously just peered into the baroness's bedchamber, which Gareth had told her was connected to the small office.

Hyacinth gulped. If he'd taken the time to inspect the bedchamber, then the closet had to be next. She burrowed farther back, scooting herself until her shoulder connected with the wall. Gareth was right there next to her, and then he was pulling her against him, moving her to the corner before covering her body with his.

He was protecting her. Shielding her so that if the closet door was opened, his would be the only body seen.

Hyacinth heard the footsteps approach. The doorknob was loose and rattly, and it clattered when a hand landed on it.

She grabbed on to Gareth, clutching his coat along the side darts. He was close, scandalously close, with his back pressed up against her so tightly she could feel the entire length of him, from her knees to her shoulders.

And everything in between.

She forced herself to breathe evenly and quietly. There was something about her position, mixed with something about her circumstance—it was a combination of fear and awareness, and the hot proximity of his body. She felt strange, queer, almost as if she were somehow suspended in time, ready to lift off her toes and float away.

She had the strangest urge to press closer, to tip her hips forward and cradle him. She was in a closet—a stranger's closet in the dead of night—and yet even as she froze with terror, she couldn't help but feel something else . . . something more powerful than fright. It was excitement, a thrill, something heady and new that set her heart racing and her blood pounding, and . . .

And something else as well. Something she wasn't quite ready to analyze or name.

Hyacinth caught her lip between her teeth.

The doorknob turned.

Her lips parted.

The door opened.

And then, amazingly, it closed again. Hyacinth felt herself sag against the back wall, felt Gareth sag against her. She wasn't sure how it was they hadn't been detected; probably Gareth had been better shielded by the clothing than she'd thought. Or maybe the light was too dim, or the man hadn't thought to look down for feet peeking out from behind the gowns. Or maybe he'd had bad eyesight, or maybe . . .

Or maybe they were just damned lucky.

They waited in silence until it was clear that the man had left the baroness's office, and then they waited for a good five minutes more, just to be sure. But finally, Gareth moved away from her, pushing through the clothes to the closet door. Hyacinth waited in back until she heard his whispered, "Let's go."

She followed him in silence, creeping through the house until they reached the window with the broken latch. Gareth leapt down ahead of her, then held out his hands so that she could balance against the wall and pull the window shut before hopping down to the ground.

"Follow me," Gareth said, taking her hand and pulling her behind him as he ran through the streets of Mayfair. Hyacinth tripped along behind him, and with each step a sliver of the fear that had gripped her back in the closet was replaced by excitement.

Exhilaration.

By the time they reached Hay Hill, Hyacinth felt as if she was almost ready to bubble over with laughter, and finally, she had to dig in her heels and say, "Stop! I can't breathe."

Gareth stopped, but he turned with stern eyes. "I need to get you home," he said.

"I know, I know, I—"

His eyes widened. "Are you laughing?"

"No! Yes. I mean"—she smiled helplessly—"I might."

"You're a madwoman."

She nodded, still grinning like a fool. "I think so."

He turned on her, hands on hips. "Have you no sense? We could have been caught back there. That was my father's butler, and trust me, he has never been in possession of a sense of humor. If he had discovered us, my father would have thrown us in gaol, and your brother would have hauled us straight to a church."

"I know," Hyacinth said, trying to appear suitably solemn.

She failed.

Miserably.

Finally, she gave up and said, "But wasn't it fun?"

For a moment she didn't think he would respond. For a moment it seemed all he was capable of was a dull, stupefied stare. But then, she heard his voice, low and disbelieving. "Fun?"

She nodded. "A little bit, at least." She pressed her lips together, working hard to turn them down at the corners. Anything to keep from bursting out with laughter.

"You're mad," he said, looking stern and shocked and—God help her—sweet, all at the same time. "You are stark, raving mad," he said. "Everyone told me, but I didn't quite believe—"

"Someone told you I was mad?" Hyacinth cut in.

"Eccentric."

"Oh." She pursed her lips together. "Well, that's true, I suppose."

"Far too much work for any sane man to take on."

"Is that what they say?" she asked, starting to feel slightly less than complimented.

"All that and more," he confirmed.

Hyacinth thought about that for a moment, then just shrugged. "Well, they haven't a lick of sense, any one of them."

"Good God," Gareth muttered. "You sound precisely like my grandmother."

"So you've mentioned," Hyacinth said. And then she couldn't resist. She just had to ask. "But tell me," she said, leaning in just a bit. "Truthfully. Weren't you just a tiny bit excited? Once the fear of discovery had worn off and you knew we would be undetected? Wasn't it," she asked, her words coming out on a sigh, "just a little bit wonderful?"

He looked down at her, and maybe it was the moonlight, or maybe just her wishful imagination, but she thought she saw something flash in his eyes. Something soft, something just a little bit indulgent.

"A little bit," he said. "But just a little bit."

Hyacinth smiled. "I knew you weren't a stick."

He looked down at her, with what had to be palpable irritation. No one had ever accused him of being stodgy before. "A stick?" he said disgustedly.

"In the mud."

"I knew what you meant."

"They why did you ask?"

"Because you, Miss Bridgerton . . ."

And so it went, the rest of the way home.

Chapter 10

The next morning. Hyacinth is still in an excellent mood. Unfortunately, her mother commented upon this so many times at breakfast that Hyacinth was finally forced to flee and barricade herself in her bedchamber.

Violet Bridgerton is an exceptionally canny woman, after all, and if anyone is going to guess that Hyacinth is falling in love, it would be her.

Probably before Hyacinth, even.

Hyacinth hummed to herself as she sat at the small desk in her bedchamber, tapping her fingers against the blotter. She had translated and retranslated the note they'd found the night before in the small green office, and she still wasn't satisfied with her results, but even that could not dampen her spirits.

She'd been a little disappointed, of course, that they had not found the diamonds the night before, but the note in the curio cabinet seemed to indicate that the jewels might still be theirs for the taking. At the very least, no one else had reached any success with the trail of clues Isabella had left behind.

Hyacinth was never happier than when she had a task, a goal, some sort of quest. She loved the challenge of solving a puzzle, analyzing a clue. And Isabella Marinzoli St. Clair had turned what would surely have been a dull and ordinary season into the most exciting spring of Hyacinth's life.

She looked down at the note, twisting her mouth to the side as she forced her mind back to the task at hand. Her translation was still only about seventy percent complete, in Hyacinth's optimistic estimation, but she rather thought she'd managed enough of a translation to justify another attempt. The next clue—or the actual diamonds, if they were lucky—was almost certainly in the library.

"In a book, I imagine," she murmured, gazing sightlessly out the window. She thought of the Bridgerton library, tucked away at her brother's Grosvenor Square home. The room itself wasn't terribly large, but the shelves lined the walls from floor to ceiling.

And books filled the shelves. Every last inch of them.

"Maybe the St. Clairs aren't much for reading," she said to herself, turning her attention once again to Isabella's note. Surely there had to be something in the cryptic words to indicate which book she had chosen as her hiding spot. Something scientific, she was fairly sure. Isabella had underlined part of her note, which led Hyacinth to think that perhaps she was referring to a book title, since it didn't seem to make sense in context that she'd have been underlining for emphasis. And the part she'd underlined had mentioned water and "things that move," which sounded a bit like physics, not that Hyacinth had ever studied it. But she'd four brothers who had attended university, and she'd overheard enough of their studies to have a vague knowledge of, if not the subject, at least what the subject meant.

Still, she wasn't nearly as certain as she'd have liked about her translation, or what it meant. Maybe if she went to Gareth with what she'd translated thus far, he could read something into it that she didn't see. After all, he was more familiar with the house and its contents than she was. He might know of an odd or interesting book, something unique or out of the ordinary.

Gareth.

She smiled to herself, a loopy, silly grin that she would have died before allowing anyone else to see.

Something had happened the night before. Something special.

Something important.

He liked her. He really liked her. They had laughed and chattered the entire way home. And when he had dropped her off at the servants' entrance to Number Five, he had looked at her in that heavy-lidded, just a little bit intense way of his. He had smiled, too, one corner of his mouth lifting as if he had a secret.

She'd shivered. She'd actually forgotten how to speak. And she'd wondered if he might kiss her again, which of course he hadn't done, but maybe . . .

Maybe soon.

She had no doubt that she still drove him a little bit mad. But she seemed to drive everyone a little bit mad, so she decided not to attach too much importance to that.

But he liked her. And he respected her intelligence as well. And if he was occasionally reluctant to demonstrate this as often as she would like . . . well, she had four brothers. She had long since learned that it took a fully formed miracle to get them to admit that a woman might be smarter than a man about anything other than fabrics, perfumed soaps, and tea.

She turned her head to look at the clock, which sat on the mantel over her small fireplace. It was already past noon. Gareth had promised that he would call on her this afternoon to see how she was faring with the note. That probably didn't mean before two, but technically it was the afternoon, and—

Her ears perked up. Was that someone at the door? Her room was at the front of the house, so she could generally hear when someone was entering or exiting. Hyacinth got up and went to the window, peeking out from behind the curtains to see if she could see anyone on the front step.

Nothing.

She went to the door and opened it just enough to listen.

Nothing.

She stepped into the hall, her heart pounding with anticipation. Truly, there was no reason to be nervous, but she hadn't been able to stop thinking about Gareth, and the diamonds, and—

"Eh, Hyacinth, what're you doing?"

She nearly jumped out of her skin.

"Sorry," said her brother Gregory, not sounding sorry at all. He was standing behind her, or rather he had been, before she'd whirled around in surprise. He looked slightly disheveled, his reddish brown hair windblown and cut just a touch too long.

"Don't *do* that," she said, placing her hand over her heart, as if that might possibly calm it down.

He just crossed his arms and leaned one shoulder against the wall. "It's what I do best," he said with a grin.

"Not something *I'd* brag about," Hyacinth returned.

He ignored the insult, instead brushing an imaginary piece of lint off the sleeve of his riding coat. "What has you skulking about?"

"I'm not skulking."

"Of course you are. It's what you do best."

She scowled at him, even though she ought to have known better. Gregory was two and a half years her elder, and he lived to vex her. He always had. The two of them were a bit cut off from the rest of the family, in terms of age. Gregory was almost four years younger than Francesca, and a full ten from Colin, the next youngest son. As a result, he and Hyacinth had always been a bit on their own, a bit of a duo.

A bickering, poking, frog-in-the-bed sort of duo, but a duo nonetheless, and even though they had outgrown the worst of their pranks, neither seemed able to resist needling the other.

"I thought I heard someone come in," Hyacinth said.

He smiled blandly. "It was me."

"I realize that *now*." She placed her hand on the doorknob and pulled. "If you will excuse me."

"*You're* in a snit today."

"I'm not in a snit."

"Of course you are. It's—"

"*Not* what I do best." Hyacinth ground out.

He grinned. "You're definitely in a snit."

"I'm—" She clamped her teeth together. She was not going to descend to the behavior of a three-year-old. "I am going back into my room now. I have a book to read."

But before she could make her escape, she heard him say, "I saw you with Gareth St. Clair the other night."

Hyacinth froze. Surely he couldn't have known . . . No one had seen them. She was sure of that.

"At Bridgerton House," Gregory continued. "Off in the corner of the ballroom."

Hyacinth let out a long, quiet breath before turning back around.

Gregory was looking at her with a casual, offhand smile, but Hyacinth could tell that there was something more to his expression, a certain shrewd look in his eye.

Most of his behavior to the contrary, her brother was not stupid. And he seemed to think it was his role in life to watch over his younger sister. Probably because he was the second youngest, and she was the only one with whom he could try to assume a superior role. The rest certainly would not have stood for it.

"I'm friends with his grandmother," Hyacinth said, since it seemed nicely neutral and dull. "You know that."

He shrugged. It was a gesture they shared, and sometimes Hyacinth felt she was looking in a mirror, which seemed mad, since he was a full foot taller than she was.

"You certainly looked to be in deep conversation about something," he said.

"It was nothing in which you'd be interested."

One of his brows arched annoyingly up. "I might surprise you."

"You rarely do."

"Are you setting your cap for him?"

"That's none of your business," she said tartly.

Gregory looked triumphant. "Then you *are*."

Hyacinth lifted her chin, looking her brother squarely in the eye. "I don't know," she said, since despite their constant bickering, he probably knew her better than anyone else in the world. And he'd know it for certain if she were lying.

Either that, or he would torture her until the truth slipped out, anyway.

Gregory's brows disappeared under the fringe of his hair, which, admittedly, was too long and constantly falling in his eyes. "Really?" he asked. "Well, *that* is news."

"For your ears only," Hyacinth warned, "and it's not really news. I haven't decided yet."

"Still."

"I mean this, Gregory," Hyacinth said. "Don't make me regret confiding in you."

"Ye of little faith."

He sounded far too flip for her comfort. Hands on hips, she said,

"I only told you this because very occasionally you're not a complete idiot and despite all common sense, I do love you."

His face sobered, and she was reminded that despite her brother's asinine (in her opinion) attempts to appear the jaunty wastrel, he was actually quite intelligent and in possession of a heart of gold.

A *devious* heart of gold.

"And don't forget," Hyacinth felt it was necessary to add, "that I said *maybe*."

His brows came together. "Did you?"

"If I didn't, then I meant to."

He motioned magnanimously with his hand. "If there's anything I can do."

"Nothing," she said firmly, horrifying visions of Gregory's meddling floating through her mind. "Absolutely nothing. *Please*."

"Surely a waste of my talents."

"Gregory!"

"Well," he said with an affected sigh, "you have my approval, at least."

"Why?" Hyacinth asked suspiciously.

"It would be an excellent match," he continued. "If nothing else, think of the children."

She knew she'd regret it, but still she had to ask. "What children?"

He grinned. "The lovely lithping children you could have together. Garethhhh and Hyathinthhhh. Hyathinth and Gareth. And the thublime Thinclair tots."

Hyacinth stared at him like he was an idiot.

Which he was, she was quite certain of it.

She shook her head. "How on earth Mother managed to give birth to seven perfectly normal children and one freak is beyond me."

"Thith way to the nurthery." Gregory laughed as she headed back into the room. "With the thcrumptious little Tharah and Thamuel Thinclair. Oh, yeth, and don't forget wee little Thuth-annah!"

Hyacinth shut the door in his face, but the wood wasn't thick enough to block his parting shot.

"You're such an easy mark, Hy." And then: "Don't forget to come down for tea."

One hour later. Gareth is about to learn what it means to belong to a large family.

For better or for worthe.

"Miss Bridgerton is taking tea," said the butler, once he'd allowed Gareth admittance to the front hall of Number Five.

Gareth followed the butler down the hall to same rose-and-cream sitting room in which he'd met Hyacinth the week before.

Good God, was it just one week? It felt a lifetime ago.

Ah, well. Skulking about, breaking the law, and very nearly ruining the reputation of a proper young lady did tend to age a man before his time.

The butler stepped into the room, intoned Gareth's name, and moved to the side so that he could walk in.

"Mr. St. Clair!"

Gareth turned with surprise to face Hyacinth's mother, who was sitting on a striped sofa, setting her teacup down in its saucer. He didn't know *why* he was surprised to see Violet Bridgerton; it certainly stood to reason that she would be home at this time in the afternoon. But for whatever reason, he had only pictured Hyacinth on the way over.

"Lady Bridgerton," he said, turning to her with a polite bow. "How lovely to see you."

"Have you met my son?" she asked.

Son? Gareth hadn't even realized anyone else was in the room.

"My brother Gregory," came Hyacinth's voice. She was sitting across from her mother, on a matching sofa. She tilted her head toward the window, where Gregory Bridgerton stood, assessing him with a scary little half smile.

The smirk of an older brother, Gareth realized. It was probably exactly how he would look if he'd had a younger sister to torture and protect.

"We've met," Gregory said.

Gareth nodded. They had crossed paths from time to time about town and had, in fact, been students at Eton at the same time. But Gareth was several years older, so they had never known each other well. "Bridgerton," Gareth murmured, giving the younger man a nod.

Gregory moved across the room and plopped himself down next to his sister. "It's good to see you," he said, directing his words at Gareth. "Hyacinth says you're her special friend."

"Gregory!" Hyacinth exclaimed. She turned quickly to Gareth. "I said no such thing."

"I'm heartbroken," Gareth said.

Hyacinth looked at him with a slightly peeved expression, then turned to her brother with a hissed, "Stop it."

"Won't you have tea, Mr. St. Clair?" Lady Bridgerton asked, glossing right over her children's squabbling as if it wasn't occurring right across from her. "It is a special blend of which I am particularly fond."

"I would be delighted." Gareth sat in the same chair he had chosen last time, mostly because it put the most room between him and Gregory, although in truth, he didn't know which Bridgerton was most likely to accidentally spill scalding tea on his lap.

But it was an odd position. He was at the short end of the low, center table, and with all the Bridgertons on the sofas, it almost felt as if he were seated at its head.

"Milk?" Lady Bridgerton asked.

"Thank you," Gareth replied. "No sugar, if you please."

"Hyacinth takes hers with three," Gregory said, reaching for a piece of shortbread.

"Why," Hyacinth ground out, "would he care?"

"Well," Gregory replied, taking a bite and chewing, "he *is* your special friend."

"He's not—" She turned to Gareth. "Ignore him."

There was something rather annoying about being condescended to by a man of lesser years, but at the same time Gregory seemed to be doing an excellent job of vexing Hyacinth, an endeavor of which Gareth could only approve.

So he decided to stay out of it and instead turned back to Lady Bridgerton, who was, as it happened, the closest person to him, anyway. "And how are you this afternoon?" he asked.

Lady Bridgerton gave him a very small smile as she handed him his cup of tea. "Smart man," she murmured.

"It's self-preservation, really," he said noncommittally.

"Don't say that. They wouldn't hurt you."

"No, but I'm sure to be injured in the cross fire."

Gareth heard a little gasp. When he looked over at Hyacinth, she was glaring daggers in his direction. Her brother was grinning.

"Sorry," he said, mostly because he thought he should. He certainly didn't mean it.

"You don't come from a large family, do you, Mr. St. Clair?" Lady Bridgerton asked.

"No," he said smoothly, taking a sip of his tea, which was of excellent quality. "Just myself and my brother." He stopped, blinking against the rush of sadness that washed over him every time he thought of George, then finished with: "He passed on late last year."

"Oh," Lady Bridgerton said, her hand coming to her mouth. "I'm so sorry. I'd forgotten completely. Please forgive me. And accept my deepest sympathies."

Her apology was so artless, and her condolences so sincere, that Gareth almost felt the need to comfort her. He looked at her, right into her eyes, and he realized that she understood.

Most people hadn't. His friends had all patted him awkwardly on the back and said they were sorry, but they hadn't understood. Grandmother Danbury had, perhaps—she'd grieved for George, too. But that was somehow different, probably because he and his grandmother were so close. Lady Bridgerton was almost a stranger, and yet, she cared.

It was touching, and almost disconcerting. Gareth couldn't remember the last time anyone had said something to him and meant it.

Except for Hyacinth, of course. She always meant what she said. But at the same time, she never laid herself bare, never made herself vulnerable.

He glanced over at her. She was sitting up straight, her hands folded neatly in her lap, watching him with a curious expression.

He couldn't fault her, he supposed. He was the exact same way.

"Thank you," he said, turning back to Lady Bridgerton. "George was an exceptional brother, and the world is poorer for his loss."

Lady Bridgerton was silent for a moment, and then, as if she could read his mind, she smiled and said, "But you do not wish to dwell on this now. We shall speak of something else."

Gareth looked at Hyacinth. She was holding herself still, but he could see her chest rise and fall in a long, impatient breath. She had worked on the translation, of that he had no doubt, and she surely wished to tell him what she'd learned.

Gareth carefully suppressed a smile. He was quite certain that Hyacinth would have feigned death if that would somehow have gotten them an interview alone.

"Lady Danbury speaks very highly of you," Lady Bridgerton said.

Gareth turned back to her. "I am fortunate to be her grandson."

"I have always liked your grandmother," Lady Bridgerton said, sipping at her tea. "I know she scares half of London—"

"Oh, more than that," Gareth said genially.

Lady Bridgerton chuckled. "So she would hope."

"Indeed."

"I, however, have always found her to be quite charming," Lady Bridgerton said. "A breath of fresh air, really. And, of course, a very shrewd and sound judge of character."

"I shall pass along your regards."

"She speaks very highly of you," Lady Bridgerton said.

She'd repeated herself. Gareth wasn't sure if it was accidental or deliberate, but either way, she couldn't have been more clear if she had taken him aside and offered him money to propose to her daughter.

Of course, she did not know that his father was not actually Lord St. Clair, or that he did not in fact know who his father was. As lovely and generous as Hyacinth's mother was, Gareth rather doubted that she'd be working so hard to bring him up to scratch if she knew that he most probably carried the blood of a footman.

"My grandmother speaks highly of you as well," Gareth said

to Lady Bridgerton. "Which is quite a compliment, as she rarely speaks highly of anyone."

"Except for Hyacinth," Gregory Bridgerton put in.

Gareth turned. He'd almost forgotten the younger man was there. "Of course," he said smoothly. "My grandmother adores your sister."

Gregory turned to Hyacinth. "Do you still read to her each Wednesday?"

"Tuesday," Hyacinth corrected.

"Oh. Thorry."

Gareth blinked. Did Hyacinth's brother have a lisp?

"Mr. St. Clair," Hyacinth said, after what Gareth was quite certain was an elbow in her brother's ribs.

"Yes?" he murmured, mostly just to be kind. She'd paused in her speech, and he had a feeling she'd uttered his name without first thinking of something to ask him.

"I understand that you are an accomplished swordsman," she finally said.

He eyed her curiously. Where was she going with this? "I like to fence, yes," he replied.

"I have always wanted to learn."

"Good God," Gregory grunted.

"I would be quite good at it," she protested.

"I'm sure you would," her brother replied, "which is why you should never be allowed within thirty feet of a sword." He turned to Gareth. "She's quite diabolical."

"Yes, I'd noticed," Gareth murmured, deciding that maybe there might be a bit more to Hyacinth's brother than he had thought.

Gregory shrugged, reaching for a piece of shortbread. "It's probably why we can't seem to get her married off."

"Gregory!" This came from Hyacinth, but that was only because Lady Bridgerton had excused herself and followed one of the footmen into the hall.

"It's a compliment!" Gregory protested. "Haven't you waited your entire life for me to agree that you're smarter than any of the poor fools who have attempted to court you?"

"You might find it difficult to believe," Hyacinth shot back, "but I haven't been going to bed each night thinking to myself—*Oh, I do wish my brother would offer me something that passes for a compliment in his twisted mind.*"

Gareth choked on his tea.

Gregory turned to Gareth. "Do you see why I call her diabolical?"

"I refuse to comment," Gareth said.

"Look who is here!" came Lady Bridgerton's voice. And just in time, Gareth thought. Ten more seconds, and Hyacinth would have quite cheerfully murdered her brother.

Gareth turned to the doorway and immediately rose to his feet. Behind Lady Bridgerton stood one of Hyacinth's older sisters, the one who had married a duke. Or at least he thought that was the one. They all looked vexingly alike, and he couldn't be sure.

"Daphne!" Hyacinth said. "Come sit by me."

"There's no room next to you," Daphne said, blinking in confusion.

"There will be," Hyacinth said with cheerful venom, "as soon as Gregory gets up."

Gregory made a great show of offering his seat to his older sister.

"Children," Lady Bridgerton said with a sigh as she retook her seat. "I am never quite certain if I'm glad I had them."

But no one could ever have mistaken the humor in her voice for anything other than love. Gareth found himself rather charmed. Hyacinth's brother was a bit of a pest, or at least he was when Hyacinth was in the vicinity, and the few times he'd heard more than two Bridgertons in the same conversation, they had talked all over each other and rarely resisted the impulse to trade sly jibes.

But they loved each other. Beneath the noise, it was startlingly clear.

"It is good to see you, your grace," Gareth said to the young duchess, once she'd seated herself next to Hyacinth.

"Please, call me Daphne," she said with a sunny smile. "There is no need to be so formal if you are a friend of Hyacinth's. Besides," she said, taking a cup and pouring herself some tea, "I cannot feel like a duchess in my mother's sitting room."

"What do you feel like, then?"

"Hmmm." She took a sip of her tea. "Just Daphne Bridgerton, I suppose. It's difficult to shed the surname in this clan. In spirit, that is."

"I hope that is a compliment," Lady Bridgerton remarked.

Daphne just smiled at her mother. "I shall never escape you, I'm afraid." She turned to Gareth. "There is nothing like one's family to make one feel like one has never grown up."

Gareth thought about his recent encounter with the baron and said, with perhaps more feeling than he ought to make verbal, "I know precisely what you mean."

"Yes," the duchess said, "I expect you do."

Gareth said nothing. His estrangement from the baron was certainly common enough knowledge, even if the reason for it was not.

"How are the children, Daphne?" Lady Bridgerton asked.

"Mischievous as always. David wants a puppy, preferably one that will grow to the size of a small pony, and Caroline is desperate to return to Benedict's." She sipped at her tea and turned to Gareth. "My daughter spent three weeks with my brother and his family last month. He has been giving her drawing lessons."

"He is an accomplished artist, is he not?"

"Two paintings in the National Gallery," Lady Bridgerton said, beaming with pride.

"He rarely comes to town, though," Hyacinth said.

"He and his wife prefer the quiet of the country," her mother said. But there was a very faint edge to her voice. A firmness meant to indicate that she did not wish to discuss the matter any further.

At least not in front of Gareth.

Gareth tried to recall if he had ever heard some sort of scandal attached to Benedict Bridgerton. He didn't think so, but then again, Gareth was at least a decade his junior, and if there was something untoward in his past, it would probably have occurred before Gareth had moved to town.

He glanced over at Hyacinth to see her reaction to her mother's words. It hadn't been a scolding, not exactly, but it was clear that she'd wanted to stop Hyacinth from speaking further.

But if Hyacinth took offense, she wasn't showing it. She turned her attention to the window and was staring out, her brows pulled slightly together as she blinked.

"Is it warm out of doors?" she asked, turning to her sister. "It looks sunny."

"It is quite," Daphne said, sipping her tea. "I walked over from Hastings House."

"I should love to go for a walk," Hyacinth announced.

It took Gareth only a second to recognize his cue. "I would be delighted to escort you, Miss Bridgerton."

"Would you?" Hyacinth said with a dazzling smile.

"I was out this morning," Lady Bridgerton said. "The crocuses are in bloom in the park. A bit past the Guard House."

Gareth almost smiled. The Guard House was at the far end of Hyde Park. It would take half the afternoon to get there and back.

He rose to his feet and offered her his arm. "Shall we see the crocuses then?"

"That would be delightful." Hyacinth stood. "I just need to fetch my maid to accompany us."

Gregory pushed himself off the windowsill, upon which he'd been leaning. "Perhaps I'll come along, too," he said.

Hyacinth threw him a glare.

"Or perhaps I won't," he murmured.

"I need you here, in any case," Lady Bridgerton said.

"Really?" Gregory smiled innocently. "Why?"

"Because I do," she ground out.

Gareth turned to Gregory. "Your sister will be safe with me," he said. "I give you my vow."

"Oh, I have no worries on that score," Gregory said with a bland smile. "The real question is—will you be safe with her?"

It was a good thing, Gareth later reflected, that Hyacinth had already quit the room to fetch her coat and her maid. She probably would have killed her brother on the spot.

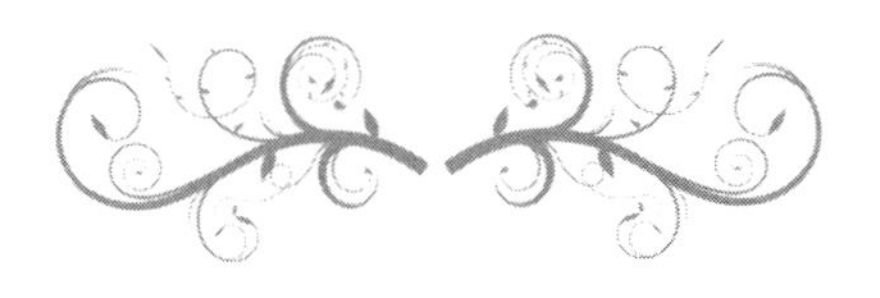

Chapter 11

A quarter of an hour later. Hyacinth is completely unaware that her life is about to change.

"Your maid is discreet?" Gareth asked, just as soon as he and Hyacinth were standing on the pavement outside of Number Five.

"Oh, don't worry about Frances," Hyacinth said, adjusting her gloves. "She and I have an understanding."

He lifted his brows in an expression of lazy humor. "Why do those words, coming from your lips, strike terror in my soul?"

"I'm sure I don't know," Hyacinth said blithely, "but I can assure you that she won't come within twenty feet of us while we're strolling. We have only to stop and get her a tin of peppermints."

"Peppermints?"

"She's easily bribed," Hyacinth explained, looking back at Frances, who had already assumed the requisite distance to the couple and was now looking quite bored. "All the best maids are."

"I wouldn't know," Gareth murmured.

"*That* I find difficult to believe," Hyacinth said. He had probably bribed maids all across London. Hyacinth couldn't imagine that he could have made it to his age, with his reputation, and not have had an affair with a woman who wanted it kept secret.

He smiled inscrutably. "A gentleman never tells."

Hyacinth decided not to pursue the topic any further. Not, of course, because she wasn't curious, but rather because she thought he'd meant what he'd said, and he wasn't going to spill any secrets, delicious though they might be.

And really, why waste one's energy if one was going to get nowhere?

"I thought we would never escape," she said, once they'd reached the end of her street. "I have much to tell you."

He turned to her with obvious interest. "Were you able to translate the note?"

Hyacinth glanced behind her. She knew she'd said Frances would remain far in back, but it was always good to check, especially as Gregory was no stranger to the concept of bribery, either.

"Yes," she said, once she was satisfied that they would not be overheard. "Well, most of it, at least. Enough to know that we need to focus our search in the library."

Gareth chuckled.

"Why is that funny?"

"Isabella was a great deal sharper than she let on. If she'd wanted to pick a room that her husband was not likely to enter, she could not have done better than the library. Except for the bedroom, I suppose, but"—he turned and gazed down at her with an annoyingly paternalistic glance—"that's not a topic for your ears."

"Stuffy man," she muttered.

"Not an accusation that is often flung my way," he said with a slightly amused smile, "but clearly you bring out the best in me."

He was so patently sarcastic that Hyacinth could do nothing but scowl.

"The library, you say," Gareth mused, after taking a moment to enjoy Hyacinth's distress. "It makes perfect sense. My father's father was no intellectual."

"I hope that means he didn't possess very many books," Hyacinth said with a frown. "I suspect that she left another clue tucked into one."

"No such luck," Gareth said with a grimace. "My grandfather might not have been fond of books, but he did care a great deal about appearances, and no self-respecting baron would have a house without a library, or a library without books."

Hyacinth let out a groan. "It will take all night to go through an entire library of books."

He gave her a sympathetic smile, and something fluttered in her stomach. She opened her mouth to speak, but all she did was inhale, and she couldn't shake the oddest feeling that she was surprised.

But by what, she had no idea.

"Perhaps, once you see what's there, something will suddenly make sense," Gareth said. He did a little one-shouldered shrug as he steered them around the corner and onto Park Lane. "That sort of thing happens to me all the time. Usually when I least expect it."

Hyacinth nodded in agreement, still a little unsettled by the strange, light-headed sensation that had just washed over her. "That's exactly what I've been hoping might happen," she said, forcing herself to reaffix her focus onto the matter at hand. "But Isabella was rather cryptic, I'm afraid. Or . . . I don't know . . . perhaps she wasn't deliberately cryptic, and it's just because I can't translate all the words. But I do think that we may assume that we will find not the diamonds but instead another clue."

"Why is that?"

She nodded thoughtfully as she spoke. "I'm almost certain that we must look in the library, specifically in a book. And I don't see how she would have fit diamonds between the pages."

"She could have hollowed the book out. Created a hiding spot."

Her breath caught. "I never thought of that," she said, her eyes widening with excitement. "We will need to redouble our efforts. I think—although I'm not certain—that the book will be one of a scientific topic."

He nodded. "That will narrow things down. It's been some time since I was in the library at Clair House, but I don't recall there being much in the way of scientific treatises."

Hyacinth screwed up her mouth a little as she tried to recall the precise words in the clue. "It was something having to do with water. But I don't think it was biological."

"Excellent work," he said, "and if I haven't said so, thank you."

Hyacinth almost stumbled, so unexpected was his compliment. "You're welcome," she replied, once she'd gotten over her initial surprise. "I'm happy to do it. To be honest, I don't know what I will do with myself when this is all over. The diary is truly a lovely distraction."

"What is it you need to be distracted from?" he asked.

Hyacinth thought about that for a moment. "I don't know," she finally said. She looked up at him, feeling her brows come together as her eyes found his. "Isn't that sad?"

He shook his head, and this time when he smiled, it wasn't condescending, and it wasn't even dry. It was just a smile. "I suspect it's rather normal," he said.

But she wasn't so convinced. Until the excitement over the diary and the search for the jewels had entered her life, she hadn't noticed how very much her days had been pressed into a mold. The same things, the same people, the same food, the same sights.

She hadn't even realized how desperately she wanted a change.

Maybe that was another curse to lay at the feet of Isabella Marinzoli St. Clair. Maybe she hadn't even wanted a change before she'd begun translating the diary. Maybe she hadn't known to want one.

But now . . . After this . . .

She had a feeling that nothing would ever be the same.

"When shall we return to Clair House?" she asked, eager to change the subject.

He sighed. Or maybe it was a groan. "I don't suppose you'd take it well if I said I was going alone."

"Very badly," she confirmed.

"I suspected as much." He gave her a sideways glance. "Is everyone in your family as obstinate as you?"

"No," she said quite freely, "although they do come close. My sister Eloise, especially. You haven't met her. And Gregory." She rolled her eyes. "He's a beast."

"Why do I suspect that whatever he's done to you, you've returned in kind, and then in tenfold?"

She cocked her head to the side, trying to look terribly dry and sophisticated. "Are you saying you don't believe I can turn the other cheek?"

"Not for a second."

"Very well, it's true," she said with a shrug. She wasn't going to be able to carry on that ruse for very long, anyway. "I can't sit still in a sermon, either."

He grinned. "Neither can I."

"Liar," she accused. "You don't even try. I have it on the best authority that you never go to church."

"The best authorities are watching out for me?" He smiled faintly. "How reassuring."

"Your grandmother."

"Ah," he said. "That explains it. Would you believe that my soul is already well past redemption?"

"Absolutely," she said, "but that's no reason to make the rest of us suffer."

He looked at her with a wicked glint in his eye. "Is it that deep a torture to be at church without my calming presence?"

"You *know* what I meant," she said. "It's not fair that I should have to attend when you do not."

"Since when are we such a pair that it's tit for tat for us?" he queried.

That stopped her short. Verbally, at least.

And he obviously couldn't resist teasing her further, because he said, "Your family certainly wasn't very subtle about it."

"Oh," she said, barely resisting a groan. "That."

"That?"

"*Them.*"

"They're not so bad," he said.

"No," she agreed. "But they *are* an acquired taste. I suppose I should apologize."

"No need," he murmured, but she suspected it was just an automatic platitude.

Hyacinth sighed. She was rather used to her family's often desperate attempts to get her married off, but she could see where it might be a bit unsettling for the poor man in question. "If it makes you feel better," she said, giving him a sympathetic glance, "you're hardly the first gentleman they've tried to foist me upon."

"How charmingly put."

"Although if you think about it," she said, "it is actually to our advantage if they do think we might make a match of it."

"How is that?"

She thought furiously. She still wasn't sure if she wished to set her cap for him, but she *was* sure that she didn't want him to *think* that she had. Because if he did, and then he rejected her . . . well, nothing could be more brutal.

Or heartbreaking.

"Well," she said, making it up as she went along, "we are going to need to spend a great deal of time in each other's company, at least until we finish with the diary. If my family thinks there might be a church at the end of the journey, they are far less likely to quibble."

He appeared to consider that. To Hyacinth's surprise, however, he didn't speak, which meant that she had to.

"The truth is," she said, trying to sound very offhand and unconcerned, "they're mad to get me off their hands."

"I don't think you're being fair to your family," he said softly.

Hyacinth's lips parted with astonishment. There was an edge to his voice, something serious and unexpected. "Oh," she said, blinking as she tried to come up with a suitable comment. "Well . . ."

He turned, and there was a strange, intense light in his eyes as he said, "You're quite lucky to have them."

She felt suddenly uncomfortable. Gareth was looking at her with such intensity—it was as if the world were dropping away around them, and they were only in Hyde Park for heaven's sake, talking about her family . . .

"Well, yes," she finally said.

When Gareth spoke, his tone was sharp. "They only love you and want what's best for you."

"Are you saying you're what's best for me?" Hyacinth teased. Because she had to tease. She didn't know how else to react to his strange mood. Anything else would reveal too much.

And maybe her joke would force him to reveal something instead.

"That's not what I meant, and you know it," he said hotly.

Hyacinth stepped back. "I'm sorry," she said, bewildered by his reaction.

But he wasn't done. He looked at her squarely, his eyes flashing with something she'd never seen there before. "You should count your blessings that you come from a large and loving family."

"I do. I—"

"Do you have any idea how many people I have in this world?" he cut in. He moved forward, closing in on her until he was uncomfortably close. "Do you?" he demanded. "One. Just one," he said, not waiting for her reply. "My grandmother. And I would lay down my life for her."

Hyacinth had never seen this sort of passion in him, hadn't even dreamed he possessed it. He was normally so calm, so unflappable. Even that night at Bridgerton House, when he'd been upset by his encounter with his father, there had still been a certain air of levity about him. And then she realized what it was about him, what had set him apart . . . He was never quite serious.

Until now.

She couldn't tear her eyes from his face, even as he turned away, leaving her only his profile. He was staring at some distant spot on the horizon, some tree or some bush that he probably couldn't even identify.

"Do you know what it means to be alone?" he asked softly, still not looking at her. "Not for an hour, not for an evening, but just to know, to absolutely know that in a few years, you will have no one."

She opened her mouth to say no, of course not, but then she realized that there had been no question mark at the end of his statement.

She waited, because she did not know what to say. And then because she recognized that if she said something, if she tried to imply that she did understand, the moment would be lost, and she would never know what he'd been thinking.

And as she stood there, staring at his face as he lost himself in his thoughts, she realized that she *desperately* wanted to know what he was thinking.

"Mr. St. Clair?" she finally whispered, after a full minute had ticked away. "Gareth?"

She saw his lips move before she heard his voice. One corner tilted up in a mocking smile, and she had the strangest sense that he'd accepted his own bad luck, that he was ready to embrace it and revel in it, because if he tried to smash it, he was simply going to have his heart broken.

"I would give the world to have one more person for whom I would lay down my life," he said.

And then Hyacinth realized that some things did come in a flash. And there were some things one simply knew without possessing the ability to explain them.

Because in that moment she knew that she was going to marry this man.

No one else would do.

Gareth St. Clair knew what was important. He was funny, he was dry, he could be arrogantly mocking, but he knew what was important.

And Hyacinth had never realized before just how important that was to *her*.

Her lips parted as she watched him. She wanted to say something, to do something. She'd finally realized just what it was she wanted in life, and it felt like she ought to leap in with both feet, work toward her goal and make sure she got it.

But she was frozen, speechless as she gazed at his profile. There was something in the way he was holding his jaw. He looked bleak, haunted. And Hyacinth had the most overpowering impulse to reach out and touch him, to let her fingers brush against his cheek, to smooth his hair where the dark blond strands of his queue rested against the collar of his coat.

But she didn't. She wasn't that courageous.

He turned suddenly, his eyes meeting hers with enough force and clarity to take her breath away. And she had the oddest sense that she was only just now seeing the man beneath the surface.

"Shall we return?" he asked, and his voice was light and disappointingly back to normal.

Whatever had happened between them, it had passed.

"Of course," Hyacinth said. Now wasn't the time to press him. "When do you wish to return to Clair . . ." Her words trailed off. Gareth had stiffened, and his eyes were focused sharply over her shoulder.

Hyacinth turned around to see what had grabbed his attention.

Her breath caught. His father was walking down the path, coming straight toward them.

She looked quickly around. They were on the less fashionable side of the park, and as such, it wasn't terribly crowded. She could see a few members of the *ton* across the clearing, but none was close enough to overhear a conversation, provided that Gareth and his father were able to remain civil.

Hyacinth looked again from one St. Clair gentleman to the other, and she realized that she had never seen them together before.

Half of her wanted to pull Gareth to the side and avoid a scene, and half was dying of curiosity. If they stayed put, and she was finally able to witness their interaction, she might finally learn the cause of their estrangement.

But it wasn't up to her. It had to be Gareth's decision. "Do you want to go?" she asked him, keeping her voice low.

His lips parted slowly as his chin rose a fraction of an inch. "No," he said, his voice strangely contemplative. "It's a public park."

Hyacinth looked from Gareth to his father and back, her head bobbing, she was sure, like a badly wielded tennis ball. "Are you certain?" she asked, but he didn't hear her. She didn't think he would have heard a cannon going off right by his ear, so focused was he on the man ambling too casually toward them.

"Father," Gareth said, giving him an oily smile. "How pleasant to see you."

A look of revulsion passed across Lord St. Clair's face before he suppressed it. "Gareth," he said, his voice even, correct, and in Hyacinth's opinion, utterly bloodless. "How . . . odd . . . to see you here with Miss Bridgerton."

Hyacinth's head jerked with surprise. He had said her name too deliberately. She hadn't expected to be drawn into their war, but it seemed that somehow it had already happened.

"Have you met my father?" Gareth drawled, directing the question to her even as his eyes did not leave the baron's face.

"We have been introduced," Hyacinth replied.

"Indeed," Lord St. Clair said, taking her hand and bending over to kiss her gloved knuckles. "You are always charming, Miss Bridgerton."

Which was enough to prove to Hyacinth that they were definitely talking about something else, because she *knew* she wasn't always charming.

"Do you enjoy my son's company?" Lord St. Clair asked her, and Hyacinth noticed that once again, someone was asking her a question without actually looking at her.

"Of course," she said, her eyes flitting back and forth between the two men. "He is a most entertaining companion." And then, because she couldn't resist, she added, "You must be very proud of him."

That got the baron's attention, and he turned to her, his eyes dancing with something that wasn't quite humor. "Proud," he murmured, his lips curving into a half smile that she thought was rather like Gareth's. "It's an interesting adjective."

"Rather straightforward, I would think," Hyacinth said coolly.

"Nothing is ever straightforward with my father," Gareth said.

The baron's eyes went hard. "What my son means to say is that I am able to see the nuance in a situation . . . when one exists." He turned to Hyacinth. "Sometimes, my dear Miss Bridgerton, the matters at hand are quite clearly black and white."

Her lips parted as she glanced to Gareth and then back at his father. What the devil were they *talking* about?

Gareth's hand on her arm tightened, but when he spoke, his voice was light and casual. Too casual. "For once my father and I are in complete agreement. Very often one *can* view the world with complete clarity."

"Right now, perhaps?" the baron murmured.

Well, *no*, Hyacinth wanted to blurt out. As far as she was concerned, this was the most abstract and muddied conversation of her life. But she held her tongue. Partly because it really wasn't her place to speak, but also partly because she didn't want to do anything to halt the unfolding scene.

She turned to Gareth. He was smiling, but his eyes were cold. "I do believe my opinions right now are clear," he said softly.

And then quite suddenly the baron shifted his attention to Hyacinth. "What about you, Miss Bridgerton?" he asked. "Do you see things in black and white, or is your world painted in shades of gray?"

"It depends," she replied, lifting her chin until she was able to look him evenly in the eye. Lord St. Clair was tall, as tall as Gareth, and he looked to be healthy and fit. His face was pleasing and surprisingly youthful, with blue eyes and high, wide cheekbones.

But Hyacinth disliked him on sight. There was something angry about him, something underhanded and cruel.

And she didn't like how he made Gareth feel.

Not that Gareth had said anything to her, but it was clear as day on his face, in his voice, even in the way he held his chin.

"A very politic answer, Miss Bridgerton," the baron said, giving her a little nod of salute.

"How funny," she replied. "I'm not often politic."

"No, you're not, are you?" he murmured. "You do have a rather . . . *candid* reputation."

Hyacinth's eyes narrowed. "It is well deserved."

The baron chuckled. "Just make certain you are in possession of all of your information before you form your opinions, Miss Bridgerton. Or"—his head moved slightly, causing his gaze to angle onto her face in strange, sly manner—"before you make any decisions."

Hyacinth opened her mouth to give him a stinging retort—one that she hoped she'd be able to make up as she went along, since she still had no idea just what he was warning her about. But before she could speak, Gareth's grip on her forearm grew painful.

"It's time to go," he said. "Your family will be expecting you."

"Do offer them my regards," Lord St. Clair said, executing a smart little bow. "They are good *ton*, your family. I'm certain they want what's best for you."

Hyacinth just stared at him. She had no idea what the subtext was in this conversation, but clearly she did not have all the facts. And she *hated* being left in the dark.

Gareth yanked on her arm, hard, and she realized that he'd already started walking away. Hyacinth tripped over a bump in the path as she fell into place at his side. "What was *that* all about?" she asked, breathless from trying to keep up with him. He was striding through the park with a speed her shorter legs simply could not match.

"Nothing," he bit off.

"It wasn't *nothing*." She glanced over her shoulder to see if Lord St. Clair was still behind them. He wasn't, and the motion set her off-balance, in any case. She stumbled, falling against Gareth, who didn't seem inclined to treat her with any exceptional tenderness and solicitude. He did stop, though, just long enough for her to regain her footing.

"It was nothing," he said, and his voice was sharp and curt and a hundred other things she'd never thought it could be.

She shouldn't have said anything else. She knew she shouldn't have said anything else, but she wasn't always cautious enough to heed her own warnings, and as he pulled her along beside him, practically dragging her east toward Mayfair, she asked, "What are we going to do?"

He stopped, so suddenly that she nearly crashed into him. "Do?" he echoed. "We?"

"We," she confirmed, although her voice didn't come out quite as firmly as she'd intended.

"*We* are not going to do anything," he said, his voice sharpening as he spoke. "*We* are going to walk back to your house, where we are going to deposit you on your doorstep, and then *we* are going to return to my small, cramped apartments and have a drink."

"Why do you hate him so much?" Hyacinth asked. Her voice was soft, but it was direct.

He didn't answer. He didn't answer, and then it became clear that he wasn't going to answer. It wasn't her business, but oh, how she wished it were.

"Shall I return you, or do you wish to walk with your maid?" he finally asked.

Hyacinth looked over her shoulder. Frances was still behind her, standing near a large elm tree. She didn't look the least bit bored.

Hyacinth sighed. She was going to need a lot of peppermints this time.

Chapter 12

Twenty minutes later, after a long and silent walk.

It was remarkable, Gareth thought with more than a little self-loathing, how one encounter with the baron could ruin a perfectly good day.

And it wasn't even so much the baron. He couldn't stand the man, that was true, but that wasn't what bothered him, what kept him up at night, mentally smacking himself for his stupidity.

He hated what his father did to him, how one conversation could turn him into a stranger. Or if not a stranger, then an astonishingly good facsimile of Gareth William St. Clair . . . at the age of fifteen. For the love of God, he was an adult now, a man of twenty-eight. He'd left home and, one hoped, grown up. He should be able to behave like an adult when in an interview with the baron. He shouldn't feel this way.

He should feel nothing. Nothing.

But it happened every time. He got angry. And snappish. And he said things just for the sake of being provoking. It was rude, and it was immature, and he didn't know how to stop it.

And this time, it had happened in front of Hyacinth.

He had walked her home in silence. He could tell she wanted to speak. Hell, even if he hadn't seen it on her face, he would have known she wanted to speak. Hyacinth always wanted to speak. But apparently she did occasionally know when to leave well enough alone, because she'd held silent throughout the long walk through Hyde Park and Mayfair. And now here they were, in front of her house, Frances the maid still trailing them by twenty feet.

"I am sorry for the scene in the park," he said swiftly, since some kind of apology was in order.

"I don't think anyone saw," she replied. "Or at the very least, I don't think anyone heard. And it wasn't your fault."

He felt himself smile. Wryly, since that was the only sort he could manage. It *was* his fault. Maybe his father had provoked him, but it was long past time that Gareth learned to ignore it.

"Will you come in?" Hyacinth asked.

He shook his head. "I'd best not."

She looked up at him, her eyes uncommonly serious. "I would like you to come in," she said.

It was a simple statement, so bare and plain that he knew he could not refuse. He gave her a nod, and together they walked up the steps. The rest of the Bridgertons had dispersed, so they entered the now-empty rose-and-cream drawing room. Hyacinth waited near the door until he reached the seating area, and then she shut it. All the way.

Gareth lifted his brows in question. In some circles, a closed door was enough to demand marriage.

"I used to think," Hyacinth said after a moment, "that the only thing that would have made my life better was a father."

He said nothing.

"Whenever I was angry with my mother," she continued, still standing by the door, "or with one of my brothers or sisters, I used to think—*If only I had a father. Everything would be perfect, and he would surely take my side.*" She looked up, and her lips were curved in an endearingly lopsided smile. "He wouldn't have done, of course, since I'm sure that most of the time I was in the wrong, but it gave me great comfort to think it."

Gareth still said nothing. All he could do was stand there and imagine himself a Bridgerton. Picture himself with all those siblings, all that laughter. And he couldn't respond, because it was too painful to think that she'd had all that and still wanted more.

"I've always been jealous of people with fathers," she said, "but no longer."

He turned sharply, his eyes snapping to hers. She returned his gaze with equal directness, and he realized he couldn't look away. Not shouldn't—couldn't.

"It's better to have no father at all than to have one such as yours, Gareth," she said quietly. "I'm so sorry."

And that was his undoing. Here was this girl who had everything—at least everything *he* thought he'd ever wanted—and somehow she still understood.

"I have memories, at least," she continued, smiling wistfully. "Or at least the memories others have told to me. I know who my father was, and I know he was a good man. He would have loved me if he'd lived. He would have loved me without reservations and without conditions."

Her lips wobbled into an expression he had never seen on her before. A little bit quirky, an awful lot self-deprecating. It was entirely unlike Hyacinth, and for that reason completely mesmerizing.

"And I know," she said, letting out a short, staccato breath, the sort one did when one couldn't quite believe what one was saying, "that it's often rather hard work to love me."

And suddenly Gareth realized that some things did come in a

flash. And there were some things one simply knew without being able to explain them. Because as he stood there watching her, all he could think was—*No.*

No.

It would be rather easy to love Hyacinth Bridgerton.

He didn't know where the thought had come from, or what strange corner of his brain had come to that conclusion, because he was quite certain it would be nearly impossible to *live* with her, but somehow he knew that it wouldn't be at all difficult to love her.

"I talk too much," she said.

He'd been lost in his own thoughts. What was she saying?

"And I'm very opinionated."

That was true, but what was—

"And I can be an absolute pill when I do not get my way, although I would like to think that most of the time I'm reasonably reasonable . . ."

Gareth started to laugh. Good God, she was cataloguing all the reasons why she was difficult to love. She was right, of course, about all of them, but none of it seemed to matter. At least not right then.

"What?" she asked suspiciously.

"Be quiet," he said, crossing the distance between them.

"Why?"

"Just be quiet."

"But—"

He placed a finger on her lips. "Grant me one favor," he said softly, "and don't say a word."

Amazingly, she complied.

For a moment he did nothing but look at her. It was so rare that she was still, that something on her face wasn't moving or speaking or expressing an opinion with nothing more than a scrunch of her nose. He just looked at her, memorizing the way her eyebrows arched into delicate wings and her eyes grew wide under the strain of keeping quiet. He savored the hot rush of her breath across his finger, and the funny little sound she made at the back of her throat without realizing it.

And then he couldn't help it. He kissed her.

He took her face in his hands, and he lowered his mouth to hers. The last time he'd been angry, and he'd seen her as little more than a piece of forbidden fruit, the one girl his father thought he couldn't have.

But this time he was going to do it right. *This* would be their first kiss.

And it would be one to remember.

His lips were soft, gentle. He waited for her to sigh, for her body to soften against his. He wouldn't take until she made it clear she was ready to give.

And then he would offer himself in return.

He brushed his mouth against hers, with just enough friction to feel the texture of her lips, to sense the heat of her body. He tickled her with his tongue, tender and sweet, until her lips parted.

And then he tasted her. She was sweet, and she was warm, and she was returning his kiss with the most devilish mix of innocence and experience he could ever have imagined. Innocence, because it was quite clear she didn't know what she was doing. And experience, because despite all that, she drove him wild.

He deepened the kiss, his hands sliding down the length of her back until one rested on the curve of her bottom and the other at the small of her back. He pulled her against him, against the rising evidence of his desire. This was insane. It was mad. They were standing in her mother's drawing room, three feet from a door that could be opened at any moment, by a brother who certainly would feel no compunction at tearing Gareth apart limb from limb.

And yet he couldn't stop.

He wanted her. He wanted all of her.

God help him, he wanted her now.

"Do you like this?" he murmured, his lips moving to her ear.

He felt her nod, heard her gasp as he took her lobe between his teeth. It emboldened him, fired him.

"Do you like this?" he whispered, taking one hand and bringing it around to the swell of her breast.

She nodded again, this time gasping a tiny little, "Yes!"

He couldn't help but smile, nor could he do anything but slide his hand inside the folds of her coat, so that the only thing between his hand and her body was the thin fabric of her dress.

"You'll like this even better," he said wickedly, skimming his palm over her until he felt her nipple harden.

She let out a moan, and he allowed himself even greater liberties, catching the nub between his fingers, rolling it just a touch, tweaking it until she moaned again, and her fingers clutched frantically at his shoulders.

She would be good in bed, he realized with a primitive satisfaction. She wouldn't know what she was doing, but it wouldn't matter. She'd learn soon enough, and he would have the time of his life teaching her.

And she would be his.

His.

And then, as his lips found hers again, as his tongue slid into her mouth and claimed her as his own, he thought—

Why not?

Why not marry her? Why n—

He pulled back, still holding her face in his hands. Some things needed to be considered with a clear mind, and the Lord knew that his head wasn't clear when he was kissing Hyacinth.

"Did I do something wrong?" she whispered.

He shook his head, unable to do anything but look at her.

"Then wh—"

He quieted her with a firm finger to her lips.

Why not marry her? Everybody seemed to want them to. His grandmother had been hinting about it for over a year, and her family was about as subtle as a sledgehammer. Furthermore, he actually rather *liked* Hyacinth, which was more than he could say for most of the women he'd met during his years as a bachelor. Certainly she drove him mad half the time, but even with that, he liked her.

Plus, it was becoming increasingly apparent that he would not be able to keep his hands off her for very much longer. Another afternoon like this, and he'd ruin her.

He could picture it, see it in his mind. Not just the two of them, but all of the people in their lives—her family, his grandmother.

His father.

Gareth almost laughed aloud. What a boon. He could marry Hyacinth, which was shaping up in his mind to be an extremely pleasant endeavor, and at the same time completely show up the baron.

It would kill him. Absolutely kill him.

But, he thought, letting his fingers trail along the line of her jaw as he pulled away, he needed to do this right. He hadn't always lived his life on the correct side of propriety, but there were some things a man had to do as a gentleman.

Hyacinth deserved no less.

"I have to go," he murmured, taking one of her hands and lifting it to his mouth in a courtly gesture of farewell.

"Where?" she blurted out, her eyes still dazed with passion.

He liked that. He liked that he befuddled her, left her without her famous self-possession.

"There are a few things I need to think about," he said, "and a few things I need to do."

"But . . . what?"

He smiled down at her. "You'll find out soon enough."

"When?"

He walked to the door. "You're a bundle of questions this afternoon, aren't you?"

"I wouldn't have to be," she retorted, clearly regaining her wits, "if you'd actually say something of substance."

"Until next time, Miss Bridgerton," he murmured, slipping out into the hall.

"But *when*?" came her exasperated voice.

He laughed all the way out.

One hour later, in the foyer of Bridgerton House. Our hero, apparently, doesn't waste any time.

"The viscount will see you now, Mr. St. Clair."

Gareth followed Lord Bridgerton's butler down the hall to a private section of the house, one which he had never seen during the handful of times he had been a guest at Bridgerton House.

"He is in his study," the butler explained.

Gareth nodded. It seemed the right place for such an interview. Lord Bridgerton would wish to appear in command, in control, and this would be emphasized by their meeting in his private sanctuary.

When Gareth had knocked upon the front door of Bridgerton

House five minutes earlier, he had not given the butler any indication as to his purpose there that day, but he had no doubt that Hyacinth's brother, the almost infamously powerful Viscount Bridgerton, knew his intentions exactly.

Why else would Gareth come calling? He had never had any cause before. And after becoming acquainted with Hyacinth's family—some of them, at least—he had no doubt that her mother had already met with her brother and discussed the possibility of their making a match.

"Mr. St. Clair," the viscount said, rising from behind his desk as Gareth entered the room. That was promising. Etiquette did not demand that the viscount come to his feet, and it was a show of respect that he did.

"Lord Bridgerton," Gareth said, nodding. Hyacinth's brother possessed the same deep chestnut hair as his sister, although his was just starting to gray at the temples. The faint sign of age did nothing to diminish him, however. He was a tall man, and probably a dozen years Gareth's senior, but he was still superbly fit and powerful. Gareth would not have wanted to meet him in a boxing ring. Or a dueling field.

The viscount motioned to a large leather chair, positioned opposite to his desk. "Sit," he said, "please."

Gareth did so, working fairly hard to hold himself still and keep his fingers from drumming nervously against the arm of the chair. He had never done this before, and damned if it wasn't the most unsettling thing. He needed to appear calm, his thoughts organized and collected. He didn't think his suit would be refused, but he'd like to come through the experience with a modicum of dignity. If he did marry Hyacinth, he was going to be seeing the viscount for the rest of his life, and he didn't need the head of the Bridgerton family thinking him a fool.

"I imagine you know why I am here," Gareth said.

The viscount, who had resumed his seat behind his large mahogany desk, tilted his head very slightly to the side. He was tapping his fingertips together, his hands making a hollow triangle. "Perhaps," he said, "to save both of us from possible embarrassment, you could state your intentions clearly."

Gareth sucked in a breath. Hyacinth's brother wasn't going to make this easy on him. But that didn't matter. He had vowed to do this right, and he would not be cowed.

He looked up, meeting the viscount's dark eyes with steady purpose. "I would like to marry Hyacinth," he said. And then, because the viscount did not say anything, because he didn't even move, Gareth added, "Er, if she'll have me."

And then about eight things happened at once. Or perhaps there were merely two or three, and it just seemed like eight, because it was all so unexpected.

First, the viscount exhaled, although that did seem to understate the case. It was more of a sigh, actually—a huge, tired, heartfelt sigh that made the man positively deflate in front of Gareth. Which was astonishing. Gareth had seen the viscount on many occasions and was quite familiar with his reputation. This was not a man who sagged or groaned.

His lips seemed to move through the whole thing, too, and if Gareth were a more suspicious man, he would have *thought* that the viscount had said, "Thank you, Lord."

Combined with the heavenward tilt of the viscount's eyes, it did seem the most likely translation.

And then, just as Gareth was taking all of this in, Lord Bridgerton let the palms of his hands fall against the desk with surprising force, and he looked Gareth squarely in the eye as he said, "Oh, she'll have you. She will definitely have you."

It wasn't quite what Gareth had expected. "I beg your pardon," he said, since truly, he could think of nothing else.

"I need a drink," the viscount said, rising to his feet. "A celebration is in order, don't you think?"

"Er . . . yes?"

Lord Bridgerton crossed the room to a recessed bookcase and plucked a cut-glass decanter off one of the shelves. "No," he said to himself, putting it haphazardly back into place, "the good stuff, I think." He turned to Gareth, his eyes taking on a strange, almost giddy light. "The good stuff, wouldn't you agree?"

"Ehhhh . . ." Gareth wasn't quite sure what to make of this.

"The good stuff," the viscount said firmly. He moved some books to the side and reached behind to pull out what looked to be a very old bottle of cognac. "Have to keep it hidden," he explained, pouring it liberally into two glasses.

"Servants?" Gareth asked.

"Brothers." He handed Gareth a glass. "Welcome to the family."

Gareth accepted the offering, almost disconcerted by how easy this had turned out to be. He wouldn't have been surprised if the viscount had somehow managed to produce a special license and a vicar right then and there. "Thank you, Lord Bridgerton, I—"

"You should call me Anthony," the viscount cut in. "We're to be brothers, after all."

"Anthony," Gareth repeated. "I just wanted . . ."

"This is a wonderful day," Anthony was muttering to himself. "A wonderful day." He looked up sharply at Gareth. "You don't have sisters, do you?"

"None," Gareth confirmed.

"I am in possession of four," Anthony said, tossing back at least a third of the contents of his glass. "Four. And now they're all off my hands. I'm done," he said, looking as if he might break into a jig at any moment. "I'm free."

"You've daughters, don't you?" Gareth could not resist reminding him.

"Just one, and she's only three. I have years before I have to go through this again. If I'm lucky, she'll convert to Catholicism and become a nun."

Gareth choked on his drink.

"It's good, isn't it?" Anthony said, looking at the bottle. "Aged twenty-four years."

"I don't believe I've ever ingested anything quite so ancient," Gareth murmured.

"Now then," Anthony said, leaning against the edge of his desk, "you'll want to discuss the settlements, I'm sure."

The truth was, Gareth hadn't even thought about the settlements, strange as that seemed for a man in possession of very few funds. He'd been so surprised by his sudden decision to marry Hyacinth that his mind hadn't even touched upon the practical aspects of such a union.

"It is common knowledge that I increased her dowry last year," Anthony said, his face growing more serious. "I will stand by that, although I would hope that it is not your primary reason for marrying her."

"Of course not," Gareth replied, bristling.

"I didn't think so," Anthony said, "but one has to ask."

"I would hardly think a man would admit it to you if it were," Gareth said.

Anthony looked up sharply. "I would like to think I can read a man's face well enough to know if he is lying."

"Of course," Gareth said, sitting back down.

But it didn't appear that the viscount had taken offense. "Now then," he said, "her portion stands at . . ."

Gareth watched with a touch of confusion as Anthony just shook his head and allowed his words to trail off. "My lord?" he murmured.

"My apologies," Anthony said, snapping back to attention. "I'm a bit unlike myself just now, I must assure you."

"Of course," Gareth murmured, since agreement was really the only acceptable course of action at that point.

"I never thought this day would come," the viscount said. "We've had offers, of course, but none I was willing to entertain, and none recently." He let out a long breath. "I had begun to despair that anyone of merit would wish to marry her."

"You seem to hold your sister in an unbecomingly low regard," Gareth said coolly.

Anthony looked up and actually smiled. Sort of. "Not at all," he said. "But nor am I blind to her . . . ah . . . unique qualities." He stood, and Gareth realized instantly that Lord Bridgerton was using his height to intimidate. He also realized that he should not misinterpret the viscount's initial display of levity and relief. This was a dangerous man, or at least he could be when he so chose, and Gareth would do well not to forget it.

"My sister Hyacinth," the viscount said slowly, walking toward the window, "is a prize. You should remember that, and if you value your skin, you will treat her as the treasure she is."

Gareth held his tongue. It didn't seem the correct time to chime in.

"But while Hyacinth may be a prize," Anthony said, turning around with the slow, deliberate steps of a man who is well familiar with his power, "she isn't easy. I will be the first one to admit to this. There aren't many men who can match wits with her, and if she is trapped into marriage with someone who does not appreciate her . . . singular personality, she will be miserable."

Still, Gareth did not speak. But he did not remove his eyes from the viscount's face.

And Anthony returned the gesture. "I will give you my permission to marry her," he said. "But you should think long and hard before you ask her yourself."

"What are you saying?" Gareth asked suspiciously, rising to his feet.

"I will not mention this interview to her. It is up to you to decide if you wish to take the final step. And if you do not . . ." The viscount shrugged, his shoulders rising and falling in an oddly Gallic gesture. "In that case," he said, sounding almost disturbingly calm, "she will never know."

How many men had the viscount scared off in this manner, Gareth wondered. Good God, was this why Hyacinth had gone unmarried for so long? He supposed he should be grateful, since it had left her free to marry him, but still, did she realize her eldest brother was a *madman*?

"If you don't make my sister happy," Anthony Bridgerton continued, his eyes just intense enough to confirm Gareth's suspicions about his sanity, "then *you* will not be happy. I will see to it myself."

Gareth opened his mouth to offer the viscount a scathing retort—to hell with treating him with kid gloves and tiptoeing around his high and mightiness. But then, just when he was about to insult his future brother-in-law, probably irreversibly, something else popped out of his mouth instead.

"You love her, don't you?"

Anthony snorted impatiently. "Of course I love her. She's my sister."

"I loved my brother," Gareth said quietly. "Besides my grandmother, he was the only person I had in this world."

"You do not intend to mend your rift with your father, then," Anthony said.

"No."

Anthony did not ask questions; he just nodded and said, "If you marry my sister, you will have all of us."

Gareth tried to speak, but he had no voice. He had no words. There were no words for what was rushing through him.

"For better or for worse," the viscount continued, with a light, self-mocking chuckle. "And I assure you, you will very often wish that Hyacinth were a foundling, left on a doorstep with not a relation to her name."

"No," Gareth said with soft resolve. "I would not wish that on anyone."

The room held silent for a moment, and then the viscount asked, "Is there anything you wish to share with me about him?"

Unease began to seep through Gareth's blood. "Who?"

"Your father."

"No."

Anthony appeared to consider this, then he asked, "Will he make trouble?"

"For me?"

"For Hyacinth."

Gareth couldn't lie. "He might."

And that was the worst of it. That was what would keep him up at night. Gareth had no idea what the baron might do. Or what he might say.

Or how the Bridgertons might feel if they learned the truth.

And in that moment, Gareth realized that he needed to do two things. First, he had to marry Hyacinth as soon as possible. She—

and her mother—would probably wish for one of those absurdly elaborate weddings that took months to plan, but he would need to put his foot down and insist that they wed quickly.

And second, as a sort of insurance, he was going to have to do something to make it impossible for her to back out, even if his father came forward with proof of Gareth's parentage.

He was going to have to compromise her. As soon as possible. There was still the matter of Isabella's diary. She might have known the truth, and if she'd written about it, Hyacinth would learn his secrets even without the intervention of the baron.

And while Gareth didn't much mind Hyacinth learning the true facts of his birth, it was vital that it not happen until after the wedding.

Or after he'd secured its eventuality with seduction.

Gareth didn't much like being backed into a corner. Nor was he especially fond of having to *have* to do anything.

But this . . .

This, he decided, would be pure pleasure.

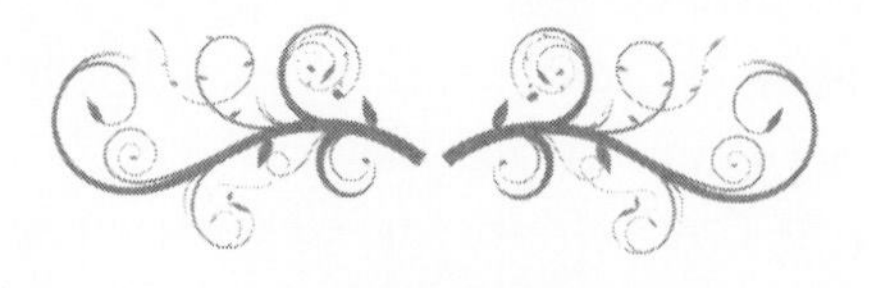

Chapter 13

Only one hour later. As we have noted, when our hero puts his mind to something . . .

And did we mention that it's a Tuesday?

"Enh?" Lady Danbury screeched. "You're not speaking loudly enough!"

Hyacinth allowed the book from which she was reading to fall closed, with just her index finger stuck inside to mark her place. "Why," she wondered aloud, "does it feel like I have heard this before?"

"You have," Lady D declared. "You never speak loudly enough."

"Funny, but my mother never makes that complaint."

"Your mother's ears aren't of the same vintage as mine," Lady Danbury said with a snort. "And where's my cane?"

Ever since she'd seen Gareth in action, Hyacinth had felt emboldened when it came to encounters with Lady Danbury's cane. "I hid it," she said with an evil smile.

Lady Danbury drew back. "Hyacinth Bridgerton, you sly cat."

"Cat?"

"I don't like dogs," Lady D said with a dismissive wave of her hand. "Or foxes, for that matter."

Hyacinth decided to take it as a compliment—always the best course of action when Lady Danbury was making no sense—and she turned back to *Miss Butterworth and the Mad Baron*, chapter seventeen. "Let's see," she murmured, "where were we . . ."

"Where did you hide it?"

"It wouldn't be hidden if I told you, now would it?" Hyacinth said, not even looking up.

"I'm trapped in this chair without it," Lady D said. "You wouldn't wish to deprive an old lady of her only means of transport, would you?"

"I would," Hyacinth said, still looking down at the book. "I absolutely would."

"You've been spending too much time with my grandson," the countess muttered.

Hyacinth kept her attention diligently on the book, but she knew she wasn't managing a completely straight face. She sucked in her lips, then pursed them, as she always did when she was trying not to look at someone, and if the temperature of her cheeks was any indication, she was blushing.

Dear God.

Lesson Number One in dealings with Lady Danbury: Never show weakness.

Lesson Number Two being, of course: When in doubt, refer to Lesson Number One.

"Hyacinth Bridgerton," Lady Danbury said, too slowly for her to be up to anything but the most devious sort of mischief, "are your cheeks pink?"

Hyacinth looked up with her blankest expression. "I can't see my cheeks."

"They *are* pink."

"If you say so." Hyacinth flipped a page with a bit more purpose than was necessary, then looked down in dismay at the small rip near the binding. Oh dear. Well, nothing she could do about it now, and Priscilla Butterworth had certainly survived worse.

"Why are you blushing?" Lady D asked.

"I'm not blushing."

"I do believe you are."

"I'm n—" Hyacinth caught herself before they started bickering like a pair of children. "I'm warm," she said, with what she felt was an admirable display of dignity and decorum.

"It's perfectly pleasant in this room," Lady Danbury said immediately. "Why are you blushing?"

Hyacinth glared at her. "Do you wish for me to read this book or not?"

"Not," Lady D said definitively. "I would much rather learn why you are blushing."

"I'm not blushing!" Hyacinth fairly yelled.

Lady Danbury smiled, an expression that on anyone else might have been pleasant but on her was diabolical. "Well, you are now," she said.

"If my cheeks are pink," Hyacinth ground out, "it is from anger."

"At me?" Lady D inquired, placing one, oh-so-innocent hand over her heart.

"I'm going to read the book now," Hyacinth announced.

"If you must," Lady D said with a sigh. She waited about a second before adding, "I believe Miss Butterworth was scrambling up the hillside."

Hyacinth turned her attention resolutely to the book in her hands.

"Well?" Lady Danbury demanded.

"I have to find my place," Hyacinth muttered. She scanned the page, trying to find Miss Butterworth and the correct hillside (there were more than one, and she'd scrambled up them all), but the words swam before her eyes, and all she saw was Gareth.

Gareth, with those rakish eyes and perfect lips. Gareth, with a dimple she was sure he'd deny if she ever pointed it out to him. Gareth . . .

Who was making her sound as foolish as Miss Butterworth. Why would he deny a dimple?

In fact . . .

Hyacinth flipped back a few pages. Yes, indeed, there it was, right in the middle of chapter sixteen:

> His eyes were rakish and his lips perfectly molded. And he possessed a dimple, right above the left corner of his mouth, that he would surely deny if she were ever brave enough to point it out to him.

"Good God," Hyacinth muttered. She didn't think Gareth even *had* a dimple.

"We're not that lost, are we?" Lady D demanded. "You've gone back three chapters, at least."

"I'm looking, I'm looking," Hyacinth said. She was going mad. That had to be it. She'd clearly lost her wits if she was now unconsciously quoting from *Miss Butterworth.*

But then again . . .

He'd kissed her.

He'd really kissed her. The first time, back in the hall at Bridgerton House—that had been something else entirely. Their lips had touched, and in truth quite a few other things had touched as well, but it hadn't been a kiss.

Not like this one.

Hyacinth sighed.

"*What* are you huffing about?" Lady Danbury demanded.

"Nothing."

Lady D's mouth clamped into a firm line. "You are not yourself this afternoon, Miss Bridgerton. Not yourself at all."

Not a point Hyacinth wished to argue. "*Miss Butterworth*," she read with more force than was necessary, "*scrambled up the hillside, her fingers digging deeper into the dirt with each step.*"

"Can fingers step?" Lady D asked.

"They can in this book." Hyacinth cleared her throat and continued: "*She could hear him behind her. He was closing the distance between them, and soon she would be caught. But for what purpose? Good or evil?*"

"Evil, I hope. It'll keep things interesting."

"I am in complete agreement," Hyacinth said. "*How would she know?*" she read on. "*How would she know? How* WOULD *she know?*" She looked up. "Emphasis mine."

"Allowed," Lady D said graciously.

"*And then she recalled the advice given to her by her mother, before the blessed lady had gone to her reward, pecked to death by pigeons—*"

"This can't be real!"

"Of course it can't. It's a novel. But I swear to you, it's right here on page 193."

"Let me see that!"

Hyacinth's eyes widened. Lady Danbury frequently accused Hyacinth of embellishment, but this was the first time she had actually demanded verification. She got up and showed the book to the countess, pointing to the paragraph in question.

"Well, I'll be," Lady Danbury said. "The poor lady did get done in by pigeons." She shook her head. "It's not how I'd like to go."

"You probably don't need to worry on that score," Hyacinth said, resuming her seat.

Lady D reached for her cane, then scowled when she realized it was gone. "Continue," she barked.

"Right," Hyacinth said to herself, looking back down at the book. "Let me see. Ah, yes . . . *gone to her reward, pecked to death by pigeons.*" She looked up, spluttering. "I'm sorry. I can't read that without laughing."

"Just read!"

Hyacinth cleared her throat several times before resuming. "*She had been only twelve, far too young for such a conversation, but perhaps her mother had anticipated her early demise.* I'm sorry," she cut in again, "but how on earth could someone anticipate something like that?"

"As you said," Lady D said dryly, "it's a novel."

Hyacinth took a breath and read on: "*Her mother had clutched her hand, and with sad, lonely eyes had said, 'Dearest, dearest Priscilla. There is nothing in this world more precious than love.'* "

Hyacinth stole a peek at Lady Danbury, who she fully expected to be snorting with disgust. But to her great surprise, the countess was rapt, hanging on her every word.

Quickly returning her attention to the book, Hyacinth read, " '*But there are deceivers, darling Priscilla, and there are men who will attempt to take advantage of you without a true meeting of the hearts.'* "

"It's true," Lady Danbury said.

Hyacinth looked up, and it was immediately apparent that Lady Danbury had not realized that she'd spoken aloud.

"Well, it is," Lady D said defensively, when she realized that Hyacinth was looking at her.

Not wishing to embarrass the countess any further, Hyacinth turned back to the book without speaking. Clearing her throat, she continued: " '*You will need to trust your instincts, dearest Priscilla, but I will give you one piece of advice. Hold it to your heart and remember it always, for I vow it is true.*' "

Hyacinth turned the page, a little embarrassed to realize that she was as captured by the book as she'd ever been.

"*Priscilla leaned forward, touching her mother's pale cheek. 'What is it, Mama?' she asked.*

" '*If you want to know if a gentleman loves you,' her mother said, 'there is only one true way to be sure.*' "

Lady Danbury leaned forward. Even Hyacinth leaned forward, and she was holding the book.

" '*It's in his kiss,' her mother whispered. 'It's all there, in his kiss.*' "

Hyacinth's lips parted, and one hand come up to touch them, without her even realizing it.

"Well," Lady Danbury declared. "That wasn't what I was expecting."

It's in his kiss. Could it be true?

"I would think," Lady D continued officiously, "that it's in his actions or his deeds, but I suppose that wouldn't have sounded romantic enough for Miss Butterworth."

"And the Mad Baron," Hyacinth murmured.

"Exactly! Who in her right mind would want a madman?"

"It's in his kiss," Hyacinth whispered to herself.

"Enh?" Lady Danbury screeched. "I can't hear you."

"It's nothing," Hyacinth said quickly, giving her head a little shake as she forced her attention back to the countess. "I was merely woolgathering."

"Pondering the intellectual dogmas laid out by Mother Butterworth?"

"Of course not." She coughed. "Shall we read some more?"

"We'd better," Lady D grumbled. "The sooner we finish this one, the sooner we can move on to another."

"We don't *need* to finish this one," Hyacinth said, although if they didn't, she was going to have to sneak it home and finish it herself.

"Don't be silly. We can't *not* finish it. I paid good money for that nonsense. And besides"—Lady D looked as sheepish as she was able when she said this, which, admittedly, wasn't very sheepish—"I wish to know how it ends."

Hyacinth smiled at her. It was as close to an expression of soft-heartedness as Lady Danbury was likely to display, and Hyacinth rather thought it should be encouraged. "Very well," she said. "If you will allow me to find my place again . . ."

"Lady Danbury," came the deep, even voice of the butler, who had entered the drawing room on silent feet, "Mr. St. Clair would like an audience."

"And he's asking for it?" Lady D inquired. "He usually just barges right in."

The butler lifted an eyebrow, more expression than Hyacinth had ever seen on a butler's face. "He has requested an audience with Miss Bridgerton," he said.

"Me?" Hyacinth squeaked.

Lady Danbury's jaw dropped. "Hyacinth!" she spluttered. "In *my* drawing room?"

"That is what he said, my lady."

"Well," Lady D declared, looking around the room even though there was no one present save Hyacinth and the butler. "Well."

"Shall I escort him in?" the butler inquired.

"Of course," Lady Danbury replied, "but I'm not going anywhere. Anything he has to say to Miss Bridgerton, he can say in front of me."

"What?" Hyacinth demanded, finally tearing her eyes off the butler and turning toward Lady Danbury. "I hardly think—"

"It's my drawing room," Lady D said, "and he's my grandson. And you're—" She clamped her mouth together as she regarded Hyacinth, her diatribe momentarily halted. "Well, you're you," she finally finished. "Hmmph."

"Miss Bridgerton," Gareth said, appearing in the doorway and filling it, to wax Butterworthian, with his marvelous presence. He turned to Lady Danbury. "Grandmother."

"Anything you have to say to Miss Bridgerton, you can say in front of me," she told him.

"I'm almost tempted to test that theory," he murmured.

"Is something amiss?" Hyacinth asked, perching at the front of her chair. After all, they'd parted ways barely two hours earlier.

"Not at all," Gareth replied. He crossed the room until he was at her side, or at least as close to it as the furniture would allow. His grandmother was staring at him with unconcealed interest, and he was beginning to doubt the wisdom of coming straight here from Bridgerton House.

But he had stepped out onto the pavement and realized that it was Tuesday. And somehow that had seemed auspicious. This had all started on a Tuesday, good heavens, was it just two weeks earlier?

Tuesdays were when Hyacinth read to his grandmother. Every Tuesday, without fail, at the same time, in the same place. Gareth had realized, as he walked down the street, pondering the new direction of his life, that he knew exactly where Hyacinth was in that moment. And if he wanted to ask her to marry him, he had only to walk the brief distance across Mayfair to Danbury House.

He probably should have waited. He probably should have picked a far more romantic time and place, something that would sweep her off her feet and leave her breathless for more. But he'd made his decision, and he didn't want to wait, and besides, after all his grandmother had done for him over the years, she deserved to be the first to know.

He hadn't, however, expected to have to make his proposal in the old lady's presence.

He glanced over at her.

"What is it?" she barked.

He should ask her to leave. He really should, although . . .

Oh, hell. She wouldn't quit the room if he got down on his knees and begged her. Not to mention that Hyacinth would have an extremely difficult time refusing him with Lady Danbury in attendance.

Not that he thought she'd say no, but it really did make sense to stack the deck in his favor.

"Gareth?" Hyacinth said softly.

He turned to her, wondering how long he'd been standing there, pondering his options. "Hyacinth," he said.

She looked at him expectantly.

"Hyacinth," he said again, this time with a bit more certitude. He smiled, letting his eyes melt into hers. "Hyacinth."

"We *know* her name," came his grandmother's voice.

Gareth ignored her and pushed a table aside so that he could drop to one knee. "Hyacinth," he said, relishing her gasp as he took her hand in his, "would you do me the very great honor of becoming my wife?"

Her eyes widened, then misted, and her lips, which he'd

been kissing so deliciously mere hours earlier, began to quiver. "I . . . I . . ."

It was unlike her to be so without words, and he was enjoying it, especially the show of emotion on her face.

"I . . . I . . ."

"Yes!" his grandmother finally yelled. "Yes! She'll marry you!"

"She can speak for herself," he said.

"No," Lady D said, "she can't. Quite obviously."

"Yes," Hyacinth said, nodding through her sniffles. "Yes, I'll marry you."

He lifted her hand to his lips. "Good."

"Well," his grandmother declared. "Well." Then she muttered, "I need my cane."

"It's behind the clock," Hyacinth said, never taking her eyes off Gareth's.

Lady Danbury blinked with surprise, then actually got up and retrieved it.

"Why?" Hyacinth asked.

Gareth smiled. "Why what?"

"Why did you ask me to marry you?"

"I should think that was clear."

"Tell her!" Lady D bellowed, thumping her cane against the carpet. She gazed down at the stick with obvious affection. "That's much better," she murmured.

Gareth and Hyacinth both turned to her, Hyacinth somewhat impatiently and Gareth with that blank stare of his that hinted of condescension without actually rubbing the recipient's face in it.

"Oh very well," Lady Danbury grumbled. "I suppose you'd like a bit of privacy."

Neither Gareth nor Hyacinth said a word.

"I'm leaving, I'm leaving," Lady D said, hobbling to the door with suspiciously less agility than she'd displayed when she'd crossed the room to retrieve the cane just moments earlier. "But don't you think," she said, pausing in the doorway, "that I'm leaving you for long. I know *you*," she said, jabbing her cane in the air toward Gareth, "and if you think I trust you with her virtue . . ."

"I'm your grandson."

"Doesn't make you a saint," she announced, then slipped out of the room, shutting the door behind her.

Gareth regarded this with a quizzical air. "I rather think she wants me to compromise you," he murmured. "She'd never have closed it all the way, otherwise."

"Don't be silly," Hyacinth said, trying for a touch of bravado under her blush, which she could feel spreading across her cheeks.

"No, I think she does," he said, taking both her hands in his and raising them to his lips. "She wants you for a granddaughter, probably more than she wants me for a grandson, and she's just underhanded enough to facilitate your ruin to ensure the outcome."

"I wouldn't back out," Hyacinth mumbled, disconcerted by his nearness. "I gave you my word."

He took one of her fingers and placed the tip between his lips. "You did, didn't you?" he murmured.

She nodded, transfixed by the sight of her finger against his mouth. "You didn't answer my question," she whispered.

His tongue found the delicate crease beneath her fingertip and flicked back and forth. "Did you ask me one?"

She nodded. It was hard to think while he was seducing her, and amazing to think that he could reduce her to such a breathless state with just one finger to his lips.

He moved, sitting beside her on the sofa, never once releasing her hand. "So lovely," he murmured. "And soon to be mine." He took her hand and turned it over, so that her palm was facing up. Hyacinth watched him watching her, watched him as he leaned over her and touched his lips to the inside of her wrist. Her breath seemed overloud in the silent room, and she wondered what it was that was most responsible for her heightened state: the feel of his mouth on her skin or the sight of him, seducing her with only a kiss.

"I like your arms," he said, holding one as if it were a precious treasure, in need of examination as much as safekeeping. "The skin first, I think," he continued, letting his fingers slide lightly along the sensitive skin above her wrist. It had been a warm day, and she'd worn a summer frock under her pelisse. The sleeves were mere caps, and—she sucked in her breath—if he continued his exploration all the way up to her shoulder, she thought she might melt right there on the sofa.

"But I like the shape of them as well," he said, gazing down at it as if it were an object of wonder. "Slim, but with just a hint of roundness and strength." He looked up, lazy humor in his eyes. "You're a bit of a sportswoman, aren't you?"

She nodded.

He curved his lips into a half smile. "I can see it in the way you walk, the way you move. Even"—he stroked her arm one last time, his fingers coming to rest near her wrist—"the shape of your arm."

He leaned in, until his face was near hers, and she felt kissed by his breath as he spoke. "You move differently than other women," he said softly. "It makes me wonder."

"What?" she whispered.

His hand was somehow on her hip, then on her leg, resting on the curve of her thigh, not quite caressing her, just reminding her of its presence with the heat and weight of it. "I think you know," he murmured.

Hyacinth felt her body flush with heat as unbidden images filled her mind. She knew what went on between a man and a woman;

she'd long since badgered the truth out of her older sisters. And she'd once found a scandalous book of erotic images in Gregory's room, filled with illustrations from the East that had made her feel very strange inside.

But nothing had prepared her for the rush of desire that she felt upon Gareth's murmured words. She couldn't help but picture him—stroking her, kissing her.

It made her weak.

It made her want him.

"Don't you wonder?" he whispered, the words hot against her ear.

She nodded. She couldn't lie. She felt bare in the moment, her very soul laid open to his gentle onslaught.

"What do you think?" he pressed.

She swallowed, trying not to notice the way her breath seemed to fill her chest differently. "I couldn't say," she finally managed.

"No, you couldn't," he said, smiling knowingly, "could you? But that's of no matter." He leaned in and kissed her, once, slowly, on the lips. "You will soon."

He rose to his feet. "I fear I must leave before my grandmother attempts to spy on us from the house across the way."

Hyacinth's eyes flew to the window in horror.

"Don't worry," Gareth said with a chuckle. "Her eyes aren't that good."

"She owns a telescope," Hyacinth said, still regarding the window with suspicion.

"Why does that not surprise me?" Gareth murmured, walking to the door.

Hyacinth watched him as he crossed the room. He had always reminded her of a lion. He still did, only now he was hers to tame.

"I shall call upon you tomorrow," Gareth said, honoring her with a small bow.

She nodded, watching as he took his leave. Then, when he was gone, she untwisted her torso so that she was once again facing front.

"Oh. My—"

"What did he say?" Lady Danbury demanded, reentering the room a scant thirty seconds after Gareth's departure.

Hyacinth just looked at her blankly.

"You asked him why he asked you to marry him," Lady D reminded her. "What did he say?"

Hyacinth opened her mouth to reply, and it was only then that she realized he had never answered her question.

"He said he couldn't not marry me," she lied. It was what she wished he'd said; it might as well be what Lady Danbury thought had transpired.

"Oh!" Lady D sighed, clasping a hand to her chest. "How lovely."

Hyacinth regarded her with a new appreciation. "You're a romantic," she said.

"Always," Lady D replied, with a secret smile that Hyacinth knew she didn't often share. "Always."

Chapter 14

Two weeks have passed. All of London now knows that Hyacinth is to become Mrs. St. Clair. Gareth is enjoying his new status as an honorary Bridgerton, but still, he can't help but wait for it all to fall apart.

The time is midnight. The place, directly below Hyacinth's bedroom window.

He had planned for everything, plotted every last detail. He'd played it out in his mind, everything but the words he'd say, since those, he knew, would come in the heat of the moment.

It would be a thing of beauty.

It would be a thing of passion.

It would be that night.

Tonight, thought Gareth, with a strange mix of calculation and delight, he would seduce Hyacinth.

He had a few vague pangs about the degree to which he was plotting her downfall, but these were quickly dismissed. It wasn't as if he was going to ruin her and leave her to the wolves. He was planning to marry the girl, for heaven's sake.

And no one would know. No one but him and Hyacinth.

And her conscience, which would never allow her to pull out of a betrothal once she'd given herself to her fiancé.

They had made plans to search Clair House that night. Hyacinth had wanted to go the week before, but Gareth had put her off. It was too soon to set his plan in motion, so he had made up a story about his father having guests. Common sense dictated that they would wish to search the emptiest house possible, after all.

Hyacinth, being the practical girl she was, had agreed immediately.

But tonight would be perfect. His father would almost certainly be at the Mottram Ball, on the off chance that they actually made it to Clair House to conduct their search. And more importantly, Hyacinth was ready.

He'd made sure she was ready.

The past two weeks had been surprisingly delightful. He'd been forced to attend an astounding number of parties and balls. He had been to the opera and the theater. But he had done it all with Hyacinth at his side, and if he'd had any doubts about the wisdom of marrying her, they were gone now. She was sometimes vexing, occasionally infuriating, but always entertaining.

She would make a fine wife. Not for most men, but for him, and that was all that mattered.

But first he had to make sure she could not back out. He had to make their agreement permanent.

He'd begun her seduction slowly, tempting her with glances, touches, and stolen kisses. He'd teased her, always leaving a hint of what might transpire next. He'd left her breathless; hell, he'd left himself breathless.

He'd started this two weeks earlier, when he had asked her to marry him, knowing all the while that theirs would need to be a hasty engagement. He'd started it with a kiss. Just a kiss. Just one little kiss.

Tonight he would show her just what a kiss could be.

All in all, Hyacinth thought as she hurried up the stairs to her bedroom, it had gone rather well.

She would have preferred to stay home that night—all the more time to prepare for her outing to Clair House, but Gareth had pointed out that if he was going to send his regrets to the Mottrams, she had best attend. Otherwise, there might be speculation as to both of their whereabouts. But after spending three hours talking and laughing and dancing, Hyacinth had located her mother and pleaded a headache. Violet was having a fine time, as Hyacinth had known she would be, and did not wish to depart, so instead she'd sent Hyacinth home in the carriage by herself.

Perfect, perfect. Everything was perfect. The carriage had not encountered any traffic on the way home, so it had to be just about midnight, which meant that Hyacinth had fifteen minutes to change her clothing and creep down to the back stairs to await Gareth.

She could hardly wait.

She wasn't certain if they would find the jewels that night. She wouldn't be surprised if Isabella had instead left more clues. But they would be one step closer to their goal.

And it would be an adventure.

Had she always possessed this reckless streak, Hyacinth wondered. Had she always thrilled to danger? Had she only been waiting for the opportunity to be wild?

She moved quietly down the upper hall to her bedroom door. The house was silent, and she certainly didn't wish to rouse any of the servants. She reached out and turned the well-oiled doorknob, then pushed the door open and slipped inside.

At last.

Now all she had to do was—

"Hyacinth."

She almost shrieked.

"Gareth?" she gasped, her eyes nearly bugging out. Good God, the man was lounging on her bed.

He smiled. "I've been waiting for you."

She looked quickly around the room. How had he got inside? "What are you doing here?" she whispered frantically.

"I arrived early," he said in a lazy voice. But his eyes were sharp and intense. "I thought I'd wait for you."

"*Here?*"

He shrugged, smiled. "It was cold outside."

Except it wasn't. It was unseasonably warm. Everyone had been remarking on it.

"How did you get in?" Good God, did the servants know? Had someone *seen* him?

"Scaled the wall."

"You scaled the—You what?" She ran to the window, peering out and down. "How did you—"

But he had risen from the bed and crept up behind her. His arms encircled her, and he murmured, low and close to her ear, "I'm very, very clever."

She let out a nervous laugh. "Or part cat."

She felt him smile. "That, too," he murmured. And then, after a pause: "I missed you."

"I—" She wanted to say that she'd missed him, too, but he was too close, and she was too warm, and her voice escaped her.

He leaned down, his lips finding the soft spot just below her ear.

He touched her, so softly she wasn't even sure it was a kiss, then murmured, "Did you enjoy yourself this evening?"

"Yes. No. I was too . . ." She swallowed, unable to withstand the touch of his lips without making a reaction. ". . . anxious."

He took her hands, kissing each in turn. "Anxious? Whyever?"

"The jewels," she reminded him. Good heavens, did every woman have this much trouble breathing when standing so close to a handsome man?

"Ah, yes." His hand found her waist, and she felt herself being pulled toward him. "The jewels."

"Don't you want—"

"Oh, I do," he murmured, holding her scandalously close. "I want. Very much."

"Gareth," she gasped. His hands were on her bottom, and his lips on her neck.

And she wasn't sure how much longer she could remain standing.

He did things to her. He made her feel things she didn't recognize. He made her gasp and moan, and all she knew was that she wanted more.

"I think about you every night," he whispered against her skin.

"You do?"

"Mmm-hmm." His voice, almost a purr, rumbled against her throat. "I lie in bed, wishing you were there beside me."

It took every ounce of her strength just to breathe. And yet some little part of her, some wicked and very wanton corner of her soul, made her say, "What do you think about?"

He chuckled, clearly pleased with her question. "I think about doing *this*," he murmured, and his hand, already cupping her bottom, tightened until she was pressed against the evidence of his desire.

She made a noise. It might have been his name.

"And I think a *lot* about doing this," he said, his expert fingers flicking open one of the buttons on the back of her gown.

Hyacinth gulped. Then she gulped again when she realized he'd undone three more in the time it took her to draw one breath.

"But most of all," he said, his voice low and smooth. "I think about doing *this*."

He swept her into his arms, her skirt swirling around her legs even as the bodice of her dress slid down, resting precariously at the top of her breasts. She clutched at his shoulders, her fingers barely making a dent in his muscles, and she wanted to say something—anything that might make her seem more sophisticated than she actually was, but all she managed was a startled little "Oh!" as she became weightless, seemingly floating through the air until he laid her down on her bed.

He lay down next to her, perched on his side, one hand idly stroking the bare skin covering her breastbone. "So pretty," he murmured. "So soft."

"What are you doing?" she whispered.

He smiled. Slowly, like a cat. "To you?"

She nodded.

"That depends," he said, leaning down and letting his tongue tease where his fingers had just been. "How does it make you feel?"

"I don't know," she admitted.

He laughed, the sound low and soft, and strangely heartwarming. "That's a good thing," he said, his fingers finding the loosened bodice of her gown. "A very good thing."

He tugged, and Hyacinth sucked in her breath as she was bared, to the air, to the night.

To him.

"So pretty," he whispered, smiling down at her, and she wondered if his touch could possibly leave her as breathless as his gaze. He did nothing but look at her, and she was taut and tense.

Eager.

"You are so beautiful," he murmured, and then he touched her, his hand skimming along the tip of her breast so lightly he might have been the wind.

Oh, yes, his touch did quite a bit more than his gaze.

She felt it in her belly, she felt it between her legs. She felt it to the tips of her toes, and she couldn't help but arch up, reaching for more, for something closer, firmer.

"I thought you'd be perfect," he said, taking his torture to her other breast. "I didn't realize. I just didn't realize."

"What?" she whispered.

His eyes locked with hers. "That you're better," he said. "Better than perfect."

"Th-that's not possible," she said, "you can't—oh!" He'd done something else, something even more wicked, and if this was a battle for her wits, she was losing desperately.

"What can't I do?" he asked innocently, his fingers rolling over her nipple, feeling it harden into an impossibly taut little nub.

"Can't make something—can't make something—"

"I can't?" He smiled deviously, trying his tricks on the other side. "I think I can. I think I just did."

"No," she gasped. "You can't make something better than perfect. It's not proper English."

And then he stilled. Completely, which took her by surprise. But his gaze still smoldered, and as his eyes swept over her, she *felt* him. She couldn't explain it; she just knew that she did.

"That's what I thought," he murmured. "Perfection is absolute, is it not? One can't be slightly unique, and one can't be more than perfect. But somehow . . . you are."

"Slightly unique?"

His smile spread slowly across his face. "Better than perfect."

She reached up, touched his cheek, then brushed a lock of his hair back and tucked it behind his ear. The moonlight glinted off the strands, making them seem more golden than usual.

She didn't know what to say, didn't know what to do. All she knew was that she loved this man.

She wasn't sure when it had happened. It hadn't been like her decision to marry him, which had been sudden and clear in an instant. This . . . this love . . . it had crept up on her, rolling along, gaining in momentum until one day it was *there.*

It was there, and it was true, and she knew it would be with her always.

And now, lying on her bed, in the secret stillness of the night, she wanted to give herself to him. She wanted to love him in every way a woman could love a man, and she wanted him to take everything she could give. It didn't matter if they weren't married; they would be soon enough.

Tonight, she couldn't wait.

"Kiss me," she whispered.

He smiled, and it was in his eyes even more than his lips. "I thought you'd never ask." He leaned down, but his lips skimmed hers for barely a second. Instead they veered downward, breathing heat across her until they found her breast. And then he—

"Ohhhh!" she moaned. He couldn't do that. Could he?

He could. And he did.

Pure pleasure shot through her, tickling to every corner of her body. She clutched his head, her hands sinking into his thick, straight hair, and she didn't know if she was pulling or pushing. She didn't think she could stand any more, and yet she didn't want him to stop.

"Gareth," she gasped. "I . . . You . . ."

His hands seemed to be everywhere, touching her, caressing her, pushing her dress down, down . . . until it was pooled around her hips, just an inch from revealing the very core of her womanhood.

Panic began to rise in Hyacinth's chest. She wanted this. She knew she wanted this, and yet she was suddenly terrified.

"I don't know what to do," she said.

"That's all right." He straightened, yanking his shirt off with enough force it was amazing buttons didn't fly. "I do."

"I know, but—"

He touched her lips with his finger. "Shhh. Let me show you." He smiled down at her, his eyes dancing with mischief. "Do I dare?" he wondered aloud. "Should I . . . Well . . . maybe . . ."

He lifted his finger from her mouth.

She spoke instantly. "But I'm afraid I will—"

He put his finger back. "I knew that would happen."

She glared at him. Or rather, she tried to. Gareth had an uncanny ability to make her laugh at herself. And she could feel her lips twitching, even as he pressed them shut.

"Will you be quiet?" he asked, smiling down at her.

She nodded.

He pretended to think about it. "I don't believe you."

She planted her hands on her hips, which had to be a ludicrous position, naked as she was from the waist up.

"All right," he acceded, "but the only words I'll allow from your mouth are 'Oh, Gareth,' and 'Yes, Gareth.'"

He lifted his finger.

"What about 'More, Gareth?'"

He almost kept a straight face. "That will be acceptable."

She felt laughter bubbling up within her. She didn't actually make a noise, but she felt it all the same—that silly, giddy feeling that tingled and danced in one's belly. And she marveled at it. She was so nervous—or rather, she had been.

He'd taken it away.

And she somehow knew that it would be all right. Maybe he'd done this before. Maybe he'd done this a hundred times before, with women a hundred times more beautiful than she.

It didn't matter. He was her first, and she was his last.

He lay down beside her, pulling her onto her side and against him for a kiss. His hands sank into her hair, pulling it free from its coils until it fell in silky waves down her back. She felt free, untamed.

Daring.

She took one hand and pressed it against his chest, exploring his skin, testing the contours of the muscles beneath. She'd never touched him, she realized. Not like this. She trailed her fingers down his side to his hip, tracing a line at the edge of his breeches.

And she could feel his reaction. His muscles leapt wherever she touched, and when she moved to his belly, to that spot between his navel and the last of his clothing, he sucked in his breath.

She smiled, feeling powerful, and so, so womanly.

She curved her fingers so that her nails would scrape his skin, lightly, softly, just enough to tickle and tease. His belly was flat, with a light dusting of hair that formed a line and disappeared below his breeches.

"Do you like this?" she whispered, taking her index finger and making a circle around his navel.

"Mmm-hmm." His voice was smooth, but she could hear his breathing growing ragged.

"What about this?" Her finger found the line of hair and slid slowly down.

He didn't say anything, but his eyes said yes.

"What about—"

"Undo the buttons," he grunted.

Her hand stilled. "Me?" Somehow it hadn't occurred to her that she might aid in their disrobing. It seemed the job of the seducer.

His hand took hers and led it to the buttons.

With trembling fingers, Hyacinth slid each disc free, but she did not pull back the fabric. That was something she was not quite ready to do.

Gareth seemed to understand her reluctance, and he hopped from the bed, for just long enough to pull off the rest of his clothing. Hyacinth averted her eyes . . . at first.

"Dear G—"

"Don't worry," he said, resuming his spot next to her. His hands found the edge of her dress and tugged it the rest of the way down. "Never"—he kissed her belly—"ever"—he kissed her hip—"worry."

Hyacinth wanted to say that she wouldn't, that she trusted him, but just then his fingers slid between her legs, and it was all she could do simply to breathe.

"Shhhh," he crooned, coaxing her apart. "Relax."

"I am," she gasped.

"No," he said, smiling down at her, "you're not."

"I *am*," she insisted.

He leaned down, dropping an indulgent kiss on her nose. "Trust me," he murmured. "Just for this moment, trust me."

And she tried to relax. She really did. But it was near impossible when he was teasing her body into such an inferno. One moment his fingers were on the inside of her thigh, and the next they'd parted her, and he was touching her where she'd never been touched before.

"Oh, m— Oh!" Her hips arched, and she didn't know what to do. She didn't know what to say.

She didn't know what to feel.

"You're perfect," he said, pressing his lips to her ear. "Perfect."

"Gareth," she gasped. "What are you—"

"Making love to you," he said. "I'm making love to you."

Her heart leapt in her chest. It wasn't quite *I love you*, but it was awfully close.

And in that moment, in that last moment of her brain actually functioning, he slid one finger inside her.

"Gareth!" She grabbed his shoulders. Hard.

"Shhhh." He did something utterly wicked. "The servants."

"I don't care," she gasped.

He gazed down at her in a most amused manner, then . . . whatever he'd done . . . did it again. "I think you do."

"No, I don't. I don't. I—"

He did something else, something on the outside, and her entire body felt it. "You're so ready," he said. "I can't believe it."

He moved, positioning himself above her. His fingers were still delivering their torture, but his face was over hers, and she was lost in the clear blue depths of his eyes.

"Gareth," she whispered, and she had no idea what she meant by it. It wasn't a question, or a plea, or really, anything but his name. But it had to be said, because it was him.

It was *him*, here with her.

And it was sacred.

His thighs settled between hers, and she felt him at her opening, large and demanding. His fingers were still between them, holding her open, readying her for his manhood.

"Please," she moaned, and this time it *was* a plea. She wanted this. She needed him.

"Please," she said again.

Slowly, he entered her, and she sucked in her breath, so startled was she by the size and feel of him.

"Relax," he said, only he didn't sound relaxed. She looked up at him. His face was strained, and his breathing was quick and shallow.

He held very still, giving her time to adjust to him, then pushed forward, just a little, but it was enough to make her gasp.

"Relax," he said again.

"I'm *trying*," she ground out.

Gareth almost smiled. There was something so quintessentially Hyacinth about the statement, and also something almost reassuring. Even now, in what had to be one of the most startling and strange experiences of her life, she was . . . the same.

She was herself.

Not many people were, he was coming to realize.

He pushed forward again, and he could feel her easing, stretching to accommodate him. The last thing he wanted was to hurt her, and he had a feeling he wouldn't be able to eliminate the pain completely, but by God, he would make this as perfect for her as he could. And if that meant nearly killing himself to go slowly, he would.

She was as stiff as a board beneath him, her teeth gritted as she anticipated his invasion. Gareth nearly groaned; he'd had her so close, so ready, and now she was trying so hard *not* to be nervous that she was about as relaxed as a wrought-iron fence.

He touched her leg. It was as rigid as a stick.

"Hyacinth," he murmured in her ear, trying not to sound amused, "I think you were enjoying yourself a bit more just a minute earlier."

There was a beat of silence, and she said, "That might be true."

He bit his lip to keep from laughing. "Do you think you might see your way to enjoying yourself again?"

Her lips pursed into that expression of hers—the one she made when she knew she was being teased and wished to return in kind. "I would like to, yes."

He had to admire her. It was a rare woman who could keep her composure in such a situation.

He flicked his tongue behind her ear, distracting her as his hand found its way between her legs. "I might be able to help you with that."

"With what?" she gasped, and he knew from the way her hips jerked that she was on her way back to oblivion.

"Oh, with that feeling," he said, stroking her almost offhandedly as he pushed farther within. "The *Oh, Gareth, Yes, Gareth, More Gareth* feeling."

"Oh," she said, letting out a high-pitched moan as his finger began to move in a delicate circle. "That feeling."

"It's a good feeling," he confirmed.

"It's going to . . . Oh!" She clenched her teeth and groaned against the sensations he was striking within her.

"It's going to what?" he asked, and now he was almost all the way in. He was going to earn a medal for this, he decided. He had to. Surely no man had ever exercised such restraint.

"Get me into trouble," she gasped.

"I certainly hope so," he said, and then he pushed forward, breaching her last barrier until he was fully sheathed. He shuddered as he felt her quiver around him. Every muscle in his body was screaming at him, demanding action, but he held still. He had to hold still. If he didn't give her time to adjust, he would hurt her, and there was no way Gareth was going to allow his bride to look back on her first intimacy with pain.

Good God, it could scar her for life.

But if Hyacinth was hurting, even she didn't know it, because her hips were starting to move beneath him, pressing up, grinding in circles, and when he looked at her face, he saw nothing but passion.

And the last strings of his control snapped.

He began to move, his body falling into its rhythm of need. His desire spiraled, until he was quite certain he could not bear it any longer, and then she would make a tiny little sound, nothing more than a moan, really, and he wanted her even more.

It seemed impossible.

It was magical.

His fingers grasped her shoulders with a force that was surely too intense, but he could not loose his hold. He was seized by an overwhelming urge to claim her, to mark her in some way as his.

"Gareth," she moaned. "Oh, Gareth."

And the sound was too much. It was all too much—the sight, the smell of her, and he felt himself shuddering toward completion.

He gritted his teeth. Not yet. Not when she was so close.

"Gareth!" she gasped.

He slid his hand between their bodies again. He found her, swollen and wet, and he pressed, probably with less finesse than he ought but certainly with as much as he was able.

And he never looked away from her face. Her eyes seemed to darken, the color turning almost marine. Her lips parted, desperately seeking breath, and her body was arching, pressing, pushing.

"Oh!" she cried out, and he quickly kissed her to swallow the sound. She was tense, she was quivering, and then she spasmed around him. Her hands grabbed at his shoulders, his neck, her fingers biting his skin.

But he didn't care. He couldn't feel it. There was nothing but the exquisite pressure of her, grabbing him, sucking him in until he quite literally exploded.

And he had to kiss her again, this time to tamp down his own cries of passion.

It had never been like this. He hadn't known it could.

"Oh, my," Hyacinth breathed, once he'd rolled off her and onto his back.

He nodded, still too spent to speak. But he took her hand in his. He wanted to touch her still. He needed the contact.

"I didn't know," she said.

"Neither did I," he somehow managed.

"Is it always—"

He squeezed her hand, and when he heard her turn to him, he shook his head.

"Oh." There was a moment of silence, then she said, "Well, it's a good thing we're getting married, then."

Gareth started to shake with laughter.

"What is it?" she demanded.

He couldn't speak. All he could do was lie there, his body shaking the entire bed.

"What's so funny?"

He caught his breath, turned and rolled until he was back on top of her, nose to nose. "You," he said.

She started to frown, but then melted into a smile.

A wicked smile.

Good Lord, but he was going to *enjoy* being married to this woman.

"I think we might need to move up the wedding date," she said.

"I'm willing to drag you off to Scotland tomorrow." And he was serious.

"I can't," she said, but he could tell she half wished she could.

"It would be an adventure," he said, sliding one hand along her hip to sweeten the deal.

"I'll talk to my mother," she promised. "If I'm sufficiently annoying, I'm sure I can get the engagement period cut in half."

"It makes me wonder," he said. "As your future husband, should I be concerned by your use of the phrase *if I'm sufficiently annoying*?"

"Not if you accede to all of my wishes."

"A sentence that concerns me even more," he murmured.

She did nothing but smile.

And then, just when he was starting to feel quite comfortable in every way, she let out an "Oh!" and wriggled out from beneath him.

"What is it?" he asked, the question muffled by his inelegant landing in the pillows.

"The jewels," she said, clutching the sheet to her chest as she sat up. "I completely forgot about them. Good heavens, what time is it? We have to get going."

"You can *move*?"

She blinked. "You can't?"

"If I didn't have to vacate this bed before morning, I'd be quite content to snore until noon."

"But the jewels! Our plans!"

He closed his eyes. "We can go tomorrow."

"No," she said, batting him on the shoulder with the heel of her hand, "we can't."

"Why not?'

"Because I already have plans for tomorrow, and my mother will grow suspicious if I keep pleading headaches. And besides, we planned on this evening."

He opened one eye. "It's not as if anyone's expecting us."

"Well, I'm going," she stated, pulling the bedsheet around her body as she climbed from the bed.

Gareth's brows rose as he pondered his naked form. He looked at Hyacinth with a masculine smile, which spread even farther when she blushed and turned away.

"I . . . ah . . . just need to wash myself," she mumbled, scooting away to her dressing room.

With a great show of reluctance (even though Hyacinth had her back to him) Gareth began to pull on his clothing. He couldn't believe she would even ponder heading out that evening. Weren't virgins supposed to be stiff and sore after their first time?

She stuck her head out of the dressing room door. "I purchased better shoes," she said in a stage whisper, "in case we have to run."

He shook his head. She was no ordinary virgin.

"Are you certain you wish to do this tonight?" he asked, once she reemerged in her black men's clothing.

"Absolutely," she said, pulling her hair into a queue at her neck. She looked up, her eyes shining with excitement. "Don't you?"

"I'm exhausted."

"Really?" She looked at him with open curiosity. "I feel quite the opposite. Energized, really."

"You *will* be the death of me, you do realize that."

She grinned. "Better me than someone else."

He sighed and headed for the window.

"Would you like me to wait for you at the bottom," she asked politely, "or would you prefer to go down the back stairs with me?"

Gareth paused, one foot on the windowsill. "Ah, the back stairs will be quite acceptable," he said.

And he followed her out.

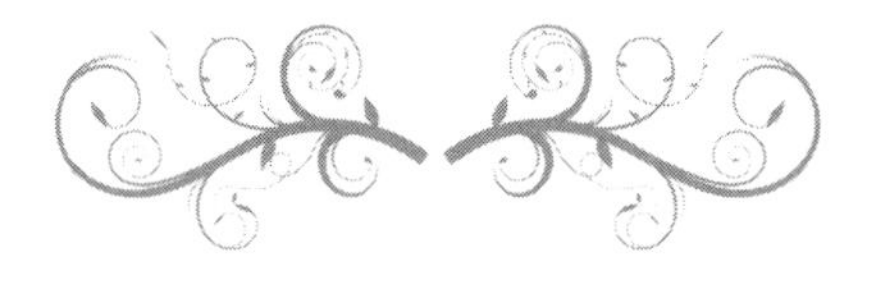

Chapter 15

Inside the Clair House library. There is little reason to chronicle the journey across Mayfair, other than to make note of Hyacinth's wellspring of energy and enthusiasm, and Gareth's lack thereof.

"Do you see anything?" Hyacinth whispered.

"Only books."

She gave him a frustrated glare but decided not to chastise him for his lack of enthusiasm. Such an argument would only distract them from the task at hand. "Do you see," she said, with as much patience as she could muster, "any sections which seem to be composed of scientific titles?" She glanced at the shelf in front of her, which contained three novels, two works of philosophy, a three-volume history of ancient Greece, and *The Care and Feeding of Swine.* "Or are they in any order at all?" she sighed.

"Somewhat," came the reply from above. Gareth was standing on a stool, investigating the upper shelves. "Not really."

Hyacinth twisted her neck, glancing up until she had a fairly good view of the underside of his chin. "What do you see?"

"Quite a bit on the topic of early Britain. But look what I found, tucked away on the end." He plucked a small book from the shelf and tossed it down.

Hyacinth caught it easily, then turned it in her hands until the title was right side up. "No!" she said.

"Hard to believe, isn't it?"

She looked back down again. Right there, in gold lettering: *Miss Davenport and the Dark Marquis.* "I don't believe it," she said.

"Perhaps you should take it home to my grandmother. No one will miss it here."

Hyacinth opened to the title page. "It was written by the same author as *Miss Butterworth.*"

"It would have to be," Gareth commented, bending his knees to better inspect the next shelf down.

"We didn't know about this one," Hyacinth said. "We've read *Miss Sainsbury and the Mysterious Colonel*, of course."

"A military tale?"

"Set in Portugal." Hyacinth resumed her inspection of the shelf in front of her. "It didn't seem terribly authentic, however. Not, of course, that I've ever been to Portugal."

He nodded, then stepped off his stool and moved it in front of the next set of shelves. Hyacinth watched as he climbed back up and began his work anew, on the highest shelf.

"Remind me," he said. "What, precisely, are we looking for?"

Hyacinth pulled the oft-folded note from her pocket. "*Discorso Intorno alle Cose che stanno in sù l'acqua.*"

He stared at her for a moment. "Which means . . . ?"

"Discussion of inside things that are in water?" She hadn't meant to say it as a question.

He looked dubious. "Inside things?"

"That are in water. Or that move," she added. "*Ò che in quella si muovono.* That's the last part of it."

"And someone would wish to read that because . . . ?"

"I have no idea," she said, shaking her head. "You're the Cantabridgian."

He cleared his throat. "Yes, well, I wasn't much for the sciences."

Hyacinth decided not to comment and turned back to the shelf in front of her, which contained a seven-volume set on the topic of English botany, two works of Shakespeare, and a rather fat book titled, simply, *Wildflowers*. "I think," she said, chewing on her lower lip for a moment as she glanced back at several of the shelves she'd already cataloged, "that perhaps these books had been in order at some point. There does seem to be *some* organization to it. If you look right here"—she motioned to one of the first shelves she'd inspected—"it's almost completely works of poetry. But then right in the middle one finds something by Plato, and over on the end, *An Illustrated History of Denmark*."

"Right," Gareth said, sounding a bit like he was grimacing. "Right."

"Right?" she echoed, looking up.

"Right." Now he sounded embarrassed. "That might have been my fault."

She blinked. "I beg your pardon?"

"It was one of my less mature moments," he admitted. "I was angry."

"You were . . . angry?"

"I rearranged the shelves."

"You *what*?" She'd have liked to yell, and frankly, she was rather proud of herself for not doing so.

He shrugged sheepishly. "It seemed impressively underhanded at the time."

Hyacinth found herself staring blankly at the shelf in front of her. "Who could have guessed it would come back to haunt you?"

"Who indeed." He moved to another shelf, tilting his head as he read the titles on the spines. "The worst of it was, it turned out to be a tad *too* underhanded. Didn't bother my father one bit."

"It would have driven me insane."

"Yes, but you read. My father never even noticed there was anything amiss."

"But someone must have been here since your little effort at reorganization." Hyacinth looked down at the book by her side. "I don't think *Miss Davenport* is more than a few years old."

Gareth shook his head. "Perhaps someone left it here. It could have been my brother's wife. I imagine one of the servants just tucked it on whichever shelf possessed the most room."

Hyacinth let out a long exhale, trying to figure out how best to proceed. "Can you remember anything about the organization of the titles?" she asked. "Anything at all? Were they grouped by author? By subject?"

Gareth shook his head. "I was in a bit of a rush. I just grabbed books at random and swapped their places." He stopped, exhaling as he planted his hands on his hips and surveyed the room. "I do recall that there was quite a bit on the topic of hounds. And over there there was . . ."

His words trailed off. Hyacinth looked up sharply and saw that he was staring at a shelf by the door. "What is it?" she asked urgently, coming to her feet.

"A section in Italian," he said, turning and striding to the opposite side of the room.

Hyacinth was right on his heels. "They must be your grandmother's books."

"And the last ones any of the St. Clairs might think to open," Gareth murmured.

"Do you see them?"

Gareth shook his head as he ran his finger along the spines of the books, searching for the ones in Italian.

"I don't suppose you thought to leave the set intact," Hyacinth murmured, crouching below him to inspect the lower shelves.

"I don't recall," he admitted. "But surely most will still be where they belong. I grew too bored of the prank to do a really good job of it. I left most in place. And in fact He suddenly straightened. "Here they are."

Hyacinth immediately stood up. "Are there many?"

"Only two shelves," he said. "I would imagine it was rather expensive to import books from Italy."

The books were right on a level with Hyacinth's face, so she had Gareth hold their candle while she scanned the titles for something that sounded like what Isabella had written in her note. Several did not have the entire title printed on the spine, and these she had to pull out to read the words on the front. Every time she did so, she could hear Gareth's sharply indrawn breath, followed by a disappointed exhale when she replaced the book on the shelf.

She reached the end of the lower shelf and then stood on her tiptoes to investigate the upper. Gareth was right behind her, standing so close that she could feel the heat of his body rippling through the air.

"Do you see anything?" he asked, his words low and warm by her ear. She didn't think he was purposefully trying to unsettle her with his nearness, but it was the end result all the same.

"Not yet," she said, shaking her head. Most of Isabella's books were poetry. A few seemed to be English poets, translated into Italian. As Hyacinth reached the midpoint of the shelf, however, the books turned to nonfiction. History, philosophy, history, history . . .

Hyacinth's breath caught.

"What is it?" Gareth demanded.

With trembling hands she pulled out a slim volume and turned it over until the front cover was visible to them both.

Galileo Galilei
Discorso intorno alle cose che stanno, in sù
l'acqua, ò che in quella si muovono

"Exactly what she wrote in the clue," Hyacinth whispered, hastily adding, "Except for the bit about Mr. Galilei. It would have been a great deal easier to find the book if we'd known the author."

Gareth waved aside her excuses and motioned to the text in her hands.

Slowly, carefully, Hyacinth opened the book to look for the telltale slip of paper. There was nothing tucked right inside, so she turned a page, then another, then another . . .

Until Gareth yanked the book from her hands. "Do you want to be here until next week?" he whispered impatiently. With no delicacy whatsoever, he grasped both the front and back covers of the book and held it open, spine-side up so that the pages formed an upside-down fan.

"Gareth, you—"

"Shush." He shook the book, bent down and peered up and inside, then shook it again, harder. And sure enough, a slip of paper came free and fell to the carpet.

"Give that to me," Hyacinth demanded, after Gareth had grabbed it. "You won't be able to read it in any case."

Obviously swayed by her logic, he handed the clue over, but he remained close, leaning over her shoulder with the candle as she opened the single fold in the paper.

"What does it say?" he asked.

She shook her head. "I don't know."

"What do you mean, you don't—"

"I don't know," she snapped, *hating* that she had to admit defeat. "I don't recognize anything. I'm not even certain this is Italian. Do you know if she spoke another language?"

"I have no idea."

Hyacinth clamped her teeth together, thoroughly discouraged by the turn of events. She hadn't necessarily thought they would find the jewels that evening, but it had never occurred to her that the next clue might lead them straight into a brick wall.

"May I see?" Gareth asked.

She handed him the note, watching as he shook his head. "I don't know what that is, but it's not Italian."

"Nor anything related to it," Hyacinth said.

Gareth swore under his breath, something that Hyacinth was fairly certain she was not meant to hear.

"With your permission," she said, using that even tone of voice she'd long since learned was required when dealing with a truculent male, "I could show it to my brother Colin. He has traveled quite extensively, and he might recognize the language, even if he lacks the ability to translate it."

Gareth appeared to hesitate, so she added, "We can trust him. I promise you."

He gave her a nod. "We'd best leave. There's nothing more we can do this night, anyway."

There was little cleaning up to be done; they had put the books back on the shelves almost as soon as they'd removed them. Hyacinth moved a stool back in place against the wall, and Gareth did the same with a chair. The drapes had remained in place this time; there was little moonlight to see by, anyway.

"Are you ready?" he asked.

She grabbed *Miss Davenport and the Dark Marquis.* "Are you certain no one will miss this?"

He tucked Isabella's clue between the pages for safekeeping. "Quite."

Hyacinth watched as he pressed his ear to the door. No one had been about when they had sneaked in a half hour earlier, but Gareth had explained that the butler never retired before the baron. And with the baron still out at the Mottram Ball, that left one man up and possibly about, and another who could return at any time.

Gareth placed one finger on his lips and motioned for her to follow him as he carefully turned the doorknob. He opened the door an inch—just enough to peer out the crack and make sure that it was safe to proceed. Together they crept into the hall, moving swiftly to the stairs that led down to the ground floor. It was dark, but Hyacinth's eyes had adjusted well enough to see where she was going, and in under a minute they were back in the drawing room—the one with the faulty window latch.

As he had the time before, Gareth climbed out first, then formed a step with his hands for Hyacinth to balance upon as she reached up and shut the window. He lowered her down, dropped a quick kiss on her nose, and said, "You need to get home."

She couldn't help but smile. "I'm already hopelessly compromised."

"Yes, but I'm the only one who knows."

Hyacinth thought it rather charming of him to be so concerned for her reputation. After all, it didn't truly matter if anyone caught them or not; she had lain with him, and she must marry him. A woman of her birth could do no less. Good heavens, there could be a baby, and even if not, she was no longer a virgin.

But she had known what she was doing when she had given herself to him. She knew the ramifications.

Together they crept down the alley to Dover Street. It was imperative, Hyacinth realized, that they move quickly. The Mottram Ball was notorious for running into the wee hours of the morning, but they'd got a late start on their search, and surely everyone would be heading home soon. There would be carriages on the streets of Mayfair, which meant that she and Gareth needed to render themselves as invisible as possible.

Hyacinth's joking aside, she didn't wish to be caught out in the middle of the night. It was true that their marriage was now an inevitability, but all the same, she didn't particularly relish the thought of being the subject of scurrilous gossip.

"Wait here," Gareth said, barring her from moving forward with his arm. Hyacinth remained in the shadows as he stepped onto Dover Street, edging as close to the corner as she dared while he made sure there was no one about. After a few seconds she saw Gareth's hand, reaching back and making a scooping, "come along" gesture.

She stepped out onto Dover Street, but she was there barely a second before she heard Gareth's sharply indrawn breath and felt herself being shoved back into the shadows.

Flattening herself against the back wall of the corner building, she clutched *Miss Davenport*—and within it, Isabella's clue—to her chest as she waited for Gareth to appear by her side.

And then she heard it.

Just one word. In his father's voice.

"*You.*"

Gareth had barely a second to react. He didn't know how it had happened, didn't know where the baron had suddenly appeared from, but somehow he managed to push Hyacinth back into the alley in the very second before he was caught.

"Greetings," he said, in his jauntiest voice, stepping forward so as to put as much distance between him and the alley as possible.

His father was already striding over, his face visibly angry, even in the dim light of the night. "What are you doing here?" he demanded.

Gareth shrugged, the same expression that had infuriated his father so many times before. Except this time he wasn't trying to provoke, he was just trying to keep the baron's attention firmly fixed. "Just making my way home," he said, with deliberate nonchalance.

His father's eyes were suspicious. "You're a bit far afield."

"I like to stop by and inspect my inheritance every now and then," Gareth said, his smile terribly bland. "Just to make sure you haven't burned the place down."

"Don't think I haven't thought about it."

"Oh, I'm sure you have."

The baron held silent for a moment, then said, "You weren't at the ball tonight."

Gareth wasn't sure how best to respond, so he just lifted his brows ever so slightly and kept his expression even.

"Miss Bridgerton wasn't there, either."

"Wasn't she?" Gareth asked mildly, hoping the lady in question possessed sufficient self-restraint not to leap out from the alley, yelling, "Yes, I was!"

"Just at the beginning," the baron admitted. "She left rather early."

Gareth shrugged again. "It's a woman's prerogative."

"To change her mind?" The baron's lips formed the tiniest of curves, and his eyes were mocking. "You had better hope she's a bit more steadfast than that."

Gareth gave him a cold stare. Somehow, amazingly, he still felt in control. Or at the very least, like the adult he liked to think that he was. He felt no childish desire to lash out, or to say something for the sole purpose of infuriating him. He'd spent half his life trying to impress the man, and the other half trying to aggravate him. But now . . . finally . . . all he wanted was to be rid of him.

He didn't quite feel the nothing he had wished for, but it was damned close.

Maybe, just maybe, it was because he'd finally found someone else to fill the void.

"You certainly didn't waste any time with her," the baron said, his voice snide.

"A gentleman must marry," Gareth said. It wasn't exactly the statement he wished to say in front of Hyacinth, but it was far more important to keep up the ruse with his father than it was to feed whatever need she might feel for romantic speech.

"Yes," the baron murmured. "A *gentleman* must."

Gareth's skin began to prickle. He knew what his father was hinting at, and even though he'd already compromised Hyacinth, he'd rather she didn't learn the truth of his birth until after the wedding. It would simply be easier that way, and maybe . . .

Well, maybe she'd never learn the truth at all. It seemed unlikely, between his father's venom and Isabella's diary, but stranger things had happened.

He needed to leave. Now. "I have to go," he said brusquely.

The baron's mouth curved into an unpleasant smile. "Yes, yes," he said mockingly. "You'll need to tidy yourself up before you go off to lick Miss Bridgerton's feet tomorrow."

Gareth spoke between his teeth. "Get out of my way."

But the baron wasn't done. "What I wonder is . . . how did you get her to say yes?"

A red haze began to wash over Gareth's eyes. "I said—"

"Did you seduce her?" his father laughingly asked. "Make sure she couldn't say no, even if—"

Gareth hadn't meant to do it. He'd meant to maintain his calm, and he would have managed it if the baron had kept his insults to him. But when he mentioned Hyacinth . . .

His fury took over, and the next thing he knew, he had his father pinned against the wall. "Do not," he warned, barely recognizing his own voice, "speak to me of her again."

"You would make the mistake of attempting to kill me here, on a public street?" The baron was gasping, but even so, his voice maintained an impressive degree of hatred.

"It's tempting."

"Ah, but you'd lose the title. And then where would you be? Oh yes," he said, practically choking on his words now, "at the end of a hangman's rope."

Gareth loosened his grip. Not because of his father's words, but because he was finally regaining his hold on his emotions. Hyacinth was listening, he reminded himself. She was right around the corner. He could not do something he might later regret.

"I knew you'd do it," his father said, just when Gareth had let go and turned to leave.

Damn. He always knew what to say, exactly which button to push to keep Gareth from doing the right thing.

"Do what?" Gareth asked, frozen in his tracks.

"Ask her to marry you."

Gareth turned slowly around. His father was grinning, supremely pleased with himself. It was a sight that made Gareth's blood run cold.

"You're so predictable," the baron said, cocking his head just an inch or so to the side. It was a gesture Gareth had seen a hundred times before, maybe a thousand. It was patronizing and it was contemptuous, and it always managed to make Gareth feel like he was a boy again, working so hard for his father's approval.

And failing every time.

"One word from me," the baron said, chuckling to himself. "Just one word from me."

Gareth chose his words very carefully. He had an audience. He had to remember that. And so, when he spoke, all he said was, "I have no idea what you're talking about."

And his father erupted with laughter. He threw back his head and roared, showing a degree of mirth that shocked Gareth into silence.

"Oh, come now," he said, wiping his eyes. "I told you you couldn't win her, and look what you did."

Gareth's chest began to feel very, very tight. What was his father saying? That he'd *wanted* him to marry Hyacinth?

"You went right out and asked her to marry you," the baron continued. "How long did that take? A day? Two? No more than a week, I'm sure."

"My proposal to Miss Bridgerton had nothing to do with you," Gareth said icily.

"Oh, please," the baron said, with utter disdain. "Everything you do is because of me. Haven't you figured that out by now?"

Gareth stared at him in horror. Was it true? Was it even a little bit true?

"Well, I do believe I shall take myself off to bed," the baron said, with an affected sigh. "It's been . . . entertaining, don't you think?"

Gareth didn't know what to think.

"Oh, and before you marry Miss Bridgerton," the baron said, tossing the remark over his shoulder as he placed his foot on the first step up to Clair House's front door, "you might want to see about clearing up your other betrothal."

"*What?*"

The baron smiled silkily. "Didn't you know? You're still betrothed to poor little Mary Winthrop. She never did marry anyone else."

"That can't be legal."

"Oh, I assure you it is." The baron leaned slightly forward. "I made sure of it."

Gareth just stood there, his mouth slack, his arms hanging limply at his sides. If his father had yanked down the moon and clocked him on the head with it he couldn't have been more stunned.

"I'll see you at the wedding," the baron called out. "Oh, silly me. Which wedding?" He laughed, taking a few more steps up toward the front door. "Do let me know, once you sort it all out." He gave a little wave, obviously pleased with himself, and slipped inside the house.

"Dear God," Gareth said to himself. And then again, because never in his life had the moment more called for blasphemy: "Dear God."

What sort of mess was he in now? A man couldn't offer marriage to more than one woman at once. And while *he* might not have offered it to Mary Winthrop, the baron had done so in his name, and had signed documents to that effect. Gareth had no idea what this meant to his plans with Hyacinth, but it couldn't be good.

Oh, bloody . . . Hyacinth.

Dear God, indeed. She'd heard every word.

Gareth started to run for the corner, then stopped himself,

glancing up at the house to make sure that his father wasn't watching for him. The windows were still dark, but that didn't mean . . .

Oh, hell. Who cared?

He ran around the corner, skidding to a halt in front of the alley, where he'd left her.

She was gone.

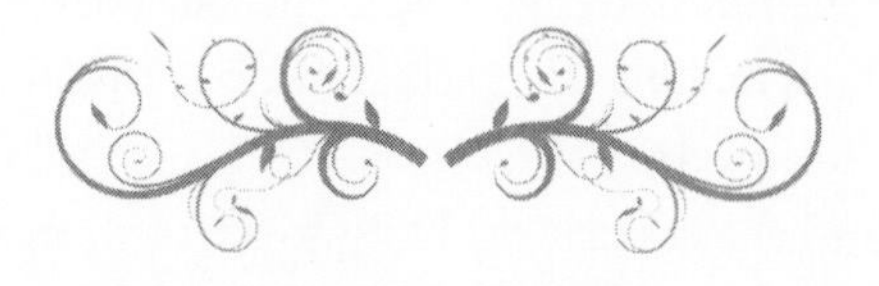

Chapter 16

Still in the alley. Gareth is staring at the spot where Hyacinth should have been standing.

He never wants to feel like this again.

Gareth's heart stopped.

Where the hell was Hyacinth?

Was she in danger? It was late, and even though they were in one of the most expensive and exclusive areas of London, thieves and cutthroats might still be about, and—

No, she couldn't have fallen prey to foul play. Not here. He would have heard something. A scuffle. A shout. Hyacinth would never be taken without a fight.

A very loud fight.

Which could only mean . . .

She must have heard his father talking about Mary Winthrop and run off. Damn the woman. She should have had more sense than that.

Gareth let out an aggravated grunt as he planted his hands on his hips and scanned the area. She could have dashed home any one of eight different ways, probably more if one counted all the alleys and mews, which he hoped she was sensible enough to avoid.

He decided to try the most direct route. It would take her right on Berkeley Street, which was a busy enough thoroughfare that there might be carriages rolling home from the Mottram Ball, but Hyacinth was probably just angry enough that her primary aim would have been to get home as quickly as possible.

Which was just fine with Gareth. He would much rather see her caught by a gossip on the main road than by a thief on a side street.

Gareth took off at a run toward Berkeley Square, slowing down at each intersection to glance up and down the cross streets.

Nothing.

Where the hell had she gone? He knew she was uncommonly athletic for a female, but good God, how fast could she run?

He dashed past Charles Street, onto the square proper. A carriage rolled by, but Gareth paid it no mind. Tomorrow's gossip would probably be filled with tales of his crazed middle-of-the-night run through the streets of Mayfair, but it was nothing his reputation couldn't withstand.

He ran along the edge of the square, and then finally he was on Bruton Street passing by Number Sixteen, Twelve, Seven . . .

There she was, running like the wind, heading around the corner so that she could enter the house from the back.

His body propelled by a strange, furious energy, Gareth took off even faster. His arms were pumping, and his legs were burning, and his shirt would surely be forever soiled with sweat, but he didn't care. He was going to catch that bloody woman before she entered her house, and when he did . . .

Hell, he didn't know what he was going to do with her, but it wasn't going to be pretty.

Hyacinth skidded around the last corner, slowing down just enough to glance over her shoulder. Her mouth opened as she spied him, and then, her entire body tensed with determination, she took off for the servants' entrance in the back.

Gareth's eyes narrowed with satisfaction. She was going to have to fumble for the key. She'd never make it now. He slowed a bit, just enough to attempt to catch his breath, then eased his gait into a stalk.

She was in for it now.

But instead of reaching behind a brick for a key, Hyacinth just opened the door.

Bloody hell. They hadn't locked the door behind them when they left.

Gareth vaulted into another sprint, and he almost made it.

Almost.

He reached the door just as she shut it in his face.

And his hand landed on the knob just in time to hear the lock click into place.

Gareth's hand formed a fist, and he itched to pound it against the door. More than anything he wanted to bellow her name, propriety be damned. All it would do was force their wedding to be held even sooner, which was his aim, anyway.

But he supposed some things were far too ingrained in a man, and he was, apparently, too much of a gentleman to destroy her reputation in such a public manner.

"Oh, no," he muttered to himself, striding back to the front of the house, "all destruction shall be strictly in private."

He planted his hands on his hips and glared up at her bedroom window. He'd got himself in once; he could do it again.

A quick glance up and down the street assured him that no one was coming, and he quickly scaled the wall, his ascent much easier this time, now that he knew exactly where to place his hands and feet. The window was still slightly open, just as he'd left it the last time—not that he'd thought he was going to have to climb in again.

He jammed it up, tumbled through, and landed with a thud on the carpet just as Hyacinth entered through the door.

"You," he growled, coming to his feet like a cat, "have some explaining to do."

"Me?" Hyacinth returned. "Me? I hardly think—" Her lips parted as she belatedly assessed the situation. "And get out of my room!"

He quirked a brow. "Shall I take the front stairs?"

"You'll go back out the window, you miserable cur."

Gareth realized that he'd never seen Hyacinth angry. Irritated, yes; annoyed, certainly. But this . . .

This was something else entirely.

"How dare you!" she fumed. "How *dare* you." And then, before he could even begin to reply, she stormed to his side and smacked him with the heels of both of her hands. "Get out!" she snarled. "Now!"

"Not until you"—he punctuated this with a pointed finger, right against her breastbone—"promise me that you will never do anything as foolish as what you did tonight."

"Unh! Unh!" She let out a choking sort of noise, the kind one makes when one cannot manage even a single intelligible syllable. And then finally, after a few more gasps of fury, she said, her voice dangerously low, "You are in no position to demand anything of me."

"No?" He lifted one of his brows and looked down at her with an arrogant half smile. "As your future husband—"

"Do not even mention that to me right now."

Gareth felt something squeeze and turn over in his chest. "Do you plan to cry off?"

"No," she said, looking at him with a furious expression, "but you took care of that this evening, didn't you? Was that your purpose? To force my hand by rendering me unmarriageable for any other man?"

It had been exactly his purpose, and for that reason Gareth didn't say anything. Not a word.

"You'll rue this," Hyacinth hissed. "You will rue the day. Trust me."

"Oh, really?"

"As your future wife," she said, her eyes flashing dangerously, "I can make your life hell on earth."

Of that, Gareth had no doubt, but he decided to deal with that problem when he came to it. "This is not about what happened between us earlier," he said, "and it is not about anything you may or may not have heard the baron say. What this is about—"

"Oh, for the love of—" Hyacinth cut herself off in the nick of time. "Who do you think you are?"

He jammed his face next to hers. "The man who is going to marry you. And you, Hyacinth Bridgerton soon-to-be St. Clair, will never *ever* wander the streets of London without a chaperone, at any time of day."

For a moment she said nothing, and he almost let himself think that she was touched by his concern for her safety. But then, she just stepped back and said, "It's a rather convenient time to develop a sense of propriety."

He resisted the urge to grab her by the shoulders and shake—barely. "Do you have any idea how I felt when I came back around the corner, and you were gone? Did you even stop to think about what might have happened to you before you ran off on your own?"

One of her brows lifted into a perfectly arrogant arch. "Nothing more than what happened to me right here."

As strikes went, it was perfectly aimed, and Gareth nearly flinched. But he held on to his temper, and his voice was cool as he said, "You don't mean that. You might think you mean it, but you don't, and I'll forgive you for it."

She stood still, utterly and completely still save for the rise and fall of her chest. Her hands were fists at her sides, and her face was growing redder and redder.

"Don't you ever," she finally said, her voice low and clipped and terribly controlled, "speak to me in that tone of voice again. And don't you ever presume to know my mind."

"Don't worry, it's a claim I'm seldom likely to make."

Hyacinth swallowed—her only show of nerves before saying, "I want you to leave."

"Not until I have your promise."

"I don't owe you anything, Mr. St. Clair. And you certainly are not in a position to make demands."

"Your promise," he repeated.

Hyacinth just stared at him. How dare he come in here and try to make this about her? *She* was the injured party. He was the one who—He—

Good God, she couldn't even *think* in full sentences.

"I want you to leave," she said again.

His reply came practically on top of her last syllable. "And I want your promise."

She clamped her mouth shut. It would have been an easy promise to make; she certainly didn't plan on any more middle-of-the-night jaunts. But a promise would have been akin to an apology, and she would not give him that satisfaction.

Call her foolish, call her juvenile, but she would not do it. Not after what he'd done to her.

"Good God," he muttered, "you're stubborn."

She gave him a sickly smile. "It is going to be a joy to be married to me."

"Hyacinth," he said, or rather, half sighed. "In the name of all that is—" He raked his hand through his hair, and he seemed to look all around the room before finally turning back to her. "I understand that you're angry . . ."

"Do not speak to me as if I were a child."

"I wasn't."

She looked at him coolly. "You were."

He gritted his teeth together and continued. "What my father said about Mary Winthrop . . ."

Her mouth fell open. "Is *that* what you think this is about?"

He stared at her, blinking twice before saying, "Isn't it?"

"Of course not," she sputtered. "Good heavens, do you take me for a fool?"

"I . . . er . . . no?"

"I hope I know you well enough to know that you would not offer marriage to two women. At least not purposefully."

"Right," he said, looking a little confused. "Then what—"

"Do you know why you asked me to marry you?" she demanded.

"What the devil are you talking about?"

"Do you know?" she repeated. She'd asked him once before, and he had not answered.

"Of course I know. It's because—" But he cut himself off, and he obviously didn't know what to say.

She shook her head, blinking back tears. "I don't want to see you right now."

"What is *wrong* with you?"

"There is nothing wrong with me," she cried out, as loudly as she dared. "I at least know why I accepted your proposal. But you—You have no idea why you rendered it."

"Then tell me," he burst out. "Tell me what it is you think is so damned important. You always seem to know what is best for everything and everyone, and now you clearly know everyone's mind as well. So tell me. Tell me, Hyacinth—"

She flinched from the venom in his voice.

"—tell me."

She swallowed. She would not back down. She might be shaking, she might be as close to tears as she had ever been in her life, but she would not back down. "You did this," she said, her voice low, to keep the tremors at bay, "you asked me . . . because of *him*."

He just stared at her, making a *please elaborate* motion with his head.

"Your father." She would have yelled it, if it hadn't been the middle of the night.

"Oh, for God's sake," he swore. "Is that what you think? This has nothing to do with him."

Hyacinth gave him a pitying look.

"I don't do anything because of him," Gareth hissed, furious that she would even suggest it. "He means nothing to me."

She shook her head. "You are deluding yourself, Gareth. Everything you do, you do because of him. I didn't realize it until he said it, but it's true."

"You'd take his word over mine?"

"This isn't about someone's *word*," she said, sounding tired, and frustrated, and maybe just a little bit bleak. "It's just about the way things are. And you . . . you asked me to marry you because you wanted to show him you could. It had *nothing* to do with me."

Gareth held himself very still. "That is not true."

"Isn't it?" She smiled, but her face looked sad, almost resigned. "I know that you wouldn't ask me to marry you if you believed yourself promised to another woman, but I also know that you would do anything to show up your father. Including marrying me."

Gareth gave his head a slow shake. "You have it all wrong," he said, but inside, his certitude was beginning to slip. He had thought, more than once and with an unbecoming gleefulness, that his father must be livid over Gareth's marital success. And he'd enjoyed it. He'd enjoyed knowing that in the chess game that was his relationship with Lord St. Clair, he had finally delivered the killing move.

Checkmate.

It had been exquisite.

But it wasn't *why* he had asked Hyacinth to marry him. He'd asked her because—Well, there had been a hundred different reasons. It had been complicated.

He liked her. Wasn't that important? He even liked her family. And she liked his grandmother. He couldn't possibly marry a woman who couldn't deal well with Lady Danbury.

And he'd wanted her. He'd wanted her with an intensity that had taken his breath away.

It had made sense to marry Hyacinth. It still made sense.

That was it. That was what he needed to articulate. He just needed to make her understand. And she would. She was no foolish girl. She was Hyacinth.

It was why he liked her so well.

He opened his mouth, motioning with his hand before any words actually emerged. He had to get this right. Or if not right, then at least not completely wrong. "If you look at this sensibly," he began.

"I am looking at it sensibly," she shot back, cutting him off before he could complete the thought. "Good heavens, if I weren't so bloody *sensible*, I would have cried off." Her jaw went rigid, and she swallowed.

And he thought to himself—*My God, she's going to cry.*

"I knew what I was doing earlier this evening," she said, her voice painfully quiet. "I knew what it meant, and I knew that it was irrevocable." Her lower lip quivered, and she looked away as she said, "I just never expected to regret it."

It was like a punch to the gut. He'd hurt her. He'd really hurt her. He hadn't meant to, and he wasn't certain that she wasn't overreacting, but he'd hurt her.

And he was stunned to realize how much that hurt *him.*

For a moment they did nothing, just stood there, warily watching the other.

Gareth wanted to say something, thought perhaps that he should say something, but he had no idea. The words just weren't there.

"Do you know how it feels to be someone's pawn?" Hyacinth asked.

"Yes," he whispered.

The corners of her mouth tightened. She didn't look angry, just . . . sad. "Then you will understand why I'm asking you to leave."

There was something primal within him that cried out to stay, something primitive that wanted to grab her and make her understand. He could use his words or he could use his body. It didn't really matter. He just wanted to make her understand.

But there was something else within him—something sad and

something lonely that knew what it was to hurt. And somehow he knew that if he stayed, if he tried to force her to understand, he would not succeed. Not this night.

And he'd lose her.

So he nodded. "We will discuss this later," he said.

She said nothing.

He walked back to the window. It seemed a bit ludicrous and anticlimactic, making his exit that way, but really, who the hell cared?

"This Mary person," Hyacinth said to his back, "whatever the problem is with her, I am certain it can be resolved. My family will pay hers, if necessary."

She was trying to gain control of herself, to tamp down her pain by focusing on practicalities. Gareth recognized this tactic; he had employed it himself, countless times.

He turned around, meeting her gaze directly. "She is the daughter of the Earl of Wrotham."

"Oh." She paused. "Well, that does change things, but I'm sure if it was a long time ago . . ."

"It was."

She swallowed before asking, "Is it the cause of your estrangement? The betrothal?"

"You're asking a rather lot of questions for someone who has demanded that I leave."

"I'm going to marry you," she said. "I will learn eventually."

"Yes, you will," he said. "But not tonight."

And with that, he swung himself through the window.

He looked up when he reached the ground, desperate for one last glimpse of her. Anything would have been nice, a silhouette, perhaps, or even just her shadowy form, moving behind the curtains.

But there was nothing.

She was gone.

Chapter 17

Teatime at Number Five. Hyacinth is alone in the drawing room with her mother, always a dangerous proposition when one is in possession of a secret.

"Is Mr. St. Clair out of town?"

Hyacinth looked up from her rather sloppy embroidery for just long enough to say, "I don't believe so, why?"

Her mother's lips tightened fleetingly before she said, "He hasn't called in several days."

Hyacinth affixed a bland expression onto her face as she said, "I believe he is busy with something or other relating to his property in Wiltshire."

It was a lie, of course. Hyacinth didn't think he possessed any property, in Wiltshire or anywhere else. But with any luck, her mother would be distracted by some other matter before she got around to inquiring about Gareth's nonexistent estates.

"I see," Violet murmured.

Hyacinth stabbed her needle into the fabric with perhaps a touch more vigor than was necessary, then looked down at her handiwork with a bit of a snarl. She was an abysmal needlewoman. She'd never had the patience or the eye for detail that it required, but she always kept an embroidery hoop going in the drawing room. One never knew when one would need it to provide an acceptable distraction from conversation.

The ruse had worked quite well for years. But now that Hyacinth was the only Bridgerton daughter living at home, teatime often consisted of just her and her mother. And unfortunately, the needlework that had kept her so neatly out of three- and four-way conversations didn't seem to do the trick so well with only two.

"Is anything amiss?" Violet asked.

"Of course not." Hyacinth didn't want to look up, but avoiding eye contact would surely make her mother suspicious, so she set her needle down and lifted her chin. In for a penny, in for a pound, she decided. If she was going to lie, she might as well make it convincing. "He's merely busy, that is all. I rather admire him for it. You wouldn't wish for me to marry a wastrel, would you?"

"No, of course not," Violet murmured, "but still, it does seem odd. You're so recently affianced."

On any other day, Hyacinth would have just turned to her mother and said, "If you have a question, just ask it."

Except then her mother would ask a question.

And Hyacinth most certainly did not wish to answer.

It had been three days since she had learned the truth about Gareth. It sounded so dramatic, melodramatic even—"learned the truth." It sounded like she'd discovered some terrible secret, uncovered some dastardly skeleton in the St. Clair family closet.

But there was no secret. Nothing dark or dangerous, or even mildly embarrassing. Just a simple truth that had been staring her in the face all along.

And she had been too blind to see it. Love did that to a woman, she supposed.

And she had most certainly fallen in love with him. That much was clear. Sometime between the moment she had agreed to marry him and the night they had made love, she'd fallen in love with him.

But she hadn't known him. Or had she? Could she really say that she'd known him, truly known the measure of the man, when she hadn't even understood the most basic element of his character?

He'd used her.

That's what it was. He had used her to win his never-ending battle with his father.

And it hurt far more than she would ever have dreamed.

She kept telling herself she was being silly, that she was splitting hairs. Shouldn't it count that he liked her, that he thought she was clever and funny and even occasionally wise? Shouldn't it count that she knew he would protect her and honor her and, despite his somewhat spotted past, be a good and faithful husband?

Why did it *matter* why he'd asked her to marry him? Shouldn't it only matter that he had?

But it did matter. She'd felt used, unimportant, as if she were just a chess piece on a much larger game board.

And the worst part of it was—she didn't even understand the game.

"That's a rather heartfelt sigh."

Hyacinth blinked her mother's face into focus. Good heavens, how long had she been sitting there, staring into space?

"Is there something you wish to tell me?" Violet asked gently.

Hyacinth shook her head. How did one share something such as this with one's mother?

—Oh, yes, by the by and in case you're interested, it has recently come to my attention that my affianced husband asked me to marry him because he wished to infuriate his father.

—Oh, and did I mention that I am no longer a virgin? No getting out of it now!

No, that wasn't going to work.

"I suspect," Violet said, taking a little sip of her tea, "that you have had your first lovers' quarrel."

Hyacinth tried *very* hard not to blush. Lovers, indeed.

"It is nothing to be ashamed about," Violet said.

"I'm not ashamed," Hyacinth said quickly.

Violet raised her brows, and Hyacinth wanted to kick herself for falling so neatly into her mother's trap.

"It's nothing," she muttered, poking at her embroidery until the yellow flower she'd been working on looked like a fuzzy little chick.

Hyacinth shrugged and pulled out some orange thread. Might as well give it some feet and a beak.

"I know that it is considered unseemly to display one's emotions," Violet said, "and certainly I would not suggest that you engage in anything that might be termed histrionic, but sometimes it does help to simply tell someone how you feel."

Hyacinth looked up, meeting her mother's gaze directly. "I rarely have difficulty telling people how I feel."

"Well, that much is true," Violet said, looking slightly disgruntled at having her theory shot to pieces.

Hyacinth turned back to her embroidery, frowning as she realized that she'd put the beak too high. Oh, very well, it was a chick in a party hat.

"Perhaps," her mother persisted, "Mr. St. Clair is the one who finds it difficult to—"

"I know how he feels," Hyacinth cut in.

"Ah." Violet pursed her lips and let out a short little exhale through her nose. "Perhaps he is not sure how to proceed. How he ought to go about approaching you."

"He knows where I live."

Violet sighed audibly. "You're not making this easy for me."

"I'm *trying* to embroider." Hyacinth held up her handiwork as proof.

"You're trying to avoid—" Her mother stopped, blinking. "I say, why does that flower have an ear?"

"It's not an ear." Hyacinth looked down. "And it's not a flower."

"Wasn't it a flower yesterday?"

"I have a very creative mind," Hyacinth ground out, giving the blasted flower another ear.

"That," Violet said, "has never been in any doubt."

Hyacinth looked down at the mess on the fabric. "It's a tabby cat," she announced. "I just need to give it a tail."

Violet held silent for a moment, then said, "You can be very hard on people."

Hyacinth's head snapped up. "I'm your daughter!" she cried out.

"Of course," Violet replied, looking somewhat shocked by the force of Hyacinth's reaction. "But—"

"Why must you assume that whatever is the matter, it must be my fault?"

"I didn't!"

"You did." And Hyacinth thought of countless spats between the Bridgerton siblings. "You always do."

Violet responded with a horrified gasp. "That is not true, Hyacinth. It's just that I know you better than I do Mr. St. Clair, and—"

"—and therefore you know all of my faults?"

"Well . . . yes." Violet appeared to be surprised by her own answer and hastened to add, "That is not to say that Mr. St. Clair is not in possession of foibles and faults of his own. It's just that . . . Well, I'm just not acquainted with them."

"They are large," Hyacinth said bitterly, "and quite possibly insurmountable."

"Oh, Hyacinth," her mother said, and there was such concern in her voice that Hyacinth very nearly burst into tears right then and there. "Whatever can be the matter?"

Hyacinth looked away. She shouldn't have said anything. Now her mother would be beside herself with worry, and Hyacinth would have to sit there, feeling terrible, wanting desperately to throw herself into her arms and be a child again.

When she was small, she had been convinced that her mother could solve any problem, make anything better with a soft word and a kiss on the forehead.

But she wasn't a child any longer, and these weren't a child's problems.

And she couldn't share them with her mother.

"Do you wish to cry off?" Violet asked, softly and very carefully.

Hyacinth gave her head a shake. She *couldn't* back out of the marriage. But . . .

She looked away, surprised by the direction of her thoughts. Did she even *want* to back out of the marriage? If she had not given herself to Gareth, if they hadn't made love, and there was nothing forcing her to remain in the betrothal, what would she do?

She had spent the last three days obsessing about that night, about that horrible moment when she'd heard Gareth's father laughingly talk about how he had manipulated him into offering for her. She'd gone over every sentence in her head, every word she could remember, and yet she was only just now asking herself what had to be the most important question. The only question that mattered, really. And she realized—

She would stay.

She repeated it in her mind, needing time for the words to sink in.

She would stay.

She loved him. Was it really as simple as that?

"I don't wish to cry off," she said, even though she'd already shaken her head. Some things needed to be said aloud.

"Then you will have to help him," Violet said. "With whatever it is that troubles him, it will be up to you to help him."

Hyacinth nodded slowly, too lost in her thoughts to offer a more meaningful reply. Could she help him? Was it possible? She had known him barely a month; he'd had a lifetime to build this hatred with his father.

He might not want help, or perhaps more likely—he might not realize that he needed it. Men never did.

"I believe he cares for you," her mother said. "I truly believe that he does."

"I know he does," Hyacinth said sadly. But not as much as he hated his father.

And when he'd gone down on one knee and asked her to spend the rest of her life with him, to take his name and bear him children, it hadn't been because of *her*.

What did that say about *him*?

She sighed, feeling very weary.

"This isn't like you," her mother said.

Hyacinth looked up.

"To be so quiet," Violet clarified, "to wait."

"To wait?" Hyacinth echoed.

"For him. I assume that is what you're doing, waiting for him to call upon you and beg your forgiveness for whatever it is he has done."

"I—" She stopped. That was exactly what she'd been doing. She hadn't even realized it. And it was probably part of the reason she was feeling so miserable. She'd placed her fate and her happiness in the hands of another, and she hated it.

"Why don't you send him a letter?" Violet suggested. "Request that he pay you a visit. He is a gentleman, and you are his fiancée. He would never refuse."

"No," Hyacinth murmured, "he wouldn't. But"—she looked up, her eyes begging for advice—"what would I say?"

It was a silly question. Violet didn't even know what the problem was, so how could she know the solution? And yet, somehow, as always, she managed to say exactly the right thing.

"Say whatever is in your heart," Violet said. Her lips twisted wryly. "And if that doesn't work, I suggest that you take a book and knock him over the head with it."

Hyacinth blinked, then blinked again. "I beg your pardon."

"I didn't say that," Violet said quickly.

Hyacinth felt herself smile. "I'm rather certain you did."

"Do you think?" Violet murmured, concealing her own smile with her teacup.

"A large book," Hyacinth queried, "or small?"

"Large, I think, don't you?"

Hyacinth nodded. "Have we *The Complete Works of Shakespeare* in the library?"

Violet's lips twitched. "I believe that we do."

Something began to bubble in Hyacinth's chest. Something very close to laughter. And it felt so good to feel it again.

"I love you, Mother," she said, suddenly consumed by the need to say it aloud. "I just wanted you to know that."

"I know, darling," Violet said, and her eyes were shining brightly. "I love you, too."

Hyacinth nodded. She'd never stopped to think how precious that was—to have the love of a parent. It was something Gareth had never had. Heaven only knew what his childhood had been like. He had never spoken of it, and Hyacinth was ashamed to realize that she'd never asked.

She'd never even noticed the omission.

Maybe, just maybe, he deserved a little understanding on her part.

He would still have to beg her forgiveness; she wasn't *that* full of kindness and charity.

But she could try to understand, and she could love him, and maybe, if she tried with everything she had, she could fill that void within him.

Whatever it was he needed, maybe she could be it.

And maybe that would be all that mattered.

But in the meantime, Hyacinth was going to have to expend a bit of energy to bring about her happy ending. And she had a feeling that a note wasn't going to be sufficient.

It was time to be brazen, time to be bold.

Time to beard the lion in his den, to—

"I say, Hyacinth," came her mother's voice, "are you quite all right?"

She shook her head, even as she said, "I'm perfectly well. Just thinking like a fool, that's all."

A fool in love.

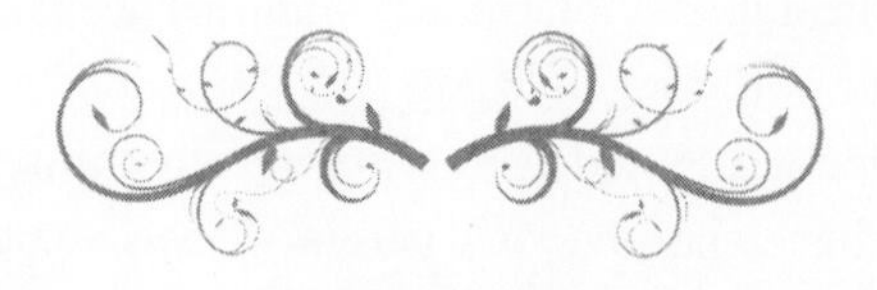

Chapter 18

Later that afternoon, in the small study in Gareth's very small suite of apartments. Our hero has come to the conclusion that he must take action.

He does not realize that Hyacinth is about to beat him to the punch.

A grand gesture.

That, Gareth decided, was what he needed. A grand gesture.

Women loved grand gestures, and while Hyacinth was certainly rather unlike any other woman he'd had dealings with, she was still a woman, and she would certainly be at least a little swayed by a grand gesture.

Wouldn't she?

Well, she'd better, Gareth thought grumpily, because he didn't know what else to do.

But the problem with grand gestures was that the grandest ones tended to require money, which was one thing Gareth had in short supply. And the ones that didn't require a great deal of money usually involved some poor sod embarrassing himself in a most public manner—reciting poetry or singing a ballad, or making some sort of sappy declaration with eight hundred witnesses.

Not, Gareth decided, anything he was likely to do.

But Hyacinth was, as he'd often noted, an uncommon sort of female, which meant that—hopefully—an uncommon sort of gesture would work with her.

He would show her he cared, and she'd forget all this nonsense about his father, and all would be well.

All had to be well.

"Mr. St. Clair, you have a visitor."

He looked up. He'd been seated behind his desk for so long it was a wonder he hadn't grown roots. His valet was standing in the doorway to his office. As Gareth could not afford a butler—and really, who needed one with only four rooms to care for—Phelps often assumed those duties as well.

"Show him in," Gareth said, somewhat absently, sliding some books over the papers currently sitting on his desk.

"Er . . ." *Cough cough. Cough cough cough.*

Gareth looked up. "Is there a problem?"

"Well . . . no . . ." The valet looked pained. Gareth tried to take pity on him. Poor Mr. Phelps hadn't realized that he would occasionally be acting as a butler when he'd interviewed for the position, and clearly he'd never been taught the butlerian skill of keeping one's face devoid of all emotion.

"Mr. Phelps?" Gareth queried.

"He is a she, Mr. St. Clair."

"A hermaphrodite, Mr. Phelps?" Gareth asked, just to see the poor fellow blush.

To his credit, the valet made no reaction save squaring his jaw. "It is Miss Bridgerton."

Gareth jumped to his feet so quickly he smacked both his thighs on the edge of the desk. "Here?" he asked. "Now?"

Phelps nodded, looking just a little bit pleased at his discomfiture. "She gave me her card. She was rather polite about it all. As if it were nothing out of the ordinary."

Gareth's mind spun, trying to figure out why on earth Hyacinth would do something so ill-advised as to call upon him at his home in the middle of the day. Not that the middle of the night would have been better, but still, any number of busybodies might have seen her entering the building.

"Ah, show her in," he said. He couldn't very well turn her out. As it was, he would certainly have to return her to her home himself. He couldn't imagine she'd come with a proper escort. She'd probably brought no one save that peppermint-eating maid of hers, and heaven knew she was no protection on the streets of London.

He crossed his arms as he waited. His rooms were set up in a square, and one could access his study from either the dining room or his bedchamber. Unfortunately, the day maid had chosen this day to provide the dining room floor with some sort of twice-yearly wax that she swore (rather vocally and on her dear mother's grave) would keep the floor clean *and* ward off disease. As a result, the table had been shoved up against the door to the study, which meant that the only way in was through his bedroom.

Gareth groaned and shook his head. The last thing he needed was to picture Hyacinth in his bedroom.

He hoped she felt awkward passing through. It was the least she deserved, coming out here on her own.

"Gareth," she said, appearing in the doorway.

And all his good intentions flew right out the window.

"What the devil are you doing here?" he demanded.

"It's nice to see you, too," she said, with such composure that he felt like a fool.

But still he plodded on. "Any number of people could have seen you. Have you no care for your reputation?"

She shrugged delicately, pulling off her gloves. "I'm engaged to be married. You can't cry off, and I don't intend to, so I doubt I'll be forever ruined if someone catches me."

Gareth tried to ignore the rush of relief he felt at her words. He had, of course, gone to great lengths to ensure that she could not cry off, and she had already said that she would not, but all the same, it was surprisingly good to hear it again.

"Very well," he said slowly, choosing his words with great care. "Why, then, are you here?"

"I am not here to discuss your father," she said briskly, "if that is what worries you."

"I'm not worried," he bit off.

She lifted one brow. Damn, but *why* had he chosen to marry the one woman in the world who could do that? Or at least the one woman of his acquaintance.

"I'm not," he said testily.

She said nothing in direct reply, but she did give him a look that said she didn't believe him for one instant. "I have come," she said, "to discuss the jewels."

"The jewels," he repeated.

"Yes," she replied, still in that prim, businesslike voice of hers. "I hope you have not forgotten about them."

"How could I?" he murmured. She was starting to irritate him, he realized. Or rather, her demeanor was. He was still roiling inside, on edge just from the very sight of her, and she was utterly cool, almost preternaturally composed.

"I hope you still intend to look for them," she said. "We have come too far to give up now."

"Have you any idea where we might begin?" he asked, keeping his voice scrupulously even. "If I recall correctly, we seem to have hit a bit of a brick wall."

She reached into her reticule and pulled out the latest clue from Isabella, which she'd had in her possession ever since they had parted a few days earlier. With careful, steady fingers she unfolded it and smoothed it open on his desk. "I took the liberty of taking this to my brother Colin," she said. She looked up and reminded him, "You had given me your permission to do so."

He gave her a brief nod of agreement.

"As I mentioned, he has traveled extensively on the Continent, and he seems to feel that it is written in a Slavic language. After consulting a map, he guessed that it is Slovene." At his blank stare, she added, "It is what they speak in Slovenia."

Gareth blinked. "Is there such a country?"

For the first time in the interview, Hyacinth smiled. "There is. I must confess, I was unaware of its existence as well. It's more of a region, really. To the north and east of Italy."

"Part of Austria-Hungary, then?"

Hyacinth nodded. "And the Holy Roman Empire before that. Was your grandmother from the north of Italy?"

Gareth suddenly realized that he had no idea. Grandmother Isabella had loved to tell him stories of her childhood in Italy, but they had been tales of food and holidays—the sorts of things a very young boy might find interesting. If she'd mentioned the town of her birth, he had been too young to take note. "I don't know," he said, feeling rather foolish—and in truth, somewhat inconsiderate—for his ignorance. "I suppose she must have been. She wasn't very dark. Her coloring was a bit like mine, actually."

Hyacinth nodded. "I had wondered about that. Neither you nor your father has much of a Mediterranean look about you."

Gareth smiled tightly. He could not speak for the baron, but there was a very good reason why *he* did not look as if he carried any Italian blood.

"Well," Hyacinth said, looking back down at the sheet of paper she had laid on his desk. "If she was from the northeast, it stands to reason that she might have lived near the Slovene border and thus been familiar with the language. Or at least familiar enough to pen two sentences in it."

"I can't imagine that she thought anyone here in England might be able to translate it, though."

"Exactly," she said, making an animated motion of agreement. When it became apparent that Gareth had no idea what she was talking about, she continued with, "If you wanted to make a clue particularly difficult, wouldn't you write it in the most obscure language possible?"

"It's really a pity I don't speak Chinese," he murmured.

She gave him a look—either of impatience or irritation; he wasn't sure which—then continued with, "I am also convinced that this must be the final clue. Anyone who had got this far would be forced to expend quite a lot of energy, and quite possibly expense as well to obtain a translation. Surely she wouldn't force someone to go through the trouble twice."

Gareth looked down at the unfamiliar words, chewing on his lower lip as he pondered this.

"Don't you agree?" Hyacinth pressed.

He looked up, shrugging. "Well, *you* would."

Her mouth fell open. "What do you mean? That's simply not—" She stopped, reflecting on his words. "Very well, I would. But I think we can both agree that, for better or for worse, I am a bit more diabolical than a typical female. Or male, for that matter," she muttered.

Gareth smiled wryly, wondering if he ought to be made more nervous by the phrase, "for better or for worse."

"Do you think your grandmother would be as devious as, er . . ."—she cleared her throat—"I?" Hyacinth seemed to lose a little steam toward the end of the question, and Gareth suddenly saw in her eyes that she was not as collected as she wished for him to believe.

"I don't know," he said quite honestly. "She passed away when I was rather young. My recollections and perceptions are those of a seven-year-old boy."

"Well," she said, tapping her fingers against the desk in a revealingly nervous gesture. "We can certainly begin our search for a speaker of Slovene." She rolled her eyes as she added, somewhat dryly, "There must be one somewhere in London."

"One would think," he murmured, mostly just to egg her on. He shouldn't do it; he should be far wiser by now, but there was something so . . . entertaining about Hyacinth when she was determined.

And as usual, she did not disappoint. "In the meantime," she stated, her voice marvelously matter-of-fact, "I believe we should return to Clair House."

"And search it from top to bottom?" he asked, so politely that it had to be clear that he thought she was mad.

"Of course not," she said with a scowl.

He almost smiled. That was much more like her.

"But it seems to me," she added, "that the jewels must be hidden in her bedchamber."

"And why would you think that?"

"Where else would she put them?"

"Her dressing room," he suggested, tilting his head to the side, "the drawing room, the attic, the butler's closet, the guest bedroom, the *other* guest bedroom—"

"But where," she cut in, looking rather annoyed with his sarcasm, "would make the most sense? Thus far, she has been keeping everything to the areas of the house least visited by your grandfather. Where better than her bedchamber?"

He eyed her thoughtfully and for long enough to make her blush. Finally, he said, "We know he visited her there at least twice."

She blinked. "Twice?"

"My father and my father's younger brother. He died at Trafalgar," he explained, even though she hadn't asked.

"Oh." That seemed to take the winds out of her sails. At least momentarily. "I'm sorry."

Gareth shrugged. "It was a long time ago, but thank you."

She nodded slowly, looking as if she wasn't quite sure what to say now. "Right," she finally said. "Well."

"Right," he echoed.

"Well."

"Well," he said softly.

"Oh, hang it all!" she burst out. "I cannot stand this. I am not *made* to sit idly by and brush things under the rug."

Gareth opened his mouth to speak, not that he had any idea of what to say, but Hyacinth wasn't done.

"I know I should be quiet, and I know I should leave well enough alone, but I can't. I just can't do it." She looked at him, and she looked like she wanted to grab his shoulders and shake. "Do you understand?"

"Not a word," he admitted.

"I have to know!" she cried out. "I have to know why you asked me to marry you."

It was a topic he did not wish to revisit. "I thought you said you didn't come here to discuss my father."

"I lied," she said. "You didn't really believe me, did you?"

"No," he realized. "I don't suppose I did."

"I just—I can't—" She wrung her hands together, looking more pained and tortured than he'd ever seen her. A few strands of her hair had come loose from its pinnings, probably the result of her anxious gestures, and her color was high.

But it was her eyes that looked the most changed. There was a desperation there, a strange discomfort that did not belong.

And he realized that that was the thing about Hyacinth, the distinguishing characteristic that set her so apart from the rest of humanity. She was always at ease in her own skin. She knew who she was, and she liked who she was, and he supposed that was a large part of why he so enjoyed her company.

And he realized that she had—and she was—so many things he'd always wanted.

She knew her place in this world. She knew where she belonged.

She knew who she belonged with.

And he wanted the same. He wanted it with an intensity that cut right down to his soul. It was a strange, almost indescribable jealousy, but it was there. And it seared him.

"If you have any feeling for me whatsoever," she said, "you will understand how bloody difficult this is for me, so for the love of God, Gareth, will you *say something*?"

"I—" He opened his mouth to speak, but the words seemed to strangle him. Why *had* he asked her to marry him? There were a hundred reasons, a thousand. He tried to remember just what it was that had pushed the idea into his mind. It had come to him suddenly—he remembered that. But he didn't recall exactly why, except that it had seemed the right thing to do.

Not because it was expected, not because it was proper, but just because it was right.

And yes, it was true that it had crossed his mind that it would be the ultimate win in this never-ending game with his father, but that wasn't *why* he'd done it.

He'd done it because he'd had to.

Because he couldn't imagine not doing it.

Because he loved her.

He felt himself slide, and thank God the desk was behind him, or he'd have ended up on the floor.

How on earth had this happened? He was in love with Hyacinth Bridgerton.

Surely someone somewhere was laughing about this.

"I'll go," she said, her voice breaking, and it was only when she reached the door that he realized he must have been silent for a full minute.

"No!" he called out, and his voice sounded impossibly hoarse. "Wait!" And then:

"Please."

She stopped, turned. Shut the door.

And he realized that he had to tell her. Not that he loved her—*that* he wasn't quite ready to reveal. But he had to tell her the truth about his birth. He couldn't trick her into marriage.

"Hyacinth, I—"

The words jammed in his throat. He'd never told anyone. Not even his grandmother. No one knew the truth except for him and the baron.

For ten years, Gareth had kept it inside, allowed it to grow and fill him until sometimes it felt like it was all that he was. Nothing but a secret. Nothing but a lie.

"I need to tell you something," he said haltingly, and she must have sensed that this was something out of the ordinary, because she went very still.

And Hyacinth was rarely still.

"I—My father . . ."

It was strange. He'd never thought to say it, had never rehearsed the words. And he didn't know how to put them together, didn't know which sentence to choose.

"He's not my father," he finally blurted out.

Hyacinth blinked. Twice.

"I don't know who my real father is."

Still, she said nothing.

"I expect I never will."

He watched her face, waited for some sort of reaction. She was expressionless, so completely devoid of movement that she didn't look like herself. And then, just when he was certain that he'd lost her forever, her mouth came together in a peevish line, and she said:

"Well. That's a relief, I must say."

His lips parted. "I beg your pardon."

"I wasn't particularly excited about my children carrying Lord St. Clair's blood." She shrugged, lifting her brows in a particularly Hyacinthish expression. "I'm happy for them to have his title—it's a handy thing to possess, after all—but his blood is quite another thing. He's remarkably bad-tempered, did you know that?"

Gareth nodded, a bubble of giddy emotion rising within him. "I'd noticed," he heard himself say.

"I suppose we'll have to keep it a secret," she said, as if she were speaking of nothing more than the idlest of gossip. "Who else knows?"

He blinked, still a little dazed by her matter-of-fact approach to the problem. "Just the baron and me, as far as I'm aware."

"And your real father."

"I hope not," Gareth said, and he realized that it was the first time he'd actually allowed himself to say the words—even, really, to think them.

"He might not have known," Hyacinth said quietly, "or he might have thought you were better off with the St. Clairs, as a child of nobility."

"I know all that," Gareth said bitterly, "and yet somehow it doesn't make it feel any better."

"Your grandmother might know more."

His eyes flew to her face.

"Isabella," she clarified. "In her diary."

"She wasn't really my grandmother."

"Did she ever act that way? As if you weren't hers?"

He shook his head. "No," he said, losing himself to the memories. "She loved me. I don't know why, but she did."

"It might be," Hyacinth said, her voice catching in the oddest manner, "because you're slightly lovable."

His heart leapt. "Then you don't wish to end the engagement," he said, somewhat cautiously.

She looked at him with an uncommonly direct gaze. "Do you?"

He shook his head.

"Then why," she said, her lips forming the barest of smiles, "would you think that I would?"

"Your family might object."

"Pffft. We're not so high in the instep as that. My brother's wife is the illegitimate daughter of the Earl of Penwood and an actress of God knows what provenance, and any one of us would lay down our lives for her." Her eyes narrowed thoughtfully. "But you are not illegitimate."

He shook his head. "To my father's everlasting despair."

"Well, then," she said, "I don't see a problem. My brother and Sophie like to live quietly in the country, in part because of her past, but we shan't be forced to do the same. Unless of course, you wish to."

"The baron could raise a huge scandal," he warned her.

She smiled. "Are you trying to talk me out of marrying you?"

"I just want you to understand—"

"Because I would hope by now you've learned that it's a tiresome endeavor to attempt to talk me out of anything."

Gareth could only smile at that.

"Your father won't say a word," she stated. "What would be the point? You were born in wedlock, so he can't take away the title, and revealing you as a bastard would only reveal *him* as a cuckold." She waved her hand through the air with great authority. "No man wants that."

His lips curved, and he felt something changing inside of him, as if he were growing lighter, more free. "And you can speak for all men?" he murmured, moving slowly in her direction.

"Would *you* wish to be known as a cuckold?"

He shook his head. "But I don't have to worry about that."

She started to look just a little unnerved—but also excited—as he closed the distance between them. "Not if you keep me happy."

"Why, Hyacinth Bridgerton, is that a threat?"

Her expression turned coy. "Perhaps."

He was only a step away now. "I can see that I have my work cut out for me."

Her chin lifted, and her chest began to rise and fall more rapidly. "I'm not a particularly easy woman."

He found her hand and lifted her fingers to his mouth. "I do enjoy a challenge."

"Then it's a good thing you're—"

He took one of her fingers and slid it into his mouth, and she gasped.

"—marrying me," she somehow finished.

He moved to another finger. "Mmm-hmm."

"I—Ah—I—Ah—"

"You do like to talk," he said with a chuckle.

"What do you—Oh!—"

He smiled to himself as he moved to the inside of her wrist.

"—mean by that?" But there wasn't much punch left in her question. She was quite literally melting against the wall, and he felt like the king of the world.

"Oh, nothing much," he murmured, tugging her close so that he could move his lips to the side of her throat. "Just that I'm looking forward to actually marrying you so that you can make as much noise as you'd like."

He couldn't see her face—he was much too busy attending to the neckline of her dress, which clearly had to be brought down—but he knew she blushed. He felt the heat beneath her skin.

"Gareth," she said in feeble protest. "We should stop."

"You don't mean that," he said, sliding his hand under the hem of her skirt once it became clear that the bodice wasn't going to budge.

"No"—she sighed—"not really."

He smiled. "Good."

She let out a moan as his fingers tickled up her leg, and then she must have grasped onto one last shred of sanity, because she said, "But we can't . . . oh."

"No, we can't," he agreed. The desk wouldn't be comfortable, there was no room on the floor, and heaven only knew if Phelps had shut the outer door to his bedroom. He pulled back and gave her a devilish smile. "But we can do other things."

Her eyes opened wide. "What other things?" she asked, sounding delightfully suspicious.

He wound his fingers in hers and then pulled both her hands over her head. "Do you trust me?"

"No," she said, "but I don't care."

Still holding her hands aloft, he leaned her against the door and came in for a kiss. She tasted like tea, and like . . .

Her.

He could count the number of times he'd kissed her on one hand, and yet he still knew, still understood, that this was the essence of her. She was unique in his arms, beneath his kiss, and he knew that no one else would ever do again.

He let go of one of her hands, stroking his way softly down the line of her arm to her shoulder . . . neck . . . jaw. And then his other hand released her and found its way back to the hem of her dress.

She moaned his name, gasping and panting as his fingers moved up her leg.

"Relax," he instructed, his lips hot against her ear.

"I can't."

"You can."

"No," she said, grabbing his face and forcing him to look at her. "I can't."

Gareth laughed aloud, enchanted by her bossiness. "Very well," he said, "don't relax." And then, before she had a chance to respond, he slid his finger past the edge of her underthings and touched her.

"Oh!"

"No relaxing now," he said with a chuckle.

"Gareth," she gasped.

"Oh, Gareth, No Gareth, or More Gareth?" he murmured.

"More," she moaned. "Please."

"I love a woman who knows when to beg," he said, redoubling his efforts.

Her head, which had been thrown back, came down so that she could look him in the eye. "You'll pay for that," she said.

He quirked a brow. "I will?"

She nodded. "Just not now."

He laughed softly. "Fair enough."

He rubbed her gently, using soft friction to bring her to a quivering peak. She was breathing erratically now, her lips parted and her eyes glazed. He loved her face, loved every little curve of it, the way the light hit her cheekbones and the shape of her jaw.

But there was something about it now, when she was lost in her own passion, that took his breath away. She was beautiful—not in a way that would launch a thousand ships, but in a more private fashion.

Her beauty was his and his alone.

And it humbled him.

He leaned down to kiss her, tenderly, with all the love he felt. He wanted to catch her gasp when she climaxed, wanted to feel her breath and her moan with his mouth. His fingers tickled and teased, and she tensed beneath him, her body trapped between his and the wall, grinding against them both.

"Gareth," she gasped, breaking free of the kiss for just long enough to say his name.

"Soon," he promised. He smiled. "Maybe now."

And then, as he captured her for one last kiss, he slid one finger inside of her, even as another continued its caress. He felt her close tight around him, felt her body practically lift off the floor with the force of her passion.

And it was only then that he realized the true measure of his own desire. He was hard and hot and desperate for her, and even so, he'd been so focused on her that he hadn't noticed.

Until now.

He looked at her. She was limp, breathless, and as near to insensible as he'd ever seen her.

Damn.

That was all right, he told himself unconvincingly. They had their whole lives ahead of them. One encounter with a tub of cold water wasn't going to kill him.

"Happy?" he murmured, gazing down at her indulgently.

She nodded, but that was all she managed.

He dropped a kiss on her nose, then remembered the papers he'd left on his desk. They weren't quite complete, but still, it seemed a good time to show them to her.

"I have a present for you," he said.

Her eyes lit up. "You do?"

He nodded. "Just keep in mind that it's the thought that counts."

She smiled, following him to his desk, then taking a seat in the chair in front of it.

Gareth pushed aside some books, then carefully lifted a piece of paper. "It's not done."

"I don't care," she said softly.

But still, he didn't show it to her. "I think it's rather obvious that we are not going to find the jewels," he said.

"No!" she protested. "We can—"

"Shhh. Let me finish."

It went against her every last impulse, but she managed to shut her mouth.

"I am not in possession of a great deal of money," he said.

"That doesn't matter."

He smiled wryly. "I'm glad you feel that way, because while we shan't want for anything, nor will we live like your brothers and sisters."

"I don't need all that," she said quickly. And she didn't. Or at least she hoped she didn't. But she knew, down to the tips of her toes, that she didn't need anything as much as she needed him.

He looked slightly grateful, and also, maybe, just a little bit uncomfortable. "It'll probably be even worse once I inherit the title," he added. "I think the baron is trying to fix it so that he can beggar me from beyond the grave."

"Are you trying to talk me out of marrying you again?"

"Oh, no," he said. "You're most definitely stuck with me now. But I did want you to know that if I could, I would give you the world." He held out the paper. "Starting with this."

She took the sheet into her hands and looked down. It was a drawing, of her.

Her eyes widened with surprise. "Did you do this?" she asked.

He nodded. "I'm not well trained, but I can—"

"It's very good," she said, cutting him off. He would never find his way into history as a famous artist, but the likeness was a good one, and she rather thought he'd captured something in her eyes, something that she'd not seen in any of the portraits of her her family had commissioned.

"I have been thinking about Isabella," he said, leaning against the edge of his desk. "And I remembered a story she told me when I was young. There was a princess, and an evil prince, and"—he smiled ruefully—"a diamond bracelet."

Hyacinth had been watching his face, mesmerized by the warmth in his eyes, but at this she looked quickly back down at the drawing. There, on her wrist, was a diamond bracelet.

"I'm sure it's nothing like what she actually hid," he said, "but it is how I remember her describing it to me, and it is what I would give to you, if only I could."

"Gareth, I—" And she felt tears, welling in her eyes, threatening to spill down her cheeks. "It is the most precious gift I have ever received."

He looked . . . not like he didn't believe her, but rather like he wasn't quite sure that he should. "You don't have to say—"

"It is," she insisted, rising to her feet.

He turned and picked another piece of paper up off the desk. "I drew it here as well," he said, "but larger, so you could see it better."

She took the second piece of paper into her hands and looked down. He'd drawn just the bracelet, as if suspended in air. "It's lovely," she said, touching the image with her fingers.

He gave her a self-deprecating smile. "If it doesn't exist, it should."

She nodded, still examining the drawing. The bracelet was lovely, each link shaped almost like a leaf. It was delicate and whimsical, and Hyacinth ached to place it on her wrist.

But she could never treasure it as much as she did these two drawings. Never.

"I—" She looked up, her lips parting with surprise. She almost said, "I love you."

"I love them," she said instead, but when she looked up at him, she rather fancied that the truth was in her eyes.

I love you.

She smiled and placed her hand over his. She wanted to say it, but she wasn't quite ready. She didn't know why, except that maybe she was afraid to say it first. She, who was afraid of almost nothing, could not quite summon the courage to utter three little words.

It was astounding.

Terrifying.

And she decided to change the mood. "I still want to look for the jewels," she said, clearing her throat until her voice emerged in its customarily efficient manner.

He groaned. "Why won't you give up?"

"Because I . . . Well, because I can't." She clamped her mouth into a frown. "I certainly don't want your father to have them now. Oh." She looked up. "Am I to call him that?"

He shrugged. "I still do. It's a difficult habit to break."

She acknowledged this with a nod. "I don't care if Isabella wasn't really your grandmother. You deserve the bracelet."

He gave her an amused smile. "And why is that?"

That stumped her for a moment. "Because you do," she finally said. "Because someone has to have it, and I don't want it to be him. Because—" She glanced longingly down at the drawing in her hands. "Because this is *gorgeous.*"

"Can't we wait to find our Slovenian translator?"

She shook her head, pointing at the note, still lying on the desk. "What if it's not in Slovene?"

"I thought you said it was," he said, clearly exasperated.

"I said my brother *thought* it was," she returned. "Do you know how many languages there are in central Europe?"

He cursed under his breath.

"I know," she said. "It's very frustrating."

He stared at her in disbelief. "That's not why I swore."

"Then why—"

"Because you are going to be the death of me," he ground out.

Hyacinth smiled, pointing her index finger and pressing it right against his chest. "Now you know why I said my family was mad to get me off their hands."

"God help me, I do."

She cocked her head to the side. "Can we go tomorrow?"

"No?"

"The next day?"

"No!"

"Please?" she tried.

He clamped his hands on her shoulders and spun her around until she faced the door. "I'm taking you home," he announced.

She turned, trying to talk over her shoulder. "Pl—"

"No!"

Hyacinth shuffled along, allowing him to push her toward the door. When she could not put it off any longer, she grasped the doorknob, but before she turned it, she twisted back one last time, opened her mouth, and—

"NO!"

"I didn't—"

"Very well," he groaned, practically throwing his arms up in exasperation. "You win."

"Oh, *thank*—"

"But you are not coming."

She froze, her mouth still open and round. "I beg your pardon," she said.

"I will go," he said, looking very much as if he'd rather have all of his teeth pulled. "But you will not."

She stared at him, trying to come up with a way to say "That's not fair" without sounding juvenile. Deciding that was impossible, she set to work attempting to figure out how to ask how she would know he'd actually gone without sounding as if she didn't trust him.

Botheration, that was a lost cause as well.

So she settled for crossing her arms and skewering him with a glare.

To no effect whatsoever. He just stared down at her and said, "No."

Hyacinth opened her mouth one last time, then gave up, sighed, and said, "Well, I suppose if I could walk all over you, you wouldn't be worth marrying."

He threw back his head and laughed. "You're going to be a fine wife, Hyacinth Bridgerton," he said, nudging her out of the room.

"Hmmph."

He groaned. "Good God, but not if you turn into my grandmother."

"It is my every aspiration," she said archly.

"Pity," he murmured, tugging at her arm so that she came to a halt before they reached his sitting room.

She turned to him, questioning with her eyes.

He curved his lips, all innocence. "Well, I can't do *this* to my grandmother."

"Oh!" she yelped. How had he gotten his hand *there?*

"Or *this*."

"Gareth!"

"Gareth, yes, or Gareth, no?"

She smiled. She couldn't help it.

"Gareth *more*."

Chapter 19

The following Tuesday.

Everything important seems to happen on a Tuesday, doesn't it?

"Look what I have!"

Hyacinth grinned as she stood in the doorway of Lady Danbury's drawing room, holding aloft *Miss Davenport and the Dark Marquis.*

"A new book?" Lady D asked from her position across the room. She was seated in her favorite chair, but from the way she held herself, it might as well have been a throne.

"Not just any book," Hyacinth said with a sly smile as she held it forth. "Look."

Lady Danbury took the book in her hands, glanced down, and positively beamed. "We haven't read this one yet," she said. She looked back up at Hyacinth. "I hope it's just as bad as the rest."

"Oh, come now, Lady Danbury," Hyacinth said, taking a seat next to her, "you shouldn't call them bad."

"I didn't say they weren't entertaining," the countess said, eagerly flipping through the pages. "How many chapters do we have left with dear Miss Butterworth?"

Hyacinth plucked the book in question off a nearby table and opened it to the spot she had marked the previous Tuesday. "Three," she said, flipping back and forth to check.

"Hmmph. I wonder how many cliffs poor Priscilla can hang from in that time."

"Two at least, I should think," Hyacinth murmured. "Provided she isn't struck with the plague."

Lady Danbury attempted to peer at the book over her shoulder. "Do you think it possible? A bit of the bubonic would do wonders for the prose."

Hyacinth chuckled. "Perhaps that should have been the subtitle. *Miss Butterworth and the Mad Baron, or*"—she lowered her voice dramatically—"*A Bit of the Bubonic.*"

"I prefer *Pecked to Death by Pigeons* myself."

"Maybe we *should* write a book," Hyacinth said with a smile, getting ready to launch into chapter eighteen.

Lady Danbury looked as if she wanted to clap Hyacinth on the head. "That is exactly what I've been telling you."

Hyacinth scrunched her nose as she shook her head. "No," she said, "it really wouldn't be much fun past the titles. Do you think anyone would wish to buy a collection of amusing book titles?"

"They would if it had my name on the cover," Lady D said with great authority. "Speaking of which, how is your translation of my grandson's other grandmother's diary coming along?"

Hyacinth's head bobbed slightly as she tried to follow Lady D's convoluted sentence structure. "I'm sorry," she finally said, "how does that have anything to do with people being compelled to purchase a book with your name on the cover?"

Lady Danbury waved her hand forcefully in the air as if Hyacinth's comment were a physical thing she could push away. "You haven't told me anything," she said.

"I'm only a little bit more than halfway through," Hyacinth admitted. "I remember far less Italian than I had thought, and I am finding it a much more difficult task than I had anticipated."

Lady D nodded. "She was a lovely woman."

Hyacinth blinked in surprise. "You knew her? Isabella?"

"Of course I did. Her son married my daughter."

"Oh. Yes," Hyacinth murmured. She didn't know why this hadn't occurred to her before. And she wondered—Did Lady Danbury know anything about the circumstances of Gareth's birth? Gareth had said that she did not, or at least that he had never spoken to her about it. But perhaps each was keeping silent on the assumption that the other did not know.

Hyacinth opened her mouth, then closed it sharply. It was not her place to say anything. It was *not*.

But—

No. She clamped her teeth together, as if that would keep her from blurting anything out. She could not reveal Gareth's secret. She absolutely, positively could not.

"Did you eat something sour?" Lady D asked, without any delicacy whatsoever. "You look rather ill."

"I'm perfectly well," Hyacinth said, pasting a sprightly smile on her face. "I was merely thinking about the diary. I brought it with me, actually. To read in the carriage." She had been working on the translation tirelessly since learning Gareth's secret earlier that week. She wasn't sure if they would ever learn the identity of Gareth's real father, but Isabella's diary seemed to be the best possible place to start the search.

"Did you?" Lady Danbury sat back in her chair, closing her eyes. "Read to me from that instead, why don't you?"

"You don't understand Italian," Hyacinth pointed out.

"I know, but it's a lovely language, so melodious and smooth. And I need to take a nap."

"Are you certain?" Hyacinth asked, reaching into her small satchel for the diary.

"That I need a nap? Yes, more's the pity. It started two years ago. Now I can't exist without one each afternoon."

"Actually, I was referring to the reading of the diary," Hyacinth murmured. "If you wish to fall asleep, there are certainly better methods than my reading to you in Italian."

"Why, Hyacinth," Lady D said, with a noise that sounded suspiciously like a cackle, "are you offering to sing me lullabies?"

Hyacinth rolled her eyes. "You're as bad as a child."

"Whence we came, my dear Miss Bridgerton. Whence we came."

Hyacinth shook her head and found her spot in the diary. She'd left off in the spring of 1793, four years before Gareth's birth. According to what she had read in the carriage on the way over, Gareth's mother was pregnant, with what Hyacinth assumed would be Gareth's older brother George. She had suffered two miscarriages before that, which had not endeared her to her husband.

What Hyacinth was finding most interesting about the tale was the disappointment Isabella expressed about her son. She loved him, yes, but she regretted the degree to which she had allowed her husband to mold him. As a result, Isabella had written, the son was just like the father. He treated his mother with disdain, and his wife fared no better.

Hyacinth was finding the entire tale to be rather sad. She liked Isabella. There was an intelligence and humor to her writing that shone through, even when Hyacinth was not able to translate every word, and Hyacinth liked to think that if they had been of an age, they would have been friends. It saddened her to realize the degree to which Isabella had been stifled and made unhappy by her husband.

And it reinforced her belief that it really did matter who one married. Not for wealth or status, although Hyacinth was not so idealistic that she would pretend those were completely unimportant.

But one only got one life, and, God willing, one husband. And how nice to actually *like* the man to whom one pledged one's troth. Isabella hadn't been beaten or misused, but she had been ignored, and her thoughts and opinions had gone unheard. Her husband sent her off to some remote country house, and he taught his sons by example. Gareth's father treated his wife the exact same way. Hyacinth supposed that Gareth's uncle would have been the same, too, if he had lived long enough to take a wife.

"Are you going to read to me or not?" Lady D asked, somewhat stridently.

Hyacinth looked over at the countess, who had not even bothered to open her eyes for her demand. "Sorry," she said, using her finger to find where she had left off. "I need just a moment to . . . ah, here we are."

Hyacinth cleared her throat and began to read in Italian. "*Si avvicina il giorno in cui nascerà il mio primo nipote. Prego che sia un maschio . . .*"

She translated in her head as she continued to read aloud in Italian:

> *The day draws near in which will be born my first grandchild. I pray that it will be a boy. I would love a little girl—I would probably be allowed to see her and love her more, but it will be better for us all if we have a boy. I am afraid to think how quickly Anne will be forced to endure the attentions of my son if she has a girl.*

I should love better my own son, but instead I worry about his wife.

Hyacinth paused, eyeing Lady Danbury for signs that she understood any of the Italian. This was her daughter she was reading about, after all. Hyacinth wondered if the countess had any idea how sad the marriage had been. But Lady D had, remarkably, started to snore.

Hyacinth blinked in surprise—and suspicion. She had never dreamed that Lady Danbury might fall asleep that quickly. She held silent for a few moments, waiting for the countess's eyes to pop open with a loud demand for her to continue.

After a minute, however, Hyacinth was confident that Lady D really had fallen asleep. So she continued reading to herself, laboriously translating each sentence in her head. The next entry was dated a few months later; Isabella expressed her relief that Anne had delivered a boy, who had been christened George. The baron was beside himself with pride, and had even given his wife the gift of a gold bracelet.

Hyacinth flipped a few pages ahead, trying to see how long it would be until Isabella reached 1797, the year of Gareth's birth. One, two, three . . . She counted the pages, passing quickly through the years. Seven, eight, nine . . . Ah, 1796. Gareth had been born in March, so if Isabella had written about his conception, it would be here, not 1797.

Ten pages away, that was all.

And it occurred to her—

Why not skip ahead? There was no law requiring her to read the diary in perfect, chronological order. She could just peek ahead to 1796 and 1797 and see if there was anything relating to Gareth and his parentage. If not, she'd go right back to where she'd left off and start reading anew.

And wasn't it Lady Danbury who'd said that patience most certainly was not a virtue?

Hyacinth glanced ruefully down at 1793, then, holding the five leaves of paper as one, shifted to 1796.

Back . . . forth . . . back . . .

Forth.

She turned to 1796, and planted her left hand down so that she wouldn't turn back again.

Definitely forth.

"*24 June 1796*," she read to herself. "*I arrived at Clair House for a summer visit, only to be informed that my son had already left for London.*"

Hyacinth quickly subtracted months in her head. Gareth was born in March of 1797. Three months took her back to December 1796, and another six to—

June.

And Gareth's father was out of town.

Barely able to breathe, Hyacinth read on:

Anne seems contented that he is gone, and little George is such a treasure. Is it so terrible to admit that I am more happy when Richard isn't here? It is such a joy to have all the persons I love so close . . .

Hyacinth scowled as she finished the entry. There was nothing out of the ordinary there. Nothing about a mysterious stranger, or an improper friend.

She glanced up at Lady Danbury, whose head was now tilted awkwardly back. Her mouth was hanging a bit open, too.

Hyacinth turned resolutely back to the diary, turning to the next entry, dated three months later.

She gasped.

Anne is carrying a child. And we all know it cannot be Richard's. He has been away for two months. Two months. I am afraid for her. He is furious. But she will not reveal the truth.

"Reveal it," Hyacinth ground out. "Reveal it."

"Enh?"

Hyacinth slammed the book shut and looked up. Lady Danbury was stirring in her seat.

"Why did you stop reading?" Lady D asked groggily.

"I didn't," Hyacinth lied, her fingers holding the diary so tightly it was a wonder she didn't burn holes through the binding. "You fell asleep."

"Did I?" Lady Danbury murmured. "I must be getting old."

Hyacinth smiled tightly.

"Very well," Lady D said with a wave of her hand. She fidgeted a bit, moving first to the left, then to the right, then back to the left again. "I'm awake now. Let's get back to Miss Butterworth."

Hyacinth was aghast. "*Now?*"

"As opposed to when?"

Hyacinth had no good answer for that. "Very well," she said, with as much patience as she could muster. She forced herself to set the diary down beside her, and she picked up *Miss Butterworth and the Mad Baron* in its stead.

"Ahem." She cleared her throat, turning to the first page of chapter Eighteen. "Ahem."

"Throat bothering you?" Lady Danbury asked. "I still have some tea in the pot."

"It's nothing," Hyacinth said. She exhaled, looked down, and read, with decidedly less animation than was usual, "*The baron was in possession of a secret. Priscilla was quite certain of that. The only question was—would the truth ever be revealed?*"

"Indeed," Hyacinth muttered.

"Enh?"

"I think something important is about to happen," Hyacinth said with a sigh.

"Something important is always about to happen, my dear girl," Lady Danbury said. "And if not, you'd do well to act as if it were. You'll enjoy life better that way."

For Lady Danbury, the comment was uncharacteristically philosophical. Hyacinth paused, considering her words.

"I have no patience with this current fashion for *ennui*," Lady Danbury continued, reaching for her cane and thumping it against the floor. "Ha. When did it become a crime to show an interest in things?"

"I beg your pardon?"

"Just read the book," Lady D said. "I think we're getting to the good part. Finally."

Hyacinth nodded. The problem was, she was getting to the good part of the *other* book. She took a breath, trying to return her attention to *Miss Butterworth*, but the words swam before her eyes. Finally, she looked up at Lady Danbury and said, "I'm sorry, but would you mind terribly if I cut our visit short? I'm not feeling quite the thing."

Lady Danbury stared at her as if she'd just announced that she was carrying Napoleon's love child.

"I would be happy to make it up to you tomorrow," Hyacinth quickly added.

Lady D blinked. "But it's Tuesday."

"I realize that. I—" Hyacinth sighed. "You *are* a creature of habit, aren't you?"

"The hallmark of civilization is routine."

"Yes, I understand, but—"

"But the sign of a truly advanced mind," Lady D cut in, "is the ability to adapt to changing circumstances."

Hyacinth's mouth fell open. Never in her wildest dreams would she have imagined Lady Danbury uttering *that.*

"Go on, dear child," Lady D said, shooing her toward the door. "Do whatever it is that has you so intrigued."

For a moment Hyacinth could do nothing but stare at her. And then, suffused with a feeling that was as lovely as it was warm, she gathered her things, rose to her feet, and crossed the room to Lady Danbury's side.

"You're going to be my grandmother," she said, leaning down and giving her a kiss on the cheek. She'd never assumed such familiarity before, but somehow it felt right.

"You silly child," Lady Danbury said, brushing at her eyes as Hyacinth walked to the door. "In my heart, I've been your grandmother for years. I've just been waiting for you to make it official."

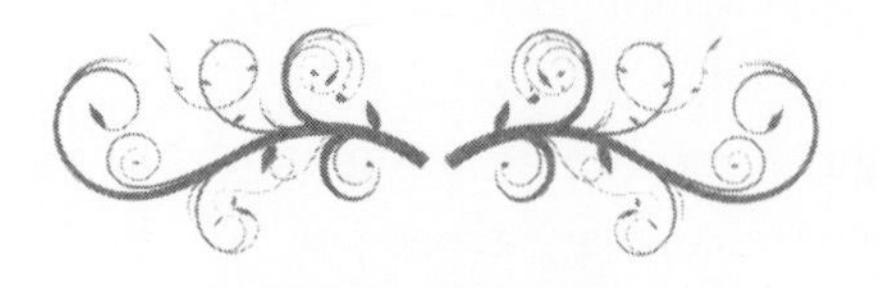

Chapter 20

Later that night. Quite a bit later, actually. Hyacinth's attempts at translation had to be postponed for a lengthy family dinner, followed by an interminable game of charades. Finally, at half eleven, she found the information she was seeking.

Excitement proved stronger than caution . . .

Another ten minutes and Gareth would not have been there to hear the knock. He had pulled on his jumper, a rough, woolen thing that his grandmother would have called dreadfully uncouth but which had the advantage of being black as night. He was just sitting on his sofa to don his most quietly soled boots when he heard it.

A knock. Soft but adamant.

A glance at the clock told him it was almost midnight. Phelps had long since gone to bed, so Gareth went to the door himself, positioning himself near the heavy wood with a, "Yes?"

"It is I," came the insistent reply.

What? No, it couldn't be . . .

He yanked the door open.

"What are you doing here?" he hissed, pulling Hyacinth into the room. She went flying by him, stumbling into a chair as he let go to peer out into the hall. "Didn't you bring someone with you?"

She shook her head. "No time to—"

"Are you mad?" he whispered furiously. "Have you gone stark, raving insane?" He'd thought he'd been angry with her last time she'd done this, running through London on her own after dark. But at least then she'd had some sort of an excuse, having been surprised by his father. This time—*This* time—

He could barely control himself. "I'm going to have to lock you up," he said, more to himself than to her. "That is it. That is the only solution. I am going to have to hold you down and—"

"If you'll just lis—"

"Get in here," he bit off, grabbing her by the arm and pulling her into his bedroom. It was the farthest from Phelps's small quarters off the drawing room. The valet usually slept like the dead, but with Gareth's luck, this would be the night he decided to awaken for a midnight snack.

"Gareth," Hyacinth whispered, scurrying behind him, "I have to tell you—"

He turned on her with furious eyes. "I don't want to hear anything from you that doesn't start with 'I'm a damned fool.' "

She crossed her arms. "Well, I'm certainly not going to say *that*."

He flexed and bent his fingers, the carefully controlled movement the only thing that was keeping him from lunging at her. The world was turning a dangerous shade of red, and all he could think of was the image of her racing across Mayfair, by herself, only to be attacked, mauled—

"I'm going to kill you," he ground out.

Hell, if anyone was going to attack or maul her, it might as well be him.

But she was just shaking her head, not listening to anything he was saying. "Gareth, I have to—"

"No," he said forcefully. "Not a word. Don't say a word. Just sit there—" He blinked, realizing that she was standing, then pointed at the bed. "Sit there," he said, "*quietly* until I figure out what the hell to do with you."

She sat, and for once she didn't look as if she was going to open her mouth to speak. In fact, she looked somewhat smug.

Which made him instantly suspicious. He had no idea how she had figured out that he had chosen that night to return to Clair House for one last search for the jewels. He must have let something slip, alluded to the trip during one of their recent conversations. He would have liked to think that he was more careful than that, but Hyacinth was fiendishly clever, and if anyone could have deduced his intentions, it would be her.

It was a damn fool endeavor in his opinion; he didn't have a clue where the diamonds might be save for Hyacinth's theory about the baroness's bedchamber. But he had promised her he would go, and he must have had a more finely tuned sense of honor than he had thought, because here he was, heading out to Clair House for the third time that month.

He glared at her.

She smiled serenely.

Sending him right over the edge. That was *it*. That was absolutely—

"All right," he said, his voice so low it was almost shaking. "We are going to lay out some rules, right here and right now."

Her spine stiffened. "I beg your pardon."

"When we are married, you will not exit the house without my permission—"

"*Ever?*" she cut in.

"Until you have proven yourself to be a responsible adult," he finished, barely recognizing himself in his own words. But if this was what it took to keep the bloody little fool safe from herself, then so be it.

She let out an impatient breath. "When did you grow so pompous?"

"When I fell in love with you!" he practically roared. Or he would have, if they hadn't been in the middle of a building of apartments, all inhabited by single men who stayed up late and liked to gossip.

"You . . . You . . . You what?"

Her mouth fell open into a fetching little oval, but Gareth was too far gone to appreciate the effect. "I love you, you idiot woman," he said, his arms jerking and flailing like a madman's. It was astonishing, what she had reduced him to. He couldn't remember the last time he'd lost his temper like this, the last time someone had made him so angry that he could barely speak.

Except for her, of course.

He ground his teeth together. "You are the most maddening, frustrating—"

"But—"

"And you *never* know when to stop talking, but God help me, I love you, anyway,—

"But, Gareth—"

"And if I have to tie you to the damned bed just to keep you safe from yourself, as God is my witness, that is what I'll do."

"But Gareth—"

"Not a word. Not a single bloody word," he said, wagging his finger toward her in an extremely impolite manner. Finally, his hand seemed to freeze, his index finger stuck into a point, and after a few jerky motions, he managed to still himself and drag his hands to his hips.

She was staring at him, her blue eyes large and filled with wonder. Gareth couldn't tear his gaze away as she slowly rose to her feet and closed the distance between them.

"You love me?" she whispered.

"It will be the death of me, I'm sure, but yes." He sighed wearily, exhausted simply by the prospect of it all. "I can't seem to help myself."

"Oh." Her lips quivered, then wobbled, and then somehow she was smiling. "Good."

"Good?" he echoed. "That's all you have to say?"

She stepped forward, touched his cheek. "I love you, too. With all my heart, with everything I am, and everything—"

He'd never know what she'd been about to say. It was lost beneath his kiss.

"Gareth," she gasped, during the bare moment when he paused for breath.

"Not now," he said, his mouth taking hers again. He couldn't stop. He'd told her, and now he had to show her.

He loved her. It was as simple as that.

"But Gareth—"

"Shhh . . ." He held her head in his hands, and he kissed her and kissed her . . . until he made the mistake of freeing her mouth by moving to her throat.

"Gareth, I have to tell you—"

"Not now," he murmured. He had other things in mind.

"But it's very important, and—"

He dragged himself away. "Good God, woman," he grunted. "What *is* it?"

"You have to listen to me," she said, and he felt somewhat vindicated that her breathing was every bit as labored as his. "I know it was mad to come here so late."

"By yourself," he saw fit to add.

"By myself," she granted him, her lips twisting peevishly. "But I swear to you, I wouldn't have done something this foolish if I hadn't needed to speak with you right away."

His mouth tilted wryly. "A note wouldn't have done?"

She shook her head. "Gareth," she said, and her face was so serious it took his breath away, "I know who your father is."

It was as if the floor were slipping away, and yet at the same time, he could not tear his eyes off of hers. He clutched her shoulders, his fingers surely digging too hard into her skin, but he couldn't move. For years to come, if anyone had asked him about that moment, he would have said that she was the only thing holding him upright.

"Who is it?" he asked, almost dreading her reply. His entire adult life he'd wanted this answer, and now that it was here, he could feel nothing but terror.

"It was your father's brother," Hyacinth whispered.

It was as if something had slammed into his chest. "Uncle Edward?"

"Yes," Hyacinth said, her eyes searching his face with a mix of love and concern. "It was in your grandmother's diary. She didn't know at first. No one did. They only knew it couldn't be your fath—er, the baron. He was in London all spring and summer. And your mother . . . wasn't."

"How did she find out?" he whispered. "And was she certain?"

"Isabella figured it out after you were born," Hyacinth said softly. "She said you looked too much like a St. Clair to be a bastard, and Edward had been in residence at Clair House. When your father was gone."

Gareth shook his head, desperately trying to comprehend this. "Did he know?"

"Your father? Or your uncle?"

"My—" He turned, a strange, humorless sound emerging from his throat. "I don't know what to call him. Either of them."

"Your father—Lord St. Clair," she corrected. "He didn't know. Or at least, Isabella didn't think he did. He didn't know that Edward had been at Clair Hall that summer. He was just out of Oxford, and—well, I'm not exactly certain what transpired, but it sounded like he was supposed to go to Scotland with friends. But then he didn't, and so he went to Clair Hall instead. Your grandmother said—" Hyacinth stopped, and her face took on a wide-eyed expression. "Your grandmother," she murmured. "She really *was* your grandmother."

He felt her hand on his shoulder, imploring him to turn, but somehow he couldn't look at her just then. It was too much. It was all too much.

"Gareth, Isabella *was* your grandmother. She really was."

He closed his eyes, trying to recall Isabella's face. It was hard to do; the memory was so old.

But she had loved him. He remembered that. She had loved him.

And she had known the truth.

Would she have told him? If she had lived to see him an adult, to know the man he had become, would she have told him the truth?

He could never know, but maybe . . . If she had seen how the baron had treated him . . . what they had both become . . .

He liked to think yes.

"Your uncle—" came Hyacinth's voice.

"He knew," Gareth said with low certitude.

"He did? How do you know? Did he say something?"

Gareth shook his head. He didn't know how he knew that Edward had been aware of the truth, but he was certain now that he had. Gareth had been eight when he'd last seen his uncle. Old enough to remember things. Old enough to realize what was important.

And Edward had loved him. Edward had loved him in a way that the baron never had. It was Edward who had taught him to ride, Edward who had given him the gift of a puppy on his seventh birthday.

Edward, who'd known the family well enough to know that the truth would destroy them all. Richard would never forgive Anne for siring a son who was not his, but if he had ever learned that her lover had been his own *brother* . . .

Gareth felt himself sink against the wall, needing support beyond his own two legs. Maybe it was a blessing that it had taken this long for the truth to be revealed.

"Gareth?"

Hyacinth was whispering his name, and he felt her come up next to him, her hand slipping into his with a soft gentleness that made his heart ache.

He didn't know what to think. He didn't know whether he should be angry or relieved. He really was a St. Clair, but after so many years of thinking himself an impostor, it was hard to grasp. And given the behavior of the baron, was that even anything of which to be proud?

He'd lost so much, spent so much time wondering who he was, where he'd come from, and—

"Gareth."

Her voice again, soft, whispering.

She squeezed his hand.

And then suddenly—

He knew.

Not that it didn't all matter, because it did.

But he knew that it didn't matter as much as she did, that the past wasn't as important as the future, and the family he'd lost wasn't nearly as dear to him as the family he would make.

"I love you," he said, his voice finally rising above a whisper. He turned, his heart, his very soul in his eyes. "I love you."

She looked confused by his sudden change in demeanor, but in the end she just smiled—looking for all the world as if she might actually laugh. It was the sort of expression one made when one had too much happiness to keep it all inside.

He wanted to make her look like that every day. Every hour. Every minute.

"I love you, too," she said.

He took her face in his hands and kissed her, once, deeply, on the mouth. "I mean," he said, "I *really* love you."

She quirked a brow. "Is this a contest?"

"It is anything you want," he promised.

She grinned, that enchanting, perfect smile that was so quintessentially hers. "I feel I must warn you, then," she said, cocking her head to the side. "When it comes to contests and games, I always win."

"Always?"

Her eyes grew sly. "Whenever it matters."

He felt himself smile, felt his soul lighten and his worries slip away. "And what, precisely, does that mean?"

"It means," she said, reaching up and undoing the buttons of her coat, "that I really *really* love you."

He backed up, crossing his arms as he gave her an assessing look. "Tell me more."

Her coat fell to the ground. "Is that enough?"

"Oh, not nearly."

She tried to look brazen, but her cheeks were starting to turn pink. "I will need help with the rest," she said, fluttering her lashes.

He was at her side in an instant. "I live to serve you."

"Is that so?" She sounded intrigued by the notion, so dangerously so that Gareth felt compelled to add, "In the bedroom." His fingers found the twin ribbons at her shoulders, and he gave them a tug, causing the bodice of her dress to loosen dangerously.

"More help, milady?" he murmured.

She nodded.

"Perhaps . . ." He looped his fingers around the neckline, preparing to ease it down, but she placed one hand over his. He looked up. She was shaking her head.

"No," she said. "You."

It took him a moment to grasp her meaning, and then a slow smile spread across his face. "But of course, milady," he said, pulling his jumper back over his head. "Anything you say."

"Anything?"

"Right now," he said silkily, "anything."

She smiled. "The buttons."

He moved to the fastenings on his shirt. "As you wish." And in a moment his shirt was on the floor, leaving him naked from the waist up.

He brought his sultry gaze to her face. Her eyes were wide, and her lips parted. He could hear the raspy sound of her breath, in perfect time with the rise and fall of her chest.

She was aroused. Gloriously so, and it was all he could do not to drag her onto the bed then and there.

"Anything else?" he murmured.

Her lips moved, and her eyes flickered toward his breeches. She was too shy, he realized with delight, still too much of an innocent to order him to remove them.

"This?" he asked, hooking his thumb under the waistband.

She nodded.

He peeled off his breeches, his gaze never leaving her face. And he smiled—at the exact moment when her eyes widened.

She wanted to be a sophisticate, but she wasn't. Not yet.

"You're overdressed," he said softly, moving closer, closer, until his face was mere inches from hers. He placed two fingers under her chin and tipped her up, leaning down for a kiss as his other hand found the neckline of her dress and tugged it down.

She fell free, and he moved his hand to the warm skin of her back, pressing her against him until her breasts flattened against his chest. His fingers lightly traced the delicate indentation of her spine, settling at the small of her back, right where her dress rested loosely around her hips.

"I love you," he said, allowing his nose to settle against hers.

"I love you, too."

"I'm so glad," he said, smiling against her ear. "Because if you didn't, this would all be so very awkward."

She laughed, but there was a slightly hesitant quality to it. "Are you saying," she asked, "that all your other women loved you?"

He drew back, taking her face in his hands. "What I am saying," he said, making sure that she was looking deeply into his eyes as he found the words, "is that I never loved them. And I don't know that I could bear it, loving you the way I do, if you didn't return the feeling."

Hyacinth watched his face, losing herself in the deep blue of his eyes. She touched his forehead, then his hair, smoothing one golden lock aside before affectionately tucking it behind his ear.

Part of her wanted to stand like this forever, just looking at his face, memorizing every plane and shadow, from the full curve of his lower lip to the exact arch of his brows. She was going to make her life with this man, give him her love and bear him children, and she was filled with the most wonderful sense of anticipation, as if she were standing at the edge of something, about to embark on a spectacular adventure.

And it all started now.

She tilted her head, leaned in, and raised herself to her toes, just so she could place one kiss on his lips.

"I love you," she said.

"You do, don't you?" he murmured, and she realized that he was just as amazed by this miracle as she was.

"Sometimes I'm going to drive you mad," she warned.

His smile was as lopsided as his shrug. "I'll go to my club."

"And you'll do the same to me," she added.

"You can have tea with your mother." One of his hands found hers as the other moved around her waist, until they were held together almost as in a waltz. "And we'll have the most marvelous time later that night, kissing and begging each other's forgiveness."

"Gareth," she said, wondering if this ought to be a more serious conversation.

"No one said we had to spend every waking moment together," he said, "but at the end of the day"—he leaned down and kissed each of her eyebrows, in turn—"and most of the time during, there is no one I would rather see, no one whose voice I would rather hear, and no one whose mind I would rather explore."

He kissed her then. Once, slowly and deeply. "I love you, Hyacinth Bridgerton. And I always will."

"Oh, Gareth." She would have liked to have said something more eloquent, but his words would have to be enough for the both of them, because in that moment she was overcome, too full of emotion to do anything more than sigh his name.

And when he scooped her into his arms and carried her to his bed, all she could do was say "Yes."

Her dress fell away before she reached the mattress, and by the time his body covered hers, they were skin against skin. There was something thrilling about being beneath him, feeling his power, his strength. He could dominate her if he so chose, hurt her even, and yet in his arms she became the most priceless of treasures.

His hands roamed her body, searing a path across her skin. Hyacinth felt every touch to the core of her being. He stroked her arm, and she felt it in her belly; he touched her shoulder, and she tingled in her toes.

He kissed her lips, and her heart sang.

He nudged her legs apart, and his body cradled itself next to hers. She could feel him, hard and insistent, but this time there was no fear, no apprehension. Just an overwhelming need to have him, to take him within her and wrap herself around him.

She wanted him. She wanted every inch of him, every bit of himself that he was able to give.

"Please," she begged, straining her hips toward his. "Please."

He didn't say anything, but she could hear his need in the roughness of his breath. He moved closer, positioning himself near her opening, and she arched herself closer to meet him.

She clutched at his shoulders, her fingers biting into his skin. There was something wild within her, something new and hungry. She needed him. She needed this. Now.

"Gareth," she gasped, desperately trying to press herself against him.

He moved a little, changing the angle, and he began to slide in.

It was what she wanted, what she'd expected, but still, the first touch of him was a shock. She stretched, she pulled, and there was even a little bit of pain, but still, it felt good, and it felt right, and she wanted more.

"Hy . . . Hy . . . Hy . . ." he was saying, his breath coming in harsh little bursts as he moved forward, each thrust filling her more completely. And then, finally, he was there, pressed so fully within her that his body met hers.

"Oh my God," she gasped, her head thrown back by the force of it all.

He moved, forward and back, the friction whipping her into insensibility. She reached, she clawed, she grasped—anything to bring him closer, anything to reach the tipping point.

She knew where she was going this time.

"Gareth!" she cried out, the noise captured by his mouth as he swooped in for a kiss.

Something within her began to tighten and coil, twisting and tensing until she was certain she'd shatter. And then, just when she couldn't possibly bear it for one second longer, it all reached its peak, and something burst within her, something amazing and true.

And as she arched, as her body threatened to shatter with the force of it, she felt Gareth grow frenzied and wild, and he buried his face in her neck as he let out a primal shout, pouring himself into her.

For a minute, maybe two, all they could do was breathe. And then, finally, Gareth rolled off of her, still holding her close as he settled onto his side.

"Oh, my," she said, because it seemed to sum up everything she was feeling. "Oh, my."

"When are we getting married?" he asked, pulling her gently until they were curved like two spoons.

"Six weeks."

"Two," he said. "Whatever you have to tell your mother, I don't care. Get it changed to two, or I'll haul you off to Gretna."

Hyacinth nodded, snuggling herself against him, reveling in the feel of him behind her. "Two," she said, the word practically a sigh. "Maybe even just one."

"Even better," he agreed.

They lay together for several minutes, enjoying the silence, and then Hyacinth twisted in his arms, craning her neck so that she could see his face. "Were you going out to Clair House this evening?"

"You didn't know?"

She shook her head. "I didn't think you were going to go again."

"I promised you I would."

"Well, yes," she said, "but I thought you were lying, just to be nice."

Gareth swore under his breath. "You are going to be the death of me. I can't believe you didn't really mean for me to go."

"Of course I meant for you to go," she said. "I just didn't think you would." And then she sat up, so suddenly that the bed shook. Her eyes widened, and they took on a dangerous glow and sparkle. "Let's go. Tonight."

Easy answer. "No."

"Oh, please. Please. As a wedding gift to me."

"No," he said.

"I understand your reluctance—"

"No," he repeated, trying to ignore the sinking feeling in his stomach. The sinking feeling that he was going to relent. "No, I don't think you do."

"But really," she said, her eyes bright and convincing, "what do we have to lose? We're getting married in two weeks—"

He lifted one brow.

"Next week," she corrected. "Next week, I promise."

He pondered that. It *was* tempting.

"Please," she said. "You know you want to."

"Why," he wondered aloud, "do I feel like I am back at university, with the most degenerate of my friends convincing me that I must drink three more glasses of gin?"

"Why would you wish to be friends with a degenerate?" she asked. Then she smiled with wicked curiosity. "And did you do it?"

Gareth pondered the wisdom of answering that; truly, he didn't wish for her to know the worst of his schoolboy excesses. But it would get her off the topic of the jewels, and—

"Let's go," she urged again. "*I* know you want to."

"I know what I want to do," he murmured, curving one hand around her bottom, "and it is not that."

"Don't you want the jewels?" she prodded.

He started to stroke her. "Mmm-hmmm."

"Gareth!" she yelped, trying to squirm away.

"Gareth yes, or Gareth—"

"No," she said firmly, somehow eluding him and wriggling to the other side of the bed. "Gareth, *no.* Not until we go to Clair House to look for the jewels."

"Good Lord," he muttered. "It's *Lysistrata*, come home to me in human form."

She tossed a triumphant smile over her shoulder as she pulled on her clothing.

He rose to his feet, knowing he was defeated. And besides, she did have a point. His main worry had been for her reputation; as long as she remained by his side, he was fully confident of his ability to keep her safe. If they were indeed going to marry in a week or two, their antics, if caught, would be brushed aside with a wink and a leer. But still, he felt like he ought to offer up at least a token of resistance, so he said, "Aren't you supposed to be tired after all this bedplay?"

"Positively energized."

He let out a weary breath. "This is the last time," he said sternly.

Her reply was immediate. "I promise."

He pulled on his clothing. "I mean it. If we do not find the jewels tonight, we don't go again until I inherit. Then you may tear the place apart, stone by stone if you like."

"It won't be necessary," she said. "We're going to find them tonight. I can feel it in my bones."

Gareth thought of several retorts, none of which was fit for her ears.

She looked down at herself with a rueful expression. "I'm not really dressed for it," she said, fingering the folds of her skirt. The fabric was dark, but it was not the boy's breeches she'd donned on their last two expeditions.

He didn't even bother to suggest that they postpone their hunt. There was no point. Not when she was practically glowing with excitement.

And sure enough, she pointed one foot out from beneath the hem of her dress, saying, "But I am wearing my most comfortable footwear, and surely that is the most important thing."

"Surely."

She ignored his peevishness. "Are you ready?"

"As I'll ever be," he said with a patently false smile. But the truth was, she'd planted the seed of excitement within him, and he was already mapping his route in his mind. If he hadn't wanted to go, if he weren't convinced of his ability to keep her safe, he would have lashed her to the bed before allowing her to take one step out into the night.

He took her hand, lifted it to his mouth, kissed her. "Shall we be off?" he asked.

She nodded and tiptoed in front of him, out into the hall. "We're going to find them," she said softly. "I know we will."

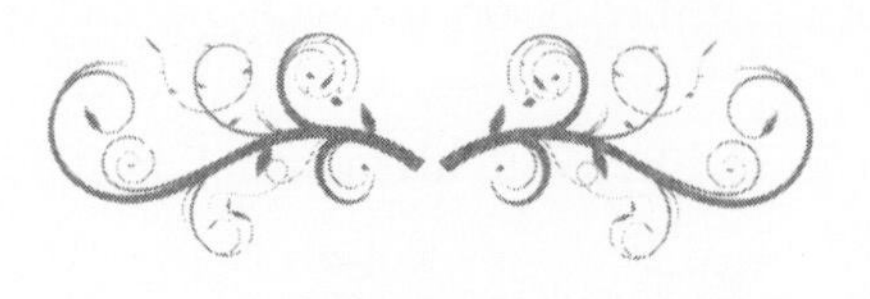

Chapter 21

One half hour later.

"We're not going to find them."

Hyacinth had her hands planted on her hips as she surveyed the baroness's bedchamber. They had spent fifteen minutes getting to Clair House, five sneaking in through the faulty window and creeping up to the bedchamber, and the last ten searching every last nook and corner.

The jewels were nowhere.

It was not like Hyacinth to admit defeat. In fact, it was so wholly out of character that the words, "We're not going to find them," had come out sounding more surprised than anything else.

It hadn't occurred to her that they might not find the jewels. She'd imagined the scene a hundred times in her head, she'd plotted and planned, she'd thought the entire scheme to death, and not once had she ever pictured herself coming up empty-handed.

She felt as if she'd slammed into a brick wall.

Maybe she had been foolishly optimistic. Maybe she had just been blind. But this time, she'd been wrong.

"Do you give up?" Gareth asked, looking up at her. He was crouching next to the bed, feeling for panels in the wall behind the headboard. And he sounded . . . not pleased, exactly, but rather somewhat *done*, if that made any sense.

He'd known that they weren't going to find anything. Or if he hadn't known it, he had been almost sure of it. And he'd come tonight mostly just to humor her. Hyacinth decided she loved him all the more for that.

But now, his expression, his aspect, everything in his voice seemed to say one thing—*We tried, we lost, can we please just move on*?

There was no satisfied smirk, no "I told you so," just a flat, matter-of-fact stare, with perhaps the barest hint of disappointment, as if a tiny corner of him had been hoping to be proven wrong.

"Hyacinth?" Gareth said, when she didn't reply.

"I . . . Well . . ." She didn't know what to say.

"We haven't much time," he cut in, his face taking on a steely expression. Clearly, her time for reflection was over. He rose to his feet, brushing his hands against each other to rid them of dust. The baroness's bedchamber had been shut off, and it didn't appear to be on a regular cleaning schedule. "Tonight is the baron's monthly meeting with his hound-breeding club."

"Hound-breeding?" Hyacinth echoed. "In London?"

"They meet on the last Tuesday of the month without fail," Gareth explained. "They have been doing it for years. To keep abreast of pertinent knowledge while they're in London."

"Does pertinent knowledge change very often?" Hyacinth asked. It was just the sort of random tidbit of information that always interested her.

"I have no idea," Gareth replied briskly. "It's probably just an excuse to get together and drink. The meetings always end at eleven, and then they spend about two hours in social discourse. Which means the baron will be home"—he pulled out his pocket watch and swore under his breath—"now."

Hyacinth nodded glumly. "I give up," she said. "I don't think I've ever uttered those words while not under duress, but I give up."

Gareth chucked her softly under her chin. "It's not the end of the world, Hy. And just think, you may resume your mission once the baron finally kicks off, and I inherit the house. Which," he added thoughtfully, "I actually have some right to." He shook his head. "Imagine that."

"Do you think Isabella meant for anyone to find them?" she asked.

"I don't know," Gareth replied. "One would think that if she had, she might have chosen a more accessible language for her final hint than Slovene."

"We should go," Hyacinth said, sighing. "I need to return home in any case. If I'm to pester my mother for a change in the wedding date, I want to do it now, while she's sleepy and easy to sway."

Gareth looked at her over his shoulder as he placed his hand on the doorknob. "You *are* diabolical."

"You didn't believe it before?"

He smiled, then gave her a nod when it was safe to creep out into the hall. Together they moved down the stairs to the drawing room with the faulty window. Swiftly and silently, they slipped outside and hopped down to the alley below.

Gareth walked in front, stopping at the alley's end and stretching one arm behind him to keep Hyacinth at a distance while he peered out onto Dover Street.

"Let's go," he whispered, jerking his head toward the street. They had come over in a hansom cab—Gareth's apartments were not quite close enough to walk—and they'd left it waiting two intersections away. It wasn't really necessary to ride back to Hyacinth's house, which was just on the other side of Mayfair, but Gareth had decided that as long as they had the cab, they might as well make use of it. There was a good spot where they could be let out, right around the corner from Number Five, that was set back in shadows and with very few windows looking out upon it.

"This way," Gareth said, taking Hyacinth's hand and tugging her along. "Come on, we can—"

He stopped, stumbled. Hyacinth had halted in her tracks.

"What is it?" he hissed, turning to look at her.

But she wasn't looking at him. Instead, her eyes were focused on something—someone—to the right.

The baron.

Gareth froze. Lord St. Clair—his father, his uncle, whatever he should call him—was standing at the top of the steps leading to Clair House. His key was in his hand, and he had obviously spotted them just as he was about to enter the building.

"This is interesting," the baron said. His eyes glittered.

Gareth felt his chest puff out, some sort of instinctive show of bravado as he pushed Hyacinth partly behind him. "Sir," he said. It was all he'd ever called the man, and some habits were hard to break.

"Imagine my curiosity," the baron murmured. "This is the second time I have run across you here in the middle of the night."

Gareth said nothing.

"And now"—Lord St. Clair motioned to Hyacinth—"you have brought your lovely betrothed with you. Unorthodox, I must say. Does her family know she is running about after midnight?"

"What do you want?" Gareth asked in a hard voice.

But the baron only chuckled. "I believe the more pertinent question is what do *you* want? Unless you intend to attempt to convince me that you are just here for the fresh night air."

Gareth stared at him, looking for signs of resemblance. They were all there—the nose, the eyes, the way they held their shoulders. It was why Gareth had never, until that fateful day in the baron's office, thought he might be a bastard. He'd been so baffled as a child; his father had treated him with such contempt. Once he'd grown old enough to understand a bit of what went on between men and women, he had wondered about it—his mother's infidelity would seem a likely explanation for his father's behavior toward him.

But he'd dismissed the notion every time. There was that damned St. Clair nose, right in the middle of his face. And then the baron had looked him in the eye and said that he was not his, that he couldn't be, that the nose was mere coincidence.

Gareth had believed him. The baron was many things, but he was not stupid, and he certainly knew how to count to nine.

Neither of them had dreamed that the nose might be something more than coincidence, that Gareth might be a St. Clair, after all.

He tried to remember—had the baron loved his brother? Had Richard and Edward St. Clair been close? Gareth couldn't recall them in each other's company, but then again, he'd been banished to the nursery most of the time, anyway.

"Well?" the baron demanded. "What do you have to say for yourself?"

And there it was, on the tip of his tongue. Gareth looked him in the eye—the man who had, for so many years, been the ruling force in his life—and he almost said—*Nothing at all, Uncle Richard.*

It would have been the best kind of direct hit, a complete surprise, designed to stagger and strike.

It would have been worth it just for the shock on the baron's face.

It would have been perfect.

Except that Gareth didn't want to do it. He didn't need to.

And *that* took his breath away.

Before, he would have tried to guess how his father might feel. Would he be relieved to know that the barony would go to a true St. Clair, or would he instead be enraged, devastated by the knowledge that he had been cuckolded by his own brother?

Before, Gareth would have weighed his options, balanced them, then gone with his instincts and tried to deliver the most crushing blow.

But now . . .

He didn't care.

He would never love the man. Hell, he would never even like him. But for the first time in his life, he was reaching a point where it just didn't matter.

And he was stunned by how good that felt.

He took Hyacinth's hand, interlocked their fingers. "We're just out for a stroll," he said smoothly. It was a patently ridiculous statement, but Gareth delivered it with his usual *savoir-faire*, in the same tone that he always used with the baron. "Come along, Miss Bridgerton," he added, turning his body to lead her down the street.

But Hyacinth didn't move. Gareth turned to look at her, and she seemed frozen into place. She looked at him with questioning eyes, and he knew she couldn't believe that he'd held silent.

Gareth looked at her, then he looked at Lord St. Clair, and then he looked within himself. And he realized that while his never-ending war with the baron might not matter, the truth did. Not because it had the power to wound, just because it was the truth, and it had to be told.

It was the secret that had defined both of their lives for so long. And it was time that they were both set free.

"I have to tell you something," Gareth said, looking the baron in the eye. It wasn't easy, being this direct. He had no experience speaking to this man without malice. He felt strange, stripped bare.

Lord St. Clair said nothing, but his expression changed slightly, became more watchful.

"I am in possession of Grandmother St. Clair's diary," Gareth said. At the baron's startled expression, he added, "Caroline found it among George's effects with a note instructing her to give it to me."

"He did not know that you are not her grandson," the baron said sharply.

Gareth opened his mouth to retort, "*But I was*," but he managed to bite off the comment. He would do this right. He had to do this right. Hyacinth was at his side, and suddenly his angry ways seemed callow, immature. He didn't want her to see him like that. He didn't want to *be* like that.

"Miss Bridgerton has some knowledge of Italian," Gareth continued, keeping his voice even. "She has assisted me in its translation."

The baron looked at Hyacinth, his piercing eyes studying her for a moment before turning back to Gareth.

"Isabella knew who my father was," Gareth said softly. "It was Uncle Edward."

The baron said nothing, not a word. Except for the slight parting of his lips, he was so still that Gareth wondered if he was even breathing.

Had he known? Had he suspected?

As Gareth and Hyacinth stood in silence, the baron turned and looked down the street, his eyes settling on some far-off point. When he turned back, he was as white as a sheet.

He cleared his throat and nodded. Just once, as an acknowledgment. "You should marry that girl," he said, motioning with his head toward Hyacinth. "The Lord knows you're going to need her dowry."

And then he walked up the rest of the steps, let himself into his home, and shut the door.

"That's *all*?" Hyacinth said, after a moment of just standing there with her mouth agape. "That's all he's going to *say*?"

Gareth felt himself begin to shake. It was laughter, he realized, almost as an aside. He was laughing.

"He can't do that," Hyacinth protested, her eyes flashing with indignation. "You just revealed the biggest secret of both of your lives, and all he does is—are you *laughing*?"

Gareth shook his head, even though it was clear that he was.

"What's so funny?" Hyacinth asked suspiciously.

And her expression was so . . . *her*. It made him laugh even harder.

"What's so funny?" she asked again, except this time she looked as if she might smile, too. "*Gareth*," she persisted, tugging on his sleeve. "Tell me."

He shrugged helplessly. "I'm happy," he said, and he realized it was true. He'd enjoyed himself in his life, and he'd certainly had many happy moments, but it had been so long since he'd felt this—happiness, complete and whole. He'd almost forgotten the sensation.

She placed her hand abruptly on his brow. "Are you feverish?" she muttered.

"I'm fine." He pulled her into his arms. "I'm better than fine."

"Gareth!" she gasped, ducking away as he swooped down for a kiss. "Are you mad? We're in the middle of Dover Street, and it's—"

He cut her off with a kiss.

"It's the middle of the night," she spluttered.

He grinned devilishly. "But I'm going to marry you next week, remember?"

"Yes, but—"

"Speaking of which," he murmured.

Hyacinth's mouth fell open as he dropped down to one knee. "What are you doing?" she squeaked, frantically looking this way and that. Lord St. Clair was surely peeking out at them, and heaven only knew who else was, too. "Someone will see," she whispered.

He seemed unconcerned. "People will say we're in love."

"I—" Good heavens, but how did a woman argue against that?

"Hyacinth Bridgerton," he said, taking her hand in his, "will you marry me?"

She blinked in confusion. "I already said I would."

"Yes, but as you said, I did not ask you for the right reasons. They were mostly the right reasons, but not all."

"I—I—" She was stumbling on the words, choking on the emotion.

He was staring up at her, his eyes glowing clear and blue in the dim light of the streetlamps. "I am asking you to marry me because I love you," he said, "because I cannot imagine living my life without you. I want to see your face in the morning, and then at night, and a hundred times in between. I want to grow old with you, I want to laugh with you, and I want to sigh to my friends about how managing you are, all the while secretly knowing I am the luckiest man in town."

"What?" she demanded.

He shrugged. "A man's got to keep up appearances. I'll be universally detested if everyone realizes how perfect you are."

"Oh." Again, how could a woman argue with *that*?

And then his eyes grew serious. "I want you to be my family. I want you to be my wife."

She stared down at him. He was gazing at her with such obvious love and devotion, she hardly knew what to do. It seemed to surround her, embrace her, and she knew that *this* was poetry, this was music.

This was love.

He smiled up at her, and all she could do was smile back, dimly aware that her cheeks were growing wet.

"Hyacinth," he said. "Hyacinth."

And she nodded. Or at least she thought she did.

He squeezed her hands as he rose to his feet. "I never thought I'd have to say this to you, of all people, but for God's sake, *say* something, woman!"

"Yes," she said. And she threw herself into his arms. "Yes!"

Epilogue

A few moments to bring us up to date . . .

Four days after the end of our tale, Gareth called upon Lord Wrotham, only to find that the earl in no way felt the betrothal was binding, especially after he related Lady Bridgerton's promise to take one of the younger Wrotham daughters under her wing the following season.

Four days after that, Gareth was informed by Lady Bridgerton, in no uncertain manner, that her youngest child would not be married in haste, and he was forced to wait two months before wedding Hyacinth in an elaborate yet tasteful ceremony at St. George's, in London.

Eleven months after that, Hyacinth gave birth to a healthy baby boy, christened George.

Two years after that, they were blessed with a daughter, christened Isabella.

Four years after that, Lord St. Clair was thrown from his horse during a fox hunt and instantly killed. Gareth assumed the title, and he and Hyacinth moved to their new town residence at Clair House.

That was six years ago. She has been looking for the jewels ever since . . .

"Haven't you already searched this room?"

Hyacinth looked up from her position on the floor of the baroness's washroom. Gareth was standing in the doorway, gazing down at her with an indulgent expression.

"Not for at least a month," she replied, testing the baseboards for loose sections—as if she hadn't yanked and prodded them countless times before.

"Darling," Gareth said, and she knew from his tone what he was thinking.

She gave him a pointed look. "Don't."

"Darling," he said again.

"No." She turned back to the baseboards. "I don't want to hear it. If it takes until the day I die, I will find these bloody jewels."

"Hyacinth."

She ignored him, pressing along the seam where the baseboard met the floor.

Gareth watched her for several seconds before remarking, "I'm quite certain you've done that before."

She spared him only the briefest of glances before rising to inspect the window frame.

"Hyacinth," he said.

She turned so suddenly that she almost lost her balance. "The note said 'Cleanliness is next to Godliness, and the Kingdom of Heaven is rich indeed.'"

"In Slovene," he said wryly.

"Three Slovenians," she reminded him. "Three Slovenians read the clue, and they all reached the same translation."

And it certainly hadn't been easy to find three Slovenians.

"Hyacinth," Gareth said, as if he hadn't already uttered her name twice . . . and countless times before that, always in the same slightly resigned tone.

"It has to be here," she said. "It has to."

Gareth shrugged. "Very well," he said, "but Isabella has translated a passage from the Italian, and she wishes for you to check her work."

Hyacinth paused, sighed, then lifted her fingers from the windowsill. At the age of eight, her daughter had announced that she wished to learn the language of her namesake, and Hyacinth and Gareth had hired a tutor to offer instruction three mornings each week. Within a year, Isabella's fluency had outstripped her mother's, and Hyacinth was forced to employ the tutor for herself the other two mornings just to keep up.

"Why is it you've never studied Italian?" she asked, as Gareth led her through the bedroom and into the hallway.

"I've no head for languages," he said blithely, "and no need for it, with my two ladies at my side."

Hyacinth rolled her eyes. "I'm not going to tell you any more naughty words," she warned.

He chuckled. "Then I'm not going to slip Signorina Orsini any more pound notes with instructions to *teach* you the naughty words."

Hyacinth turned to him in horror. "You didn't!"

"I did."

Her lips pursed. "And you don't even look the least bit remorseful about it."

"Remorseful?" He chuckled, deep in his throat, and then leaned down to press his lips against her ear. There were a few words of Italian he bothered to commit to memory; he whispered every one of them to her.

"Gareth!" she squeaked.

"Gareth, yes? Or Gareth, no?"

She sighed. She couldn't help it. "Gareth, *more*."

Isabella St. Clair tapped her pencil against the side of her head as she regarded the words she'd recently written. It was a challenge, translating from one language to another. The literal meaning never read quite right, so one had to choose one's idioms with the utmost of care. But this—she glanced over at the open page in Galileo's *Discorso intorno alle cose che stanno, in sù l'acqua, ò che in quella si muovono*—this was perfect.

Perfect perfect perfect.

Her three favorite words.

She glanced toward the door, waiting for her mother to appear. Isabella loved translating scientific texts because her mother always seemed to stumble on the technical words, and it was, of course, always good fun to watch her mum pretend that she actually knew more Italian than her daughter.

Not that Isabella was mean-spirited. She pursed her lips, considering that. She wasn't mean-spirited; the only person she adored more than her mother was her great-grandmother Danbury, who, although confined to a wheeled chair, still managed to wield her cane with almost as much accuracy as her tongue.

Isabella smiled. When she grew up, she wanted to be first exactly like her mother, and then, when she was through with that, just like Great-Grandmama.

She sighed. It would be a marvelous life.

But what was *taking* so long? It had been ages since she'd sent her father down—and it should be added that she loved him with equal fervor; it was just that he was merely a man, and she couldn't very well aspire to grow to be *him*.

She grimaced. Her mother and father were probably giggling and whispering and ducking into a darkened corner. Good heavens. It was downright embarrassing.

Isabella stood, resigning herself to a long wait. She might as well use the washroom. Carefully setting her pencil down, she glanced one last time at the door and crossed the room to the nursery washroom. Tucked high in the eaves of the old mansion, it was, somewhat unexpectedly, her favorite room in the house. Someone in years gone past had obviously taken a liking to the little room, and it had been tiled rather festively in what she could only assume was some sort of Eastern fashion. There were lovely blues and shimmering aquas and yellows that were streaks of pure sunshine.

If it had been big enough for Isabella to drag in a bed and call it her chamber, she would have done. As it was, she thought it was particularly amusing that the loveliest room in the house (in her opinion, at least) was the most humble.

The nursery washroom? Only the servants' quarters were considered of less prestige.

Isabella did her business, tucked the chamber pot back in the corner, and headed back for the door. But before she got there, something caught her eye.

A crack. Between two of the tiles.

"That wasn't there before," Isabella murmured.

She crouched, then finally lowered herself to her bottom so that she could inspect the crack, which ran from the floor to the top of the first tile, about six inches up. It wasn't the sort of thing most people would notice, but Isabella was not most people. She noticed everything.

And this was something new.

Frustrated with her inability to get really close, she shifted to her forearms and knees, then laid her cheek against the floor.

"Hmmm." She poked the tile to the right of the crack, then the left. "Hmmm."

Why would a crack suddenly open up in her bathroom wall? Surely Clair House, which was well over a hundred years old, was done with its shifting and settling. And while she'd heard that there were far distant areas where the earth shifted and shook, it didn't happen anyplace as civilized as *London.*

Had she kicked the wall without thinking? Dropped something?

She poked again. And again.

She drew back her arm, preparing to pound a little harder, but then stopped. Her mother's bathroom was directly below. If she made a terrible racket, Mummy was sure to come up and demand to know what she was doing. And although she'd sent her father down to retrieve her mother eons earlier, it was quite a good bet that Mummy was still in her washroom.

And when Mummy went into her washroom—Well, either she was out in a minute, or she was there for an hour. It was the strangest thing.

So Isabella did not want to make a lot of noise. Surely her parents would frown upon her taking the house apart.

But perhaps a little tap . . .

She did a little nursery rhyme to decide which tile to attack, chose the one to the left, and hit it a little harder. Nothing happened.

She stuck her fingernail at the edge of the crack and dug it in. A tiny piece of plaster lodged under her nail.

"Hmmm." Perhaps she could extend the crack . . .

She glanced over at her vanity table until her eyes fell upon a silver comb. That might work. She grabbed it and carefully positioned the last tooth near the edge of the crack. And then, with precise movements, she drew it back and tapped it against the plaster that ran between the tiles.

The crack snaked upward! Right before her eyes!

She did it again, this time positioning her comb over the left tile. Nothing. She tried it over the right.

And then harder.

Isabella gasped as the crack literally shot through the plaster, until it ran all the way along the top of the tile. And then she did it a few more times until it ran down the other side.

With bated breath, she dug her nails in on either side of the tile and pulled. She shifted it back and forth, shimmying and jimmying, prying with all her might.

And then, with a creak and a groan that reminded her of the way her great-grandmother moved when she managed to hoist herself from her wheeled chair into her bed, the tile gave way.

Isabella set it down carefully, then peered at what was left. Where there should have been nothing but wall, there was a little compartment, just a few inches square. Isabella reached in, pinching her fingers together to make her hand long and skinny.

She felt something soft. Like velvet.

She pulled it out. It was a little bag, held together with a soft, silky cord.

Isabella straightened quickly, crossing her legs so that she was sitting Indian style. She slid one finger inside the bag, widening the mouth, which had been pulled tight.

And then, with her right hand, she upended it, sliding the contents into her left.

"*Oh my G—*"

Isabella quickly swallowed her shriek. A veritable pool of diamonds had showered into her hand.

It was a necklace. And a bracelet. And while she did not think of herself as the sort of girl who lost her mind over baubles and clothes, *OH MY GOD* these were the most beautiful things she had ever seen.

"Isabella?"

Her mother. Oh, no. Oh no oh no oh no.

"Isabella? Where are you?"

"In—" She stopped to clear her throat; her voice had come out like a squeak. "Just in the washroom, Mummy. I'll be out in a moment."

What should she do? What should she do?

Oh, very well, she knew what she should do. But what did she *want* to do?

"Is this your translation here on the table?" came her mother's voice.

"Er, yes!" She coughed. "It's from Galileo. The original is right next to it."

"Oh." Her mother paused. Her voice sounded funny. "Why did you—Never mind."

Isabella looked frantically at the jewels. She had only a moment to decide.

"Isabella!" her mother called. "Did you remember to do your sums this morning? You're starting dancing lessons this afternoon. Did you recall?"

Dancing lessons? Isabella's face twisted, rather as if she'd swallowed lye.

"Monsieur Larouche will be here at two. Promptly. So you will need . . ."

Isabella stared at the diamonds. Hard. So hard that her peripheral vision slipped away, and the noise around her faded into nothing. Gone were the sounds of the street, floating through the open window. Gone was her mother's voice, droning on about dancing lessons and the importance of punctuality. Gone was everything but the blood rushing past her ears and the quick, uneven sound of her own breath.

Isabella looked down at the diamonds.

And then she smiled.

And put them back.

Dear Reader,

Have you ever wondered what happened to your favorite characters after you closed the final page? Wanted just a little bit more of a favorite novel? I have, and if the questions from my readers are any indication, I'm not the only one. So after countless requests from Bridgerton fans, I decided to try something a little different, and I wrote a "2nd Epilogue" for each of the novels. These are the stories that come after *the stories.*

At first, the Bridgerton 2nd Epilogues were available exclusively online; later they were published (along with a novella about Violet Bridgerton) in a collection called The Bridgertons: Happily Ever After. *Now, for the first time, each 2nd Epilogue is being included with the novel it follows. I hope you enjoy Gareth and Hyacinth as they continue their journey.*

Warmly,
Julia Quinn

It's in His Kiss: The 2nd Epilogue

1847, and all has come full circle. Truly.

Hmmph.

It was official, then.

She had become her mother.

Hyacinth St. Clair fought the urge to bury her face in her hands as she sat on the cushioned bench at Mme. Langlois, Dressmaker, by far the most fashionable modiste in all London.

She counted to ten, in three languages, and then, just for good measure, swallowed and let out an exhale. Because, really, it would not do to lose her temper in such a public setting.

No matter how desperately she wanted to *throttle* her daughter.

"Mummy." Isabella poked her head out from behind the curtain. Hyacinth noted that the word had been a statement, not a question.

"Yes?" she returned, affixing onto her face an expression of such placid serenity she might have qualified for one of those pietà paintings they had seen when last they'd traveled to Rome.

"Not the pink."

Hyacinth waved a hand. Anything to refrain from speaking.

"Not the purple, either."

"I don't believe I suggested purple," Hyacinth murmured.

"The blue's not right, and nor is the red, and frankly, I just don't understand this insistence society seems to have upon white, and well, if I might express my opinion—"

Hyacinth felt herself slump. Who knew motherhood could be so tiring? And really, shouldn't she be *used* to this by now?

"—a girl really ought to wear the color that most complements her complexion, and not what some overimportant ninny at Almack's deems fashionable."

"I agree wholeheartedly," Hyacinth said.

"You do?" Isabella's face lit up, and Hyacinth's breath positively caught, because she looked so like her own mother in that moment it was almost eerie.

"Yes," Hyacinth said, "but you're still getting at least one in white."

"But—"

"No buts!"

"But—"

"Isabella."

Isabella muttered something in Italian.

"I heard that," Hyacinth said sharply.

Isabella smiled, a curve of lips so sweet that only her own mother (certainly *not* her father, who freely admitted himself wound around her finger) would recognize the deviousness underneath. "But did you understand it?" she asked, blinking three times in rapid succession.

And because Hyacinth knew that she would be trapped by her lie, she gritted her teeth and told the truth. "No."

"I didn't think so," Isabella said. "But if you're interested, what I said was—"

"Not—" Hyacinth stopped, forcing her voice to a lower volume; panic at what Isabella might say had caused her outburst to come out overly loud. She cleared her throat. "Not now. Not here," she added meaningfully. Good heavens, her daughter had no sense of propriety. She had such opinions, and while Hyacinth was always in favor of a female with opinions, she was even more in favor of a female who knew *when* to share such opinions.

Isabella stepped out of her dressing room, clad in a lovely gown of white with sage green trimming that Hyacinth knew she'd turn her nose up at, and sat beside her on the bench. "What are you whispering about?" she asked.

"I wasn't whispering," Hyacinth said.

"Your lips were moving."

"Were they?"

"They were," Isabella confirmed.

"If you must know, I was sending off an apology to your grandmother."

"Grandmama Violet?" Isabella asked, looking around. "Is she here?"

"No, but I thought she was deserving of my remorse, nonetheless."

Isabella blinked and cocked her head to the side in question. "Why?"

"All those times," Hyacinth said, hating how tired her voice sounded. "All those times she said to me, 'I hope you have a child *just like you . . .*'?"

"And you do," Isabella said, surprising her with a light kiss to the cheek. "Isn't it just delightful?"

Hyacinth looked at her daughter. Isabella was nineteen. She'd made her debut the year before, to grand success. She was, Hyacinth thought rather objectively, far prettier than she herself had ever been. Her hair was a breathtaking strawberry blond, a throwback to some long-forgotten ancestor on heaven knew which side of the family. And the curls—oh, my, they were the bane of Isabella's existence, but Hyacinth adored them. When Isabella had been a toddler, they'd bounced in perfect little ringlets, completely untamable and always delightful.

And now . . . Sometimes Hyacinth looked at her and saw the woman she'd become, and she couldn't even breathe, so powerful was the emotion squeezing across her chest. It was a love she couldn't have imagined, so fierce and so tender, and yet at the same time the girl drove her positively batty.

Right now, for example.

Isabella was smiling innocently at her. Too innocently, truth be told, and then she looked down at the slightly poufy skirt on the dress Hyacinth loved (and Isabella would hate) and picked absently at the green ribbon trimmings.

"Mummy?" she said.

It was a question this time, not a statement, which meant that Isabella wanted something, and (for a change) wasn't quite certain how to go about getting it.

"Do you think this year—"

"No," Hyacinth said. And this time she really did send up a silent apology to her mother. Good heavens, was this what Violet had gone through? *Eight* times?

"You don't even know what I was going to ask."

"Of course I know what you were going to ask. When will you learn that I *always* know?"

"Now that is not true."

"It's more true than it is untrue."

"You can be quite supercilious, did you know that?"

Hyacinth shrugged. "I'm your mother."

Isabella's lips clamped into a line, and Hyacinth enjoyed a full four seconds of peace before she asked, "But this year, do you think we can—"

"We are not traveling."

Isabella's lips parted with surprise. Hyacinth fought the urge to let out a triumphal shout.

"How did you kn—"

Hyacinth patted her daughter's hand. "I told you, I always know. And much as I'm sure we would all enjoy a bit of travel, we will remain in London for the season, and you, my girl, will smile and dance and look for a husband."

Cue the bit about becoming her mother.

Hyacinth sighed. Violet Bridgerton was probably laughing about this, this very minute. In fact, she'd been laughing about it for nineteen years. "Just like you," Violet liked to say, grinning at Hyacinth as she tousled Isabella's curls. "Just like you."

"Just like you, Mother," Hyacinth murmured with a smile, picturing Violet's face in her mind. "And now I'm just like you."

An hour or so later. Gareth, too, has grown and changed, although, we soon shall see, not in any of the ways that matter . . .

Gareth St. Clair leaned back in his chair, pausing to savor his brandy as he glanced around his office. There really was a remarkable sense of satisfaction in a job well-done and completed on time. It wasn't a sensation he'd been used to in his youth, but it was something he'd come to enjoy on a near daily basis now.

It had taken several years to restore the St. Clair fortunes to a respectable level. His father—he'd never quite got 'round to calling him anything else—had stopped his systematic plundering and eased into a vague sort of neglect once he learned the truth about Gareth's birth. So Gareth supposed it could have been a great deal worse.

But when Gareth had assumed the title, he discovered that he'd inherited debts, mortgages, and houses that had been emptied of almost all valuables. Hyacinth's dowry, which had increased with prudent investments upon their marriage, went a long way toward fixing the situation, but still, Gareth had had to work harder and with more diligence than he'd ever dreamed possible to wrench his family out of debt.

The funny thing was, he'd enjoyed it.

Who would have thought that he, of all people, would find such satisfaction in hard work? His desk was spotless, his ledgers neat and tidy, and he could put his fingers on any important document in under a minute. His accounts always summed properly, his properties were thriving, and his tenants were healthy and prosperous.

He took another sip of his drink, letting the mellow fire roll down his throat. Heaven.

Life was perfect. Truly. Perfect.

George was finishing up at Cambridge, Isabella would surely choose a husband this year, and Hyacinth . . .

He chuckled. Hyacinth was still Hyacinth. She'd become a bit more sedate with age, or maybe it was just that motherhood had smoothed off her rough edges, but she was still the same outspoken, delightful, perfectly wonderful Hyacinth.

She drove him crazy half the time, but it was a *nice* sort of crazy, and even though he sometimes sighed to his friends and nodded tiredly when they all complained about their wives, secretly he knew he was the luckiest man in London. Hell, England even. The world.

He set his drink down, then tapped his fingers against the elegantly wrapped box sitting on the corner of his desk. He'd purchased it that morning at Mme. LaFleur, the dress shop he knew Hyacinth did not frequent, in order to spare her the embarrassment of having to deal with salespeople who knew every piece of lingerie in her wardrobe.

French silk, Belgian lace.

He smiled. Just a little bit of French silk, trimmed with a minuscule amount of Belgian lace.

It would look heavenly on her.

What there was of it.

He sat back in his chair, savoring the daydream. It was going to be a long, lovely night. Maybe even . . .

His eyebrows rose as he tried to remember his wife's schedule for the day. Maybe even a long, lovely afternoon. When *was* she due home? And would she have either of the children with her?

He closed his eyes, picturing her in various states of undress, followed by various interesting poses, followed by various *fascinating* activities.

He groaned. She was going to have to return home *very* soon, because his imagination was far too active not to be satisfied, and—

"*Gareth!*"

Not the most mellifluous of tones. The lovely erotic haze floating about his head disappeared entirely. Well, almost entirely. Hyacinth might not have looked the least bit inclined for a bit of afternoon sport as she stood in the doorway, her eyes narrowed and jaw clenched, but she was *there*, and that was half the battle.

"Shut the door," he murmured, rising to his feet.

"Do you know what your daughter did?"

"Your daughter, you mean?"

"Our daughter," she ground out. But she shut the door.

"Do I want to know?"

"Gareth!"

"Very well," he sighed, followed by a dutiful "What did she do?"

He'd had this conversation before, of course. Countless times. The answer usually had something to do with something involving marriage and Isabella's somewhat unconventional views on the subject. And of course, Hyacinth's frustration with the whole situation.

It rarely varied.

"Well, it wasn't so much what she did," Hyacinth said.

He hid his smile. This was also not unexpected.

"It's more what she won't do."

"Jump to your bidding?"

"*Gareth.*"

He halved the distance between them. "Aren't I enough?"

"I beg your pardon?"

He reached out, tugged at her hand, pulled her gently against him. "I always jump to your bidding," he murmured.

She recognized the look in his eye. "Now?" She twisted around until she could see the closed door. "Isabella is upstairs."

"She won't hear."

"But she could—"

His lips found her neck. "There's a lock on the door."

"But she'll know—"

He started working on the buttons of her frock. He was *very* good at buttons. "She's a smart girl," he said, stepping back to enjoy his handiwork as the fabric fell away. He *loved* when his wife didn't wear a chemise.

"Gareth!"

He leaned down and took one rosy-tipped breast into his mouth before she could object.

"Oh, Gareth!" And her knees went weak. Just enough for him

to scoop her up and take her to the sofa. The one with the extra-deep cushions.

"More?"

"God, yes," she groaned.

He slid his hand under her skirt until he could tickle her senseless. "Such token resistance," he murmured. "Admit it. You always want me."

"Twenty years of marriage isn't admission enough?"

"Twenty-two years, and I want to hear it from your lips."

She moaned when he slipped a finger inside of her. "Almost always," she conceded. "I almost always want you."

He sighed for dramatic effect, even as he smiled into her neck. "I shall have to work harder, then."

He looked up at her. She was gazing down at him with an arch expression, clearly over her fleeting attempt at uprightness and respectability.

"Much harder," she agreed. "And a bit faster, too, while you're at it."

He laughed out loud at that.

"Gareth!" Hyacinth might be a wanton in private, but she was always aware of the servants.

"Don't worry," he said with a smile. "I'll be quiet. I'll be very, very quiet." With one easy movement, he bunched her skirts well above her waist and slid down until his head was between her legs. "It's you, my darling, who will have to control your volume."

"Oh. Oh. Oh . . ."

"More?"

"Definitely more."

He licked her then. She tasted like heaven. And when she squirmed, it was always a treat.

"Oh my heavens. Oh my . . . Oh my . . ."

He smiled against her, then swirled a circle on her until she let out a quiet little shriek. He loved doing this to her, loved bringing her, his capable and articulate wife, to senseless abandon.

Twenty-two years. Who would have thought that after twenty-two years he'd still want this one woman, this one woman only, and this one woman so intensely?

"Oh, Gareth," she was panting. "Oh, Gareth . . . More, Gareth . . ."

He redoubled his efforts. She was close. He knew her so well, knew the curve and shape of her body, the way she moved when she was aroused, the way she breathed when she wanted him. She was close.

And then she was gone, arching and gasping until her body went limp.

He chuckled to himself as she batted him away. She always did that when she was done, saying she couldn't bear one more touch, that she'd surely die if she wasn't given the chance to float down to normalcy.

He moved, curling against her body until he could see her face.

"That was nice," she said.

He lifted a brow. "Nice?"

"Very nice."

"Nice enough to reciprocate?"

Her lips curved. "Oh, I don't know if it was *that* nice."

His hand went to his trousers. "I shall have to offer a repeat engagement, then."

Her lips parted in surprise.

"A variation on a theme, if you will."

She twisted her neck to look down. "What are you doing?"

He grinned lasciviously. "Enjoying the fruits of my labors." And then she gasped as he slid inside of her, and he gasped from the sheer pleasure of it all, and then he thought how very much he loved her.

And then he thought nothing much at all.

The following day. We didn't really think that Hyacinth would give up, did we?

Late afternoon found Hyacinth back at her second favorite pastime. Although *favorite* didn't seem quite the right adjective, nor was *pastime* the correct noun. *Compulsion* probably fit the description better, as did *miserable*, or perhaps *unrelenting. Wretched?*

Inevitable.

She sighed. Definitely inevitable. An inevitable compulsion.

How long had she lived in this house? Fifteen years?

Fifteen years. Fifteen years and a few months atop that, and she was still searching for those bloody jewels.

One would think she'd have given up by now. Certainly, anyone else would have given up by now. She was, she had to admit, the most ridiculously stubborn person of her own acquaintance.

Except, perhaps, her own daughter. Hyacinth had never told Isabella about the jewels, if only because she knew that Isabella would join in the search with an unhealthy fervor to rival her own. She hadn't told her son, George, either, because he would tell Isabella. And Hyacinth would never get that girl married off if she thought there was a fortune in jewels to be found in her home.

Not that Isabella would want the jewels for fortune's sake. Hyacinth knew her daughter well enough to realize that in some matters—possibly most—Isabella was exactly like her. And Hyacinth's search for the jewels had never been about the money they might bring. Oh, she freely admitted that she and Gareth could use the money (and could have done with it even more so a few years back). But it wasn't about that. It was the principle. It was the glory.

It was the desperate need to finally clutch those bloody rocks in her hand and shake them before her husband's face and say, "See? See? I haven't been mad all these years!"

Gareth had long since given up on the jewels. They probably didn't even exist, he told her. Someone had surely found them years earlier. They'd lived in Clair House for *fifteen years*, for heaven's sake. If Hyacinth was going to find them, she'd have located them by now, so why did she continue to torture herself??

An excellent question.

Hyacinth gritted her teeth together as she crawled across the washroom floor for what was surely the eight hundredth time in her life. She knew all that. Lord help her, she knew it, but she couldn't give up now. If she gave up now, what did that say about the past fifteen years? Wasted time? All of it, wasted time?

She couldn't bear the thought.

Plus, she really wasn't the sort to give up, was she? If she did, it would be so completely at odds with everything she knew about herself. Would that mean she was getting old?

She wasn't ready to get old. Perhaps that was the curse of being the youngest of eight children. One was never quite ready to be old.

She leaned down even lower, planting her cheek against the cool tile of the floor so that she could peer under the tub. No old lady would do *this*, would she? No old lady would—

"Ah, there you are, Hyacinth."

It was Gareth, poking his head in. He did not look the least bit surprised to find his wife in such an odd position. But he did say, "It's been several months since your last search, hasn't it?"

She looked up. "I thought of something."

"Something you hadn't already thought of??"

"Yes," she ground out, lying through her teeth.

"Checking behind the tile?" he queried politely.

"Under the tub," she said reluctantly, moving herself into a seated position.

He blinked, shifting his gaze to the large claw-footed tub. "Did you move that?" he asked, his voice incredulous.

She nodded. It was amazing the sort of strength one could summon when properly motivated.

He looked at her, then at the tub, then back again. "No," he said. "It's not possible. You didn't—"

"I did."

"You couldn't—"

"I could," she said, beginning to enjoy herself. She didn't get to surprise him these days nearly as often as she would have liked. "Just a few inches," she admitted.

He looked back over at the tub.

"Maybe just one," she allowed.

For a moment she thought he would simply shrug his shoulders and leave her to her endeavors, but then he surprised her by saying, "Would you like some help?"

It took her a few seconds to ascertain his meaning. "With the tub?" she asked.

He nodded, crossing the short distance to the edge of its basin. "If you can move it an inch by yourself," he said, "surely the two of us can triple that. Or more."

Hyacinth rose to her feet. "I thought you didn't believe that the jewels are still here."

"I don't." He planted his hands on his hips as he surveyed the tub, looking for the best grip. "But you do, and surely this must fall within the realm of husbandly duties."

"Oh." Hyacinth swallowed, feeling a little guilty for thinking him so unsupportive. "Thank you."

He motioned for her to grab a spot on the opposite side. "Did you lift?" he asked. "Or shove?"

"Shove. With my shoulder, actually." She pointed to a narrow spot between the tub and the wall. "I wedged myself in there, then hooked my shoulder right under the lip, and—"

But Gareth was already holding his hand up to stop her. "No more," he said. "Don't tell me. I beg of you."

"Why not?"

He looked at her for a long moment before answering, "I don't really know. But I don't want the details."

"Very well." She went to the spot he'd indicated and grabbed the lip. "Thank you, anyway."

"It's my—" He paused. "Well, it's not my pleasure. But it's something."

She smiled to herself. He really was the best of husbands.

Three attempts later, however, it became apparent that they were not going to budge the tub in that manner. "We're going to have to use the wedge and shove method," Hyacinth announced. "It's the only way."

Gareth gave her a resigned nod, and together they squeezed into the narrow space between the tub and the wall.

"I have to say," he said, bending his knees and planting the soles of his boots against the wall, "this is all very undignified."

Hyacinth had nothing to say to that, so she just grunted. He could interpret the noise any way he wished.

"This should really count for something," he murmured.

"I beg your pardon?"

"This." He motioned with his hand, which could have meant just about anything, as she wasn't quite certain whether he was referring to the wall, the floor, the tub, or some particle of dust floating through the air.

"As gestures go," he continued, "it's not too terribly grand, but I would think, should I ever forget your birthday, for example, that this ought to go some distance in restoring myself to your good graces."

Hyacinth lifted a brow. "You couldn't do this out of the goodness of your heart?"

He gave her a regal nod. "I could. And in fact, I am. But one never knows when one—"

"Oh, for heaven's sake," Hyacinth muttered. "You do live to torture me, don't you?"

"It keeps the mind sharp," he said affably. "Very well. Shall we have at it?"

She nodded.

"On my count," he said, bracing his shoulders. "One, two . . . *three*."

With a heave and a groan, they both put all of their weight into the task, and the tub slid recalcitrantly across the floor. The noise was horrible, all scraping and squeaking, and when Hyacinth looked down she saw unattractive white marks arcing across the tile. "Oh, dear," she murmured.

Gareth twisted around, his face creasing into a peeved expression when he saw that they'd moved the tub a mere four inches. "I would have thought we'd have made a bit more progress than that," he said.

"It's heavy," she said, rather unnecessarily.

For a moment he did nothing but blink at the small sliver of floor they'd uncovered. "What do you plan to do now?" he asked.

Her mouth twisted slightly in a somewhat stumped expression. "I'm not sure," she admitted. "Check the floor, I imagine."

"You haven't done so already?" And then, when she didn't answer in, oh, half a second, he added, "In the fifteen years since you moved here?"

"I've *felt* along the floor, of course," she said quickly, since it was quite obvious that her arm fit under the tub. "But it's just not the same as a visual inspection, and—"

"Good luck," he cut in, rising to his feet.

"You're leaving?"

"Did you wish for me to stay?"

She hadn't expected him to stay, but now that he was here . . . "Yes," she said, surprised by her own answer. "Why not?"

He smiled at her then, and the expression was so warm, and loving, and best of all, familiar. "I could buy you a diamond necklace," he said softly, sitting back down.

She reached out, placed her hand on his. "I know you could."

They sat in silence for a minute, and then Hyacinth scooted herself closer to her husband, letting out a comfortable exhale as she eased against his side, letting her head rest on his shoulder. "Do you know why I love you?" she said softly.

His fingers laced through hers. "Why?"

"You could have bought me a necklace," she said. "And you could have hidden it." She turned her head so that she could kiss the curve of his neck. "Just so that I could have found it, you could have hidden it. But you didn't."

"I—"

"And don't say you never thought of it," she said, turning back so that she was once again facing the wall, just a few inches away. But her head was on his shoulder, and he was facing the same wall, and even though they weren't looking at each other, their hands were still entwined, and somehow the position was everything a marriage should be.

"Because I know you," she said, feeling a smile growing inside. "I know you, and you know me, and it's just the loveliest thing."

He squeezed her hand, then kissed the top of her head. "If it's here, you'll find it."

She sighed. "Or die trying."

He chuckled.

"That shouldn't be funny," she informed him.

"But it is."

"I know."

"I love you," he said.

"I know."

And really, what more could she want?

Meanwhile six feet away . . .

Isabella was quite used to the antics of her parents. She accepted the fact that they tugged each other into dark corners with far more frequency than was seemly. She thought nothing of the fact that her mother was one of the most outspoken women in London or that her father was still so handsome that her own friends sighed and stammered in his presence. In fact, she rather enjoyed being the daughter of such an unconventional couple. Oh, on the outside they were all that was proper, to be sure, with only the nicest sort of reputation for high-spiritedness.

But behind the closed doors of Clair House . . . Isabella knew that her friends were not encouraged to share their opinions as she was. Most of her friends were not even encouraged to have opinions. And certainly most young ladies of her acquaintance had not been given the opportunity to study modern languages, nor to delay a social debut by one year in order to travel on the continent.

So, when all was said and done, Isabella thought herself quite fortunate as pertained to her parents, and if that meant overlooking the occasional episodes of Not Acting One's Age—well, it was worth it, and she'd learned to ignore much of their behavior.

But when she'd sought out her mother this afternoon—to acquiesce on the matter of the white gown with the dullish green trim, she might add—and instead found her parents on the washroom floor pushing a *bathtub* . . .

Well, really, that was a bit much, even for the St. Clairs.

And who would have faulted her for remaining to eavesdrop?

Not her mother, Isabella decided as she leaned in. There was no way Hyacinth St. Clair would have done the right thing and walked away. One couldn't live with the woman for nineteen years without learning *that.* And as for her father—well, Isabella rather thought he would have stayed to listen as well, especially as they were making it so *easy* for her, facing the wall as they were, with their backs to the open doorway, indeed with bathtub between them.

"What do you plan to do now?" her father was asking, his voice laced with that particular brand of amusement he seemed to reserve for her mother.

"I don't know," her mother replied, sounding uncharacteristically . . . well, not *un*sure, but certainly not as sure as usual. "Check the floor, I imagine."

Check the floor? What on earth were they talking about? Isabella leaned forward for a better listen, just in time to hear her father ask, "You haven't done so already? In the fifteen years since you moved here?"

"I've felt along the floor," her mother retorted, sounding much more like herself. "But it's not the same as a visual inspection, and—"

"Good luck," her father said, and then—*Oh, no! He was leaving!*

Isabella started to scramble, but then something must have happened because he sat back down. She inched back toward the open doorway—

Carefully, carefully now, he could get up at any moment. Holding her breath, she leaned in, unable to take her eyes off of the backs of her parents' heads.

"I could buy you a diamond necklace," her father said.

A diamond necklace?

A diamond . . .

Fifteen years.

Moving a tub?

In a washroom?

Fifteen years.

Her mother had searched for fifteen years.

For a diamond necklace?

A diamond necklace.

A diamond . . .

Oh. Dear. God.

What was she going to do? What was she going to do? She knew what she must do, but good God, *how* was she supposed to do it?

And what could she say? What could she possibly say to—

Forget that for now. Forget it because her mother was talking again and she was saying, "You could have bought me a necklace. And you could have hidden it. Just so that I could have found it, you could have hidden it. But you didn't."

There was so much love in her voice it made Isabella's heart ache. And something about it seemed to sum up everything that her parents were. To themselves, to each other.

To their children.

And suddenly the moment was too personal to spy upon, even

for her. She crept from the room, then ran to her own chamber, sagging into a chair just as soon as she closed the door.

Because she knew what her mother had been looking for for so very long.

It was sitting in the bottom drawer of her desk. And it was more than a necklace. It was an entire parure—a necklace, bracelet, and ring, a veritable shower of diamonds, each stone framed by two delicate aquamarines. Isabella had found them when she was ten, hidden in a small cavity behind one of the Turkish tiles in the nursery washroom. She *should* have said something about them. She knew that she should. But she hadn't, and she wasn't even sure why.

Maybe it was because she had found them. Maybe because she loved having a secret. Maybe it was because she hadn't thought they belonged to anyone else, or indeed, that anyone even knew of their existence. Certainly she hadn't thought that her mother had been searching for fifteen years.

Her mother!

Her mother was the last person anyone would imagine was keeping a secret. No one would think ill of Isabella for not thinking, when she'd discovered the diamonds—*Oh, surely my mother must be looking for these and has chosen, for her own devious reasons, not to tell me about it.*

Truly, when all was said and done, this was really her mother's fault. If Hyacinth had *told* her that she was searching for jewels, Isabella would immediately have confessed. Or if not immediately, then soon enough to satisfy everyone's conscience.

And now, speaking of consciences, hers was beating a nasty little tattoo in her chest. It was a most unpleasant—and unfamiliar—feeling.

It wasn't that Isabella was the soul of sweetness and light, all sugary smiles and pious platitudes. Heavens, no, she avoided such girls like the plague. But by the same token, she rarely did anything that was likely to make her feel guilty afterward, if only because perhaps—and only perhaps—her notions of propriety and morality were ever-so-slightly flexible.

But now she had a lump in the pit of her stomach, a lump with peculiar talent for sending bile up her throat. Her hands were shaking, and she felt ill. Not feverish, not even aguey, just ill. With herself.

Letting out an uneven breath, Isabella rose to her feet and crossed the room to her desk, a delicate rococo piece her namesake great-grandmother had brought over from Italy. She'd put the jewels there three years back, when she'd finally moved out of the top-floor nursery. She'd discovered a secret compartment at the back of the bottom drawer. This hadn't particularly surprised her; there seemed to be an uncommon number of secret compartments in the furniture at Clair House, much of which had been imported from Italy. But it *was* a boon and rather convenient, and so one day, when her family was off at some *ton* function they had deemed Isabella too young to attend, she'd sneaked back up to the nursery, retrieved the jewels from their hiding place behind the tile (which she had rather resourcefully plastered back up), and moved them to her desk.

They'd remained there ever since, except for the odd occasion when Isabella took them out and tried them on, thinking how nice they would look with her new gown, but *how* was she to explain their existence to her parents?

Now it seemed that no explanation would have been necessary. Or perhaps just a different sort of explanation.

A very different sort.

Settling into the desk chair, Isabella leaned down and retrieved the jewels from the secret compartment. They were still in the same corded velvet bag in which she'd found them. She slid them free, letting them pool luxuriously on the desktop. She didn't know much about jewels, but surely these had to be of the finest quality. They caught the sunlight with an indescribable magic, almost as if each stone could somehow capture the light and then send it showering off in every direction.

Isabella didn't like to think herself greedy or materialistic, but in the presence of such treasure, she understood how diamonds could make a man go a little bit mad. Or why women longed so desperately for one more piece, one more stone that was bigger, more finely cut than the last.

But these did not belong to her. Maybe they belonged to no one. But if anyone had a right to them, it was most definitely her mother. Isabella didn't know how or why Hyacinth knew of their existence, but that didn't seem to matter. Her mother had some sort of connection to the jewels, some sort of important knowledge. And if they belonged to anyone, they belonged to her.

Reluctantly, Isabella slid them back into the bag and tightened the gold cord so that none of the pieces could slip out. She knew what she had to do now. She knew exactly what she had to do.

But after that . . .

The torture would be in the waiting.

One year later

It had been two months since Hyacinth had last searched for the jewels, but Gareth was busy with some sort of estate matter, she had no good books to read, and, well, she just felt . . . itchy.

This happened from time to time. She'd go months without searching, weeks and days without even thinking about the diamonds, and then something would happen to remind her, to start her wondering, and there she was again—obsessed and frustrated, sneaking about the house so that no one would realize what she was up to.

And the truth was, she was embarrassed. No matter how one looked at it, she was at least a little bit of a fool. Either the jewels were hidden away at Clair House and she hadn't found them despite sixteen years of searching, or they weren't hidden, and she'd been chasing a delusion. She couldn't even imagine how she might explain this to her children, the servants surely thought her more than a little bit mad (they'd all caught her snooping about a washroom at one point or another), and Gareth—well, he was sweet and he humored her, but all the same, Hyacinth kept her activities to herself.

It was just better that way.

She'd chosen the nursery washroom for the afternoon's search. Not for any particular reason, of course, but she'd finished her systematic search of all of the servants' washrooms (always an endeavor that required some sensitivity and finesse), and before that she'd done her own washroom, and so the nursery seemed a good choice. After this she'd move to some of the second floor washrooms. George had moved into his own lodgings and if there really was a merciful God, Isabella would be married before long, and Hyacinth would not have to worry about anyone stumbling upon her as she poked, pried, and quite possibly pulled the tiles from the walls.

Hyacinth put her hands on her hips and took a deep breath as she surveyed the small room. She'd always liked it. The tiling was, or at least appeared to be, Turkish, and Hyacinth had to think that the Eastern peoples must enjoy far less sedate lives than the British, because the colors never failed to put her in a splendid mood—all royal blues and dreamy aquas, with streaks of yellow and orange.

Hyacinth had been to the south of Italy once, to the beach. It looked exactly like this room, sunny and sparkly in ways that the shores of England never seemed to achieve.

She squinted at the crown molding, looking for cracks or indentations, then dropped to her hands and knees for her usual inspection of the lower tiles.

She didn't know what she hoped to find, what might have suddenly made an appearance that she hadn't detected during the other, oh, at least a dozen previous searches.

But she had to keep going. She had to because she simply had no choice. There was something inside of her that just would not let go. And—

She stopped. Blinked. What was that?

Slowly, because she couldn't quite believe that she'd found anything new—it had been over a decade since any of her searches had changed in any measurable manner—she leaned in.

A crack.

It was small. It was faint. But it was definitely a crack, running from the floor to the top of the first tile, about six inches up. It wasn't the sort of thing most people would notice, but Hyacinth wasn't most people, and sad as it sounded, she had practically made a career of inspecting washrooms.

Frustrated with her inability to get really close, she shifted to her forearms and knees, then laid her cheek against the floor. She poked the tile to the right of the crack, then the left.

Nothing happened.

She stuck her fingernail at the edge of the crack, and dug it in. A tiny piece of plaster lodged under her nail.

A strange excitement began to build in her chest, squeezing, fluttering, rendering her almost incapable of drawing breath.

"Calm down," she whispered, even those words coming out on a shake. She grabbed the little chisel she always took with her on her searches. "It's probably nothing. It's probably—"

She jammed the chisel in the crack, surely with more force than was necessary. And then she twisted. If one of the tiles was loose, the torque would cause it to press outward, and—

"Oh!"

The tile quite literally popped out, landing on the floor with a clatter. Behind it was a small cavity.

Hyacinth squeezed her eyes shut. She'd waited her entire adult life for this moment, and now she couldn't even bring herself to look. "Please," she whispered. "*Please.*"

She reached in.

"Please. Oh, please."

She touched something. Something soft. Like velvet.

With shaking fingers she drew it out. It was a little bag, held together with a soft, silky cord.

Hyacinth straightened slowly, crossing her legs so that she was sitting Indian style. She slid one finger inside the bag, widening the mouth, which had been pulled tight.

And then, with her right hand, she upended it, sliding the contents into her left.

Oh my G—

"Gareth!" she shrieked. "Gareth!"

"I did it," she whispered, gazing down at the pool of jewels now spilling from her left hand. "I did it."

And then she bellowed it.

"I DID IT!!!!"

She looped the necklace around her neck, still clutching the bracelet and ring in her hand.

"I did it, I did it, I did it." She was singing it now, hopping up and down, almost dancing, almost crying. "I did it!"

"Hyacinth!" It was Gareth, out of breath from taking four flights of stairs two steps at a time.

She looked at him, and she could swear she could feel her eyes shining. "I did it!" She laughed, almost crazily. "I did it!"

For a moment he could do nothing but stare. His face grew slack, and Hyacinth thought he might actually lose his footing.

"I did it," she said again. "I did it."

And then he took her hand, took the ring, and slipped it onto her finger. "So you did," he said, leaning down to kiss her knuckles. "So you did."

Meanwhile, one floor down . . .

"*Gareth!*"

Isabella looked up from the book she was reading, glancing toward the ceiling. Her bedchamber was directly below the nursery, rather in line with the washroom, actually.

"*I did it!*"

Isabella turned back to her book.

And she smiled.

BRIDGERTON

ON THE WAY TO THE WEDDING

For Lyssa Keusch.
Because you're my editor.
Because you're my friend.

And also for Paul.
Just because.

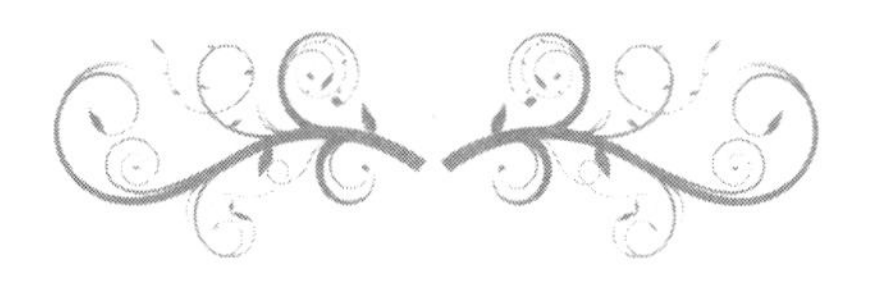

Prologue

London, not far from St. George's, Hanover Square
Summer, 1827

His lungs were on fire.

Gregory Bridgerton was running. Through the streets of London, oblivious to the curious stares of onlookers, he was running.

There was a strange, powerful rhythm to his movements—*one two three four, one two three four*—that pushed him along, propelling him forward even as his mind remained focused on one thing and one thing only.

The church.

He had to get to the church.

He had to stop the wedding.

How long had he been running? One minute? Five? He couldn't know, couldn't concentrate on anything but his destination.

The church. He had to get to the church.

It had started at eleven. This thing. This ceremony. This thing that should never have happened. But she'd done it anyway. And he had to stop it. He had to stop *her*. He didn't know how, and he certainly didn't know why, but she was doing it, and it was wrong.

She had to know that it was wrong.

She was *his*. They belonged together. She knew that. God damn it all, she knew that.

How long did a wedding ceremony take? Five minutes? Ten? Twenty? He'd never paid attention before, certainly never thought to check his watch at the beginning and end.

Never thought he'd need the information. Never thought it would matter this much.

How long had he been running? Two minutes? Ten?

He skidded around a corner and onto Regent Street, grunting something that was meant to take the place of "Excuse me," as he bumped into a respectably dressed gentleman, knocking his case to the ground.

Normally Gregory would have stopped to aid the gentleman, bent to retrieve the case, but not today, not this morning.

Not now.

The church. He had to get to the church. He could not think of anything else. He must not. He must—

Damn! He skidded to a halt as a carriage cut in front of him. Resting his hands on his thighs—not because he wanted to, but rather because his desperate body demanded it—he sucked in huge gulps of air, trying to relieve the screaming pressure in his chest, that horrible burning, tearing feeling as—

The carriage moved past and he was off again. He was close now. He could do it. It couldn't have been more than five minutes since he'd left the house. Maybe six. It felt like thirty, but it couldn't have been more than seven.

He had to stop this. It was wrong. He had to stop it. He *would* stop it.

He could see the church. Off in the distance, its gray steeple rising into the bright blue sky. Someone had hung flowers from the lanterns. He couldn't tell what kind they were—yellow and white, yellow mostly. They spilled forth with reckless abandon, bursting from the baskets. They looked celebratory, cheerful even, and it was all so wrong. This was not a cheerful day. It was not an event to be celebrated.

And he *would* stop it.

He slowed down just enough so that he could run up the steps without falling on his face, and then he wrenched the door open, wide, wider, barely hearing the slam as it crashed into the outer wall. Maybe he should have paused for breath. Maybe he should have entered quietly, giving himself a moment to assess the situation, to gauge how far along they were.

The church went silent. The priest stopped his drone, and every spine in every pew twisted until every face was turned to the back.

To him.

"Don't," Gregory gasped, but he was so short of breath, he could barely hear the word.

"Don't," he said, louder this time, clutching the edge of the pews as he staggered forward. "Don't do it."

She said nothing, but he saw her. He saw her, her mouth open with shock. He saw her bouquet slip from her hands, and he knew—by God he knew that she'd stopped breathing.

She looked so beautiful. Her golden hair seemed to catch the light, and it shone with a radiance that filled him with strength. He straightened, still breathing hard, but he could walk unassisted now, and he let go of the pew.

"Don't do it," he said again, moving toward her with the stealthy grace of a man who knows what he wants.

Who knows what should be.

Still she didn't speak. No one did. It was strange, that. Three hundred of London's biggest busybodies, gathered into one building, and no one could utter a word. No one could take his eyes off him as he walked down the aisle.

"I love you," he said, right there, right in front of everyone. Who cared? He would not keep this a secret. He would not let her marry someone else without making sure all the world knew that she owned his heart.

"I love you," he said again, and out of the corner of his eye he could see his mother and sister, seated primly in a pew, their mouths open with shock.

He kept walking. Down the aisle, each step more confident, more sure.

"Don't do it," he said, stepping out of the aisle and into the apse. "Don't marry him."

"Gregory," she whispered. "Why are you doing this?"

"I love you," he said, because it was the only thing to say. It was the only thing that mattered.

Her eyes glistened, and he could see her breath catch in her throat. She looked up at the man she was trying to marry. His brows rose as he gave her a tiny, one-shouldered shrug, as if to say, *It is your choice.*

Gregory sank to one knee. "Marry me," he said, his very soul in his words. "Marry *me.*"

He stopped breathing. The entire church stopped breathing.

She brought her eyes to his. They were huge and clear and everything he'd ever thought was good and kind and true.

"Marry me," he whispered, one last time.

Her lips were trembling, but her voice was clear when she said—

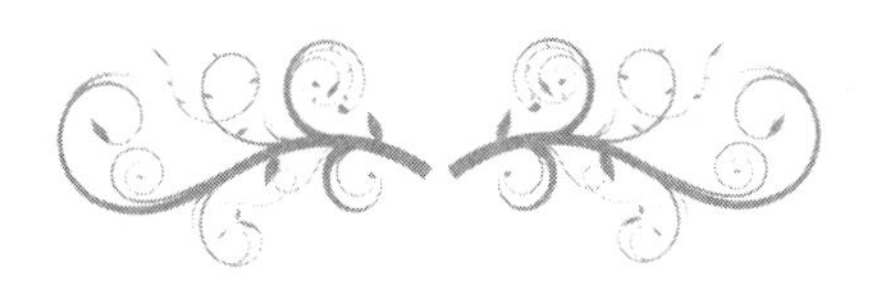

Chapter 1

In which Our Hero falls in love.

Two months earlier

Unlike most men of his acquaintance, Gregory Bridgerton believed in true love.

He'd have to have been a fool not to.

Consider the following:

His eldest brother, Anthony.

His eldest sister, Daphne.

His other brothers, Benedict and Colin, not to mention his sisters, Eloise, Francesca, and (galling but true) Hyacinth, all of whom—*all* of whom—were quite happily besotted with their spouses.

For most men, such a state of affairs would produce nothing quite so much as bile, but for Gregory, who had been born with an uncommonly cheerful, if occasionally (according to his younger sister) annoying, spirit, it simply meant that he had no choice but to believe the obvious:

Love existed.

It was not a wispy figment of the imagination, designed to keep the poets from complete starvation. It might not be something that one could see or smell or touch, but it was out there, and it was only a matter of time before he, too, found the woman of his dreams and settled down to be fruitful, multiply, and take on such baffling hobbies as papier-mâché and the collection of nutmeg graters.

Although, if one wanted to put a fine point on it, which did seem rather precise for such an abstract sort of concept, his dreams didn't exactly include a woman. Well, not one with any specific and identifiable attributes. He didn't know anything about this woman of his, the one who was supposed to transform his life completely, turning him into a happy pillar of boredom and respectability. He didn't know if she would be short or tall, dark or fair. He'd like to think she would be intelligent and in possession of a fine sense of humor, but beyond that, how was he to know? She could be shy or outspoken. She might like to sing. Or maybe not. Maybe she was a horsewoman, with a ruddy complexion born of too much time out of doors.

He didn't know. When it came to this woman, this impossible, wonderful, and currently nonexistent woman, all he really knew was that when he found her . . .

He'd know.

He didn't know how he'd know; he just knew that he would. Something this momentous, this earth-shattering and life-altering . . . well, really, it wasn't going to whisper its way into existence. It would come full and forceful, like the proverbial ton of bricks. The only question was when.

And in the meantime, he saw no reason not to have a fine time while he anticipated her arrival. One didn't need to behave like a monk while waiting for one's true love, after all.

Gregory was, by all accounts, a fairly typical man about London, with a comfortable—although by no means extravagant—allowance, plenty of friends, and a level enough head to know when to quit a gaming table. He was considered a decent enough catch on the Marriage Mart, if not precisely the top selection (fourth sons never did command a great deal of attention), and he was always in demand when the society matrons needed an eligible man to even up the numbers at dinner parties.

Which did make his aforementioned allowance stretch a bit further—always a benefit.

Perhaps he ought to have had a bit more purpose in his life. Some sort of direction, or even just a meaningful task to complete. But that could wait, couldn't it? Soon, he was sure, everything would come clear. He would know just what it was he wished to do, and whom he wished to do it with, and in the meantime, he'd—

Not have a fine time. Not just at *this* moment, at least.

To explain:

Gregory was presently sitting in a leather chair, a rather accommodating one, not that that really had any bearing on the matter other than the fact that the lack of discomfort was conducive to daydreaming, which in turn was conducive to not listening to his brother, who, it should be noted, was standing approximately four feet away, droning on about something or other, almost certainly involving some variation of the words *duty* and *responsibility*.

Gregory wasn't really paying attention. He rarely did.

Well, no, occasionally he did, but—

"Gregory? Gregory!"

He looked up, blinking. Anthony's arms were crossed, never a good sign. Anthony was the Viscount Bridgerton, and had been for more than twenty years. And while he was, Gregory would be the first to insist, the very best of brothers, he would have made a rather fine feudal lord.

"Begging your pardon for intruding upon your thoughts, such as they are," Anthony said in a dry voice, "but have you, perhaps—just perhaps—heard anything I've said?"

"Diligence," Gregory parroted, nodding with what he deemed sufficient gravity. "Direction."

"Indeed," Anthony replied, and Gregory congratulated himself on what had clearly been an inspired performance. "It was well past time that you finally sought some direction in your life."

"Of course," Gregory murmured, mostly because he'd missed supper, and he was hungry, and he'd heard that his sister-in-law was serving light refreshments in the garden. Besides, it never made sense to argue with Anthony. Never.

"You must make a change. Choose a new course."

"Indeed." Maybe there would be sandwiches. He could eat about forty of those ridiculous little ones with the crusts cut off right then.

"Gregory."

Anthony's voice held that tone. The one that, while impossible to describe, was easy enough to recognize. And Gregory knew it was time to pay attention.

"Right," he said, because truly, it was remarkable how well a single syllable could delay a proper sentence. "I expect I'll join the clergy."

That stopped Anthony cold. Dead, frozen, cold. Gregory paused to savor the moment. Too bad he had to become a bloody vicar to achieve it.

"I beg your pardon," Anthony finally murmured.

"It's not as if I've many choices," Gregory said. And as the words emerged, he realized it was the first time he'd spoken them. It somehow made them more real, more permanent. "It's the military or the clergy," he continued, "and, well, it's got to be said—I'm a beastly bad shot."

Anthony didn't say anything. They all knew it was true.

After a moment of awkward silence, Anthony murmured, "There are swords."

"Yes, but with my luck I'll be posted to the Sudan." Gregory shuddered. "Not to be overly fastidious, but really, the heat. Would *you* want to go?"

Anthony demurred immediately. "No, of course not."

"And," Gregory added, beginning to enjoy himself, "there is Mother."

There was a pause. Then: "She pertains to the Sudan . . . how?"

"She wouldn't very well like my going, and then you, you must know, will be the one who must hold her hand every time she worries, or has some ghastly nightmare about—"

"Say no more," Anthony interrupted.

Gregory allowed himself an inner smile. It really wasn't fair to his mother, who, it was only sporting to point out, had never once claimed to portend the future with anything so wispy as a dream. But she *would* hate his going to the Sudan, and Anthony *would* have to listen to her worry over it.

And as Gregory didn't particularly wish to depart England's misty shores, the point was moot, anyway.

"Right," Anthony said. "Right. I am glad, then, that we have finally been able to have this conversation."

Gregory eyed the clock.

Anthony cleared his throat, and when he spoke, there was an edge of impatience to his voice. "And that you are finally thinking toward your future."

Gregory felt something tighten at the back of his jaw. "I am but six-and-twenty," he reminded him. "Surely too young for such repeated use of the word *finally*."

Anthony just arched a brow. "Shall I contact the archbishop? See about finding you a parish?"

Gregory's chest twisted into an unexpected coughing spasm. "Er, no," he said, when he was able. "Not yet, at least."

One corner of Anthony's mouth moved. But not by much, and not, by any stretch of the definition, into a smile. "You could marry," he said softly.

"I could," Gregory agreed. "And I shall. In fact, I plan to."

"Really?"

"When I find the right woman." And then, at Anthony's dubious expression, Gregory added, "Surely you, of all people, would recommend a match of love over convenience."

Anthony was rather famously besotted with his wife, who was in turn rather inexplicably besotted with him. Anthony was also rather famously devoted to his seven younger siblings, so Gregory should not have felt such an unexpected wellspring of emotion when he softly said, "I wish you every happiness that I myself enjoy."

Gregory was saved from having to make a reply by the very loud rumbling of his stomach. He gave his brother a sheepish expression. "Sorry. I missed supper."

"I know. We expected you earlier."

Gregory avoided wincing. Just.

"Kate was somewhat put out."

That was the worst. When Anthony was disappointed that was one thing. But when he claimed that his wife had been somehow pained . . .

Well, that was when Gregory *knew* he was in trouble. "Got a late start from London," he mumbled. It was the truth, but still, no excuse for bad behavior. He had been expected at the house party in time for supper, and he had not come through. He almost said, "I shall make it up to her," but at the last moment bit his tongue. Somehow that would make it worse, he knew, almost as if he was making light of his tardiness, assuming that he could smooth over any transgression with a smile and a glib comment. Which he often could, but for some reason this time—

He didn't want to.

So instead he just said, "I'm sorry." And he meant it, too.

"She's in the garden," Anthony said gruffly. "I think she means to have dancing—on the patio, if you can believe it."

Gregory could. It sounded exactly like his sister-in-law. She wasn't the sort to let any serendipitous moment pass her by, and with the weather so uncommonly fine, why not organize an impromptu dance al fresco?

"See that you dance with whomever she wishes," Anthony said. "Kate won't like any of the young ladies to feel left out."

"Of course not," Gregory murmured.

"I will join you in a quarter of an hour," Anthony said, moving back to his desk, where several piles of paper awaited him. "I have a few items here yet to complete."

Gregory stood. "I shall pass that along to Kate." And then, the interview quite clearly at an end, he left the room and headed out to the garden.

It had been some time since he'd been to Aubrey Hall, the ancestral home of the Bridgertons. The family gathered here in Kent for Christmas, of course, but in truth, it wasn't home for Gregory, and never really had been. After his father had died, his mother had done the unconventional and uprooted her family, electing to spend most of the year in London. She had never said so, but Gregory had always suspected that the graceful old house held too many memories.

As a result, Gregory had always felt more at home in town than in the country. Bridgerton House, in London, was the home of his childhood, not Aubrey Hall. Still, he enjoyed his visits, and he was always game for bucolic pursuits, such as riding and swimming (when the lake was warm enough to permit it), and strangely enough, he liked the change of pace. He liked the way the air felt quiet and clean after months in the city.

And he liked the way he could leave it all behind when it grew *too* quiet and clean.

The night's festivities were being held on the south lawn, or so he'd been told by the butler when he'd arrived earlier that evening. It seemed a good spot for an outdoor fête—level ground, a view to the lake, and a large patio with plenty of seating for the less energetic.

As he approached the long salon that opened to the outside, he could hear the low murmur of voices buzzing in through the French doors. He wasn't certain how many people his sister-in-law had invited for her house party—probably something between twenty and thirty. Small enough to be intimate, but still large enough so that one could escape for some peace and quiet without leaving a gaping hole in the gathering.

As Gregory passed through the salon, he took a deep breath, trying in part to determine what sort of food Kate had decided to serve. There wouldn't be much, of course; she would have already overstuffed her guests at supper.

Sweets, Gregory decided, smelling a hint of cinnamon as he reached the light gray stone of the patio. He let out a disappointed breath. He was starving, and a huge slab of meat sounded like heaven right then.

But he was late, and it was nobody's fault but his own, and

Anthony would have his head if he did not join the party immediately, so cakes and biscuits it would have to be.

A warm breeze sifted across his skin as he stepped outside. It had been remarkably hot for May; everyone was talking about it. It was the sort of weather that seemed to lift the mood—so surprisingly pleasant that one couldn't help but smile. And indeed, the guests milling about seemed to be in happy spirits; the low buzz of conversation was peppered with frequent rumbles and trills of laughter.

Gregory looked around, both for the refreshments and for someone he knew, most preferably his sister-in-law Kate, whom propriety dictated he greet first. But as his eyes swept across the scene, instead he saw . . .

Her.

Her.

And he knew it. He knew that she was the one. He stood frozen, transfixed. The air didn't rush from his body; rather, it seemed to slowly escape until there was nothing left, and he just stood there, hollow, and aching for more.

He couldn't see her face, not even her profile. There was just her back, just the breathtakingly perfect curve of her neck, one lock of blond hair swirling against her shoulder.

And all he could think was—*I am wrecked.*

For all other women, he was wrecked. This intensity, this fire, this overwhelming sense of rightness—he had never felt anything like it.

Maybe it was silly. Maybe it was mad. It was probably both those things. But he'd been waiting. For this moment, for so long, he'd been waiting. And it suddenly became clear—why he hadn't joined the military or the clergy, or taken his brother up on one of his frequent offers to manage a smaller Bridgerton estate.

He'd been waiting. That's all it was. Hell, he hadn't even realized how much he'd been doing nothing but waiting for this moment.

And here it was.

There *she* was.

And he knew.

He knew.

He moved slowly across the lawn, food and Kate forgotten. He managed to murmur his greetings to the one or two people he passed on his way, still keeping his pace. He had to reach her. He had to see her face, breathe her scent, know the sound of her voice.

And then he was there, standing mere feet away. He was breathless, awed, somehow fulfilled merely to stand in her presence.

She was speaking with another young lady, with enough animation to mark them as good friends. He stood there for a moment, just watching them until they slowly turned and realized he was there.

He smiled. Softly, just a little bit. And he said . . .

"How do you do?"

Lucinda Abernathy, better known to, well, everyone who knew her, as Lucy, stifled a groan as she turned to the gentleman who had crept up on her, presumably to make calf eyes at Hermione, as did, well, everyone who met Hermione.

It was an occupational hazard of being friends with Hermione Watson. She collected broken hearts the way the old vicar down by the Abbey collected butterflies.

The only difference, being, of course, that Hermione didn't jab her collection with nasty little pins. In all fairness, Hermione didn't wish to win the hearts of gentlemen, and she certainly never set out to break any of them. It just . . . happened. Lucy was used to it by now. Hermione was Hermione, with pale blond hair the color of butter, a heart-shaped face, and huge, wide-set eyes of the most startling shade of green.

Lucy, on the other hand, was . . . Well, she wasn't Hermione, that much was clear. She was simply herself, and most of the time, that was enough.

Lucy was, in almost every visible way, just a little bit *less* than Hermione. A little less blond. A little less slender. A little less tall. Her eyes were a little less vivid in color—bluish-gray, actually, quite attractive when compared with anyone other than Hermione, but that did her little good, as she never *went* anywhere without Hermione.

She had come to this stunning conclusion one day while not paying attention to her lessons on English Composition and Literature at Miss Moss's School for Exceptional Young Ladies, where she and Hermione had been students for three years.

Lucy was a little bit less. Or perhaps, if one wanted to put a nicer sheen on it, she was simply *not quite.*

She was, she supposed, reasonably attractive, in that healthy, traditional, English rose sort of manner, but men were rarely (oh, very well, never) struck dumb in her presence.

Hermione, however . . . well, it was a good thing she was such a nice person. She would have been impossible to be friends with, otherwise.

Well, that and the fact that she simply could not dance. Waltz, quadrille, minuet—it really didn't matter. If it involved music and movement, Hermione couldn't do it.

And it was *lovely.*

Lucy didn't think herself a particularly shallow person, and she would have insisted, had anyone asked, that she would freely throw herself in front of a carriage for her dearest friend, but there was a sort of satisfying fairness in the fact that the most beautiful girl in England had two left feet, at least one of them club.

Metaphorically speaking.

And now here was another one. Man, of course, not foot. Handsome, too. Tall, although not overly so, with warm brown hair and a rather pleasing smile. And a twinkle in his eyes as well, the color of which she couldn't quite determine in the dim night air.

Not to mention that she couldn't actually *see* his eyes, as he wasn't looking at her. He was looking at Hermione, as men always did.

Lucy smiled politely, even though she couldn't imagine that he'd notice, and waited for him to bow and introduce himself.

And then he did the most astonishing thing. After disclosing his name—she should have known he was a Bridgerton from the looks of him—he leaned down and kissed *her* hand first.

Lucy's breath caught.

Then, of course, she realized what he was doing.

Oh, he was *good*. He was really good. Nothing, *nothing* would endear a man to Hermione faster than a compliment to Lucy.

Too bad for him that Hermione's heart was otherwise engaged.

Oh well. It would be amusing to watch it all play out, at least.

"I am Miss Hermione Watson," Hermione was saying, and Lucy realized that Mr. Bridgerton's tactics were doubly clever. By kissing Hermione's hand second, he could linger over it, and her, really, and then she would be the one required to make the introductions.

Lucy was almost impressed. If nothing else, it marked him as slightly more intelligent than the average gentleman.

"And this is my dearest friend," Hermione continued, "Lady Lucinda Abernathy."

She said it the way she always said it, with love and devotion, and perhaps just the barest touch of desperation, as if to say—*For heaven's sake, spare Lucy a glance, too.*

But of course they never did. Except when they wanted advice concerning Hermione, her heart, and the winning thereof. When that happened, Lucy was always in high demand.

Mr. Bridgerton—Mr. Gregory Bridgerton, Lucy mentally corrected, for there were, as far as she knew, three Mr. Bridgertons in total, not counting the viscount, of course—turned and surprised her with a winning smile and warm eyes. "How do you do, Lady Lucinda," he murmured.

"Very well, thank you," and then she could have kicked herself for she actually stammered before the V in *very*, but for heaven's sake, they never looked at her after gazing upon Hermione, never.

Could he possibly be interested in *her*?

No, impossible. They never were.

And really, did it matter? Of course it would be rather charming if a man fell madly and passionately in love with her for a change. Really, she wouldn't *mind* the attention. But the truth was, Lucy was practically engaged to Lord Haselby and had been for years and years and years, so there was no use in having a besotted admirer of her own. It wasn't as if it could lead to anything useful.

And that besides, it certainly wasn't Hermione's fault that she'd been born with the face of an angel.

So Hermione was the siren, and Lucy was the trusty friend, and all was right with the world. Or if not right, then at least quite predictable.

"May we count you among our hosts?" Lucy finally asked, since no one had said anything once they'd all finished with the requisite "Pleased to meet yous."

"I'm afraid not," Mr. Bridgerton replied. "Much as I would like to take credit for the festivities, I reside in London."

"You are very fortunate to have Aubrey Hall in your family," Hermione said politely, "even if it is your brother's."

And that was when Lucy knew. Mr. Bridgerton fancied Hermione. Forget that he'd kissed her hand first, or that he'd actually looked at her when she said something, which most men never bothered to do. One had only to see the way he regarded Hermione when she spoke to know that he, too, had joined the throngs.

His eyes had that slightly glazed look. His lips were parted. And there was an intensity there, as if he'd like to gather Hermione up and stride down the hill with her, crowds and propriety be damned.

As opposed to the way he looked at her, which could be quite easily catalogued as polite disinterest. Or perhaps it was—*Why are you blocking my way, thus preventing me from sweeping Hermione up in my arms and striding down the hill with her, crowds and propriety be damned?*

It wasn't disappointing, exactly. Just . . . not . . . un-disappointing.

There ought to be a word for that. Really, there ought.

"Lucy? Lucy?"

Lucy realized with a touch of embarrassment that she had not been paying attention to the conversation. Hermione was regarding her curiously, her head tilted in that manner of hers that men always seemed to find so fetching. Lucy had tried it once. It had made her dizzy.

"Yes?" she murmured, since some sort of verbal expression seemed to be in order.

"Mr. Bridgerton has asked me to dance," Hermione said, "but I have told him that I *cannot*."

Hermione was forever feigning twisted ankles and head colds to keep herself off the dance floor. Which was also all good and fine, except that she fobbed off all her admirers on Lucy. Which was all good and fine *at first*, but it had got so common that Lucy suspected that the gentlemen now thought they were being shoved in her direction out of pity, which couldn't have been further from the truth.

Lucy was, if she did say so herself, a rather fine dancer. And an excellent conversationalist as well.

"It would be my pleasure to lead Lady Lucinda in a dance," Mr. Bridgerton said, because, really, what else could he say?

And so Lucy smiled, not entirely heartfelt, but a smile nonetheless, and allowed him to lead her to the patio.

Chapter 2

In which Our Heroine displays a decided lack of respect for all things romantic.

Gregory was nothing if not a gentleman, and he hid his disappointment well as he offered his arm to Lady Lucinda and escorted her to the makeshift dance floor. She was, he was sure, a perfectly charming and lovely young lady, but she wasn't Miss Hermione Watson.

And he had been waiting his entire life to meet Miss Hermione Watson.

Still, this *could* be considered beneficial to his cause. Lady Lucinda was clearly Miss Watson's closest friend—Miss Watson had positively gushed about her during their brief conversation, during which time Lady Lucinda gazed off at something beyond his shoulder, apparently not listening to a word. And with four sisters, Gregory knew a thing or two about women, the most important of which was that it was always a good idea to befriend the friend, provided they really *were* friends, and not just that odd thing women did where they pretended to be friends and were actually just waiting for the perfect moment to knife each other in the ribs.

Mysterious creatures, women. If they could just learn to say what they meant, the world would be a far simpler place.

But Miss Watson and Lady Lucinda gave every appearance of friendship and devotion, Lady Lucinda's woolgathering aside. And if Gregory wished to learn more about Miss Watson, Lady Lucinda Abernathy was the obvious place to start.

"Have you been a guest at Aubrey Hall very long?" Gregory asked politely as they waited for the music to begin.

"Just since yesterday," she replied. "And you? We did not see you at any of the gatherings thus far."

"I only arrived this evening," he said. "After supper." He grimaced. Now that he was no longer gazing upon Miss Watson, he remembered that he was rather hungry.

"You must be famished," Lady Lucinda exclaimed. "Would you prefer to take a turn around the patio instead of dancing? I promise that we may stroll past the refreshment table."

Gregory could have hugged her. "You, Lady Lucinda, are a capital young lady."

She smiled, but it was an odd sort of smile, and he couldn't quite tell what it meant. She'd liked his compliment, of that he was fairly certain, but there was something else there as well, something a little bit rueful, maybe something a little bit resigned.

"You must have a brother," he said.

"I do," she confirmed, smiling at his deduction. "He is four years my elder and always hungry. I will be forever amazed we had any food in the larder when he was home from school."

Gregory fit her hand in the crook of his elbow, and together they moved to the perimeter of the patio.

"This way," Lady Lucinda said, giving his arm a little tug when he tried to steer them in a counterclockwise direction. "Unless you would prefer sweets."

Gregory felt his face light up. "Are there savories?"

"Sandwiches. They are small, but they are quite delicious, especially the egg."

He nodded, somewhat absently. He'd caught sight of Miss Watson out of the corner of his eye, and it was a bit difficult to concentrate on anything else. Especially as she had been surrounded by men. Gregory was sure they had been just waiting for someone to remove Lady Lucinda from her side before moving in for the attack.

"Er, have you known Miss Watson very long?" he asked, trying not to be too obvious.

There was a very slight pause, and then she said, "Three years. We are students together at Miss Moss's. Or rather we were students together. We completed our studies earlier this year."

"May I assume you plan to make your debuts in London later this spring?"

"Yes," she replied, nodding toward a table laden with small snacks. "We have spent the last few months preparing, as Hermione's mother likes to call it, attending house parties and small gatherings."

"Polishing yourselves?" he asked with a smile.

Her lips curved in answer. "Exactly that. I should make an excellent candlestick by now."

He found himself amused. "A mere candlestick, Lady Lucinda? Pray, do not understate your value. At the very least you are one of those extravagant silver urns everyone seems to need in their sitting rooms lately."

"I am an urn, then," she said, almost appearing to consider the idea. "What would that make Hermione, I wonder?"

A jewel. A diamond. A diamond set in gold. A diamond set in gold surrounded by . . .

He forcibly halted the direction of his thoughts. He could perform his poetic gymnastics later, when he wasn't expected to keep up one end of a conversation. A conversation with a different young lady. "I'm sure I do not know," he said lightly, offering her a plate. "I have only barely made Miss Watson's acquaintance, after all."

She said nothing, but her eyebrows rose ever so slightly. And that, of course, was when Gregory realized he was glancing over her shoulder to get a better look at Miss Watson.

Lady Lucinda let out a small sigh. "You should probably know that she is in love with someone else."

Gregory dragged his gaze back to the woman he was meant to be paying attention to. "I beg your pardon?"

She shrugged delicately as she placed a few small sandwiches on her plate. "Hermione. She is in love with someone else. I thought you would like to know."

Gregory gaped at her, and then, against every last drop of his good judgment, looked back at Miss Watson. It was the most obvious, pathetic gesture, but he couldn't help himself. He just . . . Dear God, he just wanted to look at her and look at her and never stop. If this wasn't love, he could not imagine what was.

"Ham?"

"What?"

"Ham." Lady Lucinda was holding out a little strip of sandwich with a pair of serving tongs. Her face was annoyingly serene. "Would you care for one?" she asked.

He grunted and held out his plate. And then, because he couldn't leave the matter as it was, he said stiffly, "I'm sure it is none of my business."

"About the sandwich?"

"About Miss Watson," he ground out.

Even though, of course, he meant no such thing. As far as he was concerned, Hermione Watson was very much his business, or at least she would be, very soon.

It was somewhat disconcerting that *she* had apparently not been hit by the same thunderbolt that had struck him. It had never occurred to him that when he did fall in love, his intended might not feel the same, and with equal immediacy, too. But at least this explanation—her thinking she was in love with someone else—assuaged his pride. It was much more palatable to think her infatuated with someone else than completely indifferent to him.

All that was left to do was make her realize that whoever the other man was, he was not the one for her.

Gregory was not so filled with conceit that he thought he could win any woman upon whom he set his sights, but he certainly had never had *difficulties* with the fairer sex, and given the nature of his reaction to Miss Watson, it was simply inconceivable that his feelings could go unrequited for very long. He might have to work to win her heart and hand, but that would simply make victory all the sweeter.

Or so he told himself. Truth was, a mutual thunderbolt would have been far less trouble.

"Don't feel badly," Lady Lucinda said, craning her neck slightly as she surveyed the sandwiches, looking, presumably, for something more exotic than British pig.

"I don't," he bit off, then waited for her to actually return her attention to him. When she didn't, he said again, "I don't."

She turned, gazed at him frankly, and blinked. "Well, that's refreshing, I must say. Most men are crushed."

He scowled. "What do you mean, most men are crushed?"

"Exactly what I said," she replied, giving him an impatient glance. "Or if they're not crushed, they become rather unaccountably angry." She let out a ladylike snort. "As if any of it could be considered her fault."

"Fault?" Gregory echoed, because in truth, he was having a devil of a time following her.

"You are not the first gentleman to imagine himself in love with Hermione," she said, her expression quite jaded. "It happens all the time."

"I don't *imagine* myself in love—" He cut himself off, hoping she didn't notice the stress on the word *imagine*. Good God, what was happening to him? He used to have a sense of humor. Even about himself. Especially about himself.

"You don't?" She sounded pleasantly surprised. "Well, that's refreshing."

"Why," he asked with narrowed eyes, "is that refreshing?

She returned with: "Why are you asking so many questions?"

"I'm not," he protested, even though he was.

She sighed, then utterly surprised him by saying, "I am sorry."

"I beg your pardon?"

She glanced at the egg salad sandwich on her plate, then back up at him, the order of which he did not find complimentary. He usually rated above egg salad. "I thought you would wish to speak of Hermione," she said. "I apologize if I was mistaken."

Which put Gregory in a fine quandary. He could admit that he'd fallen headlong in love with Miss Watson, which was rather embarrassing, even to a hopeless romantic such as himself. Or he could deny it all, which she clearly wouldn't believe. Or he could compromise, and admit to a mild infatuation, which he might normally regard as the best solution, except that it could only be insulting to Lady Lucinda.

He'd met the two girls at the same time, after all. And he wasn't headlong in love with *her*.

But then, as if she could read his thoughts (which frankly scared him), she waved a hand and said, "Pray do not worry yourself over my feelings. I'm quite used to this. As I said, it happens *all* the time."

Open heart, insert blunt dagger. Twist.

"Not to mention," she continued blithely, "that I am practically engaged myself." And then she took a bite of the egg salad.

Gregory found himself wondering what sort of man had found himself attached to this odd creature. He didn't pity the fellow, exactly, just . . . wondered.

And then Lady Lucinda let out a little "Oh!"

His eyes followed hers, to the spot where Miss Watson had once stood.

"I wonder where she went," Lady Lucinda said.

Gregory immediately turned toward the door, hoping to catch one last glimpse of her before she disappeared, but she was already gone. It was damned frustrating, that. What was the point of a mad, bad, immediate attraction if one couldn't do anything about it?

And forget *all* about it being one-sided. Good Lord.

He wasn't sure what one called sighing through gritted teeth, but that's exactly what he did.

"Ah, Lady Lucinda, there you are."

Gregory looked up to see his sister-in-law approaching.

And remembered that he'd forgotten all about her. Kate wouldn't take offense; she was a phenomenally good sport. But still, Gregory did usually try to have better manners with women to whom he was not blood related.

Lady Lucinda gave a pretty little curtsy. "Lady Bridgerton."

Kate smiled warmly in return. "Miss Watson has asked me to inform you that she was not feeling well and has retired for the evening."

"She has? Did she say—Oh, never mind." Lady Lucinda gave a little wave with her hand—the sort meant to convey nonchalance, but Gregory saw the barest hint of frustration pinching at the corners of her mouth.

"A head cold, I believe," Kate added.

Lady Lucinda gave a brief nod. "Yes," she said, looking a bit less sympathetic than Gregory would have imagined, given the circumstances, "it would be."

"And you," Kate continued, turning to Gregory, "have not even seen fit to greet me. How are you?"

He took her hands, kissed them as one in apology. "Tardy."

"That I knew." Her face assumed an expression that was not irritated, just a little bit exasperated. "How are you otherwise?"

"Otherwise lovely." He grinned. "As always."

"As always," she repeated, giving him a look that was a clear promise of future interrogation. "Lady Lucinda," Kate continued, her tone considerably less dry, "I trust you have made the acquaintance of my husband's brother, Mr. Gregory Bridgerton?"

"Indeed," Lady Lucinda replied. "We have been admiring the food. The sandwiches are delicious."

"Thank you," Kate said, then added, "and has Gregory promised you a dance? I cannot promise music of a professional quality, but we managed to round together a string quartet amongst our guests."

"He did," Lady Lucinda replied, "but I released him from his obligation so that he might assuage his hunger."

"You must have brothers," Kate said with a smile.

Lady Lucinda looked to Gregory with a slightly startled expression before replying, "Just one."

He turned to Kate. "I made the same observation earlier," he explained.

Kate let out a short laugh. "Great minds, to be sure." She turned to the younger woman and said, "It is well worth understanding the behavior of men, Lady Lucinda. One should never underestimate the power of food."

Lady Lucinda regarded her with wide eyes. "For the benefit of a pleasing mood?"

"Well, *that*," Kate said, almost offhandedly, "but one really shouldn't discount its uses for the purpose of winning an argument. Or simply getting what you want."

"She's barely out of the schoolroom, Kate," Gregory chided.

Kate ignored him and instead smiled widely at Lady Lucinda. "One is never too young to acquire important skills."

Lady Lucinda looked at Gregory, then at Kate, and then her eyes began to sparkle with humor. "I understand why so many look up to you, Lady Bridgerton."

Kate laughed. "You are too kind, Lady Lucinda."

"Oh, please, Kate," Gregory cut in. He turned to Lady Lucinda and added, "She will stand here all night if you keep offering compliments."

"Pay him no attention," Kate said with a grin. "He is young and foolish and knows not of what he speaks."

Gregory was about to make another comment—he couldn't very well allow Kate to get away with that—but then Lady Lucinda cut in.

"I would happily sing your praises for the rest of the evening, Lady Bridgerton, but I believe that it is time for me to retire. I should like to check on Hermione. She has been under the weather all day, and I wish to assure myself that she is well."

"Of course," Kate replied. "Please do give her my regards, and be certain to ring if you need anything. Our housekeeper fancies herself something of an herbalist, and she is always mixing potions. Some of them even work." She grinned, and the expression was so friendly that Gregory instantly realized that she approved of Lady

Lucinda. Which meant something. Kate had never suffered fools, gladly or otherwise.

"I shall walk you to the door," he said quickly. It was the least he could do to offer her this courtesy, and besides, it would not do to insult Miss Watson's closest friend.

They said their farewells, and Gregory fit her arm into the crook of his elbow. They walked in silence to the door to the drawing room, and Gregory said, "I trust you can make your way from here?"

"Of course," she replied. And then she looked up—her eyes were bluish, he noticed almost absently—and asked, "Would you like me to convey a message to Hermione?"

His lips parted with surprise. "Why would you do that?" he asked, before he could think to temper his response.

She just shrugged and said, "You are the lesser of two evils, Mr. Bridgerton."

He wanted desperately to ask her to clarify that comment, but he could not ask, not on such a flimsy acquaintance, so he instead worked to maintain an even mien as he said, "Give her my regards, that is all."

"Really?"

Damn, but that look in her eye was annoying. "Really."

She bobbed the tiniest of curtsies and was off.

Gregory stared at the doorway through which she had disappeared for a moment, then turned back to the party. The guests had begun dancing in greater numbers, and laughter was most certainly filling the air, but somehow the night felt dull and lifeless.

Food, he decided. He'd eat twenty more of those tiny little sandwiches and then he'd retire for the night as well.

All would come clear in the morning.

Lucy *knew* that Hermione didn't have a headache, or any sort of ache for that matter, and she was not at all surprised to find her sitting on her bed, poring over what appeared to be a four-page letter.

Written in an extremely compact hand.

"A footman brought it to me," Hermione said, not even looking up. "He said it arrived in today's post, but they forgot to bring it earlier."

Lucy sighed. "From Mr. Edmonds, I presume?"

Hermione nodded.

Lucy crossed the room she and Hermione were currently sharing and sat down in the chair at the vanity table. This wasn't the first piece of correspondence Hermione had received from Mr. Edmonds, and Lucy knew from experience that Hermione would need to read it twice, then once again for deeper analysis, and then finally one last time, if only to pick apart any hidden meanings in the salutation and closing.

Which meant that Lucy would have nothing to do but examine her fingernails for at least five minutes.

Which she did, not because she was terribly interested in her fingernails, nor because she was a particularly patient person, but rather because she knew a useless situation when she saw one, and she saw little reason in expending the energy to engage Hermione in conversation when Hermione was so patently uninterested in anything she had to say.

Fingernails could only occupy a girl for so long, however, especially when they were already meticulously neat and groomed, so Lucy stood and walked to the wardrobe, peering absently at her belongings.

"Oh, dash," she muttered, "I hate when she does that." Her maid had left a pair of shoes the wrong way, with the left on the right and the right on the left, and while Lucy knew there was nothing earth-shatteringly wrong with that, it did offend some strange (and extremely tidy) little corner of her sensibilities, so she righted the slippers, then stood back to inspect her handiwork, then planted her hands on her hips and turned around. "Are you finished yet?" she demanded.

"Almost," Hermione said, and it sounded as if the word had been resting on the edge of her lips the whole time, as if she'd had it ready so that she could fob off Lucy when she asked.

Lucy sat back down with a huff. It was a scene they had played out countless times before. Or at least four.

Yes, Lucy knew exactly how many letters Hermione had received from the romantic Mr. Edmonds. She would have liked *not* to have known; in fact, she was more than a little irritated that the item was taking up valuable space in her brain that might have been devoted to something useful, like botany or music, or good heavens, even another page in *DeBrett's*, but the unfortunate fact was, Mr. Edmonds's letters were nothing if not an *event*, and when Hermione had an event, well, Lucy was forced to have it, too.

They had shared a room for three years at Miss Moss's, and since Lucy had no close female relative who might help her make her bow into society, Hermione's mother had agreed to sponsor her, and so here they were, still together.

Which was lovely, really, except for the always-present (in spirit, at least) Mr. Edmonds. Lucy had made his acquaintance only once, but it certainly *felt* as if he were always there, hovering over them, causing Hermione to sigh at strange moments and gaze wistfully off into the distance as if she were committing a love sonnet to memory so that she might include it in her next reply.

"You are aware," Lucy said, even though Hermione had not indicated that she was finished reading her missive, "that your parents will never permit you to marry him."

That was enough to get Hermione to set the letter down, albeit briefly. "Yes," she said with an irritated expression, "you've said as much."

"He is a secretary," Lucy said.

"I realize that."

"A secretary," Lucy repeated, even though they'd had this conversation countless times before. "Your *father's* secretary."

Hermione had picked the letter back up in an attempt to ignore Lucy, but finally she gave up and set it back down, confirming Lucy's suspicions that she had long since finished it and was now in the first, or possibly even second, rereading.

"Mr. Edmonds is a good and honorable man," Hermione said, lips pinched.

"I'm sure he is," Lucy said, "but you can't *marry* him. Your father is a viscount. Do you really think he will allow his only daughter to marry a penniless secretary?"

"My father loves me," Hermione muttered, but her voice wasn't exactly replete with conviction.

"I am not trying to dissuade you from making a love match," Lucy began, "but—"

"That is exactly what you are trying to do," Hermione cut in.

"Not at all. I just don't see why you can't try to fall in love with someone of whom your parents might actually approve."

Hermione's lovely mouth twisted into a frustrated line. "You don't understand."

"What is there to understand? Don't you think your life might be just a touch easier if you fell in love with someone suitable?"

"Lucy, we don't get to choose who we fall in love with."

Lucy crossed her arms. "I don't see why not."

Hermione's mouth actually fell open. "Lucy Abernathy," she said, "you understand nothing."

"Yes," Lucy said dryly, "you've mentioned."

"How can you possibly think a person can choose who she falls in love with?" Hermione said passionately, although not so passionately that she was forced to rouse herself from her semireclined position on the bed. "One doesn't *choose*. It just happens. In an instant."

"Now *that* I don't believe," Lucy replied, and then added, because she could not resist, "not for an instant."

"Well, it does," Hermione insisted. "I know, because it happened to me. I wasn't *looking* to fall in love."

"Weren't you?"

"No." Hermione glared at her. "I wasn't. I fully intended to find a husband in London. Really, who would have expected to meet anyone in *Fenchley*?"

Said with the sort of disdain found only in a native Fenchleyan.

Lucy rolled her eyes and tilted her head to the side, waiting for Hermione to get on with it.

Which Hermione did not appreciate. "Don't look at me like that," she snipped.

"Like what?"

"Like *that*."

"I repeat, like what?"

Hermione's entire face pinched. "You know exactly what I'm talking about."

Lucy clapped a hand to her face. "Oh my," she gasped. "You looked *exactly* like your mother just then."

Hermione drew back with affront. "That was unkind."

"Your mother is lovely!"

"Not when her face is all pinchy."

"Your mother is lovely even with a pinchy face," Lucy said, trying to put an end to the subject. "Now, do you intend to tell me about Mr. Edmonds or not?"

"Do you plan to mock me?"

"Of course not."

Hermione lifted her brows.

"Hermione, I promise I will not mock you."

Hermione still looked dubious, but she said, "Very well. But if you do—"

"Hermione."

"As I told you," she said, giving Lucy a warning glance, "I wasn't expecting to find love. I didn't even know my father had hired a new secretary. I was just walking in the garden, deciding which of the roses I wished to have cut for the table, and then . . . *I saw him.*"

Said with enough drama to warrant a role on the stage.

"Oh, Hermione," Lucy sighed.

"You said you wouldn't mock me," Hermione said, and she actually jabbed a finger in Lucy's direction, which struck Lucy as sufficiently out of character that she quieted down.

"I didn't even see his face at first," Hermione continued. "Just the back of his head, the way his hair curled against the collar of his coat." She sighed then. She actually sighed as she turned to Lucy with the most pathetic expression. "And the color. Truly, Lucy, have you ever seen hair such a spectacular shade of blond?"

Considering the number of times Lucy had been forced to listen to gentlemen make the same statement about Hermione's hair, she thought it spoke rather well of her that she refrained from comment.

But Hermione was not done. Not nearly. "Then he turned," she said, "and I saw his profile, and I swear to you I heard music."

Lucy would have liked to point out that the Watsons' conservatory was located right next to the rose garden, but she held her tongue.

"And then he turned," Hermione said, her voice growing soft and her eyes taking on that *I'm-memorizing-a-love-sonnet* expression, "and all I could think was—*I am ruined.*"

Lucy gasped. "Don't *say* that. Don't even hint at it."

Ruin was not the sort of thing any young lady mentioned lightly.

"Not *ruined* ruined," Hermione said impatiently. "Good heavens, Lucy, I was in the rose garden, or haven't you been listening? But I knew—I *knew* that I was ruined for all other men. There could never be another to compare."

"And you knew all this from the back of his neck?" Lucy asked.

Hermione shot her an exceedingly irritated expression. "And his profile, but that's not the point."

Lucy waited patiently for the point, even though she was quite certain it wouldn't be one with which she would agree. Or probably even understand.

"The point is," Hermione said, her voice growing so soft that Lucy had to lean forward to hear her, "that I cannot possibly be happy without him. Not possibly."

"Well," Lucy said slowly, because she wasn't precisely certain how she was meant to add to *that*, "you seem happy now."

"That is only because I know he is waiting for me. And"—Hermione held up the letter—"he writes that he loves me."

"Oh dear," Lucy said to herself.

Hermione must have heard her, because her mouth tightened, but she didn't say anything. The two of them just sat there, in their respective places, for a full minute, and then Lucy cleared her throat and said, "That nice Mr. Bridgerton seemed taken with you."

Hermione shrugged.

"He's a younger son, but I believe he has a nice portion. And he is certainly from a good family."

"Lucy, I told you I am not interested."

"Well, he's very handsome," Lucy said, perhaps a bit more emphatically than she'd meant to.

"You pursue him, then," Hermione retorted.

Lucy stared at her in shock. "You know I cannot. I'm practically engaged to Lord Haselby."

"Practically," Hermione reminded her.

"It might as well be official," Lucy said. And it was true. Her uncle had discussed the matter with the Earl of Davenport, Viscount Haselby's father, years ago. Haselby was about ten years older than Lucy, and they were all simply waiting for her to grow up.

Which she supposed she'd done. Surely the wedding wouldn't be too far off now.

And it was a good match. Haselby was a perfectly pleasant fellow. He didn't speak to her as if she were an idiot, he seemed to be kind to animals, and his looks were pleasing enough, even if his hair was beginning to thin. Of course, Lucy had only actually met her intended husband three times, but everyone knew that first impressions were extremely important and usually spot-on accurate.

Besides, her uncle had been her guardian since her father had died ten years earlier, and if he hadn't exactly showered her and her brother Richard with love and affection, he had done his duty by them and raised them well, and Lucy knew it was her duty to obey his wishes and honor the betrothal he had arranged.

Or practically arranged.

Really, it didn't make much difference. She was going to marry Haselby. Everyone knew it.

"I think you use him as an excuse," Hermione said.

Lucy's spine stiffened. "I beg your pardon."

"You use Haselby as an excuse," Hermione repeated, and her face took on a lofty expression Lucy did not enjoy one bit. "So that you do not allow your heart to become engaged elsewhere."

"And just where else, precisely, might I have engaged my heart?" Lucy demanded. "The season has not even begun!"

"Perhaps," Hermione said, "but we have been out and about, getting 'polished' as you and my mother like to put it. You have not been living under a rock, Lucy. You have met any number of men."

There was really no way to point out that none of those men ever even *saw* her when Hermione was near. Hermione would try to deny it, but they would both know that she was lying in an attempt to spare Lucy's feelings. So Lucy instead grumbled something under her breath that was meant to be a reply without actually *being* a reply.

And then Hermione did not say anything; she just looked at her in that arch manner that she never used with anyone else, and finally Lucy had to defend herself.

"It's not an excuse," she said, crossing her arms, then planting her hands on her hips when that didn't feel right. "Truly, what would be the point of it? You know that I'm to marry Haselby. It's been planned for ages."

She crossed her arms again. Then dropped them. Then finally sat down.

"It's not a bad match," Lucy said. "Truthfully, after what happened to Georgiana Whiton, I should be getting down on my hands and knees and kissing my uncle's feet for making such an acceptable alliance."

There was a moment of horrified, almost reverent silence. If they had been Catholic, they would have surely crossed themselves. "There but for the grace of God," Hermione finally said.

Lucy nodded slowly. Georgiana had been married off to a wheezy seventy-year-old with gout. And not even a titled seventy-year-old with gout. Good heavens, she ought to have at least earned a "Lady" before her name for her sacrifice.

"So you see," Lucy finished, "Haselby really isn't such a bad sort. Better than most, actually."

Hermione looked at her. Closely. "Well, if it is what you wish, Lucy, you know that I shall support you unreservedly. But as for me . . ." She sighed, and her green eyes took on that faraway look that made grown men swoon. "I want something else."

"I know you do," Lucy said, trying to smile. But she couldn't even begin to imagine how Hermione would achieve her dreams. In the world they lived in, viscounts' daughters did not marry viscounts' secretaries. And it seemed to Lucy that it would make far more sense to adjust Hermione's dreams than to reshape the social order. Easier, too.

But right now she was tired. And she wanted to go to bed. She would work on Hermione in the morning. Starting with that handsome Mr. Bridgerton. He would be perfect for her friend, and heaven knew he was interested.

Hermione would come around. Lucy would make sure of it.

Chapter 3

In which Our Hero tries very, very hard.

The following morning was bright and clear, and as Gregory helped himself to breakfast, his sister-in-law appeared at his side, smiling faintly, clearly up to something.

"Good morning," she said, far too breezy and cheerful.

Gregory nodded his greeting as he heaped eggs on his plate. "Kate."

"I thought, with the weather so fine, that we might organize an excursion to the village."

"To buy ribbons and bows?"

"Exactly," she replied. "I do think it is important to support the local shopkeepers, don't you?"

"Of course," he murmured, "although I have not recently found myself in great need of ribbons and bows."

Kate appeared not to notice his sarcasm. "All of the young ladies have a bit of pin money and nowhere to spend it. If I do not send them to town they are liable to start a gaming establishment in the rose salon."

Now *that* was something he'd like to see.

"And," Kate continued quite determinedly, "if I send them to town, I will need to send them with escorts."

When Gregory did not respond quickly enough, she repeated, "*With escorts.*"

Gregory cleared his throat. "Might I assume you are asking me to walk to the village this afternoon?"

"This morning," she clarified, "*and*, since I thought to match everyone up, *and*, since you are a Bridgerton and thus my favorite gentleman of the bunch, I thought I might inquire if there happened to be anyone with whom you might prefer to be paired."

Kate was nothing if not a matchmaker, but in this case Gregory decided he ought to be grateful for her meddling tendencies. "As a matter of fact," he began, "there is—"

"Excellent!" Kate interrupted, clapping her hands together. "Lucy Abernathy it is."

Lucy Aber— "Lucy Abernathy?" he repeated, dumbfounded. "The Lady Lucinda?"

"Yes, the two of you seemed so well-matched last evening, and I must say, Gregory, I like her tremendously. She says she is practically engaged, but it is my opinion that—"

"I'm not interested in Lady Lucinda," he cut in, deciding it would be too dangerous to wait for Kate to draw breath.

"You're not?"

"No. I'm not. I—" He leaned in, even though they were the only two people in the breakfast room. Somehow it seemed odd, and yes, a little bit embarrassing to shout it out. "Hermione Watson," he said quietly. "I would like to be paired with Miss Watson."

"Really?" Kate didn't look disappointed exactly, but she did look slightly resigned. As if she'd heard this before. Repeatedly.

Damn.

"Yes," Gregory responded, and he felt a rather sizable surge of irritation washing over him. First at Kate, because, well, she was right there, and he'd fallen desperately in love and all she could do was say, "Really?" But then he realized he'd been rather irked all morning. He hadn't slept well the night before; he hadn't been able to stop thinking about Hermione and the slope of her neck, the green of her eyes, the soft lilt of her voice. He had never—never—reacted to a woman like this, and while he was in some way relieved to have finally found the woman he planned to make his wife, it was a bit disconcerting that she had not had the same reaction to *him*.

Heaven knew he'd dreamed of this moment before. Whenever he'd thought about finding his true love, she had always been fuzzy in his thoughts—nameless, faceless. But she had always felt the same grand passion. She hadn't sent him off dancing with her best friend, for God's sake.

"Hermione Watson it is, then," Kate said, exhaling in that way females did when they meant to tell you something you couldn't possibly begin to understand even if they had chosen to convey it in English, which, of course they did not.

Hermione Watson it was. Hermione Watson it would be.

Soon.

Maybe even that morning.

"Do you suppose there is anything to purchase in the village aside from bows and ribbons?" Hermione asked Lucy as they pulled on their gloves.

"I certainly hope so," Lucy responded. "They do this at every house party, don't they? Send us off with our pin money to purchase ribbons and bows. I could decorate an entire house by now. Or at the very least, a small thatched cottage."

Hermione smiled gamely. "I shall donate mine to the cause, and together we shall remake a . . ." She paused, thinking, then smiled. "A large thatched cottage!"

Lucy grinned. There was something so *loyal* about Hermione. Nobody ever saw it, of course. No one ever bothered to look past her face. Although, to be fair, Hermione rarely shared enough of herself with any of her admirers for them to realize what lay behind her pretty exterior. It wasn't that she was shy, precisely, although she certainly wasn't as outgoing as Lucy. Rather, Hermione was private. She simply did not care to share her thoughts and opinions with people she did not know.

And it drove the gentlemen mad.

Lucy peered out the window as they entered one of Aubrey Hall's many drawing rooms. Lady Bridgerton had instructed them to arrive promptly at eleven. "At least it doesn't look as if it might rain," she said. The last time they'd been sent out for fripperies it had drizzled the entire way home. The tree canopy had kept them moderately dry, but their boots had been nearly ruined. And Lucy had been sneezing for a week.

"Good morning, Lady Lucinda, Miss Watson."

It was Lady Bridgerton, their hostess, striding into the room in that confident way of hers. Her dark hair was neatly pulled back, and her eyes gleamed with brisk intelligence. "How lovely to see you both," she said. "You are the last of the ladies to arrive."

"We are?" Lucy asked, horrified. She *hated* being late. "I'm so terribly sorry. Didn't you say eleven o'clock?"

"Oh dear, I did not mean to upset you," Lady Bridgerton said. "I did indeed say eleven o'clock. But that is because I thought to send everyone out in shifts."

"In shifts?" Hermione echoed.

"Yes, it's far more entertaining that way, wouldn't you agree? I have eight ladies and eight gentlemen. If I sent the lot of you out at once, it would be impossible to have a proper conversation. Not to mention the width of the road. I would hate for you to be tripping over one another."

There was also something to be said for safety in numbers, but Lucy kept her thoughts to herself. Lady Bridgerton clearly had some sort of agenda, and as Lucy had already decided that she greatly admired the viscountess, she was rather curious as to the outcome.

"Miss Watson, you will be paired with my husband's brother. I believe you made his acquaintance last night?"

Hermione nodded politely.

Lucy smiled to herself. Mr. Bridgerton had been a busy man that morning. Well done.

"And you, Lady Lucinda," Lady Bridgerton continued, "will be escorted by Mr. Berbrooke." She smiled weakly, almost in apology. "He is a relation of sorts," she added, "and, ah, truly a good-natured fellow."

"A relation?" Lucy echoed, since she wasn't exactly certain how she was meant to respond to Lady Bridgerton's uncharacteristically hesitant tone. "Of sorts?"

"Yes. My husband's brother's wife's sister is married to his brother."

"Oh." Lucy kept her expression bland. "Then you are close?"

Lady Bridgerton laughed. "I like you, Lady Lucinda. And as for Neville . . . well, I am certain you will find him entertaining. Ah, here he is now. Neville! Neville!"

Lucy watched as Lady Bridgerton moved to greet Mr. Neville Berbrooke at the door. They had already been introduced, of course; introductions had been made for everyone at the house party. But Lucy had not yet conversed with Mr. Berbrooke, nor truly even seen him except from afar. He seemed an affable enough fellow, rather jolly-looking with a ruddy complexion and a shock of blond hair.

"Hallo, Lady Bridgerton," he said, somehow crashing into a table leg as he entered the room. "Excellent breakfast this morning. Especially the kippers."

"Thank you," Lady Bridgerton replied, glancing nervously at the Chinese vase now teetering on the tabletop. "I'm sure you remember Lady Lucinda."

The pair murmured their greetings, then Mr. Berbrooke said, "D'you like kippers?"

Lucy looked first to Hermione, then to Lady Bridgerton for guidance, but neither seemed any less baffled than she, so she just said, "Er . . . yes?"

"Excellent!" he said. "I say, is that a tufted tern out the window?"

Lucy blinked. She looked to Lady Bridgerton, only to discover that the viscountess would not make eye contact. "A tufted tern you say," Lucy finally murmured, since she could not think of any other suitable reply. Mr. Berbrooke had ambled over to the window, so she went to join him. She peered out. She could see no birds.

Meanwhile, out of the corner of her eye she could see that Mr. Bridgerton had entered the room and was doing his best to charm Hermione. Good heavens, the man had a nice smile! Even white teeth, and the expression extended to his eyes, unlike most of the bored young aristocrats Lucy had met. Mr. Bridgerton smiled as if he meant it.

Which made sense, of course, as he was smiling at Hermione, with whom he was quite obviously infatuated.

Lucy could not hear what they were saying, but she easily recognized the expression on Hermione's face. Polite, of course, since Hermione would never be impolite. And maybe no one could see it but Lucy, who knew her friend so well, but Hermione was doing no more than tolerating Mr. Bridgerton's attentions, accepting his flattery with a nod and a pretty smile while her mind was far, far elsewhere.

With that cursed Mr. Edmonds.

Lucy clenched her jaw as she pretended to look for terns, tufted or otherwise, with Mr. Berbrooke. She had no reason to think Mr. Edmonds anything but a nice young man, but the simple truth was, Hermione's parents would never countenance the match, and while Hermione might think she would be able to live happily on a secretary's salary, Lucy was quite certain that once the first bloom of marriage faded, Hermione would be miserable.

And she could do *so* much better. It was obvious that Hermione could marry anyone. Anyone. She wouldn't need to settle. She could be a queen of the *ton* if she so desired.

Lucy eyed Mr. Bridgerton, nodding and keeping one ear on Mr. Berbrooke, who was back on the subject of kippers. Mr. Bridgerton was perfect. He didn't possess a title, but Lucy was not so ruthless that she felt Hermione had to marry into the highest available rank. She just could not align herself with a secretary, for heaven's sake.

Plus, Mr. Bridgerton was extremely handsome, with dark, chestnut hair and lovely hazel eyes. And his family seemed perfectly nice and reasonable, which Lucy had to think was a point in his favor. When you married a man, you married his family, really.

Lucy couldn't imagine a better husband for Hermione. Well, she supposed she would not complain if Mr. Bridgerton were next in line for a marquisate, but really, one could not have everything. And most importantly, she was quite certain that he would make Hermione happy, even if Hermione did not yet realize this.

"I will make this happen," she said to herself.

"Eh?" from Mr. Berbrooke. "Did you find the bird?"

"Over there," Lucy said, pointing toward a tree.

He leaned forward. "Really?"

"Oh, Lucy!" came Hermione's voice.

Lucy turned around.

"Shall we be off? Mr. Bridgerton is eager to be on his way."

"I am at your service, Miss Watson," the man in question said. "We depart at your discretion."

Hermione gave Lucy a look that clearly said that *she* was eager to be on her way, so Lucy said, "Let us depart, then," and she took Mr. Berbrooke's proffered arm and allowed him to lead her to the front drive, managing to yelp only once, even though she thrice stubbed her toe on heaven knew what, but somehow, even with a nice, lovely expanse of grass, Mr. Berbrooke managed to find every tree root, rock, and bump, and lead her directly to them.

Gad.

Lucy mentally prepared herself for further injury. It was going to be a painful outing. But a productive one. By the time they returned home, Hermione would be at least a little intrigued by Mr. Bridgerton.

Lucy would make sure of it.

If Gregory had had any doubts about Miss Hermione Watson, they were banished the moment he placed her hand in the crook of his elbow. There was a rightness to it, a strange, mystical sense of two halves coming together. She fit perfectly next to him. *They* fit.

And he wanted her.

It wasn't even desire. It was strange, actually. He wasn't feeling anything so plebian as bodily desire. It was something else. Something within. He simply wanted her to be his. He wanted to look at her, and to know. To *know* that she would carry his name and bear his children and gaze lovingly at him every morning over a cup of chocolate.

He wanted to tell her all this, to share his dreams, to paint a picture of their life together, but he was no fool, and so he simply said, as he guided her down the front path, "You look exceptionally lovely this morning, Miss Watson."

"Thank you," she said.

And then said nothing else.

He cleared his throat. "Did you sleep well?"

"Yes, thank you," she said.

"Are you enjoying your stay?"

"Yes, thank you," she said.

Funny, but he'd always thought conversation with the woman he'd marry would come just a *little* bit easier.

He reminded himself that she still fancied herself in love with another man. Someone unsuitable, if Lady Lucinda's comment of the night before was any indication. What was that she had called him—the lesser of two evils?

He glanced forward. Lady Lucinda was stumbling along ahead of him on the arm of Neville Berbrooke, who had never learned to adjust his gait for a lady. She seemed to be managing well enough, although he did think he might have heard a small cry of pain at one point.

He gave his head a mental shake. It was probably just a bird. Hadn't Neville said he'd seen a flock of them through the window?

"Have you been friends with Lady Lucinda for very long?" he asked Miss Watson. He knew the answer, of course; Lady Lucinda had told him the night before. But he couldn't think of anything else to ask. And he needed a question that could not be answered with *yes, thank you* or *no, thank you*.

"Three years," Miss Watson replied. "She is my dearest friend."

And then her face finally took on a bit of animation as she said, "We ought to catch up."

"To Mr. Berbrooke and Lady Lucinda?"

"Yes," she said with a firm nod. "Yes, we ought."

The last thing Gregory wanted to do was squander his precious time alone with Miss Watson, but he dutifully called out to Berbrooke to hold up. He did, stopping so suddenly that Lady Lucinda quite literally crashed into him.

She let out a startled cry, but other than that was clearly unhurt.

Miss Watson took advantage of the moment, however, by disengaging her hand from his elbow and rushing forward. "Lucy!" she cried out. "Oh, my dearest Lucy, are you injured?"

"Not at all," Lady Lucinda replied, looking slightly confused by the extreme level of her friend's concern.

"I must take your arm," Miss Watson declared, hooking her elbow through Lady Lucinda's.

"You must?" Lady Lucinda echoed, twisting away. Or rather, attempting to. "No, truly, that is not necessary."

"I insist."

"It is not necessary," Lady Lucinda repeated, and Gregory wished he could see her face, because it *sounded* as if she were gritting her teeth.

"Heh heh," came Berbrooke's voice. "P'rhaps I'll take your arm, Bridgerton."

Gregory gave him a level look. "*No.*"

Berbrooke blinked. "It was a joke, you know."

Gregory fought the urge to sigh and somehow managed to say, "I was aware." He'd known Neville Berbrooke since they'd both been in leading strings, and he usually had more patience with him, but right now he wanted nothing so much as to fit him with a muzzle.

Meanwhile, the two girls were bickering about something, in

tones hushed enough that Gregory couldn't hope to make out what they were saying. Not that he'd likely have understood their language even if they'd been shouting it; it was clearly something bafflingly female. Lady Lucinda was still tugging her arm, and Miss Watson quite simply refused to let go.

"She is injured," Hermione said, turning and batting her eyelashes.

Batting her eyelashes? She chose *this* moment to flirt?

"I am not," Lucy returned. She turned to the two gentlemen. "I am not," she repeated. "Not in the slightest. We should continue."

Gregory couldn't quite decide if he was amused or insulted by the entire spectacle. Miss Watson quite clearly did not wish for his escort, and while some men loved to pine for the unattainable, he'd always preferred his women smiling, friendly, and willing.

Miss Watson turned then, however, and he caught sight of the back of her neck (what *was* it about the back of her neck?). He felt himself sinking again, that madly in love feeling that had captured him the night before, and he told himself not to lose heart. He hadn't even known her a full day; she merely needed time to get to know him. Love did not strike everyone with the same speed. His brother Colin, for example, had known his wife for years and years before he'd realized they were meant to be together.

Not that Gregory planned to wait years and years, but still, it did put the current situation in a better perspective.

After a few moments it became apparent that Miss Watson would not acquiesce, and the two women would be walking arm in arm. Gregory fell in step beside Miss Watson, while Berbrooke ambled on, somewhere in the vicinity of Lady Lucinda.

"You must tell us what it is like to be from such a large family," Lady Lucinda said to him, leaning forward and speaking past Miss Watson. "Hermione and I each have but one sibling."

"Have three m'self," said Berbrooke. "All boys, all of us. 'Cept for my sister, of course."

"It is . . ." Gregory was about to give his usual answer, about it being mad and crazy and usually more trouble than it was worth, but then somehow the deeper truth slipped across his lips, and he found himself saying, "Actually, it's comforting."

"Comforting?" Lady Lucinda echoed. "What an intriguing choice of word."

He looked past Miss Watson to see her regarding him with curious blue eyes.

"Yes," he said slowly, allowing his thoughts to coalesce before replying. "There is comfort in having a family, I think. It's a sense of . . . just *knowing*, I suppose."

"What do you mean?" Lucy asked, and she appeared quite sincerely interested.

"I know that they are there," Gregory said, "that should I ever be in trouble, or even simply in need of a good conversation, I can always turn to them."

And it was true. He had never really thought about it in so many words, but it was true. He was not as close to his brothers as they were to one another, but that was only natural, given the age difference. When they had been men about town, he had been a student at Eton. And now they were all three married, with families of their own.

But still, he knew that should he need them, or his sisters for that matter, he had only to ask.

He never had, of course. Not for anything important. Or even most things unimportant. But he knew that he could. It was more than most men had in this world, more than most men would ever have.

"Mr. Bridgerton?"

He blinked. Lady Lucinda was regarding him quizzically.

"My apologies," he murmured. "Woolgathering, I suppose." He offered her a smile and a nod, then glanced over at Miss Watson, who, he was surprised to see, had also turned to look at him. Her eyes seemed huge in her face, clear and dazzlingly green, and for a moment he felt an almost electric connection. She smiled, just a little, and with a touch of embarrassment at having been caught, then looked away.

Gregory's heart leaped.

And then Lady Lucinda spoke again. "That is *exactly* how I feel about Hermione," she said. "She is the sister of my heart."

"Miss Watson is truly an exceptional lady," Gregory murmured, then added, "As, of course, are you."

"She is a superb watercolorist," Lady Lucinda said.

Hermione blushed prettily. *"Lucy."*

"But you are," her friend insisted.

"Like to paint myself," came Neville Berbrooke's jovial voice. "Ruin my shirts every time, though."

Gregory glanced at him in surprise. Between his oddly revealing conversation with Lady Lucinda and his shared glance with Miss Watson, he'd almost forgotten Berbrooke was there.

"M'valet is up in arms about it," Neville continued, ambling along. "Don't know why they can't make paint that washes out of linen." He paused, apparently in deep thought. "Or wool."

"Do you like to paint?" Lady Lucinda asked Gregory.

"No talent for it," he admitted. "But my brother is an artist of some renown. Two of his paintings hang in the National Gallery."

"Oh, that is marvelous!" she exclaimed. She turned to Miss Watson. "Did you hear that, Hermione? You must ask Mr. Bridgerton to introduce you to his brother."

"I would not wish to inconvenience either Mr. Bridgerton," she said demurely.

"It would be no inconvenience at all," Gregory said, smiling down at her. "I would be delighted to make the introduction, and Benedict always loves to natter on about art. I rarely am able to follow the conversation, but he seems quite animated."

"You see," Lucy put in, patting Hermione's arm. "You and Mr. Bridgerton have a great deal in common."

Even Gregory thought that was a bit of a stretch, but he did not comment.

"Velvet," Neville suddenly declared.

Three heads swung in his direction. "I beg your pardon?" Lady Lucinda murmured.

"S'the worst," he said, nodding with great vigor. "T'get the paint out of, I mean."

Gregory could only see the back of her head, but he could well imagine her blinking as she said, "You wear velvet while you paint?"

"If it's cold."

"How . . . unique."

Neville's face lit up. "Do you think so? I've always wanted to be unique."

"You are," she said, and Gregory did not hear anything other than reassurance in her voice. "You most certainly are, Mr. Berbrooke."

Neville beamed. "Unique. I like that. Unique." He smiled anew, testing the word on his lips. "Unique. *Unique*. You-oo-oooooo-neek."

The foursome continued toward the village in amiable silence, punctuated by Gregory's occasional attempts to draw Miss Watson into a conversation. Sometimes he succeeded, but more often than not, it was Lady Lucinda who ended up chatting with him. When she wasn't trying to prod Miss Watson into conversation, that was.

And the whole time Neville chattered on, mostly carrying on a conversation with himself, mostly about his newfound uniqueness.

At last the familiar buildings of the village came into view. Neville declared himself uniquely famished, whatever that meant, so Gregory steered the group to the White Hart, a local inn that served simple but always delicious fare.

"We should have a picnic," Lady Lucinda suggested. "Wouldn't that be marvelous?"

"Capital idea," Neville exclaimed, gazing at her as if she were a goddess. Gregory was a little startled by the fervor of his expression, but Lady Lucinda seemed not to notice.

"What is your opinion, Miss Watson?" Gregory asked. But the lady in question was lost in thought, her eyes unfocused even as they remained fixed on a painting on the wall.

"Miss Watson?" he repeated, and then when he finally had her attention, he said, "Would you care to take a picnic?"

"Oh. Yes, that would be lovely." And then she went back to staring off into space, her perfect lips curved into a wistful, almost longing expression.

Gregory nodded, tamping down his disappointment, and set out making arrangements. The innkeeper, who knew his family well, gave him two clean bedsheets to lay upon the grass and promised to bring out a hamper of food when it was ready.

"Excellent work, Mr. Bridgerton," Lady Lucinda said. "Don't you agree, Hermione?"

"Yes, of course."

"Hope he brings pie," Neville said as he held the door open for the ladies. "I can always eat pie."

Gregory tucked Miss Watson's hand in the crook of his arm before she could escape. "I asked for a selection of foods," he said quietly to her. "I hope there is something that meets your cravings."

She looked up at him and he felt it again, the air swooshing from his body as he lost himself in her eyes. And he knew she felt it, too.

She had to. How could she not, when he felt as if his own legs might give out beneath him?

"I am sure that it will be delightful," she said.

"Are you in possession of a sweet tooth?"

"I am," she admitted.

"Then you are in luck," Gregory told her. "Mr. Gladdish has promised to include some of his wife's gooseberry pie, which is quite famous in this district."

"Pie?" Neville visibly perked up. He turned to Lady Lucinda. "Did he say we were getting pie?"

"I believe he did," she replied.

Neville sighed with pleasure. "Do you like pie, Lady Lucinda?"

The barest hint of exasperation washed over her features as she asked, "What sort of pie, Mr. Berbrooke?"

"Oh, any pie. Sweet, savory, fruit, meat."

"Well . . ." She cleared her throat, glancing about as if the buildings and trees might offer some guidance. "I . . . ah . . . I suppose I like most pies."

And it was in that minute that Gregory was quite certain Neville had fallen in love.

Poor Lady Lucinda.

They walked across the main thoroughfare to a grassy field, and Gregory swept open the sheets, laying them flat upon the ground. Lady Lucinda, clever girl that she was, sat first, then patted a spot for Neville that would guarantee that Gregory and Miss Watson would be forced to share the other patch of cloth.

And then Gregory set about winning her heart.

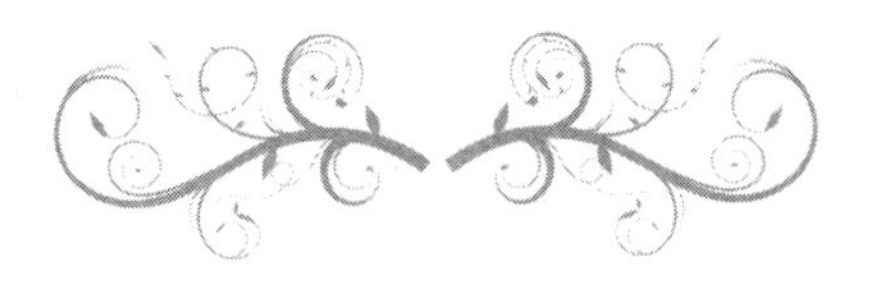

Chapter 4

In which Our Heroine offers advice,
Our Hero takes it, and everyone eats too much pie.

He was going about it all wrong.

Lucy glanced over Mr. Berbrooke's shoulder, trying not to frown. Mr. Bridgerton was making a valiant attempt to win Hermione's favor, and Lucy had to admit that under normal circumstances, with a different female, he would have succeeded handily. Lucy thought of the many girls she knew from school—any one of them would be head over heels in love with him by now. *Every* one of them, as a matter of fact.

But not Hermione.

He was trying too hard. Being too attentive, too focused, too . . . too . . . Well, too in love, quite frankly, or at least too infatuated.

Mr. Bridgerton was charming, and he was handsome, and obviously quite intelligent as well, but Hermione had *seen* all this before. Lucy could not even begin to count the number of gentlemen who had pursued her friend in much the same manner. Some were witty, some were earnest. They gave flowers, poetry, candy—one even brought Hermione a puppy (instantly refused by Hermione's mother, who had informed the poor gentleman that the natural habitat of dogs did not include Aubusson carpets, porcelain from the Orient, or herself).

But underneath they were all the same. They hung on her every word, they gazed at her as if she were a Greek goddess come down to earth, and they fell over each other in an attempt to offer the cleverest, most romantic compliments ever to rain down upon her pretty ears. And they never seemed to understand how completely unoriginal they all were.

If Mr. Bridgerton truly wished to pique Hermione's interest, he was going to need to do something different.

"More gooseberry pie, Lady Lucinda?" Mr. Berbrooke asked.

"Yes, please," Lucy murmured, if only to keep him busy with the slicing as she pondered what to do next. She really didn't want Hermione to throw her life away on Mr. Edmonds, and truly, Mr. Bridgerton was perfect. He just needed a little help.

"Oh, look!" Lucy exclaimed. "Hermione doesn't have any pie."

"No pie?" Mr. Berbrooke gasped.

Lucy batted her eyelashes at him, not a mannerism with which she had much practice or skill. "Would you be so kind as to serve her?"

As Mr. Berbrooke nodded, Lucy stood up. "I believe I will stretch my legs," she announced. "There are lovely flowers on the far side of the field. Mr. Bridgerton, do you know anything about the local flora?"

He looked up, surprised by her question. "A bit." But he didn't move.

Hermione was busy assuring Mr. Berbrooke that she adored gooseberry pie, so Lucy took advantage of the moment and jerked her head toward the flowers, giving Mr. Bridgerton the sort of urgent look that generally meant "*Come with me* now."

For a moment he appeared to be puzzled, but he quickly recovered and rose to his feet. "Will you allow me to tell you a bit about the scenery, Lady Lucinda?"

"That would be marvelous," she said, perhaps a touch too enthusiastically. Hermione was staring at her with patent suspicion. But Lucy knew that she would not offer to join them; to do so would encourage Mr. Bridgerton to believe she desired his company.

So Hermione would be left with Mr. Berbrooke and the pie. Lucy shrugged. It was only fair.

"That one, I believe, is a daisy," Mr. Bridgerton said, once they had crossed the field. "And that stalky blue one— Actually, I don't know what it's called."

"Delphinium," Lucy said briskly, "and you must know that I did not summon you to speak of flowers."

"I had an inkling."

She decided to ignore his tone. "I wished to give you some advice."

"Really," he drawled. Except it wasn't a question.

"Really."

"And what might your advice be?"

There was really no way to make it sound any better than it was, so she looked him in the eye and said, "You're going about this all wrong."

"I beg your pardon," he said stiffly.

Lucy stifled a groan. Now she'd pricked his pride, and he would surely be insufferable. "If you want to win Hermione," she said, "you have to do something different."

Mr. Bridgerton stared down at her with an expression that almost bordered on contempt. "I am well able to conduct my own courtships."

"I am sure you are . . . with other ladies. But Hermione is different."

He remained silent, and Lucy knew that she had made her point. He also thought Hermione different, else he wouldn't be making such an effort.

"Everyone does what you do," Lucy said, glancing over at the picnic to make sure that neither Hermione nor Mr. Berbrooke had got up to join them. "Everyone."

"A gentleman does love to be compared to the flock," Mr. Bridgerton murmured.

Lucy had any number of rejoinders for *that*, but she kept her mind on the task at hand and said, "You cannot act like the rest of them. You need to set yourself apart."

"And how do you propose I do that?"

She took a breath. He wasn't going to like her answer. "You must stop being so . . . devoted. Don't treat her like a princess. In fact, you should probably leave her alone for a few days."

His expression turned to distrust. "And allow all the other gentleman to rush in?"

"They will rush in anyway," she said in a matter-of-fact voice. "There is nothing you can do about that."

"Lovely."

Lucy plodded on. "If *you* withdraw, Hermione will be curious as to the reason why."

Mr. Bridgerton looked dubious, so she continued with, "Do not worry, she will know that you're interested. Heavens, after today she'd have to be an idiot not to."

He scowled at that, and Lucy herself couldn't quite believe she was speaking so frankly to a man she barely knew, but desperate times surely called for desperate measures . . . or desperate speech. "She will know, I promise you. Hermione is very intelligent. Not that anyone seems to notice. Most men can't see beyond her face."

"I would like to know her mind," he said softly.

Something in his tone hit Lucy squarely in the chest. She looked up, right into his eyes, and she had the strangest sense that she was somewhere else, and he was somewhere else, and the world was dropping away around them.

He was different from the other gentlemen she'd met. She wasn't sure how, exactly, except that there was something more to him. Something different. Something that made her ache, deep in her chest.

And for a moment she thought she might cry.

But she didn't. Because, really, she couldn't. And she wasn't that sort of female, anyway. She didn't wish to be. And she certainly did not cry when she did not know the reason for it.

"Lady Lucinda?"

She'd stayed silent too long. It was unlike her, and— "She will not wish to allow you to," she blurted out. "Know her mind, I mean. But you can . . ." She cleared her throat, blinked, regained her focus, and then planted her eyes firmly on the small patch of daisies sparkling in the sun. "You can convince her otherwise," she continued. "I am sure that you can. If you are patient. And you are true."

He didn't say anything right away. There was nothing but the faint whistle of the breeze. And then, quietly, he asked, "Why are you helping me?"

Lucy turned back to him and was relieved that this time the earth remained firmly fixed beneath her feet. She was herself again, brisk, no-nonsense, and practical to a fault. And he was just another gentleman vying for Hermione's hand.

All was normal.

"It's you or Mr. Edmonds," she said.

"Is that his name," he murmured.

"He is her father's secretary," she explained. "He is not a bad man, and I don't think he is only after her money, but any fool could see that you are the better match."

Mr. Bridgerton cocked his head to the side. "Why, I wonder, does it sound as if you have just called Miss Watson a fool?"

Lucy turned to him with steel in her eyes. "Do not *ever* question my devotion to Hermione. I could not—" She shot a quick glance at Hermione to make sure she wasn't looking before she lowered her voice and continued. "I could not love her better if she were my blood sister."

To his credit, Mr. Bridgerton gave her a respectful nod and said, "I did you a disservice. My apologies."

Lucy swallowed uncomfortably as she acknowledged his words. He looked as if he meant them, which went a long way toward mollifying her. "Hermione means the world to me," she said. She thought about the school holidays she had spent with the Watson family, and she thought about the lonely visits home. Her returns had never seemed to coincide with those of her brother, and Fennsworth Abbey was a cold and forbidding place with only her uncle for company.

Robert Abernathy had always done his duty by his two charges, but he was rather cold and forbidding as well. Home meant long walks alone, endless reading alone, even meals alone, as Uncle Robert had never shown any interest in dining with her. When he had informed Lucy that she would be attending Miss Moss's, her initial impulse had been to throw her arms around him and gush, "Thank you thank you *thank you*!"

Except that she had never hugged him before, not in the seven years he'd been her guardian. And besides that, he had been seated behind his desk and had already returned his attention to the papers in front of him. Lucy had been dismissed.

When she arrived at school, she had thrown herself into her

new life as a student. And she had adored every moment. It was so marvelous just to have people to talk to. Her brother Richard had left for Eton at the age of ten, even before their father had died, and she'd been wandering the halls of the Abbey for nearly a decade with no one but her officious governess for company.

At school people liked her. That had been the best part of all. At home she was nothing more than an afterthought, but at Miss Moss's School for Exceptional Young Ladies the other students sought her company. They asked her questions and actually waited to hear her answer. Lucy might not have been the queen bee of the school, but she had felt that she belonged, and that she had mattered.

She and Hermione had been assigned to share a room that first year at Miss Moss's, and their friendship had been almost instant. By nightfall of that first day, the two were laughing and chattering as if they had known each other all of their lives.

Hermione made her feel . . . better somehow. Not just their friendship, but the knowledge of their friendship. Lucy *liked* being someone's best friend. She liked having one, too, of course, but she really liked knowing that in all the world, there was someone who liked her best. It made her feel confident.

Comfortable.

It was rather like Mr. Bridgerton and what he'd said about his family, actually.

She knew she could count on Hermione. And Hermione knew the same was true of her. And Lucy wasn't sure that there was anyone else in the world she could say that of. Her brother, she supposed. Richard would always come to her aid if she needed him, but they saw each other so rarely these days. It was a pity, really. They had been quite close when they were small. Shut away at Fennsworth Abbey, there was rarely anyone else with whom to play, and so they'd had no choice but to turn to each other. Luckily, they'd got along, more often than not.

She forced her mind back to the present and turned to Mr. Bridgerton. He was standing quite still, regarding her with an expression of polite curiosity, and Lucy had the strangest sense that if she told him everything—about Hermione and Richard and Fennsworth Abbey and how lovely it had been to leave for school . . .

He would have understood. It seemed impossible that he could, coming from such a large and famously close family. He couldn't possibly know what it was to be lonely, to have something to say but no one to say it to. But somehow—it was his eyes, really, suddenly greener than she'd realized, and so focused on her face—

She swallowed. Good heavens, what was happening to her that she could not even finish her own thoughts?

"I only wish for Hermione's happiness," she managed to get out. "I hope you realize that."

He nodded, then flicked his eyes toward the picnic. "Shall we rejoin the others?" he asked. He smiled ruefully. "I do believe Mr. Berbrooke has fed Miss Watson three pieces of pie."

Lucy felt a laugh bubbling within her. "Oh dear."

His tone was charmingly bland as he said, "For the sake of her health, if nothing else, we ought to return."

"Will you think about what I said?" Lucy asked, allowing him to place her hand on his arm.

He nodded. "I will."

She felt herself grip him a little more tightly. "I am right about this. I promise you that I am. No one knows Hermione better than I. And no one else has watched all those gentlemen try—and fail—to win her favor."

He turned, and his eyes caught hers. For a moment they stood perfectly still, and Lucy realized that he was assessing her, taking her measure in a manner that should have been uncomfortable.

But it wasn't. And that was the oddest thing. He was staring at her as if he could see down to her very soul, and it didn't feel the least bit awkward. In fact, it felt oddly . . . nice.

"I would be honored to accept your advice regarding Miss Watson," he said, turning so that they might return to the picnic spot. "And I thank you for offering to help me win her."

"Th-thank you," Lucy stammered, because really, hadn't that been her intention?

But then she realized that she no longer felt quite so nice.

Gregory followed Lady Lucinda's directives to the letter. That evening, he did not approach Miss Watson in the drawing room, where the guests had assembled before supper. When they removed themselves to the dining room, he made no attempt to interfere with the social order and have his seat switched so that he might sit next to her. And once the gentlemen had returned from their port and joined the ladies in the conservatory for a piano recital, he took a seat at the rear, even though she and Lady Lucinda were standing quite alone, and it would have been easy—expected, even—for him to pause and murmur his greetings as he passed by.

But no, he had committed to this possibly ill-advised scheme, and so the back of the room it was. He watched as Miss Watson found a seat three rows ahead, and then settled into his chair, finally allowing himself the indulgence of gazing upon the back of her neck.

Which would have been a perfectly fulfilling pastime were he not *completely* unable to think of anything other than her absolute lack of interest. In him.

Truly, he could have grown two heads and a tail and he would have received nothing more than the polite half-smile she seemed to give everyone. If that.

It was not the sort of reaction Gregory was used to receiving from women. He did not expect universal adulation, but really, when he did make an effort, he usually saw better results than this.

It was damned irritating, actually.

And so he watched the two women, willing them to turn, to squirm, to do something to indicate that they were cognizant of his presence. Finally, after three concertos and a fugue, Lady Lucinda slowly twisted in her seat.

He could easily imagine her thoughts.

Slowly, slowly, act as if you're glancing at the door to see if someone came in. Flick your eyes ever so slightly at Mr. Bridgerton—

He lifted his glass in salute.

She gasped, or at least he hoped she did, and turned quickly around.

He smiled. He probably shouldn't take such joy in her distress, but truly, it was the only bright spot in the evening thus far.

As for Miss Watson—if she could feel the heat of his stare, she gave no indication. Gregory would have liked to have thought that she was studiously ignoring him—that at least might have indicated some sort of awareness. But as he watched her glance idly around the room, dipping her head every so often to whisper something in Lady Lucinda's ear, it became painfully clear that she wasn't ignoring him at all. That would imply that she noticed him.

Which she quite obviously did not.

Gregory felt his jaw clench. While he did not doubt the good intentions behind Lady Lucinda's advice, the advice itself had been quite patently dreadful. And with only five days remaining to the house party, he had wasted valuable time.

"You look bored."

He turned. His sister-in-law had slipped into the seat next to him and was speaking in a low undertone so as not to interfere with the performance.

"Quite a blow to my reputation as a hostess," she added dryly.

"Not at all," he murmured. "You are splendid as always."

Kate turned forward and was silent for a few moments before saying, "She's quite pretty."

Gregory did not bother to pretend that he didn't know what she was talking about. Kate was far too clever for that. But that didn't mean he had to encourage the conversation. "She is," he said simply, keeping his eyes facing front.

"My suspicion," said Kate, "is that her heart is otherwise engaged. She has not encouraged any of the gentlemen's attentions, and they have certainly all tried."

Gregory felt his jaw tense.

"I have heard," Kate continued, surely aware that she was being a bother, not that that would stop her, "that the same has been true all of this spring. The girl gives no indication that she wishes to make a match."

"She fancies her father's secretary," Gregory said. Because, really, what was the point of keeping it a secret? Kate had a way of finding everything out. And perhaps she could be of help.

"Really?" Her voice came out a bit too loud, and she was forced to murmur apologies to her guests. "Really?" she said again, more quietly. "How do you know?"

Gregory opened his mouth to reply, but Kate answered her own question. "Oh, of course," she said, "the Lady Lucinda. She would know everything."

"Everything," Gregory confirmed dryly.

Kate pondered this for a few moments, then stated the obvious. "Her parents cannot be pleased."

"I don't know that they are aware."

"Oh my." Kate sounded sufficiently impressed by this gossipy tidbit that Gregory turned to look at her. Sure enough, her eyes were wide and sparkling.

"Do try to contain yourself," he said.

"But it's the most excitement I've had all spring."

He looked her squarely in the face. "You need to find a hobby."

"Oh, Gregory," she said, giving him a little nudge with her elbow. "Don't allow love to turn you into such a stuff. You're far too much fun for that. Her parents will never allow her to marry the secretary, and she's not one to elope. You need only to wait her out."

He let out an irritated exhale.

Kate patted him comfortingly. "I know, I know, you wish to have things done. Your sort is never one for patience."

"My sort?"

She flicked her hand, which she clearly considered enough of an answer. "Truly, Gregory," she said, "this is for the best."

"That she is in love with someone else?"

"Stop being so dramatic. I meant that it will give you time to be certain of your feelings for her."

Gregory thought of the gut-punched feeling he got every time he looked at her. Good God, especially the back of her neck, strange as that seemed. He couldn't imagine he needed time. This was everything he'd ever imagined love to be. Huge, sudden, and utterly exhilarating.

And somehow crushing at the same time.

"I was surprised you didn't ask to be seated with her at supper," Kate murmured.

Gregory glared at the back of Lady Lucinda's head.

"I can arrange it for tomorrow, if you wish," Kate offered.

"Do."

Kate nodded. "Yes, I— Oh, here we are. The music is ending. Pay attention now and look like we're polite."

He stood to applaud, as did she. "Have you ever *not* chattered all the way through a music recital?" he asked, keeping his eyes front.

"I have a curious aversion to them," she said. But then her lips curved into a wicked little smile. "And a nostalgic sort of a fondness, as well."

"Really?" *Now* he was interested.

"I don't tell tales, of course," she murmured, quite purposefully not looking at him, "but really, have you ever seen me attend the opera?"

Gregory felt his brows lift. Clearly there was an opera singer somewhere in his brother's past. Where *was* his brother, anyway? Anthony seemed to have developed a remarkable talent for avoiding most of the social functions of the house party. Gregory had seen him only twice aside from their interview the night he arrived.

"Where *is* the scintillating Lord Bridgerton?" he asked.

"Oh, somewhere. I don't know. We'll find each other at the end of the day, that is all that matters." Kate turned to him with a remarkably serene smile. Annoyingly serene. "I must mingle," she said, smiling at him as if she hadn't a care in the world. "Do enjoy yourself." And she was off.

Gregory hung back, making polite conversation with a few of the other guests as he surreptitiously watched Miss Watson. She was chatting with two young gentlemen—annoying sops, the both of them—while Lady Lucinda stood politely to the side. And while Miss Watson did not appear to be flirting with either, she certainly was paying them more attention than *he'd* received that evening.

And there was Lady Lucinda, smiling prettily, taking it all in.

Gregory's eyes narrowed. Had she double-crossed him? She

didn't seem the sort. But then again, their acquaintance was barely twenty-four hours old. How well did he know her, really? She *could* have an ulterior motive. And she *might* be a very fine actress, with dark, mysterious secrets lying below the surface of her—

Oh, blast it all. He was going mad. He would bet his last penny that Lady Lucinda could not lie to save her life. She was sunny and open and most definitely *not* mysterious. She had meant well, of that much he was certain.

But her advice had been excremental.

He caught her eye. A faint expression of apology seemed to flit across her face, and he thought she might have shrugged.

Shrugged? What the hell did *that* mean?

He took a step forward.

Then he stopped.

Then he thought about taking another step.

No.

Yes.

No.

Maybe?

Damn it. He didn't know what to do. It was a singularly unpleasant sensation.

He looked back at Lady Lucinda, quite certain that his expression was not one of sweetness and light. Really, this was all her fault.

But of course now she wasn't looking at him.

He did not shift his gaze.

She turned back. Her eyes widened, hopefully with alarm.

Good. Now they were getting somewhere. If he couldn't feel the bliss of Miss Watson's regard, then at least he could make Lady Lucinda feel the misery of his.

Truly, there were times that just didn't call for maturity and tact.

He remained at the edge of the room, finally beginning to enjoy himself. There was something perversely entertaining about imagining Lady Lucinda as a small defenseless hare, not quite sure if or when she might meet her untimely end.

Not, of course, that Gregory could ever assign himself the role of hunter. His piss-poor marksmanship guaranteed that he couldn't hit anything that moved, and it was a damned good thing he wasn't responsible for acquiring his own food.

But he *could* imagine himself the fox.

He smiled, his first real one of the evening.

And then he knew that the fates were on his side, because he saw Lady Lucinda make her excuses and slip out the conservatory door, presumably to attend to her needs. As Gregory was standing on his own in the back corner, no one noticed when he exited the room through a different door.

And when Lady Lucinda passed by the doorway to the library, he was able to yank her in without making a sound.

Chapter 5

In which Our Hero and Heroine have a most intriguing conversation.

One moment Lucy was walking down the corridor, her nose scrunched in thought as she tried to recall the location of the nearest washroom, and the next she was hurtling through the air, or at the very least tripping over her feet, only to find herself bumping up against a decidedly large, decidedly warm, and decidedly human form.

"Don't scream," came a voice. One she knew.

"Mr. Bridgerton?" Good heavens, this seemed out of character. Lucy wasn't quite certain if she ought to be scared.

"We need to talk," he said, letting go of her arm. But he locked the door and pocketed the key.

"Now?" Lucy asked. Her eyes adjusted to the dim light and she realized they were in the library. "Here?" And then a more pertinent question sprang to mind. "Alone?"

He scowled. "I'm not going to ravish you, if that's what worries you."

She felt her jaw clench. She hadn't thought he *would*, but he didn't need to make his honorable behavior sound so much like an insult.

"Well, then, what is this about?" she demanded. "If I am caught here in your company, there will be the devil to pay. I'm practically engaged, you know."

"I know," he said. In *that* sort of tone. As if she'd informed him of it ad nauseam, when she knew for a fact she had not mentioned it more than once. Or possibly twice.

"Well, I am," she grumbled, just knowing that she would think of the perfect retort two hours later.

"What," he demanded, "is going on?"

"What do you mean?" she asked, even though she knew quite well what he was talking about.

"Miss Watson," he ground out.

"Hermione?" As if there was another Miss Watson. But it did buy her a bit of time.

"Your advice," he said, his gaze boring into hers, "was abysmal."

He was correct, of course, but she'd been hoping he might not have noticed.

"Right," she said, eyeing him warily as he crossed his arms. It wasn't the most welcoming of gestures, but she had to admit that he carried it off well. She'd heard that his reputation was one of joviality and fun, neither of which was presently in evidence, but, well, hell hath no fury and all that. She supposed one didn't need to be a woman to feel a tad bit underwhelmed at the prospect of unrequited love.

And as she glanced hesitantly at his handsome face, it occurred to her that he probably didn't have much experience with unrequited love. Really, who *would* say no to this gentleman?

Besides Hermione. But she said no to everyone. He shouldn't take it personally.

"Lady Lucinda?" he drawled, waiting for a response.

"Of course," she stalled, wishing he didn't seem so very *large* in the closed room. "Right. Right."

He lifted a brow. "Right."

She swallowed. His tone was one of vaguely paternal indulgence, as if she were mildly amusing but not quite worthy of notice. She knew that tone well. It was a favorite of older brothers, for use with younger sisters. And any friends they might bring home for school holidays.

She hated that tone.

But she plowed on nonetheless and said, "I agree that my plan did not turn out to be the best course of action, but truthfully, I am not certain that anything else would have been an improvement."

This did not appear to be what he wished to hear. She cleared her throat. Twice. And then again. "I'm terribly sorry," she added, because she did feel badly, and it was her experience that apologies always worked when one wasn't quite certain what to say. "But I really did think—"

"You told me," he interrupted, "that if I ignored Miss Watson—"

"I didn't tell you to *ignore* her!"

"You most certainly did."

"No. No, I did not. I told you to back away a bit. To try to be not quite so obvious in your besottedment."

It wasn't a word, but really, Lucy couldn't be bothered.

"Very well," he replied, and his tone shifted from slightly-superior-older-brother to outright condescension. "If I wasn't meant to ignore her, just what precisely do you think I should have done?"

"Well . . ." She scratched the back of her neck, which suddenly felt as if it were sprouting the most horrid of hives. Or maybe it was just nerves. She'd almost rather the hives. She didn't much like this queasy feeling growing in her stomach as she tried to think of something reasonable to say.

"Other than what I did, that is," he added.

"I'm not sure," she ground out. "I haven't *oceans* of experience with this sort of thing."

"Oh, *now* you tell me."

"Well, it was worth a try," she shot back. "Heaven knows, you certainly weren't succeeding on your own."

His mouth clamped into a line, and she allowed herself a small, satisfied smile for hitting a nerve. She wasn't *normally* a mean-spirited person, but the occasion did seem to call for just a little bit of self-congratulation.

"Very well," he said tightly, and while she would have preferred that he apologized and then said—explicitly—that she was right and he was wrong, she supposed that in *some* circles, "Very well" *might* pass for an acknowledgment of error.

And judging by his face, it was the most she was likely to receive.

She nodded regally. It seemed the best course of action. Act like a queen and maybe she would be treated like one.

"Have you any other brilliant ideas?"

Or not.

"Well," she said, pretending that he'd actually sounded as if he cared about the answer, "I don't think it's so much a question of what to do as why what you did didn't work."

He blinked.

"No one has ever given up on Hermione," Lucy said with a touch of impatience. She hated when people did not understand her meaning immediately. "Her disinterest only makes them redouble their efforts. It's embarrassing, really."

He looked vaguely affronted. "I beg your pardon."

"Not *you*," Lucy said quickly.

"My relief is palpable."

Lucy should have taken offense at his sarcasm, but his sense of humor was so like her own she couldn't help but enjoy it. "As I was saying," she continued, because she always did like to remain on the topic at hand, "no one ever seems to admit defeat and move on to a more attainable lady. Once everyone realizes that everyone *else* wants her, they seem to go mad. It's as if she's nothing but a prize to be won."

"Not to me," he said quietly.

Her eyes snapped to his face, and she realized instantly that he meant that Hermione was *more* than a prize. He cared for her. He truly cared for her. Lucy wasn't sure why, or even how, as he had barely made her friend's acquaintance. And Hermione hadn't been terribly forthcoming in her conversations, not that she ever was with the gentlemen who pursued her. But Mr. Bridgerton cared for the woman inside, not just the perfect face. Or at least he thought he did.

She nodded slowly, letting all this sink in. "I thought that perhaps if someone actually *stopped* dancing attendance on her, she might find it intriguing. Not," she hastened to assure him, "that Hermione sees all of this gentlemanly attention as her due. Quite to the contrary. To be honest, for the most part it's a nuisance."

"Your flattery knows no bounds." But he was smiling—just a little bit—as he said it.

"I've never been very skilled at flattery," she admitted.

"Apparently not."

She smiled wryly. He hadn't meant his words as an insult, and she wasn't going to take them as such. "She will come around."

"Do you think so?"

"I do. She will have to. Hermione is a romantic, but she understands how the world works. Deep down she knows she cannot marry Mr. Edmonds. It simply cannot be done. Her parents will disown her, or at the very least they will threaten to, and she is not the sort to risk that."

"If she really loved someone," he said softly, "she would risk anything."

Lucy froze. There was something in his voice. Something rough, something powerful. It shivered across her skin, raising goose-bumps, leaving her strangely unable to move.

And she had to ask. She had to. She had to *know*. "Would you?" she whispered. "Would you risk anything?"

He didn't move, but his eyes burned. And he didn't hesitate. "Anything."

Her lips parted. With surprise? Awe? Something else?

"Would *you*?" he countered.

"I . . . I'm not sure." She shook her head, and she had the queerest feeling that she didn't quite know herself any longer. Because it ought to have been an easy question. It would have been, just a few days ago. She would have said of course not, and she would have said she was far too practical for that sort of nonsense.

And most of all, she would have said that that sort of love did not exist, anyway.

But something had changed, and she didn't know what. Something had shifted within her, leaving her off-balance.

Unsure.

"I don't know," she said again. "I suppose it would depend."

"On what?" And his voice grew even softer. Impossibly soft, and yet she could make out every word.

"On . . ." She didn't know. How could she not know what it would depend upon? She felt lost, and rootless, and . . . and . . . and then the words just came. Slipped softly from her lips. "On love, I suppose."

"On love."

"Yes." Good heavens, had she ever had such a conversation? Did people actually talk about such things? And were there even any answers?

Or was she the only person in the world who didn't understand?

Something caught in her throat, and Lucy suddenly felt far too alone in her ignorance. He knew, and Hermione knew, and the poets claimed they did as well. It seemed *she* was the only lost soul, the only person who didn't understand what love was, who wasn't even sure it existed, or if it did, whether it existed for her.

"On how it felt," she finally said, because she didn't know what else to say. "On how love felt. How it feels."

His eyes met hers. "Do you think there is a variation?"

She hadn't expected another question. She was still reeling from the last one.

"How love feels," he clarified. "Do you think it could possibly be different for different people? If you loved someone, truly and deeply, wouldn't it feel like . . . like *everything*?"

She didn't know what to say.

He turned and took a few steps toward the window. "It would consume you," he said. "How could it not?"

Lucy just stared at his back, mesmerized by the way his finely cut coat stretched across his shoulders. It was the strangest thing, but she couldn't seem to pull her gaze from the little spot where his hair touched his collar.

She almost jumped when he turned around. "There would be no doubting it," he said, his voice low with the intensity of a true believer. "You would simply know. It would feel like everything you'd ever dreamed, and then it would feel like more."

He stepped toward her. Once. Then again. And then he said, "That, I think, is how love must feel."

And in that moment Lucy knew that she was not destined to feel that way. If it existed—if love existed the way Gregory Bridgerton imagined it—it did not wait for her. She couldn't imagine such a maelstrom of emotion. And she would not enjoy it. That much she knew. She didn't want to feel lost to the whirlwind, at the mercy of something beyond her control.

She didn't want misery. She didn't want despair. And if that meant she also had to forsake bliss and rapture, so be it.

She lifted her eyes to his, made breathless by the gravity of her own revelations. "It's too much," she heard herself say. "It would be too much. I wouldn't . . . I wouldn't . . ."

Slowly, he shook his head. "You would have no choice. It would be beyond your control. It just . . . happens."

Her mouth parted with surprise. "That's what she said."

"Who?"

And when she answered, her voice was strangely detached, as if the words were being drawn straight from her memory. "Hermione," she said. "That's what Hermione said about Mr. Edmonds."

Gregory's lips tightened at the corners. "Did she?"

Lucy slowly nodded. "Almost precisely. She said it just happens. In an instant."

"She said that?" The words sounded like an echo, and indeed, that was all he could do—whisper inane questions, looking for verification, hoping that maybe he had misheard, and she would reply with something entirely different.

But of course she did not. In fact, it was worse than he'd feared. She said, "She was in the garden, that's what she said, just looking at the roses, and then she saw him. And she knew."

Gregory just stared at her. His chest felt hollow, his throat tight. This wasn't what he wanted to hear. *Damn* it, this was the one thing he didn't want to hear.

She looked up at him then, and her eyes, gray in the dim light of the night, found his in an oddly intimate manner. It was as if he knew her, knew what she would say, and how her face would look when she said it. It was strange, and terrifying, and most of all, discomforting, because this wasn't the Honorable Miss Hermione Watson.

This was Lady Lucinda Abernathy, and she was not the woman with whom he intended to spend the rest of his life.

She was perfectly nice, perfectly intelligent, and certainly more than attractive. But Lucy Abernathy was not for him. And he almost laughed, because it all would have been so much easier if his heart had flipped the first time he saw *her*. She might be practically engaged, but she wasn't in love. Of that he was certain.

But Hermione Watson . . .

"What did she say?" he whispered, dreading the answer.

Lady Lucinda tilted her head to the side, and she looked nothing so much as puzzled. "She said that she didn't even see his face. Just the back of his head—"

Just the back of her neck.

"—and then he turned, and she thought she heard music, and all she could think was—"

I am wrecked.

"—'I am ruined.' That is what she said to me." She looked up at him, her head still tilting curiously to the side. "Can you imagine? Ruined? Of all things. I couldn't quite grasp it."

But *he* could. He could.

Exactly.

He looked at Lady Lucinda, and he saw that she was watching his face. She looked puzzled still. And concerned. And just a little bit bewildered when she asked, "Don't you find it odd?"

"Yes." Just one word, but with his entire heart wrapped around it. Because it *was* strange. It cut like a knife. She wasn't supposed to feel that way about someone else.

This wasn't the way it was supposed to happen.

And then, as if a spell had been broken, Lady Lucinda turned and took a few steps to the right. She peered at the bookshelves—not that she could possibly make out any of the titles in this light—then ran her fingers along the spines.

Gregory watched her hand; he didn't know why. He just watched it as it moved. She was quite elegant, he realized. It wasn't noticeable at first, because her looks were so wholesome and traditional. One expected elegance to shimmer like silk, to glow, to transfix. Elegance was an orchid, not a simple daisy.

But when Lady Lucinda moved, she looked different. She seemed to . . . flow.

She would be a good dancer. He was sure of it.

Although he wasn't quite sure why that mattered.

"I'm sorry," she said, turning quite suddenly around.

"About Miss Watson?"

"Yes. I did not mean to hurt your feelings."

"You didn't," he said, perhaps a little too sharply.

"Oh." She blinked, perhaps with surprise. "I'm glad for that. I didn't mean to."

She wouldn't mean to, he realized. She wasn't the sort.

Her lips parted, but she didn't speak right away. Her eyes seemed to focus beyond his shoulder, as if she were searching behind him for the correct words. "It was just that . . . Well, when you said what you said about love," she began, "it just sounded so familiar. I couldn't quite fathom it."

"Nor could I," he said softly.

She held silent, not quite looking at him. Her lips were pursed—

just a touch—and every now and then she would blink. Not a fluttery sort of movement but rather something quite deliberate.

She was thinking, he realized. She was the sort who *thought* about things, probably to the neverending frustration of anyone charged with the task of guiding her through life.

"What will you do now?" she asked.

"About Miss Watson?"

She nodded.

"What do you suggest I do?"

"I'm not sure," she said. "I can speak to her on your behalf, if you would like."

"No." Something about that seemed far too juvenile. And Gregory was only just now beginning to feel that he was truly a man, well and grown, ready to make his mark.

"You can wait, then," she said with a tiny shrug. "Or you can proceed and try again to woo her. She won't have the opportunity to see Mr. Edmonds for at least a month, and I would think . . . eventually . . . she would come to see . . ."

But she didn't finish. And he wanted to know. "Come to see what?" he pressed.

She looked up, as if pulled from a dream. "Why, that you . . . that you . . . just that you are so much *better* than the rest. I don't know why she cannot see it. It's quite obvious to me."

From anyone else it would have been a strange statement. Overly forward, perhaps. Maybe even a coy hint of availability.

But not from her. She was without artifice, the sort of girl a man could trust. Rather like his sisters, he supposed, with a keen wit and a sharp sense of humor. Lucy Abernathy would never inspire poetry, but she would make a very fine friend.

"It will happen," she said, her voice soft but certain. "She will realize. You . . . and Hermione . . . You will be together. I am sure of it."

He watched her lips as she spoke. He didn't know why, but the shape of them was suddenly intriguing . . . the way they moved, formed their consonants and vowels. They were ordinary lips. Nothing about them had attracted his attention before. But now, in the darkened library, with nothing in the air but the soft whisper of their voices . . .

He wondered what it would mean to kiss her.

He stepped back, feeling suddenly and overwhelmingly *wrong.*

"We should return," he said abruptly.

A flicker of hurt passed over her eyes. Damn. He hadn't meant to sound like he was so eager to be rid of her. None of this was her fault. He was just tired. And frustrated. And she was there. And the night was dark. And they were alone.

And it hadn't been desire. It couldn't be desire. He'd been waiting his entire life to react to a woman the way he had to Hermione Watson. He couldn't possibly feel desire for another woman after that. Not Lady Lucinda, not anyone.

It was nothing. *She* was nothing.

No, that was not fair. She was something. Quite a bit, actually. But not for him.

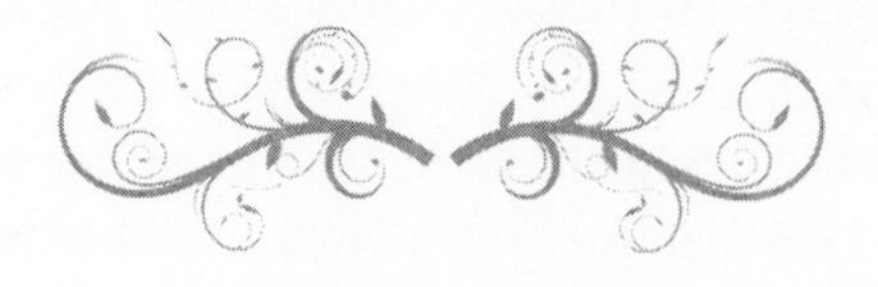

Chapter 6

In which Our Hero makes progress.

Dear God, *what* had she said?

That single thought pounded through Lucy's mind as she lay in bed that night, too horrified even to toss and turn. She lay on her back, staring at the ceiling, utterly still, utterly mortified.

And the next morning, as she peered in the mirror, sighing at the weary lavender color beneath her eyes, there it was again—

Oh, Mr. Bridgerton, you are so much better than the rest.

And every time she relived it, the voice in her memory grew higher, more simpering, until she turned into one of those awful creatures—the girls who fluttered and swooned every time someone's older brother came to visit at school.

"Lucy Abernathy," she muttered under her breath, "you silly cow."

"Did you say something?" Hermione looked up at her from her position near the bed. Lucy already had her hand on the doorknob, ready to leave for breakfast.

"Just doing sums in my head," Lucy lied.

Hermione went back to putting on her shoes. "For heaven's sake, *why*?" she said, mostly to herself.

Lucy shrugged, even though Hermione was not looking at her. She always said that she was doing sums in her head when Hermione caught her talking to herself. She had no idea why Hermione believed her; Lucy detested sums, almost as much as she hated fractions and tables. But it seemed like the sort of thing she might do, practical as she was, and Hermione had never questioned it.

Every now and then Lucy mumbled a number, just to make it more authentic.

"Are you ready to go down?" Lucy asked, twisting the knob. Not that *she* was. The last thing she wished was to see, well, anyone. Mr. Bridgerton in particular, of course, but the thought of facing the world at large was just ghastly.

But she was hungry, and she was going to have to show herself eventually, and she didn't see why her misery ought to wallow on an empty stomach.

As they walked to breakfast, Hermione peered at her curiously. "Are you well, Lucy?" she asked. "You look a little strange."

Lucy fought the urge to laugh. She *was* strange. She was an idiot, and probably shouldn't be let loose in public.

Good God, had she actually told Gregory Bridgerton that he was better than the rest?

She wanted to die. Or at the very least hide under a bed.

But no, she couldn't even manage to feign illness and have a good lying-in. It hadn't even occurred to her to try. She was so ridiculously normal and routineish that she was up and ready to depart for breakfast before she'd even managed a single coherent thought.

Aside from the pondering of her apparent madness, of course. *That* she had no trouble focusing upon.

"Well, you look very fine, anyway," Hermione said as they reached the top of the staircase. "I do like your choice of the green ribbon with the blue dress. I wouldn't have thought of it, but it's very smart. And so lovely with your eyes."

Lucy looked down at her clothing. She had no recollection of dressing herself. It was a miracle she did not look as if she had escaped from a circus.

Although . . .

She let out a little sigh. Running off with the circus sounded rather appealing just then, practical even, since she was quite certain she ought never to show her face in polite society again. Clearly she was missing an extremely important connecting vessel between her brain and her mouth, and heaven only knew what might emerge from her lips next.

Good gracious, she might as well have told Gregory Bridgerton that she thought him a god.

Which she did not. Not at all. She merely thought him a rather fine catch for Hermione. And she'd told him so. Hadn't she?

What *had* she said? Precisely, what had she said?

"Lucy?"

What she said was . . . What she said *was*—

She stopped cold.

Dear *God*. He was going to think *she* wanted him.

Hermione walked another few paces before she realized Lucy was no longer in step beside her. "Lucy?"

"Do you know," Lucy said, her voice coming out just a little bit squeaky, "I don't believe I'm hungry after all."

Hermione looked incredulous. "For breakfast?"

It *was* a bit farfetched. Lucy always ate like a sailor at breakfast.

"I . . . ah . . . I think something did not quite agree with me last night. Perhaps the salmon." She put her hand on her belly for added effect. "I think I should lie down."

And never get up.

"You do look a bit green," Hermione said.

Lucy smiled wanly, making a conscious decision to be thankful for small favors.

"Would you like me to bring you something?" Hermione asked.

"Yes," Lucy said fervently, hoping Hermione hadn't heard the rumble of her stomach.

"Oh, but I shouldn't," Hermione said, placing one thoughtful finger to her lips. "You probably shouldn't eat if you are feeling queasy. The last thing you want is to bring it all up again."

"It's not queasiness, exactly," Lucy improvised.

"It's not?"

"It's . . . ah . . . rather difficult to explain, actually. I . . ." Lucy sagged against the wall. Who knew she had it in her to be such a fine actress?

Hermione rushed to her side, concern knitting her brow. "Oh dear," she said, supporting Lucy with an arm around her back. "You look ghastly."

Lucy blinked. Maybe she *was* taking ill. Even better. That would keep her sequestered for days.

"I am returning you to bed," Hermione said, her tone brooking no argument. "And then I will summon Mother. She will know what to do."

Lucy nodded with relief. Lady Watson's remedy for any sort of ailment was chocolate and biscuits. Unorthodox, to be sure, but as it was what Hermione's mother chose whenever she claimed to be ill, she couldn't very well deny it to anyone else.

Hermione guided her back to their bedchamber, even going so far as to remove Lucy's slippers for her before she lay atop the bed. "If I didn't know you so well," Hermione said, tossing the slippers carelessly into the armoire, "I would think you were faking."

"I would never."

"Oh, you would," Hermione said. "You absolutely would. But you could never carry it off. You're far too traditional."

Traditional? What had *that* to do with anything?

Hermione let out a little huff of air. "I'm probably going to have to sit with that wearisome Mr. Bridgerton at breakfast now."

"He's not so dreadful," Lucy said, with perhaps a bit more verve than one might expect from someone with a belly full of bad salmon.

"I suppose not," Hermione acceded. "He's better than most, I daresay."

Lucy winced at the echo of her own words. *So much better than the rest. So much better than the rest.*

It was quite possibly the most appalling thing ever to cross her lips.

"But he is not for me," Hermione continued, oblivious to Lucy's distress. "He will realize it soon enough. And then he will move on to someone else."

Lucy doubted that, but she didn't say anything. What a coil. Hermione was in love with Mr. Edmonds, Mr. Bridgerton was in love with Hermione, and Lucy was *not* in love with Mr. Bridgerton.

But he thought she was.

Which was nonsense, of course. She would never allow that to happen, practically engaged as she was to Lord Haselby.

Haselby. She nearly groaned. This would all be so much easier if she could remember his face.

"Perhaps I'll ring for breakfast," Hermione said, her face lighting up as if she had just discovered a new continent. "Do you think they will send up a tray?"

Oh, blast. There went all her plans. Now Hermione had an excuse to remain in their chamber all day. And the next, too, if Lucy continued to feign illness.

"I don't know why I didn't think of it sooner," Hermione said, heading to the bellpull. "I would much rather remain here with you."

"Don't," Lucy called out, her brain spinning madly.

"Why not?"

Indeed. Lucy thought quickly. "If you have them bring a tray, you might not get what you want."

"But I know what I want. Coddled eggs and toast. Surely they can manage that."

"But *I* don't want coddled eggs and toast." Lucy tried to keep her expression as pitiful and pathetic as she could manage. "You know my taste so well. If you go to the breakfast room, I'm sure you would find something exactly right."

"But I thought you weren't going to eat."

Lucy put her hand back on her belly. "Well, I might want to eat a little."

"Oh, very well," Hermione said, by now sounding more impatient than anything else. "What do you want?"

"Er, perhaps some bacon?"

"With a fishy stomach?"

"I'm not sure it was the fish."

For the longest moment, Hermione just stood there and stared at her. "Just bacon, then?" she finally asked.

"Ehm, and anything else you think I might enjoy," Lucy said, since it would have been easy enough to ring for bacon.

Hermione let out a pent-up breath. "I shall return soon." She regarded Lucy with a slightly suspicious expression. "Don't overexert yourself."

"I won't," Lucy promised. She smiled at the door as it closed behind Hermione. She counted to ten, then hopped out of bed and ran to the wardrobe to straighten her slippers. Once that was done to her satisfaction, she snatched up a book and crawled back in to settle down and read.

All in all, it was turning out to be a lovely morning.

By the time Gregory entered the breakfast room, he was feeling much better. What had happened the night before—it was nothing. Practically forgotten.

It wasn't as if he'd *wanted* to kiss Lady Lucinda. He'd merely wondered about it, which was worlds apart.

He was just a man, after all. He'd wondered about hundreds of women, most of the time without *any* intention of even speaking to them. Everybody wondered. It was whether one acted upon it that made the difference.

What was that his brothers—his happily married brothers, he might add—had once said? Marriage didn't render them *blind.* They might not be looking for other women, but that didn't mean they didn't notice what was standing right in front of them. Whether it was a barmaid with extremely large bosoms or a proper young lady with a—well, with a pair of lips—one couldn't very well not *see* the body part in question.

And if one saw, then of course one would wonder, and—

And nothing. It all added up to nothing.

Which meant Gregory could eat his breakfast with a clear head.

Eggs were good for the soul, he decided. Bacon, too.

The only other occupant of the breakfast room was the fifty-ish and perpetually starchy Mr. Snowe, who was thankfully more interested in his newspaper than in conversation. After the obligatory grunts of greeting, Gregory sat down at the opposite end of the table and began to eat.

Excellent sausage this morning. And the toast was exceptional as well. Just the right amount of butter. A bit of salt needed for the eggs, but other than that they were rather tasty.

He tried the salted cod. Not bad. Not bad at all.

He took another bite. Chewed. Enjoyed himself. Thought very deep thoughts about politics and agriculture.

Moved on determinedly to Newtonian physics. He really should have paid more attention at Eton, because he couldn't quite recall the difference between force and work.

Let's see, work was that bit with the foot-pounds, and force was . . .

It wasn't even really *wondering*. Honestly, it could all be blamed on a trick of the light. And his mood. He'd been feeling a bit off. He'd been looking at her mouth because she'd been talking, for heaven's sake. Where else was he meant to look?

He picked up his fork with renewed vigor. Back to the cod. And his tea. Nothing washed everything away like tea.

He took a long sip, peering over the edge of his cup as he heard someone coming down the hall.

And then *she* filled the doorway.

He blinked with surprise, then glanced over her shoulder. She'd come without her extra appendage.

Now that he thought about it, he didn't think he'd ever seen Miss Watson without Lady Lucinda.

"Good morning," he called out, in precisely the right tone. Friendly enough so as not to sound bored, but not *too* friendly. A man never wanted to sound desperate.

Miss Watson looked over at him as he stood, and her face registered absolutely no emotion whatsoever. Not happiness, not ire, nothing but the barest flicker of acknowledgment. It was quite remarkable, really.

"Good morning," she murmured.

Then, hell, why not. "Will you join me?" he asked.

Her lips parted and she paused, as if not quite sure what she wished to do. And then, as if to offer perverse proof that they did in fact share some sort of higher connection, he read her mind.

Truly. He knew exactly what she was thinking.

Oh, very well, I suppose I have to eat breakfast, anyway.

It positively warmed the soul.

"I cannot stay very long," Miss Watson said. "Lucy is unwell, and I promised to bring her a tray."

It was difficult to imagine the indomitable Lady Lucinda taking ill, although Gregory didn't know why. It wasn't as if he *knew* her. Really, it had been nothing but a few conversations. If that. "I trust it is nothing serious," he murmured.

"I don't think so," she replied, taking a plate. She looked up at him, blinking those astounding green eyes. "Did you eat the fish?"

He looked down at his cod. "Now?"

"No, last night."

"I imagine so. I usually eat everything."

Her lips pursed for a moment, then she murmured, "I ate it as well."

Gregory waited for further explanation, but she didn't seem inclined to offer any. So instead he remained on his feet as she placed delicate portions of eggs and bacon on her plate. Then, after a moment's deliberation—

Am I really hungry? Because the more food I put on my plate, the longer it will take to consume it. Here. In the breakfast room. With him.

—she took a piece of toast.

Hmmm. Yes, I'm hungry.

Gregory waited until she took a seat across from him, and he sat down. Miss Watson offered him a small smile—the sort that was really nothing more than a shrug of the lips—and proceeded to eat her eggs.

"Did you sleep well?" Gregory asked.

She dabbed at her mouth with her serviette. "Very well, thank you."

"I did not," he announced. Hell, if polite conversation failed to draw her out, perhaps he ought to opt for surprise.

She looked up. "I'm so sorry." And then she looked back down. And ate.

"Terrible dream," he said. "Nightmare, really. Ghastly."

She picked up her knife and cut her bacon. "I'm so sorry," she said, seemingly unaware that she'd uttered those very same words mere moments earlier.

"I can't quite recall what it was," Gregory mused. He was making it all up, of course. He hadn't slept well, but not because of a nightmare. But he was going to get her to talk to him or die trying. "Do you remember your dreams?" he asked.

Her fork stopped midway to her mouth—and there was that delightful connection of the minds again.

In God's name, why is he asking me this?

Well, maybe not in God's name. That would require a bit more emotion than she seemed to possess. At least with him.

"Er, no," she said. "Not usually."

"Really? How intriguing. I recall mine about half of the time, I would estimate."

She nodded.

If I nod, I won't have to come up with something to say.

He plowed on. "My dream from last night was quite vivid. There was a rainstorm. Thunder and lightning. Very dramatic."

She turned her neck, ever so slowly, and looked over her shoulder.

"Miss Watson?"

She turned back. "I thought I heard someone."

I hoped I heard someone.

Really, this mind-reading talent was beginning to grow tedious.

"Right," he said. Well, where was I?"

Miss Watson began to eat very quickly.

Gregory leaned forward. She wasn't going to escape so easily. "Oh, yes, the rain," he said. "It was pouring. Absolute deluge. And the ground began to melt beneath my feet. Dragged me down."

He paused, purposefully, and then kept his eyes on her face until she was forced to say something.

After a few moments of exceedingly awkward silence, she finally moved her gaze from her food to his face. A small piece of egg trembled on the edge of her fork.

"The ground was melting," he said. And almost laughed.

"How . . . unpleasant."

"It *was*," he said, with great animation. "I thought it would swallow me whole. Have you ever felt like that, Miss Watson?"

Silence. And then— "No. No, I can't say that I have."

He idly fingered his earlobe, and then said, quite offhandedly, "I didn't much like it."

He thought she might spit her tea.

"Well, really," he continued. "Who would?"

And for the first time since he'd met her, he thought he saw the disinterested mask slip from her eyes as she said, with quite a bit of feeling, "I have no idea."

She even shook her head. Three things at once! A complete sentence, a spot of emotion, *and* a shake of the head. By George, he might be getting through to her.

"What happened next, Mr. Bridgerton?"

Good *God*, she had asked him a question. He might tumble from his chair. "Actually," he said, "I woke up."

"That's fortunate."

"I thought so as well. They say if you die in your dreams, you die in your sleep."

Her eyes widened. "They do?"

"*They* being my brothers," he admitted. "You may feel free to assess the information based upon its source."

"I have a brother," she said. "He delights in tormenting me."

Gregory offered her a grave nod. "That is what brothers are meant to do."

"Do you torment your sisters?"

"Mostly just the younger one."

"Because she's smaller."

"No, because she deserves it."

She laughed. "Mr. Bridgerton, you are terrible."

He smiled slowly. "You haven't met Hyacinth."

"If she bothers you enough to make you wish to torment her, I am sure I would adore her."

He sat back, enjoying this feeling of ease. It was nice not to have to work so hard. "Your brother is your elder, then?"

She nodded. "He *does* torment me because I'm smaller."

"You mean you don't deserve it?"

"Of course not."

He couldn't quite tell if she was being facetious. "Where is your brother now?"

"Trinity Hall." She took the last bite of her eggs. "Cambridge. Lucy's brother was there as well. He has been graduated for a year."

Gregory wasn't quite certain why she was telling him this. He wasn't interested in Lucinda Abernathy's brother.

Miss Watson cut another small piece of bacon and lifted her fork to her mouth. Gregory ate as well, stealing glances at her as he chewed. Lord, but she was lovely. He didn't think he'd ever seen another woman with her coloring. It was the skin, really. He imagined that most men thought her beauty came from her hair and eyes, and it was true that those were the features that initially stopped a man cold. But her skin was like alabaster laid over a rose petal.

He paused mid-chew. He had no idea he could be so poetic.

Miss Watson set down her fork. "Well," she said, with the tiniest of sighs, "I suppose I should prepare that plate for Lucy."

He stood immediately to assist her. Good heavens, but she actually sounded as if she didn't wish to leave. Gregory congratulated himself on an extremely productive breakfast.

"I shall find someone to carry it back for you," he said, signaling to a footman.

"Oh, that would be lovely." She smiled gratefully at him, and his heart quite literally skipped a beat. He'd thought it merely a figure of speech, but now he knew it was true. Love really could affect one's internal organs.

"Please do offer Lady Lucinda my well wishes," he said, watching curiously as Miss Watson heaped five slices of meat on the plate.

"Lucy likes bacon," she said.

"I see that."

And then she proceeded to spoon eggs, cod, potatoes, tomatoes, and then on a separate plate muffins and toast.

"Breakfast has always been her favorite meal," Miss Watson said.

"Mine as well."

"I shall tell her that."

"I can't imagine that she will be interested."

A maid had entered the room with a tray, and Miss Watson placed the heaping plates upon it. "Oh, she will," she said breezily. "Lucy is interested in everything. She does sums in her head, even. For entertainment."

"You're joking." Gregory couldn't imagine a less pleasant way to keep oneself occupied.

She placed her hand on her heart. "I swear it to you. I think she must be trying to improve her mind, because she was never very good at maths." She walked to the door, then turned to face him. "Breakfast was lovely, Mr. Bridgerton. Thank you for the company and the conversation."

He inclined his head. "The pleasure was all mine."

Except that it wasn't. She had enjoyed their time together, too. He could see it in her smile. And her eyes.

And he felt like a king.

"Did you know that if you die in your dreams, you die in your sleep?"

Lucy didn't even pause in her cutting of her bacon. "Nonsense," she said. "Who told you that?"

Hermione perched on the edge of the bed. "Mr. Bridgerton."

Now *that* rated above bacon. Lucy looked up immediately. "Then you saw him at breakfast?"

Hermione nodded. "We sat across from each other. He helped me arrange for the tray."

Lucy regarded her massive breakfast with dismay. Usually she managed to hide her ferocious appetite by dallying at the breakfast table, then getting another serving once the first wave of guests had departed.

Oh well, nothing to do about it. Gregory Bridgerton already thought her a widgeon—he might as well think her a widgeon who would weigh twelve stone by the year's end.

"He's rather amusing, actually," Hermione said, absently twirling her hair.

"I've heard he's quite charming."

"Mmmm."

Lucy watched her friend closely. Hermione was gazing out the window, and if she didn't quite have that ridiculous memorizing-a-love-sonnet look to her, she had at least worked her way up to a couplet or two.

"He is extremely handsome," Lucy said. There seemed no harm in confessing it. It wasn't as if she was planning to set her cap for him, and his looks were fine enough that it could be interpreted as a statement of fact rather than opinion.

"Do you think so?" Hermione asked. She turned back to Lucy, her head tilting thoughtfully to the side.

"Oh yes," Lucy replied. "His eyes, particularly. I'm quite partial to hazel eyes. I always have been."

Actually, she'd never considered it one way or the other, but now that she thought about it, hazel eyes *were* rather fine. Bit of brown, bit of green. Best of both worlds.

Hermione looked at her curiously. "I didn't know that."

Lucy shrugged. "I don't tell you everything."

Another lie. Hermione was privy to every boring detail of Lucy's life and had been for three years. Except, of course, for her plans to match Hermione with Mr. Bridgerton.

Mr. Bridgerton. Right. Must return the conversation to the subject of *him*.

"But you must agree," Lucy said in her most pondering of voices, "he's not *too* handsome. It's a good thing, really."

"Mr. Bridgerton?"

"Yes. His nose has a great deal of character, wouldn't you say? And his eyebrows aren't quite even." Lucy frowned. She hadn't realized she was quite so familiar with Gregory Bridgerton's face.

Hermione did nothing but nod, so Lucy continued with "I don't think I should want to be married to someone who was *too* handsome. It must be terribly intimidating. I would feel like a duck every time I opened my mouth."

Hermione giggled at that. "A duck?"

Lucy nodded and decided not to quack. She wondered if the men who courted Hermione worried about the same thing.

"He's quite dark," Hermione said.

"Not so dark." Lucy thought his hair a medium-brown.

"Yes, but Mr. Edmonds is so fair."

Mr. Edmonds did have lovely blond hair, so Lucy decided not to comment. And she knew she had to be very careful at this point. If she pushed Hermione too hard in Mr. Bridgerton's direction, Hermione would surely balk and go right back to being in love with Mr. Edmonds, which, of course, was utter disaster.

No, Lucy was going to need to be subtle. If Hermione was going to switch her devotion to Mr. Bridgerton, she was going to have to figure it out for herself. Or think she did.

"And his family is very smart," Hermione murmured.

"Mr. Edmonds's?" Lucy asked, deliberately misinterpreting.

"No, Mr. Bridgerton's, of course. I have heard such interesting things about them."

"Oh, yes," Lucy said. "I have as well. I rather admire Lady Bridgerton. She's been a marvelous hostess."

Hermione nodded her agreement. "I think she prefers you to me."

"Don't be silly."

"I don't mind," Hermione said with a shrug. "It's not as if she *doesn't* like me. She just likes you better. Women always like you better."

Lucy opened her mouth to contradict but then stopped, realizing that it was true. How odd that she had never noticed it. "Well, it's not as if you'd be marrying *her*," she said.

Hermione looked at her sharply. "I didn't say I wished to marry Mr. Bridgerton."

"No, of course not," Lucy said, mentally kicking herself. She'd known the words were a mistake the minute they'd escaped her mouth.

"But . . ." Hermione sighed and proceeded to stare off into space.

Lucy leaned forward. So this was what it meant to hang on a word.

And she hung, and she hung . . . until she could bear it no longer. "Hermione?" she finally queried.

Hermione flopped back onto the bed. "Oh, Lucy," she moaned, in tones worthy of Covent Garden, "I'm so confused."

"Confused?" Lucy smiled. This had to be a good thing.

"Yes," Hermione replied, from her decidedly inelegant position atop the bed. "When I was sitting at the table with Mr. Bridgerton—well, actually at first I thought him quite mad—but then I realized I was enjoying myself. He was funny, actually, and made me laugh."

Lucy did not speak, waiting for Hermione to gather the rest of her thoughts.

Hermione made a little noise, half-sigh, half-moan. Wholly distressed. "And then once I realized that, I looked up at him, and I—" She rolled onto her side, leaning on her elbow and propping her head up with one hand. "I *fluttered*."

Lucy was still trying to digest the *mad* comment. "Fluttered?" she echoed. "What is *fluttered*?"

"My stomach. My heart. My—my something. I don't know what."

"Similar to when you saw Mr. Edmonds for the first time?"

"No. *No*. No." Each no was said with a different emphasis, and Lucy had the distinct sense that Hermione was trying to convince herself of it.

"It wasn't the same at all," Hermione said. "But it was . . . a little bit the same. On a much smaller scale."

"I see," Lucy said, with an admirable amount of gravity, considering that she didn't understand at all. But then again, she never understood this sort of thing. And after her strange conversation with Mr. Bridgerton the night before, she was quite convinced she never would.

"But wouldn't you think—if I am so desperately in love with Mr. Edmonds—wouldn't you think I would never flutter with anyone else?"

Lucy thought about that. And then she said, "I don't see why love has to be desperate."

Hermione pushed herself up on her elbows and looked at her curiously. "That wasn't my question."

It wasn't? Oughtn't it have been?

"Well," Lucy said, choosing her words carefully, "perhaps it means—"

"I know what you are going to say," Hermione cut in. "You're going to say that it probably means I am not as in love with Mr. Edmonds as I thought. And then you will say that I need to give Mr. Bridgerton a chance. And then you will tell me that I ought to give all of the other gentlemen a chance."

"Well, not *all* of them," Lucy said. But the rest of it was rather close.

"Don't you think this has all occurred to me? Don't you realize how terribly distressing all of this is? To doubt myself so? And good heavens, Lucy, what if this is not the end of it? What if this happens again? With someone else?"

Lucy rather suspected she was not meant to answer, but still she spoke. "There is nothing wrong with doubting yourself, Hermione. Marriage is an enormous undertaking. The biggest choice you will ever make in your life. Once it's done, you can't change your mind."

Lucy took a bite of her bacon, reminding herself how grateful she was that Lord Haselby was so suitable. Her situation could have been ever so much worse. She chewed, swallowed, and said, "You need only to give yourself a bit of time, Hermione. And you should. There is never any good reason to rush into marriage."

There was a long paused before Hermione answered. "I reckon you're right."

"If you are truly meant to be with Mr. Edmonds, he will wait for you." Oh, heavens. Lucy couldn't *believe* she'd just said that.

Hermione jumped from the bed, just so that she could rush to Lucy's side and envelop her in a hug. "Oh, Lucy, that was the sweetest thing you have ever said to me. I know you don't approve of him."

"Well . . ." Lucy cleared her throat, trying to think of an acceptable reply. Something that would make her feel not *quite* so guilty for not having meant it. "It's not that—"

A knock sounded at the door.

Oh, thank goodness.

"Enter," the two girls called out in unison.

A maid came in and bobbed a quick curtsy. "M'lady," she said, looking at Lucy, "Lord Fennsworth has arrived to see you."

Lucy gaped at her. "My *brother*?"

"He is waiting in the rose salon, m'lady. Shall I tell him you will be right down?"

"Yes. Yes, of course."

"Will there be anything else?"

Lucy slowly shook her head. "No, thank you. That will be all."

The maid departed, leaving Lucy and Hermione staring at each other in shock.

"Why do you think Richard is here?" Hermione asked, her eyes wide with interest. She had met Lucy's brother on a number of occasions, and they had always got on well.

"I don't know." Lucy quickly climbed out of bed, all thoughts of feigning an upset stomach forgotten. "I hope nothing is amiss."

Hermione nodded and followed her to the wardrobe. "Has your uncle been unwell?"

"Not that I have been made aware." Lucy fished out her slippers and sat on the edge of the bed to put them back on her feet. "I had best get down to see him. If he is here, it is something important."

Hermione regarded her for a moment, then asked, "Would you like for me to accompany you? I shan't intrude upon your conversation, of course. But I will walk down with you, if you like."

Lucy nodded, and together they departed for the rose salon.

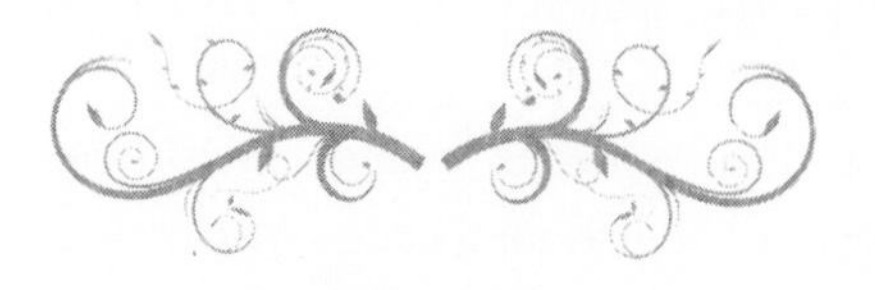

Chapter 7

In which Our Unexpected Guest delivers distressing news.

Gregory had been chatting with his sister-in-law in the breakfast room when the butler informed her of their unexpected guest, and so naturally he decided to accompany her to the rose salon to greet Lord Fennsworth, elder brother to Lady Lucinda. He had nothing better to do, and it somehow seemed he ought to go meet the young earl, given that Miss Watson had been chattering on about him a quarter of an hour earlier. Gregory knew him only by reputation; the four years' difference in their ages had ensured that they had not crossed paths at university, and Fennsworth had not yet chosen to take his place in London society.

Gregory had been expecting a studious, bookish sort; he'd heard that Fennsworth had elected to remain at Cambridge even when school was not in session. Indeed, the gentleman waiting by the window in the rose salon did possess a certain gravitas that made him seem slightly older than his years. But Lord Fennsworth was also tall, fit, and although perhaps a touch shy, he carried himself with an air of self-possession that came from something more primal than a title of nobility.

Lady Lucinda's brother knew who he was, not just what he was born to be called. Gregory liked him immediately.

Until it became obvious that he, like the rest of male humanity, was in love with Hermione Watson.

The only mystery, really, was why Gregory was surprised.

Gregory had to commend him—Fennsworth managed a full minute of inquiries about his sister's welfare before he added, "And Miss Watson? Will she be joining us as well?"

It wasn't so much the words as the tone, and even that not so much as the flicker in his eyes—that spark of eagerness, anticipation.

Oh, call a spade a spade. It was desperate longing, pure and simple. Gregory ought to know—he was quite certain it had flashed through his own eyes more than once in the past few days.

Good God.

Gregory supposed he still found Fennsworth a good enough fellow, even with his annoying infatuation, but really, the entire situation was beginning to grow tiresome.

"We are so pleased to welcome you to Aubrey Hall, Lord Fennsworth," Kate said, once she had informed him that she did not know if Miss Watson would be accompanying his sister down to the rose salon. "I do hope that your presence does not indicate an emergency at home."

"Not at all," Fennsworth replied. "But my uncle has requested that I fetch Lucy and bring her home. He wishes to speak with her on a matter of some importance."

Gregory felt one corner of his lips quirk in an upward direction. "You must be quite devoted to your sister," he said, "to come all this way yourself. Surely you could have simply sent a carriage."

To his credit, Lucy's brother did not appear flustered by the question, but at the same time, he did not have an immediate answer. "Oh no," he said, the words coming out rather quickly after the long pause. "I was more than happy to make the trip. Lucy is good company, and we have not visited for quite some time."

"Must you leave right away?" Kate asked. "I have been so enjoying your sister's company. And we would be honored to count you among our guests as well."

Gregory wondered just what she was about. Kate was going to have to locate another female to even up the numbers if Lord Fennsworth was to join the party. Although he supposed that if Lady Lucinda left, she would have to do the exact same thing.

The young earl hesitated, and Kate took advantage of the moment with a beautifully executed "Oh, do say that you will remain. Even if it cannot be for the duration of the party."

"Well," Fennsworth said, blinking as he considered the invitation. It was clear that he wanted to stay (and Gregory was quite certain he knew the reason why). But title or no, he was still young, and Gregory imagined that he answered to his uncle on all matters pertaining to the family.

And said uncle clearly desired Lady Lucinda's swift return.

"I suppose there would be no harm in taking an extra day," Fennsworth said.

Oh, dandy. He was willing to defy his uncle to gain extra time with Miss Watson. And as Lady Lucinda's brother, he was the one man who Hermione would never brush away with her usual polite boredom. Gregory readied himself for another day of tedious competition.

"Please say you will stay until Friday," Kate said. "We are planning a masked ball for Thursday evening, and I would hate for you to miss it."

Gregory made a mental note to give Kate an extremely ordinary gift for her next birthday. Rocks, maybe.

"It's only one more day," Kate said with a winning smile.

It was at that moment that Lady Lucinda and Miss Watson entered the room, the former in a morning dress of lightish blue and the latter in the same green frock she'd worn to breakfast. Lord Fennsworth took one look at the duo (more at one than the other, and suffice it to say that blood was not thicker than unrequited love), and he murmured, "Friday it is."

"Delightful," Kate said, clasping her hands together. "I shall have a room readied for you straightaway."

"Richard?" Lady Lucinda queried. "Why are you here?" She paused in the doorway and looked from person to person, apparently confused by Kate's and Gregory's presence.

"Lucy," her brother said. "It has been an age."

"Four months," she said, almost unthinkingly, as if some little part of her brain required absolute accuracy, even when it hardly mattered.

"Heavens, that is a long time," Kate said. "We will leave you now, Lord Fennsworth. I am sure you and your sister wish to have a few moments of privacy."

"There is no rush," Fennsworth said, his eyes flicking briefly to Miss Watson. "I would not wish to be rude, and I haven't yet had the opportunity to thank you for your hospitality."

"It wouldn't be rude at all," Gregory put in, anticipating a swift departure from the salon with Miss Watson on his arm.

Lord Fennsworth turned and blinked, as if he'd forgotten Gregory's presence. Not terribly surprising, as Gregory had remained uncharacteristically silent through the exchange.

"Pray do not trouble yourself," the earl said. "Lucy and I will have our conversation later."

"Richard," Lucy said, looking somewhat concerned, "are you certain? I was not expecting you, and if there is anything amiss . . ."

But her brother shook his head. "Nothing that cannot wait. Uncle Robert wishes to speak with you. He asked me to bring you home."

"Now?"

"He did not specify," Fennsworth replied, "but Lady Bridgerton has very graciously asked us to remain until Friday, and I agreed. That is"—he cleared his throat—"assuming you wish to remain."

"Of course," Lucy replied, looking confused and adrift. "But I—well . . . Uncle Robert . . ."

"We should leave," Miss Watson said firmly. "Lucy, you should have a moment with your brother."

Lucy looked at her brother, but he had taken advantage of Miss Watson's entry into the conversation by looking at *her*, and he said, "And how are you, Hermione? It has been far too long."

"Four months," Lucy said.

Miss Watson laughed and smiled warmly at the earl. "I am well, thank you. And Lucy is correct, as always. We last spoke in January, when you visited us at school."

Fennsworth dipped his chin in acknowledgment. "How could I have forgotten? It was such a pleasant few days."

Gregory would have bet his right arm that Fennsworth had known down to the minute how long it had been since he had last laid eyes on Miss Watson. But the lady in question was clearly oblivious to the infatuation, because she just smiled and said, "It was, wasn't it? It was so sweet of you to take us ice skating. You are always such good company."

Good God, how could she be so oblivious? There was no way she would have been so encouraging had she realized the nature of the earl's feelings for her. Gregory was certain of it.

But while it was obvious that Miss Watson was extremely fond of Lord Fennsworth, there was no indication that she held him in any sort of romantic esteem. Gregory consoled himself with the knowledge that the two had certainly known each other for years, and naturally she would be friendly with Fennsworth, given how close she was to Lady Lucinda.

Practically brother and sister, really.

And speaking of Lady Lucinda—Gregory turned in her direction and was not surprised to find that she was frowning. Her brother, who had traveled at least a day to reach her side, now seemed in no hurry whatsoever to speak with her.

And indeed, everyone else had fallen silent, as well. Gregory watched the awkward tableau with interest. Everyone seemed to be glancing about, waiting to see who might speak next. Even Lady Lucinda, whom no one would call shy, seemed not to know what to say.

"Lord Fennsworth," Kate said, thankfully breaking the silence, "you must be famished. Will you have some breakfast?"

"I would appreciate that greatly, Lady Bridgerton."

Kate turned to Lady Lucinda. "I did not see you at breakfast, either. Will you have something now?"

Gregory thought of the massive tray Miss Watson had had brought up for her and wondered how much of it she'd managed to wolf down before having to come meet her brother.

"Of course," Lady Lucinda murmured. "I should like to keep Richard company, in any case."

"Miss Watson," Gregory cut in smoothly, "would you care to take a turn about the gardens? I believe the peonies are in bloom. And those stalky blue things—I always forget what they are called."

"Delphinium." It was Lady Lucinda, of course. He'd known she would not be able to resist. Then she turned and looked at him, her eyes narrowing ever so slightly. "I told you that the other day."

"So you did," he murmured. "I've never had much of a head for details."

"Oh, Lucy remembers everything," Miss Watson said breezily. "And I would be delighted to view the gardens with you. That is, if Lucy and Richard do not mind."

Both assured her that they did not, although Gregory was quite certain he saw a flash of disappointment and—dare he say it—irritation in Lord Fennsworth's eyes.

Gregory smiled.

"I shall find you back in our room?" Miss Watson said to Lucy.

The other girl nodded, and with a feeling of triumph—there was nothing quite like besting one's competition—Gregory placed Miss Watson's hand in the crook of his elbow and led her out of the room.

It was going to be an excellent morning, after all.

Lucy followed her brother and Lady Bridgerton to the breakfast room, which she did not mind one bit, as she had not had a chance to eat very much of what Hermione had brought her earlier. But it did mean that she had to endure a full thirty minutes of meaningless conversation while her brain raced about, imagining all sorts of disasters that could be responsible for her unexpected summons home.

Richard couldn't very well speak to her about anything important with Lady Bridgerton and half of the house party blithering on about coddled eggs and the recent rainfall, so Lucy waited uncomplainingly while he finished (he'd always been an annoyingly slow eater), and then she tried her best not to lose her patience as they strolled out to the side lawn, Richard first asking her about school, then Hermione, and then Hermione's mother, and then her upcoming debut, and then Hermione again, with a side tangent to Hermione's brother, whom he'd apparently run across in Cambridge, and then it was back to the debut, and to what extent she was to share it with Hermione . . .

Until finally Lucy halted in her tracks, planted her hands on her hips, and demanded that he tell her why he was there.

"I told you," he said, not quite meeting her eyes. "Uncle Robert wishes to speak with you."

"But *why*?" It was not a question with an obvious answer. Uncle Robert hadn't cared to speak with her more than a handful of times in the past ten years. If he was planning to start now, there was a reason for it.

Richard cleared his throat a number of times before finally saying, "Well, Luce, I think he plans to marry you off."

"Straightaway?" Lucy whispered, and she didn't know why she was so surprised. She'd known this was coming; she'd been practically engaged for years. And she had told Hermione, on more than one occasion, that a season for her was really quite foolish—why bother with the expense when she was just going to marry Haselby in the end?

But now . . . suddenly . . . she didn't want to do it. At least not so soon. She didn't want to go from schoolgirl to wife, with nothing in between. She wasn't asking for adventure—she didn't even *want* adventure—truly, she wasn't the sort.

She wasn't asking for very much—just a few months of freedom, of laughter.

Of dancing breathlessly, spinning so fast that the candle flames streaked into long snakes of light.

Maybe she was practical. Maybe she was "that old Lucy," as so many had called her at Miss Moss's. But she liked to dance. And she wanted to do it. Now. Before she was old. Before she became Haselby's wife.

"I don't know when," Richard said, looking down at her with . . . was it regret?

Why would it be regret?

"Soon, I think," he said. "Uncle Robert seems somewhat eager to have it done."

Lucy just stared at him, wondering why she couldn't stop thinking about dancing, couldn't stop picturing herself, in a gown of silvery blue, magical and radiant, in the arms of—

"Oh!" She clapped a hand to her mouth, as if that could somehow silence her thoughts.

"What is it?"

"Nothing," she said, shaking her head. Her daydreams did not have a face. They could not. And so she said it again, more firmly, "It was nothing. Nothing at all."

Her brother stooped to examine a wildflower that had somehow missed the discerning eyes of Aubrey Hall's gardeners. It was small, blue, and just beginning to open.

"It's lovely, isn't it?" Richard murmured.

Lucy nodded. Richard had always loved flowers. Wildflowers in particular. They were different that way, she realized. She had always preferred the order of a neatly arranged bed, each bloom in its place, each pattern carefully and lovingly maintained.

But now . . .

She looked down at that little flower, small and delicate, defiantly sprouting where it didn't belong.

And she decided that she liked the wild ones, too.

"I know you were meant to have a season," Richard said apologetically. "But truly, is it so very dreadful? You never really wanted one, did you?"

Lucy swallowed. "No," she said, because she knew it was what he wanted to hear, and she didn't want him to feel any worse than he already did. And she hadn't really cared one way or the other about a season in London. At least not until recently.

Richard pulled the little blue wildflower out by the roots, looked at it quizzically, and stood. "Cheer up, Luce," he said, chucking her lightly on the chin. "Haselby's not a bad sort. You won't mind being married to him."

"I know," she said softly.

"He won't hurt you," he added, and he smiled, that slightly false sort of smile. The kind that was meant to be reassuring and somehow never was.

"I didn't think he would," Lucy said, an edge of . . . of *something* creeping into her voice. "Why would you bring such a thing up?"

"No reason at all," Richard said quickly. "But I know that it is a concern for many women. Not all men give their wives the respect with which Haselby will treat you."

Lucy nodded. Of course. It was true. She'd heard stories. They'd all heard stories.

"It won't be so bad," Richard said. "You'll probably even like him. He's quite agreeable."

Agreeable. It was a good thing. Better than disagreeable.

"He will be the Earl of Davenport someday," Richard added, even though of course she already knew that. "You will be a countess. Quite a prominent one."

There was that. Her schoolfriends had always said she was so lucky to have her prospects already settled, and with such a lofty result. She was the daughter of an earl and the sister of an earl. And she was destined to be the wife of one as well. She had nothing to complain about. Nothing.

But she felt so empty.

It wasn't a bad feeling precisely. But it was disconcerting. And unfamiliar. She felt rootless. She felt adrift.

She felt not like herself. And that was the worst of it.

"You're not surprised, are you, Luce?" Richard asked. "You knew this was coming. We all did."

She nodded. "It is nothing," she said, trying to sound her usual matter-of-fact self. "It is only that it never felt quite so immediate."

"Of course," Richard said. "It is a surprise, that is all. Once you grow used to the idea, it will all seem so much better. Normal, even. After all, you have always known you were to be Haselby's wife. And think of how much you will enjoy planning the wedding. Uncle Robert says it is to be a grand affair. In London, I believe. Davenport insists upon it."

Lucy felt herself nod. She did rather like to plan things. There was such a pleasant feeling of being in charge that came along with it.

"Hermione can be your attendant, as well," Richard added.

"Of course," Lucy murmured. Because, really, who else would she choose?

"Is there a color that doesn't favor her?" Richard asked with a frown. "Because you will be the bride. You don't want to be overshadowed."

Lucy rolled her eyes. That was a brother for you.

He seemed not to realize that he had insulted her, though, and Lucy supposed she shouldn't have been surprised. Hermione's beauty was so legendary that no one took insult with an unfavorable comparison. One would have to be delusional to think otherwise.

"I can't very well put her in black," Lucy said. It was the only hue she could think of that turned Hermione a bit sallow.

"No, no you couldn't, could you?" Richard paused, clearly pondering this, and Lucy stared at him in disbelief. Her brother, who had to be regularly informed of what was fashionable and what was not, was actually *interested* in the shade of Hermione's attendant dress.

"Hermione can wear whatever color she desires," Lucy decided. And why not? Of all the people who would be in attendance, there was no one who meant more to her than her closest friend.

"That's very kind of you," Richard said. He looked at her thoughtfully. "You're a good friend, Lucy."

Lucy knew she should have felt complimented, but instead she just wondered why it had taken him so long to realize it.

Richard gave her a smile, then looked down at the flower, still in his hands. He held it up, twirled it a few times, the stem rolling back and forth between his thumb and index finger. He blinked, his brow furrowing a touch, then he placed the flower in front of her dress. They were the same blue—slightly purple, maybe just a little bit gray.

"You should wear this color," he said. "You look quite lovely just now."

He sounded a little surprised, so Lucy knew that he was not just saying it. "Thank you," she said. She'd always thought the hue made her eyes a bit brighter. Richard was the first person besides Hermione ever to comment on it. "Perhaps I will."

"Shall we walk back to the house?" he asked. "I am sure you will wish to tell Hermione everything."

She paused, then shook her head. "No, thank you. I think I shall remain outside for a short while." She motioned to a spot near the path that led down to the lake. "There is a bench not too far away. And the sun feels rather pleasant on my face."

"Are you certain?" Richard squinted up at the sky. "You're always saying you don't want to get freckles."

"I already have freckles, Richard. And I won't be very long." She hadn't planned to come outside when she'd gone to greet him, so she had not brought her bonnet. But it was early yet in the day. A few minutes of sunshine would not destroy her complexion.

And besides that, she wanted to. Wouldn't it be nice to do something just because she wanted to, and not because it was expected?

Richard nodded. "I will see you at dinner?"

"I believe it is laid at half one."

He grinned. "You would know."

"There is nothing like a brother," she grumbled.

"And there is nothing like a sister." He leaned over and kissed her brow, catching her completely off-guard.

"Oh, Richard," she muttered, aghast at her soppy reaction. She never cried. In fact, she was known for her complete lack of flowerpot tendencies.

"Go on," he said, with enough affection to send one tear rolling down her cheek. Lucy brushed it away, embarrassed that he'd seen it, embarrassed that she'd done it.

Richard squeezed her hand and motioned with his head toward the south lawn. "Go stare at the trees and do whatever you need to do. You'll feel better after you have a few moments to yourself."

"I don't feel poorly," Lucy said quickly. "There is no need for me to feel *better.*"

"Of course not. You are merely surprised."

"Exactly."

Exactly. Exactly. Really, she was delighted, really. She'd been waiting for this moment for years. Wouldn't it be nice to have everything settled? She liked order. She liked being settled.

It was just the surprise. That was all. Rather like when one saw a friend in an unexpected location and almost didn't recognize her. She hadn't expected the announcement now. Here, at the Bridgerton house party. And that was the only reason she felt so odd.

Really.

Chapter 8

In which Our Heroine learns a truth about her brother (but does not believe it), Our Hero learns a secret about Miss Watson (but is not concerned by it), and both learn a truth about themselves (but are not aware of it).

An hour later, Gregory was still congratulating himself on the masterful combination of strategy and timing that had led to his outing with Miss Watson. They had had a perfectly lovely time, and Lord Fennsworth had—well, Fennsworth may have also had a perfectly lovely time, but if so, it had been in the company of his sister and not the lovely Hermione Watson.

Victory was indeed sweet.

As promised, Gregory had taken her on a stroll through the Aubrey Hall gardens, impressing them both with his stupendous recall of six different horticultural names. Delphinium, even, though in truth that was all Lady Lucinda's doing.

The others were, just to give credit where it was due: rose, daisy, peony, hyacinth, and grass. All in all, he thought he'd acquitted himself well. Details never had been his forte. And truly, it was all just a game by that point.

Miss Watson appeared to be warming to his company, as well. She might not have been sighing and fluttering her lashes, but the veil of polite disinterest was gone, and twice he had even made her laugh.

She hadn't made *him* laugh, but he wasn't so certain she'd been trying to, and besides, he had certainly smiled. On more than one occasion.

Which was a good thing. Really. It was rather pleasant to once again have his wits about him. He was no longer struck by that punched-in-the-chest feeling, which one would think had to be good for his respiratory health. He was discovering he rather enjoyed breathing, an undertaking he seemed to find difficult while gazing upon the back of Miss Watson's neck.

Gregory frowned, pausing in his solitary jaunt down to the lake. It *was* a rather odd reaction. And surely he'd seen the back of her neck that morning. Hadn't she run ahead to smell one of the flowers?

Hmmm. Perhaps not. He couldn't quite recall.

"Good day, Mr. Bridgerton."

He turned, surprised to see Lady Lucinda sitting by herself on a nearby stone bench. It was an odd location for a bench, he'd always thought, facing nothing but a bunch of trees. But maybe that was the point. Turning one's back on the house—and its many inhabitants. His sister Francesca had often said that after a day or two with the entire Bridgerton family, trees could be quite good company.

Lady Lucinda smiled faintly in greeting, and it struck him that she didn't look quite herself. Her eyes seemed tired, and her posture was not quite straight.

She looks vulnerable, he thought, rather unexpectedly. Her brother must have brought unhappy tidings.

"You're wearing a somber expression," he said, walking politely to her side. "May I join you?"

She nodded, offering him a bit of a smile. But it wasn't a smile. Not quite.

He took a seat beside her. "Did you have an opportunity to visit with your brother?"

She nodded. "He passed along some family news. It was . . . not important."

Gregory tilted his head as he regarded her. She was lying, clearly. But he did not press further. If she'd wanted to share, she would have done. And besides, it wasn't his business in any case.

He was curious, though.

She stared off in the distance, presumably at some tree. "It's quite pleasant here."

It was an oddly bland statement, coming from her.

"Yes," he said. "The lake is just a short walk beyond these trees. I often come in this direction when I wish to think."

She turned suddenly. "You do?"

"Why are you so surprised?"

"I—I don't know." She shrugged. "I suppose you don't seem the sort."

"To think?" Well, really.

"Of course not," she said, giving him a peevish look. "I meant the sort who needed to get away to do so."

"Pardon my presumptuousness, but you don't seem the sort, either."

She thought about that for a moment. "I'm not."

He chuckled at that. "You must have had quite a conversation with your brother."

She blinked in surprise. But she didn't elaborate. Which again didn't seem like her. "What are you here to think about?" she asked.

He opened his mouth to reply, but before he could utter a word, she said, "Hermione, I suppose."

There seemed little point in denying it. "Your brother is in love with her."

That seemed to snap her out of her fog. "*Richard?* Don't be daft."

Gregory looked at her in disbelief. "I can't believe you haven't seen it."

"I can't believe you *have*. For heaven's sake, she thinks of him as a brother."

"That may well be true, but he does not return the sentiment."

"Mr. Br—"

But he halted her with a lifted hand. "Now, now, Lady Lucinda, I daresay I have been witness to more fools in love than you have—"

The laughter quite literally exploded from her mouth. "Mr. Bridgerton," she said, once she was able, "I have been constant companion these last three years to Hermione Watson. *Hermione Watson*," she added, just in case he hadn't understood her meaning. "Trust me when I tell you there is no one who has been witness to more lovesick fools than I."

For a moment Gregory did not know how to respond. She did have a point.

"Richard is not in love with Hermione," she said with a dismissive shake of her head. And a snort. A ladylike one, but still. She *snorted* at him.

"I beg to differ," he said, because he had seven siblings, and he certainly did not know how to gracefully bow out of an argument.

"He can't be in love with her," she said, sounding quite certain of her statement. "There is someone else."

"Oh, really?" Gregory didn't even bother to get his hopes up.

"Really. He's always nattering on about a girl he met through one of his friends," she said. "I think it was someone's sister. I can't recall her name. Mary, perhaps."

Mary. Hmmph. He *knew* that Fennsworth had no imagination.

"Ergo," Lady Lucinda continued, "he is not in love with Hermione."

At least she seemed rather more like herself. The world seemed a bit steadier with Lucy Abernathy yipping along like a terrier. He'd felt almost off-balance when she'd been staring morosely at the trees.

"Believe what you will," Gregory said with a lofty sigh. "But know this: your brother will be nursing a broken heart ere long."

"Oh, really?" she scoffed. "Because you are so convinced of your own success?"

"Because I'm convinced of his lack of it."

"You don't even know him."

"And now you are defending him? Just moments ago you said he wasn't interested."

"He's not." She bit her lip. "But he is my brother. And if he *were* interested, I would have to support him, wouldn't you think?"

Gregory lifted a brow. "My, how quickly your loyalties shift."

She looked almost apologetic. "He *is* an earl. And you . . . are not."

"You shall make a fine society mama."

Her back stiffened. "I beg your pardon."

"Auctioning your friend off to the highest bidder. You'll be well-practiced by the time you have a daughter."

She jumped to her feet, her eyes flashing with anger and indignation. "That is a terrible thing to say. My most important consideration has always been Hermione's happiness. And if she can be made happy by an earl . . . who happens to be my *brother* . . ."

Oh, brilliant. Now she was going to *try* to match Hermione with Fennsworth. Well done, Gregory. Well done, indeed.

"She can be made happy by me," he said, rising to his feet. And it was true. He'd made her laugh twice this morning, even if she had not done the same for him.

"Of course she can," Lady Lucinda said. "And heavens, she probably will if you don't muck it up. Richard is too young to marry, anyway. He's only two-and-twenty."

Gregory eyed her curiously. Now she sounded as if she were back to him as the best candidate. What was she about, anyway?

"And," she added, impatiently tucking a lock of her dark blond hair behind her ear when the wind whipped it into her face, "he is *not* in love with her. I'm quite certain of it."

Neither one of them seemed to have anything to add to *that*, so, since they were both already on their feet, Gregory motioned toward the house. "Shall we return?"

She nodded, and they departed at a leisurely pace.

"This still does not solve the problem of Mr. Edmonds," Gregory remarked.

She gave him a funny look.

"What was that for?" he demanded.

And she actually giggled. Well, perhaps not a giggle, but she did do that breathy thing with her nose people did when they were rather amused. "It was nothing," she said, still smiling. "I'm rather impressed, actually, that you didn't pretend to not remember his name."

"What, should I have called him Mr. Edwards, and then Mr. Ellington, and then Mr. Edifice, and—"

Lucy gave him an arch look. "You would have lost all of my respect, I assure you."

"The horror. Oh, the horror," he said, laying one hand over his heart.

She glanced at him over her shoulder with a mischievous smile. "It was a near miss."

He looked unconcerned. "I'm a terrible shot, but I do know how to dodge a bullet."

Now *that* made her curious. "I've never known a man who would admit to being a bad shot."

He shrugged. "There are some things one simply can't avoid. I shall always be the Bridgerton who can be bested at close range by his sister."

"The one you told me about?"

"All of them," he admitted.

"Oh." She frowned. There ought to be some sort of prescribed statement for such a situation. What *did* one say when a gentleman confessed to a shortcoming? She couldn't recall ever hearing one do so before, but surely, sometime in the course of history, some gentleman had. And someone would have had to make a reply.

She blinked, waiting for something meaningful to come to mind. Nothing did.

And then—

"Hermione can't dance." It just popped out of her mouth, with no direction whatsoever from her head.

Good gracious, *that* was meant to be meaningful?

He stopped, turning to her with a curious expression. Or maybe it was more that he was startled. Probably both. And he said the only thing she imagined one *could* say under the circumstances:

"I beg your pardon?"

Lucy repeated it, since she couldn't take it back. "She can't dance. That's why she won't dance. Because she can't."

And then she waited for a hole to open up in the ground so that she could jump into it. It didn't help that he was presently staring at her as if she were slightly deranged.

She managed a feeble smile, which was all that filled the impossibly long moment until he finally said, "There must be a reason you are telling this to me."

Lucy let out a nervous exhale. He didn't sound angry—more curious than anything else. And she hadn't *meant* to insult Hermione. But when he said he couldn't shoot, it just seemed to make an odd sort of sense to tell him that Hermione couldn't dance. It fit, really. Men were supposed to shoot, and women were supposed to dance, and trusty best friends were supposed to keep their foolish mouths shut.

Clearly, all three of them needed a bit of instruction.

"I thought to make you feel better," Lucy finally said. "Because you can't shoot."

"Oh, I can *shoot*," he said. "That's the easy part. I just can't aim."

Lucy grinned. She couldn't help herself. "I could show you."

His head swung around. "Oh, *gad*. Don't tell me *you* know how to shoot."

She perked up. "Quite well, actually."

He shook his head. "The day only needed this."

"It's an admirable skill," she protested.

"I'm sure it is, but I've already four females in my life who can best me. The last thing I need is—oh, gad *again*, please don't say Miss Watson is a crack shot as well."

Lucy blinked. "Do you know, I'm not sure."

"Well, there is still hope there, then."

"Isn't that peculiar?" she murmured.

He gave her a deadpan look. "That I have hope?"

"No, that—" She couldn't say it. Good heavens, it sounded silly even to her.

"Ah, then you must think it peculiar that you don't know whether Miss Watson can shoot."

And there it was. He guessed it, anyway. "Yes," she admitted. "But then again, why would I? Marksmanship wasn't a part of the curriculum at Miss Moss's."

"To the great relief of gentlemen everywhere, I assure you." He gave her a lopsided smile. "Who did teach you?"

"My father," she said, and it was strange, because her lips parted before she answered. For a moment she thought she'd been surprised by the question, but it hadn't been that.

She'd been surprised by her answer.

"Good heavens," he responded, "were you even out of leading strings?"

"Just barely," Lucy said, still puzzling over her odd reaction. It was probably just because she didn't often think of her father. He had been gone so long that there weren't many questions to which the late Earl of Fennsworth constituted the reply.

"He thought it an important skill," she continued. "Even for girls. Our home is near the Dover coast, and there were always smugglers. Most of them were friendly—everyone knew who they were, even the magistrate."

"He must have enjoyed French brandy," Mr. Bridgerton murmured.

Lucy smiled in recollection. "As did my father. But not all of the smugglers were known to us. Some, I'm sure, were quite dangerous. And . . ." She leaned toward him. One really couldn't say something like this without leaning in. Where would the fun be in that?

"And . . . ?" he prompted.

She lowered her voice. "I think there were spies."

"In Dover? Ten years ago? Absolutely there were spies. Although I do wonder at the advisability of arming the infant population."

Lucy laughed. "I was a bit older than *that*. I believe we began when I was seven. Richard continued the lessons once my father had passed on."

"I suppose he's a brilliant marksman as well."

She nodded ruefully. "Sorry."

They resumed their stroll toward the house. "I won't challenge him to a duel, then," he said, somewhat offhandedly.

"I'd rather you didn't."

He turned to her with an expression that could only be called sly. "Why, Lady Lucinda, I do believe you have just declared your affection for me."

Her mouth flapped open like an inarticulate fish. "I have n—what could possibly lead you to that conclusion?" And *why* did her cheeks feel so suddenly hot?

"It could never be a fair match," he said, sounding remarkably at ease with his shortcomings. "Although in all truth, I don't know that there is a man in Britain with whom I could have a fair match."

She still felt somewhat light-headed after her previous surprise, but she managed to say, "I'm sure you overstate."

"No," he said, almost casually. "Your brother would surely leave a bullet in my shoulder." He paused, considering this. "Assuming he wasn't of a mind to put one in my heart."

"Oh, don't be silly."

He shrugged. "Regardless, you must be more concerned for my welfare than you were aware."

"I'm concerned for everybody's welfare," she muttered.

"Yes," he murmured, "you would be."

Lucy drew back. "Why does that sound like an insult?"

"Did it? I can assure you it wasn't meant to."

She stared at him suspiciously for so long that he finally lifted his hands in surrender. "It was a compliment, I swear to you," he said.

"Grudgingly given."

"Not at all!" He glanced over at her, quite obviously unable to suppress a smile.

"You're laughing at me."

"No," he insisted, and then of course he laughed. "Sorry. Now I am."

"You could at least *attempt* to be kind and say that you are laughing *with* me."

"I could." He grinned, and his eyes turned positively devilish. "But it would be a lie."

She almost smacked him on the shoulder. "Oh, you are terrible."

"Bane of my brothers' existence, I assure you."

"Really?" Lucy had never been the bane of anyone's existence, and right then it sounded rather appealing. "How so?"

"Oh, the same as always. I need to settle down, find purpose, apply myself."

"Get married?"

"That, too."

"Is that why you are so enamored of Hermione?"

He paused—just for a moment. But it was there. Lucy felt it.

"No," he said. "It was something else entirely."

"Of course," she said quickly, feeling foolish for having asked. He'd told her all about it the night before—about love just happening, having no choice in the matter. He didn't want Hermione to please his brother; he wanted Hermione because he couldn't *not* want her.

And it made her feel just a little bit more alone.

"We are returned," he said, motioning to the door to the drawing room, which she had not even realized they had reached.

"Yes, of course." She looked at the door, then looked at him, then wondered why it felt so awkward now that they had to say goodbye. "Thank you for the company."

"The pleasure was all mine."

Lucy took a step toward the door, then turned back to face him with a little "Oh!"

His brows rose. "Is something wrong?"

"No. But I must apologize—I turned you quite around. You said you like to go that way—down toward the lake—when you need to think. And you never got to."

He looked at her curiously, his head tilting ever so slightly to the side. And his eyes—oh, she wished she could describe what she saw there. Because she didn't understand it, didn't quite comprehend how it made her tilt her head in concert with his, how it made her feel as if the moment were stretching . . . longer . . . longer . . . until it could last a lifetime.

"Didn't you wish for time for yourself?" she asked, softly . . . so softly it was almost a whisper.

Slowly, he shook his head. "I did," he said, sounding as if the words were coming to him at that very moment, as if the thought itself was new and not quite what he had expected.

"I did," he said again, "but now I don't."

She looked at him, and he looked at her. And the thought quite suddenly popped into her head—

He doesn't know why.

He didn't know why he no longer wanted to be by himself.

And she didn't know why that was meaningful.

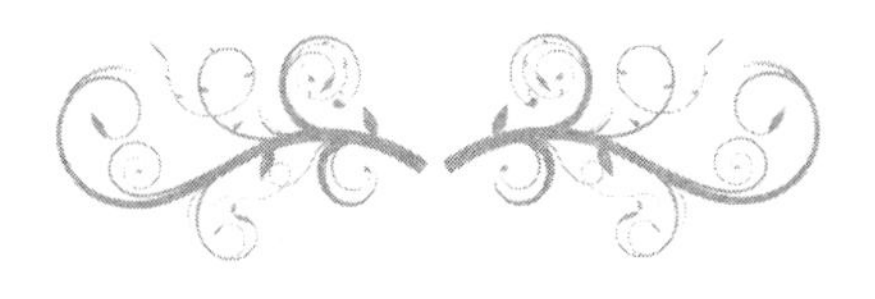

Chapter 9

In which Our Story takes a turn.

The following night was the masked ball. It was to be a grand affair, not *too* grand, of course—Gregory's brother Anthony wouldn't stand for that much disruption of his comfortable life in the country. But nevertheless, it was to be the pinnacle of the house party events. All the guests would be there, along with another hundred or so extra attendees—some down from London, others straight from their homes in the country. Every last bedchamber had been aired out and prepared for occupants, and even with that, a good number of partygoers were staying at the homes of neighbors, or, for an unlucky few, at nearby inns.

Kate's original intention had been to throw a fancy dress party—she'd been longing to fashion herself as Medusa (to the surprise of no one)—but she had finally abandoned the idea after Anthony informed her that if she had her way with this, *he* would choose his own costume.

The look he gave her was apparently enough for her to declare an immediate retreat.

She later told Gregory that he had still not forgiven her for costuming him as Cupid at the Billington fancy dress ball the previous year.

"Costume too cherubic?" Gregory murmured.

"But on the bright side," she had replied, "I now know exactly how he must have looked as a baby. Quite darling, actually."

"Until this moment," Gregory said with a wince, "I'm not sure I understood exactly how much my brother loves you."

"Quite a bit." She smiled and nodded. "Quite a bit indeed."

And so a compromise was reached. No costumes, just masks. Anthony didn't mind that one bit, as it would enable him to abandon his duties as host entirely if he so chose (who would notice his absence, after all?), and Kate set to work designing a mask with Medusaish snakes jumping out in every direction. (She was unsuccessful.)

At Kate's insistence, Gregory arrived in the ballroom at precisely half eight, the ball's announced start. It meant, of course, that the only guests in attendance were he, his brother, and Kate, but there were enough servants milling about to make it seem not quite so empty, and Anthony declared himself delighted with the gathering.

"It's a much better party without everyone else jostling about," he said happily.

"When did you grow so opposed to social discourse?" Gregory asked, plucking a champagne flute off a proffered tray.

"It's not that at all," Anthony answered with a shrug. "I've simply lost patience for stupidity of any kind."

"He is not aging well," his wife confirmed.

If Anthony took any exception to her comment, he made no show of it. "I simply refuse to deal with idiots," he told Gregory. His face brightened. "It has cut my social obligations in half."

"What's the point of possessing a title if one cannot refuse one's invitations?" Gregory murmured wryly.

"Indeed," was Anthony's reply. "Indeed."

Gregory turned to Kate. "You have no arguments with this?"

"Oh, I have many arguments," she answered, craning her neck as she examined the ballroom for any last-minute disasters. "I always have arguments."

"It's true," Anthony said. "But she knows when she cannot win."

Kate turned to Gregory even though her words were quite clearly directed at her husband. "What I *know* is how to choose my battles."

"Pay her no mind," Anthony said. "That is just her way of admitting defeat."

"And yet he continues," Kate said to no one in particular, "even though he knows that I always win in the end."

Anthony shrugged and gave his brother an uncharacteristically sheepish grin. "She's right, of course." He finished his drink. "But there is no point in surrendering without a fight."

Gregory could only smile. Two bigger fools in love had yet to be born. It was endearing to watch, even if it did leave him with a slight pang of jealousy.

"How fares your courtship?" Kate asked him.

Anthony's ears perked up. "Your courtship?" he echoed, his face assuming its usual *obey-me-I-am-the-viscount* expression. "Who is she?"

Gregory shot Kate an aggravated look. He had not shared his feelings with his brother. He wasn't sure why; surely in part because he hadn't actually *seen* much of Anthony in the past few days. But there was more. It just didn't seem like the sort of thing one wished to share with one's brother. Especially one who was considerably more father than brother.

Not to mention . . . If he didn't succeed . . .

Well, he didn't particularly wish for his family to know.

But he *would* succeed. Why was he doubting himself? Even earlier, when Miss Watson was still treating him like a minor nuisance, he had been sure of the outcome. It made no sense that now—with their friendship growing—he should suddenly doubt himself.

Kate, predictably, ignored Gregory's irritation. "I just adore it when you don't know something," she said to her husband. "Especially when I do."

Anthony turned to Gregory. "You're sure you want to marry one of these?"

"Not that one precisely," Gregory answered. "Something rather like it, though."

Kate's expression turned somewhat pinched at having been called an "it," but she recovered quickly, turning to Anthony and saying, "He has declared his love for—" She let one of her hands flutter in the air as if waving away a foolish idea. "Oh, never mind, I think I won't tell you."

Her phrasing was a bit suspect. She probably had meant to keep it from him all along. Gregory wasn't sure which he found more satisfying—that Kate had honored his secret or that Anthony had been flummoxed.

"See if you can guess," Kate said to Anthony with an arch smile. "That should lend your evening a sense of purpose."

Anthony turned to Gregory with a level stare. "Who is it?"

Gregory shrugged. He always sided with Kate when it came to thwarting his brother. "Far be it from me to deny you a sense of purpose."

Anthony muttered, "Arrogant pup," and Gregory knew that the evening was off to a fine start.

The guests began to trickle in, and within an hour, the ballroom sang with the low buzz of conversation and laughter. Everyone seemed a bit more adventurous with a mask on their face, and soon the banter grew more risqué, the jokes more ribald.

And the laughter . . . It was difficult to put the right word on it, but it was different. There was more than merriment in the air. There was an edge to the excitement, as if the partygoers somehow knew that this was the night to be daring.

To break free.

Because in the morning, no one would know.

All in all, Gregory liked nights like these.

By half nine, however, he was growing frustrated. He could not be positive, but he was almost certain that Miss Watson had not made an appearance. Even with a mask, she would find it nearly impossible to keep her identity a secret. Her hair was too startling, too ethereal in the candlelight for her to pass as anyone else.

But Lady Lucinda, on the other hand . . . She would have no trouble blending in. Her hair was certainly a lovely shade of honeyish blond, but it was nothing unexpected or unique. Half the ladies of the *ton* probably had hair that color.

He glanced around the ballroom. Very well, not half. And maybe not even a quarter. But it wasn't the spun moonlight of her friend's.

He frowned. Miss Watson really ought to have been present by then. As a member of the house party, she need not deal with muddy roads or lame horses or even the long line of carriages waiting out front to deliver the guests. And while he doubted she would have wished to arrive as early as he had done, surely she would not come over an hour late.

If nothing else, Lady Lucinda would not have tolerated it. She was clearly a punctual sort.

In a good way.

As opposed to an insufferable, nagging way.

He smiled to himself. She wasn't like that.

Lady Lucinda was more like Kate, or at least she would be, once she was a bit older. Intelligent, no-nonsense, just a little bit sly.

Rather good fun, actually. She was a good sport, Lady Lucinda was.

But he didn't see her among the guests, either. Or at least he didn't think he did. He couldn't be quite sure. He did see several ladies with hair the approximate shade of hers, but none of them seemed quite right. One of them moved the wrong way—too clunky, maybe even a little bit lumbering. And another was the wrong height. Not very wrong, probably just a few inches. But he could tell.

It wasn't she.

She was probably wherever Miss Watson was. Which he did find somewhat reassuring. Miss Watson could not possibly get into trouble with Lady Lucinda about.

His stomach growled, and he decided to abandon his search for the time being and instead seek sustenance. Kate had, as always, provided a hearty selection of food for her guests to nibble upon during the course of the evening. He went directly to the plate of sandwiches—they looked rather like the ones she'd served the night he'd arrived, and he'd liked those quite well. Ten of them ought to do the trick.

Hmmm. He saw cucumber—a waste of bread if ever he saw one. Cheese—no, not what he was looking for. Perhaps—

"Mr. Bridgerton?"

Lady Lucinda. He'd know that voice anywhere.

He turned. There she was. He congratulated himself. He'd been right about those other masked honey blonds. He definitely hadn't come across her yet this evening.

Her eyes widened, and he realized that her mask, covered with slate blue felt, was the exact color of her eyes. He wondered if Miss Watson had obtained a similar one in green.

"It *is* you, isn't it?"

"How did you know?" he returned.

She blinked. "I don't know. I just did." Then her lips parted—just enough to reveal a tiny little gleam of white teeth, and she said, "It's Lucy. Lady Lucinda."

"I know," he murmured, still looking at her mouth. What was it about masks? It was as if by covering up the top, the bottom was made more intriguing.

Almost mesmerizing.

How was it he hadn't noticed the way her lips tilted ever so slightly up at the corners? Or the freckles on her nose. There were seven of them. Precisely seven, all shaped like ovals, except for that last one, which looked rather like Ireland, actually.

"Were you hungry?" she asked.

He blinked, forced his eyes back to hers.

She motioned to the sandwiches. "The ham is very nice. As is the cucumber. I'm not normally partial to cucumber sandwiches—they never seem to satisfy although I do like the crunch—but these have a bit of soft cheese on them instead of just butter. It was a rather nice surprise."

She paused and looked at him, tilting her head to the side as she awaited his reply.

And he smiled. He couldn't help it. There was something so uncommonly entertaining about her when she was prattling on about food.

He reached out and placed a cucumber sandwich on his plate. "With such a recommendation," he said, "how could I refuse?"

"Well, the ham is nice, too, if you don't like it."

Again, so like her. Wanting everyone to be happy. *Try this. And if you don't like it, try this or this or this or this. And if that doesn't work, have mine.*

She'd never said it, of course, but somehow he knew she would.

She looked down at the serving platter. "I do wish they weren't all mixed up."

He looked at her quizzically. "I beg your pardon?"

"Well," she said—that singular sort of *well* that foretold a long and heartfelt explanation. "Don't you think it would have made far more sense to separate the different types of sandwiches? To put each on its own smaller plate? That way, if you found one you liked, you would know exactly where to go to get another. *Or*"—at this she grew even more animated, as if she were attacking a problem of great societal importance—"*if* there was another. Consider it." She waved at the platter. "There might not be a single ham sandwich left in the stack. And you couldn't very well sift through them all, looking. It would be most impolite."

He regarded her thoughtfully, then said, "You like things to be orderly, don't you?"

"Oh, I do," she said with feeling. "I really do."

Gregory considered his own disorganized ways. He tossed shoes in the wardrobe, left invitations strewn about . . . The year before, he had released his valet-secretary from service for a week to visit his ailing father, and when the poor man had come back, the chaos on Gregory's desk alone had nearly done him in.

Gregory looked at Lady Lucinda's earnest expression and chuckled. He'd probably drive her mad in under a week as well.

"Do you like the sandwich?" she asked, once he'd taken a bite. "The cucumber?"

"Very intriguing," he murmured.

"I wonder, is food meant to be intriguing?"

He finished the sandwich. "I'm not certain."

She nodded absently, then said, "The ham is nice."

They lapsed into a companionable silence as they glanced out across the room. The musicians were playing a lively waltz, and the ladies' skirts were billowing like silken bells as they spun and twirled. It was impossible to watch the scene and not feel as if the night itself were alive . . . restless with energy . . . waiting to make its move.

Something would happen that night. Gregory was sure of it. Someone's life would change.

If he was lucky, it would be his.

His hands began to tingle. His feet, too. It was taking everything he had just to stand still. He wanted to move, he wanted to *do* something. He wanted to set his life in motion, reach out and capture his dreams.

He wanted to move. He couldn't stand still. He—

"Would you like to dance?"

He hadn't meant to ask. But he'd turned, and Lucy was right there beside him, and the words just tumbled out.

Her eyes lit up. Even with the mask, he could see that she was delighted. "Yes," she said, almost sighing as she added, "I love to dance."

He took her hand and led her to the floor. The waltz was in full swing, and they quickly found their place in the music. It seemed to lift them, render them as one. Gregory needed only to press his hand at her waist, and she moved, exactly as he anticipated. They spun, they twirled, the air rushing past their faces so quickly that they had to laugh.

It was perfect. It was breathless. It was as if the music had crept under their skin and was guiding their every movement.

And then it was over.

So quickly. *Too* quickly. The music ended, and for a moment they stood, still in each other's arms, still wrapped in the memory of the music.

"Oh, that was lovely," Lady Lucinda said, and her eyes shone.

Gregory released her and bowed. "You are a superb dancer, Lady Lucinda. I knew you would be."

"Thank you, I—" Her eyes snapped to his. "You did?"

"I—" Why had he said that? He hadn't meant to say that. "You're quite graceful," he finally said, leading her back to the ballroom's perimeter. Far more graceful than Miss Watson, actually, although that did make sense given what Lucy had said about her friend's dancing ability.

"It is in the way you walk," he added, since she seemed to be expecting a more detailed explanation.

And that would have to do, since he wasn't about to examine the notion any further.

"Oh." And her lips moved. Just a little. But it was enough. And it struck him—she looked happy. And he realized that most people didn't. They looked amused, or entertained, or satisfied.

Lady Lucinda looked happy.

He rather liked that.

"I wonder where Hermione is," she said, looking this way and that.

"She didn't arrive with you?" Gregory asked, surprised.

"She did. But then we saw Richard. And he asked her to dance. *Not*," she added with great emphasis, "because he is in love with her. He was merely being polite. That is what one does for one's sister's friends."

"I have four sisters," he reminded her. "I know." But then he remembered. "I thought Miss Watson does not dance."

"She doesn't. But Richard does not know that. No one does. Except me. And you." She looked at him with some urgency. "Please do *not* tell anyone. I beg of you. Hermione would be mortified."

"My lips are sealed," he promised.

"I imagine they went off to find something to drink," Lucy said, leaning slightly to one side as she tried to catch a glimpse of the lemonade table. "Hermione made a comment about being overheated. It is her favorite excuse. It almost always works when someone asks her to dance."

"I don't see them," Gregory said, following her gaze.

"No, you wouldn't." She turned back to face him, giving her head a little shake. "I don't know why I was looking. It was some time ago."

"Longer than one can sip at a drink?"

She chuckled. "No, Hermione can make a glass of lemonade last an entire evening when she needs to. But I think Richard would have lost patience."

It was Gregory's opinion that her brother would gladly cut off his right arm just for the chance to gaze upon Miss Watson while she pretended to drink lemonade, but there was little point in trying to convince Lucy of that.

"I imagine they decided to take a stroll," Lucy said, quite obviously unconcerned.

But Gregory immediately felt an unease. "Outside?"

She shrugged. "I suppose. They are certainly not here in the ballroom. Hermione cannot hide in a crowd. Her hair, you know."

"But do you think it is wise for them to be off alone?" Gregory pressed.

Lady Lucinda looked at him as if she couldn't quite understand the urgency in his voice. "They're hardly off alone," she said. "There are at least two dozen people outside. I looked out through the French doors."

Gregory forced himself to stand perfectly still while he considered what to do. Clearly he needed to find Miss Watson, and quickly, before she was subjected to anything that might be considered irrevocable.

Irrevocable.

Jesus.

Lives could turn on a single moment. If Miss Watson really was off with Lucy's brother . . . If someone caught them . . .

A strange heat began to rise within him, something angry and jealous and entirely unpleasant. Miss Watson might be in danger . . . or she might not. Maybe she welcomed Fennsworth's advances . . .

No. No, she did not. He practically forced the thought down his throat. Miss Watson thought she was in love with that ridiculous Mr. Edmonds, whoever he was. She wouldn't welcome advances from Gregory *or* Lord Fennsworth.

But had Lucy's brother seized an opportunity that *he* had missed? It rankled, lodged itself in his chest like a hot cannonball—this *feeling*, this emotion, this bloody . . . awful . . . pissish . . .

"Mr. Bridgerton?"

Foul. Definitely foul.

"Mr. Bridgerton, is something wrong?"

He moved his head the inch required to face Lady Lucinda, but even so, it took several seconds for him to focus on her features. Her eyes were concerned, her mouth pressed into a worried line.

"You don't look well," she said.

"I'm fine," he ground out.

"But—"

"*Fine*," he positively snapped.

She drew back. "Of course you are."

How had Fennsworth done it? How had he got Miss Watson off alone? He was still wet behind the ears, for God's sake, barely out of university and never come down to London. And Gregory was . . . Well, more experienced than that.

He should have been paying more attention.

He should never have allowed this.

"Perhaps I'll look for Hermione," Lucy said, inching away. "I can see that you would prefer to be alone."

"No," he blurted out, with a bit more force than was strictly polite. "I will join you. We shall search together."

"Do you think that's wise?"

"Why wouldn't it be wise?"

"I . . . don't know." She stopped, stared at him with wide, unblinking eyes, finally saying, "I just don't think it is. You yourself just questioned the wisdom of Richard and Hermione going off together."

"You certainly cannot search the house by yourself."

"Of course not," she said, as if he were foolish for even having suggested it. "I was going to find Lady Bridgerton."

Kate? Good God. "Don't do *that*," he said quickly. And perhaps a bit disdainfully as well, although that hadn't been his intention.

But she clearly took umbrage because her voice was clipped as she asked, "And why not?"

He leaned in, his tone low and urgent. "If Kate finds them, and they are not as they should be, they will be married in less than a fortnight. Mark my words."

"Don't be absurd. Of course they will be as they should," she hissed, and it took him aback, actually, because it never occurred to him that she might stand up for herself with quite so much vigor.

"Hermione would never behave in an untoward manner," she continued furiously, "and neither would Richard, for that matter. He is my brother. My *brother*."

"He loves her," Gregory said simply.

"No. He. *Doesn't.*" Good God, she looked ready to explode. "And even if he did," she railed on, "which he does not, he would *never* dishonor her. Never. He wouldn't. He wouldn't—"

"He wouldn't what?"

She swallowed. "He wouldn't do that to *me.*"

Gregory could not believe her naiveté. "He's not thinking of *you*, Lady Lucinda. In fact, I believe it would be safe to say that you have not crossed his mind even once."

"That is a terrible thing to say."

Gregory shrugged. "He's a man in love. Hence, he is a man insensible."

"Oh, is *that* how it works?" she retorted. "Does that render *you* insensible as well?"

"No," he said tersely, and he realized it was actually true. He had already grown accustomed to this strange fervor. He'd regained his equilibrium. And as a gentleman of considerably more experience, he was, even when Miss Watson was not an issue, more easily in possession of his wits than Fennsworth.

Lady Lucinda gave him a look of disdainful impatience. "Richard is not in love with her. I don't know how many ways I can explain that to you."

"You're wrong," he said flatly. He'd been watching Fennsworth for two days. He'd been watching him watching Miss Watson. Laughing at her jokes. Fetching her a cool drink.

Picking a wildflower, tucking it behind her ear.

If that wasn't love, then Richard Abernathy was the most attentive, caring, and unselfish older brother in the history of man.

And as an older brother himself—one who had frequently been pressed into service dancing attendance upon his sisters' friends—

Gregory could categorically say that there did not exist an older brother with such levels of thoughtfulness and devotion.

One loved one's sister, of course, but one did not sacrifice one's every waking minute for the sake of her best friend without some sort of compensation.

Unless a pathetic and unrequited love factored into the equation.

"I am not wrong," Lady Lucinda said, looking very much as if she would like to cross her arms. "And I'm getting Lady Bridgerton."

Gregory closed his hand around her wrist. "That would be a mistake of magnificent proportions."

She yanked, but he did not let go. "Don't patronize me," she hissed.

"I'm not. I'm instructing you."

Her mouth fell open. Really, truly, flappingly open.

Gregory would have enjoyed the sight, were he not so furious with everything else in the world just then.

"You are insufferable," she said, once she'd recovered.

He shrugged. "Occasionally."

"*And* delusional."

"Well done, Lady Lucinda." As one of eight, Gregory could not help but admire any well-placed quip or retort. "But I would be far more likely to admire your verbal skills if I were not trying to stop you from doing something monumentally stupid."

She looked at him through narrowed eyes, and then she said, "I don't care to speak to you any longer."

"Ever?"

"I'm getting Lady Bridgerton," she announced.

"You're getting me? What is the occasion?"

It was the last voice Gregory wanted to hear.

He turned. Kate was standing in front of them both, regarding the tableau with a single lifted brow.

No one spoke.

Kate glanced pointedly at Gregory's hand, still on Lady Lucinda's wrist. He dropped it, quickly stepping back.

"Is there something I should know about?" Kate asked, and her voice was that perfectly awful mix of cultured inquiry and moral authority. Gregory was reminded that his sister-in-law could be a formidable presence when she so chose.

Lady Lucinda—*of course*—spoke immediately. "Mr. Bridgerton seems to feel that Hermione might be in danger."

Kate's demeanor changed instantly. "Danger? Here?"

"No," Gregory ground out, although what he really meant was—*I am going to* kill *you*. Lady Lucinda, to be precise.

"I haven't seen her for some time," the annoying twit continued. "We arrived together, but that was nearly an hour ago."

Kate glanced about, her gaze finally settling on the doors leading outside. "Couldn't she be in the garden? Much of the party has moved abroad."

Lady Lucinda shook her head. "I didn't see her. I looked."

Gregory said nothing. It was as if he were watching the world destructing before his very eyes. And really, what could he possibly say to stop it?

"Not outside?" Kate said.

"I didn't think anything was amiss," Lady Lucinda said, rather officiously. "But Mr. Bridgerton was instantly concerned."

"He was?" Kate's head snapped to face him. "You were? Why?"

"May we speak of this at another time?" Gregory ground out.

Kate immediately dismissed him and looked squarely at Lucy. "Why was he concerned?"

Lucy swallowed. And then she whispered, "I think she might be with my brother."

Kate blanched. "That is not good."

"Richard would never do anything improper," Lucy insisted. "I promise you."

"He is in love with her," Kate said.

Gregory said nothing. Vindication had never felt less sweet.

Lucy looked from Kate to Gregory, her expression almost bordering on panic. "No," she whispered. "No, you're wrong."

"I'm not wrong," Kate said in a serious voice. "And we need to find them. Quickly."

She turned and immediately strode toward the door. Gregory followed, his long legs keeping pace with ease. Lady Lucinda seemed momentarily frozen, and then, jumping into action, she scurried after them both. "He would never do anything against Hermione's will," she said urgently. "I promise you."

Kate stopped. Turned around. Looked at Lucy, her expression frank and perhaps a little sad as well, as if she recognized that the younger woman was, in that moment, losing a bit of her innocence and that she, Kate, regretted having to be the one to deliver the blow.

"He might not have to," Kate said quietly.

Force her. Kate didn't say it, but the words hung in the air all the same.

"He might not have— What do you—"

Gregory saw the moment she realized it. Her eyes, always so changeable, had never looked more gray.

Stricken.

"We have to find them," Lucy whispered.

Kate nodded, and the three of them silently left the room.

Chapter 10

In which love is triumphant—
but not for Our Hero and Heroine.

Lucy followed Lady Bridgerton and Gregory into the hallway, trying to stem the anxiety she felt building within her. Her belly felt queer, her breath not quite right.

And her mind wouldn't quite clear. She needed to focus on the matter at hand. She knew she needed to give her full attention to the search, but it felt as if a portion of her mind kept pulling away—dizzy, panicked, and unable to escape a horrible sense of foreboding.

Which she did not understand. Didn't she *want* Hermione to marry her brother? Hadn't she just told Mr. Bridgerton that the match, while improbable, would be superb? Hermione would be her sister in name, not just in feeling, and Lucy could not imagine anything more fitting. But still, she felt . . .

Uneasy.

And a little bit angry as well.

And guilty. Of course. Because what right did she have to feel angry?

"We should search separately," Mr. Bridgerton directed, once they had turned several corners, and the sounds of the masked ball had receded into the distance. He yanked off his mask, and the two ladies followed suit, leaving all three on a small lamp table that was tucked into a recessed nook in the hallway.

Lady Bridgerton shook her head. "We can't. *You* certainly can't find them by yourself," she said to him. "I don't wish to even ponder the consequences of Miss Watson being alone with two unmarried gentlemen."

Not to mention his reaction, Lucy thought. Mr. Bridgerton struck her as an even-tempered man; she wasn't sure that he could come across the pair alone without thinking he had to spout off about honor and the defense of virtue, which always led to disaster. Always. Although given the depth of his feelings for Hermione, his reaction might be a little less honor and virtue and a little more jealous rage.

Even worse, while Mr. Bridgerton might lack the ability to shoot a straight bullet, Lucy had no doubt that he could blacken an eye with lethal speed.

"And *she* can't be alone," Lady Bridgerton continued, motioning in Lucy's direction. "It's dark. And empty. The gentlemen are wearing masks, for heaven's sake. It does loosen the conscience."

"I wouldn't know where to look, either," Lucy added. It was a large house. She'd been there nearly a week, but she doubted she'd seen even half of it.

"We shall remain together," Lady Bridgerton said firmly.

Mr. Bridgerton looked as if he wanted to argue, but he held his temper in check and instead bit off, "Fine. Let's not waste time, then." He strode off, his long legs establishing a pace that neither of the two women was going to find easy to keep up with.

He wrenched open doors and then left them hanging ajar, too

driven to reach the next room to leave things as he'd found them. Lucy scrambled behind him, trying rooms on the other side of the hall. Lady Bridgerton was just up ahead, doing the same.

"Oh!" Lucy jumped back, slamming a door shut.

"Did you find them?" Mr. Bridgerton demanded. Both he and Lady Bridgerton immediately moved to her side.

"No," Lucy said, blushing madly. She swallowed. "Someone else."

Lady Bridgerton groaned. "Good God. Please say it wasn't an unmarried lady."

Lucy opened her mouth, but several seconds passed before she said, "I don't know. The masks, you realize."

"They were wearing masks?" Lady Bridgerton asked. "They're married, then. And not to each other."

Lucy desperately wanted to ask how she had reached that conclusion, but she couldn't bring herself to do so, and besides, Mr. Bridgerton quite diverted her thoughts by cutting in front of her and yanking the door open. A feminine shriek split the air, followed by an angry male voice, uttering words Lucy dare not repeat.

"Sorry," Mr. Bridgerton grunted. "Carry on." He shut the door. "Morley," he announced, "and Whitmore's wife."

"Oh," Lady Bridgerton said, her lips parting with surprise. "I had no idea."

"Should we do something?" Lucy asked. Good heavens, there were people committing *adultery* not ten feet away from her.

"It's Whitmore's problem," Mr. Bridgerton said grimly. "We have our own matters to attend to."

Lucy's feet remained rooted to the spot as he took off again, striding down the hallway. Lady Bridgerton glanced at the door, looking very much as if she wanted to open it and peek inside, but in the end she sighed and followed her brother-in-law.

Lucy just stared at the door, trying to figure out just what it was that was niggling at her mind. The couple on the table—on the *table*, for God's sake—had been a shock, but something else was bothering her. Something about the scene wasn't quite right. Out of place. Out of context.

Or maybe something was sparking a memory.

What *was* it?

"Are you coming?" Lady Bridgerton called.

"Yes," Lucy replied. And then she took advantage of her innocence and youth, and added, "The shock, you know. I just need a moment."

Lady Bridgerton gave her a sympathetic look and nodded, but she carried on her work, inspecting the rooms on the left side of the hall.

What had she seen? There was the man and the woman, of course, and the aforementioned table. Two chairs, pink. One sofa, striped. And one end table, with a vase of cut flowers . . .

Flowers.

That was it.

She knew where they were.

If she was wrong and everybody else was right, and her brother really was in love with Hermione, there was only one place he would have taken her to try to convince her to return the emotion.

The orangery. It was on the other side of the house, far from the ballroom. And it was filled, not just with orange trees, but with flowers. Gorgeous tropical plants that must have cost Lord Bridgerton a fortune to import. Elegant orchids. Rare roses. Even humble wildflowers, brought in and replanted with care and devotion.

There was no place more romantic in the moonlight, and no place her brother would feel more at ease. He loved flowers. He always had, and he possessed an astounding memory for their names, scientific and common. He was always picking something up, rattling off some sort of informational tidbit—this one only opened in the moonlight, that one was related to some such plant brought in from Asia. Lucy had always found it somewhat tedious, but she could see how it might seem romantic, if it weren't one's brother doing the talking.

She looked up the hall. The Bridgertons had stopped to speak to each other, and Lucy could see by their postures that the conversation was intensely felt.

Wouldn't it be best if she were the one to find them? Without *any* of the Bridgertons?

If Lucy found them, she could warn them and avert disaster. If Hermione wanted to marry her brother . . . well, it could be her choice, not something she had to do because she'd been caught unawares.

Lucy knew how to get to the orangery. She could be there in minutes.

She took a cautious step back toward the ballroom. Neither Gregory nor Lady Bridgerton seemed to notice her.

She made her decision.

Six quiet steps, backing up carefully to the corner. And then—one last quick glance thrown down the hall—she stepped out of sight.

And ran.

She picked up her skirts and ran like the wind, or at the very least, as fast as she possibly could in her heavy velvet ball gown. She had no idea how long she would have before the Bridgertons noticed her absence, and while they would not know her destination, she had no doubt that they would find her. All Lucy had to do was find Hermione and Richard first. If she could get to them, warn them, she could push Hermione out the door and claim she'd come across Richard alone.

She would not have much time, but she could do it. She knew she could.

Lucy made it to the main hall, slowing her pace as much as she dared as she passed through. There were servants about, and probably a few late-arriving guests as well, and she couldn't afford to arouse suspicion by running.

She slipped out and into the west hallway, skidding around a corner as she took off again at a run. Her lungs began to burn, and her skin grew damp with perspiration beneath her gown. But she did not slow down. It wasn't far now. She could do it.

She knew she could.

She had to.

And then, amazingly, she was there, at the heavy double doors that led out to the orangery. Her hand landed heavily on one of the doorknobs, and she meant to turn it, but instead she found herself bent over, struggling to catch her breath.

Her eyes stung, and she tried to stand, but when she did she was hit with what felt like a wall of panic. It was physical, palpable, and it rushed at her so quickly that she had to grab on to the wall for support.

Dear God, she didn't want to open that door. She didn't want to see them. She didn't want to know what they had been doing, didn't want to know how or why. She didn't want this, any of this. She wanted it all back as it was, just three days earlier.

Couldn't she have that back? It was just *three days*. Three days, and Hermione would still be in love with Mr. Edmonds, which really wasn't such a problem since nothing would come of it, and Lucy would still be—

She would still be herself, happy and confident, and only practically engaged.

Why did everything have to *change*? Lucy's life had been perfectly acceptable the way it was. Everyone had his place, and all was in perfect order, and she hadn't had to *think* so hard about everything. She hadn't cared about what love meant or how it felt, and her brother wasn't secretly pining for her best friend, and her wedding was a hazy plan for the future, and she had been happy. She had been happy.

And she wanted it all back.

She grasped the knob more tightly, tried to turn it, but her hand wouldn't move. The panic was still there, freezing her muscles, pressing at her chest. She couldn't focus. She couldn't think.

And her legs began to tremble.

Oh, dear God, she was going to fall. Right there in the hallway, inches from her goal, she was going to crumple to the floor. And then—

"Lucy!"

It was Mr. Bridgerton, and he was running to her, and it occurred to her that she'd failed.

She'd failed.

She'd made it to the orangery. She'd made it in time, but then she'd just stood at the door. Like an idiot, she'd stood there, with her fingers on the bloody knob and—

"My God, Lucy, what were you thinking?"

He grabbed her by the shoulders, and Lucy leaned into his strength. She wanted to fall into him and forget. "I'm sorry," she whispered. "I'm sorry."

She did not know what she was sorry for, but she said it all the same.

"This is no place for a woman alone," he said, and his voice sounded different. Hoarse. "Men have been drinking. They use the masks as a license to—"

He fell silent. And then— "People are not themselves."

She nodded, and she finally looked up, pulling her eyes from the floor to his face. And then she saw him. Just saw him. His face, which had become so familiar to her. She seemed to know every feature, from the slight curl of his hair to the tiny scar near his left ear.

She swallowed. Breathed. Not quite the way she was meant to, but she breathed. More slowly, closer to normal.

"I'm sorry," she said again, because she didn't know what else to say.

"My God," he swore, searching her face with urgent eyes, "what happened to you? Are you all right? Did someone—"

His grip loosened slightly as he looked frantically around. "Who did this?" he demanded. "Who made you—"

"No," Lucy said, shaking her head. "It was no one. It was just me. I—I wanted to find them. I thought if I— Well, I didn't want you to— And then I— And then I got here, and I—"

Gregory's eyes moved quickly to the doors to the orangery. "Are they in there?"

"I don't know," Lucy admitted. "I think so. I couldn't—" The panic was finally receding, almost gone, really, and it all seemed so silly now. She felt so stupid. She'd stood there at the door, and she'd done nothing. Nothing.

"I couldn't open the door," she finally whispered. Because she had to tell him. She couldn't explain it—she didn't even understand it—but she had to tell him what had happened.

Because he'd found her.

And that had made the difference.

"Gregory!" Lady Bridgerton burst on the scene, practically hurtling against them, quite clearly out of breath from having tried to keep up. "Lady Lucinda! Why did you— Are you all right?"

She sounded so concerned that Lucy wondered what she looked like. She felt pale. She felt small, actually, but what could possibly be in her face that would cause Lady Bridgerton to look upon her with such obvious worry.

"I'm fine," Lucy said, relieved that she had not seen her as Mr. Bridgerton had. "Just a bit overset. I think I ran too quickly. It was foolish of me. I'm sorry."

"When we turned around and you were gone—" Lady Bridgerton looked as if she were trying to be stern, but worry was creasing her brow, and her eyes were so very kind.

Lucy wanted to cry. No one had ever looked at her like that. Hermione loved her, and Lucy took great comfort in that, but this was different. Lady Bridgerton couldn't have been that much older than she was—ten years, maybe fifteen—but the way she was looking at her . . .

It was almost as if she had a mother.

It was just for a moment. Just a few seconds, really, but she could pretend. And maybe wish, just a little.

Lady Bridgerton hurried closer and put an arm around Lucy's shoulders, drawing her away from Gregory, who allowed his arms to return to his sides. "Are you certain you are all right?" she asked.

Lucy nodded. "I am. Now."

Lady Bridgerton looked over to Gregory. He nodded. Once.

Lucy didn't know what that meant.

"I think they might be in the orangery," she said, and she wasn't quite certain what had caught at her voice—resignation or regret.

"Very well," Lady Bridgerton said, her shoulders pushing back as she went to the door. "There's nothing for it, is there?"

Lucy shook her head. Gregory did nothing.

Lady Bridgerton took a deep breath and pulled open the door. Lucy and Gregory immediately moved forward to peer inside, but the orangery was dark, the only light the moon, shining through the expansive windows.

"Damn."

Lucy's chin drew back in surprise. She'd never heard a woman curse before.

For a moment the trio stood still, and then Lady Bridgerton stepped forward and called out, "Lord Fennsworth! Lord Fennsworth, please reply. Are you here?"

Lucy started to call out for Hermione, but Gregory clamped a hand over her mouth.

"Don't," he whispered in her ear. "If someone else is here, we don't want them to realize we're looking for them both."

Lucy nodded, feeling painfully green. She'd thought she'd known something of the world, but as each day passed, it seemed she understood less and less. Mr. Bridgerton stepped away, moving farther into the room. He stood with his hands on his hips, his stance wide as he scanned the orangery for occupants.

"Lord Fennsworth!" Lady Bridgerton called out again.

This time they heard a rustling. But soft. And slow. As if someone were trying to conceal his presence.

Lucy turned toward the sound, but no one came forward. She bit her lip. Maybe it was just an animal. There were several cats at Aubrey Hall. They slept in a little hutch near the door to the kitchen, but maybe one of them had lost its way and got locked in the orangery.

It had to be a cat. If it were Richard, he'd have come forward when he heard his name.

She looked at Lady Bridgerton, waiting to see what she would do next. The viscountess was looking intently at her brother-in-law, mouthing something and motioning with her hands and pointing in the direction of the noise.

Gregory gave her a nod, then moved forward on silent feet, his long legs crossing the room with impressive speed, until—

Lucy gasped. Before she had time to blink, Gregory had charged forward, a strange, primal sound ripping from his throat. Then he positively leaped through the air, coming down with a thud and a grunt of "I have you!"

"Oh no." Lucy's hand rose to cover her mouth. Mr. Bridgerton had someone pinned to the floor, and his hands looked to be very close to his captive's throat.

Lady Bridgerton rushed toward them, and Lucy, seeing her, finally remembered her own feet and ran to the scene. If it was Richard—*oh, please don't let it be Richard*—she needed to reach him before Mr. Bridgerton killed him.

"Let . . . me . . . *go*!"

"Richard!" Lucy called out shrilly. It was his voice. There could be no mistaking it.

The figure on the floor of the orangery twisted, and then she could see his face.

"Lucy?" He looked stunned.

"Oh, Richard." There was a world of disappointment in those two words.

"Where is she?" Gregory demanded.

"Where is who?"

Lucy felt sick. Richard was feigning ignorance. She knew him too well. He was lying.

"Miss Watson," Gregory ground out.

"I don't know what y—"

A horrible gurgling noise came from Richard's throat.

"Gregory!" Lady Bridgerton grabbed his arm. "Stop!"

He loosened his hold. Barely.

"Maybe she's not here," Lucy said. She knew it wasn't true, but somehow it seemed the best way to salvage the situation. "Richard loves flowers. He always has. And he doesn't like parties."

"It's true," Richard gasped.

"Gregory," Lady Bridgerton said, "you must let him up."

Lucy turned to face her as she spoke, and that was when she saw it. Behind Lady Bridgerton.

Pink. Just a flash. More of a strip, actually, just barely visible through the plants.

Hermione was wearing pink. That very shade.

Lucy's eyes widened. Maybe it was just a flower. There were heaps of pink flowers. She turned back to Richard. Quickly.

Too quickly. Mr. Bridgerton saw her head snapping around.

"What did you see?" he demanded.

"Nothing."

But he didn't believe her. He let go of Richard and began to move in the direction Lucy was looking, but Richard rolled to the side and grabbed one of his ankles. Gregory went down with a yell, and he quickly retaliated, catching hold of Richard's shirt and yanking with enough force to scrape his head along the floor.

"Don't!" Lucy cried, rushing forward. Good God, they were going to kill each other. First Mr. Bridgerton was on top, then Richard, then Mr. Bridgerton, then she couldn't tell *who* was winning, and the whole time they were just *pummeling* each other.

Lucy wanted desperately to separate them, but she didn't see how without risking injury to herself. The two of them were beyond noticing anything so mundane as a human being.

Maybe Lady Bridgerton could stop them. It was her home, and the guests her responsibility. She could attack the situation with more authority than Lucy could hope to muster.

Lucy turned. "Lady Br—"

The words evaporated in her throat. Lady Bridgerton was not where she had been just moments earlier.

Oh *no.*

Lucy twisted frantically about. "Lady Bridgerton? Lady Bridgerton?"

And then there she was, moving back toward Lucy, making her way through the plants, her hand wrapped tightly around Hermione's wrist. Hermione's hair was mussed, and her dress was wrinkled and dirty, and—dear God above—she looked as if she might cry.

"Hermione?" Lucy whispered. What had happened? What had Richard done?

For a moment Hermione did nothing. She just stood there like a guilty puppy, her arm stretched limply in front of her, almost as if she'd forgotten that Lady Bridgerton still had her by the wrist.

"Hermione, what happened?"

Lady Bridgerton let go, and it was almost as if Hermione were water, let loose from a dam. "Oh, Lucy," she cried, her voice catching as she rushed forward. "I'm so sorry."

Lucy stood in shock, embracing her . . . but not quite. Hermione was clutching her like a child, but Lucy didn't quite know what to do with herself. Her arms felt foreign, not quite attached. She looked past Hermione's shoulder, down to the floor. The men had finally stopped thrashing about, but she wasn't sure she cared any longer.

"Hermione?" Lucy stepped back, far enough so that she could see her face. "What happened?"

"Oh, Lucy," Hermione said. *"I fluttered."*

An hour later, Hermione and Richard were engaged to be married. Lady Lucinda had been returned to the party, not that she would be able to concentrate on anything anyone was saying, but Kate had insisted.

Gregory was drunk. Or at the very least, doing his best to get there.

He supposed the night had brought a few small favors. He hadn't actually come across Lord Fennsworth and Miss Watson in flagrante delicto. Whatever they'd been doing—and Gregory was expending a great deal of energy to *not* imagine it—they had stopped when Kate had bellowed Fennsworth's name.

Even now, it all felt like a farce. Hermione had apologized, then Lucy had apologized, then *Kate* had apologized, which had seemed remarkably out of character until she finished her sentence with, "but you are, as of this moment, engaged to be married."

Fennsworth had looked delighted, the annoying little sod, and then he'd had the gall to give Gregory a triumphant little smirk.

Gregory had kneed him in the balls.

Not *too* hard.

It could have been an accident. Really. They were still on the floor, locked into a stalemate position. It was entirely plausible that his knee could have slipped.

Up.

Whatever the case, Fennsworth had grunted and collapsed.

Gregory rolled to the side the second the earl's grip loosened, and he moved fluidly to his feet.

"So sorry," he'd said to the ladies. "I'm not certain what's come over him."

And that, apparently, was that. Miss Watson had apologized to him—after apologizing to first Lucy, then Kate, then Fennsworth, although heaven knew why, as he'd clearly won the evening.

"No apology is needed," Gregory had said tightly.

"No, but I—" She looked distressed, but Gregory didn't much care just then.

"I did have a lovely time at breakfast," she said to him. "I just wanted you to know that."

Why? Why would she *say* that? Did she think it would make him feel better?

Gregory hadn't said a word. He gave her a single nod, and then walked away. The rest of them could sort the details out themselves. He had no ties to the newly affianced couple, no responsibilities to them or to propriety. He didn't care when or how the families were informed.

It was not his concern. None of it was.

So he left. He had a bottle of brandy to locate.

And now here he was. In his brother's office, drinking his brother's liquor, wondering what the hell this all meant. Miss Watson was lost to him now, that much was clear. Unless of course he wanted to kidnap the girl.

Which he did not. Most assuredly. She'd probably squeal like an idiot the whole way. Not to mention the little matter of her possibly having given herself to Fennsworth. Oh, and Gregory destroying his good reputation. There was that. One did not kidnap a gently bred female—especially one affianced to an earl—and expect to emerge with one's good name intact.

He wondered what Fennsworth had said to get her off alone.

He wondered what Hermione had meant when she'd said she fluttered.

He wondered if they would invite him to the wedding.

Hmmm. Probably. Lucy would insist upon it, wouldn't she? Stickler for propriety, that one. Good manners all around.

So what now? After so many years of feeling slightly aimless, of waiting waiting waiting for the pieces of his life to fall into place, he'd thought he finally had it all figured out. He'd found Miss Watson and he was ready to move forward and conquer.

The world had been bright and good and shining with promise.

Oh, very well, the world had been perfectly bright and good and shining with promise before. He hadn't been unhappy in the least. In fact, he hadn't really minded the waiting. He wasn't even sure he'd wanted to find his bride so soon. Just because he knew his true love existed didn't mean he wanted her right away.

He'd had a very pleasant existence before. Hell, most men would give their eyeteeth to trade places.

Not Fennsworth, of course.

Bloody little bugger was probably plotting every last detail of his wedding night that very minute.

Sodding little b—

He tossed back his drink and poured another.

So what did it mean? What did it mean when you met the woman who made you forget how to breathe and she up and married someone else? What was he supposed to do now? Sit and wait until the back of someone else's neck sent him into raptures?

He took another sip. He'd had it with necks. They were highly overrated.

He sat back, plunking his feet on his brother's desk. Anthony would hate it, of course, but was he in the room? No. Had he just discovered the woman he'd hoped to marry in the arms of another man? No. More to the immediate point, had his face recently served as a punching bag for a surprisingly fit young earl?

Definitely not.

Gregory gingerly touched his left cheekbone. And his right eye.

He was not going to look attractive tomorrow, that was for sure.

But neither would Fennsworth, he thought happily.

Happily? He was happy? Who'd have thought?

He let out a long sigh, attempting to assess his sobriety. It had to be the brandy. Happiness was not on the agenda for the evening.

Although . . .

Gregory stood. Just as a test. Bit of scientific inquiry. Could he stand?

He could.

Could he walk?

Yes!

Ah, but could he walk straight?

Almost.

Hmmm. He wasn't nearly as foxed as he'd thought.

He might as well go out. No sense in wasting an unexpectedly fine mood.

He made his way to the door and put his hand on the knob. He stopped, cocking his head in thought.

It had to be the brandy. Really, there was no other explanation for it.

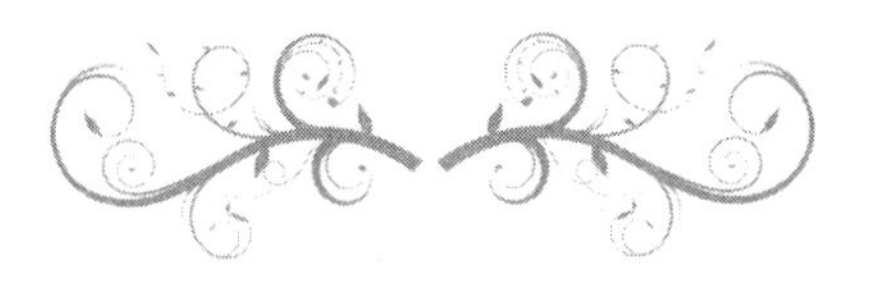

Chapter 11

In which Our Hero does the one thing he would never have anticipated.

The irony of the evening was not lost on Lucy as she made her way back to her room.

Alone.

After Mr. Bridgerton's panic over Hermione's disappearance . . . after Lucy had been thoroughly scolded for running off by herself in the middle of what was turning out to be a somewhat raucous evening . . . after one couple had been forced to become engaged, for heaven's sake—no one had noticed when Lucy left the masked ball by herself.

She still couldn't believe that Lady Bridgerton had insisted upon returning her to the party. She had practically led Lucy back by the collar, depositing her in the care of someone or other's maiden aunt before retrieving Hermione's mother, who, it must be presumed, had no idea of the excitement that lay in wait for her.

And so Lucy had stood at the edge of the ballroom like a fool, staring at the rest of the guests, wondering how they could possibly not be aware of the events of the evening. It seemed inconceivable that three lives could be upended so completely, and the rest of the world was carrying on as usual.

No, she thought, rather sadly, actually—it was four; there was Mr. Bridgerton to be considered. His plans for the future had been decidedly different at the outset of the evening.

But no, everyone else appeared perfectly normal. They danced, they laughed, they ate sandwiches that were still distressingly mixed up on a single serving platter.

It was the strangest sight. Shouldn't something seem different? Shouldn't someone come up to Lucy and say, eyes quizzical—*You look somewhat altered. Ah, I know. Your brother must have seduced your closest friend.*

No one did, of course, and when Lucy caught sight of herself in a mirror, she was startled to see that she appeared entirely unchanged. A little tired, perhaps, maybe a little pale, but other than that, the same old Lucy.

Blond hair, not *too* blond. Blue eyes—again, not too blue. Awkwardly shaped mouth that never quite held still the way she wanted it to, and the same nondescript nose with the same seven freckles, including the one close to her eye that no one ever noticed but her.

It looked like Ireland. She didn't know why that interested her, but it always had.

She sighed. She'd never been to Ireland, and she probably never would. It seemed silly that this would suddenly bother her, as she didn't even want to go to Ireland.

But if she did wish to, she'd have to ask Lord Haselby, wouldn't she? It wasn't much different from having to ask Uncle Robert for permission to do, well, anything, but somehow . . .

She shook her head. Enough. It had been a strange night, and now she was in a strange mood, stuck in all her strangeness in the middle of a masked ball.

Clearly what she needed to do was go to bed.

And so, after thirty minutes of trying to look as if she were enjoying herself, it finally became apparent that the maiden aunt entrusted with her care did not quite understand the scope of the assignment. It wasn't difficult to deduce; when Lucy had attempted to speak to her, she had squinted through her mask and screeched, "Lift your chin, gel! Do I know you?"

Lucy decided that this was not an opportunity to be wasted, and so she had replied, "I'm sorry. I thought you were someone else," and walked right out of the ballroom.

Alone.

Really, it was almost funny.

Almost.

She wasn't foolish, however, and she'd traversed enough of the house that evening to know that while the guests had spilled to the west and south of the ballroom, they had not ventured to the north wing, where the family kept their private rooms. Strictly speaking, Lucy ought not to go that way, either, but after what she'd been through in the past few hours, she rather thought she deserved a bit of latitude.

But when she reached the long hall that led to the north, she saw a closed door. Lucy blinked with surprise; she'd never noticed a door there before. She supposed the Bridgertons normally left it open. Then her heart sank. Surely it would be locked—what was the purpose of a closed door if not to keep people out?

But the doorknob turned with ease. Lucy carefully shut the door behind her, practically melting with relief. She couldn't face going back to the party. She just wanted to crawl into bed, curl up under the covers, close her eyes, and sleep sleep sleep.

It sounded like heaven. And with any luck, Hermione would not yet have returned. Or better yet, her mother would insist upon her remaining overnight in her room.

Yes, privacy sounded extremely appealing just then.

It was dark as she walked, and quiet, too. After a minute or so, Lucy's eyes adjusted to the dim light. There were no lanterns or candles to illuminate the way, but a few doors had been left open, allowing pale shafts of moonlight to make parallelograms on the carpet. She walked slowly, and with an odd sort of deliberation, each step carefully measured and aimed, as if she were balancing on a thin line, stretching right down the center of the hall.

One, two . . .

Nothing out of the ordinary. She frequently counted her steps. And *always* on the stairs. She'd been surprised when she got to school and realized that other people did not.

. . . three, four . . .

The runner carpet looked monochromatic in the moonlight, but Lucy knew that the big diamonds were red, and the smaller ones were gold. She wondered if it were possible to step only on gold.

. . . five, six . . .

Or maybe red. Red would be easier. This wasn't a night to challenge herself.

. . . seven, eight, n—

"Oomph!"

She crashed into something. Or dear heaven, some*one*. She'd been looking down, following the red diamonds, and she hadn't seen . . . but shouldn't the other person have seen *her*?

Strong hands caught her by the arms and steadied her. And then—"Lady Lucinda?"

She froze. "Mr. Bridgerton?"

His voice was low and smooth in the darkness. "Now *this* is a coincidence."

She carefully disentangled herself—he had grabbed her by the arms to keep her from falling—and stepped back. He seemed very large in the close confines of the hall. "What are you doing here?" she asked.

He offered her a suspiciously easy grin. "What're *you* doing here?"

"Going to bed. This hallway seemed the best route," she explained, then added with a wry expression, "given my state of unaccompaniment."

He cocked his head. Scrunched his brow. Blinked. And finally: "Is that a word?"

For some reason that made her smile. Not her lips, exactly, but on the inside, where it counted. "I don't think so," she replied, "but really, I can't be bothered."

He smiled faintly, then motioned with his head to the room he must have just exited. "I was in my brother's office. Pondering."

"Pondering?"

"Quite a bit to ponder this evening, wouldn't you say?"

"Yes." She looked around the hall. Just in case there was someone else about, even though she was quite certain there was not. "I really shouldn't be here alone with you."

He nodded gravely. "I wouldn't want to disrupt your practical engagement."

Lucy hadn't even been thinking of *that*. "I meant after what happened with Hermione and—" And then it seemed somehow insensitive to spell it out. "Well, I'm sure you're aware."

"Indeed."

She swallowed, then tried to make it appear as if she weren't looking at his face to see if he was upset.

He just blinked, then he shrugged, and his expression was . . .

Nonchalant?

She chewed on her lip. No, that couldn't be. She must have misread him. He had been a man in love. He had told her so.

But this was none of her business. This required a certain measure of self-remindering (to add another word to her rapidly growing collection), but there it was. It was none of her business. Not one bit.

Well, except for the part about her brother and her best friend. No one could say that *that* didn't concern her. If it had just been Hermione, or just been Richard, there *might* have been an argument that she should keep her nose out of it, but with the both of them—well, clearly she was involved.

As regarded Mr. Bridgerton, however . . . *none* of her business.

She looked at him. His shirt collar was loosened, and she could see a tiny scrap of skin where she knew she ought not look.

None. None! Business. Of hers. None of it.

"Right," she said, ruining her determined tone with a decidedly involuntary cough. Spasm. Coughing spasm. Vaguely punctuated by: "Should be going."

But it came out more like . . . Well, it came out like something that she was quite certain could not be spelled with the twenty-six letters of the English language. Cyrillic might do it. Or possibly Hebrew.

"Are you all right?" he queried.

"Perfectly well," she gasped, then realized she was back to looking at that spot that wasn't even his neck. It was more his chest, which meant that it was more someplace decidedly unsuitable.

She yanked her eyes away, then coughed again, this time on purpose. Because she had to do *some*thing. Otherwise her eyes would be right back where they ought not be.

He watched her, almost a bit owlish in his regard, as she recovered. "Better?"

She nodded.

"I'm glad."

Glad? *Glad?* What did *that* mean?

He shrugged. "I hate it when that happens."

Just that he is a human being, Lucy you dolt. One who knows what a scratchy throat feels like.

She was going mad. She was quite certain of it.

"I should go," she blurted out.

"You should."

"I really should."

But she just stood there.

He was looking at her in the *strangest* way. His eyes were narrowed—not in that angry way people usually associated with squinty eyes, but rather as if he were thinking exceptionally hard about something.

Pondering. That was it. He was pondering, just as he'd said.

Except that he was pondering *her.*

"Mr. Bridgerton?" she asked hesitantly. Not that she knew what she might inquire of him when he acknowledged her.

"Do you drink, Lady Lucinda?"

Drink? "I beg your pardon?"

He gave her a sheepish half-smile. "Brandy. I know where my brother keeps the good stuff."

"Oh." *Goodness.* "No, of course not."

"Pity," he murmured.

"I really couldn't," she added, because, well, she felt as if she had to explain.

Even though *of course* she did not drink spirits.

And *of course* he would know that.

He shrugged. "Don't know why I asked."

"I should go," she said.

But he didn't move.

And neither did she.

She wondered what brandy tasted like.

And she wondered if she would ever know.

"How did you enjoy the party?" he asked.

"The party?"

"Weren't you forced to go back?"

She nodded, rolling her eyes. "It was strongly suggested."

"Ah, so then she dragged you."

To Lucy's great surprise, she chuckled. "Rather close to it. And I didn't have my mask, which made me stick out a bit."

"Like a mushroom?"

"Like a—?"

He looked at her dress and nodded at the color. "A blue mushroom."

She glanced at herself and then at him. "Mr. Bridgerton, are you intoxicated?"

He leaned forward with a sly and slightly silly smile. He held up his hand, his thumb and index finger measuring an inch between them. "Just a little bit."

She eyed him dubiously. "Really?"

He looked down at his fingers with a furrowed brow, then added another inch or so to the space between them. "Well, perhaps this much."

Lucy didn't know much about men or much about spirits, but she knew enough about the two of them together to ask, "Isn't that always the case?"

"No." He lifted his brows and stared down his nose at her. "I usually know exactly how drunk I am."

Lucy had no idea what to say to that.

"But do you know, tonight I'm not sure." And he sounded surprised at that.

"Oh." Because she was at her articulate best this evening.

He smiled.

Her stomach felt strange.

She tried to smile back. She really should be going.

So naturally, she did not move.

His head tilted to the side and he let out a thoughtful exhale, and it occurred to her that he was doing exactly what he'd said he'd been doing—pondering. "I was thinking," he said slowly, "that given the events of the evening . . ."

She leaned forward expectantly. Why did people always let their voices trail off just when they were about to say something meaningful? "Mr. Bridgerton?" she nudged, because now he was just staring at some painting on the wall.

His lips twisted thoughtfully. "Wouldn't you think I ought to be a bit more upset?"

Her lips parted with surprise. "You're not upset?" How was that possible?

He shrugged. "Not as much as I should be, given that my heart practically stopped beating the first time I saw Miss Watson."

Lucy smiled tightly.

His head went back to vertical, and he looked at her and blinked—perfectly clear-eyed, as if he had just reached an obvious conclusion. "Which is why I suspect the brandy."

"I see." She didn't, of course, but what else could she say? "You . . . ah . . . you certainly seemed upset."

"I was cross," he explained.

"You're not any longer?"

He thought about that. "Oh, I'm still cross."

And Lucy felt the need to apologize. Which she *knew* was ridiculous, because none of this was her fault. But it was so ingrained in her, this need to apologize for everything. She couldn't help it. She wanted everyone to be happy. She always had. It was neater that way. More orderly.

"I'm sorry I didn't believe you about my brother," she said. "I didn't know. Truly, I didn't know."

He looked down at her, and his eyes were kind. She wasn't sure when it had happened, because a moment ago, he'd been flip and nonchalant. But now . . . he was different.

"I know you didn't," he said. "And there is no need to apologize."

"I was just as startled when we found them as you were."

"I wasn't very startled," he said. Gently, as if he were trying to spare her feelings. Make her feel not such a dunce for not seeing the obvious.

She nodded. "No, I suppose you wouldn't have been. You realized what was happening, and I did not." And truly, she did feel like a half-wit. How could she have been so completely unaware? It was Hermione and her brother, for heaven's sake. If anyone were to detect a budding romance, it ought to have been she.

There was a pause—an awkward one—and then he said, "I will be well."

"Oh, of course you will," Lucy said reassuringly. And then *she* felt reassured, because it felt so lovely and *normal* to be the one trying to make everything right. That's what she did. She scurried about. She made sure everyone was happy and comfortable.

That was who she was.

But then he asked —oh *why* did he ask—"Will you?"

She said nothing.

"Be well," he clarified. "Will you be well"—he paused, then shrugged— "as well?"

"Of course," she said, a little too quickly.

She thought that was the end of it, but then he said, "Are you certain? Because you seemed a little . . ."

She swallowed, waiting uncomfortably for his assessment.

". . . overset," he finished.

"Well, I was surprised," she said, glad to have an answer. "And so naturally I was somewhat disconcerted." But she heard a slight stammer in her voice, and she was wondering which one of them she was trying to convince.

He didn't say anything.

She swallowed. It was uncomfortable. *She* was uncomfortable, and yet she kept talking, kept explaining it all. And she said, "I'm not entirely certain what happened."

Still, he did not speak.

"I felt a little . . . Right here . . ." Her hand went to her chest, to the spot where she had felt so paralyzed. She looked up at him, practically begging him with her eyes to say something, to change the subject and end the conversation.

But he didn't. And the silence made her explain.

If he'd asked a question, said even one comforting word, she wouldn't have told him. But the silence was too much. It had to be filled.

"I couldn't move," she said, testing out the words as they left her lips. It was as if by speaking, she was finally confirming what had happened. "I reached the door, and I couldn't open it."

She looked up at him, searching for answers. But of course he did not have any.

"I—I don't know why I was so overcome." Her voice sounded breathy, nervous even. "I mean—it was Hermione. And my brother. I—I'm sorry for your pain, but this is all rather tidy, really. It's nice. Or at least it should be. Hermione will be my sister. I have always wanted a sister."

"They are occasionally entertaining." He said it with a half-smile, and it did make Lucy feel better. It was remarkable how much it did. And it was just enough to cause her words to spill out, this time without hesitation, without even a stammer.

"I could not believe they had gone off together. They should have said something. They should have told me that they cared for one another. I shouldn't have had to discover it that way. It's not right." She grabbed his arm and looked up at him, her eyes earnest and urgent. "It's not right, Mr. Bridgerton. It's not right."

He shook his head, but only slightly. His chin barely moved, and neither did his lips as he said, "No."

"Everything is changing," she whispered, and she wasn't talking about Hermione any longer. But it didn't matter, except that she didn't want to think anymore. Not about that. Not about the future. "It's all changing," she whispered, "and I can't stop it."

Somehow his face was closer as he said, again, "No."

"It's too much." She couldn't stop looking at him, couldn't move her eyes from his, and she was still whispering it—"It's all too much"—when there was no more distance between them.

And his lips . . . they touched hers.

It was a kiss.

She had been kissed.

Her. Lucy. For once it was about her. She was at the center of her world. It was life. And it was happening to *her*.

It was remarkable, because it all felt so *big*, so transforming. And yet it was just a little kiss—soft, just a brush, so light it almost tickled. She felt a rush, a shiver, a tingly lightness in her chest. Her body seemed to come alive, and at the same time freeze into place, as if afraid that the wrong movement might make it all go away.

But she didn't want it to go away. God help her, she wanted this.

She wanted this moment, and she wanted this memory, and she wanted . . .

She just *wanted.*

Everything. Anything she could get.

Anything she could feel.

His arms came around her, and she leaned in, sighing against his mouth as her body came into contact with his. This was it, she thought dimly. This was the music. This was a symphony.

This was a flutter. More than a flutter.

His mouth grew more urgent, and she opened to him, reveling in the warmth of his kiss. It spoke to her, called to her soul. His hands were holding her tighter, tighter, and her own snaked around him, finally resting where his hair met his collar.

She hadn't meant to touch him, hadn't even thought about it. Her hands seemed to know where to go, how to find him, bring him closer. Her back arched, and the heat between them grew.

And the kiss went on . . . and on.

She felt it in her belly, she felt it in her toes. This kiss seemed to be everywhere, all across her skin, straight down to her soul.

"Lucy," he whispered, his lips finally leaving hers to blaze a hot trail along her jaw to her ear. "My God, Lucy."

She didn't want to speak, didn't want to do anything to break the moment. She didn't know what to call him, couldn't quite say *Gregory*, but *Mr. Bridgerton* was no longer right.

He was more than that now. More to her.

She'd been right earlier. Everything *was* changing. She didn't feel the same. She felt . . .

Awakened.

Her neck arched as he nipped at her earlobe, and she moaned—soft, incoherent sounds that slid from her lips like a song. She wanted to sink into him. She wanted to slide to the carpet and take him with her. She wanted the weight of him, the heat of him, and she wanted to *touch* him—she wanted to *do* something. She wanted to act. She wanted to be daring.

She moved her hands to his hair, sinking her fingers into the silky strands. He let out a little groan, and just the sound of his voice was enough to make her heart beat faster. He was doing remarkable things to her neck—his lips, his tongue, his teeth—she didn't know which, but one of them was setting her on fire.

His lips moved down the column of her throat, raining fire along her skin. And his hands—they had moved. They were cupping her, pressing her against him, and everything felt so *urgent.*

This was no longer about what she wanted. It was about what she needed.

Was this what had happened to Hermione? Had she innocently gone for a stroll with Richard and then . . . *this*?

Lucy understood it now. She understood what it meant to want something you knew was wrong, to allow it to happen even though it could lead to scandal and—

And then she said it. She tried it. "Gregory," she whispered, testing the name on her lips. It felt like an endearment, an intimacy, almost as if she could change the world and everything around her with one single word.

If she said his name, then he could be hers, and she could forget everything else, she could forget—

Haselby.

Dear God, she was engaged. It was not just an understanding any longer. The papers had been signed. And she was—

"No," she said, pressing her hands on his chest. "No, I can't."

He allowed her to push him away. She turned her head, afraid to look at him. She knew . . . if she saw his face . . .

She was weak. She wouldn't be able to resist.

"Lucy," he said, and she realized that the sound of him was just as hard to bear as his face would have been.

"I can't do this." She shook her head, still not looking at him. "It's wrong."

"Lucy." And this time she felt his fingers on her chin, gently urging her to face him.

"Please allow me to escort you upstairs," he said.

"No!" It came out too loud, and she stopped, swallowing uncomfortably. "I can't risk it," she said, finally allowing her eyes to meet his.

It was a mistake. The way he was looking at her— His eyes were stern, but there was more. A hint of softness, a touch of warmth. And curiosity. As if . . . As if he wasn't quite sure what he was seeing. As if he were looking at her for the very first time.

Dear heaven, that was the part she couldn't bear. She wasn't even sure why. Maybe it was because he was looking at *her*. Maybe it was because the expression was so . . . *him*. Maybe it was both.

Maybe it didn't matter.

But it terrified her all the same.

"I will not be deterred," he said. "Your safety is my responsibility."

Lucy wondered what had happened to the slightly intoxicated, rather jolly man with whom she'd been conversing just moments earlier. In his place was someone else entirely. Someone quite in charge.

"Lucy," he said, and it wasn't exactly a question, more of a reminder. He would have his way in this, and she would have to acknowledge it.

"My room isn't far," she said, trying one last time, anyway. "Truly, I don't need your assistance. It's just up those stairs."

And down the hall and around a corner, but he didn't need to know that.

"I will walk you to the stairs, then."

Lucy knew better than to argue. He would not relent. His voice was quiet, but it had an edge she wasn't quite certain she'd heard there before.

"And I will remain there until you reach your room."

"That's not necessary."

He ignored her. "Knock three times when you do so."

"I'm not going to—"

"If I don't hear your knock, I will come upstairs and personally assure myself of your welfare."

He crossed his arms, and as she looked at him she wondered if he'd have been the same man had he been the firstborn son. There was an unexpected imperiousness to him. He would have made a fine viscount, she decided, although she wasn't certain she would have liked him so well. Lord Bridgerton quite frankly terrified her, although he must have had a softer side, adoring his wife and children as he so obviously did.

Still . . .

"Lucy."

She swallowed and gritted her teeth, hating to have to admit that she'd lied. "Very well," she said grudgingly. "If you wish to hear my knock, you had better come to the top of the stairs."

He nodded and followed her, all the way to the top of the seventeen steps.

"I will see you tomorrow," he said.

Lucy said nothing. She had a feeling that would be unwise.

"I will see you tomorrow," he repeated.

She nodded, since it seemed to be required, and she didn't see how she was meant to avoid him, anyway.

And she wanted to see him. She shouldn't want to, and she *knew* she shouldn't do it, but she couldn't help herself.

"I suspect we will be leaving," she said. "I'm meant to return to my uncle, and Richard . . . Well, he will have matters to attend to."

But her explanations did not change his expression. His face was still resolute, his eyes so firmly fixed on hers that she shivered.

"I will see you in the morning," was all he said.

She nodded again, and then left, as quickly as she could without breaking into a run. She rounded the corner and finally saw her room, just three doors down.

But she stopped. Right there at the corner, just out of his sight.

And she knocked three times.

Just because she could.

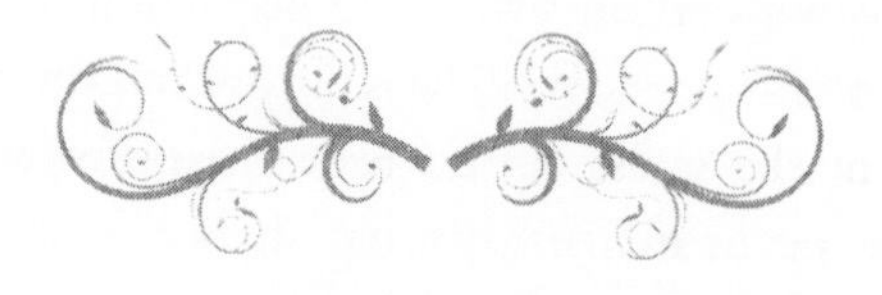

Chapter 12

In which nothing is resolved.

When Gregory sat down to breakfast the next day, Kate was already there, grim-faced and weary.

"I'm so sorry," was the first thing she said when she took the seat next to him.

What *was* it with apologies? he wondered. They were positively rampant these past few days.

"I know you had hoped—"

"It is nothing," he interrupted, flicking a glance at the plate of food she'd left on the other side of the table. Two seats down.

"But—"

"Kate," he said, and even he didn't quite recognize his own voice. He sounded older, if that was possible. Harder.

She fell silent, her lips still parted, as if her words had been frozen on her tongue.

"It's nothing," he said again, and turned back to his eggs. He didn't want to talk about it, he didn't want to listen to explanations. What was done was done, and there was nothing he could do about it.

Gregory was not certain what Kate was doing while he concentrated on his food—presumably looking around the room, gauging whether any of the guests could hear their conversation. Every now and then he heard her shifting in her seat, unconsciously changing her position in anticipation of saying something.

He moved on to his bacon.

And then—he knew she would not be able to keep her mouth shut for long—"But are you—"

He turned. Looked at her hard. And said one word.

"Don't."

For a moment her expression remained blank. Then her eyes widened, and one corner of her mouth tilted up. Just a little. "How old were you when we met?" she asked.

What the devil was she about? "I don't know," he said impatiently, trying to recall her wedding to his brother. There had been a bloody lot of flowers. He'd been sneezing for weeks, it seemed. "Thirteen, perhaps. Twelve?"

She regarded him curiously. "It must be difficult, I think, to be so very much younger than your brothers."

He set his fork down.

"Anthony and Benedict and Colin—they are all right in a row. Like ducks, I've always thought, although I'm not so foolish to say so. And then—hmmm. How many years between you and Colin?"

"Ten."

"Is that all?" Kate looked surprised, which he wasn't sure he found particularly complimentary.

"It's a full six years from Colin to Anthony," she continued, pressing one finger against her chin as if that were to indicate deep thought. "A bit more than that, actually. But I suppose they are more commonly lumped together, what with Benedict in the middle."

He waited.

"Well, no matter," she said briskly. "Everyone finds his place in life, after all. Now then—"

He stared at her in amazement. How could she change the subject like that? Before he had any idea what she was talking about.

"—I suppose I should inform you of the remainder of the events of last night. After you left." Kate sighed—groaned really—shaking her head. "Lady Watson was a bit put out that her daughter had not been closely supervised, although really, whose fault is that? And *then* she was put out that Miss Watson's London season was over before she had a chance to spend money on a new wardrobe. Because, after all, it is not as if she will make a debut now."

Kate paused, waiting for Gregory to say something. He lifted his brows in the tiniest of shrugs, just enough to say that he had nothing to add to the conversation.

Kate gave him one more second, then continued with: "Lady Watson did come about rather quickly when it was pointed out that Fennsworth is an earl, however young."

She paused, twisting her lips. "He *is* rather young, isn't he?"

"Not so much younger than I am," Gregory said, even though he'd thought Fennsworth the veriest infant the night before.

Kate appeared to give that some thought. "No," she said slowly, "there's a difference. He's not . . . Well, I don't know. Anyway—"

Why did she keep changing the subject just when she started to say something he actually wanted to hear?

"—the betrothal is done," she continued, picking up speed with that, "and I believe that all parties involved are content."

Gregory supposed he did not count as an involved party. But then again, he felt more irritation than anything else. He did not like being beaten. At anything.

Well, except for shooting. He'd long since given up on that.

How was it that it never occurred to him, not even once, that he might not win Miss Watson in the end? He had accepted that it would not be easy, but to him, it was a fait accompli. Predestined.

He'd actually been making progress with her. She had laughed with him, by gad. Laughed. Surely that had to have meant something.

"They are leaving today," Kate said. "All of them. Separately, of course. Lady and Miss Watson are off to prepare for the wedding, and Lord Fennsworth is taking his sister home. It's why he came, after all."

Lucy. He had to see Lucy.

He'd been trying not to think about her.

With mixed results.

But she was there, all the time, hovering at the back of his mind, even while he was stewing over the loss of Miss Watson.

Lucy. It was impossible now to think of her as Lady Lucinda. Even if he hadn't kissed her, she would be Lucy. It was who she was. It fit her perfectly.

But he *had* kissed her. And it had been magnificent.

But most of all, unexpected.

Everything about it had surprised him, even the very fact that he'd done it. It was Lucy. He wasn't supposed to kiss *Lucy*.

But she'd been holding his arm. And her eyes—what was it about her eyes? She'd been looking up at him, searching for something.

Searching *him* for something.

He hadn't meant to do it. It just happened. He'd felt pulled, inexorably tugged toward her, and the space between them had grown smaller and smaller . . .

And then there she was. In his arms.

He'd wanted to melt to the floor, lose himself in her and never let go.

He'd wanted to kiss her until they both fell apart from the passion of it.

He'd wanted to—

Well. He'd wanted to do quite a bit, to tell the truth. But he'd also been a little bit drunk.

Not very. But enough to doubt the veracity of his response.

And he'd been angry. And off-balance.

Not with Lucy, of course, but he was quite certain it had impaired his judgment.

Still, he should see her. She was a gently bred young lady. One didn't kiss one of *those* without making explanations. And he ought to apologize as well, although that didn't really feel like what he wanted to do.

But it was what he *should* do.

He looked up at Kate. "When are they leaving?"

"Lady and Miss Watson? This afternoon, I believe."

No, he almost blurted out, *I meant Lady Lucinda*. But he caught himself and kept his voice unconcerned as he said instead, "And Fennsworth?"

"Soon, I think. Lady Lucinda has already been down for breakfast." Kate thought for a moment. "I believe Fennsworth said he wished to be home by supper. But they can make the journey in one day. They don't live too very far away."

"Near Dover," Gregory murmured absently.

Kate's brow furrowed. "I think you're right."

Gregory frowned at his food. He'd thought to wait here for Lucy; she would not be able to miss breakfast. But if she'd already eaten, then the time of her departure would be growing near.

And he needed to find her.

He stood. A bit abruptly—he knocked his thigh against the

edge of the table, causing Kate to look up at him with a startled expression.

"You're not going to finish your breakfast?" she asked.

He shook his head. "I'm not hungry."

She looked at him with patent disbelief. She'd been a member of the family for over ten years, after all. "How is that possible?"

He ignored the question. "I bid you a lovely morning."

"Gregory?"

He turned. He didn't want to, but there was a slight edge to her voice, just enough for him to know he needed to pay attention.

Kate's eyes filled with compassion—and apprehension. "You're not going to seek out Miss Watson, are you?"

"No," he said, and it was almost funny, because that was the last thing on his mind.

Lucy stared at her packed trunks, feeling tired. And sad. And confused.

And heaven knew what else.

Wrung out. That was how she felt. She'd watched the maids with the bath towels, how they twisted and twisted to wring out every last drop of water.

So it had come to this.

She was a bath towel.

"Lucy?"

It was Hermione, quietly entering their room. Lucy had already been asleep when Hermione had returned the night before, and Hermione had been asleep when Lucy had left for breakfast.

When Lucy had returned, Hermione had been gone. In many ways, Lucy had been grateful for that.

"I was with my mother," Hermione explained. "We depart this afternoon."

Lucy nodded. Lady Bridgerton had found her at breakfast and informed her of everyone's plans. By the time she had returned to her bedchamber, her belongings were all packed and ready to be loaded onto a carriage.

That was it, then.

"I wanted to talk with you," Hermione said, perching on the edge of the bed but keeping a respectful distance from Lucy. "I wanted to explain."

Lucy's gaze remained fixed on her trunks. "There is nothing to explain. I'm very happy that you will be marrying Richard." She managed a weary smile. "You shall be my sister now."

"You don't sound happy."

"I'm tired."

Hermione was quiet for a moment, and then, when it was apparent that Lucy was done speaking, she said, "I wanted to make sure that you knew that I was not keeping secrets from you. I would never do that. I hope you know I would never do that."

Lucy nodded, because she did know, even if she had felt abandoned, and perhaps even a little betrayed the night before.

Hermione swallowed, and then her jaw tightened, and then she took a breath. And Lucy knew in that moment that she had been rehearsing her words for hours, tossing them back and forth in her mind, looking for the exact right combination to say what she felt.

It was exactly what Lucy would have done, and yet somehow it made her want to cry.

But for all Hermione's practice, when she spoke she was still changing her mind, choosing new words and phrases. "I really did love— No. No," she said, talking more to herself than to Lucy. "What I mean is, I really did *think* I loved Mr. Edmonds. But I reckon I didn't. Because first there was Mr. Bridgerton, and then . . . Richard."

Lucy looked sharply up. "What do you mean, first there was Mr. Bridgerton?"

"I . . . I'm not sure, actually," Hermione answered, flustered by the question. "When I shared breakfast with him it was as if I was awakened from a long, strange dream. Do you remember, I spoke to you about it? Oh, I didn't hear music or any some such, and I did not even feel . . . Well, I don't know how to explain it, but even though I was not in any way *overcome*—as I was with Mr. Edmonds—I . . . I wondered. About him. And whether maybe I *could* feel something. If I tried. And I did not see how I could possibly be in love with Mr. Edmonds if Mr. Bridgerton made me wonder."

Lucy nodded. Gregory Bridgerton made her wonder, too. But not about whether she could. That she knew. She just wanted to know how to make herself *not*.

But Hermione did not see her distress. Or perhaps Lucy hid it well. Either way, Hermione just continued with her explanation. "And then . . ." she said, "with Richard . . . I'm not certain how it happened, but we were walking, and we were talking, and it all felt so pleasant. But more than pleasant," she hastily added. "Pleasant sounds dull, and it wasn't that. I felt . . . right. Like I'd come home."

Hermione smiled, almost helplessly, as if she couldn't quite believe her good fortune. And Lucy was glad for her. She really was. But she wondered how it was possible to feel so happy and so sad at the same time. Because she was never going to feel that way. And even if she hadn't believed in it before, she did now. And that made it so much worse.

"I am sorry if I did not appear happy for you last night," Lucy said softly. "I am. Very much so. It was the shock, that is all. So many changes all at one time."

"But *good* changes, Lucy," Hermione said, her eyes shining. "Good changes."

Lucy wished she could share her confidence. She wanted to embrace Hermione's optimism, but instead she felt overwhelmed. But she could not say that to her friend. Not now, when she was glowing with happiness.

So Lucy smiled and said, "You will have a good life with Richard." And she meant it, too.

Hermione grasped her hand with both of her own, squeezing tightly with all the friendship and excitement inside of her. "Oh, Lucy, I know it. I have known him for so long, and he's *your* brother, so he has always made me feel safe. Comfortable, really. I don't have to worry about what he thinks of me. You've surely already told him everything, good and bad, and he still believes I'm rather fine."

"He doesn't know you can't dance," Lucy admitted.

"He doesn't?" Hermione shrugged. "I will tell him, then. Perhaps he can teach me. Does he have any talent for it?"

Lucy shook her head.

"Do you see?" Hermione said, her smile wistful and hopeful and joyful all at once. "We are perfectly matched. It has all become so clear. It is so easy to talk with him, and last night . . . I was laughing, and he was laughing, and it just felt so . . . *lovely*. I can't really explain."

But she didn't have to explain. Lucy was terrified that she knew exactly what Hermione meant.

"And then we were in the orangery, and it was so beautiful with the moonlight shining through the glass. It was all dappled and blurry and . . . and then I looked at him." Hermione's eyes grew misty and unfocused, and Lucy knew that she was lost in the memory.

Lost and happy.

"I looked at him," Hermione said again, "and he was looking down at me. I could not look away. I simply could not. And then we kissed. It was . . . I didn't even think about it. It just happened. It was just the most natural, wonderful thing in the world."

Lucy nodded sadly.

"I realized that I didn't understand before. With Mr. Edmonds—oh, I thought myself so violently in love with him, but I did not know what love was. He was so handsome, and he made me feel shy and excited, but I never longed to kiss him. I never looked at him and leaned in, not because I wanted to, but just because . . . because . . ."

Because what? Lucy wanted to scream. But even if she'd had the inclination, she lacked the energy.

"Because it was where I belonged," Hermione finished softly, and she looked amazed, as if she hadn't herself realized it until that very moment.

Lucy suddenly began to feel very queer. Her muscles felt twitchy, and she had the most insane desire to wrap her hands into fists. What did she *mean*? Why was she saying this? Everyone had spent so much time telling her that love was a thing of magic, something wild and uncontrollable that came like a thunderstorm.

And now it was something else? It was just *comfort*? Something peaceful? Something that actually sounded *nice*? "What happened to hearing music?" she heard herself demand. "To seeing the back of his head and *knowing*?"

Hermione gave her a helpless shrug. "I don't know. But I shouldn't trust it, if I were you."

Lucy closed her eyes in agony. She didn't need Hermione's warning. She would never have trusted that sort of feeling. She wasn't the sort who memorized love sonnets, and she never would be. But the other kind—the one with the laughing, the comfort, the feeling *nice*—that she would trust in a heartbeat.

And dear God, that was what she'd felt with Mr. Bridgerton.

All that and music, too.

Lucy felt the blood drain from her face. She'd heard *music* when she kissed him. It had been a veritable symphony, with soaring crescendos and pounding percussion and even that pulsing little underbeat one never noticed until it crept up and took over the rhythm of one's heart.

Lucy had floated. She'd tingled. She'd felt all those things Hermione had said she'd felt with Mr. Edmonds—and everything she'd said she felt with Richard, as well.

All with one person.

She was in love with him. She was in love with Gregory Bridgerton. The realization couldn't have been more clear . . . or more cruel.

"Lucy?" Hermione asked hesitantly. And then again—"Luce?"

"When is the wedding?" Lucy asked abruptly. Because changing the subject was the only thing she could do. She turned, looked directly at Hermione and held her gaze for the first time in the conversation. "Have you begun making plans? Will it be in Fenchley?"

Details. Details were her salvation. They always had been.

Hermione's expression grew confused, then concerned, and then she said, "I . . . no, I believe it is to be at the Abbey. It's a bit more grand. And . . . are you certain you're all right?"

"Quite well," Lucy said briskly, and she *sounded* like herself, so maybe that would mean she would begin to feel that way, too. "But you did not mention when."

"Oh. Soon. I'm told there were people near the orangery last night. I am not certain what was heard—or repeated—but the whispering has begun, so we will need to have it all settled post-haste." Hermione gave her a sweet smile. "I don't mind. And I don't think Richard does, either."

Lucy wondered which of them would reach the altar first. She hoped it was Hermione.

A knock sounded on the door. It was a maid, followed by two footmen, there to remove Lucy's trunks.

"Richard desires an early start," Lucy explained, even though she had not seen her brother since the events of the previous night. Hermione probably knew more about their plans than she did.

"Think of it, Lucy," Hermione said, walking her to the door. "We shall both be countesses. I of Fennsworth, and you of Davenport. We shall cut quite a dash, we two."

Lucy knew that she was trying to cheer her up, so she used every ounce of her energy to force her smile to reach her eyes as she said, "It will be great fun, won't it?"

Hermione took her hand and squeezed it. "Oh, it will, Lucy. You shall see. We are at the dawn of a new day, and it will be bright, indeed."

Lucy gave her friend a hug. It was the only way she could think to hide her face from view.

Because there was no way she could feign a smile this time.

Gregory found her just in time. She was in the front drive, surprisingly alone, save for the handful of servants scurrying about. He could see her profile, chin tipped slightly up as she watched her trunks being loaded onto the carriage. She looked . . . composed. Carefully held.

"Lady Lucinda," he called out.

She went quite still before she turned. And when she did, her eyes looked pained.

"I am glad I caught you," he said, although he was no longer sure that he was. She was not happy to see him. He had not been expecting that.

"Mr. Bridgerton," she said. Her lips were pinched at the corners, as if she thought she was smiling.

There were a hundred different things he could have said, so of course he chose the least meaningful and most obvious. "You're leaving."

"Yes," she said, after the barest of pauses. "Richard desires an early start."

Gregory looked around. "Is he here?"

"Not yet. I imagine he is saying goodbye to Hermione."

"Ah. Yes." He cleared his throat. "Of course."

He looked at her, and she looked at him, and they were quiet.

Awkward.

"I wanted to say that I am sorry," he said.

She . . . she didn't smile. He wasn't sure what her expression was, but it wasn't a smile. "Of course," she said.

Of course? *Of course?*

"I accept." She looked slightly over his shoulder. "Please, do not think of it again."

It was what she had to say, to be sure, but it still niggled at Gregory. He had kissed her, and it had been stupendous, and if he wished to remember it, he damned well would.

"Will I see you in London?" he asked.

She looked up at him then, her eyes finally meeting his. She was searching for something. She was searching for something in him, and he did not think she found it.

She looked too somber, too tired.

Too not like *her.*

"I expect you shall," she replied. "But it won't be the same. I am engaged, you see."

"*Practically* engaged," he reminded her, smiling.

"No." She shook her head, slow and resigned. "I truly am now. That is why Richard came to fetch me home. My uncle has finalized the agreements. I believe the banns will be read soon. It is done."

His lips parted with surprise. "I see," he said, and his mind raced. And raced and raced, and got absolutely nowhere. "I wish you the best," he said, because what else could he say?

She nodded, then tilted her head toward the wide green lawn in front of the house. "I believe I shall take a turn around the garden. I have a long ride ahead of me."

"Of course," he said, giving her a polite bow. She did not wish for his company. She could not have made herself more clear if she had spoken the words.

"It has been lovely knowing you," she said. Her eyes caught his, and for the first time in the conversation, he *saw* her, saw right down to everything inside of her, weary and bruised.

And he saw that she was saying goodbye.

"I am sorry . . ." She stopped, looked to the side. At a stone wall. "I am sorry that everything did not work out as you had hoped."

I'm not, he thought, and he realized that it was true. He had a sudden flash of his life married to Hermione Watson, and he was . . .

Bored.

Good God, how was it he was only just now realizing it? He and Miss Watson were not suited at all, and in truth, he had made a narrow escape.

He wasn't likely to trust his judgment next time when it came to matters of the heart, but that seemed far more preferable to a dull marriage. He supposed he had Lady Lucinda to thank for that, although he wasn't sure why. She had not prevented his marriage to Miss Watson; in fact, she had encouraged it at every turn.

But somehow she was responsible for his coming to his senses. If there was any one true thing to be known that morning, that was it.

Lucy motioned to the lawn again. "I shall take that stroll," she said.

He nodded his greeting and watched her as she walked off. Her hair was smoothed neatly into a bun, the blond strands catching the sunlight like honey and butter.

He waited for quite some time, not because he expected her to turn around, or even because he hoped she would.

It was just in case.

Because she might. She might turn around, and she might have something to say to him, and then he might reply, and she might—

But she didn't. She kept on walking. She did not turn, did not look back, and so he spent his final minutes watching the back of her neck. And all he could think was—

Something is not right.

But for the life of him, he did not know what.

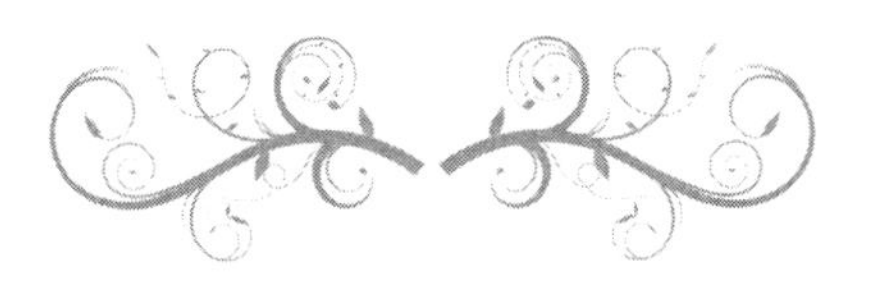

Chapter 13

In which Our Heroine sees a glimpse of her future.

One month later

The food was exquisite, the table settings magnificent, the surroundings beyond opulent.

Lucy, however, was miserable.

Lord Haselby and his father, the Earl of Davenport, had come to Fennsworth House in London for supper. It had been Lucy's idea, a fact which she now found painfully ironic. Her wedding was a mere week away, and yet until this night she hadn't even seen her future husband. Not since the wedding had shifted from probable to imminent, anyway.

She and her uncle had arrived in London a fortnight earlier, and after eleven days had passed without a glimpse of her intended, she had approached her uncle and asked if they might arrange some sort of gathering. He had looked rather irritated, although not, Lucy was fairly certain, because he thought the request foolish. No, her mere presence was all it required to bring on such an expression. She was standing in front of him, and he had been forced to look up.

Uncle Robert did not like to be interrupted.

But he apparently saw the wisdom in allowing an affianced couple to share a word or two before they met at a church, so he had curtly told her that he would make the arrangements.

Buoyed by her small victory, Lucy had also asked if she might attend one of the many social events that were taking place practically right outside her door. The London social season had begun, and each night Lucy stood at her window, watching the elegant carriages roll by. Once there had been a party directly across St. James's Square from Fennsworth House. The line of carriages had snaked around the square, and Lucy had snuffed the candles in her room so that she would not be silhouetted in the window as she watched the proceedings. A number of partygoers had grown impatient with the wait, and since the weather was so fine, they had disembarked on her side of the square and walked the rest of the way.

Lucy had told herself that she just wanted to see the gowns, but in her heart she knew the truth.

She was looking for Mr. Bridgerton.

She didn't know what she would do if she actually *saw* him. Duck out of sight, she supposed. He had to know that this was her home, and surely he would be curious enough to glance at the façade, even if her presence in London was not a widely known fact.

But he didn't attend that party, or if he did, his carriage had deposited him right at the front doorstep.

Or maybe he wasn't in London at all. Lucy had no way of knowing. She was trapped in the house with her uncle and her aging, slightly deaf aunt Harriet, who had been brought in for the sake of propriety. Lucy left the house for trips to the dressmaker and walks in the park, but other than that, she was completely on her own, with an uncle who did not speak, and an aunt who could not hear.

So she was not generally privy to gossip. About Gregory Bridgerton or anyone, for that matter.

And even on the odd occasion when she did see someone she knew, she couldn't very well *ask* after him. People would think she was interested, which of course she was, but no one, absolutely no one, could ever know of it.

She was marrying someone else. In a week. And even if she weren't, Gregory Bridgerton had shown no sign that he might be interested in taking Haselby's place.

He had kissed her, that was true, and he had seemed concerned for her welfare, but if he was of the belief that a kiss demanded a proposal of marriage, he had made no indication. He had not known that her engagement to Haselby had been finalized—not when he'd kissed her, and not the following morning when they had stood awkwardly in the drive. He could only have believed that he was kissing a girl who was entirely unattached. One simply did not *do* such a thing unless one was ready and willing to step up to the altar.

But not Gregory. When she *had* finally told him, he hadn't looked stricken. He hadn't even looked mildly upset. There had been no pleas to reconsider, or to try to find a way out of it. All she'd seen in his face—and she had *looked*, oh, how she'd looked—was . . . nothing.

His face, his eyes—they had been almost blank. Maybe a touch of surprise, but no sorrow or relief. Nothing to indicate that her engagement meant anything to him, one way or another.

Oh, she did not think him a cad, and she was quite sure he would have married her, had it been necessary. But no one had seen them, and thus, as far as the rest of the world was concerned, it had never happened.

There were no consequences. For either of them.

But wouldn't it have been nice if he'd seemed just a little bit upset? He'd kissed her, and the earth had *shook*—surely he'd felt it. Shouldn't he have wanted more? Shouldn't he have wanted, if not to marry her, then at least the possibility of doing so?

Instead he'd said, "I wish you the best," and it had sounded so final. As she'd stood there, watching her trunks being loaded into the carriage, she had *felt* her heart breaking. Felt it, right there in her chest. It had *hurt.* And as she walked away, it had just got worse, pressing and squeezing until she thought it would steal her very breath. She'd begun to move faster—as fast as she could while maintaining a normal gait, and then finally she rounded a corner and collapsed onto a bench, letting her face fall helplessly into her hands.

And prayed that no one saw her.

She'd wanted to look back. She'd wanted to steal one last glance at him and memorize his stance—that singular way he held himself when he stood, hands behind his back, legs slightly apart. Lucy knew that hundreds of men stood the same way, but on him it was different. He could be facing the other direction, yards and yards away, and she would know it was he.

He walked differently, too, a little bit loose and easygoing, as if a small part of his heart was still seven years old. It was in the shoulders, the hips maybe—the sort of thing almost no one would notice, but Lucy had always paid attention to details.

But she hadn't looked back. It would have only made it worse. He probably wasn't watching her, but if he were . . . and he saw her turn around . . .

It would have been devastating. She wasn't sure why, but it would.

She didn't want him to see her face. She had managed to remain composed through their conversation, but once she turned away, she had felt herself change. Her lips had parted, and she'd sucked in a huge breath, and it was as if she had hollowed herself out.

It was awful. And she didn't want him to see it.

Besides, he wasn't interested. He had all but fallen over himself to apologize for the kiss. She knew it was what he had to do; society dictated it (or if not that, then a quick trip to the altar). But it hurt all the same. She'd wanted to think he'd felt at least a tiny fraction of what she had. Not that anything could come of it, but it would have made her feel better.

Or maybe worse.

And in the end, it didn't matter. It didn't matter what her heart did or didn't know, because she couldn't do anything with it. What was the point of feelings if one couldn't use them toward a tangible end? She had to be practical. It was what she was. It was her only constant in a world that was spinning far too quickly for her comfort.

But still—here in London—she wanted to see him. It was silly and it was foolish and it was most certainly unadvisable, but she wanted it all the same. She didn't even have to speak with him. In fact she probably *shouldn't* speak with him. But a glimpse . . .

A glimpse wouldn't hurt anyone.

But when she had asked Uncle Robert if she might attend a party, he had refused, stating that there was little point in wasting time or money on the season when she was already in possession of the desired outcome—a proposal of marriage.

Furthermore, he informed her, Lord Davenport wished for Lucy to be introduced to society as Lady Haselby, not as Lady Lucinda Abernathy. Lucy wasn't sure why this was important, especially as quite a few members of society already knew her as Lady Lucinda

Abernathy, both from school and the "polishing" she and Hermione had undergone that spring. But Uncle Robert had indicated (in his inimitable manner, that is to say, without a word) that the interview was over, and he had already returned his attention to the papers on his desk.

For a brief moment, Lucy had remained in place. If she said his name, he might look up. Or he might not. But if he did, his patience would be thin, and she would feel like an annoyance, and she wouldn't receive any answers to her questions, anyway.

So she just nodded and left the room. Although heaven only knew why she had bothered to nod. Uncle Robert never looked back up once he dismissed her.

And now here she was, at the supper she herself had requested, and she was wishing—fervently—that she had never opened her mouth. Haselby was fine, perfectly pleasant even. But his father . . .

Lucy prayed that she would not be living at the Davenport residence. Please *please* let Haselby have his own home.

In Wales. Or maybe France.

Lord Davenport had, after complaining about the weather, the House of Commons, and the opera (which he found, respectively, rainy, full of ill-bred idiots, and *by God not even in English!*) then turned his critical eye on her.

It had taken all of Lucy's fortitude not to back up as he descended upon her. He looked rather like an overweight fish, with bulbous eyes and thick, fleshy lips. Truly, Lucy would not have been surprised if he had torn off his shirt to reveal gills and scales.

And then . . . *eeeeuhh* . . . she shuddered just to remember it. He stepped close, so close that his hot, stale breath puffed around her face.

She stood rigidly, with the perfect posture that had been drilled into her since birth.

He told her to show her teeth.

It had been humiliating.

Lord Davenport had inspected her like a broodmare, even going so far as to place his hands on her hips to measure them for potential childbirth! Lucy had gasped and glanced frantically at her uncle for help, but he was stone-faced and staring resolutely at a spot that was not her face.

And now that they had sat to eat . . . good heavens! Lord Davenport was *interrogating* her. He had asked every conceivable question about her health, covering areas she was quite certain were not suitable for mixed company, and then, just when she thought the worst of it was over—

"Can you do your tables?"

Lucy blinked. "I beg your pardon?"

"Your tables," he said impatiently. "Sixes, sevens."

For a moment Lucy could not speak. He wanted her to do *maths*?

"Well?" he demanded.

"Of course," she stammered. She looked again to her uncle, but he was maintaining his expression of determined disinterest.

"Show me." Davenport's mouth settled into a firm line in his jowly cheeks. "Sevens will do."

"I . . . ah . . ." Utterly desperate, she even tried to catch Aunt Harriet's eye, but she was completely oblivious to the proceedings and in fact had not uttered a word since the evening had begun.

"Father," Haselby interrupted, "surely you—"

"It's all about breeding," Lord Davenport said curtly. "The future of the family lies in her womb. We have a right to know what we're getting."

Lucy's lips parted in shock. Then she realized she'd moved a hand to her abdomen. Hastily she allowed it to drop. Her eyes shot back and forth between father and son, not sure whether she was supposed to speak.

"The last thing you want is a woman who thinks too much," Lord Davenport was saying, "but she ought to be able to do something as basic as multiplication. Good God, son, think of the ramifications."

Lucy looked to Haselby. He looked back. Apologetically.

She swallowed and shut her eyes for a fortifying moment. When she opened them, Lord Davenport was staring straight at her, and his lips were parting, and she realized he was going to speak again, which she positively could not bear, and—

"Seven, fourteen, twenty-one," she blurted out, cutting him off as best she could. "Twenty-eight, thirty-five, forty-two . . ."

She wondered what he would do if she botched it. Would he call off the marriage?

". . . forty-nine, fifty-six . . ."

It was tempting. So tempting.

". . . sixty-three, seventy, seventy-seven . . ."

She looked at her uncle. He was eating. He wasn't even looking at her.

". . . eighty-two, eighty-nine . . ."

"Eh, that's enough," Lord Davenport announced, coming in right atop the *eighty-two*.

The giddy feeling in her chest quickly drained away. She'd rebelled—possibly for the first time in her entire life—and no one had noticed. She'd waited too long.

She wondered what else she should have done already.

"Well done," Haselby said, with an encouraging smile.

Lucy managed a little smile in return. He really wasn't bad.

In fact, if not for Gregory, she would have thought him a rather fine choice. Haselby's hair was perhaps a little thin, and actually *he* was a little thin as well, but that wasn't really anything to complain about. Especially as his personality—surely the most important aspect of any man—was perfectly agreeable. They had managed a short conversation before supper while his father and her uncle were discussing politics, and he had been quite charming. He'd even made a dry, sideways sort of joke about his father, accompanied by a roll of the eyes that had made Lucy chuckle.

Truly, she shouldn't complain.

And she didn't. She wouldn't. She just wished for something else.

"I trust you acquitted yourself acceptably at Miss Moss's?" Lord Davenport asked, his eyes narrowed just enough to make his query not precisely friendly.

"Yes, of course," Lucy replied, blinking with surprise. She'd thought the conversation had veered away from her.

"Excellent institution," Davenport said, chewing on a piece of roasted lamb. "They know what a girl should and should not know. Winslow's daughter went there. Fordham's, too."

"Yes," Lucy murmured, since a reply seemed to be expected. "They are both very sweet girls," she lied. Sybilla Winslow was a nasty little tyrant who thought it good fun to pinch the upper arms of the younger students.

But for the first time that evening, Lord Davenport appeared to be pleased with her. "You know them well, then?" he asked.

"Er, somewhat," Lucy hedged. "Lady Joanna was a bit older, but it's not a large school. One can't really *not* know the other students."

"Good." Lord Davenport nodded approvingly, his jowls quivering with the movement.

Lucy tried not to look.

"These are the people you will need to know," he went on. "Connections that you must cultivate."

Lucy nodded dutifully, all the while making a mental list of all the places she would rather be. Paris, Venice, Greece, although weren't they at war? No matter. She would still rather be in Greece.

". . . responsibility to the name . . . certain standards of behavior . . ."

Was it very hot in the Orient? She'd always admired Chinese vases.

". . . will not tolerate any deviation from . . ."

What was the name of that dreadful section of town? St. Giles? Yes, she'd rather be there as well.

". . . obligations. Obligations!"

This last was accompanied by a fist on the table, causing the silver to rattle and Lucy to jerk in her seat. Even Aunt Harriet looked up from her food.

Lucy snapped to attention, and because all eyes were on her, she said, "Yes?"

Lord Davenport leaned in, almost menacingly. "Someday you will be Lady Davenport. You will have obligations. Many obligations."

Lucy managed to stretch her lips just enough to count as a response. Dear God, when would this evening end?

Lord Davenport leaned in, and even though the table was wide and laden with food, Lucy instinctively backed away. "You cannot take lightly your responsibilities," he continued, his voice rising scarily in volume. "Do you understand me, gel?"

Lucy wondered what would happen if she clasped her hands to her head and shouted it out.

God in heaven, put an end to this torture!!!

Yes, she thought, almost analytically, that might very well put him off. Maybe he would judge her unsound of mind and—

"Of course, Lord Davenport," she heard herself say.

She was a coward. A miserable coward.

And then, as if he were some sort of wind-up toy that someone had twisted off, Lord Davenport sat back in his seat, perfectly composed. "I am glad to hear of it," he said dabbing at the corner of his mouth with his serviette. "I am reassured to see that they still teach deference and respect at Miss Moss's. I do not regret my choice in having sent you there."

Lucy's fork halted halfway to her mouth. "I did not realize you had made the arrangements."

"I had to do something," he grunted, looking at her as if she were of feeble mind. "You haven't a mother to make sure you are properly schooled for your role in life. There are things you will need to know to be a countess. Skills you must possess."

"Of course," she said deferentially, having decided that a show of absolute meekness and obedience would be the quickest way to put an end to the torture. "Er, and thank you."

"For what?" Haselby asked.

Lucy turned to her fiancé. He appeared to be genuinely curious.

"Why, for having me sent to Miss Moss's," she explained, carefully directing her answer at Haselby. Maybe if she didn't *look* at Lord Davenport, he would forget she was there.

"Did you enjoy it, then?" Haselby asked.

"Yes, very much," she replied, somewhat surprised at how very *nice* it felt to be asked a polite question. "It was lovely. I was extremely happy there."

Haselby opened his mouth to reply, but to Lucy's horror, the voice that emerged was that of his father.

"It's not about what makes one happy!" came Lord Davenport's blustery roar.

Lucy could not take her eyes off the sight of Haselby's still-open mouth. *Really*, she thought, in a strange moment of absolute calm, *that had been almost frightening.*

Haselby shut his mouth and turned to his father with a tight smile. "What is about, then?" he inquired, and Lucy could not help but be impressed at the absolute lack of displeasure in his voice.

"It is about what one learns," his father answered, letting one of his fists bang down on the table in a most unseemly manner. "And who one befriends."

"Well, I did master the multiplication tables," Lucy put in mildly, not that anyone was listening to her.

"She will be a countess," Davenport boomed. "A countess!"

Haselby regarded his father equably. "She will only be a countess when you die," he murmured.

Lucy's mouth fell open.

"So really," Haselby continued, casually popping a minuscule bite of fish into his mouth, "it won't matter much to you, will it?"

Lucy turned to Lord Davenport, her eyes very very wide.

The earl's skin flushed. It was a horrible color—angry, dusky, and deep, made worse by the vein that was positively jumping in his left temple. He was staring at Haselby, his eyes narrowed with rage. There was no malice there, no wish to do ill or harm, but although it made absolutely no sense, Lucy would have sworn in that moment that Davenport hated his son.

And Haselby just said, "Fine weather we're having." And he smiled.

Smiled!

Lucy gaped at him. It was pouring and had been for days. But more to the point, didn't he realize that his father was one cheeky comment away from an apoplectic fit? Lord Davenport looked ready to spit, and Lucy was quite certain she could hear his teeth grinding from across the table.

And then, as the room practically pulsed with fury, Uncle Robert stepped into the breach. "I am pleased we have decided to hold the wedding here in London," he said, his voice even and smooth and tinged with finality, as if to say—*We are done with that, then.* "As you know," he continued, while everyone else regained his composure, "Fennsworth was married at the Abbey just two weeks ago, and while it does put one in the mind of ancestral history—I believe the last seven earls held their weddings in residence—really, hardly anyone was able to attend."

Lucy suspected that had as much to do with the hurried nature of the event as with its location, but this didn't seem the time to weigh in on the topic. And she had loved the wedding for its smallness. Richard and Hermione had been so very happy, and everyone in attendance had come out of love and friendship. It had truly been a joyous occasion.

Until they had left the next day for their honeymoon trip to Brighton. Lucy had never felt so miserable and alone as when she'd stood in the drive and waved them away.

They would be back soon, she reminded herself. Before her own wedding. Hermione would be her only attendant, and Richard was to give her away.

And in the meantime she had Aunt Harriet to keep her company. And Lord Davenport. And Haselby, who was either utterly brilliant or completely insane.

A bubble of laughter—ironic, absurd, and highly inappropriate—pressed in her throat, escaping through her nose with an inelegant snort.

"Enh?" Lord Davenport grunted.

"It is nothing," she hastily said, coughing as best she could. "A bit of food. Fishbone, probably."

It was almost funny. It would have been funny, even, if she'd been reading it in a book. It would have had to have been a satire, she decided, because it certainly wasn't a romance.

And she couldn't bear to think it might turn out a tragedy.

She looked around the table at the three men who presently made up her life. She was going to have to make the best of it. There was nothing else to do. There was no sense in remaining miserable, no matter how difficult it was to look on the bright side. And truly, it could have been worse.

So she did what she did best and tried to look at it all from a practical standpoint, mentally cataloguing all the ways it could have been worse.

But instead, Gregory Bridgerton's face kept coming to mind—and all the ways it could have been better.

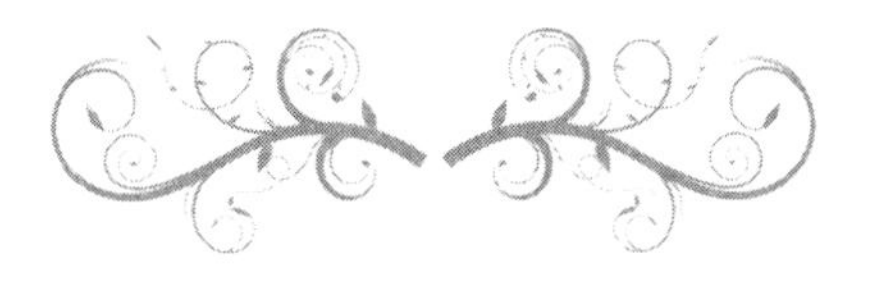

Chapter 14

In which Our Hero and Heroine are reunited, and the birds of London are ecstatic.

When Gregory saw her, right there in Hyde Park his first day back in London, his first thought was—

Well, of course.

It seemed only natural that he would come across Lucy Abernathy in what was literally his first hour out and about in London. He didn't know *why*; there was no logical reason for them to cross paths. But she had been much in his thoughts since they had parted ways in Kent. And even though he'd thought her still off at Fennsworth, he was strangely unsurprised that hers would be the first familiar face he'd see upon his return after a month in the country.

He'd arrived in town the night before, uncommonly weary after a long trip on flooded roads, and he'd gone straight to bed. When he woke—rather earlier than usual, actually—the world was still wet from the rains, but the sun had popped out and was shining brightly.

Gregory had immediately dressed to go out. He loved the way

the air smelled clean after a good, stormy rain—even in London. No, *especially* in London. It was the only time the city smelled like that—thick and fresh, almost like leaves.

Gregory kept a small suite of rooms in a tidy little building in Marylebone, and though his furnishings were spare and simple, he rather liked the place. It felt like home.

His brother and his mother had, on multiple occasions, invited him to live with them. His friends thought him mad to refuse; both residences were considerably more opulent and more to the point, better staffed than his humble abode. But he preferred his independence. It wasn't that he minded them telling him what to do—they knew he wasn't going to listen, and he knew he wasn't going to listen, but for the most part, everyone remained rather good-natured about it.

It was the scrutiny he couldn't quite tolerate. Even if his mother was pretending not to interfere in his life, he knew that she was always watching him, taking note of his social schedule.

And *commenting* on it. Violet Bridgerton could, when the inclination struck, converse on the topic of young ladies, dance cards, and the intersection thereof (as pertained to her unmarried son) with a speed and facility that could make a grown man's head spin.

And frequently did.

There was this young lady and that young lady and would he please be sure to dance with both of them—twice—at the next soiree, and above all, he must never, ever forget the *other* young lady. The one off by the wall, didn't he see her, standing by herself. Her aunt, he must recall, was a close personal friend.

Gregory's mother had a lot of close personal friends.

Violet Bridgerton had successfully ushered seven of her eight children into happy marriages, and now Gregory was bearing the sole brunt of her matchmaking fervor. He adored her, of course, and he adored that she cared so much for his well-being and happiness, but at times she made him want to pull his hair out.

And Anthony was worse. He didn't even have to *say* anything. His mere presence was usually enough to make Gregory feel that he was somehow not living up to the family name. It was difficult to make one's way in the world with the mighty Lord Bridgerton constantly looking over one's shoulder. As far as Gregory could determine, his eldest brother had never made a mistake in his life.

Which made his own all the more egregious.

But, as luck would have it, this was a problem more easily solved than not. Gregory had simply moved out. It required a fair portion of his allowance to maintain his own residence, small though it was, but it was worth it, every last penny.

Even something as simple as this—just leaving the house without anyone wondering why or where (or in his mother's case, to *whom*)—it was lovely. Fortifying. It was strange how a mere stroll could make one feel like one's own man, but it did.

And then there she was. Lucy Abernathy. In Hyde Park when by all rights she ought to still be in Kent.

She was sitting on a bench, tossing bits of bread at a scruffy lot of birds, and Gregory was reminded of that day he'd stumbled upon her at the back of Aubrey Hall. She had been sitting on a bench then as well, and she had seemed so subdued. In retrospect, Gregory realized that her brother had probably just told her that her engagement had been finalized.

He wondered why she hadn't said anything to him.

He wished she'd said something to him.

If he had known that she was spoken for, he would never have kissed her. It went against every code of conduct to which he held himself. A gentleman did not poach upon another man's bride. It was simply not done. If he had known the truth, he would have stepped away from her that night, and he would have—

He froze. He didn't know what he would have done. How was it that he had rewritten the scene in his mind countless times, and he only now realized that he had never quite got to the point where he pushed her away?

If he had known, would he have set her on her way right at that first moment? He'd had to take hold of her arms to steady her, but he could have shifted her toward her destination when he let go. It would not have been difficult—just a little shuffle of the feet. He could have ended it then, before anything had had a chance to begin.

But instead, he had smiled, and he had asked her what she was doing there, and then—good *God*, what had he been thinking—he'd asked her if she drank brandy.

After that—well, he wasn't sure how it had happened, but he remembered it all. Every last detail. The way she was looking at him, her hand on his arm. She'd been clutching him, and for a moment it had almost felt like she needed him. He could be her rock, her center.

He had never been anyone's center.

But it wasn't that. He hadn't kissed her for that. He'd kissed her because . . .

Because . . .

Hell, he didn't know *why* he'd kissed her. There had just been that moment—that strange, inscrutable moment—and it had all been so quiet—a fabulous, magical, mesmerizing silence that seemed to seep into him and steal his breath.

The house had been full, teeming with guests, even, but the hallway had been theirs alone. Lucy had been gazing up at him, her eyes searching, and then . . . somehow . . . she was closer. He didn't recall moving, or lowering his head, but her face was just a few inches away. And the next thing he knew . . .

He was kissing her.

From that moment on, he had been quite simply gone. It was as if he'd lost all knowledge of words, of rationality and thought. His mind had become a strange, preverbal thing. The world was color and sound, heat and sensation. It was as if his mind had been subsumed by his body.

And now he wondered—when he let himself wonder—if he could have stopped it. If she hadn't said no, if she hadn't pressed her hands to his chest and told him to stop—

Would he have done so on his own?

Could he have done so?

He straightened his shoulders. Squared his jaw. Of course he could have. She was Lucy, for heaven's sake. She was quite wonderful, in quite a number of ways, but she wasn't the sort men lost their heads over. It had been a temporary aberration. Momentary insanity brought on by a strange and unsettling evening.

Even now, sitting on a bench in Hyde Park with a small fleet of pigeons at her feet, she was clearly the same old Lucy. She hadn't seen him yet, and it felt almost luxurious just to observe. She was on her own, save for her maid, who was twiddling her thumbs two benches over.

And her mouth was moving.

Gregory smiled. Lucy was talking to the birds. Telling them something. Most likely she was giving them directions, perhaps setting a date for future bread-tossing engagements.

Or telling them to chew with their beaks closed.

He chuckled. He couldn't help himself.

She turned. She turned, and she saw him. Her eyes widened, and her lips parted, and it hit him squarely in the chest—

It was *good* to see her.

Which struck him as a rather odd sort of reaction, given how they'd parted.

"Lady Lucinda," he said, walking forward. "This is a surprise. I had not thought you were in London."

For a moment it seemed she could not decide how to act, and then she smiled—perhaps a bit more hesitantly than he was accustomed to—and held forward a slice of bread.

"For the pigeons?" he murmured. "Or me?"

Her smile changed, grew more familiar. "Whichever you prefer. Although I should warn you—it's a bit stale."

His lips twitched. "You've tried it, then?"

And then it was as if none of it had happened. The kiss, the awkward conversation the morning after . . . it was gone. They were back to their odd little friendship, and all was right with the world.

Her mouth was pursed, as if she thought she ought to be scolding him, and he was chuckling, because it was such good fun to bait her.

"It's my second breakfast," she said, utterly deadpan.

He sat on the opposite end of the bench and began to tear his bread into bits. When he had a good-sized handful, he tossed them all at once, then sat back to watch the ensuing frenzy of beaks and feathers.

Lucy, he noticed, was tossing her crumbs methodically, one after another, precisely three seconds apart.

He counted. How could he not?

"The flock has abandoned me," she said with a frown.

Gregory grinned as the last pigeon hopped to the feast of Bridgerton. He threw down another handful. "I always host the best parties."

She turned, her chin dipping as she gave him a dry glance over her shoulder. "You are insufferable."

He gave her a wicked look. "It is one of my finest qualities."

"According to whom?"

"Well, my mother seems to like me quite well," he said modestly.

She sputtered with laughter.

It felt like a victory.

"My sister . . . not as much."

One of her brows lifted. "The one you are fond of torturing?"

"I don't torture her because I *like* to," he said, in a rather instructing sort of tone. "I do it because it is *necessary*."

"To whom?"

"To all Britain," he said. "Trust me."

She looked at him dubiously. "She can't be that bad."

"I suppose not," he said. "My mother seems to like her quite well, much as that baffles me."

She laughed again, and the sound was . . . *good.* A nondescript word, to be sure, but somehow it got right to the heart of it. Her laughter came from within—warm, rich, and true.

Then she turned, and her eyes grew quite serious. "You like to tease, but I would bet all that I have that you would lay down your life for her."

He pretended to consider this. "How much do you have?"

"For shame, Mr. Bridgerton. You're avoiding the question."

"Of course I would," he said quietly. "She's my little sister. Mine to torture and mine to protect."

"Isn't she married now?"

He shrugged, gazing out across the park. "Yes, I suppose St. Clair can take care of her now, God help him." He turned, flashing her a lopsided smile. "Sorry."

But she wasn't so high in the instep as to take offense. And in fact, she surprised him utterly by saying—with considerable feeling, "There is no need to apologize. There are times when only the Lord's name will properly convey one's desperation."

"Why do I feel you are speaking from recent experience?"

"Last night," she confirmed.

"Really?" He leaned in, terribly interested. "What happened?"

But she just shook her head. "It was nothing."

"Not if *you* were blaspheming."

She sighed. "I did tell you you were insufferable, didn't I?"

"Once today, and almost certainly several times before."

She gave him a dry look, the blue of her eyes sharpening as they fixed upon him. "You've been counting?"

He paused. It was an odd question, not because she'd asked it—for heaven's sake, he would have asked the very thing, had he been given the same bait. Rather, it was odd because he had the eerie feeling that if he thought about it long enough, he might actually know the answer.

He liked talking with Lucy Abernathy. And when she said something to him . . .

He remembered it.

Peculiar, that.

"I wonder," he said, since it seemed a good time to change the topic. "Is *sufferable* a word?"

She considered that. "I think it must be, don't you?"

"No one has ever uttered it in my presence."

"This surprises you?"

He smiled slowly. With appreciation. "You, Lady Lucinda, have a smart mouth."

Her brows arched, and in that moment she was positively devilish. "It is one of my best-kept secrets."

He started to laugh.

"I'm more than just a busybody, you know."

The laughter grew. Deep in his belly it rumbled, until he was shaking with it.

She was watching him with an indulgent smile, and for some reason he found that calming. She looked warm . . . peaceful, even.

And he was happy to be with her. Here on this bench. It was rather pleasant simply to be in her company. So he turned. Smiled. "Do you have another piece of bread?"

She handed him three. "I brought the entire loaf."

He started tearing them up. "Are you trying to fatten the flock?"

"I have a taste for pigeon pie," she returned, resuming her slow, miserly feeding schedule.

Gregory was quite sure it was his imagination, but he would have sworn the birds were looking longingly in his direction. "Do you come here often?" he asked.

She didn't answer right away, and her head tilted, almost as if she had to think about her answer.

Which was odd, as it was a rather simple question.

"I like to feed the birds," she said. "It's relaxing."

He hurled another handful of bread chunks and quirked a smile. "Do you think so?"

Her eyes narrowed and she tossed her next piece with a precise, almost military little flick of her wrist. The following piece went out the same way. And the one after that, as well. She turned to him with pursed lips. "It is if you're not trying to incite a riot."

"Me?" he returned, all innocence. "You are the one forcing them to battle to the death, all for one pathetic crumb of stale bread."

"It's a very fine loaf of bread, well-baked and extremely tasty, I'll have you know."

"On matters of nourishment," he said with overdone graciousness, "I shall always defer to you."

Lucy regarded him dryly. "Most women would not find that complimentary."

"Ah, but you are not most women. And," he added, "I have seen you eat breakfast."

Her lips parted, but before she could gasp her indignation, he cut in with: "That was a compliment, by the way."

Lucy shook her head. He really was insufferable. And she was *so* thankful for that. When she'd first seen him, just standing there watching her as she fed the birds, her stomach had dropped, and she'd felt queasy, and she didn't know what to say or how to act, or really, anything.

But then he'd ambled forward, and he'd been so . . . *himself.* He'd put her immediately at ease, which, under the circumstances, was really quite astonishing.

She was, after all, in love with him.

But then he'd smiled, that lazy, familiar smile of his, and he'd made some sort of joke about the pigeons, and before she knew it, she was smiling in return. And she felt like herself, which was so reassuring.

She hadn't felt like herself for weeks.

And so, in the spirit of making the best of things, she had decided not to dwell upon her inappropriate affection for him and instead be thankful that she could be in his presence without turning into an awkward, stammering fool.

There *were* small favors left in the world, apparently.

"Have you been in London all this time?" she asked him, quite determined to maintain a pleasant and perfectly normal conversation.

He drew back in surprise. Clearly, he had not expected that question. "No. I only just returned last night."

"I see." Lucy paused to digest that. It was strange, but she hadn't even considered that he might not be in town. But it would explain—Well, she wasn't sure what it would explain. That she hadn't caught a glimpse of him? It wasn't as if she'd been anywhere besides her home, the park, and the dressmaker. "Were you at Aubrey Hall, then?"

"No, I left shortly after you departed and went to visit my brother. He lives with his wife and children off in Wiltshire, quite blissfully away from all that is civilized."

"Wiltshire isn't so very far away."

He shrugged. "Half the time they don't even receive the *Times*. They claim they are not interested."

"How odd." Lucy didn't know anyone who did not receive the newspaper, even in the most remote of counties.

He nodded. "I found it rather refreshing this time, however. I have no idea what anyone is doing, and I don't mind it a bit."

"Are you normally such a gossip?"

He gave her a sideways look. "Men don't gossip. We talk."

"I see," she said. "That explains so much."

He chuckled. "Have *you* been in town long? I had assumed you were also rusticating."

"Two weeks," she replied. "We arrived just after the wedding."

"We? Are your brother and Miss Watson here, then?"

She hated that she was listening for eagerness in his voice, but she supposed it couldn't be helped. "She is Lady Fennsworth now, and no, they are on their honeymoon trip. I am here with my uncle."

"For the season?"

"For my wedding."

That stopped the easy flow of conversation.

She reached into her bag and pulled out another slice of bread. "It is to take place in a week."

He stared at her in shock. "That soon?"

"Uncle Robert says there is no point in dragging it out."

"I see."

And maybe he did. Maybe there was some sort of etiquette to all this that she, sheltered girl from the country that she was, had not been taught. Maybe there *was* no point in postponing the inevitable. Maybe it was all a part of that making the best of things philosophy she was working so diligently to espouse.

"Well," he said. He blinked a few times, and she realized that he did not know what to say. It was a most uncharacteristic response and one she found gratifying. It was a bit like Hermione not knowing how to dance. If Gregory Bridgerton could be at a loss for words, then there was hope for the rest of humanity.

Finally he settled upon: "My felicitations."

"Thank you." She wondered if he had received an invitation. Uncle Robert and Lord Davenport were determined to hold the ceremony in front of absolutely everyone. It was, they said, to be her grand debut, and they wanted all the world to know that she was Haselby's wife.

"It is to be at St. George's," she said, for no reason whatsoever.

"Here in London?" He sounded surprised. "I would have thought you would marry from Fennsworth Abbey."

It was most peculiar, Lucy thought, how *not* painful this was—discussing her upcoming wedding with him. She felt more numb, actually. "It was what my uncle wanted," she explained, reaching into her basket for another slice of bread.

"Your uncle remains the head of the household?" Gregory asked, regarding her with mild curiosity. "Your brother is the earl. Hasn't he reached his majority?"

Lucy tossed the entire slice to the ground, then watched with morbid interest as the pigeons went a bit mad. "He has," she replied. "Last year. But he was content to allow my uncle to handle the family's affairs while he was conducting his postgraduate studies at Cambridge. I expect that he will assume his place soon now that he is"—she offered him an apologetic smile—"married."

"Do not worry over my sensibilities," he assured her. "I am quite recovered."

"Truly?"

He gave her a small, one-shouldered shrug. "Truth be told, I count myself lucky."

She pulled out another slice of bread, but her fingers froze before pinching off a piece. "You do?" she asked, turning to him with interest. "How is that possible?"

He blinked with surprise. "You *are* direct, aren't you?"

And she blushed. She felt it, pink and warm and just *horrible* on her cheeks. "I'm sorry," she said. "That was terribly rude of me. It is only that you were so very much—"

"Say no more," he cut her off, and then she felt even worse, because she had been about to describe—probably in meticulous detail—how lovesick he'd been over Hermione. Which, had she been in his position, she'd not wish recounted.

"I'm sorry," she said.

He turned. Regarded her with a contemplative sort of curiosity. "You say that quite frequently."

"I'm sorry?"

"Yes."

"I . . . I don't know." Her teeth ground together, and she felt quite tense. Uncomfortable. Why would he point out such a thing? "It's what I do," she said, and she said it firmly, because . . . Well, because. That ought to be enough of a reason.

He nodded. And that made her feel even worse. "It's who I am," she added defensively, even though he'd been agreeing with her, for heaven's sake. "I smooth things over and I make things right."

And at that, she hurled the last piece of bread to the ground.

His brows rose, and they both turned in unison to watch the ensuing chaos. "Well done," he murmured.

"I make the best of things," she said. "Always."

"It's a commendable trait," he said softly.

And at that, somehow, she was angry. Really, truly, beastly angry. She didn't want to be commended for knowing how to settle for second-best. That was like winning a prize for the prettiest shoes in a footrace. Irrelevant and *not* the point.

"And what of you?" she asked, her voice growing strident. "Do you make the best of things? Is that why you claim yourself recovered? Weren't you the one who waxed rhapsodic over the mere thought of love? You said it was *everything*, that it gave you no choice. You said—"

She cut herself off, horrified by her tone. He was staring at her as if she'd gone mad, and maybe she had.

"You said many things," she mumbled, hoping that might end the conversation.

She ought to go. She had been sitting on the bench for at least fifteen minutes before he'd arrived, and it was damp and breezy, and her maid wasn't dressed warmly enough, and if she thought long and hard enough about it, she probably had a hundred things she needed to do at home.

Or at least a book she could read.

"I am sorry if I upset you," Gregory said quietly.

She couldn't quite bring herself to look at him.

"But I did not lie to you," he said. "Truthfully, I no longer think of Miss—excuse me, Lady Fennsworth—with any great frequency, except, perhaps, to realize that we should not have been well-suited after all."

She turned to him, and she realized she wanted to believe him. She really did.

Because if he could forget Hermione, maybe she could forget him.

"I don't know how to explain it," he said, and he shook his head, as if he were every bit as perplexed as she. "But if ever you fall madly and inexplicably in love . . ."

Lucy froze. *He wasn't going to say it. Surely, he couldn't say it.*

He shrugged. "Well, I shouldn't trust it."

Dear God. Hermione's words. Exactly.

She tried to remember how she had replied to Hermione. Because she had to say something. Otherwise, he would notice the silence, and then he'd turn, and he'd see her looking so unnerved. And then he would ask questions, and she wouldn't know the answers, and—

"It's not likely to happen to me," she said, the words practically pouring from her mouth.

He turned, but she kept her face scrupulously forward. And she wished desperately that she had not tossed out all the bread. It would be far easier to avoid looking at him if she could pretend to be involved with something else.

"You don't believe that you will fall in love?" he asked.

"Well, perhaps," she said, trying to sound blithe and sophisticated. "But not *that.*"

"That?"

She took a breath, hating that he was forcing her to explain. "That desperate sort of thing you and Hermione now disavow," she said. "I'm not the sort, don't you think?"

She bit her lip, then finally allowed herself to turn in his direction. Because what if he could tell that she was lying? What if he sensed that she was already in love—with him? She would be embarrassed beyond comprehension, but wouldn't it be better to *know* that he knew? At least then, she wouldn't have to wonder.

Ignorance wasn't bliss. Not for someone like her.

"It is all beside the point, anyway," she continued, because she couldn't bear the silence. "I am marrying Lord Haselby in one week, and I would *never* stray from my vows. I—"

"Haselby?" Gregory's entire body twisted as he swung around to face her. "You're marrying *Haselby*?"

"Yes," she said, blinking furiously. What sort of reaction was *that*? "I thought you knew."

"No. I didn't—" He looked shocked. Stupefied.

Good heavens.

He shook his head. "I can't imagine why I didn't know."

"It wasn't a secret."

"No," he said, a bit forcefully. "I mean, no. No, of course not. I did not mean to imply."

"Do you hold Lord Haselby in low esteem?" she asked, choosing her words with extreme care.

"No," Gregory replied, shaking his head—but just a little, as if he were not quite aware that he was doing it. "No. I've known him for a number of years. We were at college together. And university."

"Are you of an age, then?" Lucy asked, and it occurred to her that something was a bit wrong if she did not know the age of her fiancé. But then again, she wasn't certain of Gregory's age, either.

He nodded. "He's quite . . . affable. He will treat you well." He cleared his throat. "Gently."

"Gently?" she echoed. It seemed an odd choice of words.

His eyes met hers, and it was only then that she realized he had not precisely looked at her since she'd told him the name of her fiancé. But he didn't speak. Instead he just stared at her, his eyes so intense that they seemed to change color. They were brown with green, then green with brown, and then it all seemed almost to blur.

"What is it?" she whispered.

"It is of no account," he said, but he did not sound like himself. "I . . ." And then he turned away, broke the spell. "My sister," he said, clearing his throat. "She is hosting a soiree tomorrow evening. Would you like to attend?"

"Oh yes, that would be lovely," Lucy said, even though she knew she should not. But it had been so long since she'd had any sort of social interaction, and she wasn't going to be able to spend time in his company once she was married. She ought not torture herself now, longing for something she could not have, but she couldn't help it.

Gather ye rosebuds.

Now. Because really, when else—

"Oh, but I *can't*," she said, disappointment turning her voice to nearly a whine.

"Why not?"

"It is my uncle," she replied, sighing. "And Lord Davenport—Haselby's father."

"I know who he is."

"Of course. I'm sor—" She cut herself off. She wasn't going to say it. "They don't wish for me to make my bow yet."

"I beg your pardon. Why?"

Lucy shrugged. "There is no point in my being introduced to society as Lady Lucinda Abernathy when I'm to be Lady Haselby in a week."

"That's ridiculous."

"It is what they say." She frowned. "And I don't think they wish to suffer the expense, either."

"You will attend tomorrow evening," Gregory said firmly. "I shall see to it."

"You?" Lucy asked dubiously.

"Not *me*," he answered, as if she'd gone mad. "My mother. Trust me, when it comes to matters of social discourse and niceties, she can accomplish anything. Have you a chaperone?"

Lucy nodded. "My aunt Harriet. She is a bit frail, but I am certain she could attend a party if my uncle allowed it."

"He will allow it," Gregory said confidently. "The sister in question is my eldest. Daphne." He then clarified: "Her grace the Duchess of Hastings. Your uncle would not say no to a duchess, would he?"

"I don't think so," she said slowly. Lucy could not think of anyone who would say no to a duchess.

"It's settled, then," Gregory said. "You shall be hearing from Daphne by afternoon." He stood, offering his hand to help her up.

She swallowed. It would be bittersweet to touch him, but she placed her hand in his. It felt warm, and comfortable. And safe.

"Thank you," she murmured, taking her hand back so that she might wrap both around the handle of her basket. She nodded at her maid, who immediately began walking to her side.

"Until tomorrow," he said, bowing almost formally as he bade her farewell.

"Until tomorrow," Lucy echoed, wondering if it were true. She had never known her uncle to change his mind before. But maybe . . .

Possibly.

Hopefully.

Chapter 15

In which Our Hero learns that he is not, and probably never will be, as wise as his mother.

One hour later, Gregory was waiting in the drawing room at Number Five, Bruton Street, his mother's London home since she had insisted upon vacating Bridgerton House upon Anthony's marriage. It had been his home, too, until he had found his own lodgings several years earlier. His mother lived there alone now, ever since his younger sister had married. Gregory made a point of calling upon her at least twice a week when he was in London, but it never ceased to surprise him how quiet the house seemed now.

"Darling!" his mother exclaimed, sailing into the room with a wide smile. "I had not thought to see you until this evening. How was your journey? And tell me everything about Benedict and Sophie and the children. It is a crime how infrequently I see my grandchildren."

Gregory smiled indulgently. His mother had visited Wiltshire just one month earlier, and did so several times per year. He dutifully passed along news of Benedict's four children, with added emphasis on little Violet, her namesake. Then, once she had exhausted her supply of questions, he said, "Actually, Mother, I have a favor to ask of you."

Violet's posture was always superb, but still, she seemed to straighten a bit. "You do? What is it you need?"

He told her about Lucy, keeping the tale as brief as possible, lest she reach any inappropriate conclusions about his interest in her.

His mother tended to view any unmarried female as a potential bride. Even those with a wedding scheduled for the week's end.

"Of course I will assist you," she said. "This will be easy."

"Her uncle is determined to keep her sequestered," Gregory reminded her.

She waved away his warning. "Child's play, my dear son. Leave this to me. I shall make short work of it."

Gregory decided not to pursue the subject further. If his mother said she knew how to ensure someone's attendance at a ball, then he believed her. Continued questioning would only lead her to believe he had an ulterior motive.

Which he did not.

He simply liked Lucy. Considered her a friend. And he wished for her to have a bit of fun.

It was admirable, really.

"I shall have your sister send an invitation with a personal note," Violet mused. "And perhaps I shall call upon her uncle directly. I shall lie and tell him I met her in the park."

"Lie?" Gregory's lips twitched. "You?"

His mother's smile was positively diabolical. "It won't matter if he does not believe me. It is one of the advantages of advanced years. No one dares to countermand an old dragon like me."

Gregory lifted his brows, refusing to fall for her bait. Violet Bridgerton might have been the mother of eight adult children, but with her milky, unlined complexion and wide smile, she did not look like anyone who could be termed old. In fact, Gregory had often wondered why she did not remarry. There was no shortage of dashing widowers clamoring to take her in to supper or stand up for a dance. Gregory suspected any one of them would have leaped at the chance to marry his mother, if only she would indicate interest.

But she did not, and Gregory had to admit that he was rather selfishly glad of it. Despite her meddling, there was something quite comforting in her single-minded devotion to her children and grandchildren.

His father had been dead for over two dozen years. Gregory hadn't even the slightest memory of the man. But his mother had spoken of him often, and whenever she did, her voice changed. Her eyes softened, and the corners of her lips moved—just a little, just enough for Gregory to see the memories on her face.

It was in those moments that he understood why she was so adamant that her children choose their spouses for love.

He'd always planned to comply. It was ironic, really, given the farce with Miss Watson.

Just then a maid arrived with a tea tray, which she set on the low table between them.

"Cook made your favorite biscuits," his mother said, handing him a cup prepared exactly as he liked it—no sugar, one tiny splash of milk.

"You anticipated my visit?" he asked.

"Not this afternoon, no," Violet said, taking a sip of her own tea. "But I knew you could not stay away for long. Eventually you would need sustenance."

Gregory offered her a lopsided smile. It was true. Like many men of his age and status, he did not have room in his apartments for a proper kitchen. He ate at parties, and at his club, and, of course, at the homes of his mother and siblings.

"Thank you," he murmured, accepting the plate onto which she'd piled six biscuits.

Violet regarded the tea tray for a moment, her head cocked slightly to the side, then placed two on her own plate. "I am quite touched," she said, looking up at him, "that you seek my assistance with Lady Lucinda."

"Are you?" he asked curiously. "Who else would I turn to with such a matter?"

She took a delicate bite of her biscuit. "No, I am the obvious choice, of course, but you must realize that you rarely turn to your family when you need something."

Gregory went still, then turned slowly in her direction. His mother's eyes—so blue and so unsettlingly perceptive—were fixed on his face. What could she possibly have meant by that? No one could love his family better than he did.

"That cannot be true," he finally said.

But his mother just smiled. "Do you think not?"

His jaw clenched. "I *do* think not."

"Oh, do not take offense," she said, reaching across the table to pat him on the arm. "I do not mean to say that you do not love us. But you do prefer to do things for yourself."

"Such as?"

"Oh, finding yourself a wife—"

He cut her off right then and there. "Are you trying to tell me that Anthony, Benedict, and Colin welcomed your interference when they were looking for wives?"

"No, of course not. No man does. But—" She flitted one of her hands through the air, as if she could erase the sentence. "Forgive me. It was a poor example."

She let out a small sigh as she gazed out the window, and Gregory realized that she was prepared to let the subject drop. To his surprise, however, he was not.

"What is wrong with preferring to do things for oneself?" he asked.

She turned to him, looking for all the world as if she had not just introduced a potentially discomforting topic. "Why, nothing. I am quite proud that I raised such self-sufficient sons. After all, three of you must make your own way in the world." She paused, considering this, then added, "With some help from Anthony, of course. I should be quite disappointed if he did not watch out for the rest of you."

"Anthony is exceedingly generous," Gregory said quietly.

"Yes, he is, isn't he?" Violet said, smiling. "With his money *and* his time. He is quite like your father in this way." She looked at him with wistful eyes. "I am so sorry you never knew him."

"Anthony was a good father to me." Gregory said it because he knew it would bring her joy, but he also said it because it was true.

His mother's lips pursed and tightened, and for a moment Gregory thought she might cry. He immediately retrieved his handkerchief and held it out to her.

"No, no, that's not necessary," she said, even as she took it and dabbed her eyes. "I am quite all right. Merely a little—" She swallowed, then smiled. But her eyes still glistened. "Someday you will understand—when you have children of your own—how lovely it was to hear that."

She set the handkerchief down and picked up her tea. Sipping it thoughtfully, she let out a little sigh of contentment.

Gregory smiled to himself. His mother adored tea. It went quite beyond the usual British devotion. She claimed it helped her to think, which he would normally have lauded as a good thing, except that all too often *he* was the subject of her thoughts, and after her third cup she had usually devised a frighteningly thorough plan to marry him off to the daughter of whichever friend she had most recently paid a morning call to.

But this time, apparently, her mind was not on marriage. She set her cup down, and, just when he thought she was ready to change the subject, she said, "But he is not your father."

He paused, his own teacup halfway to his mouth. "I beg your pardon."

"Anthony. He is not your father."

"Yes?" he said slowly, because really, what could possibly be her point?

"He is your brother," she continued. "As are Benedict and Colin, and when you were small—oh, how you wished to be a part of their affairs."

Gregory held himself very still.

"But of course they were not interested in bringing you along, and really, who can blame them?"

"Who indeed?" he murmured tightly.

"Oh, do not take offense, Gregory," his mother said, turning to him with an expression that was a little bit contrite and little bit impatient. "They were wonderful brothers, and truly, very patient most of the time."

"Most of the time?"

"Some of the time," she amended. "But you were so much smaller than they were. There simply wasn't much in common for you to do. And then when you grew older, well . . ."

Her words trailed off, and she sighed. Gregory leaned forward. "Well?" he prompted.

"Oh, it's nothing."

"Mother."

"Very well," she said, and he knew right then and there that she knew *exactly* what she was saying, and that any sighs and lingering words were entirely for effect.

"I think that you think you must prove yourself to them," Violet said.

He regarded her with surprise. "Don't I?"

His mother's lips parted, but she made no sound for several seconds. "No," she finally said. "Why would you think you would?"

What a silly question. It was because— It was because—

"It's not the sort of thing one can easily put into words," he muttered.

"Really?" She sipped at her tea. "I must say, that was not the sort of reaction I had anticipated."

Gregory felt his jaw clench. "What, precisely, did you anticipate?"

"Precisely?" She looked up at him with just enough humor in her eyes to completely irritate him. "I'm not certain that I can be precise, but I suppose I had expected you to deny it."

"Just because I do not wish it to be the case does not render it untrue," he said with a deliberately casual shrug.

"Your brothers respect you," Violet said.

"I did not say they do not."

"They recognize that you are your own man."

That, Gregory thought, was not precisely true.

"It is not a sign of weakness to ask for help," Violet continued.

"I have never believed that it was," he replied. "Didn't I just seek your assistance?"

"With a matter that could only be handled by a female," she said, somewhat dismissively. "You had no choice but to call on me."

It was true, so Gregory made no comment.

"You are used to having things done for you," she said.

"Mother."

"Hyacinth is the same way," she said quickly. "I think it must be a symptom of being the youngest. And truly, I did not mean to imply that either of you is lazy or spoiled or mean-spirited in any way."

"What did you mean, then?" he asked.

She looked up with a slightly mischievous smile. "Precisely?"

He felt a bit of his tension slipping away. "Precisely," he said, with a nod to acknowledge her wordplay.

"I merely meant that you have never had to work particularly hard for anything. You're quite lucky that way. Good things seem to happen to you."

"And as my mother, you are bothered by this . . . how?"

"Oh, Gregory," she said with a sigh. "I am not bothered at all. I wish you nothing but good things. You know that."

He wasn't quite sure what the proper response might be to this, so he held silent, merely lifting his brows in question.

"I've made a muddle of this, haven't I?" Violet said with a frown. "All I am trying to say is that you have never had to expend much of an effort to achieve your goals. Whether that is a result of your abilities or your goals, I am not certain."

He did not speak. His eyes found a particularly intricate spot in the patterned fabric covering the walls, and he was riveted, unable to focus on anything else as his mind churned.

And yearned.

And then, before he even realized what he was thinking, he asked, "What has this to do with my brothers?"

She blinked uncomprehendingly, and then finally murmured, "Oh, you mean about your feeling the need to prove yourself?"

He nodded.

She pursed her lips. Thought. And then said, "I'm not sure."

He opened his mouth. That was not the answer he had been expecting.

"I don't know everything," she said, and he suspected it was the first time that particular collection of words had ever crossed her lips.

"I suppose," she said, slowly and thoughtfully, "that you . . . Well, it's an odd combination, I should think. Or perhaps not so odd, when one has so many older brothers and sisters."

Gregory waited as she collected her thoughts. The room was quiet, the air utterly still, and yet it felt as if something were bearing down on him, pressing at him from all sides.

He did not know what she was going to say, but somehow . . .

He knew . . .

It mattered.

Maybe more than anything else he'd ever heard.

"You don't wish to ask for help," his mother said, "because it is so important to you that your brothers see you as a man grown. And yet at the same time . . . Well, life has come easily to you, and so I think sometimes you don't try."

His lips parted.

"It is not that you refuse to try," she hastened to add. "Just that most of the time you don't have to. And when something is going to require too much effort . . . If it is something you cannot manage yourself, you decide that it is not worth the bother."

Gregory found his eyes pulling back toward that spot on the wall, the one where the vine twisted so curiously. "I know what it means to work for something," he said in a quiet voice. He turned to her then, looking her full in the face. "To want it desperately and to know that it might not be yours."

"Do you? I'm glad." She reached for her tea, then apparently changed her mind and looked up. "Did you get it?"

"No."

Her eyes turned a little bit sad. "I'm sorry."

"I'm not," he said stiffly. "Not any longer."

"Oh. Well." She shifted in her seat. "Then I am not sorry. I imagine you are a better man for it now."

Gregory's initial impulse leaned toward offense, but to his great surprise, he found himself saying, "I believe you are correct."

To his even greater surprise, he meant it.

His mother smiled wisely. "I am so glad you are able to see it in that light. Most men cannot." She glanced up at the clock and let out a chirp of surprise. "Oh dear, the time. I promised Portia Featherington that I would call upon her this afternoon."

Gregory stood as his mother rose to her feet.

"Do not worry about Lady Lucinda," she said, hurrying to the door. "I shall take care of everything. And please, finish your tea. I do worry about you, living all by yourself with no woman to care for you. Another year of this, and you will waste away to skin and bones."

He walked her to the door. "As nudges toward matrimony go, that was particularly unsubtle."

"Was it?" She gave him an arch look. "How nice for me that I no longer even try for subtlety. I have found that most men do not notice anything that is not clearly spelled out, anyway."

"Even your sons."

"*Especially* my sons."

He smiled wryly. "I asked for that, didn't I?"

"You practically wrote me an invitation."

He tried to accompany her to the main hall, but she shooed him away. "No, no, that's not necessary. Go and finish your tea. I asked the kitchen to bring up sandwiches when you were announced. They should arrive at any moment and will surely go to waste if you don't eat them."

Gregory's stomach grumbled at that exact moment, so he bowed and said, "You are a superb mother, did you know that?"

"Because I feed you?"

"Well, yes, but perhaps for a few other things as well."

She stood on her toes and kissed him on the cheek. "You are no longer my darling boy, are you?"

Gregory smiled. It had been her endearment for him for as long as he remembered. "I am for as long as you wish it, Mother. As long as you wish it."

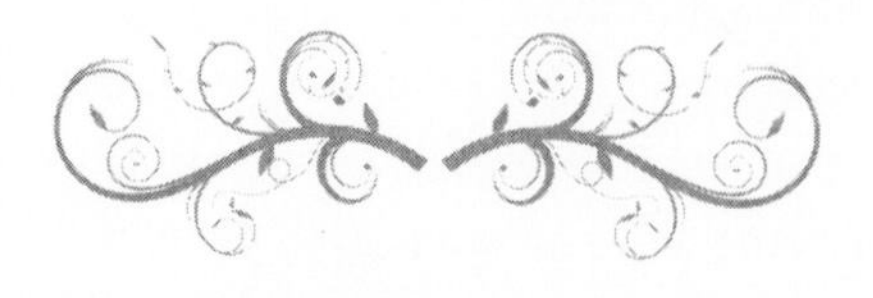

Chapter 16

In which Our Hero falls in love. Again.

When it came to social machinations, Violet Bridgerton was every bit as accomplished as she claimed, and indeed, when Gregory arrived at Hastings House the following evening, his sister Daphne, the current Duchess of Hastings, informed him that Lady Lucinda Abernathy would indeed be attending the ball.

He found himself rather unaccountably pleased at the outcome. Lucy had looked so disappointed when she'd told him that she would not be able to go, and really, shouldn't the girl enjoy one last night of revelry before she married Haselby?

Haselby.

Gregory still couldn't quite believe it. How could he have not known that she was marrying Haselby? There was nothing he could do to stop it, and really, it wasn't his place, but dear God, it was *Haselby.*

Shouldn't Lucy be told?

Haselby was a perfectly amiable fellow, and, Gregory had to allow, in possession of a more than acceptable wit. He wouldn't beat her, and he wouldn't be unkind, but he didn't . . . he couldn't . . .

He would not be a husband to her.

Just the thought of it left him grim. Lucy wasn't going to have a regular marriage, because Haselby didn't *like* women. Not the way a man was meant to.

Haselby would be kind to her, and he'd probably provide her with an exceedingly generous allowance, which was more than many women had in their marriages, regardless of their husbands' proclivities.

But it did not seem fair that, of all people, Lucy was destined for such a life. She deserved so much more. A house full of children. And dogs. Perhaps a cat or two. She seemed the sort who'd want a menagerie.

And flowers. In Lucy's home there would be flowers everywhere, he was certain of it. Pink peonies, yellow roses, and that stalky blue thing she liked so well.

Delphinium. That was it.

He paused. Remembered. Delphinium.

Lucy might claim that her brother was the horticulturalist of the family, but Gregory could not imagine her living in a home without color.

There would be laughter and noise and splendid disarray—despite her attempts to keep every corner of her life neat and tidy. He could see her easily in his mind's eye, fussing and organizing, trying to keep everyone on a proper schedule.

It almost made him laugh aloud, just to think of it. It wouldn't matter if there was a fleet of servants dusting and straightening and shining and sweeping. With children nothing was ever quite where one put it.

Lucy was a manager. It was what made her happy, and she ought to have a household to manage.

Children. Lots of them.

Maybe eight.

He glanced around the ballroom, which was slowly beginning to fill. He didn't see Lucy, and it wasn't so crowded yet that he might miss her. He did, however, see his mother.

She was heading his way.

"Gregory," she said, reaching out to him with both hands when she reached him, "you look especially handsome this evening."

He took her hands and raised them to his lips. "Said with all the honesty and impartiality of a mother," he murmured.

"Nonsense," she said with a smile. "It is a fact that all of my children are exceedingly intelligent and good-looking. If it were merely my opinion, don't you think someone would have corrected me by now?"

"As if any would dare."

"Well, yes, I suppose," she replied, maintaining an impressively impassive face. "But I shall be stubborn and insist that the point is moot."

"As you wish, Mother," he said with perfect solemnity. "As you wish."

"Has Lady Lucinda arrived?"

Gregory shook his head. "Not yet."

"Isn't it odd that I haven't met her," she mused. "One would think, if she has been in town a fortnight already . . . Ah well, it matters not. I am certain I will find her delightful if you made such an effort to secure her attendance this evening."

Gregory gave her a look. He knew this tone. It was a perfect blend of nonchalance and utter precision, usually utilized whilst digging for information. His mother was a master at it.

And sure enough, she was discreetly patting her hair and not quite looking at him as she said, "You said you were introduced while you were visiting Anthony, did you not?"

He saw no reason to pretend he did not know what she was about.

"She is engaged to be married, Mother," he said with great emphasis. And then for good measure he added, "In one week."

"Yes, yes, I know. To Lord Davenport's son. It is a long-standing match, I understand."

Gregory nodded. He couldn't imagine that his mother knew the truth about Haselby. It was not a well-known fact. There were whispers, of course. There were always whispers. But none would dare repeat them in the presence of ladies.

"I received an invitation to the wedding," Violet said.

"Did you?"

"It's to be a very large affair, I understand."

Gregory clenched his teeth a bit. "She is to be a countess."

"Yes, I suppose. It's not the sort of thing one can do up small."

"No."

Violet sighed. "I adore weddings."

"Do you?"

"Yes." She sighed again, with even more drama, not that Gregory would have imagined it possible. "It is all so romantic," she added. "The bride, the groom . . ."

"Both are considered standard in the ceremony, I understand."

His mother shot him a peevish look. "How could I have raised a son who is so unromantic?"

Gregory decided there could not possibly be an answer to that.

"Fie on you, then," Violet said, "I plan to attend. I almost never refuse an invitation to a wedding."

And then came *the voice*. "Who is getting married?"

Gregory turned. It was his younger sister, Hyacinth. Dressed in blue and poking her nose into everyone else's business as usual.

"Lord Haselby and Lady Lucinda Abernathy," Violet answered.

"Oh yes." Hyacinth frowned. "I received an invitation. At St. George's, is it not?"

Violet nodded. "Followed by a reception at Fennsworth House."

Hyacinth glanced around the room. She did that quite frequently, even when she was not searching for anyone in particular. "Isn't it odd that I haven't met her? She is sister to the Earl of Fennsworth, is she not?" She shrugged. "Odd that I have not met him, either."

"I don't believe Lady Lucinda is 'out,'" Gregory said. "Not formally, at least."

"Then tonight will be her debut," his mother said. "How exciting for us all."

Hyacinth turned to her brother with razor-sharp eyes. "And how is it that you are acquainted with Lady Lucinda, Gregory?"

He opened his mouth, but she was already saying, "And do not say that you are not, because Daphne has already told me everything."

"Then why are you asking?"

Hyacinth scowled. "She did not tell me how you *met*."

"You might wish to revisit your understanding of the word *everything*." Gregory turned to his mother. "Vocabulary and comprehension were never her strong suits."

Violet rolled her eyes. "Every day I marvel that the two of you managed to reach adulthood."

"Afraid we'd kill each other?" Gregory quipped.

"No, that I'd do the job myself."

"Well," Hyacinth stated, as if the previous minute of conversation had never taken place, "Daphne said that you were most anxious that Lady Lucinda receive an invitation, and Mother, I understand, even penned a note saying how much she enjoys her company, which as we all know is a baldfaced lie, as none of us has ever met the—"

"Do you ever cease talking?" Gregory interrupted.

"Not for you," Hyacinth replied. "How *do* you know her? And more to the point, how well? *And* why are you so eager to extend an invitation to a woman who will be married in a week?"

And then, amazingly, Hyacinth *did* stop talking.

"I was wondering that myself," Violet murmured.

Gregory looked from his sister to his mother and decided he hadn't meant any of that rot he'd said to Lucy about large families being a comfort. They were a nuisance and an intrusion and a whole host of other things, the words for which he could not quite retrieve at that moment.

Which may have been for the best, as none of them were likely to have been polite.

Nonetheless, he turned to the two women with extreme patience and said, "I was introduced to Lady Lucinda in Kent. At Kate and Anthony's house party last month. And I asked Daphne to invite her this evening because she is an amiable young lady, and I happened upon her yesterday in the park. Her uncle has denied her a season, and I thought it would be a kind deed to provide her with an opportunity to escape for one evening."

He lifted his brows, silently daring them to respond.

They did, of course. Not with words—words would never have been as effective as the dubious stares they were hurling in his direction.

"Oh, for heaven's sake," he nearly burst out. "She is *engaged.* To be married."

This had little visible effect.

Gregory scowled. "Do I appear to be attempting to put a halt to the nuptials?"

Hyacinth blinked. Several times, the way she always did when she was thinking far too hard about something not her affair. But to his great surprise, she let out a little *hmm* of acquiescence and said, "I suppose not." She glanced about the room. "I should like to meet her, though."

"I'm sure you will," Gregory replied, and he congratulated himself, as he did at least once a month, on not strangling his sister.

"Kate wrote that she is lovely," Violet said.

Gregory turned to her with a sinking feeling. "*Kate* wrote to you?" Good God, what had she revealed? It was bad enough that Anthony knew about the fiasco with Miss Watson—he had figured it out, of course—but if his mother found out, his life would be utter hell.

She would kill him with kindness. He was sure of it.

"Kate writes twice a month," Violet replied with a delicate, one-shouldered shrug. "She tells me everything."

"Is Anthony aware?" Gregory muttered.

"I have no idea," Violet said, giving him a superior look. "It's really none of his business."

Good God.

Gregory just managed to not say it aloud.

"I gather," his mother continued, "that her brother was caught in a compromising position with Lord Watson's daughter."

"*Really?*" Hyacinth had been perusing the crowd, but she swung back for that.

Violet nodded thoughtfully. "I had wondered why that wedding was so rushed."

"Well, that's why," Gregory said, a little bit like a grunt.

"Hmmmm." This, from Hyacinth.

It was the sort of sound one never wished to hear from Hyacinth.

Violet turned to her daughter and said, "It was quite the to-do."

"Actually," Gregory said, growing more irritated by the second, "it was all handled discreetly."

"There are always whispers," Hyacinth said.

"Don't you add to them," Violet warned her.

"I won't say a word," Hyacinth promised, waving her hand as if she had never spoken out of turn in her life.

Gregory let out a snort. "Oh, *please.*"

"I won't," she protested. "I am superb with a secret as long as I *know* it is a secret."

"Ah, so what you mean, then, is that you possess no sense of discretion?"

Hyacinth narrowed her eyes.

Gregory lifted his brows.

"How *old* are you?" Violet interjected. "Goodness, the two of you haven't changed a bit since you were in leading strings. I half expect you to start pulling each other's hair right on the spot."

Gregory clamped his jaw into a line and stared resolutely ahead. There was nothing quite like a rebuke from one's mother to make one feel three feet tall.

"Oh, don't be a stuff, Mother," Hyacinth said, taking the scolding with a smile. "He knows I only tease him so because I love him best." She smiled up at him, sunny and warm.

Gregory sighed, because it was true, and because he felt the same way, and because it was, nonetheless, exhausting to be her brother. But the two of them were quite a bit younger than the rest of their siblings, and as a result, had always been a bit of a pair.

"He returns the sentiment, by the way," Hyacinth said to Violet, "but as a man, he would never say as much."

Violet nodded. "It's true."

Hyacinth turned to Gregory. "And just to be perfectly clear, I never pulled your hair."

Surely his signal to leave. Or lose his sanity. Really, it was up to him.

"Hyacinth," Gregory said, "I adore you. You know it. Mother, I adore you as well. And now I am leaving."

"Wait!" Violet called out.

He turned around. He should have known it wouldn't be that easy.

"Would you be my escort?"

"To what?"

"Why, to the wedding, of course."

Gad, *what* was that awful taste in his mouth? "Whose wedding? Lady Lucinda's?"

His mother gazed at him with the most innocent blue eyes. "I shouldn't like to go alone."

He jerked his head in his sister's direction. "Take Hyacinth."

"She'll wish to go with Gareth," Violet replied.

Gareth St. Clair was Hyacinth's husband of nearly four years. Gregory liked him immensely, and the two had developed a rather fine friendship, which was how he knew that Gareth would rather peel his eyelids back (and leave them that way for an indefinite amount of time) than sit through a long, drawn-out, all-day society affair.

Whereas Hyacinth was, as she did not mind putting it, *always* interested in gossip, which meant that she surely would not wish to miss such an important wedding. Someone would drink too much, and someone else would dance too close, and Hyacinth would *hate* to be the last to hear of it.

"Gregory?" his mother prompted.

"I'm not going."

"But—"

"I wasn't invited."

"Surely an oversight. One that will be corrected, I am certain, after your efforts this evening."

"Mother, as much as I would like to wish Lady Lucinda well, I have no desire to attend her or anyone's wedding. They are such sentimental affairs."

Silence.

Never a good sign.

He looked at Hyacinth. She was regarding him with large owlish eyes. "You like weddings," she said.

He grunted. It seemed the best response.

"You do," she said. "At my wedding, you—"

"Hyacinth, you are my sister. It is different."

"Yes, but you also attended Felicity Albansdale's wedding, and I distinctly recall—"

Gregory turned his back on her before she could recount his merriness. "Mother," he said, "thank you for the invitation, but I do not wish to attend Lady Lucinda's wedding."

Violet opened her mouth as if to ask a question, but then she closed it. "Very well," she said.

Gregory was instantly suspicious. It was not like his mother to capitulate so quickly. Further prying into her motives, however, would eliminate any chance of a quick escape.

It was an easy decision.

"I bid you both *adieu*," he said.

"Where you going?" Hyacinth demanded. "And why are you speaking French?"

He turned to his mother. "She is all yours."

"Yes," Violet sighed. "I know."

Hyacinth immediately turned on her. "What does *that* mean?"

"Oh, for heaven's sake, Hyacinth, you—"

Gregory took advantage of the moment and slipped away while their attention was fixed on each other.

The party was growing more crowded, and it occurred to him

that Lucy might very well have arrived while he was speaking with his mother and sister. If so, she wouldn't have made it very far into the ballroom, however, and so he began to make his way toward the receiving line. It was a slow process; he had been out of town for over a month, and everyone seemed to have something to say to him, none of it remotely of interest.

"Best of luck with it," he murmured to Lord Trevelstam, who was trying to interest him in a horse he could not afford. "I am sure you will have no difficulty—"

His voice left him.

He could not speak.

He could not *think*.

Good God, not again.

"Bridgerton?"

Across the room, just by the door. Three gentlemen, an elderly lady, two matrons, and—

Her.

It was her. And he was being pulled, as sure as if there were a rope between them. He needed to reach her side.

"Bridgerton, is something—"

"I beg your pardon," Gregory managed to say, brushing past Trevelstam.

It was her. Except . . .

It was a different her. It wasn't Hermione Watson. It was— He wasn't sure who she was; he could see her only from the back. But there it was—that same splendid and terrible feeling. It made him dizzy. It made him ecstatic. His lungs were hollow. *He* was hollow.

And he wanted her.

It was just as he'd always imagined it—that magical, almost incandescent sense of knowing that his life was complete, that *she* was the one.

Except that he'd done this before. And Hermione Watson *hadn't* been the one.

Dear God, could a man fall insanely, stupidly in love twice?

Hadn't he just told Lucy to be wary and scared, that if she was ever overcome with such a feeling, she should not trust it?

And yet . . .

And yet there she was.

And there *he* was.

And it was happening all over again.

It was just as it had been with Hermione. No, it was worse. His body tingled; he couldn't keep his toes still in his boots. He wanted to jump out of his skin, rush across the room and . . . just . . . just . . .

Just *see* her.

He wanted her to turn. He wanted to see her face. He wanted to know who she was.

He wanted to know *her.*

No.

No, he told himself, trying to force his feet in the other direction. This was madness. He should leave. He should leave right now.

But he couldn't. Even with every rational corner of his soul screaming at him to turn around and walk away, he was rooted to the spot, waiting for her to turn.

Praying for her to turn.

And then she did.

And she was—

Lucy.

He stumbled as if struck.

Lucy?

No. It couldn't be possible. He knew Lucy.

She did not do this to him.

He had seen her dozens of times, kissed her even, and never once felt like this, as if the world might swallow him whole if he did not reach her side and take her hand in his.

There had to be an explanation. He had felt this way before. With Hermione.

But this time—it wasn't quite the same. With Hermione it had been dizzying, new. There had been the thrill of discovery, of conquest. But this was Lucy.

It was Lucy, and—

It all came flooding back. The tilt of her head as she explained why sandwiches ought to be properly sorted. The delightfully peeved look on her face when she had tried to explain to him why he was doing everything wrong in his courtship of Miss Watson.

The way it had felt so right simply to sit on a bench with her in Hyde Park and throw bread at the pigeons.

And the kiss. Dear God, *the kiss.*

He still dreamed about that kiss.

And he wanted her to dream about it, too.

He took a step. Just one—slightly forward and to the side so that he could better see her profile. It was all so familiar now—the tilt of her head, the way her lips moved when she spoke. How could he not have recognized her instantly, even from the back? The memories had been there, tucked away in the recesses of his mind, but he hadn't wanted—no he hadn't allowed himself—to acknowledge his presence.

And then she saw him. Lucy saw him. He saw it first in her eyes, which widened and sparkled, and then in the curve of her lips.

She smiled. For him.

It filled him. To near bursting, it filled him. It was just one smile, but it was all he needed.

He began to walk. He could barely feel his feet, had almost no conscious control over his body. He simply moved, knowing from deep within that he had to reach her.

"Lucy," he said, once he was next to her, forgetting that they were surrounded by strangers, and worse, friends, and he should not presume to use her given name.

But nothing else felt right on his lips.

"Mr. Bridgerton," she said, but her eyes said, *Gregory*.

And he knew.

He loved her.

It was the strangest, most wonderful sensation. It was exhilarating. It was as if the world had suddenly become open to him. Clear. He understood. He understood everything he needed to know, and it was all right there in her eyes.

"Lady Lucinda," he said, bowing deeply over her hand. "May I have this dance?"

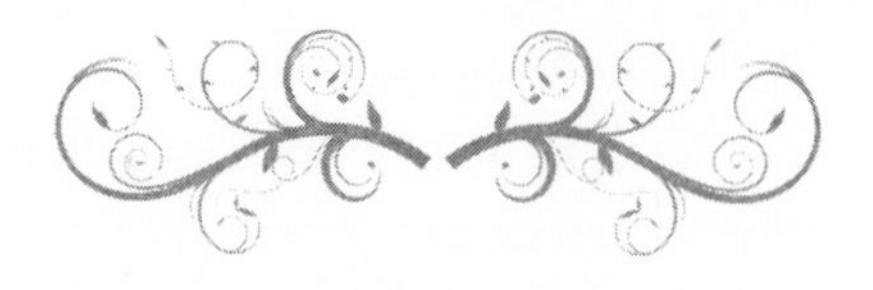

Chapter 17

In which Our Hero's sister moves things along.

It was heaven.

Forget angels, forget St. Peter and glittering harpsichords. Heaven was a dance in the arms of one's true love. And when the one in question had a mere week before marrying someone else entirely, the aforementioned one had to grab heaven tightly, with both hands.

Metaphorically speaking.

Lucy grinned as she bobbed and twirled. Now there was an image. What would people say if she charged forward and grabbed him with both hands?

And never let go.

Most would say she was mad. A few that she was in love. The shrewd would say both.

"What are you thinking about?" Gregory asked. He was looking at her . . . differently.

She turned away, turned back. She felt daring, almost magical. "Wouldn't you care to know?"

He stepped around the lady to his left and returned to his place. "I would," he answered, smiling wolfishly at her.

But she just smiled and shook her head. Right now she wanted to pretend she was someone else. Someone a little less conventional. Someone a great deal more impulsive.

She did not want to be the same old Lucy. Not tonight. She was sick of planning, sick of placating, sick of never doing anything without first thinking through every possibility and consequence.

If I do this, then that will happen, but if I do that, then this, this, and the other thing will happen, which will yield an entirely different result, which could mean that—

It was enough to make a girl dizzy. It was enough to make her feel paralyzed, unable to take the reins of her own life.

But not tonight. Tonight, somehow, through some amazing miracle named the Duchess of Hastings—or perhaps the dowager Lady Bridgerton, Lucy was not quite certain—she was wearing a gown of the most exquisite green silk, attending the most glittering ball she could ever have imagined.

And she was dancing with the man she was quite certain she would love until the end of time.

"You look different," he said.

"I feel different." She touched his hand as they stepped past each other. His fingers gripped hers when they should have just brushed by. She looked up and saw that he was gazing at her. His eyes were warm and intense and he was watching her the same way—

Dear God, he was watching her the way he'd watched Hermione.

Her body began to tingle. She felt it in the tips of her toes, in places she did not dare to contemplate.

They stepped past each other again, but this time he leaned in, perhaps a bit more than he ought, and said, "I feel different as well."

Her head snapped around, but he had already turned so that his back was to her. How was he different? Why? What did he *mean*?

She circled around the gentleman to her left, then moved past Gregory.

"Are you glad you attended this evening?" he murmured.

She nodded, since she had moved too far away to answer without speaking too loudly.

But then they were together again, and he whispered, "So am I."

They moved back to their original places and held still as a different couple began to process. Lucy looked up. At him. At his eyes.

They never moved from her face.

And even in the flickering light of the night—the hundreds of candles and torches that lit the glittering ballroom—she could see the gleam there. The way he was looking at her—it was hot and possessive and proud.

It made her shiver.

It made her doubt her ability to stand.

And then the music was done, and Lucy realized that some things must truly be ingrained because she was curtsying and smiling and nodding at the woman next to her as if her entire life had not been altered in the course of the previous dance.

Gregory took her hand and led her to the side of the ballroom, back to where the chaperones milled about, watching their charges over the rims of their glasses of lemonade. But before they reached their destination, he leaned down and whispered in her ear.

"*I need to speak with you.*"

Her eyes flew to his.

"Privately," he added.

She felt him slow their pace, presumably to allow them more time to speak before she was returned to Aunt Harriet. "What is it?" she asked. "Is something amiss?"

He shook his head. "Not any longer."

And she let herself hope. Just a little, because she could not bear to ponder the heartbreak if she was wrong, but maybe . . . Maybe he loved her. Maybe he wished to marry her. Her wedding was less than a week away, but she had not said her vows.

Maybe there was a chance. Maybe there was a way.

She searched Gregory's face for clues, for answers. But when she pressed him for more information, he just shook his head and whispered, "The library. It is two doors down from the ladies' retiring room. Meet me there in thirty minutes."

"Are you mad?"

He smiled. "Just a little."

"Gregory, I—"

He gazed into her eyes, and it silenced her. The way he was looking at her—

It took her breath away.

"I cannot," she whispered, because no matter what they might feel for each other, she was still engaged to another man. And even if she were not, such behavior could only lead to scandal. "I can't be alone with you. You know that."

"You must."

She tried to shake her head, but she could not make herself move.

"Lucy," he said, "you must."

She nodded. It was probably the biggest mistake she would ever make, but she could not say no.

"Mrs. Abernathy," Gregory said, his voice sounding overly loud as he greeted her aunt Harriet. "I return Lady Lucinda to your care."

Aunt Harriet nodded, even though Lucy suspected she had no idea what Gregory had said to her, and then she turned to Lucy and yelled, "I'm sitting down!"

Gregory chuckled, then said, "I must dance with others."

"Of course," Lucy replied, even though she rather suspected she was not wholly cognizant of the various intricacies involved in scheduling an illicit meeting. "I see someone I know," she lied, and then, to her great relief, she actually did see someone she knew—an acquaintance from school. Not a good friend, but still, a familiar enough face to offer greetings.

But before Lucy could even flex her foot, she heard a female voice call out Gregory's name.

Lucy could not see who it was, but she could see Gregory. He had shut his eyes and looked quite pained.

"Gregory!"

The voice had drawn close, and so Lucy turned to her left to see a young woman who could only be one of Gregory's sisters. The younger one, most probably, else she was remarkably well-preserved.

"This must be Lady Lucinda," the woman said. Her hair, Lucy noted, was the precise shade of Gregory's—a rich, warm chestnut. But her eyes were blue, sharp and acute.

"Lady Lucinda," Gregory said, sounding a bit like a man with a chore, "may I present my sister, Lady St. Clair."

"Hyacinth," she said firmly. "We must dispense with the formalities. I am certain we shall be great friends. Now then, you must tell me all about yourself. And then I wish to hear about Anthony and Kate's party last month. I had wished to go, but we had a previous engagement. I heard it was vastly entertaining."

Startled by the human whirlwind in front of her, Lucy looked to Gregory for advice, but he just shrugged and said, "This would be the one I am fond of torturing."

Hyacinth turned to him. "I beg your pardon."

Gregory bowed. "I must go."

And then Hyacinth Bridgerton St. Clair did the oddest thing.

Her eyes narrowed, and she looked from her brother to Lucy and back again. And then again. And then one more time. And then she said, "You'll need my help."

"Hy—" Gregory began.

"You will," she cut in. "You have plans. Do not try to deny it."

Lucy could not believe that Hyacinth had deduced all that from one bow and an *I must go*. She opened her mouth to ask a question, but all she got out was, "How—" before Gregory cut her off with a warning look.

"I know that you have something up your sleeve," Hyacinth said to Gregory. "Else you would not have gone to such lengths to secure her attendance this evening."

"He was just being kind," Lucy tried to say.

"Don't be silly," Hyacinth said, giving her a reassuring pat on the arm. "He would never do that."

"That's not true," Lucy protested. Gregory might be a bit of a devil, but his heart was good and true, and she would not countenance anyone—even his sister—saying otherwise.

Hyacinth regarded her with a delighted smile. "I like you," she said slowly, as if she were deciding upon it right then and there. "You are wrong, of course, but I like you, anyway." She turned to her brother. "I like her."

"Yes, you've said as much."

"And you need my help."

Lucy watched as brother and sister exchanged a glance that she couldn't begin to understand.

"You will need my help," Hyacinth said softly. "Tonight, and later, too."

Gregory stared at his sister intently, and then he said, in a voice so quiet that Lucy had to lean forward to hear it, "I need to speak with Lady Lucinda. Alone."

Hyacinth smiled. Just a touch. "I can arrange that."

Lucy had a feeling she could do anything.

"When?" Hyacinth asked.

"Whenever is easiest," Gregory replied.

Hyacinth glanced around the room, although for the life of her, Lucy could not imagine what sort of information she was gleaning that could possibly be pertinent to the decision at hand.

"One hour," she announced, with all the precision of a military general. "Gregory, you go off and do whatever it is you do at these affairs. Dance. Fetch lemonade. Be seen with that Whitford girl whose parents have been dangling after you for months.

"You," Hyacinth continued, turning to Lucy with an authoritarian gleam in her eye, "shall remain with me. I shall introduce you to everyone you need to know."

"Who do I need to know?" Lucy asked.

"I'm not sure yet. It really doesn't matter."

Lucy could only stare at her in awe.

"In precisely fifty-five minutes," Hyacinth said, "Lady Lucinda will tear her dress."

"I will?"

"*I* will," Hyacinth replied. "I'm good at that sort of thing."

"You're going to tear her dress?" Gregory asked doubtfully. "Right here in the ballroom?"

"Don't worry over the details," Hyacinth said, waving him off dismissively. "Just go and do your part, and meet her in Daphne's dressing room in one hour."

"In the duchess's bedchamber?" Lucy croaked. She couldn't possibly.

"She's Daphne to us," Hyacinth said. "Now then, everyone, off with you."

Lucy just stared at her and blinked. Wasn't she meant to stay at Hyacinth's side?

"That means him," Hyacinth said.

And then Gregory did the most startling thing. He took Lucy's hand. Right there, in the middle of the ballroom where anyone might see, he took her hand and kissed it. "I leave you in good hands," he told her, stepping back with a polite nod. He gave his sister a look of warning before adding, "As difficult as that might be to believe."

Then he went off, presumably to dote on some poor unsuspecting female who had no idea she was nothing but an innocent pawn in his sister's master plan.

Lucy looked back at Hyacinth, somewhat exhausted by the entire encounter. Hyacinth was beaming at her.

"Well done," she said, although to Lucy it sounded more like she was congratulating herself. "Now then," she continued, "why does my brother need to speak with you? And don't say that you have no idea, because I will not believe you."

Lucy pondered the wisdom of various replies and finally decided upon "I have no idea." It wasn't precisely the truth, but she wasn't about to divulge her most secret hopes and dreams to a woman she'd met only minutes earlier, no matter whose sister she might be.

And it made her feel as if she might have won the point.

"Really?" Hyacinth looked suspicious.

"Really."

Hyacinth was clearly unconvinced. "Well, you're clever, at least. I shall grant you that."

Lucy decided she would not be cowed. "Do you know," she said, "I thought I was the most organized and managing person I knew, but I think you're worse."

Hyacinth laughed. "Oh, I am not at all organized. But I *am* managing. And we shall get on famously." She looped her arm through Lucy's. "Like sisters."

One hour later, Lucy had realized three things about Hyacinth, Lady St. Clair.

First, she knew everyone. And everything about everyone.

Second, she was a wealth of information about her brother. Lucy had not needed to ask a single question, but by the time they left the ballroom, she knew Gregory's favorite color (blue) and food (cheese, any sort), and that as a child he had spoken with a lisp.

Lucy had also learned that one should never make the mistake of underestimating Gregory's younger sister. Not only had Hyacinth torn Lucy's dress, she had carried it out with enough flair and cunning so that four people were aware of the mishap (and the need for repair). And she had done all her damage to the hem, so as to conveniently preserve Lucy's modesty.

It was really quite impressive.

"I've done this before," Hyacinth confided as she guided her out of the ballroom.

Lucy was unsurprised.

"It's a useful talent," Hyacinth added, sounding utterly serious. "Here, this way."

Lucy followed her up a back staircase.

"There are very few excuses available to women who wish to leave a social function," Hyacinth continued, displaying a remarkable talent for sticking to her chosen topic like glue. "It behooves us to master every weapon in our arsenal."

Lucy was beginning to believe that she'd led a very sheltered life.

"Ah, here we are." Hyacinth pushed open a door. She peered in. "He's not here yet. Good. That gives me time."

"For what?"

"To mend your dress. I confess I forgot that detail when I formulated my plan. But I know where Daphne keeps needles."

Lucy watched as Hyacinth strode to a dressing table and opened a drawer.

"Right where I thought they were," Hyacinth said with a triumphant smile. "I do love it when I am right. It makes life so much more convenient, wouldn't you agree?"

Lucy nodded, but her mind was on her own question. And then she asked it—"Why are you helping me?"

Hyacinth looked at her as if she were daft. "You can't go back in with a torn dress. Not after we told everyone we'd gone off to mend it."

"No, not that."

"Oh." Hyacinth held up a needle and regarded it thoughtfully. "This will do. What color thread, do you think?"

"White, and you did not answer my question."

Hyacinth ripped a piece of thread off a spool and slid it through the eye of the needle. "I like you," she said. "And I love my brother."

"You know that I am engaged to be married," Lucy said quietly.

"I know." Hyacinth knelt at Lucy's feet, and with quick, sloppy stitches began to sew.

"In a *week*. Less than a week."

"I know. I was invited."

"Oh." Lucy supposed she ought to have known that. "Erm, do you plan to attend?"

Hyacinth looked up. "Do you?"

Lucy's lips parted. Until that moment, the idea of not marrying Haselby was a wispy, far-fetched thing, more of an *oh-how-I-wish-*

I-did-not-have-to-marry-him sort of feeling. But now, with Hyacinth watching her so carefully, it began to feel a bit more firm. Still impossible, of course, or at least . . .

Well, maybe . . .

Maybe not quite impossible. Maybe only mostly impossible.

"The papers are signed," Lucy said.

Hyacinth turned back to her sewing. "Are they?"

"My uncle *chose* him," Lucy said, wondering just who she was trying to convince. "It has been arranged for ages."

"Mmmm."

Mmmm? What the devil did *that* mean?

"And he hasn't . . . Your brother hasn't . . ." Lucy fought for words, mortified that she was unburdening herself to a near stranger, to Gregory's own sister, for heaven's sake. But Hyacinth wasn't *saying* anything; she was just sitting there with her eyes focused on the needle looping in and out of Lucy's hem. And if Hyacinth didn't say anything, then Lucy had to. Because— Because—

Well, because she did.

"He has made me no promises," Lucy said, her voice nearly shaking with it. "He stated no intentions."

At that, Hyacinth did look up. She glanced around the room, as if to say, *Look at us, mending your gown in the bedchamber of the Duchess of Hastings*. And she murmured, "Hasn't he?"

Lucy closed her eyes in agony. She was not like Hyacinth St. Clair. One needed only a quarter of an hour in her company to know that she would dare anything, take any chance to secure her own happiness. She would defy convention, stand up to the harshest of critics, and emerge entirely intact, in body and spirit.

Lucy was not so hardy. She wasn't ruled by passions. Her muse had always been good sense. Pragmatism.

Hadn't she been the one to tell Hermione that she needed to marry a man of whom her parents would approve?

Hadn't she told Gregory that she didn't want a violent, overwhelming love? That she just wasn't the sort?

She wasn't that kind of person. She wasn't. When her governess had made line drawings for her to fill, she had always colored between the lines.

"I don't think I can do it," Lucy whispered.

Hyacinth held her gaze for an agonizingly long moment before turning back to her sewing. "I misjudged you," she said softly.

It hit Lucy like a slap in the face.

"Wh . . . wh . . ."

What did you say?

But Lucy's lips would not form the words. She did not wish to hear the answer. And Hyacinth was back to her brisk self, looking up with an irritated expression as she said, "Don't fidget so much."

"Sorry," Lucy mumbled. And she thought—*I've said it again. I am so predictable, so utterly conventional and unimaginative.*

"You're still moving."

"Oh." Good God, could she do nothing right this evening? "Sorry."

Hyacinth jabbed her with the needle. "You're *still* moving."

"I am not!" Lucy almost yelled.

Hyacinth smiled to herself. "That's better."

Lucy looked down and scowled. "Am I bleeding?"

"If you are," Hyacinth said, rising to her feet, "it's nobody's fault but your own."

"I beg your pardon."

But Hyacinth was already standing, a satisfied smile on her face.

"There," she announced, motioning to her handiwork. "Certainly not as good as new, but it will pass any inspection this evening."

Lucy knelt to inspect her hem. Hyacinth had been generous in her self-praise. The stitching was a mess.

"I've never been gifted with a needle," Hyacinth said with an unconcerned shrug.

Lucy stood, fighting the impulse to rip the stitches out and fix them herself. "You might have told me," she muttered.

Hyacinth's lips curved into a slow, sly smile. "My, my," she said, "you've turned prickly all of a sudden."

And then Lucy shocked herself by saying, "*You've* been hurtful."

"Possibly," Hyacinth replied, sounding as if she didn't much care one way or the other. She glanced toward the door with a quizzical expression. "He ought to have been here by now."

Lucy's heart thumped strangely in her chest. "You still plan to help me?" she whispered.

Hyacinth turned back. "I am hoping," she replied, her eyes meeting Lucy's with cool assessment, "that you have misjudged yourself."

Gregory was ten minutes late to the assignation. It couldn't be helped; once he had danced with one young lady, it had become apparent that he was required to repeat the favor for a half-dozen others. And although it was difficult to keep his attention on the conversations he was meant to be conducting, he did not mind the delay. It meant that Lucy and Hyacinth were well gone before he slipped out the door. He intended to find some way to make Lucy his wife, but there was no need to go looking for scandal.

He made his way to his sister's bedchamber; he had spent countless hours at Hastings House and knew his way around. When he reached his destination, he entered without knocking, the well-oiled hinges of the door giving way without a sound.

"Gregory."

Hyacinth's voice came first. She was standing next to Lucy, who looked . . .

Stricken.

What had Hyacinth done to her?

"Lucy?" he asked, rushing forward. "Is something wrong?"

Lucy shook her head. "It is of no account."

He turned to his sister with accusing eyes.

Hyacinth shrugged. "I will be in the next room."

"Listening at the door?"

"I shall wait at Daphne's escritoire," she said. "It is halfway across the room, and before you make an objection, I cannot go farther. If someone comes you will need me to rush in to make everything respectable."

Her point was a valid one, loath as Gregory was to admit it, so he gave her a curt nod and watched her leave the room, waiting for the click of the door latch before speaking.

"Did she say something unkind?" he asked Lucy. "She can be disgracefully tactless, but her heart is usually in the right place."

Lucy shook her head. "No," she said softly. "I think she might have said exactly the right thing."

"Lucy?" He stared at her in question.

Her eyes, which had seemed so cloudy, appeared to focus. "What was it you needed to tell me?" she asked.

"Lucy," he said, wondering how best to approach this. He'd been rehearsing speeches in his mind the entire time he'd been dancing downstairs, but now that he was here, he didn't know what to say.

Or rather, he did. But he didn't know the order, and he didn't know the tone. Did he tell her he loved her? Bare his heart to a woman who intended to marry another? Or did he opt for the safer route and explain why she could not marry Haselby?

A month ago, the choice would have been obvious. He was a romantic, fond of grand gestures. He would have declared his love, certain of a happy reception. He would have taken her hand. Dropped to his knees.

He would have kissed her.

But now . . .

He was no longer quite so certain. He trusted Lucy, but he did not trust fate.

"You can't marry Haselby," he said.

Her eyes widened. "What do you mean?"

"You can't marry him," he replied, avoiding the question. "It will be a disaster. It will . . . You must trust me. You must not marry him."

She shook her head. "Why are you telling me this?"

Because I want you for myself.

"Because . . . because . . ." He fought for words. "Because you have become my friend. And I wish for your happiness. He will not be a good husband to you, Lucy."

"Why not?" Her voice was low, hollow, and heartbreakingly unlike her.

"He . . ." Dear God, how did he say it? Would she even understand what he meant?

"He doesn't . . ." He swallowed. There had to be a gentle way to say it. "He doesn't . . . Some people . . ."

He looked at her. Her lower lip was quivering.

"He prefers men," he said, getting the words out as quickly as he was able. "To women. Some men are like that."

And then he waited. For the longest moment she made no reaction, just stood there like a tragic statue. Every now and then she would blink, but beyond that, nothing. And then finally—

"Why?"

Why? He didn't understand. "Why is he—"

"No," she said forcefully. "Why did you tell me? Why would you say it?"

"I told you—"

"No, you didn't do it to be kind. Why did you tell me? Was it just to be cruel? To make me feel the way you feel, because Hermione married my brother and not you?"

"No!" The word burst out of him, and he was holding her, his hands wrapped around her upper arms. "No, Lucy," he said again. "I would never. I want you to be happy. I want . . ."

Her. He wanted her, and he didn't know how to say it. Not then, not when she was looking at him as if he'd broken her heart.

"I could have been happy with him," she whispered.

"No. No, you couldn't. You don't understand, he—"

"Yes, I could," she cried out. "Maybe I wouldn't have loved him, but I could have been happy. It was what I expected. Do you understand, it was what I was prepared for. And you . . . you . . ." She wrenched herself away, turning until he could no longer see her face. "You ruined it."

"How?"

She raised her eyes to his, and the look in them was so stark, so deep, he could not breathe. And she said, "Because you made me want you instead."

His heart slammed in his chest. "Lucy," he said, because he could not say anything else. "Lucy."

"I don't know what to do," she confessed.

"Kiss me." He took her face in his hands. "Just kiss me."

This time, when he kissed her, it was different. She was the same woman in his arms, but *he* was not the same man. His need for her was deeper, more elemental.

He loved her.

He kissed her with everything he had, every breath, every last beat of his heart. His lips found her cheek, her brow, her ears, and all the while, he whispered her name like a prayer—

Lucy Lucy Lucy.

He wanted her. He needed her.

She was like air.

Food.

Water.

His mouth moved to her neck, then down to the lacy edge of her bodice. Her skin burned hot beneath him, and as his fingers slid the gown from one of her shoulders, she gasped—

But she did not stop him.

"Gregory," she whispered, her fingers digging into his hair as his lips moved along her collarbone. "Gregory, oh my G— Gregory."

His hand moved reverently over the curve of her shoulder. Her skin glowed pale and milky smooth in the candlelight, and he was struck by an intense sense of possession. Of pride.

No other man had seen her thus, and he prayed that no other man ever would.

"You can't marry him, Lucy," he whispered urgently, his words hot against her skin.

"Gregory, don't," she moaned.

"You can't." And then, because he knew he could not allow this to go any further, he straightened, pressing one last kiss against her lips before setting her back, forcing her to look him in the eye.

"You cannot marry him," he said again.

"Gregory, what can I—"

He gripped her arms. Hard. And he said it.

"*I love you.*"

Her lips parted. She could not speak.

"I love you," he said again.

Lucy had suspected—she'd hoped—but she hadn't really allowed herself to believe. And so, when she finally found words of her own, they were: "You do?"

He smiled, and then he laughed, and then he rested his forehead on hers. "With all of my heart," he vowed. "I only just realized it. I'm a fool. A blind man. A—"

"No," she cut in, shaking her head. "Do not berate yourself. No one ever notices me straightaway when Hermione is about."

His fingers gripped her all the tighter. "She does not hold a candle to you."

A warm feeling began to spread through her bones. Not desire, not passion, just pure, unadulterated happiness. "You really mean it," she whispered.

"Enough to move heaven and earth to make sure you do not go through with your wedding to Haselby."

She blanched.

"Lucy?"

No. She could do it. She would do it. It was almost funny, really. She had spent three years telling Hermione that she had to be practical, follow the rules. She'd scoffed when Hermione had gone on about love and passion and hearing music. And now . . .

She took a deep, fortifying breath. And now she was going to break her engagement.

That had been arranged for years.

To the son of an earl.

Five days before the wedding.

Dear God, the scandal.

She stepped back, lifting her chin so that she could see Gregory's face. His eyes were watching her with all the love she herself felt.

"I love you," she whispered, because she had not yet said it. "I love you, too."

For once she was going to stop thinking about everyone else. She wasn't going to take what she was given and make the best of it. She was going to reach for her own happiness, make her own destiny.

She was not going to do what was expected.

She was going to do what *she* wanted.

It was time.

She squeezed Gregory's hands. And she smiled. It was no tentative thing, but wide and confident, full of her hopes, full of her dreams—and the knowledge that she would achieve them all.

It would be difficult. It would be frightening.

But it would be worth it.

"I will speak with my uncle," she said, the words firm and sure. "Tomorrow."

Gregory pulled her against him for one last kiss, quick and passionate with promise. "Shall I accompany you?" he asked. "Call upon him so that I might reassure him of my intentions?"

The new Lucy, the daring and bold Lucy, asked, "And what *are* your intentions?"

Gregory's eyes widened with surprise, then approval, and then his hands took hers.

She felt what he was doing before she realized it by sight. His hands seemed to slide along hers as he descended . . .

Until he was on one knee, looking up at her as if there could be no more beautiful woman in all creation.

Her hand flew to her mouth, and she realized she was shaking.

"Lady Lucinda Abernathy," he said, his voice fervent and sure, "will you do me the very great honor of becoming my wife?"

She tried to speak. She tried to nod.

"Marry me, Lucy," he said. "Marry me."

And this time she did. "Yes." And then, "Yes! Oh, yes!"

"I will make you happy," he said, standing to embrace her. "I promise you."

"There is no need to promise." She shook her head, blinking back the tears. "There is no way you could not."

He opened his mouth, presumably to say more, but he was cut off by a knock at the door, soft but quick.

Hyacinth.

"Go," Gregory said. "Let Hyacinth take you back to the ballroom. I will follow later."

Lucy nodded, tugging at her gown until everything was back in its proper place. "My hair," she whispered, her eyes flying to his.

"It's lovely," he assured her. "You look perfect."

She hurried to the door. "Are you certain?"

I love you, he mouthed. And his eyes said the same.

Lucy pulled open the door, and Hyacinth rushed in. "Good heavens, the two of you are slow," she said. "We need to be getting back. Now."

She strode to the door to the corridor, then stopped, looking first at Lucy, then at her brother. Her gaze settled on Lucy, and she lifted one brow in question.

Lucy held herself tall. "You did not misjudge me," she said quietly.

Hyacinth's eyes widened, and then her lips curved. "Good."

And it was, Lucy realized. It was very good, indeed.

Chapter 18

In which Our Heroine makes a terrible discovery.

She could do this.

She could.

She needed only to knock.

And yet there she stood, outside her uncle's study door, her fingers curled into a fist, as if *ready* to knock on the door.

But not quite.

How long had she stood like this? Five minutes? Ten? Either way, it was enough to brand her a ridiculous ninny. A coward.

How did this happen? *Why* did it happen? At school she had been known as capable and pragmatic. She was the girl who knew how to get things done. She was not shy. She was not fearful.

But when it came to Uncle Robert . . .

She sighed. She had always been like this with her uncle. He was so stern, so taciturn.

So unlike her own laughing father had been.

She'd felt like a butterfly when she left for school, but whenever she returned, it was as if she had been stuffed right back in her tight little cocoon. She became drab, quiet.

Lonely.

But not this time. She took a breath, squared her shoulders. This time she would say what she needed to say. She would make herself heard.

She lifted her hand. She knocked.

She waited.

"Enter."

"Uncle Robert," she said, letting herself into his study. It felt dark, even with the late afternoon sunlight slanting in through the window.

"Lucinda," he said, glancing briefly up before returning to his papers. "What is it?"

"I need to speak with you."

He made a notation, scowled at his handiwork, then blotted his ink. "Speak."

Lucy cleared her throat. This would be a great deal easier if he would just *look up* at her. She hated speaking to the top of his head, hated it.

"Uncle Robert," she said again.

He grunted a response but kept on writing.

"Uncle Robert."

She saw his movements slow, and then, finally, he looked up. "What is it, Lucinda?" he asked, clearly annoyed.

"We need to have a conversation about Lord Haselby." There. She had said it.

"Is there a problem?" he asked slowly.

"No," she heard herself say, even though that wasn't at all the truth. But it was what she always said if someone asked if there was a problem. It was one of those things that just came out, like *Excuse me*, or *I beg your pardon.*

It was what she'd been trained to say.

Is there a problem?

No, of course not. No, don't mind my wishes. No, please don't worry yourself on my account.

"Lucinda?" Her uncle's voice was sharp, almost jarring.

"No," she said again, louder this time, as if the volume would give her courage. "I mean yes, there is a problem. And I need to speak with you about it."

Her uncle gave her a bored look.

"Uncle Robert," she began, feeling as if she were tiptoeing through a field of hedgehogs, "did you know . . ." She bit her lip, glancing everywhere but at his face. "That is to say, were you aware . . ."

"Out with it," he snapped.

"Lord Haselby," Lucy said quickly, desperate just to get it over with. "He doesn't like women."

For a moment Uncle Robert did nothing but stare. And then he . . .

Laughed.

He *laughed.*

"Uncle Robert?" Lucy's heart began to beat far too quickly. "Did you know this?"

"Of course I knew it," he snapped. "Why do you think his father is so eager to have you? He knows you won't talk."

Why wouldn't she talk?

"You should be thanking me," Uncle Robert said harshly, cutting into her thoughts. "Half the men of the *ton* are brutes. I'm giving you to the only one who won't bother you."

"But—"

"Do you have any idea how many women would love to take your place?"

"That is not the point, Uncle Robert."

His eyes turned to ice. "I beg your pardon."

Lucy stood perfectly still, suddenly realizing that this was it. This was her moment. She had never countermanded him before, and she probably never would again.

She swallowed. And then she said it. "I do not wish to marry Lord Haselby."

Silence. But his eyes . . .

His eyes were thunderous.

Lucy met his stare with cool detachment. She could feel a strange new strength growing inside of her. She would not back down. Not now, not when the rest of her life was at stake.

Her uncle's lips pursed and twisted, even as the rest of his face seemed to be made of stone. Finally, just when Lucy was certain that the silence would break her, he asked, his voice clipped, "May I ask why?"

"I—I want children," Lucy said, latching on to the first excuse she could think of.

"Oh, you'll have them," he said.

He smiled then, and her blood turned to ice.

"Uncle Robert?" she whispered.

"He may not like women, but he will be able to do the job often enough to sire a brat off you. And if he can't . . ." He shrugged.

"What?" Lucy felt panic rising in her chest. "What do you mean?"

"Davenport will take care of it."

"His father?" Lucy gasped.

"Either way, it is a direct male heir, and that is all that is important."

Lucy's hand flew to her mouth. "Oh, I can't. I can't." She thought of Lord Davenport, with his horrible breath and jiggly jowls. And his cruel, cruel eyes. He would not be kind. She didn't know how she knew, but he wouldn't be kind.

Her uncle leaned forward in his seat, his eyes narrowing menacingly. "We all have our positions in life, Lucinda, and yours is to be a nobleman's wife. Your duty is to provide an heir. And you will do it, in whatever fashion Davenport deems necessary."

Lucy swallowed. She had always done as she was told. She had always accepted that the world worked in certain ways. Dreams could be adjusted; the social order could not.

Take what you are given, and make the best of things.

It was what she had always said. It was what she had always done.

But not this time.

She looked up, directly into her uncle's eyes. "I won't do it," she said, and her voice did not waver. "I won't marry him."

"What . . . did . . . you . . . say?" Each word came out like its own little sentence, pointy and cold.

Lucy swallowed. "I said—"

"I know what you said!" he roared, slamming his hands on his desk as he rose to his feet. "How dare you question me? I have raised you, fed you, given you every bloody thing you need. I have looked after and protected this family for ten years, when none of it—*none of it*—will come to me."

"Uncle Robert," she tried to say. But she could barely hear her own voice. Every word he had said was true. He did not own this house. He did not own the Abbey or any of the other Fennsworth holdings. He had nothing other than what Richard might choose to give him once he fully assumed his position as earl.

"I am your guardian," her uncle said, his voice so low it shook. "Do you understand? You will marry Haselby, and we will never speak of this again."

Lucy stared at her uncle in horror. He had been her guardian for ten years, and in all that time, she had never seen him lose his temper. His displeasure was always served cold.

"It's that Bridgerton idiot, isn't it?" he bit off, angrily swiping at some books on his desk. They tumbled to the floor with a loud thud.

Lucy jumped back.

"Tell me!"

She said nothing, watching her uncle warily as he advanced upon her.

"Tell me!" he roared.

"Yes," she said quickly, taking another step back. "How did you— How did you know?"

"Do you think I'm an idiot? His mother and his sister *both* beg the favor of your company on the same day?" He swore under his breath. "They were obviously plotting to steal you away."

"But you let me go to the ball."

"Because his sister is a duchess, you little fool! Even Davenport agreed that you had to attend."

"But—"

"Christ above," Uncle Robert swore, shocking Lucy into silence. "I cannot believe your stupidity. Has he even promised marriage? Are you really prepared to toss over the heir to an earldom for the *possibility* of a viscount's fourth son?"

"Yes," Lucy whispered.

Her uncle must have seen the determination on her face, because he paled. "What have you done?" he demanded. "Have you let him touch you?"

Lucy thought of their kiss, and she blushed.

"You stupid cow," he hissed. "Well, lucky for you Haselby won't know how to tell a virgin from a whore."

"Uncle Robert!" Lucy shook with horror. She had not grown so bold that she could brazenly allow him to think her impure. "I would never— I didn't— How could you think it of me?"

"Because you are acting like a bloody idiot," he snapped. "As of this minute, you will not leave this house until you leave for your wedding. If I have to post guards at your bedchamber door, I will."

"No!" Lucy cried out. "How could you do this to me? What does it matter? We don't need their money. We don't need their connections. Why can't I marry for love?"

At first her uncle did not react. He stood as if frozen, the only movement a vein pounding in his temple. And then, just when Lucy thought she might begin to breathe again, he cursed violently and lunged toward her, pinning her against the wall.

"Uncle Robert!" she gasped. His hand was on her chin, forcing her head into an unnatural position. She tried to swallow, but it was almost impossible with her neck arched so tightly. "Don't," she managed to get out, but it was barely a whimper. "Please . . . Stop."

But his grip only tightened, and his forearm pressed against her collarbone, the bones of his wrist digging painfully into her skin.

"You will marry Lord Haselby," he hissed. "You'll marry him, and I will tell you why."

Lucy said nothing, just stared at him with frantic eyes.

"You, my dear Lucinda, are the final payment of a long-standing debt to Lord Davenport."

"What do you mean?" she whispered.

"Blackmail," Uncle Robert said in a grim voice. "We have been paying Davenport for years."

"But why?" Lucy asked. What could they have possibly done to warrant blackmail?

Her uncle's lip curled mockingly. "Your father, the beloved eighth Earl of Fennsworth, was a traitor."

Lucy gasped, and it felt as if her throat were tightening, tying itself into a knot. It couldn't be true. She'd thought perhaps an extramarital affair. Maybe an earl who wasn't really an Abernathy. But treason? Dear God . . . *no.*

"Uncle Robert," she said, trying to reason with him. "There must be a mistake. A misunderstanding. My father . . . He was not a traitor."

"Oh, I assure you he was, and Davenport knows it."

Lucy thought of her father. She could still see him in her mind—tall, handsome, with laughing blue eyes. He had spent money far too freely; even as a small child she had known that. But he was not a traitor. He could not have been. He had a gentleman's honor. She remembered that. It was in the way he'd stood, the things he'd taught her.

"You are lying," she said, the words burning in her throat. "Or misinformed."

"There is proof," her uncle said, abruptly releasing her and striding across the room to his decanter of brandy. He poured a glass and took a long gulp. "And Davenport has it."

"How?"

"I don't know how," he snapped. "I only know that he does. I have seen it."

Lucy swallowed and hugged her arms to her chest, still trying to absorb what he was telling her. "What sort of proof?"

"Letters," he said grimly. "Written in your father's hand."

"They could be forged."

"They have his seal!" he thundered, slamming his glass down.

Lucy's eyes widened as she watched the brandy slosh over the side of the glass and off the edge of the desk.

"Do you think I would accept something like this without verifying it myself?" her uncle demanded. "There was information—details—things only your father could have known. Do you think I would have paid Davenport's blackmail all these years if there was a chance it was false?"

Lucy shook her head. Her uncle was many things, but he was not a fool.

"He came to me six months after your father died. I have been paying him ever since."

"But why me?" she asked.

Her uncle chuckled bitterly. "Because you will be the perfect upstanding, obedient bride. You will make up for Haselby's deficiencies. Davenport had to get the boy married to someone, and he needed a family that would not talk." He gave her a level stare. "Which we will not. We cannot. And he knows it."

She nodded her head in agreement. She would never speak of such things, whether she was Haselby's wife or not. She *liked* Haselby. She did not wish to make life difficult for him. But neither did she wish to be his wife.

"If you do not marry him," her uncle said slowly, "the entire Abernathy family will be ruined. Do you understand?"

Lucy stood frozen.

"We are not speaking of a childhood transgression, a black sheep in the family tree. Your father committed high treason. He sold state secrets to the French, passed them off to agents posing as smugglers on the coast."

"But why?" Lucy whispered. "We didn't need the money."

"How do you think we *got* the money?" her uncle returned caustically. "And your father—" He swore under his breath. "He always had a taste for danger. He probably did it for the thrill of it. Isn't that a joke upon us all? The very earldom is in danger, and all because your father wanted a spot of adventure."

"Father wasn't like that," Lucy said, but inside she wasn't so sure. She had been just eight when he had been killed by a footpad in London. She had been told that he had come to the defense of a lady, but what if that, too, was a lie? Had he been killed because of his traitorous actions? He was her father, but how much did she truly know of him?

But Uncle Robert didn't appear to have heard her comment. "If you do not marry Haselby," he said, his words low and precise, "Lord Davenport will reveal the truth about your father, and you will bring shame upon the entire house of Fennsworth."

Lucy shook her head. Surely there was another way. This couldn't rest all upon her shoulders.

"You think not?" Uncle Robert laughed scornfully. "Who do you think will suffer, Lucinda? You? Well, yes, I suppose you will suffer, but we can always pack you off to some school and let you moulder away as an instructor. You'd probably enjoy it."

He took a few steps in her direction, his eyes never leaving her face. "But do think of your brother," he said. "How will he fare as the son of a known traitor? The king will almost certainly strip him of his title. And most of his fortune as well."

"No," Lucy said. *No*. She didn't want to believe it. Richard had done nothing wrong. Surely he couldn't be blamed for his father's sins.

She sank into a chair, desperately trying to sort through her thoughts and emotions.

Treason. How could her father have done such a thing? It went against everything she'd been brought up to believe in. Hadn't her father loved England? Hadn't he told her that the Abernathys had a sacred duty to all Britain?

Or had that been Uncle Robert? Lucy shut her eyes tightly, trying to remember. Someone had said that to her. She was sure of it. She could remember where she'd stood, in front of the portrait of the first earl. She remembered the smell of the air, and the exact words, and—blast it all, she remembered everything save the person who'd spoken them.

She opened her eyes and looked at her uncle. It had probably been he. It sounded like something he would say. He did not choose to speak with her very often, but when he did, duty was always a popular topic.

"Oh, Father," she whispered. How could he have done this? To sell secrets to Napoleon—he'd jeopardized the lives of thousands of British soldiers. Or even—

Her stomach churned. Dear God, he may have been responsible for their deaths. Who knew what he had revealed to the enemy, how many lives had been lost because of his actions?

"It is up to you, Lucinda," her uncle said. "It is the only way to end it."

She shook her head, uncomprehending. "What do you mean?"

"Once you are a Davenport, there can be no more blackmail. Any shame they bring upon us would fall on their shoulders as well." He walked to the window, leaning heavily on the sill as he looked out. "After ten years, I will finally—*We* will finally be free."

Lucy said nothing. There was nothing to say. Uncle Robert peered at her over his shoulder, then turned and walked toward her, watching her closely the entire way. "I see you finally grasp the gravity of the situation," he said.

She looked at him with haunted eyes. There was no compassion in his face, no sympathy or affection. Just a cold mask of duty. He had done what was expected of him, and she would have to do the same.

She thought of Gregory, of his face when he had asked her to marry him. He loved her. She did not know what manner of miracle had brought it about, but he loved her.

And she loved him.

God above, it was almost funny. She, who had always mocked romantic love, had fallen. Completely and hopelessly, she'd fallen in love—enough to throw aside everything she'd thought she believed in. For Gregory she was willing to step into scandal and chaos. For Gregory she would brave the gossip and the whispers and the innuendo.

She, who went mad when her shoes were out of order in her wardrobe, was prepared to jilt the son of an earl four days before the wedding! If that wasn't love, she did not know what was.

Except now it was over. Her hopes, her dreams, the risks she longed to take—they were all over.

She had no choice. If she defied Lord Davenport, her family would be ruined. She thought of Richard and Hermione—so happy, so in love. How could she consign them to a life of shame and poverty?

If she married Haselby her life would not be what she wanted for herself, but she would not suffer. Haselby was reasonable. He was kind. If she appealed to him, surely he would protect her from his father. And her life would be . . .

Comfortable.

Routine.

Far better than Richard and Hermione would fare if her father's shame was made public. Her sacrifice was nothing compared to what her family would be forced to endure if she refused.

Hadn't she once wanted nothing more than comfort and routine? Couldn't she learn to want this again?

"I will marry him," she said, sightlessly gazing at the window. It was raining. When had it begun to rain?

"Good."

Lucy sat in her chair, utterly still. She could feel the energy draining from her body, sliding through her limbs, seeping out her fingers and toes. Lord, she was tired. Weary. And she kept thinking that she wanted to cry.

But she had no tears. Even after she'd risen and walked slowly back to her room—she had no tears.

The next day, when the butler asked her if she was at home for Mr. Bridgerton, and she shook her head—she had no tears.

And the day after that, when she was forced to repeat the same gesture—she had no tears.

But the day after that, after spending twenty-hours holding his calling card, gently sliding her finger over his name, of tracing each letter—*The Hon. Gregory Bridgerton*—she began to feel them, pricking behind her eyes.

Then she caught sight of him standing on the pavement, looking up at the façade of Fennsworth House.

And he saw her. She knew he did; his eyes widened and his body tensed, and she could feel it, every ounce of his bewilderment and anger.

She let the curtain drop. Quickly. And she stood there, trembling, shaking, and yet still unable to move. Her feet were frozen to the floor, and she began to feel it again—that awful rushing panic in her belly.

It was wrong. It was all so wrong, and yet she knew she was doing what had to be done.

She stood there. At the window, staring at the ripples in the curtain. She stood there as her limbs grew tense and tight, and she stood there as she forced herself to breathe. She stood there as her heart began to squeeze, harder and harder, and she stood there as it all slowly began to subside.

Then, somehow, she made her way to the bed and lay down.

And then, finally, she found her tears.

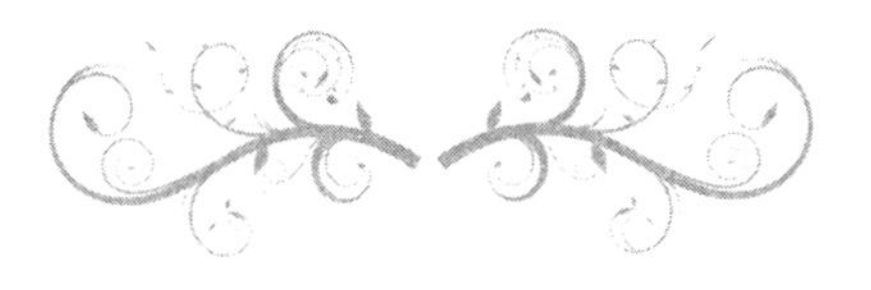

Chapter 19

In which Our Hero takes matters—
and Our Heroine—into his own hands.

By Friday Gregory was desperate.

Thrice he'd called upon Lucy at Fennsworth House. Thrice he'd been turned away.

He was running out of time.

They were running out of time.

What the *hell* was going on? Even if Lucy's uncle had denied her request to stop the wedding—and he could not have been pleased; she was, after all, attempting to jilt a future earl—surely Lucy would have attempted to contact him.

She loved him.

He knew it the way he knew his own voice, his own heart. He knew it the way he knew the earth was round and her eyes were blue and that two plus two would always *always* be four.

Lucy loved him. She did not lie. She could not lie.

She *would* not lie. Not about something like this.

Which meant that something was wrong. There could be no other explanation.

He had looked for her in the park, waiting for hours at the bench where she liked to feed pigeons, but she had not appeared. He had watched her door, hoping he might intercept her on her way to carry out errands, but she had not ventured outside.

And then, after the third time he had been refused entry, he saw her. Just a glimpse through the window; she'd let the curtains fall quickly. But it had been enough. He'd not been able to see her face—not well enough to gauge her expression. But there had been something in the way she moved, in the hurried, almost frantic release of the curtains.

Something was wrong.

Was she being held against her will? Had she been drugged? Gregory's mind raced with the possibilities, each more dire than the last.

And now it was Friday night. Her wedding was in less than twelve hours. And there was not a whisper—not a peep—of gossip. If there were even a hint that the Haselby-Abernathy wedding might not take place as planned, Gregory would have heard about it. If nothing else, Hyacinth would have said something. Hyacinth knew everything, usually before the subjects of the rumors themselves.

Gregory stood in the shadows across the street from Fennsworth House and leaned against the trunk of a tree, staring, just staring. Was that her window? The one through which he'd seen her earlier that day? There was no candlelight peeking through, but the draperies were probably heavy and thick. Or perhaps she'd gone to bed. It was late.

And she had a wedding in the morning.

Good God.

He could not let her marry Lord Haselby. He could not. If there was one thing he knew in his heart, it was that he and Lucinda Abernathy were meant to be husband and wife. Hers was the face he was supposed to gaze upon over eggs and bacon and kippers and cod and toast every morning.

A snort of laughter pressed through his nose, but it was that nervous, desperate kind of laughter, the sound one made when the only alternative was to cry. Lucy had to marry him, if only so that they could eat masses and masses of food together every morning.

He looked at her window.

What he *hoped* was her window. With his luck he was mooning over the servants' washroom.

How long he stood there he did not know. For the first time in his memory, he felt powerless, and at least this—watching a bloody window—was something he could control.

He thought about his life. Charmed, for sure. Plenty of money, lovely family, scads of friends. He had his health, he had his sanity, and until the fiasco with Hermione Watson, an unshakable belief in his own sense of judgment. He might not be the most disciplined of men, and perhaps he should have paid more attention to all those things Anthony liked to pester him about, but he knew what was right, and he knew what was wrong, and he'd known—he had absolutely *known*—that his life would play out on a happy and contented canvas.

He was simply that sort of person.

He wasn't melancholy. He wasn't given to fits of temper.

And he'd never had to work very hard.

He looked up at the window, thoughtfully.

He'd grown complacent. So sure of his own happy ending that he hadn't believed—he *still* couldn't quite believe—that he might not get what he wanted.

He had proposed. She had accepted. True, she had been promised to Haselby, and still was, for that matter.

But wasn't true love supposed to triumph? Hadn't it done so for all his brothers and sisters? Why the hell was he so unlucky?

He thought about his mother, remembered the look on her face when she had so skillfully dissected his character. She had got most everything right, he realized.

But only most.

It was true that he had never had to work very hard at anything. But that was only part of the story. He was not indolent. He would work his fingers to the very bone if only . . .

If only he had a reason.

He stared at the window.

He had a reason now.

He'd been waiting, he realized. Waiting for Lucy to convince her uncle to release her from her engagement. Waiting for the puzzle pieces that made up his life to fall into position so that he could fit the last one in its place with a triumphant "Aha!"

Waiting.

Waiting for love. Waiting for a calling.

Waiting for clarity, for that moment when he would know exactly how to proceed.

It was time to stop waiting, time to forget about fate and destiny.

It was time to act. To work.

Hard.

No one was going to hand him that second-to-last piece of the puzzle; he had to find it for himself.

He needed to see Lucy. And it had to be now, since it appeared he was forbidden to call upon her in a more conventional manner.

He crossed the street, then slipped around the corner to the back of the house. The ground floor windows were tightly shut, and all was dark. Higher on the façade, a few curtains fluttered in the breeze, but there was no way Gregory could scale the building without killing himself.

He took stock of his surroundings. To the left, the street. To the right, the alley and mews. And in front of him . . .

The servants' entrance.

He regarded it thoughtfully. Well, why not?

He stepped forward and placed his hand on the knob.

It turned.

Gregory almost laughed with delight. At the very least, he went back to believing—well, perhaps just a little—about fate and destiny and all that rot. Surely this was not a usual occurrence. A servant must have sneaked out, perhaps to make his own assignation. If the door was unlocked, then clearly Gregory was meant to go inside.

Or he was mad in the head.

He decided to believe in fate.

Gregory shut the door quietly behind him, then gave his eyes a minute to become accustomed to the dark. He appeared to be in a large pantry, with the kitchen off to the right. There was a decent chance that some of the lower servants slept nearby, so he removed his boots, carrying them in one hand as he ventured deeper into the house.

His stockinged feet were silent as he crept up the back stairs, making his way to the second floor—the one he thought housed Lucy's bedchamber. He paused on the landing, stopping for a brief moment of sanity before stepping out into the hall.

What was he thinking? He hadn't the slightest clue what might happen if he were caught here. Was he breaking a law? Probably. He couldn't imagine how he might not be. And while his position as brother to a viscount would keep him from the gallows, it would not wipe his slate clean when the home he'd chosen to invade belonged to an earl.

But he had to see Lucy. He was done with waiting.

He took a moment on the landing to orient himself, then walked toward the front of the house. There were two doors at the end. He paused, painting a picture of the house's façade in his mind, then reached for the one on the left. If Lucy had indeed been in her own room when he'd seen her, then this was the correct door. If not . . .

Well, then, he hadn't a clue. Not a clue. And here he was, prowling in the Earl of Fennsworth's house after midnight.

Good God.

He turned the knob slowly, letting out a relieved breath when it made no clicks or squeaks. He opened the door just far enough to fit his body through the opening, then carefully shut it behind him, only then taking the time to examine the room.

It was dark, with scarcely any moonlight filtering in around the window coverings. His eyes had already adjusted to the dimness, however, and he could make out various pieces of furniture—a dressing table, a wardrobe . . .

A bed.

It was a heavy, substantial thing, with a canopy and full drapes that closed around it. If there was indeed someone inside, she slept quietly—no snoring, no rustling, nothing.

That's how Lucy would sleep, he suddenly thought. Like the dead. She was no delicate flower, his Lucy, and she would not tolerate anything less than a perfectly restful night. It seemed odd that he would be so certain of this, but he was.

He *knew* her, he realized. He truly knew her. Not just the usual things. In fact, he *didn't* know the usual things. He did not know her favorite color. Nor could he guess her favorite animal or food.

But somehow it didn't matter if he didn't know if she preferred pink or blue or purple or black. He knew her heart. He *wanted* her heart.

And he could not allow her to marry someone else.

Carefully, he drew back the curtains.

There was no one there.

Gregory swore under his breath, until he realized that the sheets were mussed, the pillow with a fresh indent of someone's head.

He whirled around just in time to see a candlestick swinging wildly through the air at him.

Letting out a surprised grunt, he ducked, but not fast enough to avoid a glancing blow to his temple. He swore again, this time in full voice, and then he heard—

"Gregory?"

He blinked. "Lucy?"

She rushed forward. "What are you doing here?"

He motioned impatiently toward the bed. "Why aren't you asleep?"

"Because I'm getting married tomorrow."

"Well, that's why I'm here."

She stared at him dumbly, as if his presence was so unexpected that she could not muster the correct reaction. "I thought you were an intruder," she finally said, motioning to the candlestick.

He allowed himself the tiniest of smiles. "Not to put too fine a point on it," he murmured, "but I am."

For a moment it looked as if she might return the smile. But instead she hugged her arms to her chest and said, "You must go. Right now."

"Not until you speak with me."

Her eyes slid to a point over his shoulder. "There is nothing to say."

"What about 'I love you'?"

"Don't say that," she whispered.

He stepped forward. "I love you."

"Gregory, please."

Even closer. "I love you."

She took a breath. Squared her shoulders. "I am marrying Lord Haselby tomorrow."

"No," he said, "you're not."

Her lips parted.

He reached out and captured her hand in his. She did not pull away.

"Lucy," he whispered.

She closed her eyes.

"Be with me," he said.

Slowly, she shook her head. "Please don't."

He tugged her closer and pulled the candlestick from her slackening fingers. "Be with me, Lucy Abernathy. Be my love, be my wife."

She opened her eyes, but she held his gaze for only a moment before twisting away. "You're making it so much worse," she whispered.

The pain in her voice was unbearable. "Lucy," he said, touching her cheek, "let me help you."

She shook her head, but she paused as her cheek settled into his palm. Not for long. Barely a second. But he felt it.

"You can't marry him," he said, tilting her face toward his. "You won't be happy."

Her eyes glistened as they met his. In the dim light of the night, they looked a dark, dark gray, and achingly sad. He could imagine the entire world there, in the depths of her gaze. Everything he needed to know, everything he might *ever* need to know—it was there, within her.

"You won't be happy, Lucy," he whispered. "You know that you won't."

Still, she didn't speak. The only sound was her breath, moving quietly across her lips. And then, finally—

"I will be content."

"*Content?*" he echoed. His hand dropped from her face, falling to his side as he stepped back. "You will be content?"

She nodded.

"And that's *enough*?"

She nodded again, but smaller this time.

Anger began to spark within him. She was willing to toss him away for that? Why wasn't she willing to fight?

She loved him, but did she love him enough?

"Is it his position?" he demanded. "Does it mean so much to you to be a countess?"

She waited too long before replying, and he knew she was lying when she said, "Yes."

"I don't believe you," he said, and his voice sounded terrible. Wounded. Angry. He looked at his hand, blinking with surprise as he realized he was still holding the candlestick. He wanted to hurl it at the wall. Instead he set it down. His hands were not quite steady, he saw.

He looked at her. She said nothing.

"Lucy," he begged, "just tell me. Let me help you."

She swallowed, and he realized she was no longer looking at his face.

He took her hands in his. She tensed, but she did not pull away. Their bodies were facing each other, and he could see the ragged rise and fall of her chest.

It matched what he felt in his own.

"I love you," he said. Because if he kept saying it, maybe it would be enough. Maybe the words would fill the room, surround her and sneak beneath her skin. Maybe she would finally realize that there were certain things that could not be denied.

"We belong together," he said. "For eternity."

Her eyes closed. One single, heavy blink. But when she opened them again, she looked shattered.

"Lucy," he said, trying to put his very soul into one single word. "Lucy, tell me—"

"Please don't say that," she said, turning her head so that she was not quite looking at him. Her voice caught and shook. "Say anything else, but not that."

"Why not?"

And then she whispered, "Because it's true."

His breath caught, and in one swift movement he pulled her to him. It was not an embrace; not quite. Their fingers were entwined, their arms bent so that their hands met between their shoulders.

He whispered her name.

Lucy's lips parted.

He whispered it again, so soft that the words were more of a motion than a sound.

Lucy Lucy.

She held still, barely breathing. His body was so close to hers, yet not quite touching. There was heat, though, filling the space between them, swirling through her nightgown, trembling along her skin.

She tingled.

"Let me kiss you," he whispered. "One more time. Let me kiss you one more time, and if you tell me to go, I swear that I will."

Lucy could feel herself slipping, sliding into need, falling into a hazy place of love and desire where right was not quite so identifiable from wrong.

She loved him. She loved him so much, and he could not be hers. Her heart was racing, her breath was shaking, and all she could think was that she would never feel this way again. No one would ever look at her the way Gregory was, right at that very moment. In less than a day she was to marry a man who wouldn't even wish to kiss her.

She would never feel this strange curling in the core of her womanhood, the fluttering in her belly. This was the last time she'd stare at someone's lips and *ache* for them to touch hers.

Dear God, she wanted him. She wanted *this.* Before it was too late.

And he loved her. He loved her. He'd said it, and even though she couldn't quite believe it, she believed *him.*

She licked her lips.

"Lucy," he whispered, her name a question, a statement, and a plea—all in one.

She nodded. And then, because she knew she could not lie to herself or to him, she said the words.

"Kiss me."

There would be no pretending later, no claiming she had been swept away by passion, stripped of her ability to think. The decision was hers. And she'd made it.

For a moment Gregory did not move, but she knew that he heard her. His breath sucked raggedly into him, and his eyes turned positively liquid as he gazed at her. "Lucy," he said, his voice husky and deep and rough and a hundred other things that turned her bones to milk.

His lips found the hollow where her jaw met her neck. "Lucy," he murmured.

She wanted to say something in return, but she could not. It had taken all she had just to ask for his kiss.

"I love you," he whispered, trailing the words along her neck to her collarbone. "I love you. I love you."

They were the most painful, wonderful, horrible, magnificent words he could have said. She wanted to cry—with happiness *and* sorrow.

Pleasure and pain.

And she understood—for the first time in her life—she understood the prickly joy of complete selfishness. She shouldn't be doing this. She knew she shouldn't, and she knew he probably thought that this meant that she would find a way out of her commitment to Haselby.

She was lying to him. As surely as if she'd said the words.

But she could not help herself.

This was her moment. Her one moment to hold bliss in her hands. And it would have to last a lifetime.

Emboldened by the fire within her, she pressed her hands roughly to his cheeks, pulling his mouth against hers for a torrid kiss. She had no idea what she was doing—she was sure there must be rules to all this, but she did not care. She just wanted to kiss him. She couldn't stop herself.

One of his hands moved to her hip, burning through the thin fabric of her nightgown. Then it stole around to her bottom, squeezing and cupping, and there was no more space between them. She felt herself sliding down, and then they were on the bed, and she was on her back, his body pressed against hers, the heat and the weight of it exquisitely male.

She felt like a woman.

She felt like a goddess.

She felt like she could wrap herself around him and never let go.

"Gregory," she whispered, finding her voice as she twined her fingers in his hair.

He stilled, and she knew he was waiting for her to say more.

"I love you," she said, because it was true, and because she needed *some*thing to be true. Tomorrow he would hate her. Tomorrow she would betray him, but in this, at least, she would not lie.

"I want you," she said, when he lifted his head to gaze into her eyes. He stared at her long and hard, and she knew that he was giving her one last chance to back out.

"I want you," she said again, because she wanted him beyond words. She wanted him to kiss her, to take her, and to forget that she was not whispering words of love.

"Lu—"

She placed a finger to his mouth. And she whispered, "I want to be yours." And then she added, "Tonight."

His body shuddered, his breath moving audibly over his lips. He groaned something, maybe her name, and then his mouth met hers in a kiss that gave and took and burned and consumed until Lucy could not help but move underneath him. Her hands slid to his neck, then inside his coat, her fingers desperately seeking heat and skin. With a roughly mumbled curse, he rose up, still straddling her, and yanked off the coat and cravat.

She stared at him with wide eyes. He was removing his shirt, not slowly or with finesse, but with a frantic speed that underscored his desire.

He was not in control. She might not be in control, but neither was he. He was as much a slave to this fire as she was.

He tossed his shirt aside, and she gasped at the sight of him, the light sprinkling of hair across his chest, the muscles that sculpted and stretched under his skin.

He was beautiful. She hadn't realized a man could be beautiful, but it was the only word that could possibly describe him. She lifted one hand and gingerly placed it against his skin. His blood leaped and pulsed beneath, and she nearly pulled away.

"No," he said, covering her hand with his own. He wrapped his fingers around hers and then took her to his heart.

He looked into her eyes.

She could not look away.

And then he was back, his body hard and hot against hers, his hands everywhere and his lips everywhere else. And her nightgown—It no longer seemed to be covering quite so much of her. It was up against her thighs, then pooled around her waist. He was touching her—not *there*, but close. Skimming along her belly, scorching her skin.

"Gregory," she gasped, because somehow his fingers had found her breast.

"Oh, Lucy," he groaned, cupping her, squeezing, tickling the tip, and—

Oh, dear God. How was it possible that she felt it *there*?

Her hips arched and bucked, and she needed to be closer. She needed something she couldn't quite identify, something that would fill her, complete her.

He was tugging at her nightgown now, and it slipped over her head, leaving her scandalously bare. One of her hands instinctively rose to cover her, but he grabbed her wrist and held it against his own chest. He was straddling her, sitting upright, staring down at her as if . . . as if . . .

As if she were beautiful.

He was looking at her the way men always looked at Hermione, except somehow there was *more*. More passion, more desire.

She felt worshipped.

"Lucy," he murmured, lightly caressing the side of her breast. "I feel . . . I think . . ."

His lips parted, and he shook his head. Slowly, as if he did not quite understand what was happening to him. "I have been waiting for this," he whispered. "For my entire life. I didn't even know. I didn't know."

She took his hand and brought it to her mouth, kissing the palm. She understood.

His breath quickened, and then he slid off her, his hands moving to the fastenings of his breeches.

Her eyes widened, and she watched.

"I will be gentle," hce vowed. "I promise you."

"I'm not worried," she said, managing a wobbly smile.

His lips curved in return. "You look worried."

"I'm not." But still, her eyes wandered.

Gregory chuckled, lying down beside her. "It might hurt. I'm told it does at the beginning."

She shook her head. "I don't care."

He let his hand wander down her arm. "Just remember, if there is pain, it will get better."

She felt it beginning again, that slow burning in her belly. "How much better?" she asked, her voice breathy and unfamiliar.

He smiled as his fingers found her hip. "Quite a bit, I'm told."

"Quite a bit," she asked, now barely able to speak, "or . . . rather a lot?"

He moved over her, his skin finding every inch of hers. It was wicked.

It was bliss.

"Rather a lot," he answered, nipping lightly at her neck. "More than rather a lot, actually."

She felt her legs slide open, and his body nestled in the space between them. She could feel him, hard and hot and pressing against her. She stiffened, and he must have felt it, because his lips crooned a soft, "Shhhh," at her ear.

From there he moved down.

And down.

And down.

His mouth trailed fire along her neck to the hollow of her shoulder, and then—

Oh, dear God.

His hand was cupping her breast, making it round and plump, and his mouth found the tip.

She jerked beneath him.

He chuckled, and his other hand found her shoulder, holding her immobile while he continued his torture, pausing only to move to the other side.

"Gregory," Lucy whimpered, because she did not know what else to say. She was lost to the sensation, completely helpless against his sensual onslaught. She couldn't explain, she couldn't fix or rationalize. She could only feel, and it was the most terrifying, thrilling thing imaginable.

With one last nip, he released her breast and brought his face back up to hers. His breathing was ragged, his muscles tense.

"Touch me," he said hoarsely.

Her lips parted, and her eyes found his.

"Anywhere," he begged.

It was only then that Lucy realized that her hands were at her sides, gripping the sheets as if they could keep her sane. "I'm sorry," she said, and then, amazingly, she began to laugh.

One side of his mouth curved up. "We're going to have to break you of that habit," he murmured.

She brought her hands to his back, lightly exploring his skin. "You don't want me to apologize?" she asked. When he joked, when he teased—it made her comfortable. It made her bold.

"Not for this," he groaned.

She rubbed her feet against his calves. "Ever?"

And then his hands started doing unspeakable things. "Do you want me to apologize?"

"No," she gasped. He was touching her intimately, in ways she didn't know she could be touched. It should have been the most awful thing in the world, but it wasn't. It made her stretch, arch, squirm. She had no idea what it was she was feeling—she couldn't have described it with Shakespeare himself at her disposal.

But she wanted more. It was her only thought, the only thing she knew.

Gregory was leading her somewhere. She felt pulled, taken, transported.

And she wanted it all.

"Please," she begged, the word slipping unbidden from her lips. "Please . . ."

But Gregory, too, was beyond words. He said her name. Over and over he said it, as if his lips had lost the memory of anything else.

"Lucy," he whispered, his mouth moving to the hollow between her breasts.

"Lucy," he moaned, slipping one finger inside of her.

And then he gasped it. *"Lucy!"*

She had touched him. Softly, tentatively.

But it was she. It was her hand, her caress, and it felt as if he'd been set on fire.

"I'm sorry," she said, yanking her hand away.

"*Don't* apologize," he ground out, not because he was angry but because he could barely speak. He found her hand and dragged it back. "This is how much I want you," he said, wrapping her around him. "With everything I have, everything I am."

His nose was barely an inch from hers. Their breath mingled, and their eyes . . .

It was like they were one.

"I love you," he murmured, moving into position. Her hand slid away, then moved to his back.

"I love you, too," she whispered, and then her eyes widened, as if she were stunned that she'd said it.

But he didn't care. It didn't matter if she'd meant to tell him or not. She'd said it, and she could never take it back. She was his.

And he was hers. As he held himself still, pressing ever so softly at her entrance, he realized that he was at the edge of a precipice. His life was now one of two parts: before and after.

He would never love another woman again.

He *could* never love another woman again.

Not after this. Not as long as Lucy walked the same earth. There could be no one else.

It was terrifying, this precipice. Terrifying, and thrilling, and—

He jumped.

She let out a little gasp as he pushed forward, but when he looked down at her, she did not seem to be in pain. Her head was thrown back, and each breath was accompanied by a little moan, as if she could not quite keep her desire inside.

Her legs wrapped around his, feet running down the length of his calves. And her hips were arching, pressing, begging him to continue.

"I don't want to hurt you," he said, every muscle in his body straining to move forward. He had never wanted anything the way he wanted her in that moment. And yet he had never felt less greedy. This had to be for her. He could not hurt her.

"You're not," she groaned, and then he couldn't help himself. He captured her breast in his mouth as he pushed through her final barrier, embedding himself fully within her.

If she'd felt pain, she didn't care. She let out a quiet shriek of pleasure, and her hands grabbed wildly at his head. She writhed beneath him, and when he attempted to move to her other breast, her fingers grew merciless, holding him in place with a ferocious intensity.

And all the while, his body claiming her, moving in a rhythm that was beyond thought or control.

"Lucy Lucy Lucy," he moaned, finally tearing himself away from her breast. It was too hard. It was too much. He needed room to breathe, to gasp, to suck in the air that never quite seemed to make it to his lungs.

"Lucy!"

He should wait. He was trying to wait. But she was grabbing at him, digging her nails into his shoulders, and her body was arching off the bed with enough strength to lift him as well.

And then he felt her. Tensing, squeezing, shuddering around him, and he let go.

He let go, and the world quite simply exploded.

"I love you," he gasped as he collapsed atop her. He'd thought himself beyond words, but there they were.

They were his companion now. Three little words.

I love you.

He would never be without them.

And that was a splendid thing.

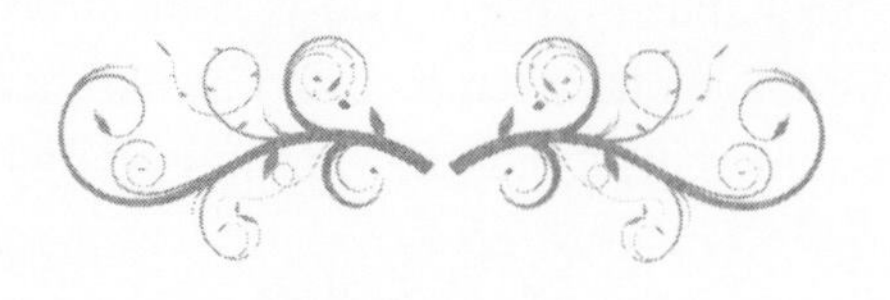

Chapter 20

In which Our Hero has a very bad morning.

Sometime later, after sleep, and then more passion, and then not quite sleep, but a peaceful quiet and stillness, and then more passion—because they just could not help themselves—it was time for Gregory to go.

It was the most difficult thing he had ever done, and yet he was still able to do it with joy in his heart because he knew that this was not the end. It was not even goodbye; it was nothing so permanent as that. But the hour was growing dangerous. Dawn would arrive shortly, and while he had every intention of marrying Lucy as soon as he could manage it, he would not put her through the shame of being caught in bed with him on the morning of her wedding to another man.

There was also Haselby to consider. Gregory did not know him well, but he had always seemed an affable fellow and did not deserve the public humiliation that would follow.

"Lucy," Gregory whispered, nudging her cheek with his nose, "it is near to morning."

She made a sleepy sound, then turned her head. "Yes," she said.

Just *Yes*, not *It's all so unfair* or *It shouldn't have to be this way*. But that was Lucy. She was pragmatic and prudent and charmingly reasonable, and he loved her for all that and more. She didn't want to change the world. She just wanted to make it lovely and wonderful for the people she loved.

The fact that she had done this—that she had let him make love to her and was planning to call off her wedding *now*, the very morning of the ceremony—it only showed him how deeply she cared for him. Lucy didn't look for attention and drama. She craved stability and routine, and for her to make the leap she was preparing for—

It humbled him.

"You should come with me," he said. "Now. We should leave together before the household wakes."

Her bottom lip stretched a bit from side to side in an *oh dear*–ish expression that was so fetching he simply had to kiss her. Lightly, since he had no time to get carried away, and just a little peck on the corner of her mouth. Nothing that interfered with her answer, which was a disappointing "I cannot."

He drew back. "You cannot remain."

But she was shaking her head. "I . . . I must do the right thing."

He looked at her quizzically.

"I must behave with honor," she explained. She sat then, her fingers clutching the bedclothes so tightly that her knuckles turned white. She looked nervous, which he supposed made sense. He felt on the edge of a brand-new dawn, whereas she—

She still had a rather large mountain to scale before she reached her happy ending.

He reached out, trying to take one of her hands, but she was not receptive. It wasn't that she was tugging away from him; rather, it almost felt as if she was not even aware of his touch.

"I cannot sneak away and allow Lord Haselby to wait in vain at the church," she said, the words rushing out, tumbling from her lips as her eyes turned to his, wide and imploring.

But just for a moment.

Then she turned away.

She swallowed. He could not see her face, but he could see it in the way she moved.

She said, softly, "Surely you understand that."

And he did. It was one of the things he loved best about her. She had such a strong sense of right and wrong, sometimes to the point of intractability. But she was never moralistic, never condescending.

"I will watch for you," he said.

Her head turned sharply, and her eyes widened in question.

"You may need my assistance," he said softly.

"No, it won't be necessary. I'm sure I can—"

"I insist," he said, with enough force to silence her. "This shall be our signal." He held up his hand, fingers together, palm out. He twisted at the wrist then, once, to bring his palm around to face him, and then again, to return it to its original position. "I shall watch for you. If you need my help, come to the window and make the signal."

She opened her mouth, as if she might protest one more time, but in the end she merely nodded.

He stood then, opening the heavy draperies that ringed her bed as he searched for his clothing. His garments were strewn about—his breeches here, his shirt remarkably over there, but he quickly gathered what he needed and dressed.

Lucy remained in bed, sitting up with the sheets tucked under her arm. He found her modesty charming, and he almost teased her for it. But instead he decided just to offer an amused smile. It had been a momentous night for her; she should not be made to feel embarrassed for her innocence.

He walked to the window to peer out. Dawn had not yet broken, but the sky hung with anticipation, the horizon painted with that faint shimmer of light one saw only before the sunrise. It glowed gently, a serene purplish-blue, and was so beautiful he beckoned to her to join him. He turned his back while she donned her nightgown and then, once she had padded across the room in her bare feet, he pulled her gently against him, her back to his chest. He rested his chin on top of her head.

"Look," he whispered.

The night seemed to dance, sparkling and tingling, as if the air itself understood that nothing would ever be the same. Dawn was waiting on the other side of the horizon, and already the stars were beginning to look less bright in the sky.

If he could have frozen time, he would have done so. Never had he experienced a single moment that was so magical, so . . . full. Everything was there, everything that was good and honest and true. And he finally understood the difference between happiness and contentment, and how lucky and blessed he was to feel both, in such breathtaking quantities.

It was Lucy. She completed him. She made his life everything he had known it could someday be.

This was his dream. It was coming true, all around him, right there in his arms.

And then, right as they were standing at the window, one of the stars shot through the sky. It made a wide, shallow arc, and it almost seemed to Gregory that he heard it as it traveled, sparking and crackling until it disappeared from sight.

It made him kiss her. He supposed a rainbow would do the same, or a four-leafed clover, or even a simple snowflake, landing on his sleeve without melting. It was simply impossible to enjoy one of nature's small miracles and *not* kiss her. He kissed her neck, and then he turned her around in his arms so that he could kiss her mouth, and her brow, and even her nose.

All seven freckles, too. God, he loved her freckles.

"I love you," he whispered.

She laid her cheek against his chest, and her voice was hoarse, almost choked as she said, "I love you, too."

"Are you certain you will not come with me now?" He knew her answer, but he asked, anyway.

As expected, she nodded. "I must do this myself."

"How will your uncle react?"

"I'm . . . not sure."

He stepped back, taking her by the shoulders and even bending at the knees so that his eyes would not lose contact with hers. "Will he hurt you?"

"No," she said, quickly enough so that he believed her. "No. I promise you."

"Will he try to force you to marry Haselby? Lock you in your room? Because I could stay. If you think you will need me, I could remain right here." It would create an even worse scandal than what currently lay ahead for them, but if it was a question of her safety . . .

There was nothing he would not do.

"Gregory—"

He silenced her with a shake of his head. "Do you understand," he began, "how completely and utterly this goes against my every instinct, leaving you here to face this by yourself?"

Her lips parted and her eyes—

They filled with tears.

"I have sworn in my heart to protect you," he said, his voice passionate and fierce and maybe even a little bit revelatory. Because today, he realized, was the day he truly became a man. After twenty-six years of an amiable and, yes, aimless existence, he had finally found his purpose.

He finally knew why he had been born.

"I have sworn it in my heart," he said, "and I will swear it before God just as soon as we are able. And it is like acid in my chest to leave you alone."

His hand found hers, and their fingers twined.

"It is not right," he said, his words low but fierce.

Slowly, she nodded her agreement. "But it is what must be done."

"If there is a problem," he said, "if you sense danger, you must promise to signal. I will come for you. You can take refuge with my mother. Or any one of my sisters. They won't mind the scandal. They would care only for your happiness."

She swallowed, and then she smiled, and her eyes grew wistful. "Your family must be lovely."

He took her hands and squeezed them. "They are *your* family now." He waited for her to say something, but she did not. He brought her hands to his lips and kissed them each in turn. "Soon," he whispered, "this will all be behind us."

She nodded, then glanced over her shoulder at the door. "The servants will be waking shortly."

And he left. He slipped out the door, boots in hand, and crept out the way he'd come in.

It was still dark when he reached the small park that filled the square across from her home. There were hours yet before the wedding, and surely he had enough time to return home to change his clothing.

But he was not prepared to chance it. He had told her he would protect her, and he would never break that promise.

But then it occurred to him—he did not need to do this alone. In fact, he should not do it alone. If Lucy needed him, she would need him well and full. If Gregory had to resort to force, he could certainly use an extra set of hands.

He had never gone to his brothers for help, never begged them to extricate him from a tight spot. He was a relatively young man. He had drunk spirits, gambled, dallied with women.

But he had never drunk too much, or gambled more than he had, or, until the previous night, dallied with a woman who risked her reputation to be with him.

He had not sought responsibility, but neither had he chased trouble.

His brothers had always seen him as a boy. Even now, in his twenty-sixth year, he suspected they did not view him as quite fully grown. And so he did not ask for help. He did not place himself in any position where he might need it.

Until now.

One of his older brothers lived not very far away. Less than a quarter of a mile, certainly, maybe even closer to an eighth. Gregory could be there and back in twenty minutes, including the time it took to yank Colin from his bed.

Gregory had just rolled his shoulders back and forth, loosening up in preparation for a sprint, when he spied a chimney sweep, walking across the street. He was young—twelve, maybe thirteen—and certainly eager for a guinea.

And the promise of another, should he deliver Gregory's message to his brother.

Gregory watched him tear around the corner, then he crossed back to the public garden. There was no place to sit, no place even to stand where he might not be immediately visible from Fennsworth House.

And so he climbed a tree. He sat on a low, thick branch, leaned against the trunk, and waited.

Someday, he told himself, he would laugh about this. Someday they would tell this tale to their grandchildren, and it would all sound very romantic and exciting.

As for now . . .

Romantic, yes. Exciting, not so much.

He rubbed his hands together.

Most of all, it was cold.

He shrugged, waiting for himself to stop noticing it. He never did, but he didn't care. What were a few blue fingertips against the rest of his life?

He smiled, lifting his gaze to her window. There she was, he thought. Right there, behind that curtain. And he loved her.

He loved her.

He thought of his friends, most of them cynics, always casting a bored eye over the latest selection of debutantes, sighing that marriage was such a chore, that ladies were interchangeable, and that love was best left to the poets.

Fools, the lot of them.

Love existed.

It was right there, in the air, in the wind, in the water. One only had to wait for it.

To watch for it.

And fight for it.

And he would. As God was his witness, he would. Lucy had only to signal, and he would retrieve her.

He was a man in love.

Nothing could stop him.

"This is not, you realize, how I had intended to spend my Saturday morning."

Gregory answered only with a nod. His brother had arrived four hours earlier, greeting him with a characteristically understated "This is interesting."

Gregory had told Colin everything, even down to the events of the night before. He did not like telling tales of Lucy, but one really could not ask one's brother to sit in a tree for hours without explaining why. And Gregory had found a certain comfort in unburdening himself to Colin. He had not lectured. He had not judged.

In fact, he had understood.

When Gregory had finished his tale, tersely explaining why he was waiting outside Fennsworth House, Colin had simply nodded and said, "I don't suppose you have something to eat."

Gregory shook his head and grinned.

It was good to have a brother.

"Rather poor planning on your part," Colin muttered. But he was smiling, too.

They turned back to the house, which had long since begun to show signs of life. Curtains had been pulled back, candles lit and then snuffed as dawn had given way to morning.

"Shouldn't she have come out by now?" Colin asked, squinting at the door.

Gregory frowned. He had been wondering the same thing. He had been telling himself that her absence boded well. If her uncle were going to force her to marry Haselby, wouldn't she have left for the church by now? By his pocket watch, which admittedly wasn't the most accurate of timepieces, the ceremony was due to begin in less than an hour.

But she had not signaled for his help, either.

And that did not sit well with him.

Suddenly Colin perked up.

"What is it?"

Colin motioned to the right with his head. "A carriage," he said, "being brought 'round from the mews."

Gregory's eyes widened with horror as the front door to Fennsworth House opened. Servants spilled out, laughing and cheering as the vehicle came to a stop in front of Fennsworth House.

It was white, open, and festooned with perfectly pink flowers and wide rosy ribbons, trailing behind, fluttering in the light breeze.

It was a wedding carriage.

And no one seemed to find that odd.

Gregory's skin began to tingle. His muscles burned.

"Not yet," Colin said, placing a restraining hand on Gregory's arm.

Gregory shook his head. His peripheral vision was beginning to fade from view, and all he could see was that damned carriage.

"I have to get her," he said. "I have to go."

"Wait," Colin instructed. "Wait to see what happens. She might not come out. She might—"

But she did come out.

Not first. That was her brother, his new wife on his arm.

Then came an older man—her uncle, most probably—and that ancient woman Gregory had met at his sister's ball.

And then . . .

Lucy.

In a wedding dress.

"Dear God," he whispered.

She was walking freely. No one was forcing her.

Hermione said something to her, whispered in her ear.

And Lucy smiled.

She smiled.

Gregory began to gasp.

The pain was palpable. Real. It shot through his gut, squeezed at his organs until he could no longer move.

He could only stare.

And think.

"Did she tell you she wasn't going to go through with it?" Colin whispered.

Gregory tried to say yes, but the word strangled him. He tried to recall their last conversation, every last word of it. She had said she must behave with honor. She had said she must do what was right. She had said that she loved him.

But she had never said that she would not marry Haselby.

"Oh my God," he whispered.

His brother laid his hand over his own. "I'm sorry," he said.

Gregory watched as Lucy stepped up into the open carriage. The servants were still cheering. Hermione was fussing with her hair, adjusting the veil, then laughing when the wind lifted the gauzy fabric in the air.

This could not be happening.

There had to be an explanation.

"No," Gregory said, because it was the only word he could think to say. "No."

Then he remembered. The hand signal. The wave. She would do it. She would signal to him. Whatever had transpired in the house, she had not been able to halt the proceedings. But now, out in the open, where he could see, she would signal.

She had to. She knew he could see her.

She knew he was out there.

Watching her.

He swallowed convulsively, never taking his eyes off her right hand.

"Is everyone here?" he heard Lucy's brother call out.

He did not hear Lucy's voice in the chorus of replies, but no one was questioning her presence.

She was the bride.

And he was a fool, watching her ride away.

"I'm sorry," Colin said quietly, as they watched the carriage disappear around the corner.

"It doesn't make sense," Gregory whispered.

Colin jumped down out of the tree and silently held out his hand to Gregory.

"It doesn't make sense," Gregory said again, too bewildered to do anything but let his brother help him down. "She wouldn't do this. She loves me."

He looked at Colin. His eyes were kind, but pitying.

"No," Gregory said. "No. You don't know her. She would not— No. You don't know her."

And Colin, whose only experience with Lady Lucinda Abernathy was the moment in which she had broken his brother's heart, asked, "Do *you* know her?"

Gregory stepped back as if struck. "Yes," he said. "Yes, I do."

Colin didn't say anything, but his brows rose, as if to ask, *Well, then?*

Gregory turned, his eyes moving to the corner around which Lucy had so recently disappeared. For a moment he stood absolutely still, his only movement a deliberate, thoughtful blink of his eyes.

He turned back around, looked his brother in the face. "I know her," he said. "I do."

Colin's lips drew together, as if trying to form a question, but Gregory had already turned away.

He was looking at that corner again.

And then he began to run.

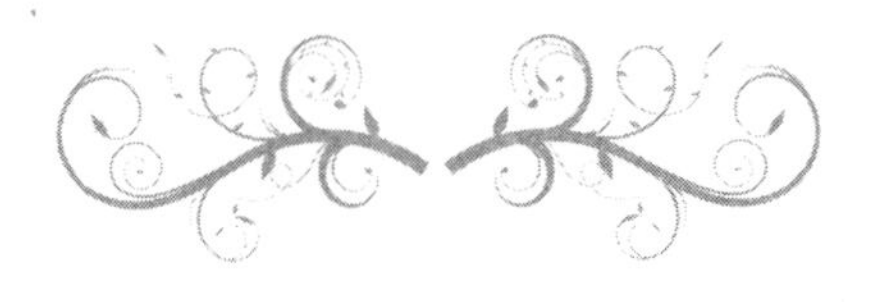

Chapter 21

In which Our Hero risks everything.

"Are you ready?"

Lucy regarded the splendid interior of St. George's—the bright stained glass, the elegant arches, the piles and piles of flowers brought in to celebrate her marriage.

She thought about Lord Haselby, standing with the priest at the altar.

She thought about the guests, all more-than-three-hundred of them, all waiting for her to enter on her brother's arm.

And she thought about Gregory, who had surely seen her climb up into the bridal carriage, dressed in her wedding finery.

"Lucy," Hermione repeated, "are you ready?"

Lucy wondered what Hermione might do if she said no.

Hermione was a romantic.

Impractical.

She would probably tell Lucy that she did not have to go through with it, that it did not matter that they were standing just outside the doors to the church sanctuary, or that the prime minister himself was seated inside.

Hermione would tell her that it did not matter that papers had been signed and banns had been read, in three different parishes. It did not matter that by fleeing the church Lucy would create the scandal of the decade. She would tell Lucy that she did not have to do it, that she should not settle for a marriage of convenience when she could have one of passion and love. She would say—

"Lucy?"

(Is what she actually said.)

Lucy turned, blinking in confusion, because the Hermione of her imagination had been giving quite an impassioned speech.

Hermione smiled gently. "Are you ready?"

And Lucy, because she was Lucy, because she would always be Lucy, nodded.

She could do nothing else.

Richard joined them. "I cannot believe you are getting married," he said to Lucy, but not before gazing warmly at his wife.

"I am not so very much younger than you are, Richard," Lucy reminded him. She tilted her head toward the new Lady Fennsworth. "And I am two months older than Hermione."

Richard grinned boyishly. "Yes, but she is not my sister."

Lucy smiled at that, and she was grateful for it. She needed smiles. Every last one she could manage.

It was her wedding day. She had been bathed and perfumed and dressed in what had to be the most luxurious gown she had ever laid eyes upon, and she felt . . .

Empty.

She could not imagine what Gregory thought of her. She had deliberately allowed him to think that she planned to call off the wedding. It was terrible of her, cruel and dishonest, but she did not know what else to do. She was a coward, and she could not bear to see his face when she told him she still intended to marry Haselby.

Good God, how could she have explained it? He would have insisted that there was another way, but he was an idealist, and he had never faced true adversity. There *wasn't* another way. Not this time. Not without sacrificing her family.

She let out a long breath. She could do this. Truly. She could. She could.

She closed her eyes, her head bobbing a half inch or so as the words echoed in her mind.

I can do this. I can. I can.

"Lucy?" came Hermione's concerned voice. "Are you unwell?"

Lucy opened her eyes, and said the only thing Hermione would possibly believe. "Just doing sums in my head."

Hermione shook her head. "I hope Lord Haselby likes maths, because I vow, Lucy, you are mad."

"Perhaps."

Hermione looked at her quizzically.

"What is it?" Lucy asked.

Hermione blinked several times before finally replying. "It is nothing, really," she said. "Just that that sounded quite unlike you."

"I don't know what you mean."

"To agree with me when I call you mad? That's not at all what you would say."

"Well, it's obviously what I did say," Lucy grumbled, "so I don't know what—"

"Oh, pish. The Lucy I know would say something like, 'Mathematics is a very extremely important endeavor, and really, Hermione, you ought to consider practicing sums yourself.' "

Lucy winced. "Am I truly so officious?"

"Yes," Hermione replied, as if she were mad even to question it. "But it's what I love best about you."

And Lucy managed another smile.

Maybe everything would be all right. Maybe she would be happy. If she could manage two smiles in one morning, then surely it couldn't be that bad. She needed only to keep moving forward, in her mind and her body. She needed to have this thing done, to make it permanent, so she could place Gregory in her past and at least pretend to embrace her new life as Lord Haselby's wife.

But Hermione was asking Richard if she might have a moment alone with Lucy, and then she was taking her hands, leaning in and whispering, "Lucy, are you certain you wish to do this?"

Lucy looked up at her in surprise. Why was Hermione asking her this? Right at the moment when she most wanted to run.

Hadn't she been smiling? Hadn't Hermione seen her smiling?

Lucy swallowed. She tried to straighten her shoulders. "Yes," she said. "Yes, of course. Why would you ask such a thing?"

Hermione did not answer right away. But her eyes—those huge, green eyes that rendered grown men senseless—they answered for her.

Lucy swallowed and turned away, unable to bear what she saw there.

And Hermione whispered, *"Lucy."*

That was all. Just Lucy.

Lucy turned back. She wanted to ask Hermione what she meant. She wanted to ask why she said her name as if it were a tragedy. But she didn't. She couldn't. And so she hoped Hermione saw her questions in her eyes.

She did. Hermione touched her cheek, smiling sadly. "You look like the saddest bride I've ever seen."

Lucy closed her eyes. "I'm not sad. I just feel . . ."

But she didn't know what she felt. What was she supposed to feel? No one had trained her for this. In all her education, with her nurse, and governess, and three years at Miss Moss's, no one had given her lessons in *this*.

Why hadn't anyone realized that this was far more important than needlework or country dances?

"I feel . . ." And then she understood. "I feel like I'm saying goodbye."

Hermione blinked with surprise. "To whom?"

To myself.

And she was. She was saying goodbye to herself, and everything she might have become.

She felt her brother's hand on her arm. "It's time to begin," he said.

She nodded.

"Where is your bouquet?" Hermione asked, then answered herself with, "Oh. Right there." She retrieved the flowers, along with her own, from a nearby table and handed them to Lucy. "You shall be happy," she whispered, as she kissed Lucy's cheek. "You must. I simply will not tolerate a world in which you are not."

Lucy's lips wobbled.

"Oh dear," Hermione said. "I sound like you now. Do you see what a good influence you are?" And then, with one last blown kiss, she entered the chapel.

"Your turn," Richard said.

"Almost," Lucy answered.

And then it was.

She was in the church, walking down the aisle. She was at the front, nodding at the priest, looking at Haselby and reminding herself that despite . . . well, despite certain habits she did not quite understand, he would make a perfectly acceptable husband.

This was what she had to do.

If she said no . . .

She could not say no.

She could see Hermione out of the corner of her eye, standing beside her with a serene smile. She and Richard had arrived in London two nights earlier, and they had been so *happy*. They laughed and they teased and they spoke of the improvements they planned to make at Fennsworth Abbey. An orangery, they had laughed. They wanted an orangery. And a nursery.

How could Lucy take that from them? How could she cast them into a life of shame and poverty?

She heard Haselby's voice, answering, "I will," and then it was her turn.

Wilt thou have this Man to thy Wedded Husband, to live together after God's ordinance in the holy estate of Matrimony? Wilt thou obey him, and serve him, love, honor, and keep him in sickness and in health; and, forsaking all other, keep thee only unto him, so long as ye both shall live?

She swallowed and tried not to think of Gregory. "I will."

She had given her consent. Was it done, then? She didn't feel different. She was still the same old Lucy, except she was standing in front of more people than she ever cared to stand in front of again, and her brother was giving her away.

The priest placed her right hand in Haselby's, and he pledged his troth, his voice loud, firm, and clear.

They separated, and then Lucy took his hand.

I, Lucinda Margaret Catherine . . .

"I, Lucinda Margaret Catherine . . ."

. . . take thee, Arthur Fitzwilliam George . . .

". . . take thee, Arthur Fitzwilliam George . . ."

She said it. She repeated after the priest, word for word. She said her part, right up until she meant to give Haselby her troth, right up until—

The doors to the chapel slammed open.

She turned around. Everyone turned around.

Gregory.

Dear God.

He looked like a madman, breathing so hard he was barely able to speak.

He staggered forward, clutching the edges of the pew for support, and she heard him say—

"Don't."

Lucy's heart stopped.

"Don't do it."

Her bouquet slipped from her hands. She couldn't move, couldn't speak, couldn't do anything but stand there like a statue as he walked toward her, seemingly oblivious to the hundreds of people staring at him.

"Don't do it," he said again.

And no one was talking. Why was no one talking? Surely someone would rush forward, grab Gregory by the arms, haul him away—

But no one did. It was a spectacle. It was theater, and it seemed no one wanted to miss the ending.

And then—

Right there.

Right there in front of everyone, he stopped.

He stopped. And he said, "I love you."

Beside her Hermione murmured, "Oh my goodness."

Lucy wanted to cry.

"I love you," he said again, and he just kept walking, his eyes never leaving her face.

"Don't do it," he said, finally reaching the front of the church. "Don't marry him."

"Gregory," she whispered, "why are you doing this?"

"I love you," he said, as if there could be no other explanation.

A little moan choked in her throat. Tears burned her eyes, and her entire body felt stiff. Stiff and frozen. One little wind, one little *breath* would knock her over. And she couldn't manage to think anything but *Why*?

And *No.*

And *Please.*

And—oh heavens, *Lord Haselby*!

She looked up at him, at the groom who had found himself demoted to a supporting role. He had been standing silently this entire time, watching the unfolding drama with as much interest as the audience. With her eyes she pleaded with him for guidance, but he just shook his head. It was a tiny movement, far too subtle for anyone else to discern, but she saw it, and she knew what it meant.

It is up to you.

She turned back to Gregory. His eyes burned, and he sank to one knee.

Don't, she tried to say. But she could not move her lips. She could not find her voice.

"Marry me," Gregory said, and she *felt* him in his voice. It wrapped around her body, kissed her, embraced her. "Marry *me*."

And oh dear Lord, she wanted to. More than anything, she wanted to sink to her knees and take his face in her hands. She wanted to kiss him, she wanted to shout out her love for him—here, in front of everyone she knew, possibly everyone she ever would know.

But she had wanted all of that the day before, and the day before that. Nothing had changed. Her world had become more public, but it had not changed.

Her father was still a traitor.

Her family was still being blackmailed.

The fate of her brother and Hermione was still in her hands.

She looked at Gregory, aching for him, aching for them both.

"Marry me," he whispered.

Her lips parted, and she said—

"No."

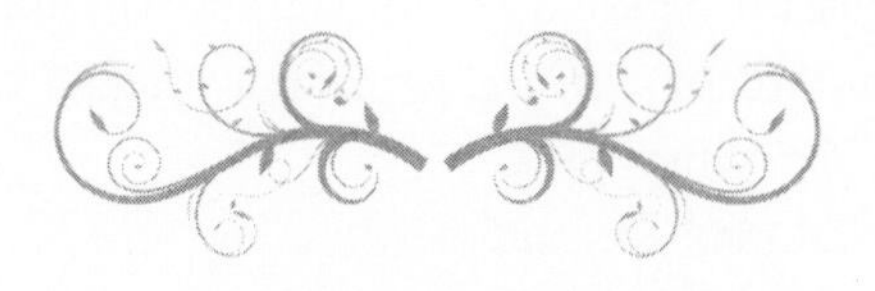

Chapter 22

In which all hell breaks loose.

All hell broke loose.

Lord Davenport charged forward, as did Lucy's uncle and Gregory's brother, who had just tripped up the steps to the church after chasing Gregory across Mayfair.

Lucy's brother dashed forward to move both Lucy and Hermione from the melee, but Lord Haselby, who had been watching the events with the air of an intrigued spectator, calmly took the arm of his intended and said, "I will see to her."

As for Lucy, she stumbled backward, her mouth open with shock as Lord Davenport leaped atop Gregory, landing belly down like a—well, like nothing Lucy had ever seen.

"I have him!" Davenport yelled triumphantly, only to be smacked soundly with a reticule belonging to Hyacinth St. Clair.

Lucy closed her eyes.

"Not the wedding of your dreams, I imagine," Haselby murmured in her ear.

Lucy shook her head, too numb to do anything else. She should help Gregory. Really, she should. But she felt positively drained of energy, and besides, she was too cowardly to face him again.

What if he rejected her?

What if she could not resist him?

"I do hope he will be able to get out from under my father," Haselby continued, his tone as mild as if he were watching a not-terribly-exciting horse race. "The man weighs twenty stone, not that he would admit it."

Lucy turned to him, unable to believe how calm he was given the near riot that had broken out in the church. Even the prime minister appeared to be fending off a largish, plumpish lady in an elaborately fruited bonnet who was swatting at anyone who moved.

"I don't think she can see," Haselby said, following Lucy's gaze. "Her grapes are drooping."

Who *was* this man she had—dear heavens, had she married him yet? They had agreed to something, of that she was certain, but no one had declared them man and wife. But either way, Haselby was bizarrely calm, given the events of the morning.

"Why didn't you say anything?" Lucy asked.

He turned, regarding her curiously. "You mean while your Mr. Bridgerton was professing his love?"

No, while the priest was droning on about the sacrament of marriage, she wanted to snap.

Instead, she nodded.

Haselby cocked his head to the side. "I suppose I wanted to see what you'd do."

She stared at him in disbelief. What would he have done if she'd said yes?

"I am honored, by the way," Haselby said. "And I shall be a kind husband to you. You needn't worry on that score."

But Lucy could not speak. Lord Davenport had been removed from Gregory, and even though some other gentleman she did not recognize was pulling him back, he was struggling to reach her.

"Please," she whispered, even though no one could possibly hear her, not even Haselby, who had stepped down to aid the prime minister. "Please don't."

But Gregory was unrelenting, and even with two men pulling at him, one friendly and one not, he managed to reach the bottom of the steps. He lifted his face, and his eyes burned into hers. They were raw, stark with anguish and incomprehension, and Lucy nearly stumbled from the unleashed pain she saw there.

"Why?" he demanded.

Her entire body began to shake. Could she lie to him? Could she do it? Here, in a church, after she had hurt him in the most personal and the most public way imaginable.

"Why?"

"Because I had to," she whispered.

His eyes flared with something—disappointment? No. Hope? No, not that, either. It was something else. Something she could not quite identify.

He opened his mouth to speak, to ask her something, but it was at that moment that the two men holding him were joined by a third, and together they managed to haul him from the church.

Lucy hugged her arms to her body, barely able to stand as she watched him being dragged away.

"How could you?"

She turned. Hyacinth St. Clair had crept up behind her and was glaring at her as if she were the very devil.

"You don't understand," Lucy said.

But Hyacinth's eyes blazed with fury. "You are weak," she hissed. "You do not deserve him."

Lucy shook her head, not quite sure if she was agreeing with her or not.

"I hope you—"

"Hyacinth!"

Lucy's eyes darted to the side. Another woman had approached. It was Gregory's mother. They had been introduced at the ball at Hastings House.

"That will be enough," she said sternly.

Lucy swallowed, blinking back tears.

Lady Bridgerton turned to her. "Forgive us," she said, pulling her daughter away.

Lucy watched them depart, and she had the strangest sense that all this was happening to someone else, that maybe it was just a dream, just a nightmare, or perhaps she was caught up in a scene from a lurid novel. Maybe her entire life was a figment of someone else's imagination. Maybe if she just closed her eyes—

"Shall we get on with it?"

She swallowed. It was Lord Haselby. His father was next to him, uttering the same sentiment, but in far less gracious words.

Lucy nodded.

"Good," Davenport grunted. "Sensible girl."

Lucy wondered what it meant to be complimented by Lord Davenport. Surely nothing good.

But still, she allowed him to lead her back to the altar. And she stood there in front of half of the congregation who had not elected to follow the spectacle outside.

And she married Haselby.

"What were you thinking?"

It took Gregory a moment to realize that his mother was demanding this of Colin, and not of him. They were seated in her carriage, to which he had been dragged once they had left the church. Gregory did not know where they were going. In random circles, most probably. Anywhere that wasn't St. George's.

"I tried to stop him," Colin protested.

Violet Bridgerton looked as angry as any of them had ever seen her. "You obviously did not try hard enough."

"Do you have any idea how fast he can run?"

"Very fast," Hyacinth confirmed without looking at them. She was seated diagonally to Gregory, staring out the window through narrowed eyes.

Gregory said nothing.

"Oh, Gregory," Violet sighed. "Oh, my poor son."

"You shall have to leave town," Hyacinth said.

"She is right," their mother put in. "It can't be helped."

Gregory said nothing. What had Lucy meant—*Because I had to?* What did that *mean*?

"I shall never receive her," Hyacinth growled.

"She will be a countess," Colin reminded her.

"I don't care if she is the bloody queen of—"

"Hyacinth!" This, from their mother.

"Well, I don't," Hyacinth snapped. "No one has the right to treat my brother like that. No one!"

Violet and Colin stared at her. Colin looked amused. Violet, alarmed.

"I shall ruin her," Hyacinth continued.

"No," Gregory said in a low voice, "you won't."

The rest of his family fell silent, and Gregory suspected that they had not, until the moment he'd spoken, realized that he had not been taking part in the conversation.

"You will leave her alone," he said.

Hyacinth ground her teeth together.

He brought his eyes to hers, hard and steely with purpose. "And if your paths should ever cross," he continued, "you shall be all that is amiable and kind. Do you understand me?"

Hyacinth said nothing.

"Do you understand me?" he roared.

His family stared at him in shock. He never lost his temper. Never.

And then Hyacinth, who'd never possessed a highly developed sense of tact, said, "No, as a matter of fact."

"I beg your pardon?" Gregory, said, his voice dripping ice at the very moment Colin turned to her and hissed, "Shut *up*."

"I don't understand you," Hyacinth continued, jamming her elbow into Colin's ribs. "How can you possibly possess sympathy for her? If this had happened to me, wouldn't you—"

"This didn't happen to you," Gregory bit off. "And you do not know her. You do not know the reasons for her actions."

"Do *you*?" Hyacinth demanded.

He didn't. And it was killing him.

"Turn the other cheek, Hyacinth," her mother said softly.

Hyacinth sat back, her bearing tense with anger, but she held her tongue.

"Perhaps you could stay with Benedict and Sophie in Wiltshire," Violet suggested. "I believe Anthony and Kate are expected in town soon, so you cannot go to Aubrey Hall, although I am sure they would not mind if you resided there in their absence."

Gregory just stared out the window. He did not wish to go to the country.

"You could travel," Colin said. "Italy is particularly pleasant this time of year. And you haven't been, have you?"

Gregory shook his head, only half listening. He did not wish to go to Italy.

Because I had to, she'd said.

Not because she wished it. Not because it was sensible.

Because she had to.

What did that mean?

Had she been forced? Was she being blackmailed?

What could she have possibly done to warrant blackmail?

"It would have been very difficult for her not to go through with it," Violet suddenly said, placing a sympathetic hand on his arm. "Lord Davenport is not a man anyone would wish as an enemy. And really, right there in the church, with everyone looking on . . . Well," she said with a resigned sigh, "one would have to be extremely brave. And resilient." She paused, shaking her head. "And prepared."

"Prepared?" Colin queried.

"For what came next," Violet clarified. "It would have been a huge scandal."

"It already is a huge scandal," Gregory muttered.

"Yes, but not as much as if she'd said yes," his mother said. "Not that I am glad for the outcome. You know I wish you nothing but your heart's happiness. But she will be looked upon approvingly for her choice. She will be viewed as a sensible girl."

Gregory felt one corner of his mouth lift into a wry smile. "And I, a lovesick fool."

No one contradicted him.

After a moment his mother said, "You are taking this rather well, I must say."

Indeed.

"I would have thought—" She broke off. "Well, it matters not what I would have thought, merely what actually is."

"No," Gregory said, turning sharply to look at her. "What would you have thought? How should I be acting?"

"It is not a question of *should*," his mother said, clearly flustered by the sudden questions. "Merely that I would have thought you would seem . . . angrier."

He stared at her for a long moment, then turned back to the window. They were traveling along Piccadilly, heading west toward Hyde Park. Why *wasn't* he angrier? Why wasn't he putting his fist through the wall? He'd had to be dragged from the church and forcibly stuffed into the carriage, but once that had been done, he had been overcome by a bizarre, almost preternatural calm.

And then something his mother had said echoed in his mind.

You know I wish you nothing but your heart's happiness.

His heart's happiness.

Lucy loved him. He was certain of it. He had seen it in her eyes, even in the moment she'd refused him. He knew it because she had told him so, and she did not lie about such things. He had felt it in the way she had kissed him, and in the warmth of her embrace.

She loved him. And whatever had made her go ahead with her marriage to Haselby, it was bigger than she was. Stronger.

She needed his help.

"Gregory?" his mother said softly.

He turned. Blinked.

"You started in your seat," she said.

Had he? He hadn't even noticed. But his senses had sharpened, and when he looked down, he saw that he was flexing his fingers.

"Stop the carriage."

Everyone turned to face him. Even Hyacinth, who had been determinedly glaring out the window.

"Stop the carriage," he said again.

"Why?" his mother asked, clearly suspicious.

"I need air," he replied, and it wasn't even a lie.

Colin knocked on the wall. "I'll walk with you."

"No. I prefer to be alone."

His mother's eyes widened. "Gregory . . . You don't plan to . . ."

"Storm the church?" he finished for her. He leaned back, giving her a casually lopsided smile. "I believe I've embarrassed myself enough for one day, wouldn't you think?"

"They'll have said their vows by now, anyway," Hyacinth put in.

Gregory fought the urge to glare at his sister, who never seemed to miss an opportunity to poke, prod, or twist. "Precisely," he replied.

"I would feel better if you weren't alone," Violet said, her blue eyes still filled with concern.

"Let him go," Colin said softly.

Gregory turned to his older brother in surprise. He had not expected to be championed by him.

"He is a man," Colin added. "He can make his own decisions."

Even Hyacinth did not attempt to contradict.

The carriage had already come to a halt, and the driver was waiting outside the door. At Colin's nod, he opened it.

"I wish you wouldn't go," Violet said.

Gregory kissed her cheek. "I need air," he said. "That is all."

He hopped down, but before he could shut the door, Colin leaned out.

"Don't do anything foolish," Colin said quietly.

"Nothing foolish," Gregory promised him, "only what is necessary."

He took stock of his location, and then, as his mother's carriage had not moved, deliberately set off to the south.

Away from St. George's.

But once he reached the next street he doubled around.

Running.

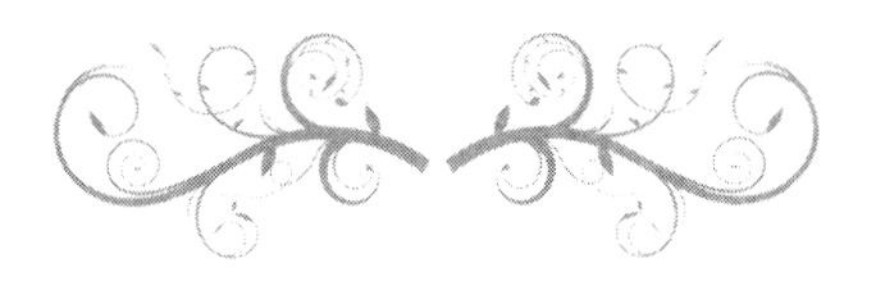

Chapter 23

In which Our Hero risks everything. Again.

In the ten years since her uncle had become her guardian, Lucy had never known him to host a party. He was not one to smile upon any sort of unnecessary expense—in truth, he was not one to smile at all. So it was with some suspicion that she approached the lavish fête being thrown in her honor at Fennsworth House following the wedding ceremony.

Lord Davenport had surely insisted upon it. Uncle Robert would have been content to serve tea cakes at the church and be done with it.

But no, the wedding must be an event, in the most extravagant sense of the word, and so as soon as the ceremony was over, Lucy was whisked to her soon-to-be-former home and given just enough time in her soon-to-be-former bedchamber to splash some cool water on her face before she was summoned to greet her guests below.

It was remarkable, she thought as she nodded and received the well wishes of the attendees, just how good the *ton* was at pretending nothing had happened.

Oh, they would be speaking of nothing else tomorrow, and she could probably look forward to being the main topic of conversation for the next few months, even. And certainly for the next year no one would say her name without appending, "You know the one. With the *wedding*."

Which would surely be followed by, "Ohhhhhhhh. *She's* the one."

But for now, to her face, there was nothing but "Such a happy occasion," and "You make a beautiful bride." And of course, for the sly and daring—"Lovely ceremony, Lady Haselby."

Lady Haselby.

She tested it out in her mind. She was Lady Haselby now.

She could have been Mrs. Bridgerton.

Lady Lucinda Bridgerton, she supposed, as she was not required to surrender her honorific upon marriage to a commoner. It was a nice name—not as lofty as Lady Haselby, perhaps, and certainly nothing compared to the Countess of Davenport, but—

She swallowed, somehow managing not to dislodge the smile she'd affixed to her face five minutes earlier.

She would have liked to have been Lady Lucinda Bridgerton.

She *liked* Lady Lucinda Bridgerton. She was a happy sort, with a ready smile and a life that was full and complete. She had a dog, maybe two, and several children. Her house was warm and cozy, she drank tea with her friends, and she laughed.

Lady Lucinda Bridgerton laughed.

But she would never be that woman. She had married Lord Haselby, and now she was his wife, and try as she might, she could not picture where her life might lead. She did not know what it meant to be Lady Haselby.

The party hummed along, and Lucy danced her obligatory dance with her new husband, who was, she was relieved to note, quite accomplished. Then she danced with her brother, which nearly made her cry, and then her uncle, because it was expected.

"You did the right thing, Lucy," he said.

She said nothing. She didn't trust herself to do so.

"I am proud of you."

She almost laughed. "You have never been proud of me before."

"I am now."

It did not escape her notice that this was not a contradiction.

Her uncle returned her to the side of the ballroom floor, and then—dear *God*—she had to dance with Lord Davenport.

Which she did, because she knew her duty. On this day, especially, she knew her duty.

At least she did not have to speak. Lord Davenport was at his most effusive, and more than carried the conversation for the both of them. He was delighted with Lucy. She was a magnificent asset to the family.

And so on and so forth until Lucy realized that she had managed to endear herself to him in the most indelible manner possible. She had not simply agreed to marry his dubiously reputationed son; she had affirmed the decision in front of the entire *ton* in a scene worthy of Drury Lane.

Lucy moved her head discreetly to the side. When Lord Davenport was excited, spittle tended to fly from his mouth with alarming speed and accuracy. Truly, she wasn't sure which was worse—Lord Davenport's disdain or his everlasting gratitude.

But Lucy managed to avoid her new father-in-law for most of the festivities, thank heavens. She managed to avoid most everyone, which was surprisingly undifficult, given that she was the bride. She didn't want to see Lord Davenport, because she detested him, and she didn't want to see her uncle, because she rather suspected she detested him, as well. She didn't want to see Lord Haselby, because that would only lead to thoughts of her upcoming wedding night, and she didn't want to see Hermione, because she would ask questions, and then Lucy would cry.

And she didn't want to see her brother, because he was sure to be with Hermione, and besides that, she was feeling rather bitter, alternating with feeling rather guilty for feeling bitter. It wasn't Richard's fault that he was deliriously happy and she was not.

But all the same, she'd rather not have to see him.

Which left the guests, most of whom she did not know. And none of whom she wished to meet.

So she found a spot in the corner, and after a couple of hours, everyone had drunk so much that no one seemed to notice that the bride was sitting by herself.

And certainly no one took note when she escaped to her bedchamber to take a short rest. It was probably very bad manners for a bride to avoid her own party, but at that moment, Lucy simply did not care. People would think she'd gone off to relieve herself, if anyone noticed her absence. And somehow it seemed appropriate for her to be alone on this day.

She slipped up the back stairs, lest she come across any wandering guests, and with a sigh of relief, she stepped into her room and shut the door behind her.

She leaned her back against the door, slowly deflating until it felt like there was nothing left within her.

And she thought—*Now I shall cry.*

She wanted to. Truly, she did. She felt as if she'd been holding it inside for hours, just waiting for a private moment. But the tears would not come. She was too numb, too dazed by the events of the last twenty-four hours. And so she stood there, staring at her bed.

Remembering.

Dear heaven, had it been only twelve hours earlier that she had lain there, wrapped in his arms? It seemed like years. It was as if her life were now neatly divided in two, and she was most firmly in *after*.

She closed her eyes. Maybe if she didn't see it, it would go away. Maybe if she—

"Lucy."

She froze. Dear God, *no*.

"Lucy."

Slowly, she opened her eyes. And whispered, "Gregory?"

He looked a mess, windblown and dirty as only a mad ride on horseback could do to a man. He must have sneaked in the same way he'd done the night before. He must have been waiting for her.

She opened her mouth, tried to speak.

"Lucy," he said again, and his voice flowed through her, melted around her.

She swallowed. "Why are you here?"

He stepped toward her, and her heart just *ached* from it. His face was so handsome, and so dear, and so perfectly wonderfully familiar. She knew the slope of his cheeks, and the exact shade of his eyes, brownish near the iris, melting into green at the edge.

And his mouth—she knew that mouth, the look of it, the feel of it. She knew his smile, and she knew his frown, and she knew—

She knew far too much.

"You shouldn't be here," she said, the catch in her voice belying the stillness of her posture.

He took another step in her direction. There was no anger in his eyes, which she did not understand. But the way he was looking at her—it was hot, and it was possessive, and it was nothing a married woman should ever allow from a man who was not her husband.

"I had to know why," he said. "I couldn't let you go. Not until I knew why."

"Don't," she whispered. "Please don't do this."

Please don't make me regret. Please don't make me long and wish and wonder.

She hugged her arms to her chest, as if maybe . . . maybe she could squeeze so tight that she could pull herself inside out. And then she wouldn't have to see, she wouldn't have to hear. She could just be alone, and—

"Lucy—"

"Don't," she said again, sharply this time.

Don't.

Don't make me believe in love.

But he moved ever closer. Slowly, but without hesitation. "Lucy," he said, his voice warm and full of purpose. "Just tell me why. That is all I ask. I will walk away and promise never to approach you again, but I must know why."

She shook her head. "I can't tell you."

"You won't tell me," he corrected.

"No," she cried out, choking on the word. "I can't! Please, Gregory. You must go."

For a long moment he said nothing. He just watched her face, and she could practically *see* him thinking.

She shouldn't allow this, she thought, a bubble of panic beginning to rise within her. She should scream. Have him ejected. She should run from the room before he could ruin her careful plans for the future. But instead she just stood there, and he said—

"You're being blackmailed."

It wasn't a question.

She did not answer, but she knew that her face gave her away.

"Lucy," he said, his voice soft and careful, "I can help you. Whatever it is, I can make it right."

"No," she said, "you can't, and you're a fool to—" She cut herself off, too furious to speak. What made him think he could rush in and fix things when he knew nothing of her travails? Did he think she had given in for something small? Something that could be easily overcome?

She was not that weak.

"You don't know," she said. "You have no idea."

"Then tell me."

Her muscles were shaking, and she felt hot . . . cold . . . everything in between.

"Lucy," he said, and his voice was so calm, so even—it was like a fork, poking her right where she could least tolerate it.

"You can't fix this," she ground out.

"That is not true. There is nothing anyone could hold over you that could not be overcome."

"By what?" she demanded. "Rainbows and sprites and the everlasting good wishes of your family? It won't work, Gregory. It won't. The Bridgertons may be powerful, but you cannot change the past, and you cannot bend the future to suit your whims."

"Lucy," he said, reaching out for her.

"No. No!" She pushed him away, rejected his offer of comfort. "You don't understand. You can't possibly. You are all so happy, so perfect."

"We are not."

"You *are*. You don't even know that you are, and you can't conceive that the rest of us are not, that we might struggle and try and be good and still not receive what we wish for."

Through it all, he watched her. Just watched her and let her stand by herself, hugging her arms to her body, looking small and pale and heartbreakingly alone.

And then he asked it.

"Do you love me?"

She closed her eyes. "Don't ask me that."

"Do you?"

He saw her jaw tighten, saw the way her shoulders tensed and rose, and he knew she was trying to shake her head.

Gregory walked toward her—slowly, respectfully.

She was hurting. She was hurting so much that it spread through the air, wrapped around him, around his heart. He ached for her. It was a physical thing, terrible and sharp, and for the first time he was beginning to doubt his own ability to make it go away.

"Do you love me?" he asked.

"Gregory—"

"Do you love me?"

"I can't—"

He placed his hands on her shoulders. She flinched, but she did not move away.

He touched her chin, nudged her face until he could lose himself in the blue of her eyes. "Do you love me?"

"Yes," she sobbed, collapsing into his arms. "But I can't. Don't you understand? I shouldn't. I have to make it stop."

For a moment Gregory could not move. Her admission should have come as a relief, and in a way it did, but more than that, he felt his blood begin to race.

He believed in love.

Wasn't that the one thing that had been a constant in his life?

He believed in love.

He believed in its power, in its fundamental goodness, its rightness.

He revered it for its strength, respected it for its rarity.

And he knew, right then, right there, as she cried in his arms, that he would dare anything for it.

For love.

"Lucy," he whispered, an idea beginning to form in his mind. It was mad, bad, and thoroughly inadvisable, but he could not escape the one thought that was rushing through his brain.

She had not consummated her marriage.

They still had a chance.

"Lucy."

She pulled away. "I must return. They will be missing me."

But he captured her hand. "Don't go back."

Her eyes grew huge. "What do you mean?"

"Come with me. Come with me now." He felt giddy, dangerous, and just a little bit mad. "You are not his wife yet. You can have it annulled."

"Oh no." She shook her head, tugging her arm away from him. "No, Gregory."

"Yes. Yes." And the more he thought about it, the more it made sense. They hadn't much time; after this evening it would be impossible for her to say that she was untouched. Gregory's own actions had made sure of that. If they had any chance of being together, it had to be now.

He couldn't kidnap her; there was no way he could remove her from the house without raising an alarm. But he could buy them a bit of time. Enough so that he could sort out what to do.

He pulled her closer.

"No," she said, her voice growing louder. She started really yanking on her arm now, and he could see the panic growing in her eyes.

"Lucy, yes," he said.

"I will scream," she said.

"No one will hear you."

She stared at him in shock, and even he could not believe what he was saying.

"Are you threatening me?" she asked.

He shook his head. "No. I'm saving you." And then, before he had the opportunity to reconsider his actions, he grabbed her around her middle, threw her over his shoulder, and ran from the room.

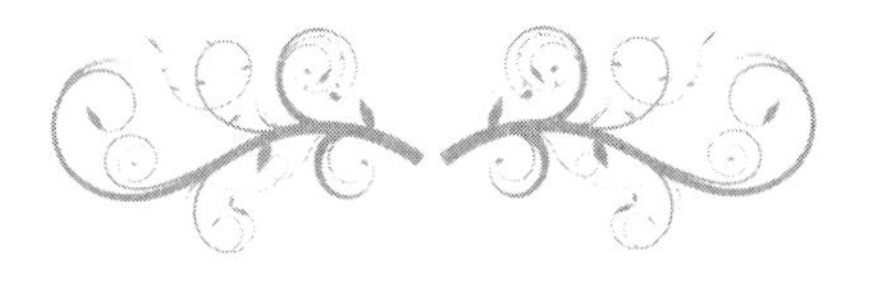

Chapter 24

In which Our Hero leaves
Our Heroine in an awkward position.

"You are tying me to a *water closet*?"

"Sorry," he said, tying two scarves into such expert knots that she almost worried that he had done this before. "I couldn't very well leave you in your room. That's the first place anyone would look." He tightened the knots, then tested them for strength. "It was the first place *I* looked."

"But a water closet!"

"On the third floor," he added helpfully. "It will take hours before anyone finds you here."

Lucy clenched her jaw, desperately trying to contain the fury that was rising within her.

He had lashed her hands together. *Behind her back.*

Good Lord, she had not known it was possible to be so angry with another person.

It wasn't just an emotional reaction—her entire body had erupted with it. She felt hot and prickly, and even though she knew it would do no good, she jerked her arms against the piping of the water closet, grinding her teeth and letting out a frustrated grunt when it did nothing but produce a dull clang.

"Please don't struggle," he said, dropping a kiss on the top of her head. "It is only going to leave you tired and sore." He looked up, examining the structure of the water closet. "Or you'll break the pipe, and surely that cannot be a hygienic prospect."

"Gregory, you have to let me go."

He crouched so that his face was on a level with hers. "I cannot," he said. "Not while there is still a chance for us to be together."

"Please," she pleaded, "this is madness. You must return me. I will be ruined."

"I will marry you," he said.

"I'm already married!"

"Not quite," he said with a wolfish smile.

"I said my vows!"

"But you did not consummate them. You can still get an annulment."

"That is not the point!" she cried out, struggling fruitlessly as he stood and walked to the door. "You don't understand the situation, and you are selfishly putting your own needs and happiness above those of others."

At that, he stopped. His hand was on the doorknob, but he stopped, and when he turned around, the look in his eyes nearly broke her heart.

"You're happy?" he asked. Softly, and with such love that she wanted to cry.

"No," she whispered, "but—"

"I've never seen a bride who looked so sad."

She closed her eyes, deflated. It was an echo of what Hermione had said, and she knew it was true. And even then, as she looked up at him, her shoulders aching, she could not escape the beatings of her own heart.

She loved him.

She would always love him.

And she hated him, too, for making her want what she could not have. She hated him for loving her so much that he would risk everything to be together. And most of all, she hated him for turning her into the instrument that would destroy her family.

Until she'd met Gregory, Hermione and Richard were the only two people in the world for whom she truly cared. And now they would be ruined, brought far lower and into greater unhappiness than Lucy could ever imagine with Haselby.

Gregory thought that it would take hours for someone to find her here, but she knew better. No one would locate her for days. She could not remember the last time anyone had wandered up here. She was in the nanny's washroom—but Fennsworth House had not had a nanny in residence for years.

When her disappearance was noticed, first they would check her room. Then they'd try a few sensible alternatives—the library, the sitting room, a washroom that had not been in disuse for half a decade . . .

And then, when she was not found, it would be assumed that she'd run off. And after what had happened at the church, no one would think she'd left on her own.

She would be ruined. And so would everyone else.

"It is not a question of my own happiness," she finally said, her voice quiet, almost broken. "Gregory, I beg of you, please don't do this. This is not just about me. My family— We will be ruined, all of us."

He walked to her side and sat. And then he said, simply, "Tell me."

She did. He would not give in otherwise, of that she was certain.

She told him everything. About her father, and the written proof of his treason. She told him about the blackmail. She told him how she was the final payment and the only thing that would keep her brother from being stripped of his title.

Lucy stared straight ahead throughout the telling, and for that, Gregory was grateful. Because what she said—it shook him to his very core.

All day Gregory had been trying to imagine what terrible secret could possibly induce her to marry Haselby. He'd run twice through London, first to the church and then here, to Fennsworth House. He had had plenty of time to think, to wonder. But never—not once—had his imagination led him to this.

"So you see," she said, "it is nothing so common as an illegitimate child, nothing so racy as an extramarital affair. My father—an earl of the realm—committed treason. *Treason*." And then she laughed. *Laughed*.

The way people did when what they really wanted was to cry.

"It's an ugly thing," she finished, her voice low and resigned. "There is no escaping it."

She turned to him for a response, but he had none.

Treason. Good God, he could not think of anything worse. There were many ways—many *many* ways—one could get oneself thrown out of society, but nothing was as unforgivable as treason. There wasn't a man, woman, or child in Britain who had not lost someone to Napoleon. The wounds were still too fresh, and even if they weren't . . .

It was *treason*.

A gentleman did not forsake his country.

It was ingrained in the soul of every man of Britain.

If the truth about Lucy's father were known, the earldom of

Fennsworth would be dissolved. Lucy's brother would be left destitute. He and Hermione would almost certainly have to emigrate.

And Lucy would . . .

Well, Lucy would probably survive the scandal, especially if her surname was changed to Bridgerton, but she would never forgive herself. Of that, Gregory was certain.

And finally, he understood.

He looked at her. She was pale and drawn, and her hands were clenched tightly in her lap. "My family has been good and true," she said, her voice shaking with emotion. "The Abernathys have been loyal to the crown since the first earl was invested in the fifteenth century. And my father has shamed us all. I cannot allow it to be revealed. I cannot." She swallowed awkwardly and then sadly said, "You should see your face. Even you don't want me now."

"No," he said, almost blurting out the word. "No. That is not true. That could never be true." He took her hands, held them in his own, savoring the shape of them, the arch of her fingers and the delicate heat of her skin.

"I am sorry," he said. "It should not have taken me so long to collect myself. I had not imagined treason."

She shook her head. "How could you?"

"But it does not change how I feel." He took her face in his hands, aching to kiss her but knowing he could not.

Not yet.

"What your father did— It is reprehensible. It is—" He swore under his breath. "I will be honest with you. It leaves me sick. But you—*you*, Lucy—you are innocent. You did nothing wrong, and you should not have to pay for his sins."

"Neither should my brother," she said quietly, "but if I do not complete my marriage to Haselby, Richard will—"

"Shhh." Gregory pressed a finger to her lips. "Listen to me. I love you."

Her eyes filled with tears.

"I love you," he said again. "There is nothing in this world or the next that could ever make me stop loving you."

"You felt that way about Hermione," she whispered.

"No," he said, almost smiling at how silly it all seemed now. "I had been waiting so long to fall in love that I wanted the love more than the woman. I never loved Hermione, just the idea of her. But with you . . . It's different, Lucy. It's deeper. It's . . . it's . . ."

He struggled for words, but there were none. Words simply did not exist to explain what he felt for her. "It's *me*," he finally said, appalled at the inelegance of it. "Without you, I . . . I am . . ."

"Gregory," she whispered, "you don't have to—"

"I am nothing," he cut in, because he wasn't going to allow her to tell him that he didn't have to explain. "Without you, I am nothing."

She smiled. It was a sad smile, but it was true, and it felt as if he'd been waiting years for that smile. "That's not true," she said. "You know that it's not."

He shook his head. "An exaggeration, perhaps, but that is all. You make me better, Lucy. You make me wish, and hope, and aspire. You make me want to *do* things."

Tears began to trickle down her cheeks.

With the pads of his thumbs he brushed them away. "You are the finest person I know," he said, "the most honorable human being I have ever met. You make me laugh. And you make me *think*. And I . . ." He took a deep breath. "I love you."

And again. "I love you."

And again. "I love you." He shook his head helplessly. "I don't know how else to say it."

She turned away then, twisting her head so that his hands slid from her face to her shoulders, and finally, away from her body completely. Gregory could not see her face, but he could hear her—the quiet, broken sound of her breathing, the soft whimper in her voice.

"I love you," she finally answered, still not looking at him. "You know that I do. I will not demean us both by lying about it. And if it were only me, I would do anything—anything for that love. I would risk poverty, ruin. I would move to America, I would move to Timbuktu if that were the only way to be with you."

She let out a long, shaky breath. "I cannot be so selfish as to bring down the two people who have loved me so well and for so long."

"Lucy . . ." He had no idea what he wanted to tell her, just that he didn't want her to finish. He knew he did not want to hear what she had to say.

But she cut him off with—"Don't, Gregory. Please. I'm sorry. I cannot do it, and if you love me as you say you do, you will bring me back now, before Lord Davenport realizes I've gone missing."

Gregory squeezed his fingers into fists, then flexed them wide and straight. He knew what he should do. He should release her, let her run downstairs to the party. He should sneak back out the servants' door and vow never to approach her again.

She had promised to love, honor, and obey another man. She was supposed to forsake all others.

Surely, he fell under that aegis.

And yet he couldn't give up.

Not yet.

"One hour," he said, moving into a crouching position beside her. "Just give me one hour."

She turned, her eyes doubtful and astonished and maybe—

maybe—just a little bit hopeful as well. "One hour?" she echoed. "What do you think you can—"

"I don't know," he said honestly. "But I will promise you this. If I cannot find a way to free you from this blackmail in one hour, I will return for you. And I will release you."

"To return to Haselby?" she whispered, and she sounded—

Did she sound disappointed? Even a little?

"Yes," he said. Because in truth it was the only thing he could say. Much as he wished to throw caution to the wind, he knew that he could not steal her away. She would be respectable, as he would marry her as soon as Haselby agreed to the annulment, but she would never be happy.

And he knew that he could not live with himself.

"You will not be ruined if you go missing for one hour," he said to her. "You can simply tell people you were overset. You wished to take a nap. I am sure that Hermione will corroborate your story if you ask her to."

Lucy nodded. "Will you release my bindings?"

He gave his head a tiny shake and stood. "I would trust you with my life, Lucy, but not with your own. You're far too honorable for your own good."

"Gregory!"

He shrugged as he walked to the door. "Your conscience will get the better of you. You know that it will."

"What if I promise—"

"Sorry." One corner of his mouth stretched into a not quite apologetic expression. "I won't believe you."

He took one last look at her before he left. And he had to smile, which seemed ludicrous, given that he had one hour to neutralize the blackmail threat against Lucy's family and extract her from her marriage. During her wedding reception.

By comparison, moving heaven and earth seemed a far better prospect.

But when he turned to Lucy, and saw her sitting there, on the floor, she looked . . .

Like herself again.

"Gregory," she said, "you cannot leave me here. What if someone finds you and removes you from the house? Who will know I am here? And what if . . . and what if . . . and then what if . . ."

He smiled, enjoying her officiousness too much to actually listen to her words. She was definitely herself again.

"When this is all over," he said, "I shall bring you a sandwich."

That stopped her short. "A sandwich? A *sandwich*?"

He twisted the doorknob but didn't yet pull. "You want a sandwich, don't you? You always want a sandwich."

"You've gone mad," she said.

He couldn't believe she'd only just come to the conclusion. "Don't yell," he warned.

"You know I can't," she muttered.

It was true. The last thing she wanted was to be found. If Gregory was not successful, she would need to be able to slip back into the party with as little fuss as possible.

"Goodbye, Lucy," he said. "I love you."

She looked up. And she whispered, "One hour. Do you really think you can do it?"

He nodded. It was what she needed to see, and it was what he needed to pretend.

And as he closed the door behind him, he could have sworn he heard her murmur, "Good luck."

He paused for one deep breath before heading for the stairs. He was going to need more than luck; he was going to need a bloody miracle.

The odds were against him. The odds were *extremely* against him. But Gregory had always been one to cheer for the underdog. And if there was any sense of justice in the world, any existential fairness floating through the air . . . If *Do unto others* offered any sort of payback, surely he was due.

Love existed.

He knew that it did. And he would be damned if it did not exist for him.

Gregory's first stop was Lucy's bedchamber, on the second floor. He couldn't very well stroll into the ballroom and request an audience with one of the guests, but he thought there was a chance that someone had noticed Lucy's absence and gone off looking for her. God willing it would be someone sympathetic to their cause, someone who actually cared about Lucy's happiness.

But when Gregory slipped inside the room, all was exactly as he'd left it. "Damn," he muttered, striding back to the door. Now he was going to have to figure out how to speak to her brother—or Haselby, he supposed—without attracting attention.

He placed his hand on the knob and yanked, but the weight of the door was all wrong, and Gregory wasn't certain which happened first—the feminine shriek of surprise or the soft, warm body tumbling into his.

"You!"

"You!" he said in return. "Thank God."

It was Hermione. The one person he *knew* cared for Lucy's happiness above all else.

"What are you doing here?" she hissed. But she closed the door to the corridor, surely a good sign.

"I had to talk to Lucy."

"She married Lord Haselby."

He shook his head. "It has not been consummated."

Her mouth quite literally fell open. "Good God, you don't mean to—"

"I will be honest with you," he cut in. "I don't know what I mean to do, other than find a way to free her."

Hermione stared at him for several seconds. And then, seemingly out of nowhere, she said, "She loves you."

"She told you that?"

She shook her head. "No, but it's obvious. Or at least with hindsight it is." She paced the room, then turned suddenly around. "Then why did she marry Lord Haselby? I know she feels strongly about honoring commitments, but surely she could have ended it before today."

"She is being blackmailed," Gregory said grimly.

Hermione's eyes grew very large. "With what?"

"I can't tell you."

To her credit, she did not waste time protesting. Instead, she looked up at him, her eyes sharp and steady. "What can I do to help?"

Five minutes later, Gregory found himself in the company of both Lord Haselby and Lucy's brother. He would have preferred to have done without the latter, who looked as if he might cheerfully decapitate Gregory were it not for the presence of his wife.

Who had his arm in a viselike grip.

"Where is Lucy?" Richard demanded.

"She is safe," Gregory replied.

"Pardon me if I am not reassured," Richard retorted.

"Richard, stop," Hermione cut in, forcibly pulling him back. "Mr. Bridgerton is not going to hurt her. He has her best interests at heart."

"Oh, really?" Richard drawled.

Hermione glared at him with more animation than Gregory had ever seen on her pretty face. "He loves her," she declared.

"Indeed."

All eyes turned to Lord Haselby, who had been standing by the door, watching the scene with a strange expression of amusement.

No one seemed to know what to say.

"Well, he certainly made it clear this morning," Haselby continued, settling into a chair with remarkably easy grace. "Wouldn't you agree?"

"Er, yes?" Richard answered, and Gregory couldn't really blame him for his uncertain tone. Haselby did seem to be taking this in a most uncommon manner. Calm. So calm that Gregory's pulse seemed to feel the need to race twice as fast, if only to make up for Haselby's shortcomings.

"She loves me," Gregory told him, balling his hand into a fist behind his back—not in preparation for violence, but rather because if he didn't move *some* part of his body, he was liable to jump out of his skin. "I'm sorry to say it, but—"

"No, no, not at all," Haselby said with a wave. "I'm quite aware she doesn't love *me*. Which is really for the best, as I'm sure we can all agree."

Gregory wasn't sure whether he was meant to answer that. Richard was flushing madly, and Hermione looked completely confused.

"Will you release her?" Gregory asked. He did not have time to dance around the subject.

"If I weren't willing to do that, do you really think I'd be standing here speaking with you in the same tones I use to discuss the weather?"

"Er . . . no?"

Haselby smiled. Slightly. "My father will not be pleased. A state of affairs which normally brings me great joy, to be sure, but it does present a host of difficulties. We shall have to proceed with caution."

"Shouldn't Lucy be here?" Hermione asked.

Richard resumed his glaring. "Where *is* my sister?"

"Upstairs," Gregory said curtly. That narrowed it down to only thirty-odd rooms.

"Upstairs *where*?" Richard ground out.

Gregory ignored the question. It really wasn't the best time to reveal that she was presently tied to a water closet.

He turned back to Haselby, who was still seated, one leg crossed casually over the other. He was examining his fingernails.

Gregory felt ready to climb the walls. How could the bloody man sit there so calmly? This was the single most critical conversation either of them would ever have, and all he could do was inspect his *manicure*?

"Will you release her?" Gregory ground out.

Haselby looked up at him and blinked. "I said I would."

"But will you reveal her secrets?"

At that, Haselby's entire demeanor changed. His body seemed to tighten, and his eyes grew deadly sharp. "I have no idea what you're talking about," he said, each word crisp and precise.

"Nor do I," Richard added, stepping close.

Gregory turned briefly in his direction. "She is being blackmailed."

"Not," Haselby said sharply, "by me."

"My apologies," Gregory said quietly. Blackmail was an ugly thing. "I did not mean to imply."

"I always wondered why she agreed to marry me," Haselby said softly.

"It *was* arranged by her uncle," Hermione put in. Then, when everyone turned to her in mild surprise, she added, "Well, you know Lucy. She's not the sort to rebel. She *likes* order."

"All the same," Haselby said, "she did have a rather dramatic opportunity to get out of it." He paused, cocking his head to the side. "It's my father, isn't it?"

Gregory's chin jerked in a single, grim nod.

"That is not surprising. He is rather eager to have me married. Well, then—" Haselby brought his hands together, twining his fingers and squeezing them down. "What shall we do? Call his bluff, I imagine."

Gregory shook his head. "We can't."

"Oh, come now. It can't be that bad. What on earth could Lady Lucinda have done?"

"We really should get her," Hermione said again. And then, when the three men turned to her again, she added, "How would you like your fate to be discussed in your absence?"

Richard stepped in front of Gregory. "Tell me," he said.

Gregory did not pretend to misunderstand. "It is bad."

"Tell me."

"It is your father," Gregory said in a quiet voice. And he proceeded to relate what Lucy had told to him.

"She did it for us," Hermione whispered once Gregory was done. She turned to her husband, clutching his hand. "She did it to save us. Oh, *Lucy*."

But Richard just shook his head. "It's not true," he said.

Gregory tried to keep the pity out of his eyes as he said, "There is proof."

"Oh, really? What sort of proof?"

"Lucy says there is written proof."

"Has she seen it?" Richard demanded. "Would she even know how to tell if something were faked?"

Gregory took a long breath. He could not blame Lucy's brother for his reaction. He supposed he would be the same, were such a thing to come to light about his own father.

"Lucy doesn't know," Richard continued, still shaking his head. "She was too young. Father wouldn't have done such a thing. It is inconceivable."

"You were young as well," Gregory said gently.

"I was old enough to know my own father," Richard snapped, "and he was not a traitor. Someone has deceived Lucy."

Gregory turned to Haselby. "Your father?"

"Is not that clever," Haselby finished. "He would cheerfully commit blackmail, but he would do it with the truth, not a lie. He is intelligent, but he is not creative."

Richard stepped forward. "But my uncle is."

Gregory turned to him with urgency. "Do you think he has lied to Lucy?"

"He certainly said the one thing to her that would guarantee that she would not back out of the marriage," Richard said bitterly.

"But why does *he* need her to marry Lord Haselby?" Hermione asked.

They all looked to the man in question.

"I have no idea," he said.

"He must have secrets of his own," Gregory said.

Richard shook his head. "Not debts."

"He's not getting any money in the settlement," Haselby remarked.

Everyone turned to look at him.

"I may have let my father choose my bride," he said with a shrug, "but I wasn't about to marry without reading the contracts."

"Secrets, then," Gregory said.

"Perhaps in concert with Lord Davenport," Hermione added. She turned to Haselby. "So sorry."

He waved off her apology. "Think nothing of it."

"What should we do now?" Richard asked.

"Get Lucy," Hermione immediately answered.

Gregory nodded briskly. "She is right."

"No," said Haselby, rising to his feet. "We need my father."

"Your father?" Richard bit off. "He's hardly sympathetic to our cause."

"Perhaps, and I'm the first to say he's intolerable for more than three minutes at a time, but he will have answers. And for all of his venom, he is mostly harmless."

"Mostly?" Hermione echoed.

Haselby appeared to consider that. "Mostly."

"We need to act," Gregory said. "Now. Haselby, you and Fennsworth will locate your father and interrogate him. Find out the truth. Lady Fennsworth and I will retrieve Lucy and bring her back here, where Lady Fennsworth will remain with her." He turned to Richard. "I apologize for the arrangements, but I must have your wife with me to safeguard Lucy's reputation should someone discover us. She's been gone nearly an hour now. Someone is bound to notice."

Richard gave him a curt nod, but it was clear he was not happy with the situation. Still, he had no choice. His honor demanded that he be the one to question Lord Davenport.

"Good," Gregory said. "Then we are agreed. I will meet the two of you back in . . ."

He paused. Aside from Lucy's room and the upstairs washroom, he had no knowledge of the layout of the house.

"Meet us in the library," Richard instructed. "It is on the ground floor, facing east." He took a step toward the door, then turned back and said to Gregory, "Wait here. I will return in a moment."

Gregory was eager to be off, but Richard's grave expression had been enough to convince him to remain in place. Sure enough, when Lucy's brother returned, barely a minute later, he carried with him two guns.

He held one out to Gregory.

Good God.

"You may need this," Richard said.

"Heaven help us if I do," Gregory said under his breath.

"Beg pardon?"

Gregory shook his head.

"Godspeed, then." Richard nodded at Haselby, and the two of them departed, moving swiftly down the hall.

Gregory beckoned to Hermione. "Let us go," he said, leading her in the opposite direction. "And do try not to judge me when you see where I am leading you."

He heard her chuckle as they ascended the stairs. "Why," she said, "do I suspect that, if anything, I shall judge you very clever indeed?"

"I did not trust her to remain in place," Gregory confessed, taking the steps two at a time. When they reached the top, he turned to face her. "It was heavy-handed, but there was nothing else I could do. All I needed was a bit of time."

Hermione nodded. "Where are we going?"

"To the nanny's washroom," he confessed. "I tied her to the water closet."

"You tied her to the—Oh my, I cannot wait to see this."

But when they opened the door to the small washroom, Lucy was gone.

And every indication was that she had not left willingly.

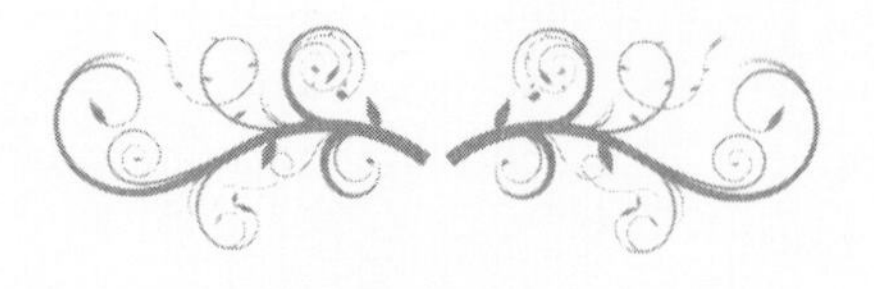

Chapter 25

In which we learn what happened,
a mere ten minutes earlier.

Had it been an hour? Surely it had been an hour.

Lucy took a deep breath and tried to calm her racing nerves. Why hadn't anyone thought to install a clock in the washroom? Shouldn't someone have realized that *eventually* someone would find herself tied to the water closet and *might* wish to know the hour?

Really, it was just a matter of time.

Lucy drummed the fingers of her right hand against the floor. Quickly, quickly, index to pinky, index to pinky. Her left hand was tied so that the pads of her fingers faced up, so she flexed, then bent, then flexed, then bent, then—

"Eeeeeuuuuuhhh!"

Lucy groaned with frustration.

Groaned? Grunted.

Groanted.

It should have been a word.

Surely it had been an hour. It must have been an hour.

And then . . .

Footsteps.

Lucy jerked to attention, glaring at the door. She was furious. And hopeful. And terrified. And nervous. And—

Good God, she wasn't meant to possess this many simultaneous emotions. One at a time was all she could manage. Maybe two.

The knob turned and the door jerked backward, and—

Jerked? Lucy had about one second to sense the wrongness of this. Gregory wouldn't jerk the door open. He would have—

"Uncle Robert?"

"You," he said, his voice low and furious.

"I—"

"You little whore," he bit off.

Lucy flinched. She knew he held no great affection for her, but still, it hurt.

"You don't understand," she blurted out, because she had no idea what she should say, and she refused—she absolutely *refused* to say, "I'm sorry."

She was done with apologizing. Done.

"Oh, really?" he spat out, crouching down to her level. "Just what don't I understand? The part about your fleeing your wedding?"

"I didn't flee," she shot back. "I was abducted! Or didn't you notice that I am *tied to the water closet*?"

His eyes narrowed menacingly. And Lucy began to feel scared.

She shrank back, her breath growing shallow. She had long feared her uncle—the ice of his temper, the cold, flat stare of his disdain.

But she had never felt frightened.

"Where is he?" her uncle demanded.

Lucy did not pretend to misunderstand. "I don't know."

"Tell me!"

"I don't know!" she protested. "Do you think he would have tied me up if he trusted me?"

Her uncle stood and cursed. "It doesn't make sense."

"What do you mean?" Lucy asked carefully. She wasn't sure what was going on, and she wasn't sure just whose wife she would be, at the end of the proverbial day, but she was fairly certain that she ought to stall for time.

And reveal nothing. Nothing of import.

"This! You!" her uncle spat out. "Why would he abduct you and leave you here, in Fennsworth House?"

"Well," Lucy said slowly. "I don't think he could have got me out without someone seeing."

"He couldn't have got into the party without someone seeing, either."

"I'm not sure what you mean."

"How," her uncle demanded, leaning down and putting his face far too close to hers, "did he grab you without your consent?"

Lucy let out a short puff of a breath. The truth was easy. And innocuous. "I went to my room to lie down," she said. "He was waiting for me there."

"He knew which room was yours?"

She swallowed. "Apparently."

Her uncle stared at her for an uncomfortably long moment. "People have begun to notice your absence," he muttered.

Lucy said nothing.

"It can't be helped, though."

She blinked. What was he talking about?

He shook his head. "It's the only way."

"I—I beg your pardon?" And then she realized—he wasn't talking to her. He was talking to himself.

"Uncle Robert?" she whispered.

But he was already slicing through her bindings.

Slicing? *Slicing?* Why did he have a knife?

"Let's go," he grunted.

"Back to the party?"

He let out a grim chuckle. "You'd like that, wouldn't you?"

Panic began to rise in her chest. "Where are you taking me?"

He yanked her to her feet, one of his arms wrapped viselike around her. "To your husband."

She managed to twist just far enough to look at his face. "My—Lord Haselby?"

"Have you another husband?"

"But isn't he at the party?"

"Stop asking so many questions."

She looked frantically about. "But where are you taking me?"

"You are not going to ruin this for me," he hissed. "Do you understand?"

"No," she pleaded. Because she didn't. She no longer understood anything.

He yanked her hard against him. "I want you to listen to me, because I will say this only once."

She nodded. She wasn't facing him, but she knew he could feel her head move against his chest.

"This marriage will go forward," he said, his voice deadly and low. "And I will personally see to it that it is consummated tonight."

"What?"

"*Don't* argue with me."

"But—" She dug her heels in as he started to drag her to the door.

"For God's sake, don't fight me," he muttered. "It's nothing that you wouldn't have had to do, anyway. The only difference is that you will have an audience."

"An audience?"

"Indelicate, but I will have my proof."

She began to struggle in earnest, managing to free one arm long enough to swing wildly through the air. He quickly restrained her, but his momentary shift in posture allowed her to kick him hard in the shins.

"God *damn* it," he muttered, wrenching her close. "Cease!"

She kicked out again, knocking over an empty chamber pot.

"Stop it!" He jammed something against her ribs. "Now!"

Lucy stilled instantly. "Is that a knife?" she whispered.

"Remember this," he said, his words hot and ugly against her ear. "I cannot kill you, but I can cause you great pain."

She swallowed a sob. "I am your niece."

"I don't care."

She swallowed and asked, her voice quiet, "Did you ever?"

He nudged her toward the door. "Care?"

She nodded.

For a moment there was silence, and Lucy was left with no means to interpret it. She could not see her uncle's face, could sense no change in his stance. She could do nothing but stare at the door, at his hand as he reached for the knob.

And then he said, "No."

She had her answer, then.

"You were a duty," he clarified. "One I fulfilled, and one I am pleased to discharge. Now come with me, and don't say a word."

Lucy nodded. His knife was pressing ever harder against her

ribs and already she had heard a soft crunching sound as it poked through the stiff fabric of her bodice.

She let him move her along the corridor and down the stairs. Gregory was here, she kept telling herself. He was here, and he would find her. Fennsworth House was large, but it was not massive. There were only so many places her uncle could stash her.

And there were hundreds of guests on the ground floor.

And Lord Haselby—surely he would not consent to such a scheme.

There were at least a dozen reasons her uncle would not succeed in this.

A dozen. Twelve. Maybe more. And she needed only one—just one to foil his plot.

But this was of little comfort when he stopped and yanked a blindfold over her eyes.

And even less when he threw her into a room and tied her up.

"I will be back," he bit off, leaving her on her bottom in the corner, hands tied tightly in front of her.

She heard his footsteps move across the room, and then it burst from her lips—a single word, the only word that mattered—

"Why?"

His footsteps stopped.

"Why, Uncle Robert?"

This couldn't be just about the family honor. Hadn't she already proved herself on that score? Shouldn't he trust her for that?

"Why?" she asked again, praying he had a conscience. Surely he couldn't have looked after her and Richard for so many years without some sense of right and wrong.

"You know why," he finally said, but she knew that he was lying. He had waited far too long before answering.

"Go, then," she said bitterly. There was no point in stalling him. It would be far better if Gregory found her alone.

But he didn't move. And even through her blindfold she could feel his suspicion.

"What are you waiting for?" she cried out.

"I'm not sure," he said slowly. And then she heard him turn.

His footsteps drew closer.

Slowly.

Slowly . . .

And then—

"Where is she?" Hermione gasped.

Gregory strode into the small room, his eyes taking in everything—the cut bindings, the overturned chamber pot. "Someone took her," he said grimly.

"Her uncle?"

"Or Davenport. They are the only two with reason to—" He shook his head. "No, they cannot do her harm. They need the marriage to be legal and binding. And long-standing. Davenport wants an heir off Lucy."

Hermione nodded.

Gregory turned to her. "You know the house. Where could she be?"

Hermione was shaking her head. "I don't know. I don't know. If it's her uncle—"

"Assume it's her uncle," Gregory ordered. He wasn't sure that Davenport was agile enough to abduct Lucy, and besides that, if what Haselby had said about his father was true, then Robert Abernathy was the man with secrets.

He was the man with something to lose.

"His study," Hermione whispered. "He is always in his study."

"Where is it?"

"On the ground floor. It looks out the back."

"He wouldn't risk it," Gregory said. "Too close to the ballroom."

"Then his bedchamber. If he means to avoid the public rooms, then that is where he would take her. That or her own chamber."

Gregory took her arm and preceded her out the door. They made their way down one flight of stairs, pausing before opening the door that led from the servants' stairs to the second floor landing.

"Point out his door to me," he said, "and then go."

"I'm not—"

"Find your husband," he ordered. "Bring him back."

Hermione looked conflicted, but she nodded and did as he asked.

"Go," he said, once he knew where to go. "Quickly."

She ran down the stairs as Gregory crept along the hall. He reached the door Hermione had indicated and carefully pressed his ear to it.

"What are you waiting for?"

It was Lucy. Muffled through the heavy wood door, but it was she.

"I don't know," came a male voice, and Gregory realized that he could not identify it. He'd had few conversations with Lord Davenport and none with her uncle. He had no idea who was holding her hostage.

He held his breath and slowly turned the knob.

With his left hand.

With his right hand he pulled out his gun.

God help them all if he had to use it.

He managed to get the door open a crack—just enough to peer in without being noticed.

His heart stopped.

Lucy was bound and blindfolded, huddled in the far corner of the room. Her uncle was standing in front of her, a gun pointed between her eyes.

"What are you up to?" he asked her, his voice chilling in its softness.

Lucy did not say anything, but her chin shook, as if she was trying too hard to hold her head steady.

"Why do you wish for me to leave?" her uncle demanded.

"I don't know."

"Tell me." He lunged forward, jamming his gun between her ribs. And then, when she did not answer quickly enough, he yanked up her blindfold, leaving them nose to nose. "Tell me!"

"Because I can't bear the waiting," she whispered, her voice quivering. "Because—"

Gregory stepped quietly into the room and pointed his gun at the center of Robert Abernathy's back. *"Release her."*

Lucy's uncle froze.

Gregory's hand tightened around the trigger. "Release Lucy and step slowly away."

"I don't think so," Abernathy said, and he turned just enough so that Gregory could see that his gun was now resting against Lucy's temple.

Somehow, Gregory held steady. He would never know how, but his arm held firm. His hand did not quiver.

"Drop your gun," her uncle ordered.

Gregory did not move. His eyes flicked to Lucy, then back to her uncle. Would he hurt her? Could he? Gregory still wasn't certain just why, precisely, Robert Abernathy needed Lucy to marry Haselby, but it was clear that he did.

Which meant that he could not kill her.

Gregory gritted his teeth and tightened his finger on the trigger. "Release Lucy," he said, his voice low, strong, and steady.

"Drop your gun!" Abernathy roared, and a horrible, choking sound flew from Lucy's mouth as one of his arms jammed up and under her ribs.

Good God, he was mad. His eyes were wild, darting around the room, and his hand—the one with the gun—was shaking.

He would shoot her. Gregory realized that in one sickening flash. Whatever Robert Abernathy had done—he thought he had nothing left to lose. And he would not care whom he brought down with him.

Gregory began to bend at his knees, never taking his eyes off Lucy's uncle.

"Don't do it," Lucy cried out. "He won't hurt me. He can't."

"Oh, I can," her uncle replied, and he smiled.

Gregory's blood ran cold. He would try—dear God, he would try with everything he had to make sure that they both came through this alive and unhurt, but if there was a choice—if only one of them was to walk out the door . . .

It would be Lucy.

This, he realized, was love. It was that sense of rightness, yes. And it was the passion, too, and the lovely knowledge that he could happily wake up next to her for the rest of his life.

But it was more than all that. It was this feeling, this knowledge, this *certainty* that he would give his life for her. There was no question. No hesitation. If he dropped his gun, Robert Abernathy would surely shoot him.

But Lucy would live.

Gregory lowered himself into a crouch. "Don't hurt her," he said softly.

"Don't let go!" Lucy cried out. "He won't—"

"Shut up!" her uncle snapped, and the barrel of his gun pressed even harder against her.

"Not another word, Lucy," Gregory warned. He still wasn't sure how the hell he was going to get out of this, but he knew that the key was to keep Robert Abernathy as calm and as sane as possible.

Lucy's lips parted, but then their eyes met . . .

And she closed them.

She trusted him. Dear God, she trusted him to keep her safe, to keep them both safe, and he felt like a fraud, because all he was doing was stalling for time, keeping all the bullets in all the guns until someone else arrived.

"I won't hurt you, Abernathy," Gregory said.

"Then drop the gun."

He kept his arm outstretched, the gun now positioned sideways so he could lay it down.

But he did not let go.

And he did not take his eyes off Robert Abernathy's face as he asked, "Why do you need her to marry Lord Haselby?"

"She didn't tell you?" he sneered.

"She told me what you told her."

Lucy's uncle began to shake.

"I spoke with Lord Fennsworth," Gregory said quietly. "He was somewhat surprised by your characterization of his father."

Lucy's uncle did not respond, but his throat moved, his Adam's apple shifting up and down in a convulsive swallow.

"In fact," Gregory continued, "he was quite convinced that you must be in error." He kept his voice smooth, even. Unmocking. He spoke as if at a dinner party. He did not wish to provoke; he only wished to converse.

"Richard knows nothing," Lucy's uncle replied.

"I spoke with Lord Haselby as well," Gregory said. "He was also surprised. He did not realize that his father had been blackmailing you."

Lucy's uncle glared at him.

"He is speaking with him now," Gregory said softly.

No one spoke. No one moved. Gregory's muscles were screaming. He had been in his crouch for several minutes, balancing on the balls of his feet. His arm, still outstretched, still holding the gun sideways but steady, felt like it was on fire.

He looked at the gun.

He looked at Lucy.

She was shaking her head. Slowly, and with small motions. Her lips made no sound, but he could easily make out her words.

Go.

And *please.*

Amazingly, Gregory felt himself smile. He shook his head, and he whispered, "Never."

"What did you say?" Abernathy demanded.

Gregory said the only thing that came to mind. "I love your niece."

Abernathy looked at him as if he'd gone mad. "I don't care."

Gregory took a gamble. "I love her enough to keep your secrets."

Robert Abernathy blanched. He went absolutely bloodless, and utterly still.

"It was you," Gregory said softly.

Lucy twisted. "Uncle Robert?"

"Shut up," he snapped.

"Did you lie to me?" she asked, and her voice sounded almost wounded. "Did you?"

"Lucy, *don't*," Gregory said.

But she was already shaking her head. "It wasn't my father, was it? It was *you*. Lord Davenport was blackmailing you for your *own* misdeeds."

Her uncle said nothing, but they all saw the truth in his eyes.

"Oh, Uncle Robert," she whispered sadly, "how could you?"

"I had nothing," he hissed. "Nothing. Just your father's droppings and leftovers."

Lucy turned ashen. "Did you kill him?"

"No," her uncle replied. Nothing else. Just no.

"Please," she said, her voice small and pained. "Do not lie to me. Not about this."

Her uncle let out an aggravated breath and said, "I know only what the authorities told me. He was found near a gambling hell, shot in the chest and robbed of all of his valuables."

Lucy watched him for a moment, and then, her eyes brimming with tears, gave a little nod.

Gregory rose slowly to his feet. "It is over, Abernathy," he said. "Haselby knows, as does Fennsworth. You cannot force Lucy to do your bidding."

Lucy's uncle gripped her more tightly. "I can use her to get away."

"Indeed you can. By letting her go."

Abernathy laughed at that. It was a bitter, caustic sound.

"We have nothing to gain by exposing you," Gregory said carefully. "Better to allow you to quietly leave the country."

"It will never be quiet," Lucy's uncle mocked. "If she does not marry that freakish fop, Davenport will shout it from here to Scotland. And the family will be ruined."

"No." Gregory shook his head. "They won't. You were never the earl. You were never their father. There will be a scandal; that cannot be avoided. But Lucy's brother will not lose his title, and it will all blow over when people begin to recall that they'd never quite liked you."

In the blink of an eye, Lucy's uncle moved the gun from her belly to her neck. "You watch what you say," he snapped.

Gregory blanched and took a step back.

And then they all heard it.

A thunder of footsteps. Moving quickly down the hall.

"Put the gun down," Gregory said. "You have only a moment before—"

The doorway filled with people. Richard, Haselby, Davenport, Hermione—they all dashed in, unaware of the deadly confrontation taking place.

Lucy's uncle jumped back, wildly pointing his gun at the lot of them. "Stay away," he yelled. "Get out! All of you!" His eyes flashed like those of a cornered animal, and his arm waved back and forth, leaving no one untargeted.

But Richard stepped forward. "You bastard," he hissed. "I will see you in—"

A gun fired.

Gregory watched in horror as Lucy fell to the ground. A guttural cry ripped from his throat; his own gun rose.

He aimed.

He fired.

And for the first time in his life, he hit his mark.

Well, almost.

Lucy's uncle was not a large man, but nonetheless, when he landed on top of her, it hurt. The air was forced completely from her lungs, leaving her gasping and choking, her eyes squeezed shut from the pain.

"Lucy!"

It was Gregory, tearing her uncle from atop her.

"Where are you hurt?" he demanded, and his hands were everywhere, frantic in their motions as he searched for a wound.

"I didn't—" She fought for breath. "He didn't—" She managed to look at her chest. It was covered with blood. "Oh my heavens."

"I can't find it," Gregory said. He took her chin, positioning her face so that she was looking directly into his eyes.

And she almost didn't recognize him.

His eyes . . . his beautiful hazel eyes . . . they looked lost, nearly empty. And it almost seemed to take away whatever it was that made him . . . *him*.

"Lucy," he said, his voice hoarse with emotion, "*please*. Speak to me."

"I'm not hurt," she finally got out, and she held up her hands, silently asking him to untie her.

He immediately got to work on the knot. "The blood," he said.

"It's not mine." She looked up at him and brought her hand to his cheek. He was shaking. Oh dear God, he was shaking. She had never seen him thus, never imagined he could be brought to this point.

The look in his eyes— She realized it now. It had been terror.

"I'm not hurt," she whispered. "Please . . . don't . . . it's all right, darling." She didn't know what she was saying; she only wanted to comfort him.

His breath was ragged, and when he spoke, his words were broken, unfinished. "I thought I'd— I don't know what I thought."

Something wet touched her finger, and she brushed it gently away. "It's over now," she said. "It's over now, and—"

And suddenly she became aware of the rest of the people in the room. "Well, I think it's over," she said hesitantly, pushing herself into a seated position. Was her uncle dead? She knew he'd been shot. By Gregory or Richard, she did not know which. Both had fired their weapons.

But Uncle Robert had not been mortally wounded. He had pulled himself to the side of the room and was propped up against the wall, clutching his shoulder and staring ahead with a defeated expression.

Lucy scowled at him. "You're lucky he's not a better shot."

Gregory made a rather strange, snorting sound.

Over in the corner, Richard and Hermione were clutching each other, but they both appeared unharmed. Lord Davenport was bellowing about something, she wasn't sure what, and Lord Haselby—good God, her *husband*—was leaning idly against the doorjamb, watching the scene.

He caught her eye and smiled. Just a bit. No teeth, of course; he never smiled quite so broadly.

"I'm sorry," she said.

"Don't be."

Gregory rose to his knees beside her, one arm draped protectively over her shoulder. Haselby viewed the tableau with patent amusement, and perhaps just a touch of pleasure as well.

"Do you still desire that annulment?" he asked.

Lucy nodded.

"I'll have the papers drawn up tomorrow."

"Are you certain?" Lucy asked, concerned. He was a lovely man, really. She didn't want his reputation to suffer.

"Lucy!"

She turned quickly to Gregory. "Sorry. I didn't mean— I just—"

Haselby gave her a wave. "Please, don't trouble yourself. It was the best thing that could possibly have happened. Shootings, blackmail, treason . . . No one will ever look to *me* as the cause of the annulment now."

"Oh. Well, that's good," Lucy said brightly. She rose to her feet because, well, it seemed only polite, given how generous he was being. "But do you still wish for a wife? Because I could help you find one, once I'm settled, that is."

Gregory's eyes practically rolled back in his head. "Good *God*, Lucy."

She watched as he stood. "I feel I must make this right. He thought he was getting a wife. In a way, it's not precisely fair."

Gregory closed his eyes for a long moment. "It is a good thing I love you so well," he said wearily, "because otherwise, I should have to fit you with a muzzle."

Lucy's mouth fell open. "Gregory!" And then, "Hermione!"

"Sorry!" Hermione said, one hand still clapped over her mouth to muffle her laughter. "But you *are* well-matched."

Haselby strolled into the room and handed her uncle a handkerchief. "You'll want to staunch that," he murmured. He turned back to Lucy. "I don't really want a wife, as I'm sure you're aware, but I suppose I must find some way to procreate or the title'll go to my odious cousin. Which would be a shame, really. The House of Lords would surely elect to disband if ever he decided to take up his seat."

Lucy just looked at him and blinked.

Haselby smiled. "So, yes, I should be grateful if you found someone suitable."

"Of course," she murmured.

"You'll need my approval, too," Lord Davenport blustered, marching forward.

Gregory turned to him with unveiled disgust. "You," he bit off, "may shut up. Immediately."

Davenport drew back in a huff. "Do you have any idea to whom you are speaking, you little whelp?"

Gregory's eyes narrowed and he rose to his feet. "To a man in a very precarious position."

"I beg your pardon."

"You will cease your blackmail immediately," Gregory said sharply.

Lord Davenport jerked his head toward Lucy's uncle. "He was a traitor!"

"And you chose not to turn him in," Gregory snapped, "which I would imagine the king would find equally reprehensible."

Lord Davenport staggered back as if struck.

Gregory rose to his feet, pulling Lucy up along with him. "You," he said to Lucy's uncle, "will leave the country. Tomorrow. Don't return."

"I shall pay his passage," Richard bit off. "No more."

"You are more generous than I would have been," Gregory muttered.

"I want him gone," Richard said in a tight voice. "If I can hasten his departure, I am happy to bear the expense."

Gregory turned to Lord Davenport. "You will never breathe a word of this. Do you understand?"

"And you," Gregory said, turning to Haselby. "Thank you."

Haselby acknowledged him with a gracious nod. "I can't help it. I'm a romantic." He shrugged. "It does get one in trouble from time to time, but we can't change our nature, can we?"

Gregory let his head shake slowly from side to side as a wide smile began to spread across his face.

"You have no idea," he murmured, taking Lucy's hand. He couldn't quite bear to be separated from her just then, even by a few inches.

Their fingers twined, and he looked down at her. Her eyes were shining with love, and Gregory had the most overwhelming, absurd desire to laugh. Just because he could.

Just because he loved her.

But then he noticed that her lips were tightening, too. Around the corners, stifling her own laughter.

And right there, in front of the oddest assortment of witnesses, he swept her into his arms and kissed her with every last drop of his hopelessly romantic soul.

Eventually—very eventually—Lord Haselby cleared his throat.

Hermione pretended to look away, and Richard said, "About that wedding . . ."

With great reluctance, Gregory pulled away. He looked to the left. He looked to the right. He looked back at Lucy.

And he kissed her again.

Because, really, it had been a long day.

And he deserved a little indulgence.

And God only knew how long it would be before he could actually marry her.

But mostly, he kissed her because . . .

Because . . .

He smiled, taking her head in his hands and letting his nose rest against hers. "I love you, you know."

She smiled back. "I know."

And he finally realized why he was going to kiss her again.

Just because.

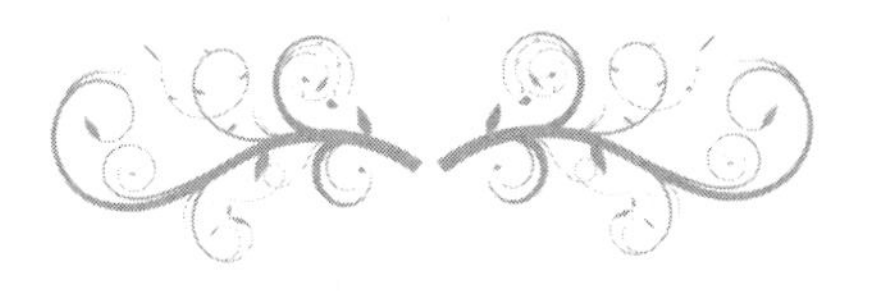

Epilogue

In which Our Hero and Heroine exhibit the industriousness of which we knew they were capable.

The first time, Gregory had been a wreck.

The second time was even worse. The memory of the first time had done little to calm his nerves. Just the opposite, in fact. Now that he had a better understanding of what was happening (Lucy had spared him no detail, a pox on her meticulous little soul) every little noise was subject to morbid scrutiny and speculation.

It was a damned good thing men couldn't have children. Gregory took no shame in admitting that the human race would have died out generations earlier.

Or at the very least, *he* would not have contributed to the current batch of mischievous little Bridgertons.

But Lucy seemed not to mind childbirth, as long as she could later describe the experience to him in relentless detail.

Whenever she wished.

And so by the third time, Gregory was a little more himself. He still sat outside the door, and he still held his breath when he heard a particularly unpleasant groan, but all in all, he wasn't wracked with anxiety.

The fourth time he brought a book.

The fifth, just a newspaper. (It did seem to be getting quicker with every child. Convenient, that.)

The sixth child caught him completely unawares. He'd popped out for a quick visit with a friend, and by the time he'd returned, Lucy was sitting up with the babe in her arms, a cheerful and not the least bit tired smile on her face.

Lucy frequently reminded him of his absence, however, so he took great care to be present for the arrival of number seven. Which he was, as long as one did not deduct points for his having abandoned his post outside her door in search of a middle-of-the-night snack.

At seven, Gregory thought they ought to be done. Seven was a perfectly fine number of children, and, as he told Lucy, he could barely recall what she looked like when she wasn't expecting.

"Well enough for you to make sure I'm expecting again," Lucy had replied pertly.

He couldn't very well argue with that, so he'd kissed her on the forehead and gone off to visit Hyacinth, to expound upon the many reasons seven was the ideal number of children. (Hyacinth was not amused.)

But then, sure enough, six months after the seventh, Lucy sheepishly told him that she was expecting another baby.

"No more," Gregory announced. "We can scarcely afford the ones we already possess." (This was not true; Lucy's dowry had been exceedingly generous, and Gregory had discovered that he possessed a shrewd eye for investments.)

But really, eight *had* to be enough.

Not that he was willing to curtail his nocturnal activities with Lucy, but there *were* things a man could do—things he probably already should have done, to tell the truth.

And so, since he was convinced that this would be his final child, he decided he might as well see what this was all about, and despite the horrified reaction of the midwife, he remained at Lucy's side through the birth (at her shoulder, of course).

"She's an expert at this," the doctor said, lifting the sheet to take a peek. "Truly, I'm superfluous at this point."

Gregory looked at Lucy. She had brought her embroidery.

She shrugged. "It really does get easier every time."

And sure enough, when the time came, Lucy laid down her work, gave a little grunt, and—

Whoosh!

Gregory blinked as he looked at the squalling infant, all wrinkled and red. "Well, that was much less involved than I'd expected," he said.

Lucy gave him a peevish expression. "If you'd been present the first time, you would have—ohhhhhhh!"

Gregory snapped back to face her. "What is it?"

"I don't know," Lucy replied, her eyes filling with panic. "But this is not right."

"Now, now," the midwife said, "you're just—"

"I know what I am supposed to feel," Lucy snapped. "And this is not it."

The doctor handed the new baby—a girl, Gregory was pleased to learn—to the midwife and returned to Lucy's side. He laid his hands upon her belly. "Hmmmm."

"Hmmmm?" Lucy returned. And not with a great deal of patience.

The doctor lifted the sheet and peered below.

"Gah!" Gregory let out, returning to Lucy's shoulder. "Didn't mean to see that."

"What is going on?" Lucy demanded. "What do you—ohhhhhhh!"

Whoosh!

"Good heavens," the midwife exclaimed. "There are two."

No, Gregory thought, feeling decidedly queasy, there were nine.

Nine children.

Nine.

It was only one less than ten.

Which possessed two digits. If he did this again, he would be in the double-digits of fatherhood.

"Oh dear Lord," he whispered.

"Gregory?" Lucy said.

"I need to sit down."

Lucy smiled wanly. "Well, your mother will be pleased, at the very least."

He nodded, barely able to think. Nine children. What did one do with nine children?

Love them, he supposed.

He looked at his wife. Her hair was disheveled, her face was puffy, and the bags under her eyes had bypassed lavender and were well on their way to purplish-gray.

He thought she was beautiful.

Love existed, he thought to himself.

And it was grand.

He smiled.

Nine times grand.

Which was very grand, indeed.

Dear Reader,

Have you ever wondered what happened to your favorite characters after you closed the final page? Wanted just a little bit more of a favorite novel? I have, and if the questions from my readers are any indication, I'm not the only one. So after countless requests from Bridgerton fans, I decided to try something a little different, and I wrote a "2nd Epilogue" for each of the novels. These are the stories that come after *the stories.*

At first, the Bridgerton 2nd Epilogues were available exclusively online; later they were published (along with a novella about Violet Bridgerton) in a collection called The Bridgertons: Happily Ever After. *Now, for the first time, each 2nd Epilogue is being included with the novel it follows. I hope you enjoy Gregory and Lucinda as they continue their journey.*

Warmly,
Julia Quinn

On the Way to the Wedding: The 2nd Epilogue

21 June 1840
Cutbank Manor
Nr Winkfield, Berks.

My dearest Gareth—

I hope this letter finds you well. I can hardly believe it has been almost a fortnight since I departed Clair House for Berkshire. Lucy is quite enormous; it seems impossible that she has not delivered yet. If I had grown so large with George or Isabella, I am sure I should have been complaining endlessly.

(I am also sure that you will not remind me of any complaints I may have uttered whilst in a similar state.)

Lucy does claim that this feels quite unlike her previous confinements. I find I must believe her. I saw her right before she gave birth to Ben, and I swear she was dancing a jig. I would confess to an intense jealousy, but it would be uncouth and unmaternal to admit to such an emotion, and as we know, I am Always Couth. And occasionally maternal.

Speaking of our progeny, Isabella is having a fine time. I do believe she would be content to remain with her cousins throughout the summer. She has been teaching them how to curse in Italian. I made a feeble effort to scold her, but I'm sure she realized I was secretly delighted. Every woman should know how to curse in another language since polite society has deemed English unavailable to us.

I am not certain when I will be home. At this rate, I should not be surprised if Lucy holds out until July. And then of course I have promised to remain for a bit of time after the baby arrives. Perhaps you should send George out for a visit? I don't think anyone would notice if one more child was added to the current horde.

Your devoted wife,
Hyacinth

Postscript—'Tis a good thing I did not seal the letter yet. Lucy just delivered twins. Twins! Good heavens, what on earth are they going to do with two more children? The mind boggles.

"I can't do this again."

Lucy Bridgerton had said it before, seven times, to be precise, but this time she really meant it. It wasn't so much that she had given birth to her ninth child just thirty minutes earlier; she'd grown rather expert at delivering babies and could pop one out with a minimum of discomfort. It was just that . . . Twins! Why hadn't anyone told her she might be carrying twins? No wonder she'd been so bloody uncomfortable these last few months. She'd had two babies in her belly, clearly engaged in a boxing match.

"Two girls," her husband was saying. Gregory looked over at her with a grin. "Well, that tips the scales. The boys will be disappointed."

"The boys will get to own property, vote, and wear trousers," said Gregory's sister Hyacinth, who had come to help Lucy toward the end of her confinement. "They shall endure."

Lucy managed a small chuckle. Trust Hyacinth to get to the heart of the matter.

"Does your husband know you've become a crusader?" Gregory asked.

"My husband supports me in all things," Hyacinth said sweetly, not taking her eyes off the tiny swaddled infant in her arms. "Always."

"Your husband is a saint," Gregory remarked, cooing at his own little bundle. "Or perhaps merely insane. Either way, we are eternally grateful to him for marrying you."

"*How* do you put up with him?" Hyacinth asked, leaning over Lucy, who was really beginning to feel quite strange. Lucy opened her mouth to make a reply, but Gregory beat her to it.

"I make her life an endless delight," he said. "Full of sweetness and light, and everything perfect and good."

Hyacinth looked as if she might like to throw up.

"You are simply jealous," Gregory said to her.

"Of what?" Hyacinth demanded.

With a wave of his hand, he dismissed the inquiry as inconsequential. Lucy closed her eyes and smiled, enjoying the interplay. Gregory and Hyacinth were always poking fun at each other—even now that they were both nearing their fortieth birthdays. Still, despite the constant needling—or maybe because of it—there was a rock-solid bond between them. Hyacinth in particular was viciously loyal; it had taken her two years to warm to Lucy after her marriage to Gregory.

Lucy supposed Hyacinth had had some just cause. Lucy had come so close to marrying the wrong man. Well, no, she *had* married the wrong man, but luckily for her, the combined influence of a viscount and an earl (along with a hefty donation to the Church of England) had made an annulment possible when, technically speaking, it shouldn't have been.

But that was all water under the bridge. Hyacinth was now a sister to her, as were all of Gregory's sisters. It had been marvelous marrying into a large family. It was probably why Lucy was so delighted that she and Gregory had ended up having such a large brood themselves.

"Nine," she said softly, opening her eyes to look at the two bundles that still needed names. And hair. "Who would have thought we'd have nine?"

"My mother will surely say that any sensible person would have stopped at eight," Gregory said. He smiled down at Lucy. "Would you like to hold one?"

She felt that familiar rush of maternal bliss wash over her. "Oh, yes."

The midwife helped her into a more upright position, and Lucy held out her arms to hold one of her new daughters. "She's very pink," she murmured, nestling the little bundle close to her chest. The tiny girl was screaming like a banshee. It was, Lucy decided, a marvelous sound.

"Pink is an excellent color," Gregory declared. "My lucky hue."

"This one has quite a grip," Hyacinth remarked, turning to the side so that everyone could see her little finger, captured in the baby's tiny fist.

"They are both very healthy," the midwife said. "Twins often aren't, you know."

Gregory leaned down to kiss Lucy on her forehead. "I am a very fortunate man," he murmured.

Lucy smiled weakly. She felt fortunate, too, almost miraculously so, but she was simply too tired to say anything other than "I think we must be done. Please tell me we're done."

Gregory smiled lovingly. "We're done," he declared. "Or at least as done as I can ensure."

Lucy nodded gratefully. She, too, was not willing to give up the comforts of the marital bed, but truly, there had to be something they could do to end the constant stream of babies.

"What shall we name them?" Gregory asked, making silly eyes at the baby in Hyacinth's arms.

Lucy nodded at the midwife and handed her the baby so that she could lie back down. Her arms were feeling shaky, she didn't trust herself to safely hold the baby, even here on her bed. "Didn't you want Eloise?" she murmured, closing her eyes. They'd named all of their children for their siblings: Katharine, Richard, Hermione, Daphne, Anthony, Benedict, and Colin. Eloise was the obvious next choice for a girl.

"I know," Gregory said, and she could hear his smile in his voice. "But I wasn't planning for *two*."

At that, Hyacinth turned around with a gasp. "You're going to name the other one Francesca," she accused.

"Well," Gregory said, sounding perhaps just a little bit smug, "she *is* next in line."

Hyacinth stood openmouthed, and Lucy would not have been at all surprised if steam began to shoot forth from her ears. "I can't believe it," she said, now positively glaring at Gregory. "You will have named your children after every possible sibling except me."

"It's a happy accident, I assure you," Gregory said. "I thought for sure that Francesca would be left out as well."

"Even Kate got a namesake!"

"Kate was rather instrumental in our falling in love," Gregory reminded her. "Whereas you attacked Lucy at the church."

Lucy would have snorted with laughter, had she the energy.

Hyacinth, however, was unamused. "She was *marrying* someone else."

"You do hold a grudge, dear sister." Gregory turned to Lucy. "She just can't let go, can she?" He was holding one of the babies again, although which one, Lucy had no idea. He probably didn't know, either. "She's beautiful," he said, looking up to smile at Lucy. "Small, though. Smaller than the others were, I think."

"Twins are always small," the midwife said.

"Oh, of course," he murmured.

"They didn't feel small," Lucy said. She tried to push herself back up so she could hold the other baby, but her arms gave out. "I'm so tired," she said.

The midwife frowned. "It wasn't such a long labor."

"There were two babies," Gregory reminded her.

"Yes, but she's had so many before," the midwife replied in a brisk voice. "Birthing does get easier the more babies one has."

"I don't feel right," Lucy said.

Gregory handed the baby to a maid and peered over at her. "What's wrong?"

"She looks pale," Lucy heard Hyacinth say.

But she didn't sound the way she ought. Her voice was tinny, and it sounded as if she were speaking through a long, skinny tube.

"Lucy? Lucy?"

She tried to answer. She thought she was answering. But if her lips were moving, she couldn't tell, and she definitely did not hear her own voice.

"Something's wrong," Gregory said. He sounded sharp. He sounded scared. "Where's Dr. Jarvis?"

"He left," the midwife answered. "There was another baby . . . the solicitor's wife."

Lucy tried to open her eyes. She wanted to see his face, to tell him that she was fine. Except that she wasn't fine. She didn't hurt, exactly; well, not any more than a body usually hurt after delivering a baby. She couldn't really describe it. She simply felt *wrong*.

"Lucy?" Gregory's voice fought its way through her haze. "Lucy!" He took her hand, squeezed it, then shook it.

She wanted to reassure him, but she felt so far away. And that wrong feeling was spreading throughout, sliding from her belly to her limbs, straight down to her toes.

It wasn't so bad if she kept herself perfectly still. Maybe if she slept . . .

"What's wrong with her?" Gregory demanded. Behind him the babies were squalling, but at least they were wriggling and pink, whereas Lucy—

"Lucy?" He tried to make his voice urgent, but to him it just sounded like terror. "Lucy?"

Her face was pasty; her lips, bloodless. She wasn't exactly unconscious, but she wasn't responsive, either.

"What is *wrong* with her?"

The midwife hurried to the foot of the bed and looked under the covers. She gasped, and when she looked up, her face was nearly as pale as Lucy's.

Gregory looked down, just in time to see a crimson stain seeping along the bedsheet.

"Get me more towels," the midwife snapped, and Gregory did not think twice before doing her bidding.

"I'll need more than this," she said grimly. She shoved several under Lucy's hips. "Go, go!"

"I'll go," Hyacinth said. "You stay."

She dashed out to the hall, leaving Gregory standing at the midwife's side, feeling helpless and incompetent. What kind of man stood still while his wife bled?

But he didn't know what to do. He didn't know how to do anything except hand the towels to the midwife, who was jamming them against Lucy with brutal force.

He opened his mouth to say . . . something. He might have got a word out. He wasn't sure. It might have just been a sound, an awful, terrified sound that burst up from deep within him.

"Where are the towels?" the midwife demanded.

Gregory nodded and ran into the hall, relieved to be given a task. "Hyacinth! Hya—"

Lucy screamed.

"Oh my God." Gregory swayed, holding the frame of the door for support. It wasn't the blood; he could handle the blood. It was the scream. He had never heard a human being make such a sound.

"What are you doing to her?" he asked. His voice was shaky as he pushed himself away from the wall. It was hard to watch, and even harder to hear, but maybe he could hold Lucy's hand.

"I'm manipulating her belly," the midwife grunted. She pressed down hard, then squeezed. Lucy let out another scream and nearly took off Gregory's fingers.

"I don't think that's such a good idea," he said. "You're pushing out her blood. She can't lose—"

"You'll have to trust me," the midwife said curtly. "I have seen this before. More times than I care to count."

Gregory felt his lips form the question—*Did they live?* But he didn't ask it. The midwife's face was far too grim. He didn't want to know the answer.

By now Lucy's screams had disintegrated into moans, but somehow this was even worse. Her breath was fast and shallow, her eyes squeezed shut against the pain of the midwife's jabs. "Please, make her stop," she whimpered.

Gregory looked frantically at the midwife. She was now using both hands, one reaching up—

"Oh, God." He turned back. He couldn't watch. "You have to let her help you," he said to Lucy.

"I have the towels!" Hyacinth said, bursting into the room. She stopped short, staring at Lucy. "Oh my God." Her voice wavered. "Gregory?"

"Shut *up*." He didn't want to hear his sister. He didn't want to talk to her, he didn't want to answer her questions. He didn't *know*. For the love of God, couldn't she see that he didn't know what was happening?

And to force him to admit that out loud would have been the cruelest sort of torture.

"It hurts," Lucy whimpered. "It *hurts*."

"I know. I know. If I could do it for you, I would. I swear to you." He clutched her hand in both of his, willing some of his own strength to pass into her. Her grip was growing feeble, tightening only when the midwife made a particularly vigorous movement.

And then Lucy's hand went slack.

Gregory stopped breathing. He looked over at the midwife in horror. She was still standing at the base of the bed, her face a mask of grim determination as she worked. Then she stopped, her eyes narrowing as she took a step back. She didn't say anything.

Hyacinth stood frozen, the towels still stacked up in her arms. "What . . . what . . ." But her voice wasn't even a whisper, lacking the strength to complete her thought.

The midwife reached a hand out, touching the bloodied bed near Lucy. "I think . . . that's all," she said.

Gregory looked down at his wife, who lay terrifyingly still. Then he turned back to the midwife. He could see her chest rise and fall, taking in all the great gulps of air she hadn't allowed herself while she was working on Lucy.

"What do you mean," he asked, barely able to force the words across his lips, "'That's all'?"

"The bleeding's done."

Gregory turned slowly back to Lucy. The bleeding was done. What did that mean? Didn't all bleeding stop . . . eventually?

Why was the midwife just standing there? Shouldn't she be doing something? Shouldn't *he* be doing something? Or was Lucy—

He turned back to the midwife, his anguish palpable.

"She's not dead," the midwife said quickly. "At least I don't think so."

"You don't *think* so?" he echoed, his voice rising in volume.

The midwife staggered forward. She was covered with blood, and she looked exhausted, but Gregory didn't give a sodding damn if she was ready to drop. "*Help her*," he demanded.

The midwife took Lucy's wrist and felt for a pulse. She gave him a quick nod when she found one, but then she said, "I've done everything I can."

"No," Gregory said, because he refused to believe that this was it. There was always something one could do. "No," he said again. "*No!*"

"Gregory," Hyacinth said, touching his arm.

He shook her off. "Do something," he said, taking a menacing step toward the midwife. "You have to do something."

"She's lost a great deal of blood," the midwife said, sagging back against the wall. "We can only wait. I have no way of knowing which way she'll go. Some women recover. Others . . ." Her voice trailed off. It might have been because she didn't want to say it. Or it might have been the expression on Gregory's face.

Gregory swallowed. He didn't have much of a temper; he'd always been a reasonable man. But the urge to lash out, to scream or beat the walls, to find some way to gather up all that blood and push it back into her . . .

He could barely breathe against the force of it.

Hyacinth moved quietly to his side. Her hand found his, and without thinking he entwined his fingers in hers. He waited for her to say something like: *She's going to be fine.* Or: *All will be well, just have faith.*

But she didn't. This was Hyacinth, and she never lied. But she was here. Thank God she was here.

She squeezed his hand, and he knew she would stay however long he needed her.

He blinked at the midwife, trying to find his voice. "What if—" *No.* "What *when*," he said haltingly. "What do we do *when* she wakes up?"

The midwife looked at Hyacinth first, which for some reason irritated him. "She'll be very weak," she said.

"But she'll be all right?" he asked, practically jumping on top of her words.

The midwife looked at him with an awful expression. It was something bordering on pity. With sorrow. And resignation. "It's hard to say," she finally said.

Gregory searched her face, desperate for something that wasn't a platitude or half answer. "What the devil does that mean?"

The midwife looked somewhere that wasn't quite his eyes. "There could be an infection. It happens frequently in cases like this."

"Why?"

The midwife blinked.

"Why?" he practically roared. Hyacinth's hand tightened around his.

"I don't know." The midwife backed up a step. "It just does."

Gregory turned back to Lucy, unable to look at the midwife any longer. She was covered in blood—Lucy's blood—and maybe this wasn't her fault—maybe it wasn't anyone's fault—but he couldn't bear to look at her for another moment.

"Dr. Jarvis must return," he said in a low voice, picking up Lucy's limp hand.

"I will see to it," Hyacinth said. "And I will have someone come for the sheets."

Gregory did not look up.

"I will be going now as well," the midwife said.

He did not reply. He heard feet moving along the floor, followed by the gentle click of the door closing, but he kept his gaze on Lucy's face the whole time.

"Lucy," he whispered, trying to force his voice into a teasing tone. "La la la Lucy." It was a silly refrain, one their daughter Hermione had made up when she was four. "La la la Lucy."

He searched her face. Did she just smile? He thought he saw her expression change a touch.

"La la la Lucy." His voice wobbled, but he kept it up. "La la la Lucy."

He felt like an idiot. He *sounded* like an idiot, but he had no idea what else to say. Normally, he was never at a loss for words. Certainly not with Lucy. But now . . . what did one say at such a time?

So he sat there. He sat there for what felt like hours. He sat there and tried to remember to breathe. He sat there and covered his mouth every time he felt a huge choking sob coming on, because he didn't want her to hear it. He sat there and tried desperately not to think about what his life might be without her.

She had been his entire world. Then they had children, and she was no longer everything to him, but still, she was at the center of it all. The sun. His sun, around which everything important revolved.

Lucy. She was the girl he hadn't realized he adored until it was almost too late. She was so perfect, so utterly his other half that he had almost overlooked her. He'd been waiting for a love fraught with passion and drama; it hadn't even occurred to him that true love might be something that was utterly comfortable and just plain easy.

With Lucy he could sit for hours and not say a word. Or they could chatter like magpies. He could say something stupid and not care. He could make love to her all night or go several weeks spending his nights simply snuggled up next to her.

It didn't matter. None of it mattered because they both *knew*.

"I can't do it without you," he blurted out. Bloody hell, he went an hour without speaking and *this* was the first thing he said? "I mean, I can, because I would have to, but it'll be awful, and honestly, I won't do such a good job. I'm a good father, but only because you are such a good mother."

If she died . . .

He shut his eyes tightly, trying to banish the thought. He'd been trying so hard to keep those three words from his mind.

Three words. "Three words" was supposed to mean *I love you*. Not—

He took a deep, shuddering breath. He had to stop thinking this way.

The window had been cracked open to allow a slight breeze, and Gregory heard a joyful shriek from outside. One of his children—one of the boys from the sound of it. It was sunny, and he imagined they were playing some sort of racing game on the lawn.

Lucy loved to watch them run about outside. She loved to run *with* them, too, even when she was so pregnant that she moved like a duck.

"Lucy," he whispered, trying to keep his voice from shaking. "Don't leave me. Please don't leave me.

"They need you more," he choked out, shifting his position so that he could hold her hand in both of his. "The children. They need *you* more. I know you know that. You would never say it, but you know it. And *I* need you. I think you know that, too."

But she didn't reply. She didn't move.

But she breathed. At least, thank God, she breathed.

"Father?"

Gregory started at the voice of his eldest child, and he quickly turned away, desperate for a moment to compose himself.

"I went to see the babies," Katharine said as she entered the room. "Aunt Hyacinth said I could."

He nodded, not trusting himself to speak.

"They're very sweet," Katharine said. "The babies, I mean. Not Aunt Hyacinth."

To his utter shock, Gregory felt himself smile. "No," he said, "no one would call Aunt Hyacinth sweet."

"But I do love her," Katharine said quickly.

"I know," he replied, finally turning to look at her. Ever loyal, his Katharine was. "I do, too."

Katharine took a few steps forward, pausing near the foot of the bed. "Why is Mama still sleeping?"

He swallowed. "Well, she's very tired, pet. It takes a great deal of energy to have a baby. Double for two."

Katharine nodded solemnly, but he wasn't sure if she believed him. She was looking at her mother with a furrowed brow—not quite concerned, but very, very curious. "She's pale," she finally said.

"Do you think so?" Gregory responded.

"She's white as a sheet."

His opinion precisely, but he was trying not to sound worried, so he merely said, "Perhaps a little more pale than usual."

Katharine regarded him for a moment, then took a seat in the chair next to him. She sat straight, her hands folded neatly in her lap, and Gregory could not help marveling at the miracle of her. Almost twelve years ago Katharine Hazel Bridgerton had entered this world, and he had become a father. It was, he had realized the instant she had been put into his arms, his one true vocation. He was a younger son; he was not going to hold a title, and he was not suited for the military or the clergy. His place in life was to be a gentleman farmer.

And a father.

When he'd looked down at baby Katharine, her eyes still that dark baby gray that all of his children had had when they were tiny, he knew. Why he was here, what he was meant for . . . that was when he knew. He existed to shepherd this miraculous little creature to adulthood, to protect her and keep her well.

He adored all of his children, but he would always have a special bond with Katharine, because she was the one who had taught him who he was meant to be.

"The others want to see her," she said. She was looking down, watching her right foot as she kicked it back and forth.

"She still needs her rest, pet."

"I know."

Gregory waited for more. She wasn't saying what she was really thinking. He had a feeling that it was Katharine who wanted to see her mother. She wanted to sit on the side of the bed and laugh and giggle and then explain every last nuance of the nature walk she'd undertaken with her governess.

The others—the littler ones—were probably oblivious.

But Katharine had always been incredibly close to Lucy. They were like two peas in a pod. They looked nothing alike; Katharine was remarkably like her namesake, Gregory's sister-in-law, the current Viscountess Bridgerton. It made absolutely no sense, as theirs was not a blood connection, but both Katharines had the same dark hair and oval face. The eyes were not the same color, but the shape was identical.

On the inside, however, Katharine—*his* Katharine—was just like Lucy. She craved order. She needed to see the pattern in things. If she were able to tell her mother about yesterday's nature walk, she would have started with which flowers they'd seen. She would not have remembered all of them, but she would definitely have known how many there had been of each color. And Gregory would not be surprised if the governess came to him later and said that Katharine had insisted they go for an extra mile so that the "pinks" caught up with the "yellows."

Fairness in all things, that was his Katharine.

"Mimsy says the babies are to be named after Aunt Eloise and Aunt Francesca," Katharine said, after kicking her foot back and forth thirty-two times.

(He'd counted. Gregory could not believe he'd counted. He was growing more like Lucy every day.)

"As usual," he replied, "Mimsy is correct." Mimsy was the children's nanny and nurse, and a candidate for sainthood if he'd ever met one.

"She did not know what their middle names might be."

Gregory frowned. "I don't think we got 'round to deciding upon that."

Katharine looked at him with an unsettlingly direct gaze. "Before Mama needed her nap?"

"Er, yes," Gregory replied, his gaze sliding from hers. He was not proud that he'd looked away, but it was his only choice if he wanted to keep from crying in front of his child.

"I think one of them ought to be named Hyacinth," Katharine announced.

He nodded. "Eloise Hyacinth or Francesca Hyacinth?"

Katharine's lips pressed together in thought, then she said, rather firmly, "Francesca Hyacinth. It has a lovely ring to it. Although . . ."

Gregory waited for her to finish her thought, and when she did not he prompted, "Although . . . ? "

"It *is* a little flowery."

"I'm not certain how one can avoid that with a name like Hyacinth."

"True," Katharine said thoughtfully, "but what if she does not turn out to be sweet and delicate?"

"Like your Aunt Hyacinth?" he murmured. Some things really did beg to be said.

"She *is* rather fierce," Katharine said, without an ounce of sarcasm.

"Fierce or fearsome?"

"Oh, only fierce. Aunt Hyacinth is not at all fearsome."

"Don't tell *her* that."

Katharine blinked with incomprehension. "You think she wants to be fearsome?"

"*And* fierce."

"How odd," she murmured. Then she looked up with especially bright eyes. "I think Aunt Hyacinth is going to love having a baby named after her."

Gregory felt himself smile. A real one, not something conjured to make his child feel safe. "Yes," he said quietly, "she will."

"She probably thought she wasn't going to get one," Katharine continued, "since you and Mama were going in order. We all knew would be Eloise for a girl."

"And who would have expected twins?"

"Even so," Katharine said, "there is Aunt Francesca to consider. Mama would have had to have had triplets for one to be named after Aunt Hyacinth."

Triplets. Gregory was not a Catholic, but it was difficult to suppress the urge to cross himself.

"And they would have all had to have been girls," Katharine added, "which does seem to be a mathematical improbability."

"Indeed," he murmured.

She smiled. And he smiled. And they held hands.

"I was thinking . . ." Katharine began.

"Yes, pet?"

"If Francesca is to be Francesca Hyacinth, then Eloise ought to be Eloise Lucy. Because Mama is the very best of mothers."

Gregory fought against the lump rising in his throat. "Yes," he said hoarsely, "she is."

"I think Mama would like that," Katharine said. "Don't you?"

Somehow, he managed to nod. "She would probably say that we should name the baby for someone else. She's quite generous that way."

"I know. That's why we must do it while she is still asleep. Before she has a chance to argue. Because she will, you know."

Gregory chuckled.

"She'll say we shouldn't have done it," Katharine said, "but secretly she will be delighted."

Gregory swallowed another lump in his throat, but this one, thankfully, was born of paternal love. "I think you're right."

Katharine beamed.

He ruffled her hair. Soon she'd be too old for such affections; she'd tell him not to muss her coiffure. But for now, he was taking all the hair ruffling he could get. He smiled down at her. "How do you know your mama so well?"

She looked up at him with an indulgent expression. They had had this conversation before. "Because I'm exactly like her."

"Exactly," he agreed. They held hands for a few more moments until something occurred to him. "Lucy or Lucinda?"

"Oh, Lucy," Katharine said, knowing instantly what he was talking about. "She's not *really* a Lucinda."

Gregory sighed and looked over at his wife, still sleeping in her bed. "No," he said quietly, "she's not." He felt his daughter's hand slip into his, small and warm.

"La la la Lucy," Katharine said, and he could hear her quiet smile in her voice.

"La la la Lucy," he repeated. And amazingly, he heard a smile in his own voice, too.

A few hours later Dr. Jarvis returned, tired and rumpled after delivering another baby down in the village. Gregory knew the doctor well; Peter Jarvis had been fresh from his studies when Gregory and Lucy had decided to take up residence near Winkfield, and he had served as the family doctor ever since. He and Gregory were of a similar age, and they had shared many a supper together over the years. Mrs. Jarvis, too, was a good friend of Lucy's, and their children had played together often.

But in all their years of friendship, Gregory had never seen such an expression on Peter's face. His lips were pinched at the corners, and there were none of the usual pleasantries before he examined Lucy.

Hyacinth was there, too, having insisted that Lucy needed the support of another woman in the room. "As if either of you could possibly understand the rigors of childbirth," she'd said, with some disdain.

Gregory hadn't said a word. He'd just stepped aside to allow his sister inside. There was something comforting in her fierce presence. Or maybe inspiring. Hyacinth was such a force; one almost believed she could *will* Lucy to heal herself.

They both stood back as the doctor took Lucy's pulse and listened to her heart. And then, to Gregory's complete shock, Peter grabbed her roughly by the shoulder and began to shake.

"What are you doing?" Gregory cried, leaping forward to intervene.

"Waking her up," Peter said resolutely.

"But doesn't she need her rest?"

"She needs to wake up more."

"But—" Gregory didn't know just what he was protesting, and the truth was, it didn't matter, because when Peter cut him off, it was to say:

"For God's sake, Bridgerton, we need to know that she *can* wake up." He shook her again, and this time, he said loudly, "Lady Lucinda! Lady Lucinda!"

"She's not a Lucinda," Gregory heard himself say, and then he stepped forward and called out, "Lucy? Lucy?"

She shifted position, mumbling something in her sleep.

Gregory looked sharply over at Peter, every question in the world hanging in his eyes.

"See if you can get her to answer you," Peter said.

"Let me try," Hyacinth said forcefully. Gregory watched as she leaned down and said something into Lucy's ear.

"What are you saying?" he asked.

Hyacinth shook her head. "You don't want to know."

"Oh, for God's sake," he muttered, pushing her aside. He picked up Lucy's hand and squeezed it with more force than he'd done earlier. "Lucy! How many steps are there in the back staircase from the kitchen to the first floor?"

She didn't open her eyes, but she did make a sound that he thought sounded like—

"Did you say fifteen?" he asked her.

She snorted, and this time he heard her clearly. "Sixteen."

"Oh, thank God." Gregory let go of her hand and collapsed into the chair by her bed. "There," he said. "There. She's all right. She will be all right."

"Gregory . . ." But Peter's voice was not reassuring.

"You told me we had to awaken her."

"We did," Peter said with stiff acknowledgment. "And it was a very good sign that we were able to. But it doesn't mean—"

"Don't say it," Gregory said in a low voice.

"But you must—"

"*Don't say it!*"

Peter went silent. He just stood there, looking at him with an awful expression. It was pity and compassion and regret and nothing he ever wanted to see on a doctor's face.

Gregory slumped. He'd done what had been asked of him. He'd woken Lucy, if only for a moment. She was sleeping again, now curled on her side, facing in the other direction.

"I did what you asked," he said softly. He looked back up at Peter. "I did what you asked," he repeated, sharply this time.

"I know," Peter said gently, "and I can't tell you how reassuring it is that she spoke. But we cannot count that as a guarantee."

Gregory tried to speak, but his throat was closing. That awful choking feeling was rushing through him again, and all he could manage was to breathe. If he could just breathe, and do nothing else, he might be able to keep from crying in front of his friend.

"The body needs to regain its strength after a blood loss," Peter explained. "She may sleep a while yet. And she might—" He cleared his throat. "She might not wake up again."

"Of course she will wake up," Hyacinth said sharply. "She's done it once, she can do it again."

The doctor gave her a fleeting glance before turning his attention back to Gregory. "If all goes well, I would think we could expect a fairly ordinary recovery. It might take some time," he warned. "I can't be sure how much blood she's lost. It can take months for the body to reconstitute its necessary fluids."

Gregory nodded slowly.

"She'll be weak. I should think she'd need to remain in bed for at least a month."

"She won't like that."

Peter cleared his throat. Awkwardly. "You will send someone if there is a change?"

Gregory nodded dumbly.

"No," Hyacinth said, stepping forth to bar the door. "I have more questions."

"I'm sorry," the doctor said quietly. "I have no more answers."

And even Hyacinth could not argue with that.

When morning came, bright and unfathomably cheery, Gregory woke in Lucy's sickroom, still in the chair next to her bed. She was sleeping, but she was restless, making her usual sleepy sounds as she shifted position. And then, amazingly, she opened her eyes.

"Lucy?" Gregory clutched her hand, then had to force himself to loosen his grip.

"I'm thirsty," she said weakly.

He nodded and rushed to get her a glass of water. "You had me so—I didn't—" But he couldn't say anything more. His voice broke into a thousand pieces, and all that came out was a wrenching sob. He froze, his back to her as he tried to regain his composure. His hand shook; the water splashed onto his sleeve.

He heard Lucy try to say his name, and he knew he had to get ahold of himself. *She* was the one who had nearly died; he did not get to collapse while she needed him.

He took a deep breath. Then another. "Here you are," he said, trying to keep his voice bright as he turned around. He brought the glass to her, then immediately realized his mistake. She was too weak to hold the glass, much less push herself up into a sitting position.

He set it down on a nearby table, then put his arms around her in a gentle embrace so that he could help her up. "Let me just fix the pillows," he murmured, shifting and fluffing until he was satisfied that she had adequate support. He held the glass to her lips and gave it the tiniest of tips. Lucy took a bit, then sat back, breathing hard from the effort of drinking.

Gregory watched her silently. He couldn't imagine she'd gotten more than a few drops into her. "You should drink more," he said.

She nodded, almost imperceptibly, then said, "In a moment."

"Would it be easier with a spoon?"

She closed her eyes and gave another weak nod.

He looked around the room. Someone had brought him tea the night before and they hadn't come to clean it up. Probably hadn't wanted to disturb him. Gregory decided that expeditiousness was more important than cleanliness, and he plucked the spoon from the sugar dish. Then he thought—she could probably use a bit of sugar, so he brought the whole thing over.

"Here you are," he murmured, giving her a spoonful of water. "Do you want some sugar, too?"

She nodded, and so he put a bit on her tongue.

"What happened?" she asked.

He stared at her in shock. "You don't know?"

She blinked a few times. "Was I bleeding?"

"Quite a lot," he choked out. He couldn't possibly have elaborated. He didn't want to describe the rush of blood he had witnessed. He didn't want her to know, and to be honest, he wanted to forget.

Her brow wrinkled, and her head tipped to the side. After a few moments Gregory realized she was trying to look toward the foot of the bed.

"We cleaned it up," he said, his lips finding a tiny smile. That was so like Lucy, making certain that all was in order.

She gave a little nod. Then she said, "I'm tired."

"Dr. Jarvis said you will be weak for several months. I would imagine you will be confined to bed for some time."

She let out a groan, but even this was a feeble sound. "I hate bed rest."

He smiled. Lucy was a doer; she always had been. She liked to fix things, to make things, to make everyone happy. Inactivity just about killed her.

A bad metaphor. But still.

He leaned toward her with a stern expression. "You will stay in bed if I have to tie you down."

"You're not the sort," she said, moving her chin ever so slightly. He thought she was trying for an insouciant expression, but it took energy to be cheeky, apparently. She closed her eyes again, letting out a soft sigh.

"I did once," he said.

She made a funny sound that he thought might actually be a laugh. "You did, didn't you?"

He leaned down and kissed her very gently on the lips. "I saved the day."

"You always save the day."

"No." He swallowed. "That's you."

Their eyes met, the gaze between them deep and strong. Gregory felt something wrenching within him, and for a moment he was sure he was going to sob again. But then, just as he felt himself begin to come apart, she gave a little shrug and said, "I couldn't move now, anyway."

His equilibrium somewhat restored, he got up to scavenge a left-over biscuit from the tea tray. "Remember that in a week." He had no doubt that she would be trying to get out of bed long before it was recommended.

"Where are the babies?"

Gregory paused, then turned around. "I don't know," he replied slowly. Good heavens, he'd completely forgotten. "In the nursery, I imagine. They are both perfect. Pink and loud and everything they are supposed to be."

Lucy smiled weakly and let out another tired sound. "May I see them?"

"Of course. I'll have someone fetch them immediately."

"Not the others, though," Lucy said, her eyes clouding. "I don't want them to see me like this."

"I think you look beautiful," he said. He came over and perched on the side of the bed. "I think you might be the most beautiful thing I have ever seen."

"Stop," she said, since Lucy never had been terribly good at receiving compliments. But he saw her lips wobble a bit, hovering between a smile and a sob.

"Katharine was here yesterday," he told her.

Her eyes flew open.

"No, no, don't worry," he said quickly. "I told her you were merely sleeping. Which is what you were doing. She isn't concerned."

"Are you sure?"

He nodded. "She called you La la la Lucy."

Lucy smiled. "She is marvelous."

"She is just like you."

"That's not why she is marv—"

"It is exactly why," he interrupted with a grin. "And I almost forgot to tell you. She named the babies."

"I thought you named the babies."

"I did. Here have some more water." He paused for a moment to get some more liquid into her. Distraction was going to be the key, he decided. A little bit here and a little bit there, and they'd get through a full glass of water. "Katharine thought of their second names. Francesca Hyacinth and Eloise Lucy."

"Eloise . . . ? "

"Lucy," he finished for her. "Eloise Lucy. Isn't it lovely?"

To his surprise, she didn't protest. She just nodded, the motion barely perceptible, her eyes filling with tears.

"She said it was because you are the best mother in the world," he added softly.

She did cry then, big silent tears rolling from her eyes.

"Would you like me to bring you the babies now?" he asked.

She nodded. "Please. And . . ." She paused, and Gregory saw her throat work. "And bring the rest, too."

"Are you certain?"

She nodded again. "If you can help me to sit up a little straighter, I think I can manage hugs and kisses."

His tears, the ones he had been trying so hard to suppress, slid from his eyes. "I can't think of anything that might help you to get better more quickly." He walked to the door, then turned around when his hand was on the knob. "I love you, La la la Lucy."

"I love you, too."

•

Gregory must have told the children to behave with extra decorum, Lucy decided, because when they filed into her room (rather adorably from oldest to youngest, the tops of their heads making a charming little staircase) they did so very quietly, finding their places against the wall, their hands clasped sweetly in front of their bodies.

Lucy had no idea who *these* children were. *Her* children had never stood so still.

"It's lonely over here," she said, and there would have been a mass tumble onto the bed except that Gregory leapt into the riot with a forceful "Gently!"

Although in retrospect, it was not so much his verbal order that held the chaos at bay as his arms, which prevented at least three children from cannonballing onto the mattress.

"Mimsy won't let me see the babies," four-year-old Ben muttered.

"It's because you haven't taken a bath in a month," retorted Anthony, two years his elder, almost to the day.

"How is that possible?" Gregory wondered aloud.

"He's very sneaky," Daphne informed him. She was trying to worm her way closer to Lucy, though, so her words were muffled.

"How sneaky can one be with a stench like that?" Hermione asked.

"I roll in flowers every single day," Ben said archly.

Lucy paused for a moment, then decided it might be best not to reflect too carefully on what her son had just said. "Er, which flowers are those?"

"Well, not the rosebush," he told her, sounding as if he could not believe she'd even asked.

Daphne leaned toward him and gave a delicate sniff. "Peonies," she announced.

"You can't tell that by sniffing him," Hermione said indignantly. The two girls were separated by only a year and a half, and when they weren't whispering secrets they were bickering like . . .

Well, bickering like Bridgertons, really.

"I have a very good nose," Daphne said. She looked up, waiting for someone to confirm this.

"The scent of peonies is very distinctive," Katharine confirmed. She was sitting down by the foot of the bed with Richard. Lucy wondered when the two of them had decided they were too old for piling together at the pillows. They were getting so big, all of them. Even little Colin didn't look like a baby any longer.

"Mama?" he said mournfully.

"Come here, sweetling," she murmured, reaching out for him. He was a little butterball, all chubby cheeks and wobbly knees, and she'd really thought he was going to be her last. But now she had two more, swaddled up in their cradles, getting ready to grow into their names.

Eloise Lucy and Francesca Hyacinth. They had quite the namesakes.

"I love you, Mama," Colin said, his warm little face finding the curve of her neck.

"I love you, too," Lucy choked out. "I love all of you."

"When will you get out of bed?" Ben asked.

"I'm not sure yet. I'm still terribly tired. It might be a few weeks."

"A few *weeks*?" he echoed, clearly aghast.

"We'll see," she murmured. Then she smiled. "I'm feeling so much better already."

And she was. She was still tired, more so than she could ever remember. Her arms were heavy, and her legs felt like logs, but her heart was light and full of song.

"I love everybody," she suddenly announced. "You," she said to Katharine, "and you and you and you and you and you and you. And the two babies in the nursery, too."

"You don't even know them yet," Hermione pointed out.

"I know that I love them." She looked over at Gregory. He was standing by the door, back where none of the children would see him. Tears were streaming down his face. "And I know that I love you," she said softly.

He nodded, then wiped his face with the back of his hand. "Your mother needs her rest," he said, and Lucy wondered if the children heard the choke in his voice.

But if they did, they didn't say anything. They grumbled a bit, but they filed out with almost as much decorum as they'd shown filing in. Gregory was last, poking his head back into the room before shutting the door. "I'll be back soon," he said.

She nodded her response, then sank back down into bed. "I love everybody," she said again, liking the way the words made her smile. "I love everybody."

And it was true. She did.

23 June 1840
Cutbank Manor
Nr Winkfield, Berks.

Dear Gareth—

I am delayed in Berkshire. The twins' arrival was quite dramatic, and Lucy must remain in bed for at least a month. My brother says that he can manage without me, but this is so untrue as to be laughable. Lucy herself begged me to remain—out of his earshot, to be sure; one must always take into account the tender sensibilities of the men of our species. (I know you will indulge me in this sentiment; even you must confess that women are far more useful in a sickroom.)

It is a very good thing that I was here. I am not certain she would have survived the birth without me. She lost a great deal of blood, and there were moments when we were not sure she would regain wakefulness. I took it upon myself to give her a few private, stern words. I do not recall the precise phrasing, but I might have threatened to maim her. I also might have given emphasis to the threat by adding, "You know I will do it."

I was, of course, speaking on the assumption that she would be too weak to locate the essential contradiction in such a statement—if she did not wake up, it would be of very little use to maim her.

You are laughing at me right now, I am sure. But she did cast a wary look in my direction when she awakened. And she did whisper a most heartfelt "Thank you."

So here I will be for a bit more time. I do miss you dreadfully. It is times like these that remind one of what is truly important. Lucy recently announced that she loves everybody. I believe we both know that I will never possess the patience for that, but I certainly love you. And I love her. And Isabella and George. And Gregory. And really, quite a lot of people.

I am a lucky woman, indeed.

Your loving wife,
Hyacinth

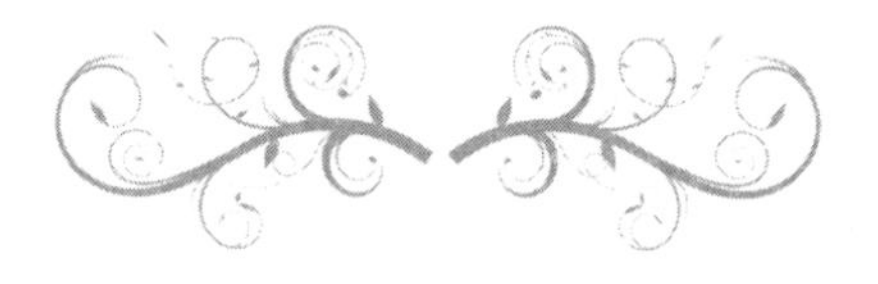

About the Author

#1 *New York Times* bestselling author JULIA QUINN began writing one month after graduating from college and, aside from a brief stint in medical school, she has been tapping away at her keyboard ever since. Her novels have been translated into forty-three languages and are beloved the world over. A graduate of Harvard and Radcliffe Colleges, she lives with her family in the Pacific Northwest.